THE WAR OF THE
DWARVES

In front of the gateway, the lead orcs were locked in combat with the dwarves, who were fighting valiantly but ineffectually against the invaders. Meanwhile, some of the smaller orcs were trying to sneak past and attack from behind, trapping the defenders between two fronts.

Tungdil glanced at the orcish leader. "It's time he went," he said, deciding that a change of tactics was in order. "We need to kill their chief."

Ireheart, brown eyes glinting manically, had fought himself into a frenzy. At the mercy of his fiery spirit, he threw himself on the enemy, windmilling his axes at incredible speed.

"Boïndil!" shouted Tungdil. "I said we need to kill their chief!" He had to repeat himself several more times before Boïndil finally heard.

The group set off toward Runshak, who spotted the approaching threat and turned to the älfar, hoping to enlist their bows in his defense. Suddenly his grin froze, his mouth falling open in horror.

Tungdil saw the fear on his ugly green face and turned to discover its source.

THE WAR OF THE
DWARVES

MARKUS HEITZ

Translated by Sally-Ann Spencer

www.orbitbooks.net

ORBIT

First English-language edition 2010
Originally published in Germany as *Der Krieg der Zwerge* by
Heyne Verlag, 2004
First published in Great Britain in 2010 by Orbit
Reprinted 2010 (twice), 2011 (twice), 2012

Copyright © 2004 by Piper Verlag GmbH, Munich
English translation copyright © 2010 by Sally-Ann Spencer

Excerpt from *Winterbirth* by Brian Ruckley
Copyright © 2006 by Brian Ruckley

The moral right of the author has been asserted.

A CIP catalogue record for this book
is available from the British Library.

ISBN 978-1-84149-573-6

Typeset in Sabon by Palimpsest Book Production Limited
Grangemouth, Stirlingshire
Printed and bound by CPI Group (UK) Ltd, Croydon, CR0 4YY

Papers used by Orbit are from well-managed forests
and other responsible sources.

MIX
Paper from
responsible sources
FSC® C104740

Orbit
An imprint of
Little, Brown Book Group
100 Victoria Embankment
London EC4Y 0DY

An Hachette UK Company
www.hachette.co.uk

www.orbitbooks.net

*For those who understand the grandeur
of the dwarven folks*

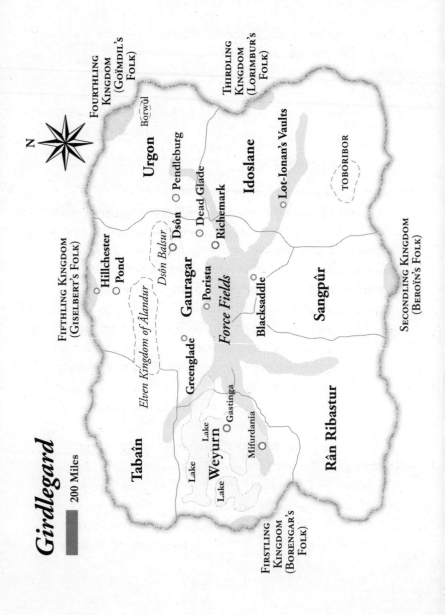

Girdlegard

200 Miles

N

FOURTHLING KINGDOM (GOÏMDIL'S FOLK)

THIRDLING KINGDOM (LORIMBUR'S FOLK)

FIFTHLING KINGDOM (GISELBERT'S FOLK)

Urgon

Borwôl

Pendleburg

Dsôn

Dead Glade

Richemark

Idoslane

Lot-Ionan's Vaults

TOBORIBOR

Hillchester

Pond

Dsôn Balsur

Elven Kingdom of Âlandur

Gauragar

Porista

Force Fields

Blacksaddle

Sangpûr

SECONDLING KINGDOM (BEROÏN'S FOLK)

Tabaîn

Greenglade

Gastinga

Mifurdania

Lake Weyurn

Lake

Lake

Rân Ribastur

FIRSTLING KINGDOM (BORENGAR'S FOLK)

"At the battle of the Blacksaddle, trolls were wailing, orcs whimpering, and our battle-hardened warriors were close to despair, but I never saw a dwarf lose heart."

—Palduríl, personal guard to Liútasil of Âlandur, lord of the elves.

"On the Nature of Dwarves.
Commonly found in gloomy mountain caverns, these diminutive creatures will fell an Orcus Gigantus with a single blow of their deadly axes, for no weapon in Girdlegard can match the finely fashioned ax of the dwarves. Afterward, they will drink beer by the barrelful without discernible effect. Such is the resilience of the dwarven female . . ."

—From "Notes on the Races of Girdlegard: Singularities and Oddities" from the archive of Viransiénsis, Kingdom of Tabaîn, compiled by the Master of Folklore M.A. Het in the 4299th Solar Cycle.

"Death came for the dwarf and tried to take him, whereupon the warrior squared his shoulders, dug his heels against the granite floor, and told him to go. Death turned around and left."

—Apologue from the southern provinces of Sangpûr.

PART ONE

Prologue

Borengar's Folk,
Eastern Border of the Firstling Kingdom,
Girdlegard,
Winter, 6234th Solar Cycle

S wirling and dancing like giddy ballerinas, snowflakes tumbled from the sky. Carried by the wind, they scattered over the mountains and came to rest among their fellows, covering the Red Range like a great white cloth.

Snow had been falling for many orbits, and the gray clouds continued to unburden themselves, burying the slopes. Some of the drifts were deep enough for ten dwarves to stand on each other's shoulders and disappear from view.

From his vantage point on the second highest of nine towers, Boëndal Hookhand of the clan of the Swinging Axes gazed out to the east.

Dressed in chain mail and a thick fur coat to protect him from the cold, the secondling warrior from Beroïn's folk was standing watch in East Ironhald. The stronghold, built by the firstlings on the eastern border of their kingdom, was protected by twin ramparts as wide as houses that rose out of the mountainside, enclosing eight watchtowers connected by bridges at a dizzying height. Further back, the ninth tower stood alone. A single bridge, broad enough to accommodate a unit of dwarves, led into the mountainside where the firstlings had made their home. The western flanks of the Red Range were protected by another stronghold almost identical in structure. The formidable defenses of West Ironhald were a bulwark against the orcs and other creatures seeking entry from the Outer Lands.

Boëndal, stranded for orbits in the firstling kingdom, was impatient to leave. *How much longer, Vraccas?* He fought back a yawn. On clear nights, the white slopes shimmered prettily in the moonlight, but Boëndal was inured to the view. Besides, there was something menacing about the glistening blanket of snow. Battlements, watchtowers, and bridges had to be cleared on a regular basis to protect the masonry from its crippling weight. The stronghold had been built to withstand the fury of invading trolls, boulders the size of an orc, and battering rams powered by ogres, but no one had reckoned with so much snow.

"Weather's coming from the west," muttered one of the sentries, peering balefully at the sky. His breath turned to miniature clouds that froze against his bushy beard and covered his whiskers in a layer of ice. Sniffing loudly, he walked to the brazier and filled his tankard from the vat of spiced beer that was simmering at the perfect temperature—pleasantly warm, but not hot enough for the alcohol to boil away.

In no time, the tankard was empty. The sentry burped, refilled the vessel, and offered it to Boëndal. "With a storm like this, you'd expect the weather to be coming from the north."

Boëndal clasped the tankard gratefully. On crisp winter nights, warm beer was the best antidote against the creeping chill. His chain mail shifted noisily over his leather jerkin as he lifted his arm to drink. He winced. The wounds in his back were healing nicely, but the slightest movement had him gasping with pain.

The sentry shot him an anxious look. "Are you all right? I've heard stories about älvish arrows—they leave terrible wounds."

"The pain is a reminder that I'm lucky to be alive. Vraccas had his work cut out to save me." The events of that orbit were vivid in his mind. He and his companions had been riding toward East Ironhald when the älfar attacked from behind. Two black-fletched älvish arrows had ripped through his chain mail, tunneling into his back. The physicians had struggled for hours to stem the blood.

"I owe my life to Vraccas and your kinsmen. They took me in and tended my wounds." There was a brief silence before he enquired, "How about you? Have you ever done battle with an älf?"

"I've fought orcs and ogres, but we seldom see älfar in these parts. Is it true that they look like elves?"

Boëndal nodded. "They're the spitting image of their cousins—tall, slender, and fleet-footed—but their hearts are full of hate."

"We should have killed the ones who brought you down. It won't be easy for your friends with a pair of älfar on their tail." The firstling shifted his gaze to the northeast. The dwarves' last hope, the Dragon Fire furnace, was burning in the fifthling kingdom, where Boëndal's companions were forging a weapon to kill the dark magus, whose tyranny had bought Girdlegard to its knees.

"Tungdil will manage," Boëndal assured him. "My twin

brother Boïndil and the rest of the company will forge the ax and kill Nôd'onn."

"I've heard of Keenfire, but what use is an ax against a wizard?" The firstling's voice was tinged with doubt.

"Keenfire has the power to destroy demonic spirits. It says in an ancient book that the blade will slay Nôd'onn and kill the evil inside him. Nature's order will be restored." Boëndal looked the firstling in the eye. "We can't fail, and we won't. Vraccas created us to protect the people of Girdlegard—and we won't let him down." He took a sip of spiced beer and felt the warmth spreading through him. "What of your queen?" he asked to dispel the silence. "Is there news of Xamtys?"

Orbits earlier, the firstling queen had set off on an underground journey through Girdlegard. The five dwarven kingdoms were connected by a network of tunnels with wagons that ran on metal rails. The system, a masterpiece of ancient dwarven engineering, enabled the folks to travel at speed in any direction by means of artificial gradients, switching points, and ramps.

"We don't know where she is," the firstling muttered unhappily, pulling on his beard. "She left here for a meeting, not to do battle with Nôd'onn. We're praying to Vraccas that she and our kinsmen are safe." He continued to tug on his beard while his left hand rested lightly on the parapet. "I can't stand the waiting." He looked at Boëndal. "But who am I telling? You're here every time I'm on watch: morning, noon, and night. Don't you sleep?"

Boëndal gulped down the rest of the beer. "My companions are risking their lives to save Girdlegard; I couldn't sleep if I wanted to." He returned the tankard to the firstling. "Thank you. It's given me strength and warmth."

He pulled his fur cloak around him and gazed at the unbroken expanse of snow. His eyes settled on the gully, the only route into the stronghold from Girdlegard. Secretly he hoped that if he looked carefully he would see his brother and the rest of the company hurrying toward him through the snow.

The most important mission in history, and they had to go without me, he thought gloomily. The wounds in his back and the blood loss had conspired to keep him to his bed, and by the time he recovered, his friends had departed. It was too late to chase after them now.

Boëndal, who was famous for his skill with a crow's beak, knew his strength would be missed in the battle against Nôd'onn. *You wanted me to stay here, didn't you, Vraccas?* He clenched his fists. *I expect you've got your reasons, but I'd rather be with Boïndil.*

Closing his eyes, he pictured his friends.

First he saw Bavragor Hammerfist, the one-eyed mason who liked to drink and sing. Bavragor had tricked his way into the company with customary cheek. Then came little Goïmgar Shimmerbeard, the nervous fourthling diamond cutter whose beard glittered brightly with the dust of countless gems. The company's leader was Tungdil, the kind-hearted, brown-haired outsider, whom Boëndal and his brother had befriended when he was a foundling with a scraggy beard. The twins had taught him how to be a proper dwarf, and the three of them were very close. After a rocky start, Tungdil had proven himself as an able leader. Boëndal didn't know much about their new smith, Balyndis Steelfinger, a firstling who had joined the expedition while he was ill. And the fifth dwarf was his twin brother, Boïndil Doubleblade, known as Ireheart because of his hot blood. Boïndil was thickset and muscular with shaven cheeks, a black beard, and long hair that reached to his knees in a plait. Most of the time he seemed a little crazy. His fiery spirit gave him formidable strength on the battlefield, but it was also a curse.

Boëndal opened his eyes. It was reassuring to think that his battle-hardened twin was with Tungdil. *Vraccas, lend them your strength.*

Wind gusted over the mountains, circling the battlements with a high-pitched whistle, through which Boëndal detected a jangling of chain mail. Someone was hurrying toward them.

He turned to see a messenger running along the battlements. It was obvious from his labored breathing that he had raced to the top of the watchtower to deliver the news.

"It's over!" he shouted through the snow, his voice swelling with excitement and pride. "The news just arrived from the Blacksaddle. Our warriors routed Nôd'onn's army with the help of the elves and men."

On hearing the good tidings, the other sentries abandoned their posts and crowded around the messenger. "Nôd'onn and his demon are dead, and the curse of the Perished Land has been lifted." He scanned the sentries' faces and discovered Boëndal in the crowd. "They said to tell you that Tungdil and your brother are on their way. Tungdil wants you both to go to the Gray Range. You're to rebuild Giselbert's kingdom for the dwarves."

Gripping the parapet, Boëndal blinked back tears of relief. For a moment he just stood there, thanking Vraccas with all his heart for helping the dwarves to prevail. Then, remembering the warm beer, he snatched a tankard from the frame above the brazier and dipped it into the vat.

"Three cheers for the dwarves!" he shouted excitedly. The others joined in and helped themselves to beer, the last of the sentries picking up the vat and draining it enthusiastically so that nothing would go to waste.

"Three cheers for the children of the Smith! Three cheers for the dwarves who killed Nôd'onn and banished the evil from our lands!" shouted Boëndal. The sentries banged the hafts of their axes against the battlements, clinked tankards, and downed the last of their beer.

The messenger smiled. "There'll be plenty of time for celebration when Her Majesty is home. I've seen the proclamation: She wants us to feast and make merry for three orbits as soon as she returns."

"I've got nothing against that kind of order," laughed the sentry whom Boëndal had talked to earlier. He stepped back to his post and winked at Boëndal. "You should get some sleep. The messenger said your brother is safe and well."

The worry was gone, replaced by tiredness. A mantle of fatigue weighed on Boëndal's shoulders, and he longed for his bed. "Yes, I suppose I should get some rest," he said smilingly. He took a last look eastward, imagining where his brother might be. "At least all the suffering was worthwhile. Tungdil and the others have been through such a lot." He filled his lungs with cold air. It tasted somehow purer and better than before. "Do you know what's strange? I always thought Tungdil would do it, but now that it's actually over . . . I suppose it takes a while to digest."

The sentry nodded. "I know what you mean. It's like setting out every orbit to fight a dragon, only to wake up one morning and find that he's dead. I don't know how you celebrate a thing like that." He rested his back against the tower and smiled. "Although a bit of drinking and feasting won't go amiss."

"I wonder what will happen to Girdlegard," said Boëndal after a time. "Maybe we'll see a new era of friendship. With the elves and the dwarves on the same side, we've never been more united. A victory like this could put a stop to our feuding."

A look of skepticism crossed the sentry's bearded face. He rubbed his nose doubtfully. "And rabbits might fly," he said in a low voice.

"Girdlegard would be stronger if we were united," countered Boëndal. "Tion's beasts have been plaguing our borders for cycles. Just because Nôd'onn has been defeated doesn't mean our kingdoms are safe." He smiled at the sentry. "It's not as if we'd move in with them or anything— perish the thought! I'm just saying we ought to talk to them, maybe meet with them every cycle. It might help us get along."

The sentry burped and spat over the wall. A blob of saliva flew through the air, turning into a tiny ball of ice as soon as it left his mouth, and plopping into the snow-covered fortifications below. "I suppose so," he said hesitantly. "But the high king can take care of it. I don't want to meet any pointy-ears. They're too—"

"Arrogant? Conceited?" suggested Boëndal.

"Girly," said the sentry, pleased to have found the right word. "The humans think the elves are so *creative*, so *arty*, but what's the point of being arty if you can't defend your forests from an älf?" He thumped Boëndal on the back. "You and I are made of rock. We're the opposite of girly. The pointy-ears wouldn't have stood a chance at the Blacksaddle if it hadn't been for us."

Boëndal was about to venture a different opinion when he glimpsed something in the distance. He peered through the snow: A comet, no bigger than a coin, was shooting toward them from the east, blazing a trail through the sky.

"Look," he said to the sentry. The comet was getting closer and closer, changing from white to pink as it hurtled their way. Suddenly it flared up, dazzling them with bright red light, then burst apart. Nothing remained except a cluster of crimson dots that faded and were swallowed gradually by the dark night sky.

Boëndal was reminded of spattered blood.

"Was it a good omen or a bad omen, do you think?" asked the sentry uncertainly.

"Well, it didn't hit us," said Boëndal dryly, "which in my book makes it a good omen. Maybe Vraccas sent a spark from the eternal smithy to . . ."

Just then a second comet shot into view. Whooshing toward them from the east, it arced through the sky, falling toward the firstling kingdom. This time it didn't burst apart.

"By the fire of Vraccas," stammered the sentry, gripping his shield as if a rectangle of wood and metal could protect him from a blazing orb. "Are you sure they're sparks from Vraccas's smithy and not Tion's revenge?"

"Look!" shouted another sentry, alarmed. "It's falling! The burning star is falling!"

"It's the sun!" a dwarf cried fearfully. "She's rolled out of her cradle—we need to wake her up!" He brought his ax against his shield, banging frantically.

The comet, which seconds ago had been no bigger than a coin, grew to the size of a leather pouch. In no time at all, it was larger than a windmill with vanes ablaze.

With a roar, the comet burned through the cloud, swooping toward the stronghold in an arc of crimson light and bathing everything beneath it—walls, watchtowers, and dwarves—in a strange red glow. In the fearsome heat, dancing snowflakes turned to raindrops and froze where they fell.

Before the dwarves could draw breath, the battlements, bridges, and staircases were glazed with thick ice.

"Run for cover!" shouted Boëndal, diving across the flagstones. A sheet of ice had formed on his chain mail, fusing his helmet to his back; it shattered with a high-pitched tinkle.

Skidding on his stomach across the ice, he grabbed hold of a corner of the brazier and came to a halt. The scars on his back were telling him to be careful, but he cursed them impatiently and gritted his teeth.

Some of the dwarves followed his example and dived for cover, while others stared at the sky in horrified fascination, unable to move or look away. A few of the sentries, convinced that the sun had fallen from its cradle, banged their weapons against their shields to rouse the burning orb.

In a shower of sparks, the shooting star sped toward them, screeching and thundering through the sky. Boëndal braced himself for the impact, but the comet swooped over the stronghold and disappeared beyond the mountains to the west.

But the danger hadn't passed.

The tail of the comet blazed red in the sky, showering debris large enough to crush a human house. The dwarves heard a drawn-out whistle, then an ear-splitting bang. The ground shook and trembled like a frightened beast. Plumes of snow shot upward, looming like luminous towers in the dark night sky. The air hissed and angry clouds of moisture rose from the vaporizing snow. Thick white fog wrapped itself around Boëndal like a blindfold.

"To the stronghold!" he commanded, realizing that watchtowers and battlements were no match for celestial might. "We'll be safer inside!" Bracing himself against the brazier, he tried to get to his feet; a moment later, one of the sentries was beside him, pulling him up.

Boëndal lost his bearings in the strange-smelling fog, but his companion knew the way without seeing. They ran, skidding and sliding every few paces until they resigned themselves to crawling and pulling themselves forward on their axes. "Quick, we need to . . ."

Boëndal's command was cut off by a droning from above. He knew exactly what it meant: The battlements were about to be hit by a volley of burning rock.

There was no time to shout a warning. The fog had already turned a muddy orange, darkening to black-streaked red as an unbearable screeching filled the air.

Vraccas protect us! Boëndal closed his eyes as a gigantic

slab of burning rock hurtled toward him. A moment later, it slammed into the solid stone walkway. Boëndal heard faint shrieks as dwarves in front of him tumbled to their deaths. He couldn't see where the rock had landed because of the fog.

"Turn back!" shouted Boëndal, crawling away from the shattered stone. Hampered by his injured back, he longed for his old agility. "To the northern walkway!"

Flagstones quaked beneath their feet as the colossal towers swayed like reeds in the breeze. Cracks opened in the groaning masonry and sections of battlement plummeted to the ground.

The bombardment continued as they hurried along the northern walkway to the highest tower. Skidding and sliding, they came to a halt at the bridge. The single-span arch construction was the only way into the kingdom and the safety of the firstling halls. Beneath the bridge was a yawning chasm, two hundred paces deep.

A gusty wind swept the watchtowers, chasing away the mist. At last they could see the gates leading into the mountain—and safety.

"Vraccas forfend!" cried one of the sentries, who had turned and was pointing back at the lifting mist.

The fortifications of East Ironhald were in ruins.

Only four of the nine towers were still standing; the rest had been crushed, toppled or flattened, leaving five rings of masonry protruding like rotten tooth stumps from the ground. The mighty ramparts, hewn from the mountain by dwarven masons, were riven with cracks wide enough for a band of trolls to breach the defenses with ease.

"Keep moving!" Boëndal urged them. "You can worry about the ramparts as soon as we've got to safety. Walls can be rebuilt."

He and the others had barely set foot on the bridge when they heard a low rumbling like distant thunder. Then the earth moved again.

The falling boulders from the comet's tail had shaken the fortifications and caused the walkways to quake, but this time the tremor was deeper and more powerful, causing walls, towers, dwarves, peaks, and ridges to shudder and sway.

The Red Range had stood firm for thousands of cycles, but nothing could withstand the violent quake.

Most of the dwarves were knocked off their feet, hitting the flagstones in a jangling of chain mail. Axes flew through the air and clattered to the ground, while helmets collided with stone. Two of the surviving towers collapsed with a deafening bang, raising clouds of dust that shrouded the rubble.

Boëndal thought of the vast orb that had passed overhead. He had only one explanation for the tremor: The comet had landed in the mountains to the west, sending shockwaves through the ground. He tried not to imagine what was happening in the underground halls and passageways; how many firstlings were dying, how many dead.

The rumbling grew fainter, the quaking subsided, and at last it was still. The dwarves held their breath, waiting for what was next.

An acrid smell burned their throats. The air was thick with dust from the ruined masonry, and smoke rose from scattered fires.

The fearsome heat had passed with the comet, and it was snowing again. From a distance, the stillness could have been mistaken for tranquility, but it was born of destruction. Death had visited the Red Range and ravaged the firstlings' home.

"Vraccas have mercy," whispered Boëndal's companion, his voice as sorrowful and defenseless as a child's.

Boëndal knew what he was thinking. Dwarves were fearless: They threw themselves into battle regardless of the odds and defended Girdlegard against the invading hordes. Their axes and hammers brought death to the most monstrous of Tion's beasts, but no dwarven weapon could match a foe like this. "We couldn't have stopped it," he told him. "Even Vraccas can't catch a falling star."

Leaning over the bridge, he realized that the base of the tower was seriously unstable. Cracks, each as wide as an outstretched arm, had opened in the stone and were spreading through the masonry. He could almost hear it breaking. "Quick, before the tower collapses and takes us with it!" He set off quickly across the bridge, followed by a handful of survivors.

They were almost halfway when a large clump of snow struck Boëndal on the neck. *What a time to play stupid games . . .* He brushed away the snow and kept walking.

The second snowball hit his left shoulder, showering him with snow. He whirled round to confront the hapless prankster. "By the hammer of Beroïn, I'll—"

Before he could finish, the dark sky opened up and pelted him with clumps of snow. Powdery snowballs hit the bridge, his helmet, and the other dwarves. Boëndal heard a faint rumbling and the bombardment intensified; he knew what it was.

The mountains, not his companions, had started the assault.

Boëndal's stomach lurched as he scanned the peaks around him. Although the comet had hit the ground many miles to the west, it had called forth a monster that lurked above the dwarven halls. Boëndal had seen it hundreds of times while standing watch in the secondling kingdom. The White Death, roused by the rain and the tremors, had mounted its steed near the summit and was galloping down the slopes. In the space of two breaths it filled the mountainside, crushing and consuming everything in its path.

Like a vast wave, the snow rolled down the mountain, throwing up powdery spray. Everything before it was toppled, stifled, and dragged on its downward plunge.

"Run!" shouted Boëndal. His legs seemed to move of their own accord. After a few paces, he slipped over, but someone grabbed him by the plait and he stumbled to his feet. Two dwarves slotted their hands under his armpits and pulled him on. Driven by fear, they stumbled over the bridge, more skating than running.

Even as the gates swung back to admit them, the White Death reeled them in.

Hurling itself triumphantly over the precipice, it fell on the dwarves like a starving animal. Its icy body smacked into the bridge, knocking them into the chasm.

Boëndal's shouts were drowned out by the roaring, thundering beast. His mouth filled with snow. He clutched at the air until his right hand grabbed a falling shield, which he clung to as if he were drowning.

His descent was fast—so fast that his stomach was spinning in all directions. He had no way of orienting himself in the snow, but the shield cut through the powder like a spade.

Tiring of the dwarf, the White Death dumped him and covered him over. The weight of the cold beast's body pushed the air from his lungs.

A little while later Boëndal blacked out. Night descended on his consciousness and his soul was ready to be summoned to Vraccas's smithy. At least it would be warm.

I

A rivulet of sweat left his greasy hair, slid down his forehead, and slithered over his soot and lard-slathered skin, zigzagging past clumps of solid dirt. It ran down the bridge of his green nose, dribbled onto his upper lip, and was licked up greedily by his thick black tongue. His vile mouth stayed open as he panted for breath, exposing the full length of his tattooed tusks, a sign of high rank. His vast jaws twitched.

"Runshak!" he thundered, gesturing for his henchman to join him.

The troop leader, putting on a burst of speed to over-take the column of marching orcs, left the path to reach the mound where his chieftain was waiting.

The long march north had started at the Blacksaddle, where the orcs had been defeated by an alliance of dwarves, elves, and men. They were heading for their new homeland in the Gray Range: Eight hundred and fifty torturous miles still separated them from the Stone Gateway at the border with the Outer Lands.

For now they were intent on destroying their cousins, who were somewhere on the road ahead.

Runshak marched up the slope and came to a halt in

front of his chieftain, the great Prince Ushnotz, one-time commander of a third of Toboribor, the southern orcish kingdom. "Are we catching them?"

"Look," boomed Ushnotz, pointing to a flat expanse of grassland amid the rolling hills. The field, a mile and a half across, was scarred with thin black lines—narrow channels cut by melt water that ran toward the eastern corner, seeping gradually into the soil. Although the field was grassing over, the trees and bushes were still bare, offering little protection from the wind—or shelter from enemies.

Hordes of tiny black figures had taken up residence on the usually peaceful land.

Runshak estimated their numbers at more than two thousand. They had set up camp and were going about their business as if they had nothing to fear. Dead wood and branches had been stacked in large pyres from which smoke was rising in thick black columns, clearly visible in the cloudless sky.

Ushnotz raised a hand to his massive forehead, shielding his eyes as he focused on the activity below. Most of the milling figures were orcs; the others, shorter and less powerful, bögnilim. What they lacked in stature, they made up for in speed, but bögnilim were cowardly creatures that had to be whipped into shape. "Northern orcs and bögnilim," he grunted scornfully. "An alliance of fools." The northern orcs, summoned by Nôd'onn to secure the human kingdoms, had demonstrated a fatal lack of discipline at the Blacksaddle, scrapping like wolves, while Ushnotz's troopers, no less ferocious or powerful, obeyed his orders like well-trained dogs. The orcish chieftain despised the northerners, but bögnilim were worse. "Prepare to attack. We'll strike when they've filled their fat bellies and they're snoring by the fire."

Runshak nodded and charged down the slope, barking orders at the pack leaders, who relayed them in similarly boorish fashion. With a clunking of armor and jangling of chain mail the mighty army of five thousand orcs rearranged itself into smaller units. The archers made their way to the back; those bearing spears and lances stood shoulder to shoulder at the front.

The orcish chieftain followed the preparations approvingly, his thick black lips curling back to reveal his magnificent tusks. He was well pleased with what he saw. A growly laugh sounded from his throat.

He took a deep breath and let out an almighty roar. The shuffling and stomping came to a halt. Nobody said a word.

"Nôd'onn broke faith with us and abandoned us to our fate. The fleshlings think we're going south, but our route will take us north—to found a new kingdom," he proclaimed, confident that the prospect of a new homeland would make them forget their tiredness and spur them into battle. He drew his notched sword and pointed at the enemy below. "Nôd'onn's northern lapdogs are in our way. We had to flee our homes because of those cretins. Destroy them, and the Gray Range will be ours. We'll be in our new kingdom before the fleshling soldiers are in sight of the peaks." He laughed malevolently. "I hope they send their cavalry after us—we could do with some meat."

His troopers grunted and snarled excitedly, pounding the hafts of their spears on the ground and banging swords against shields.

He raised his arm and the noise stopped abruptly. The silence was broken by a question. "Couldn't we march past the northerners instead?"

Ushnotz, who had excellent hearing, knew at once which of the five thousand troopers had spoken the treasonous words. Kashbugg was a troublemaker who took after his father, Raggshor.

Raggshor had met his death shortly before the battle of the Blacksaddle in circumstances not dissimilar to these, after questioning the wisdom of laying siege to a mountain. Ushnotz had thought him an excellent tactician, but criticism—especially when voiced in public—was not to be tolerated. Besides, Ushnotz made the decisions and he always knew best. He had killed Raggshor on the spot, and he was contemplating a similar fate for Kashbugg.

"Silence!" he bellowed, throwing back his head in an intimidating roar.

The display made little impression on the offending orc, who stepped forward, sword in hand, shield raised defensively. "Why not march past them and get there first? We can occupy the halls while they dash out their brains on the gates." He stood with his legs apart, bracing himself for the blow that was bound to follow. "It's time we did things differently, Ushnotz. After what happened at the Blacksaddle, we're not as strong as we were. Maybe if you'd listened to my father, we'd be back in our kingdom by now."

Several orcs grunted approvingly.

For Ushnotz, the interruption was unwelcome: The sweet smell of victory had soured, replaced by the reek of rebellion. He drew himself up to his full height, bared his tusks and tensed his muscles. Then he took off, bounding down the slope, and thundering to a stop in front of Kashbugg.

"I've got a better plan," he snarled, squaring his shoulders. There was a nasty glint in his yellow eyes. He made a feint with his sword; then, ducking beneath Kashbugg's raised shield, he whipped out his dagger, rammed it into the trooper's armpit and pierced his heart. Green blood gushed from the wound and the insolent trooper thudded to the ground. "My plan is this: Kashbugg dies first, just like his know-it-all father at the Blacksaddle." He glared at the others, challenging them to object. "Anyone else want to talk tactics?"

He wasn't surprised when no one stepped forward. The real shock came a moment later when the dead orc stood up. Kashbugg reached to his armpit and touched the wound with his claws; it healed straightaway.

Ushnotz got over his confusion faster than Kashbugg, who was clearly amazed to be alive. He rammed his sword horizontally into the injured orc's torso. The trooper sat down heavily and stared at the blood. He still showed no signs of dying.

"I'm sick of your troublemaking!" shrieked Ushnotz, grabbing him by the collar and dragging him to his feet. "How dare you defy orders? I told you to die!" The notched sword cut into the trooper's torso, but the damage was far from fatal. Kashbugg opened his mouth, dribbling blood and saliva; then he laughed.

Straightening up, he gave the chieftain a shove. "Tion has made his choice. Why else would he make me immortal? My father's death must be avenged!" He raised his shield and sword. "Tion wants me to lead the orcs to victory; the northern kingdom will be mine!"

"Why would Tion favor a boneheaded simpleton like you?" growled Ushnotz, preparing to fight. None of his troopers dared to take sides: Orcs were always arguing, but this was different. "You're hiding something, aren't you?"

"He drank dark water from the ditch!" called one of the troopers.

"It was hallowed water; I knew as soon as I saw it!" said Kashbugg, thumping the leather container on his belt. "I filled my pouch with it." He struck out at the chieftain, who blocked the blow and smashed the hilt of his sword into his face. Kashbugg stumbled backward, groaning.

"Dark water?" barked Ushnotz. He had noticed it as well: murky puddles on either side of the track. Nothing would have induced him to drink it.

"It's the blood of the Perished Land," said his challenger. "And I, Kashbugg, was elected to find it!" He sprang forward, swinging his sword.

Ushnotz flung himself to the ground and drove both boots into the trooper's knees, smashing the joints. Kashbugg screeched. The noise ended suddenly as Ushnotz dealt a long sweeping blow to his neck. The trooper's head fell one way, his body the other. This time Kashbugg was dead.

Ushnotz bent over the corpse, unhooked the water pouch and signaled to one of his underlings. "Here, drink this," he said. The trooper took the pouch.

Screwing up his face in disgust, he took a sip. Black

water dribbled from his mouth, and he coughed. "It tastes like the smell of troll's piss, only wor—"

Ushnotz stabbed him, ramming the dagger into his heart. He watched impassively as the trooper fell to the ground. The blade was still embedded in his flesh. After a while, his eyelids fluttered and he raised his head. The blood stopped pouring from his chest.

"Well?" asked Ushnotz suspiciously.

"I'm . . . I'm alive," said the orc, his voice a mixture of horror and pain. Then he realized his newfound power. Roaring with triumph, he bared his tusks and brandished the pouch. "I'm alive! The dark water made me—"

Ushnotz took hold of his dagger, pulled it out of the screaming orc's chest, and lopped off his head. He caught the pouch quickly and raised it to his lips, draining its contents. Then he hurled it to the ground. He didn't feel any different, but he was certain of the effect. As a former prince of Toboribor, he deserved to be immortal. *A leader like me needs an indestructible army*. He decided to obtain more of the water for his troops.

Leaving the troopers without a word, he lumbered up the slope to survey the enemy camp and wait for an opportunity to attack.

The northern orcs were gorging themselves on human flesh. Ushnotz, his stomach rumbling, breathed in the smell of roasting meat. He and his troopers had been nourishing themselves on whatever crossed their path—animals, snails, and beetles. Fleshlings were a rare delicacy because the northerners seldom left anything in their wake. The inhabitants of three villages, a small town, and a hamlet had been slaughtered and eaten by the marauding troops.

Ushnotz was surprised at their pillaging; it was bound to provoke the fury of the fleshling kings.

The fleshlings on their own weren't much of a threat— Ushnotz thought them feeble and clumsy—but it was imperative for his troops to reach the Gray Range before the united army of Girdlegard noticed and hunted them down. If it came to a battle, he wanted to be protected by the sturdy defenses of a dwarven stronghold at the heart of a mountain range. With any luck, the other princes of Toboribor would keep Girdlegard's warriors busy for a while.

The sun, tired from another long orbit, was dropping toward the horizon. Soon she would retire to bed, making way for the stars to populate the heavens. The time for battle was approaching. Ushnotz bellowed for Runshak and briefed him on the plan of attack.

Just then the wind changed, blowing a new smell to the hilltop where Ushnotz and Runshak were stationed. They sniffed enquiringly, their broad nostrils flaring until at last they were sure. The air smelled of horses, armor, and sweat—fleshling sweat.

"They're coming from the south," snarled Runshak, turning to face the string of hills to their right. "Confounded fleshlings."

The united army! Although Ushnotz could smell but not see the new arrivals, he knew at once that his troopers were outnumbered. Even as he resigned himself to beating a hasty retreat he realized that the enemy was hounding a different quarry. "We'll wait," he said.

"You mean, they haven't seen us?" asked Runshak, surprised.

"It's not us they're looking for; they're after the orcs who left those tracks." He grinned. A few miles earlier, he had decided to stop tailing the northerners and lead his troopers across a river. The fast-flowing water had washed away their scent. Clearly, the fleshling scouts hadn't thought to look for two separate armies or his troopers would surely have been attacked. He congratulated himself on his guile.

Runshak growled uneasily and raised his nose to the wind. "The smell's getting stronger. They're still advancing; it won't be much longer until they attack." He looked expectantly at Ushnotz. "As soon as they've started fighting, we'll jump in and teach those fleshlings a lesson."

"No," said Ushnotz. "The northerners can deal with them. We'll see how they fare." He took a silent decision to resume the march that night if the united army proved victorious. It suited his purposes for the soft-skinned fleshlings to believe that this part of Girdlegard had been purged of his race.

He would never admit as much to Runshak, but Kashbugg had been right in one respect. The battle of the Blacksaddle had weakened his army. It was time to change tactics, but Ushnotz knew how to develop his own strategies without a jumped-up trooper telling him so.

"We'll stay out of sight. The fleshlings won't know we're here, and they'll head south. As soon as it's safe, we'll march north and find more of that water—enough for all of us. No army will be powerful enough to defeat us and when we're ready, we'll claim the lives that we spared tonight."

He turned his head, looking over the fat-encrusted

surface of his epaulette. His yellow eyes focused on the troublemaker's corpse and he grunted contentedly. Kashbugg and the ill-fated victim of his experiment with the water would be the only troopers to die that night.

Prince Mallen was waiting with his cavalry fifty or so paces from the brow of the hill.

The enemy was camped on the other side, watched by two of his scouts who were crouched on the hilltop, assessing the size of the army, which had been known to them only by the boot prints on the ground.

Mallen had decided to hunt down the fleeing orcs and bögnilim and put a stop to their pillaging. From what he had seen over the past few orbits, the beasts had lived too long already. They left nothing but carnage in their wake.

The first of the scouts crawled backward down the hillside to make his report. "Two thousand of them, Prince Mallen. They've been feasting, by the looks of it, and now they're dozing around their fires."

"So there aren't five thousand as we thought?" said Mallen, sitting upright in the saddle. His mount snorted gratefully, glad of the shift in weight. After a long ride without any rest to speak of, the horses were wearier than the men.

Until that moment, the wind had been blowing toward them, but now it buffeted them from behind. The air was mild and smelled of the coming spring.

"The ground was muddy, remember," said the scout. "The soil is soggy with melting snow; you sink deeper than usual. Besides, the green-hided beasts are bigger than us and their armor is heavy." His eyes swept the rows of horsemen. "Two thousand of them, Prince Mallen—no more than two thousand and no fewer."

The Ido flag, carried proudly by one of Mallen's riders, was fluttering in the wind, betraying the southerly change. Mallen cursed. Orcs had an excellent sense of smell and could sniff out their victims from a distance; they were bound to detect the waiting men.

Mallen's finely crafted armor, engraved with the insignia of the Ido, gleamed in the light of the setting sun. He unbuckled his old-fashioned helmet from his belt, set it on his head and fastened the chinstrap. His careful handling of the headpiece showed his respect for the royal crest, which had been in his family for generations, surviving the centuries unchanged.

His riders, seeing the prince's blond hair disappear beneath his helmet, prepared themselves for battle. Mallen heard the clunking of weaponry and jangling of armor behind him and gave the order to attack.

"Archers to the front," he said resolutely. "Advance to the hilltop, but stay out of sight. Foot soldiers go with them." He turned to the right. "First unit ride in and attack. Slash, jab, and do whatever you can to bait them—but turn and flee as soon as they fight back. The dolts will follow, and we'll be waiting for them. Don't let any escape."

He nodded briskly, and the first 150 riders charged up the hill, exploding over the crest and careering down the other side to blast through the enemy camp like a hoofed gust of death.

Eyes closed, Mallen listened to their progress. He heard pounding hooves, cries of terror from the orcs and high-pitched screams from the cowardly bögnilim. A moment later, swords met with armor and shields.

The clamor intensified. One hundred voices became a thousand as the excited beasts threw themselves wildly on the small band of riders who had ventured foolishly into their camp.

The thundering horseshoes grew louder, accompanied by shouts and jeers from the pursuing beasts.

Mallen raised his arm, lifting his sword high in the air. He heard the archers nock their arrows and level their bows.

The first beasts had yet to crest the hill when Mallen brought his sword down sharply and three hundred arrows soared through the air, falling steeply over the hilltop and raining vertically on the startled wave of orcs and bögnilim.

The first flurry was followed by a second and a third. Mallen listened in satisfaction to the beasts' dying screams. Meanwhile, the riders galloped back and took their place among the ranks.

"Ride!" he shouted. "Death to the beasts of Tion! Ride!" Opening his eyes, he took a deep breath. "For Ido and for Girdlegard!" He reached back to tap his horse with the flat of his sword, and they galloped away.

The whinnying steed was joined by five hundred others. The prince's cavalry poured over the hill in a stream of glittering silver. The drumming of two thousand hooves shook the earth, striking fear into the hearts of the approaching beasts.

The orcs and bögnilim turned tail and fled, but there was no escape from the onslaught of spears, armored horses, and steel. The stragglers were the first to die; the rest were trampled a few paces later. The air was wet with green blood, but neither the screams of the dying nor the sight of the wounded could slow the riders' advance.

He could have waited for us," grumbled Boïndil Double-blade of the clan of the Swinging Axes. The secondling warrior was making his way to the surface with incredible speed. "The cavalry has attacked; I can hear the horses." He gripped the metal rungs with his powerful fingers, climbing hand over hand. The only light in the shaft came from chinks around the doorway. It was barely enough to illuminate the ladder, but Boïndil—like all dwarves—was accustomed to seeing in the gloom. "What if the long-uns finish them off before we get there?" he said anxiously.

Tungdil Goldhand, climbing behind him, tried not to laugh. He knew that his friend was desperate to fight. The hot-blooded Boïndil, known to his kinsfolk as Ireheart, pursued his enemies with a vengeance and was bent on waging war. "I had a word with Prince Mallen; he promised to leave some for you."

Ireheart snorted, his long black plait swinging across his back. "You shouldn't make fun of me," he called back grouchily, climbing faster than before. He let out an excited shriek. "I think they're right above us; I can smell their stinking armor!" The weight of his chain mail, shield, and axes seemed not to bother him. One hand was already reaching for the door; a moment later, he found the bolt and opened the hatch. He poked his helmed head tentatively into the open.

"What can you see?" panted Tungdil, whose muscles were tiring. "Any sign of the orcs?"

"We've died and gone to Vraccas's smithy," whooped Boïndil. With a bloodcurdling "oink", he catapulted himself out of the shaft like a dwarven cannonball. "Stand clear, you little runts, I'm coming!"

Craning his neck, Tungdil looked up and saw the secondling silhouetted against the light. He seemed to be brandishing both axes as he flew through the air. Tungdil turned back to the others. "Quick, after him!" He hauled himself out of the shaft.

He hadn't expected the situation to be good, but it was worse than he had imagined. He was standing in an encampment of shrieking bögnilim and angry orcs. Tungdil's notion of the eternal smithy was rather different.

As soon as he was clear of the shaft, he reached behind him and drew his ax from the sheath on his back. The diamond-encrusted blade glittered fiercely in the crimson light of the dying sun.

At the sight of Keenfire, the orcs pulled up abruptly, grunting and shuffling back. They knew they were dealing with no ordinary warrior. Every beast in Girdlegard had heard how Tungdil Goldhand had slain the dark magus and sliced the demon in half with a glittering blade.

Crafted by the best dwarven artisans, with a blade made from the purest steel and forged in the fieriest furnace, encrusted with diamonds and inlaid with precious metals and tionium, Keenfire was a weapon of untold power and strength. The beasts were right to be afraid.

Summoning his courage, an orc stepped forward to challenge its bearer. He swung his cudgel with a snarl.

"Ah, a hero," growled Tungdil, dodging the blow. He hoisted Keenfire above his head, whirled round, and drew the ax across the orc's belly. The blade sliced through the fat-smeared armor as if it weren't there, spilling green gore and intestines. The disemboweled orc groaned and toppled to the ground. Tungdil raised his ax. "Any more takers?"

The orcs shrank away and hollered for their archers.

The dwarves behind Tungdil seized their chance and clambered out of the shaft. Soon there were thirty of them standing shoulder to shoulder in a circle, weapons hefted and ready to counter an enemy attack.

Meanwhile, Ireheart was rampaging through the hordes. He darted and bounded between the orcs and bögnilim, felling beast after beast. Tungdil lost sight of him, but he could hear the secondling's frenzied laughter as he baited the enemy by oinking like a runt.

Glancing up, Tungdil caught sight of Prince Mallen's cavalry approaching from the north. The riders were charging down the hillside in a line measuring five hundred paces across. Beasts and bögnilim were trampled to the ground.

"Get back, Boïndil!" he shouted anxiously. Behind him, the last of the dwarves were clambering out of the shaft: Tungdil's troop of a hundred warriors was complete.

"Aren't you coming?" called Boïndil cheerfully from somewhere in the scrum. His voice was barely audible amid the sound of buckling armor and the shrieks of the dying beasts.

Tungdil gripped the haft of Keenfire with both hands and squared his shoulders. His eyebrows knitted together in a determined frown. "I'm coming," he murmured softly. Then he raised his voice to a shout. "Drive them forward!"

His warriors let out a fearsome battle cry and fanned out,

brandishing their hammers and axes as they threw themselves on the startled beasts. Tungdil and Keenfire led the attack. Nothing could stop the formidable blade as it sang through the air, slicing shields, hewing armor and chain mail, severing limbs, and killing strings of orcs with every blow.

The dwarves carved a path through the hordes, undeterred by the stinking blood and the vile smell of their enemies' grease-encrusted armor. Green gore splashed from gushing wounds, and dismembered limbs thudded to the ground to be trampled underfoot by the indomitable dwarves. Soon the warriors at the rear were clambering over enemy corpses, but they pressed on regardless, determined to free Girdlegard from the pestilent orcs.

The resistance soon dried up. The bravest beasts died in combat, while those of a less courageous nature fled at the sight of the grim-faced dwarves.

"After them!" shouted Tungdil. The strategy paid off: Driven forward by the dwarves, the orcs and bögnilim collided with their comrades, who were running from Mallen and his men. The beasts were doomed.

Swinging his ax, Tungdil took aim at a couple of orcs. Even as the blade swung toward them, the beasts keeled over, felled by an invisible hand. To Tungdil's astonishment, Ireheart popped up from behind the corpses. He was soaked with the blood of countless orcs and his eyes were glinting dangerously.

"I was wondering where you'd got to," he said cheerfully. "What kept you? Don't tell me you were having trouble with the runts."

"I was yelling at you to come back," scolded Tungdil, shaking his head.

"Oh," said Boïndil. "I assumed you were talking to them." He pointed to the fleeing beasts. Sighing contentedly, he contemplated the battle. "A good end to the orbit, eh?" He raised his gore-spattered axes. "Come on, we're not finished yet." Suddenly a shadow crossed his face. "To be honest, scholar, it isn't much fun without my brother. The two of us would have wiped the floor with the runty little beasts. The next twenty are for him . . ." He charged off, bellowing ferociously at the top of his voice.

"His fiery spirit will be the death of him," murmured the dwarf next to Tungdil. Soon he too was slashing his way through the orcs.

Please, Vraccas, prayed Tungdil. *Don't let Boïndil come to any harm.* He dropped back a few paces and placed the bugle to his lips, playing a sequence of notes that Mallen would recognize as a signal that the dwarves had arrived and were closing in from the opposite side. There was a danger that Mallen's archers would loose their deadly arrows at the dwarven warriors, who were hard to spot from a distance, especially when surrounded by orcs. He waited for Mallen's bugle to reply, then caught up with the rest of his company, and launched himself into the fray.

The dwarves were still fighting at sundown and Mallen's infantry joined the action, which didn't please Boïndil at all. Some of the orcs and bögnilim were intent on escaping, but Mallen was ready for them, and the attempt to leave the battlefield was blocked by a unit of riders with lances.

By nightfall, there was barely room to step around the corpses and the channels of melt water were awash with green blood.

The dwarves and men met on the southernmost hill above Prince Mallen's camp. The prince turned his horse and cantered over to Tungdil, dismounted and held out his hand. Save for a nick in his forearm and some damage to his armor, he seemed to be unscathed. "Tungdil Goldhand," he said respectfully. "Praise the gods for your safe arrival."

It wasn't often that an ordinary dwarf was greeted so courteously by a human king. Tungdil grinned and took Mallen's hand. "Another decisive victory for the men and the dwarves." They gazed down at the battlefield; every last orc had been destroyed. "The good folk of Gauragar can sleep easy tonight."

The prince's face darkened. "Some are sleeping an eternal slumber. We saw plundered villages and burned-out houses on our way." He turned his face to the darkening sky and stared at the glittering stars. "You're right, though. The people of Gauragar need fear no more."

"Trust the long-uns to start without us," grumbled Boïndil in a voice that, while quieter than usual, was loud enough for the prince to hear. "You can't startle the runts with your horses and expect them to put up a fight!" Slowly, he crossed his powerful arms in an exaggerated movement in front of his chest and glared accusingly at the riders.

Mallen knew how to handle the hot-blooded warrior. Realizing that Boïndil hadn't intended him to hear, he decided not to argue. "We'll wait for you next time," he promised. "It's a shame you were late."

"*Late?*" echoed Boïndil indignantly, sticking his chin in the air and setting his beard aquiver. "It's a wonder we got here at all! The confounded earthquake caused havoc in the tunnels. Warped rails, boulders on the line— some of them bigger than a troll's backside! Just be thankful we—"

"That's enough, Boïndil," ruled Tungdil, interrupting the warrior's outburst. "He's right, you know: We were late." He turned to the prince and rolled his eyes apologetically, signaling that Mallen should let the matter lie. "Luckily for us, it didn't make any difference: We triumphed in the end."

Tungdil could see the amusement in the ruler's eyes. "What a victory for Girdlegard," agreed Mallen with an earnest nod. "We'd still be fighting if it weren't for the dwarves." It was unusual for him to tolerate rudeness, but no one had overheard the conversation, and Boïndil was a special case.

Boïndil considered the prince's conciliatory words and perked up considerably. He pulled off his helmet, letting his long black plait unfurl down his back, and rubbed his stubbly cheeks. Sweat was trickling down his face. "I suppose you're right," he said. "We had our fun with the orcs, and Vraccas will be happy with us for wiping out the beasts." He cleared his throat. "Sorry about my temper, Mallen," he mumbled, forgetting that it was customary to address a prince with more respect.

"Apology accepted," the ruler of Idoslane said magnani- mously. He pointed to the collection of tents where his army was camped. "I see the supply wagons have arrived. There's plenty of dark ale for everyone; perhaps you'll join us in celebrating the destruction of the beasts?"

"Don't mind if I do," said Boïndil, setting off toward

the tents. His thirst led him straight to the beer barrels, which were several times the standard size. The other dwarves looked questioningly at Tungdil, who nodded for them to follow. Mallen's men, buoyed by the prospect of a night without marching, hurried back to camp.

Mallen and Tungdil lingered on the hilltop, watching the victorious warriors gather around the campfires to eat and make merry.

"A cycle ago I was an exile," the prince said slowly. "I never thought I'd wear the crown of my forefathers. And I never imagined the rulers of Girdlegard would join together in an alliance of men, elves, and dwarves."

Tungdil thought about all that had happened to him. After traveling across Girdlegard on an errand for his magus, he had been nominated against his wishes as the high king's successor and journeyed to the Blacksaddle without realizing that Vraccas had chosen him to wield Keenfire and kill Nôd'onn on behalf of the dwarves. "Adversity brought us together. A cycle ago my kinsfolk were ready to wage war on the elves."

Mallen laughed grimly. "At least Nôd'onn was good for something: He put an end to our feuding."

Tungdil nodded. "Nôd'onn gave us the spark of solidarity, but it's our responsibility to keep it alive." He leaned forward, resting his weight on Keenfire. "We need an everlasting flame in which the bonds between us can be reforged." He looked down at the feasting and merriment below. "How many did you lose?"

"Fifty men and as many horses," said Mallen. "More were wounded, but we were heavily outnumbered. It could have been worse."

"We were lucky—a few gashes and a couple of broken bones, but nothing to speak of. I think Vraccas wanted us to live. He lost so many of his children at the Blacksaddle that his smithy must be full."

The prince laid a hand on the dwarf's shoulder. "Come, Tungdil Goldhand, we should celebrate our victory before the long journey home."

Tungdil knew he was right. Tomorrow he would set off through the tunnels, pack up his things at the secondling kingdom, and head west to the firstlings in the Red Range.

From there he would journey north with the dwarves who had elected to join him, and set up home in the ancient fifthling kingdom. In time, a new folk, descended from Borengar, Beroïn, and Goïmdil, would populate the Gray Range and Tungdil's promise to Giselbert Ironeye, founding father of the fifthlings, would be fulfilled.

He knew it wouldn't be easy. While the Stone Gateway was open, there was nothing to stop orcs and other beasts crossing into Girdlegard and taking up residence in the abandoned dwarven halls.

Don't let there be too many of them, he begged his creator as he walked down the hillside with Mallen. *We can't keep fighting forever.*

They were still some distance away when they heard Boïndil's voice. He was singing a ballad that their dead companion Bavragor Hammerfist had often sung.

At least Boïndil will be happy if we're overrun with beasts.

Tungdil took the beer offered to him by Mallen, and they clinked tankards to the warriors' claps and cheers. Tungdil was well pleased: It seemed the friendship pledged at the Blacksaddle had become a reality for the dwarves and men.

He watched as the assorted warriors sat around the fires and tucked into something that smelled tantalizingly of roasted meat and soup. Conversation focused on the recent victory. The men described how they felled an orc or killed a bögnil, waving their spoons as they talked. When they were done, the dwarves laughed appreciatively, lifted their bowls to slurp their soup and shared some good-humored banter with their new friends.

To think it took Nôd'onn to bring us together! Tungdil smiled and picked his way between the groups. He heard deep dwarven voices describing the beauty of their mountain homelands. A few paces further, a couple of Mallen's soldiers were teaching battle songs to a cluster of dwarves.

He watched and listened contentedly. *If only Balyndis were here as well . . .* Balyndis, the expedition's comely smith, had kindled the fires of his furnace, filling him with longing and desire. *At least I'd be able to—*

"I'm telling you, it's not just one," he heard a soldier say softly. The urgency in his voice distracted Tungdil from his thoughts. "It's spreading. I've seen three of them already."

Tungdil stopped beside him. "What's spreading?" he asked. "Three of what?" He noticed the badge on the man's lightweight leather armor; he was a scout.

"Dead glades," the man said hesitantly. "At least, that's what I call them." He pointed to the hills and ran a hand over the stubby blades of new grass. "It's like this: The Perished Land lost its power when Nôd'onn died. Palandiell blessed the earth and gave it new life, but the evil is buried below the surface." He glanced at the little group of men and dwarves who were putting away their food with varying regard to politeness. Everyone was listening attentively, especially the dwarves. "You haven't seen what I've seen," he continued. "There are pockets of Girdlegard where the evil has taken root."

"You mean the Perished Land is lurking below the surface?" said Tungdil, all other thoughts forgotten.

The scout nodded. "I talked to the locals near one of the glades. They told me about a few poor devils who strayed among the trees. Only three came back, and they attacked their neighbors, fighting and raging with the strength of ten until the villagers chopped off their heads. King Bruron heard about it and issued a decree. Now the dead glades are blocked with palisades, walls, and moats. No one can enter or leave—on punishment of death." He reached for his tankard. "Mark my words: It's spreading through the land."

Tungdil opened his mouth to reply but was rudely interrupted.

"There you are, scholar! Still moping about?" boomed Boïndil. At the sight of his friend, Tungdil stopped worrying about the insidious powers of the glades.

"You're not thinking about womenfolk, are you?" continued Boïndil. "I must say, for someone who doesn't know a thing about dwarf-women, you've bagged yourself a lovely lass!" He clinked tankards with Tungdil. "To the finest firstling smith! May she bring you true happiness." He paused, and when he continued, his voice was tinged with sadness. "I reckon you deserve it."

"You'll find someone who makes you happy soon

enough," said Tungdil, remembering his friend's tragic past. He raised his tankard. "How about a toast to Boëndal? I dare say I miss him as much as you do. He must be fit for battle by now."

Boïndil gulped down the rest of his beer. "I killed my happiness," he said slowly, his left hand tightening around the haft of his ax. "I killed it with my own hands." He stared absently into the fire. The flames flickered over his furrowed features, revealing his inner torment. "Now all I can do is fight."

They sat in silence until Boïndil started singing. One by one, the other dwarves joined in. It was another of Bavragor's songs.

> *On they march the orc invaders*
> *Driven by greed and lust*
> *Tion loves to plague our borders*
> *It was ever thus*
> *But the dwarves are here to fight them*
> *It was ever thus*
> *Dwarven axes, dwarven hammers*
> *Smash their skulls and spill their blood*
> *Until the orcs are slain and vanquished*
> *It was ever thus*
>
> *Tirelessly we guard our borders*
> *Doughty children of the Smith*
> *And when our kinsmen fall in battle*
> *It was ever thus*
> *Our souls are summoned to Vraccas's smithy*
> *It was ever thus*

Eternal warmth, eternal fire
It was ever thus

We seek no praise, we need no thanks
It was ever thus
We do our duty, we do it gladly
It was ever thus
Our ax is sharp, our chain mail glistens
It was ever thus
No beast can breach the dwarves' defenses
It was ever thus.

Mallen's men sat in hushed silence while the deep sonorous voices sung of honor, loyalty, and service to Girdlegard. The men, although ignorant of the dwarven language, had no trouble understanding the music, which seemed to come straight from the soul.

The chorus of voices echoed over the hills, carried across the valleys and soared to the stars.

The singing stirred the hearts and minds of everyone in the camp. Tungdil's thoughts were still buzzing when he made his way to bed. He remembered the scout's description of the dead glades. *What new evil is this, Vraccas? It seems our worries aren't over yet.* He decided to investigate further as soon as he had the chance. A moment later, he was asleep.

The next morning, it was time for the men and dwarves to part.

Tungdil and his warriors would travel underground through the network of tunnels to the secondling kingdom, while Mallen's men would make their way on foot, in carriages or on horseback to Idoslane.

The dwarves tramped through the battlefield and lowered themselves into the shaft, glad to get away from the circling ravens and the overwhelming stench.

Boïndil led the way. With every rung of the ladder he seemed to shed a little of the sorrow from the previous night. He was looking forward to the journey and to being reunited with his brother whom they had left in the care of the firstlings to recover from the älfar attack.

"It's the longest we've ever been parted," he said as Tungdil reached the bottom of the ladder. They set off toward the wagons that would carry them through the underground network.

"How are you coping?"

Boïndil tugged his braided beard and pulled out a stray leaf that didn't belong there. "It's hard," he admitted with a sigh. "You curb my temper better than anyone except Boëndal, but I'm calmer when he's around." He thought for a moment. "It's like hobbling around on one leg: I can manage, but part of me is missing. Boëndal knows what I'm thinking before I do. I'm not the same without him—even fighting doesn't help."

Tungdil sensed that he was holding back. "What is it, Boïndil? Something was bothering you last night."

"I . . . I'm not sure how to describe it," said Boïndil, considering. "I've got a bad feeling, almost like a chill. The worst of the winter is over, but my insides are frozen. What if Boëndal is in danger?"

They turned a corner and stopped abruptly. Tungdil, forgetting what he was about to say, gaped at the devastation.

The roof of the tunnel had caved in, and a wall of rubble blocked their way. Worse still, their wagons were buried beneath the rock.

Growling indignantly, Boïndil bent down and reached for a scrap of metal protruding from the mess. He pulled on it casually; then, muscles tensing, he gave it an almighty tug. The warped piece of wagon came away in his hand. "It was their blasted horses," he said irritably. "Their stupid clodhopping made the tunnel collapse." He tossed the metal away carelessly.

Tungdil suspected that the real blame lay with the quake. After Nôd'onn's defeat, the Blacksaddle had been hit by a terrible tremor that, judging by reports from the allies' scouts, had shaken every village in Girdlegard. It stood to reason that the ancient network of tunnels would be damaged.

I hope the dwarven kingdoms fared better. "Change of plan," he said to the others. He gestured to the surface. "We'll have to look for another entrance."

His confident manner belied his concern. Strictly speaking, it wasn't safe to travel through the tunnels until the structure had been checked. Certain sections of the network could be negotiated only by swooping downhill, and a collision would result in certain death.

Maybe we should do the whole journey on foot or by pony trap, he thought as they clambered to the surface.

It was three hundred miles to the Blacksaddle and another six hundred to the secondling kingdom in the Blue Range. Traveling underground, the distance could be covered in a matter of orbits; walking would take an eternity.

Does someone want to stop us getting to the firstlings?

Is Girdlegard in danger? His vague misgivings hardened into an unshakable sense of dread that yesterday's victory could do nothing to allay. At last they reached the surface and he hauled himself out of the shaft. "I want everyone moving as fast as possible. Get together in pairs or groups to carry the wounded. It's time we got home."

They used the sun to find their bearings and headed east. On reaching the crest of a hill above the battlefield, they came to a sudden halt.

"By Beroïn's beard, it's a camp!" exclaimed Boïndil, peering down the far slope. He sniffed the air and examined the ground; the earth had been churned up by thousands of boots. "Another army of runts," he growled. He set off at a run, followed by the others, and stopped at the bottom of the hill. Bending down, he ran a hand over the footprints, sniffed the soil and spat. "I'll give them a taste of my axes," he vowed, fixing his eyes on the broad channel of muddy earth that the orcish troopers had left in their wake. "They're heading north."

Tungdil looked in vain for evidence of a campfire. Two of his warriors called to him from a knoll; there were more orcish footprints and a couple of dead troopers under a tree. Ravens had clustered over the bodies and were squawking and fighting for their share of the prey. Judging by the evidence, the orcs had been killed the previous orbit. The birds had ripped away the dark green flesh, exposing the bone.

"They were watching us," said Tungdil, praying that Boïndil wouldn't chase after them. "They must have waited up here while their cousins were dying. They saw which way the battle was going, and left."

"Miserable cowards," snapped Ireheart, aiming a kick at one of the corpses. The nearest raven hopped away awkwardly, flapping its wings. "Trust the runty villains to hide from us. I wouldn't have minded a proper fight." He turned to Tungdil. "Four thousand of them, minimum. They're on their way north."

"It doesn't make sense," said Tungdil, baffled. He picked up an empty water pouch and dropped it hurriedly because of the awful smell. "The odds were in their favor; you'd expect them to attack." He paused, deciding what to do. "I want to see what they're up to," he announced, knowing that his plan would meet with the secondling's approval. "We'll follow them." Dwarves weren't particularly fleet of foot and orcs were naturally faster, but it was probably worth a shot.

"Huzzah!" whooped Ireheart. "Five score of us, four thousand of them: that's four hundred for every . . ." He broke off, remembering his brother in the firstling kingdom. Their reunion would be delayed. His face dropped.

"Hang on," said Tungdil. "We're not going to fight them; we're going to see what they're up to." He dispatched a couple of messengers to chase after Mallen and tell him the news. Another twenty warriors were instructed to spread out in all directions and warn the villagers of Gauragar about the orcish army. "Tell them to take to the hills or seek refuge in the towns," Tungdil instructed them.

"Do you see that?" said Boïndil, pointing at the orcish corpses. "Whoever beheaded them was wasting his time. They were stabbed to death first."

"I expect their chief was making an example of them," reasoned Tungdil. "He probably wanted to bring his troopers into line."

"Maybe," Boïndil said doubtfully, "but this one was stabbed three times before they chopped off his head. A chief would kill with a single strike." He raised his arm and made a noise like a whooshing ax. "It's a sign of strength—and precision."

"I suppose you've got a better explanation,' said Tungdil.

Boïndil was unconvinced by Tungdil's theory, but he couldn't think how else to explain the troopers' wounds. The discussion ended there.

They set off toward the north of Gauragar, the terrain becoming craggier and more barren with every mile. Green meadows gave way to bare earth, rocks, and the occasional tuft of grass. Thankfully, the orcs had left an unmistakable trail of food scraps and boot prints, which saved the dwarves the trouble of checking their route.

"I wonder if we'll see a dead glade," murmured Tungdil. "Did you hear what Mallen's scout was saying?"

Boïndil looked at him blankly. "A dead glade? Sounds like something to be avoided."

Tungdil filled him in on what the scout had said. "Dead glades are patches of forest inhabited by the Perished Land. King Bruron banned his subjects from approaching them because the evil affects their brains. You can tell a dead glade by the color of the trees—they're completely black."

"I thought the Perished Land had retreated," growled Boïndil. "We can't let it hide in the trees."

Tungdil kept his eyes on the churned-up path. "I'll ask

Andôkai to deal with it. The Perished Land is a canker. Who knows how far it might spread?"

Slowing his pace, the secondling fell back and instructed the rest of the company to look out for black trees. Anything suspicious should be reported to King Bruron.

During the second orbit of marching, the tracks turned sharply to the east, heading straight for the highest hill. The sudden change in direction and the unnecessary ascent indicated that the orcs had left their original course.

On the third orbit of marching, the dwarves, defying the odds, succeeded in closing on the longer-legged, faster orcs. They watched from a distance of barely two miles as the beasts swarmed up a hill and disappeared over the crest.

"Oink, oink!" grunted Boïndil in excitement.

Tungdil shot him a warning look. "We're not going to fight them," he said, laying a restraining hand on the secondling's arm. "We wouldn't stand a chance."

They set off in pursuit, this time taking care to stay hidden. They ascended the steep, stony slope and stopped just short of the crest.

Tungdil took off his helmet and his long brown hair billowed in the breeze. Keeping low to the ground, he edged forward and lifted his head slowly so that only his eyes and his crown were visible over the summit. Boïndil crawled across the trampled ground to join him.

Their excitement turned to alarm. The orcs were streaming into a dark, wooded area. Tungdil stared at the trees with their black trunks and bare branches. The beasts were heading for a pool of water, the inky content of which was lapping against the stony shore and staining it black.

Tungdil had a fair idea what he was looking at. "A dead glade," he whispered. "It stands to reason, I suppose."

Boïndil peered at the orcs incredulously. "What are they doing? Surely they don't mean to stay there? Even by orcish standards it's a hellhole."

Tungdil could tell that his friend was itching for a fight. "We're not going in," he said sternly. "We'll tell King Bruron that we've found another dead glade. He'll make sure that the orcs stay where they are—they won't be leaving here alive."

Raising his head a little, he surveyed the bare treetops and tried to gauge the size of the glade. It measured at least a mile in each direction, a vast blotch of foreboding and death. Just then a familiar odor came to him on the wind. He wrinkled his nose in disgust; it was the smell of brackish water that had permeated the drinking pouch, but this time it was coming from the sinister pool. "Fancy a sip?"

Boïndil made retching noises. "I'd sooner die than drink it."

Tungdil broke into a cold sweat as he remembered what the scout had said. *The humans who strayed into the dead glades were beheaded by their fellow men.* He stared at the inky pool. *What if the two dead orcs had drunk the fetid water and gone mad? Was that why they were stabbed and beheaded?* For want of an answer, he stopped worrying and crawled down the slope to make his report to the other dwarves. After a long wait, a delegation of Bruron's men arrived and Tungdil gave them a detailed account of what he had witnessed.

"It's time we went home," he announced. Even Boïndil

was happy with the change of plan. The prospect of seeing his brother outweighed the appeal of another battle, and he was looking forward to a solid dwarven meal, washed down with a tankard of Girdlegard's finest beer.

They set off on the long journey home.

Lorimbur's Folk,
Thirdling Kingdom,
Girdlegard,
Winter, 6234th/6235th Solar Cycle

Bislipur overreached himself," said a deep voice. The lofty walls threw back the words as a toneless echo, then it was quiet in the chamber. Only the fire continued to spit and crackle. An armored hand balled itself into a fist, the articulated fingers creaking as the spikes on the knuckles rose menacingly. "Cycles of plotting, and for what? I knew it would come to nothing."

"The other folks are weak, Your Majesty. Hundreds died at the Blacksaddle. The situation can still be turned to our advantage." The red glow from the fire accentuated the terrible scars on his gleaming scalp. Contrary to appearances, the lines had been cut by a thirdling tattooist, not an enemy sword. The sequence of dwarven runes spelled death and destruction to the enemies of his kingdom, and his artfully chiseled skull was fearsome to behold. "They lost their best warriors in the battle with Nôd'onn's hordes. It left them crippled and toothless."

His kinsman leaned forward. His long black hair was streaked with gray and braided into three plaits that sat neatly against his scalp. "We're not ready for open warfare."

The thirdling commander-in-chief shrugged, causing his tunic—a finely crafted shirt of interlocking plates and chain mail—to jangle. "Name me a better time, Lorimbas Steelheart. We haven't been as strong as this in two hundred cycles."

"My plan is more subtle, Salfalur Shieldbreaker," replied the thirdling king. His beard was stiff with dye, hanging like an overstarched pennant from his chin. Even when he talked, the red, gray, and brown whiskers stayed perfectly rigid. He leaned over the table and studied a map of Girdlegard. "Bislipur's mistake was to move too slowly. My goal shall be achieved within a decade." He rose from his marble chair and signaled for his commander-in-chief to follow. The hall where they held their briefings was dimly lit, with specks of iron pyrite glittering weakly in the dark stone walls. The two dwarves seemed to be walking through nothingness with only a smattering of sparkling stars.

A line of triangular pillars hewn from the flesh of the mountain stretched toward a set of stairs. Lorimbas ascended them quickly and threw open the doors to reveal a golden shrine.

Lorimbur, founding father of the thirdlings, rested here. His coffin stood upright, his marble likeness staring out from the lid. Dwarven runes made of diamonds, precious stones, and gems praised his deeds and exhorted his descendants to avenge and destroy.

Lorimbas bowed his head respectfully. "Too long have we endured their scorn," he muttered absently. He reached out with his right hand and caressed the cold effigy. "Too many times have we failed in our duty to avenge the injustices suffered by our founder. The time is ripe, thirdling father. Your bidding will be done, and your faithful son, Lorimbas Steelheart of the clan of the Stone Grinders, ruler of your children, will drive the descendants of Beroïn, Borengar, Goïmdil, and Giselbert from their kingdoms." He kneeled down, unhooked a three-flanged mace from his belt, and held it toward the dead king. "This I promise on my life."

Salfalur joined him at the coffin and dropped to his knees. There was no need for him to speak: Lorimbas had given full expression to the passion that burned wordlessly in his soul. Head bowed, with the lethal spike of his double-headed hammer inclined respectfully to the coffin, Salfalur vowed silently to uphold the thirdling cause.

Hours passed as they prayed together, so absorbed in their devotion that their aching arms and bruised knees barely registered in their minds.

At last Lorimbas rose, kissed the sacred boots of his ancestor and locked the shrine.

Salfalur lingered for a moment, gazing at the shimmering gold doors. Like all thirdlings, he loved the founder of his kingdom better than Vraccas, who had forsaken his bold-minded son.

Lorimbur's crime was to insist on his right to choose his own name. The flint-willed dwarf, who possessed a special measure of that dwarven quality referred to as obduracy, had argued until he achieved his purpose, but in so doing he displeased the dwarven god. His brothers each received a talent, but Lorimbur was condemned to mediocrity, and his descendants never fully mastered the dwarven arts.

Salfalur leaned forward and studied the doors. In his eyes, the inscriptions looked beautiful, but a firstling would compare the metalwork to the imperfect efforts of a human smith.

They'll pay for their arrogance, he vowed darkly, flexing his muscles. He wore heavy vambraces equipped with knives to protect his arms in battle. "What did you have in mind, Your Majesty?" he asked, bowing his head as he descended backward from the shrine.

The king followed him down the steps and they returned to the marble table to study the map. "We'll drive a wedge between them and shatter their alliance," said the king, reaching for a pitcher and filling their silver tankards with beer. The index finger of his right hand hovered over the Blacksaddle. "The thirdlings built that stronghold, and I intend to get it back. It's ours by right." He raised his tankard. "To our cousins, for restoring its defenses." He drank thirstily and replaced the tankard on the table with a noisy clunk. "Well?" he prompted, eying his silent commander. "What do you say?"

The plan made little sense to Salafur, who didn't mind airing his concerns. "What use is the stronghold, Your Majesty? If it's the tunnels you're interested in, we've got access to them here."

Lorimbas smiled. "The tunnels . . . exactly. Remember when we first heard how our stronghold had been taken over by the dwarven army? I sent our scholars to do some digging in the archives. They came back with some fascinating information about the Blacksaddle. Our dwarven cousins have no idea."

Salfalur sipped his beer and looked at the king intently. "They've been ensconced in the stronghold for orbits. How can you be sure?"

"Trust me, faithful warrior, they know nothing. If our cousins had discovered the Blacksaddle's secret, every dwarf in Girdlegard would know of it by now. News like this travels fast, and our eyes and ears are everywhere. Our spies tell us everything—and they're more subtle than Bislipur." He handed Salfalur the archivists' findings: a packet of manuscripts tied with a ribbon and a stack of engraved tablets.

The commander-in-chief glanced at them briefly and waved his hand dismissively. "They're in the old tongue," he snapped. "I can't read them."

Lorimbas stared at Salfalur's bloodshot left eye, the distinguishing feature of the Red Eye clan, and nodded in satisfaction. "That's the beauty of it—hardly anyone can read the ancient script. The Blacksaddle will be in our hands before anyone fathoms its secret."

"True," said Salfalur slowly. He took a deep breath. "But how will we persuade the other folks to leave the stronghold? To fight them would be—"

"None of our kinsmen will lose their lives." The king laughed cruelly and leaned back in his chair. "We won't be doing the fighting. We'll get someone to do it for us."

"Who would fight for the thirdling cause?"

"King Bruron of Gauragar."

Salfalur's bushy brown eyebrows knitted together in a frown. "This is worthy of Bislipur," he said reprovingly.

"I thought we'd agreed that scheming is useless. So far I can't see the merit of the plan." He wrapped his hands around the haft of his hammer, an imposing weapon that almost matched him in height.

"I should have explained myself more clearly from the start," the king said soothingly. "Our archives turned out to be most instructive. The scholars found an ancient treaty dating back to the end of the 4000th cycle. It seems our ancestors signed a pact with Gauragar, which grants our kingdom everlasting ownership of Cloudpiercer in payment for our help."

"You mean, the Blacksaddle?" Salfalur knew the stories about the mountain's history. According to legend, the Blacksaddle was once a mighty peak named Cloudpiercer, the summit of which stretched thousands of paces into the sky. Cloudpiercer stood taller and prouder than any other peak in Girdlegard. It was tipped with snow throughout the seasons and its loftiest flanks were made of pure gold. After trying and failing to mine the treasure, the people of Gauragar had called on the dwarves to help them.

"Are you saying our kinsmen helped the humans to mine the gold, just like the legend says?"

"Exactly. The dwarves of Lorimbur were the first to send a delegation to Gauragar." Lorimbas gestured to the map. "They arrived at Cloudpiercer and succeeded in burrowing their way through the mountain and digging a tunnel to the top. They hollowed out the mountain and carried off the gold. In return for their help, they demanded a share of the treasure and ownership of the mountain. The king of Gauragar signed a treaty to that effect."

Salfalur knew the rest from a song that his aunt had taught him as a child. The dwarves and men had quarreled over the gold, prompting Cloudpiercer to erupt in fury and shake the miners from its core. The rest of the mountain was riddled with tunnels and the peak collapsed. From that moment on, the mountain simmered with hatred and harbored a murderous grudge against the races of dwarves and men.

"What if the mountain recognizes us and tries to bury us under its weight?" he asked nervously.

"That part of the story is almost certainly hogwash, but we'll be careful all the same." The king was still staring at the map. "Bruron should receive my missive in the next few orbits."

"Bruron is a man without principles. He'll never honor the word of his ancestors," Salfalur predicted dourly. "Besides, without the help of the other folks, his kingdom would have fallen to the magus. He'll deny all knowledge of our agreement rather than risk the anger of the dwarves."

"Humans will do anything for gold; it's simply a case of scale. A single coin won't buy a sovereign's loyalty, so I'm offering two full chests. How can he refuse? His kingdom was ransacked by orcs and his people will be hungry. He needs money to buy grain." Lorimbas sat back and folded his hands across his chest. "You see, Salfalur, I can fight with my head as well as my mace. I can outscheme poor Bislipur."

Salfalur's tattoos snaked across his face as he ground his teeth. "I don't doubt it, Your Majesty. But what did Bislipur *achieve*?"

"Patience, old friend. The first stage of the plan deals only with Bruron."

"Where would you strike next?"

Lorimbas's finger hovered over the map and landed on the kingdom of Idoslane. "Orcs are marauding through Mallen's kingdom. He'll want to destroy them, or drive them into Toboribor. We'll wait until he's busy; then we'll pay him a visit."

"Mallen and Goldhand are friends. All the money in Girdlegard won't change his allegiance." The commander-in-chief frowned. "I'm sorry, Your Majesty, but scheming won't get you further than poor Bislipur."

"You'd rather we went to war," the king said coldly, fixing his commander with his dark brown eyes. "I don't doubt that the odds have never seemed better. Our army is strong, and the others are weak from their battle with Nôd'onn." He broke off and raised a warning finger. "But numbers count for nothing while the alliance still holds. We need to kindle the hatred between our cousins and the elves. Once we've stoked the fires of enmity, we'll forge new wedges—wedges that will isolate Gandogar and the others from the humans and the elves."

It took more than flashing eyes and a raised voice to intimidate Salfalur. "I wish you every success," he said, undaunted. "What are my orders?"

"Tell our mercenaries to listen for the codeword *Lorimbur's Revenge*. When the time comes, they must lay down their arms and fight only in self-defense. Tell them not to be tempted by offers of gold." The king rested his chin on his hands and fell silent. Dark thoughts forced their way into his mind, swamping him with fear, self-doubt, and despair.

"Are you worried about your daughter?"

Lorimbas sat up sharply, startled from his thoughts. Salfalur was right; he was worried about his daughter, who had been missing for half a cycle. "Still no news," he said with a shake of the head. There had been no message, no sighting, not the slightest indication of where she was or whether she was alive. "I'd sooner carry all the peaks in Girdlegard than endure this silence."

"Have faith, Lorimbas. She's a good daughter, and an excellent wife." Salfalur's face softened for the first time that orbit. "I trained her in the art of combat, and you taught her to dissemble; she won't let us down." He stared at the fireplace, watching the flickering flames. "It's time she sent word." His left hand clenched into a fist, his gauntlet creaking.

Lorimbas sighed. *A single word, a single syllable would calm our fears . . .* "It's hard, I know. I miss my daughter, you miss your wife—but what choice did we have? No one else could achieve our purpose without arousing their suspicions." He was trying to drown out the voice of his conscience, which reminded him that he was endangering his youngest daughter by sending her on a mission that relied on total secrecy. He bowed his head and closed his eyes. "I had no choice," he whispered.

II

Beroïn's Folk,
Secondling Kingdom,
Girdlegard,
Winter, 6234th/6235th Solar Cycle

It's still a horse—just a small one, that's all," grumbled Boïndil, sliding down from the pony's saddle. He gave himself a good shake, showering sand from his clothes and beard. "If Vraccas had wanted us to be riders, he would have given us better padding." He winced as he rubbed his backside.

"You'd be complaining about your blisters if we'd walked," retorted Tungdil with a smile. Like Boïndil, he was coated from head to toe with sand, fine grains of which had snuck through his garments, clinging to the fabric and rubbing against his skin. He dismounted and ran a hand over his pony's mane. "Don't listen to the old curmudgeon," he told the pony. "You did an excellent job."

They were standing on the outermost terrace of Ogre's Death, one of the most imposing strongholds in Girdlegard, home to the secondling dwarves. Its keep had been hewn into the rock, with battlements extending down the mountainside in four separate terraces.

Until recently, no one had believed that Ogre's Death would ever be conquered, but Nôd'onn had proved that the defenses could be breached. With the help of the treacherous Bislipur, the magus's beasts had stormed the stronghold and laid waste to the secondlings' halls.

Now the stronghold was a hive of activity. Cranes were lifting, wheels turning, winches hoisting, and saws slicing through the rock. Dust filled the air, and the Blue Range echoed with a thousand hammers and chisels as hordes of industrious masons rebuilt what the beasts had destroyed. The rubble from the ruined battlements had been carted away and the fortifications were rising again, only this time the defenses would be bigger, heavier, stronger. Soon the secondlings would be safe from invaders once more.

It's good to see order returning to the kingdom, thought Tungdil, trying to overcome his nagging fears. *I shouldn't worry so much . . .*

Boïndil interrupted his thoughts. "Ha, look at Ogre's Death, rising from the ruins," he said proudly. "The secondling flags are flying from the stronghold, and the bones of the invaders have been scattered across the range. They thought they'd destroyed us, but our spirit can't be crushed." Quickening his pace, he made straight for the vast gateway, eight paces wide and ten paces high, leading from the uppermost terrace to the underground halls.

Tungdil looked up at the flagpoles. On the last stage of their journey through Sangpûr, the flags had been visible as tiny squares of cloth, but now he could make out the details. The colors of the firstlings and fourthlings flew proudly beside the crests of the seventeen secondling clans.

He tapped his forehead. *The assembly meeting!* It had slipped his mind entirely. "By my beard, Boïndil," he called out to the secondling, who was practically at the gateway. "Another orbit, and we would have missed the coronation."

Boïndil stopped in his tracks. "To think a pack of orcs and bögnilim could make us forget a thing like that! It wouldn't have happened if Boëndal had been with us." A look of consternation crossed his face and he sniffed the air anxiously. "It's all right," he declared. "We haven't missed anything important. They haven't brought out the food."

The other dwarves caught up and they set off together through the gateway, into the secondling kingdom. The passageway delved through the mountain, leading to ornately carved chambers supported by soaring columns. Ahead of them towered an enormous stone statue of Beroïn seated on a white marble throne. They filed between his feet and entered the corridor leading to the assembly hall.

"Remember what happened last time?" Boïndil asked softly.

"How could I forget?" Every detail of that orbit was etched on Tungdil's mind. On arriving at Ogre's Death, he and the twins had entered the great hall to find the delegates warring among themselves. Soon after, he had embarked on a long journey—a journey that turned him into a proper dwarf.

"It's a mercy to be out of the light," said Boïndil, whose hair had been bleached by the harsh desert sun. "We belong in the mountains, as Vraccas intended." He gave his plait a good shake to dislodge the sand. "Do you think the delegates will be arguing again?"

Tungdil shook his head. "Gandogar is the legitimate heir, and no one could dispute his right to the throne.

He proved his character as soon as he freed himself from Bislipur's wiles."

The secondling grinned. "Not as much as you proved yours."

"I don't want to be high king, Boïndil. My calling lies elsewhere." Raising his hand decisively, he knocked three times, took a deep breath, and pushed open the mighty stone doors.

Light streamed toward them. Blinking, Tungdil gazed in horror at the ruins of the hall.

Barely half of the towering cylindrical columns had survived the beasts' invasion, and it was only thanks to the secondlings' expert masonry that the ceiling hadn't collapsed.

Tungdil's heart sank as he looked at the desecrated tablets and bas-reliefs on the walls. The orcs had attacked the artwork with clubs and cudgels, smashing the marble and destroying the carefully chiseled chronicle of past victories and heroic deeds.

Glancing at his companion, he saw the secondling's expression change from horror to fury. Boïndil, already a ferocious orc-slayer, was planning his revenge.

Lanterns and braziers lit the chamber, casting a warm glow over five magnificent chairs, one for each folk, arranged in a semi-circle around a marble table.

Tungdil spotted Gandogar Silverbeard, ruler of the fourthlings and head of Goïmdil's line. Seated beside him were Xamtys II of the clan of the Stubborn Streaks, queen of the firstlings and ruler of Borengar's folk, and Balendilín Onearm of the clan of the Strong Fingers, former counselor to Gundrabur Whitecrown, the late high king. Balendilín had been crowned king of the secondlings after Gundrabur's death. The remaining delegates—chieftains and elders from the firstling, secondling, and fourthling kingdoms—had taken their places in the elegantly carved pews behind their leaders and were talking among themselves.

Scanning the ranks of the firstlings, Tungdil found Balyndis and gave her a special smile. Then it was time to address the assembly. Orbits earlier, he had reached a decision regarding his future, and he intended to see it through.

His eyes lingered on the two unoccupied chairs and the empty pews behind them.

One of the chairs was reserved for the king of the thirdlings, although none of their number was likely to attend. The other belonged to the late king of the fifthlings, whose folk were no more.

If everything went to plan, one of the chairs would soon be filled.

"Monarchs, elders, chieftains," he began loudly, although his heart was beating furiously in his chest. "I salute the assembly."

"Can't you talk normally?" hissed Boïndil, rolling his eyes. He was secretly in awe of his friend, who spoke with the authority and facility of a king. Tungdil's sixty cycles in Lot-Ionan's school had expanded his mind and honed his reason, making him wiser and more knowledgeable than most dwarves twice his age.

"The finest and best dwarves of the three dwarven folks are gathered here for the second time in four hundred cycles to elect a new high king." Tungdil stepped away from the doors and took up position in front of the table where the dwarven rulers were seated. He kept his right hand on Keenfire to steady his nerves. "This time there won't be any last-minute challenges—at least not from me."

A faint smile crossed Balendilín's timeworn features, and downy-cheeked Xamtys raised her eyebrows in surprise. To everyone's relief, Gandogar laughed good-humoredly, allowing the other delegates to chuckle as well.

Tungdil pointed to the empty chair belonging to the fifthlings. "Most of you know by now that I'm a thirdling. I'd give anything not to be descended from Lorimbur, but a dwarf can't choose his lineage. My heart doesn't burn with vengeance, and maybe, Vraccas willing, there are other thirdlings like me who weren't born with hatred in their blood. I feel a bond with my fellow dwarves—one of them, especially." He turned to look at Balyndis and allowed himself to bask for a moment in her dazzling smile. Then he strode to the empty chair on Gandogar's right.

"Some of you think I belong in the thirdling kingdom," he continued, placing his hands on his diamond-studded weapons belt, a gift from Giselbert Ironeye. He paused for a moment, remembering his parting conversation with the fifthling monarch. "But I see my place elsewhere."

Leaving the chair, he made his way to the fifthling benches and stepped onto the front pew for everyone to see him.

"I made a promise to Giselbert Ironeye. He asked me to drive the orcs from his kingdom and rebuild his halls." Pausing, he allowed the delegates a few moments to imagine the revival of the fifthling folk. "Giselbert gave me this belt in remembrance of the fifthlings, who defended their kingdom to the last. Their spirit was stronger than the curse of the Perished Land, and they served the Smith in death and beyond. For a thousand cycles they tended the Dragon Fire furnace and kept its flames alive. Without the fifthlings, Keenfire would never have been forged." He drew the ax and held it aloft for the delegates to see. "Your Majesties," he began, turning to the dwarven rulers, "you promised me enough masons and warriors to rebuild the fifthling kingdom and seal the Northern Pass. It was a truly generous offer, but no dwarf should be forced to leave his kingdom at his monarch's command. Those who wish to remain with their clansfolk should do so, but those who want to join me will be welcomed with open arms."

He sat down on the pew, placing Keenfire in front of him. The ax head jangled against the marble, echoing through the hall.

He wasn't surprised to see Boïndil striding purposefully toward him. The secondling plumped down beside him, and a moment later, Balyndis took a seat on his right.

Tungdil was thrilled to see one delegate after another stand up and join him. At last, half of the fifthling pews were taken. Among Tungdil's new companions were seven chieftains, who promised to ask the rest of their clansmen to make their homes in the fifthling halls.

Balendilín sat up in his chair, the marble trinkets in his graying beard clinking softly. "Tungdil Goldhand, your wisdom is proof, if proof be needed, that you belong among Girdlegard's monarchs, not on the pews. I know that you are not inclined to push yourself forward, but the dwarves of the fifthling kingdom will recognize your qualities. At our

next meeting, you will be seated among the rulers, I'm sure."
He turned to the delegates, his long gray hair curling about
his shoulders like silvery wool. "We are gathered here
today to settle a matter of great importance. Gundrabur
Whitecrown, the late high king, was called to Vraccas's
smithy, leaving an empty throne. The new high king must
be a strong leader who will set our course through good
times and bad." He unfurled a roll of parchment with his
one good hand. "Gandogar Silverbeard of the clan of the
Silver Beards, ruler of the fourthlings and head of Goïmdil's
line, are you ready to assert your claim to the high king's
throne?" he asked, repeating the words that he had spoken
at an earlier assembly, many orbits ago.

The fourthling monarch rose. "Unyielding as the rock
from which we were created and keen as this blade is my
will to defend our race against its foes," came his solemn
reply. "Bislipur cast a shadow over my mind, but I have
driven out the darkness. With a clear heart and mind I
swear loyalty to the dwarven folks whose welfare will be
my guiding concern. Let Vraccas and the dwarven monarchs
witness my oath."

Balendilín nodded. "Gandogar Silverbeard has asserted
his claim." He raised his voice. "Will anyone challenge
him?"

"What are you waiting for?" hissed Boïndil, prodding
Tungdil in the ribs. "Another of your fancy speeches, and
the throne will be yours."

The one-armed king dropped the parchment onto the
table. "The succession is uncontested: Gandogar shall be
crowned." He sounded his bugle, producing a long, drawn-
out tone.

The doors opened, and a procession of warriors from the folks of Beroïn, Borengar, and Goïmdil marched into the hall, bearing the crown and ceremonial hammer on an ornamental shield. Studded with gemstones, etched with magnificent runes, and inlaid with intarsia of vraccasium, silver, and gold, the hammer brought together the finest artisanship from all the folks, symbolizing the high king's power.

The procession stopped in the middle of the hall and the warriors got down on one knee. Balendilín walked over to them and signaled for Gandogar to approach. "Chosen by the united will of the folks to reign over us," he said solemnly, lowering the crown gently onto the fourthling's head. "Gandogar Silverbeard of the clan of the Silver Beards, ruler of the fourthlings, head of Goïmdil's line—dwarf of all dwarves." He signaled for Gandogar to take the hammer.

Reverently, the new high king reached forward and wrapped his fingers around the handle. The hammer was heavier than he had expected, and it took both hands to pick it up.

The delegates left their pews and dropped on one knee, raising their weapons and hailing the new king as they had once hailed King Gundrabur.

Tungdil listened to the jangling chain mail and scanned the faces of the delegates, his kinsfolk, the children of the Smith, united as never before. He felt a shiver of excitement.

Gandogar raised the hammer and brought it down sharply against the marble, signaling for the delegates to rise. "Monarchs, chieftains, and elders, you have heard my oath. If, in time, my actions give the lie to my intentions, I call on you to remind me of these words."

He left the table and stopped at the place where five marble tablets bearing Vraccas's commandments had been destroyed by Bislipur's ax. "That which was brought down by treason will rise again in an era of unity and peace." He ascended the dais and sat on his throne. "Together we will rebuild our kingdoms—but first we must celebrate. Let the feasting begin!"

The assembled dwarves erupted in cheers and applause, shouting their approval and banging their weapons against their shields. The jubilation showed no sign of stopping, but at last the clamor gave way to hearty laughter, spontaneous singing, and a round of toasts as stewards arrived with pitchers and platters, and the rest of the secondling folk poured into the hall.

Horns sounded, and the music began, the drummers beating out a lively rhythm. The exuberance was catching, and soon heavy-booted Boïndil was tapping his feet in time with the songs. For once he forgot all thought of battle and stopped worrying about his brother in the distant Red Range. Tankard in hand, he watched the festivities and enjoyed the brief respite.

Tungdil looked around for Balyndis. "They're dancing the gloomy memories from their souls," said a voice behind him.

"It's time they enjoyed themselves, don't you think?" said Tungdil, looking into Balendilín's worried eyes. Balendilín was a new king, but an old dwarf, and his face was worn with care. "Maybe you should join them."

Balendilín chuckled softly and stroked his beard.

"Why not? The orcs were kind enough to leave me both legs—I'll find myself a maiden and twirl her around the dance floor like a freshly hewn dwarf."

"What's the matter?" asked Tungdil. "Bad news from abroad?"

"*No* news," said the king, sighing. He glanced in Boïndil's direction to make sure he wasn't listening. "I haven't heard anything from the Red Range in orbits. It's possible that the tunnels are blocked, but . . ." He left the sentence hanging, but it was clear that he suspected something worse.

Balyndis, overhearing their conversation, looked alarmed. "Are you talking about Nôd'onn?" She searched their faces. "He warned us about a danger in the west." She took a deep breath, forcing down her fear. "It's all right, though—West Ironhald is unassailable. Nothing will cross the border with my kinsmen standing guard."

Tungdil reached for her hand. "I'm sure you're right," he said, trying to mask his trepidation. "The firstlings are strong enough to see off any threat." Balyndis saw through his attempt to reassure her, but she was comforted that he had tried.

There was silence for a moment. Everyone was remembering how Nôd'onn, after killing four magi and terrorizing all Girdlegard, had spoken with terror of the threat from the west.

"Queen Xamtys will leave for the Red Range tomorrow," said Balendilín at last. "She's worried as well."

"We'll go too," decided Tungdil. He gave Balyndis's hand a reassuring squeeze. "Her Majesty will be glad of some company, and it's a chance for us to recruit any firstlings who want to follow their chieftains to the Gray Range."

There was a third reason for accompanying Xamtys that he didn't mention to the others. He wanted to be on hand with Keenfire in case the firstling kingdom was really in danger. The diamond-encrusted blade had proved its worth against Nôd'onn, and he was sure that it would make short work of any threat.

Balyndis looked at him gratefully and gave him a quick kiss while Balendilín wasn't looking.

"You can't fool me," said Boïndil, joining the little group. "You're worried about something. It's the Red Range, isn't it?"

"What do you mean?" asked Balyndis anxiously.

"It was this, um . . . It was the thing that fell from the sky." Boïndil put his tankard to his lips. Dark beer trickled down his beard, mingling with the dust from the journey. "Something happened that night." His voice was so low that the others could barely hear him through the music and laughter. "Boëndal is my twin; I can tell if he's in trouble."

Balyndis didn't want to hear any more, but she found herself asking, "What sort of trouble?"

Boïndil took another draft of beer. "He was fine at first—the firstlings looked after him well, and the arrow wounds were healing." He put down the empty tankard and wiped the froth from his lips. "That was before the comet." He paused and swallowed. "I don't know what's happened to him; I just feel cold."

Balyndis gasped. "Vraccas protect us."

Tungdil was angry with himself for not having listened

more carefully when Boïndil brought up the subject before. "Why didn't you tell me sooner?" he asked him, laying a hand on his shoulder. Boïndil's chain mail felt strangely cold.

"We had to see off the runts. Vraccas knows I wanted to go to Boëndal, but our duty lay elsewhere. I've been too worried to sleep, too worried to think—and now the beasts have been dealt with and we're free to go." A shadow crossed his face. "At least we'll know for certain before too long." Excusing himself with a nod, he picked up his tankard and went in search of beer to wash away his gloomy thoughts.

Balendilín gazed after him anxiously. "Knowledge can be worse than uncertainty. I hope his fears prove unfounded." He laid a hand on Tungdil's wrist. "Do you need anything for the journey?" he asked more brightly. "The orcs spoiled most of our provisions, but I'm sure I can find you a bit of cheese, some pickled camla-moss, and a few dried pharu-mushrooms to keep you going." His brown eyes settled on Balyndis, and he smiled at her encouragingly.

Tungdil decided it was time to tell the others about the orcs who had escaped the allied army. He described the dead glade. "It was almost as if they were being drawn there. What if the Perished Land is gathering its troops?"

"They must have a reason for stopping there," the secondling king said doubtfully. "You'd think they'd find themselves a better hiding place—it's too small for an army of orcs, and there can't be much food. Bruron's men will starve them out in no time. The beasts would be better off in Toboribor, holed up in their caves."

"I don't see the sense in it either," admitted Tungdil. "Mallen's scout said that dead glades have the power to drive humans insane. If I didn't have the fifthling kingdom to worry about, I'd look into it myself."

Balendilín shook his head. "Bruron and Mallen can take care of the orcs. The beasts are their concern; the Gray Range is yours." He took his leave.

Balyndis sighed. "I thought killing Nôd'onn would put an end to our problems, but Vraccas hasn't finished with us yet."

Tungdil smiled and ran a hand tenderly over her face. Like all dwarf-women, she had a fine layer of down on her cheeks. It generally got thicker and more noticeable with age. "I can't tell you how good it is to see you. I dreamed about you while I was away." He paused. "To be honest, I couldn't stop thinking about you." He noticed that she was wearing a new necklace, a finely forged chain of steel links studded with tiny gold balls. He knew at once who had made it.

"You obviously weren't as busy as me," she said with a smile, watching the slow, stately movements of twelve dwarves who were performing a dance in honor of the dwarven miner. "We had the furnaces roaring from morning till night; I barely left the anvil." She raised an arm. "See those muscles? They're twice their usual size. The orcs made such a mess that I could stay a hundred cycles and still have work to do. I haven't had time for dreaming."

He pointed to her necklace. "Oh, really," he said teasingly. "But you found a few spare seconds to forge yourself a chain?"

She smiled. "You noticed!" The krummhorns fell silent and Balyndis joined the enthusiastic applause.

Tungdil laid an arm around her shoulders. "I'd rather you didn't spend the next hundred cycles at the secondlings' anvils; I need you in the Gray Range with me." He looked her in the eye. "I'm not asking because I need a good smith; I'm asking because I need *you*. The past few orbits have made me realize that I never want to be away from you again."

Balyndis, unaccustomed to such frankness, searched his face. "Tungdil Goldhand, what you're proposing isn't to be taken lightly."

"I know," he said, meeting her gaze. "But think of the memories we share already—and our adventures aren't over yet. I want us to still be talking and remembering in four hundred cycles' time. And of course we'll tell the stories to our children, who'll think we're making it up." He kissed her on the top of the head. "Balyndis Steelfinger of the clan of the Steel Fingers, daughter of Borengar and smith of the firstling kingdom, what would you say if a thirdling of unknown origin and no proper dwarven upbringing were to ask you to be joined with him by the iron band?"

Balyndis was so overwhelmed that she took a while to answer. "We'll never be apart again," she said at last. "Our hearts are joined already—they've been joined for a while."

She started forward and threw her arms around him. Hugging her close, Tungdil pressed his face against her skin, filling his nostrils with her scent. He was still hugging her, eyes shut and perfectly contented, when he heard her say, "Yes, Tungdil Goldhand. I want to be with you always."

It wouldn't have mattered if the great hall had caved in on him or all the beasts in Girdlegard had torn him apart or a hundred arrows had pierced his chest; he would have died a happy dwarf.

23 Miles Southwest of Dsôn Balsur,
Kingdom of Gauragar,
Girdlegard,
Winter, 6234th/6235th Solar Cycle

Looking out from the top of the highest watchtower, Liútasil surveyed row upon row of brightly colored tents, ordered strictly by unit and rank. He ran a comb through his hair. The filigree teeth, inlaid with mother-of-pearl to stop them snagging on his fine auburn hair, separated the long shimmering strands, easing the occasional tangle.

The elven lord had ordered his warriors to pitch their tents and put up a palisade around the camp's perimeter, bounded by a moat seven paces deep and seven paces wide. Here, on the outskirts of the älfar kingdom, neither man nor elf would sleep soundly unless every measure had been taken to make the camp secure.

The allied strategy had been decided at the Blacksaddle. Mallen was to deal with the orcs and bögnilim, using the superior speed of his cavalry to chase the fleeing beasts, while Liútasil and the other human generals marched north to attack the elves' dark cousins in Dsôn Balsur and drive them out of Girdlegard.

The lord of Âlandur monitored the activity in the camp. His sharp ears picked up snatches of conversation carried to him by the wind, and his sensitive nostrils detected the odor of humans and horses, mixed with smoke from campfires where men and women were roasting meat. Some of the soldiers were preparing for battle, whetting swords, sharpening lances, and dipping arrowheads into animal excrement to ensure that every missile, whether it pierced a heart, grazed a shoulder, or nicked an ankle, had a chance of causing death. A few of the men, desperate to forget their fear of the älfar, were swigging wine, while others lolled drunkenly on their bedrolls.

"Humans," he said pityingly, putting away his comb. Elves knew better than to waste their strength before a battle, but human soldiers did everything in their power to incapacitate themselves.

Without them, though, the campaign would never succeed. The elves were outnumbered by the älfar, and they didn't have the means to conquer Dsôn Balsur on their own.

Liútasil knew how much he owed to the humans and his traditional enemies, the dwarves. Before the battle of the Blacksaddle, no one had doubted that Âlandur would fall to the älfar, but now, with the enemy retreating, his kingdom was safe. The last few skirmishes had been rearguard actions on the part of the älfar, summoned to Dsôn Balsur to defend their home.

Sitalia, grant me patience, he prayed. Down below, a group of men were brawling over the last skin of wine. Order was restored when their superior had them beaten into their tents by his guards.

On occasions such as this, Liútasil despaired of his new allies, who had nothing in common with the elves. He sometimes questioned the wisdom of fighting side by side with humans and dwarves, but Sitalia seemed to approve of the alliance. *I'll trust in your will . . .*

He left the wooden platform and swiftly descended the ladder. On reaching the ground, he strode past the rows of canvas toward the purple assembly tent to debrief his scouts.

Seated at the conference table were the military commanders of Gauragar, Tabaîn, Weyurn, Sangpûr, Urgon, and Rân Ribastur. The generals were waiting in silence, sipping tumblers of water served by their guards. Liútasil was thankful that none were drinking wine or brandy.

Three elves in leather armor were standing in a corner of the tent. They were scouts, newly returned from the field. The filth of Dsôn Balsur clung to their boots, and their lightweight armor was torn and bloodied. News of the älfar didn't come cheap.

Liútasil greeted the generals with a nod and signaled that he was ready. The scouts began their report in elvish and he summarized the intelligence for the men. "Our enemies have withdrawn to the heart of their kingdom. Traps are in place to hinder our advance. The Perished Land has taken root around Dsôn Balsur and the trees are black with malice. Our first challenge is to pass through the forest unharmed."

"I say we wait," interrupted the commander of Sangpûr's army. "The Perished Land is retreating from Girdlegard and the forest may yet recover. A march through whipping branches and twisting trunks would be a disaster for the men's morale. I can't put them through it." The other generals nodded in agreement.

"I understand your concerns," said Liútasil, sitting down and resting his arms on the table. "But I know the forest in question. The land once belonged to my people, and the trees are too old. Even if the soil recovers, the forest has been drinking the poison for hundreds of cycles, and the evil has blackened its soul. With the defeat of the Perished Land, the forest is dying and turning to stone, but it's a slow process and we can't afford to wait. We routed the älfar at the Blacksaddle; we need to attack straightaway."

His speech met with silence from the generals. Realizing they needed time to consider and reach a decision, Liútasil left them and asked a few final questions of his scouts before entrusting them to the care of a physician, who was waiting to dress their wounds.

He accompanied them outside and stood in the doorway, leaning against a tent pole and gazing at the dark night sky.

Hidden in the stars were the faces of his forebears—wise, brave, clear-sighted elves whom Sitalia had elevated to the firmament to watch over their descendants and send them visions and signs.

Liútasil focused on the face of Fantur, second ruler of Âlandur and brother of Veïnsa, one-time mistress of the Golden Plains. *I need your help*, he prayed, tracing the invisible lines of the constellation. *Tell me how to dissuade them from delaying*. He returned to the conference table. "What is your decision?"

"The trees in this forest," began the commander of Rân Ribastur's army. "Are they made of ordinary wood?"

Liútasil nodded.

"In that case," continued the general, "we can burn them. I say we blaze a path to the heart of their kingdom."

"They'll know exactly where we are," objected Liútasil. "We'd be a sitting target for their arrows. We'd lose hundreds and hundreds of—"

The man shrugged. "Who cares if they know where we are? Our army is vastly superior; we'll show them our strength. If they're too scared to fight us, we'll raze their accursed kingdom to the ground. I don't think anyone will be sorry to see the Perished Land in flames."

The other generals thumped the table and grunted their support.

Liútasil realized that they were unlikely to be dissuaded from the plan. "Maybe the dwarves will have a better suggestion," he said lightly. "I've sent a party of scouts to meet them, and one of my best elves, Shanamil, is guiding them here as we speak. They'll be with us in a couple of orbits."

"Dwarves are fine for tunneling and fighting under-ground," said one of the generals. "Palandiell knows they're brave and their axes are lethal—but they don't know a thing about fighting in the open. I'm in favor of burning the forest." He looked at the others. "Who's with me?" Most of the other generals raised their hands in support.

"Let's see what the dwarves have to say," ruled Liútasil, friendly but unyielding. "Go to bed. The new dawn might bring us better counsel."

The men filed out, leaving Liútasil alone. He untied his red hair, letting it fall freely around his shoulders.

He couldn't help feeling uneasy about the campaign. Älfar liked to ambush their enemies, killing ruthlessly without exposing themselves to counterattack. Blazing a path through a forest was a dangerous tactic—as the generals would surely discover to their cost.

He picked up the map and calculated the distance from the outskirts of the forest to the capital of Dsôn Balsur— fifty-one miles. In the best-case scenario, they would lose fifty men for every mile. *I tried to warn them.*

32 Miles Southwest of Dsôn Balsur,
Kingdom of Gauragar,
Girdlegard,
Winter, 6234th/6235th Solar Cycle

Trust the long-uns and the pointy-ears to forge ahead without us. They should have waited!" grumbled Gisgurd, looking from Bundror to Gimdur. "It's not our fault that it's taken an age to get here. We'd have made it to camp orbits ago if the tunnels hadn't caved in."

"I hope you didn't say *pointy-ears*," scolded Bundror with a twinkle in his eye. "We're one big family, remember."

Gimdur tore off two large strips of dried mushroom and stuck them together with a morsel of cheese that was melting over the fire. "Since when are we supposed to *like* our families? My sister and I can't get on." He turned to Gisgurd and took a bite of his snack. "You should be grateful they made it to camp before we did," he said, mumbling through his mouthful. "They'll have dug their own trenches and saved us some work."

"Elves can't dig trenches," said Bundror scornfully. "They can't lift their shovels higher than their boots! They're good on the lute and not bad with their arrows, but when it comes to handling a shovel . . . And they don't know a thing about food—not to mention proper beer!"

Gisgurd clapped him on the back. "Too right!" he agreed enthusiastically. "When all's said and done, they're *elves*." He paused for a moment, hoping Bundror would notice that he had referred to their confederates by their proper name. "I know we're on the same side, but how are we supposed to trust them? We hated each other for cycles. You can't just bury the past."

"No one's asking you to bury the past, master dwarf," said a singsong voice from the shadows. "For my part, I'm looking forward to a future of peace and friendship." A figure stepped out of the darkness toward the three dwarves. The firelight revealed a slender elf, her dark hair blowing in the breeze. "I'm glad it didn't take long to find you, although next time you camp near Dsôn Balsur you might want to post a few sentries. Your campfire is visible for miles."

Already Gisgurd, Bundror, and Gimdur were on their feet, axes raised and ready to strike. A shout went up, waking the rest of the unit. Three hundred dwarves prepared to fight.

"The älfar don't scare us," Gisgurd said grimly. "We gave them a good thrashing at the Blacksaddle." He eyed the stranger suspiciously, his distrust deepening when nine others appeared at her side. "Who are you and what do you want?"

"My name is Shanamil, sent by Lord Liútasil to bring you to him. He wants us at the camp by dawn."

"Nice try," growled the dwarf. "And my name is Balyndis Steelfinger, sent by Vraccas to forge the mighty blade. Prove you're telling the truth or I'll . . ." He stopped short, realizing that if the stranger was who she said she was, he was likely to cause offense.

Gimdur was only too happy to take over. "You pointy-ears all look the same in the dark. How do we know you're not an älf?"

She unfastened her necklace and showed them a gold pendant bearing the seal of Lord Liútasil. "I'm his envoy," she said, throwing the pendant to Gisgurd and taking a seat by the fire. "Kill me if you don't believe me. I'm sure Lord Liútasil will understand."

Bundror positioned himself next to Gisgurd and examined the seal. "It's elven, all right. One of the bowmen at the Blacksaddle was wearing one just like it. A bögnil killed him and tried to make off with his chain—I buried my ax in his back."

Shanamil inclined her head toward him. "Thank you for avenging my kinsman. Your forebears would have danced on his grave." Her gray eyes rested on him kindly.

Bundror, convinced of her integrity, lowered his weapons. "I'll vouch for them," he whispered to Gisgurd. "They're elves from Âlandur."

Gisgurd and Gimdur inspected the maiden's companions, studying their armor, their weapons, their slender faces, as pure as they were fair. The dwarves relaxed their guard.

"Fine," said Gisgurd finally. "We're prepared to believe that Liútasil sent you—but don't expect us to trust you properly until we've seen your eyes in the light. When the sun rises over the plains tomorrow, we'll know if you're monsters or elves."

The elf maiden took the speech with good grace. "You're right to be wary," she said calmly. "It would be just like the älfar to trick you into trusting them. A unit of ten älfar could kill three hundred warriors by slitting their throats in the dark." She motioned for her companions to sit beside her at the fire. "No, I don't blame you at all. It's a good thing the älfar won't be around for much longer—you'll know who you're dealing with when you meet an elf at night." She reached for her drinking flask. "How were you planning to find the allied camp?"

Gisgurd sat down, and Bundror and Gimdur followed suit. "We thought we'd head for the spot where the sun is at its zenith. I think we were roughly on course; it's not easy finding our bearings on the surface."

"I'd be lost underground," she said with a smile that revealed two rows of even white teeth.

Gisgurd felt a deep, almost physical aversion toward her. Her beauty offended his eyes. The elves were created from earth, dew, and sunlight, which explained why he found her abhorrent; sunlight was anathema to the deep-dwelling dwarves. It confirmed his belief that he could never really be friends with one of her kind. But at least the maiden didn't seem as arrogant as the rest of the elves, an observation that he shared with her candidly.

"I suppose we're all reviewing our opinions," she said. She produced a hunk of bread from her bag and started eating. "To be honest, I was expecting a rowdy pack of stinking, drunken groundlings, not a disciplined unit of warriors with a healthy distrust of strangers." She smiled. "Although I still think a few sentries wouldn't go amiss." She tore off another hunk of bread and her companions unpacked their victuals. "Balyndis Steelfinger isn't your real name, is it?" she asked suddenly, turning to Gisgurd.

Bundror roared with laughter. "Well spotted," he said, shaking his head. He proceeded to tell her how Tungdil Goldhand and his companions had traveled to the Gray Range, overcoming innumerable obstacles to reach the fifthlings' smithy and forge Keenfire while the enemy was pounding on the door.

"Just orcs, or älfar as well?" asked the elf.

"Both," he said, explaining how Tungdil and the secondling twins had killed their first älf in Greenglade, long before the expedition proper had begun. Later, they had put an end to two of their dogged pursuers, Sinthoras and Caphalor. "They were the most dangerous älfar in the whole of Dsôn Balsur."

The elf clapped her hands appreciatively and Bundror's companions, who had listened attentively to his narrative, joined the applause. "You're an excellent storyteller," she praised him. "But soon tales about fighting the älfar will be a thing of the past."

"More's the pity," murmured Gisgurd to the others' amusement.

Gimdur ran a hand through his thick black hair. "I've always wondered how the älfar were created. Perhaps you can tell us . . ."

Shanamil nodded, crossed her legs, and looked from

one dwarf to the next. In spite of their venerable age and wrinkled skin, there was something childlike about their upturned faces.

Inàste was the daughter of Elria the Helpful, who ruled over the water.

Inspired by the beautiful creatures fashioned by Sitalia, daughter of Palandiell, Inàste set to work. Taking dew, soil, and light, she called into being a new race of elves.

But Palandiell, afraid that Sitalia's work would be eclipsed, seized the new elves and threatened to destroy them.

Inàste pleaded with Elria to intervene, but her mother was unbending. After a furious argument, Inàste swore eternal vengeance on her mother and Palandiell.

Turning her back on the other deities, she opened her chamber to Samusin, and bore him a son, a beautiful baby who resembled an elf in appearance but who burned with his mother's hatred of Palandiell and Elria.

In time, he grew up to become the first älf, and Inàste gave him weapons and sent him to live among the elves.

Palandiell lost patience with the murdering, treacherous älf, and cast him over the mountains to the north where he took up with Tion's creatures, spreading his seed throughout the Outer Lands.

Patiently, he bided his time, waiting for a chance to cross the border and wage war against his cousins.

Since then, he and his descendants have served the
Perished Land devotedly, driven by their determination to wipe out the elves.

No one clapped.

It wasn't because the dwarves hadn't appreciated the
story; on the contrary, they were under the legend's spell.
Enchanted by the elf's soft, singsong voice, they waited in
vain for her to continue. Shanamil stayed silent and bowed
her head.

"I see," said Gisgurd after a while. He cleared his throat.
"So Inàste and Samusin are to blame for the älfar."

"What about Palandiell, Elria, and Sitalia?" objected
Bundror. "They shouldn't have argued with Inàste." He
shook his head vigorously, making his beard swing from
side to side. "Vraccas would never have behaved like that.
Nothing good ever comes of a quarrel."

"It's a legend, remember," said Gimdur. "An interesting
legend—but I bet if you asked the älfar, they'd tell you a
different story and say the elves were to blame." He looked
at the envoy. "What do you say to that?"

Shanamil looked at him evenly. "I've told you our
version of the story, and I believe it—just as you believe
that the dwarves were hewn from the mountain by Vraccas.
Anyway, it's as well you're made of the hardest granite,"
she said, changing the subject. "Our army could do with
your strength and persistence. What of the dwarven heroes
you spoke of? Are they here?"

"You mean Tungdil and his companions?" Bundror
laughed. "No, he hasn't got time to bother with Dsôn
Balsur's pointy-ears." He stopped suddenly, realizing what

he'd said. Frowning, he looked at the maiden. "You don't mind if I call them pointy-ears, do you?" He took her smile as permission to refer to the älfar as he pleased.

"Mind?" growled Gimdur. "I'm sorry, elf, but I'm not going to stop insulting my enemies just because they're related to my friends." He got out his pipe and stuffed it with tobacco, still grumbling under his breath.

"In any case," said Bundror, picking up his thread. "Our task is to help Lord Liútasil and the human generals in the struggle against Inàste's pointy-ears." He lingered over the words, relishing the chance to use the insult—especially in combination with his newly acquired knowledge about the älfar's origins. "Tungdil and the others are heading north."

"What a pity," said Shanamil. "I should have liked to meet him. I'm surprised he's not here. If we had a warrior with a legendary weapon, we'd send him wherever he was needed most."

"That's why he's gone north," said Gimdur. He dropped a glowing ember into the bowl of his pipe and waited for the tobacco to catch light. Clouds of dark blue smoke rose into the air. "He's going to rebuild the fifthling halls and seal the Stone Gateway."

"On his own?" asked the maiden. "I'm impressed." The dwarves roared with laughter.

"Of course not! The best warriors and artisans from Beroïn, Borengar, and Goïmdil are going to help," explained Gimdur, puffing away on his pipe. "And some of his old companions will be there too." He jabbed the stem of his pipe at Shanamil's chest. "Not a single beast will pass through the gateway while our kinsfolk are keeping watch. You can bet on it."

In the silence that followed, Gisgurd rose to his feet. "I don't mean to be discourteous, but my warriors need some sleep." He dispatched a dozen dwarves to stand guard with their shields and axes around the makeshift camp and protect the sleeping unit from invaders. He didn't want another set of visitors that night.

"We'll need to be up early if we're to cover the rest of the journey by dawn," said Shanamil. "If you don't mind, we'll sleep here as well. You can ask one of your sentries to keep an eye on us—unless you've decided to trust us, of course." She lay down on her side, facing the fire. With a flick of her wrist, she threw her cloak over her body and drew it around her like a blanket. "We're scouts— we sleep in the open all the time." Her companions settled down for the night as well.

"They're not very demanding, are they?" whispered Bundror. "I'd never have thought an elf would consent to sleeping on the ground."

"Where did you think they'd sleep?" enquired Gisgurd. "On perfumed sheets with satin pillows and embroidered quilts?"

"We forgot to bring our pillows with us," said Shanamil, who had overheard the whispered conversation. "And we didn't have room for our four-poster beds." She closed her eyes, but her lips were smiling.

"Blast," muttered Bundror. "Their ears are sharp as well as pointy."

The hours wore on. After a time, the moon reached its highest point, bathing the camp in light and turning the dwarves into silvery statues.

Only Bundror, twitching and moaning in his sleep, was plagued by nightmares. He woke with a start.

Terrible images lingered in his mind. The camp had been overrun with älfar and the dwarves had fallen one by one. He too had looked into a pair of cruel, empty eyes and felt the lethal blade of a sword swishing toward his unprotected throat. Mercifully, he had woken in the instant before he died.

His heart was still pounding. He raised a hand to his face and realized that sweat was pouring from his forehead and trickling into his beard.

It's because we're so close to Dsôn Balsur, he told himself firmly. At home in the fourthling kingdom he was never haunted by such visions.

He threw off his blankets and sat up. The fire had burned low and his comrades were sleeping peacefully. *You can bet they're not dreaming of älfar*, he thought wryly. Mindful of his bladder, he got up, collected his ax, and stomped through the narrow corridor of bodies.

A few paces beyond the perimeter of the camp he found a suitable bush and stopped to relieve himself. Dwarven water cascaded to the ground.

Just then he was struck by a worrying thought.

For the most part, people's ideas about dwarves are false, but occasionally some of the folklore is based on fact. No one who has been in the vicinity of a sleeping dwarf would deny that dwarven breathing is curiously loud. A human would refer to the phenomenon as *snoring*; in elven forests, it was practically unknown. But among Bundror's kinsfolk, it was as natural and inevitable as swallowing one's food.

He frowned and strained his ears, hearing the patter of his water, the creaking of his boots, and the jangling of his mail. Beyond that, there was nothing—no coughing, no throat clearing, not even the familiar, reassuring chorus of snores.

The crease in his brow deepened to a furrow. He buttoned his breeches, raised his ax, and scanned his surroundings, looking for an explanation for the unnatural hush.

Tightening his grip on the ax, he tiptoed to the left toward a sentry. The dwarf was gazing over the moonlit plains. His loose hair was blowing in the wind, but he was otherwise still.

"Anything unusual to report?" enquired Boëndal. "It's horribly quiet without their snoring." The sentry paid him no attention.

"I know you're on duty," said Bundror irritably, "but if a comrade asks a question, it's polite to reply." He pushed past the dwarf, stopped abruptly, and raised his weapon with a terrible curse.

The sentry wasn't standing of his own accord.

Someone had rammed a branch through his chain mail and into his chest, skewering him through the middle and preventing him from falling. Propped up by the bloodsoaked stake, the dwarf looked almost alive, but his unseeing eyes stared at the ground and his features were etched with suffering. He had witnessed untold horrors in the instant before his death.

There was no smell of orcs, from which Bundror surmised that the sentry had been murdered by älfar. He raised his shield, drumming against it with all his might to sound the alarm and wake his sleeping comrades.

The others slept on, seemingly oblivious to the ear-splitting noise. Even the elves showed no sign of stirring.

"Wake up, wake—" He broke off, his throat constricting with panic as a terrible thought entered his mind.

Darting over to the nearest dwarf, he seized him by the shoulder, rolled him onto his back, and cried out in horror. The dwarf's body came away from his head, which lay motionless on the ground, neck and beard cleft neatly in two. Bundror's gaze settled on the pool of blood glimmering darkly in the moonlight.

"Save yourself the effort, groundling," whispered a voice to his left. "You won't raise your comrades—unless you can raise the dead."

Bundror whirled round, striking out with his ax as he turned. His blade connected with something hard—his blow had been parried by a quarterstaff of black metal.

Before he knew it, the lower end of the quarterstaff was speeding toward his helmet. He took a blow to the nose guard. The metal cut into his face, pressing against his nose and breaking the bone with an audible crack.

Eyes watering and warm blood pouring down his face, Bundror stumbled away. Dazed, he took another step back and tumbled over the corpse of a comrade. "Come on, then!" he shouted furiously, still clutching his ax. He straightened up, braced his legs, and looked around for his assailant. "Try that again, älf, and I'll cut you in two!"

The challenge met with no response. The älf had melted into the darkness and the moon wasn't strong enough, or maybe brave enough, to deliver the shadowy figure to the dwarf's vengeful eyes.

Bundror was under no illusions. The älf's knowledge

of dark arts exceeded his axmanship, but he was spurred on by hatred for the villain who had murdered his comrades.

The next blow came from nowhere. Hearing a low swish, Bundror ducked just in time. The quarterstaff slashed the air above him, only to swing round suddenly and knock him off his feet. A blade cut into his forearm, and pain stabbed through his arm, forcing his fingers apart. His heavy ax, his only protection against the murderous älf, fell from his grip.

He looked up to see the sole of a narrow boot. A moment later, he felt the pressure on his throat.

"Did you really think you were a match for me, groundling?"

Gasping for breath, he peered up and saw a tall, slim figure clad in armor. A mask of tionium covered the top half of the älf's face, and a veil of black gauze covered the nose, mouth and chin. The älf's features were framed by a hood attached to a dark gray cape.

"Count yourself lucky," he spat back, struggling for breath. "If you hadn't lurked in the shadows like a coward, I'd have cut you in two."

"You want to fight me, do you?" laughed the voice behind the veil. The black gauze rippled gently. "Is that your dying wish?"

"Yes," he spluttered.

The boot lifted from his throat. "Granted."

Bundror staggered to his feet, reached for his ax, and saw blood streaming from the gash in his forearm. Hiding his pain determinedly, he gritted his teeth and squared his shoulders. From the voice, he guessed that his antagonist was female, but the mask, cloak, and armor made it impossible to tell. "Vraccas will give me the strength to prevail." He glanced round hurriedly, but there was no sign of an älvish army. *Surely there must be others? How could she kill a whole unit by herself? Can she work magic?*

"You'll see my warriors when they want to be seen," she said coldly, as if he had spoken aloud. She windmilled her quarterstaff. "I'm waiting, groundling."

He charged toward her and hurled his ax—only for her to deflect it with her staff.

Still, the tactic worked; it gave him a fraction of a second in which to act.

Bending down, he borrowed a less cumbersome ax from one of his dead companions and snatched up a shield. Thus equipped, he charged again at the älf, hoping that the lighter weapon would lend him the necessary speed.

The duel that unfolded among the corpses of his companions was hopelessly one-sided.

Both ends of the quarterstaff seemed to jab toward Bundror at once, striking him here and there, clattering against his wooden shield, slamming into his chain mail, forcing the air from his lungs, and breaking the occasional rib. He fought back whenever he had the opportunity, which was seldom enough—and each time the agile älf parried the blow or batted away his weapon, leaving him to grunt in frustration.

Bundror soon realized that it was hopeless and he was destined to die. He decided to try another, very dwarven, approach. *Vraccas be with me.* He hurled the ax toward her, forcing her to skip aside, then picked up his shield with both hands and sprinted in her direction, hollering at the top of his voice.

The unconventional tactic took her by surprise. The shield slammed into her, and he heard a thud as he knocked her, groaning, to the ground.

"Take that, you pointy-eared scumbag!" he shouted, his voice mingling hatred and delight. "I'll cleave your head from your shoulders." He bounded through the air and hurled himself at her chest, the lower edge of his shield pointing toward her throat.

Just then two things happened.

From her supine position, the älf managed to plant the lower end of the quarterstaff into the ground and point it toward him like a lance. Under other circumstances, Bundror would have done his utmost to avoid it, but a large black shadow swept toward him and he was caught.

He heard a gravelly roar and saw a pair of glimmering red eyes. The creature opened its mighty jaws, enveloping him in foul-smelling breath. Even as he realized that the teeth were impossibly close, something rammed into his belly, passed through the links of his chain mail, and exited the other side. His mind closed down.

The corpse-strewn field was bobbing around him, and he felt himself rising and falling as if he were impaled on a moving palisade. His helmet flew off, followed by his shield, weapons belt, and one of his boots. He felt the jerk of something leaving his belly, and he was free.

He flew through the air and landed on a corpse. Through a haze of blood he saw that it was Gisgurd.

It won't be long, my friend. Fire up the furnace, I'm on my way. He rolled over. His mouth filled with a coppery-tasting liquid that seeped into his beard and fell in thick, viscous drops onto his chest. *I must warn the others*.

His fingers scrabbled over Gisgurd's rucksack and, summoning the last of his strength, he lifted the mighty bugle and put it to his shredded lips. The effort of drawing breath caused his lungs to fill with blood, but nothing could turn him from his purpose.

A single, piercing note left the bugle of the butchered dwarf and echoed over the hills. His lifeblood trickled into the instrument, and silence returned. Bundror hoped that the elves in Liútasil's camp would recognize the signal and sound the alarm.

The heavy bugle fell from his hand as his strength ebbed away. He looked up to see the tionium mask of his antagonist. "You won't achieve anything by attacking our allies," he spluttered determinedly. "They've been warned."

"Perhaps, but they won't have heard your bugle in the Gray Range." She bent down and lifted her mask to reveal her face. It was the elf maiden who had sat and conversed with them by the fire. "Look at me," she said menacingly. "Ondori is your death, and I will take your life as your kinsfolk killed my parents. May your soul wander helplessly for the rest of time." A scythe-like blade glinted in the light of the stars, and the älf muttered something in a low, sinister voice.

Bundror guessed the meaning of the incantation and prayed for help.

He was still begging Vraccas to gather him to the eternal smithy when the blade slashed his throat, severing his last fragile link to the world of the living.

III

Tungdil looked searchingly at the firstling queen. Muffled in warm furs and perched reluctantly on a pony, Xamtys was staring at the snowy peaks of the Red Range. She was looking for a sign, a hint of a threat, evidence of a catastrophe that had occurred in her absence and shrouded the stronghold in silence.

The snow-covered mountains towered into the sky, sometimes vanishing behind the fast-moving cloud. Here and there, a gentle ray of spring sunshine broke through the cloud and caressed the flanks of the mountain, revealing patches of fiery red rock where the snow had melted.

"They're still here," said Tungdil. "The mountains are still standing, Your Majesty."

She turned to face him. "I can't rejoice until I've seen my kinsmen," she said anxiously. "Remember the state of the tunnels? Who knows what damage has been done to my halls."

The tunnels to the east of the firstling kingdom had collapsed, hence the reason for traveling overland. It had taken sixty orbits to make the journey on foot. In some places the snow was too deep, in others too soft and sticky. The roads and tracks were covered in slush, and the dwarves and ponies had disappeared up to their knees, which slowed their progress and sapped their strength. Tungdil, Balyndis, and Boïndil were accustomed to the rigors of marching, but the rest of the company had struggled with the difficult terrain.

"It looks too peaceful," murmured Boïndil, who was marching at Tungdil's side, having turned down the offer of a pony. "I'm not going to let the mountains trick me into thinking everything is all right." With a loud splash, his right foot landed in a puddle. Cursing, he pulled it out and wiped it on the grass. "Smooth floors and nice solid ceilings, that's what I want," he grumbled.

"We're nearly there, Boïndil," said Balyndis, pointing to the mouth of a narrow gully that snaked toward one of the peaks. "See the entrance over there?"

They suddenly became aware of a gray mist that seemed to thicken as they approached, swirling around them until they could barely see. It was almost as if it wanted them to lose their bearings.

Tungdil pictured the six fortified walls that intersected the gully, blocking the entrance and each of its sweeping curves. At the far end of the gully lay the imposing firstling stronghold and its nine soaring towers.

"I can't see a thing," he said, disappointed. "I was hoping to see East Ironhald in full . . ." He tailed off as the mist lifted to reveal a landscape littered with vast slabs of stone. Some were black with soot, others had fractured or crumbled.

Xamtys tugged on the reins, and her pony snorted and stopped. "Vraccas be with us," she cried, staring at the remains of the defenses. Anyone wishing to enter the gully had once been obliged to scale a wall forty paces high or read the password inscribed on the metal door, which required a good knowledge of dwarfish. Neither the wall nor the door was still standing.

Three paces from the queen's feet, the ground dropped away, and a yawning black crater filled the path. There was no sign of the cause, but something had evidently hit the ground with tremendous force, crushing the masonry, scorching the rock, and turning the imposing door into an unremarkable scrap of warped metal.

"It's not possible," whispered Balyndis. Even the most powerful siege engine, designed by the best dwarven engineer to fell the most monstrous of Tion's beasts, was incapable of causing damage such as this. "What could have . . . ? Maybe it's magic. Do you think Nôd'onn somehow . . ." She suddenly remembered what she and Tungdil had seen on the night of the battle. "The comet!"

Boïndil let out an ear-piercing shriek and charged into the mist, which, it now dawned on them, smelled strongly of scorched earth. Calling his brother's name, the hot-blooded dwarf dispensed with caution and vanished in the direction of the firstling stronghold, desperate to find his twin.

"Come back!" shouted Xamtys.

Tungdil knew that his friend was in no mood to listen. Fearing that there might be dangers lurking in the fog, he chased after him. Balyndis followed without hesitation.

They relied on their ears to guide them. The sound of Boïndil's jangling chain mail and the rattling of his helmet echoed noisily through the otherwise silent gully, which made the business of locating him very easy indeed.

But the devastation around them filled them with fear.

The gully was pitted with craters, some the size of wagon wheels, others large enough to accommodate eight ponies side by side. The ground had proven the weaker element in the encounter and some of the indentations were seven paces deep. For the dwarves, it meant lowering themselves into potholes and climbing out the other side. The snow was gone from this part of the mountain, and there was no sign of melt water, just a thin layer of frozen crystals. It was as if the snow had vaporized, leaving a revolting smell.

Hurrying as best they could, Tungdil and Balyndis followed the jangling chain mail, eventually reaching the end of the gully where the stronghold would normally come into view.

They took another few steps and felt snow beneath their boots. Suddenly, the fog lifted to reveal Boïndil, standing at the foot of a mound of recrystallized snow that towered above him, too high and sheer to climb. The mist cleared further, revealing the full extent of the tragedy.

Of the stronghold's nine towers, only one was visible above the snow. The avalanche had swept away its parapet, but the tower itself was standing.

The other eight towers had disappeared entirely. The twin ramparts and cleverly designed lifts and pulleys lay buried beneath the gray mound of snow—together with the ruins of East Ironhald and, as the three dwarves suspected, the bodies of the dead.

Balyndis peered at the tower, looking for the bridge that led to the stronghold. "It's gone," she said tremulously. "The White Death has swallowed the bridge."

Tungdil was too horrified to speak.

Hooves approached from behind; the rest of the company had arrived. The sight of the ruined stronghold drew curses, cries of horror, and wails of grief from the stricken dwarves.

Xamtys dismounted and walked to the mound. She reached out and thrust her hand into the snow to pull out a battered helmet. The headwear, made of the strongest dwarven metal, evidently hadn't protected its owner from the weight of the snow.

"Worthy Vraccas, your children have paid dearly for the salvation of Girdlegard," she said gravely and without a hint of reproach. "Or is this the beginning of a new and unknown threat?" Her brown eyes settled on the surviving tower and tears trickled down her cheeks, rolling through her wispy hair and plumping onto her armored chest. "My tears mark the passing of those who died here. You have my word that nothing will stop me rebuilding my ravaged kingdom. This time the stronghold will be more imposing, more splendid than before, and evil will never triumph against us—not now, not ever, not even if I have to rebuild East Ironhald on my own." She held the helmet on high. "May the memory of the dead stay with us forever. Long live the children of the Smith!"

"The children of the Smith!" came the shout from a hundred different throats. The words were still echoing when a bugle call replied.

"The side entrance!" Balyndis told Tungdil. "It means they'll meet us at the side entrance!"

"Which side entrance?" demanded Boïndil with a glint in his eyes that Tungdil knew and feared. The secondling warrior seized Balyndis roughly by the hand. "What are you waiting for? Lead the way!"

Balyndis didn't usually take orders from Boïndil, or anyone

else for that matter, but she had witnessed his temper before. Taking heed of Tungdil's silent warning, she set off without a murmur, while Boïndil and the others followed close behind.

They picked their way around the edges of the avalanche and came to what looked like a sheer wall.

"It's in case of a siege—we wanted to be able to attack on the flank," explained Balyndis. "It's never been used."

"Until now," said Tungdil, watching as cracks appeared in the rock, forming the outlines of a door four paces high and four paces wide. It swung open, revealing a dozen waiting dwarves. Tungdil glanced nervously at Boïndil and prayed that Vraccas had held his protective shield over his twin. *Boïndil will finish what the White Death started if Boëndal has come to any harm.*

The secondling stepped forward. "Where's my brother?" he demanded. Naturally, the firstlings were more interested in welcoming their queen and took a moment to respond. Ireheart grabbed the nearest sentry by the collar and shook him roughly. "Where's Boëndal?" he roared, tightening his grip until the sentry's face went purple.

Tungdil laid a hand on Ireheart's arm. "You'll hurt him!"

"Boëndal?" gasped the poor sentry. "He's in bed. We dug him out of the snow, but . . ."

"But what?" asked Boïndil sharply, letting go of his jerkin. "For the sake of Vraccas, speak clearly."

"We can't wake him. His skin feels like ice and it's a wonder that his heart is still beating. It might stop at any moment," said the firstling, backing away quickly until he was out of the warrior's reach.

Boïndil's eyebrows formed an angry black line. "Where is he?" he asked.

In the interests of averting an incident, Xamtys overlooked his rude behavior and ordered one of the firstlings to show him to his brother's bed. Tungdil and Balyndis followed, while the queen stayed behind to quiz the guards.

The party of four dwarves strode through plain-walled corridors connecting the side entrance to the stronghold proper. The design was entirely functional—unlike the secondlings, the firstlings took little interest in fancy masonry and left the walls of little-used tunnels unadorned, preferring to focus their efforts on metalworking.

"The damage was devastating," said the guard when they asked about the quake. "We think the falling star was to blame. It came from the east, raining burning boulders from its tail. Most of our fortifications were razed to the ground— then the White Death came and swallowed the rest."

"How many were killed?" asked Balyndis. "What about the Steel Fingers?"

"They're fine, I think, but we haven't heard anything from the clans on the western border, closest to where the comet fell." The firstling led them to a wooden platform connected to a pulley system. They got on, and the lift shot up, whizzing past hundreds of steps before stopping to let them out in the eastern halls of the kingdom. "I'm just pleased that our queen has returned. Four hundred of our kinsmen lost their lives in the disaster, but Xamtys will give us the strength to carry on."

They saw straightaway that the dwarf's description of the damage was no exaggeration. The passageways were riven with cracks, some no wider than a whisker, others big enough for Tungdil to slot his fingers inside. He noticed that the metal bridges, sturdy enough to carry hundreds of dwarves across rivers and chasms, had buckled in places.

"We lost one hall entirely and the ceiling in the throne room is sagging," said the sentry. "It nearly buried our precious sculptures and statues. It was terrible."

They ascended a staircase and reached the chamber where they had left the wounded Boëndal many orbits earlier on their way to the Dragon Fire furnace. He was lying in much the same position, swaddled in blankets, in a marble bed with a thick mattress.

Boïndil threw himself on his brother and flung his arms around him. He lowered his ear to his chest and listened to his heart. "He's cold as a fish," he said softly. "Anyone would think he was . . ." He tailed off and a smile spread across his careworn face. "A heartbeat! A good, strong heartbeat!" His joy evaporated. "Nothing again . . ."

"It's what I was trying to explain," whispered the firstling. "We think his blood might be frozen. His poor heart is pumping ice through his veins."

A firstling appeared at the door with a tray. "He wasn't the only one we found in the snow, but the others weren't so lucky." She put down a pot of steaming tea by the bed.

"Lucky?" said Tungdil, shaking his head. "He's barely alive."

"Some of our kinsmen looked like they'd been flattened by a giant hammer when we pulled their poor, crushed bodies from the snow. The rest died from lack of air. Boëndal survived, which goes to show that Vraccas wanted him to live."

She stood at Boëndal's bedside, decanted the piping hot tea into a leather drinking pouch, and raised it to his half-open lips. Boïndil stopped her and laid a muscular hand on the pouch. "What are you giving him?"

"A herbal infusion. It will thaw his insides," she said. She went to raise the pouch, but Boïndil tightened his grip.

"An infusion? A tankard of warm beer will thaw his insides faster than a bunch of herbs."

"No," she said firmly. "The herbs have a medicinal effect, especially in combination with hot water."

"Wouldn't it be more effective to give him a bath?" threw in Tungdil. He had read about methods for treating hypothermia in one of Lot-Ionan's books. The author was principally concerned with reviving humans who had fallen into lakes, but there was no reason why the remedy wouldn't work on a dwarf.

"An excellent suggestion," she said brusquely. "But I'm afraid we tried it and it didn't work." She snatched the pouch away from Boïndil. "You're a warrior and I'm a physician. You do your job, and I'll do mine. I wouldn't dream of telling you how to use an ax." Boïndil complied begrudgingly, but refused to leave his brother's side.

"I scoured our archives, and the infusion is our only hope. Nothing else will work."

Tungdil knew that she was holding something back. "Is there something we can try?" he probed. "Tell me what to do, and I'll do it. I owe my life to Boëndal."

The firstling looked away. "It's a legend, nothing more."

"Listen to me," shouted Boïndil, as if he were interrogating a spy. "By the beard of Vraccas, I'll do anything—anything—to rekindle my brother's furnace and make his spirit burn as brightly as before." The glint in his dark brown eyes testified to his determination to make his brother well.

"The oldest records in our archives were chiseled by the ancients on tablets of stone. They're thousands of cycles old," said the firstling. "According to one of the tablets, it's possible to fire up the soul of a frozen dwarf by kindling the embers of his furnace with white-hot sparks."

"What do you think it means?" asked Balyndis. "Surely you can't use real fire to warm a soul?" She turned to Tungdil. "Do you think we should cut him open and put sparks in his heart?"

"The wound would kill him," said Tungdil. The legend reminded him of something, but he couldn't quite make the connection.

"Trust a blacksmith to come up with a stupid idea like that," growled Boïndil. "We can't feed him with fire or put lava into his veins."

The firstling glared at him. "For your information, the tablets came from Giselbert's folk. I've told you what I know, and besides, it's just a legend."

"Dwarven legends are usually true," said Balyndis, who wasn't prepared to give up on the idea, no matter how unlikely it sounded. "So you've tried warm baths and hot drinks. How else can you warm his blood?"

The firstling stared at the floor. "I can't. All I can do is keep giving him the infusion and praying to Vraccas to make him well."

"Can't?" Boïndil was so incensed by the plight of his frozen twin that his fiery spirit was burning out of control. "Isn't there any proper medicine in this joke of a kingdom?"

"Dragon Fire!" broke in Tungdil, who had finally worked out the connection between the legend and its provenance. "A white-hot spark! It's a reference to the fieriest furnace in Girdlegard!" He saw his friends' puzzled faces. "I think the Dragon Fire furnace might be able to help. It was lit by the mighty Branbausìl, remember?"

Neither he nor Balyndis would ever forget the power of the furnace: In all their experience of the smithy, they had never encountered such tremendous heat. The white-hot flames of Dragon Fire were powerful enough to melt any metal, from pure white palandium, made by Palandiell, to the black element of tionium, created by Tion, and the red metal of vraccasium, element of the dwarves.

"That's all very well," said the physician, "but how would it work?" She put down the pouch and laid a hand on her patient's forehead. "We'd need proper instructions."

Tungdil looked at the secondling's rigid body. "The key to the legend lies in the fifthling kingdom. My friends and I are going there anyway, and we'll take Boëndal with us." He turned to the physician. "You've done everything you can for him, but he won't get better here." After a short silence, he went over to Boïndil. "I'm not giving up on him," he said, laying a hand on his shoulder. "Vraccas cured him of the arrow wounds and rescued him from the avalanche, and now it's our task to wake him from his sleep. You mark my words: The Dragon Fire furnace holds the answer, and I'll scour the fifthlings' archives to find out how. The old Boëndal will be back before you know it."

Boïndil took his hand and squeezed it gratefully. "We're lucky to have a scholarly friend like you." He loosened his grip and stroked his brother's cheek. Then he fetched a stool and settled down to wait.

"You should get some rest," said Tungdil, following Balyndis out of the room.

"So should you," she said firmly. She asked the physician to fetch some provisions for Boïndil and make sure he had somewhere to sleep. "Come on," she said to Tungdil. "Let's get some food and go to bed."

"Not until we've spoken to Xamtys."

Balyndis's plaits whirled around in circles as she shook her head vigorously. "The queen will send for us when she needs us. Her advisors will be briefing her on the damage to the stronghold and it won't be long before she retires to bed. The rest can wait till the morning." She pulled him through the corridors to her chamber.

It was the first time that he had seen her quarters in the firstling kingdom. Someone had obviously taken care of the cleaning in her absence because the chamber was neat and tidy. Balyndis took a couple of blankets from the closet and laid them over the bed.

Then they kneeled in front of the shrine that Balyndis had erected in Vraccas's honor in the corner of her room. After praying to the Smith on Boëndal's behalf, they took off their heavy mail shirts, undressed to their undergarments, and lay down in bed.

Balyndis looked at Tungdil, her eyes filled with love. He gazed back at her tenderly, returning her unspoken affection with a kiss on the lips.

"They're talking about us, you know," she said with a tired smile.

"No wonder—we're famous."

She burst out laughing. "Not because of *that*. They're talking about us because we don't hide our love." She realized from his expression that he didn't understand. "I think the twins may have forgotten a couple of things when they were teaching you to be a dwarf. Our union hasn't been sanctioned, Tungdil. We're not supposed to show affection for one another until we've been melded. Any word or gesture that oversteps the bounds of friendship is a violation of our mores. Strictly, you shouldn't be here at all."

He grinned at her. "It's all right, Balyndis, the rules are different for heroes. Besides, it won't be long until we're joined by the iron band."

Balyndis wasn't the least reassured. "Even heroes are bound by our mores. It's a serious matter, and that's why my kinsfolk are talking. Besides, no one shows affection in public—it isn't the dwarven way."

"I don't remember the twins saying anything about that," said Tungdil, nestling closer. "Let them gossip, if they want to; we'll soon be melded."

They snuggled up to each other and fell asleep.

It was exactly as Balyndis had predicted.

Queen Xamtys II allowed them to sleep off their tiredness and sent word that she expected them in the throne room in the course of the following orbit.

In the meantime, they took the opportunity to have a long bath—in separate bathtubs because they hadn't been melded. Tungdil didn't care if his kinsfolk gossiped about them, but he tried not to cause a scandal for Balyndis's sake.

Later, she cooked for him and, in the course of conversation, it came out that she had almost been melded to someone else. Her clan had picked a partner for her, but the poor dwarf had fallen in battle before they could forge the iron band. It was lucky for Tungdil because a dwarven union was permanent unless both parties agreed to break the band, which, as far as Balyndis could remember, had never happened in the history of the dwarves.

"And then you turned up and stole my heart," she said, turning her attention to the stove. After orbits of dried food, she couldn't wait to have a proper dwarven meal. Soon their plates were piled high with steaming potatoes in mushroom ragout. Fried fudi-fungi slices and cranberry compote were served on the side. After a while Balyndis noticed that Tungdil had hardly touched his food. "Isn't it spicy enough?"

"It tastes delicious," he said quickly, "but I'm not accustomed to dwarven food." He glanced round the kitchen. "I was thinking of adding a pinch of that cheese."

She glared at him in disbelief. "You mean the stinking cheese that the twins always eat? It tastes as bad as it smells!"

"I like it," he said, offended that she was sneering at the one dwarven victual that he actually liked. He headed off an argument by changing the subject. "So your clansfolk don't know that we're . . ."

"No. How was I supposed to tell them? I'll talk to them when I see them."

He scratched his beard. "You don't think they'll mind?" Tungdil, who had been living quite happily in ignorance of dwarven sensitivities, saw himself up against all kinds of awkward rules.

"That's another matter," she conceded, helping herself to a potato. "Maidens aren't supposed to choose their partners. Widows are allowed to, but I'm only half a widow at best."

Tungdil took another serving of mushroom ragout to show that he appreciated Balyndis's food. A horrible thought had occurred to him, and he simply had to ask. "What if your clansfolk refuse?"

Balyndis put down her spoon and reached for his hand. "Listen to me, Tungdil: I'm coming with you to the Gray

Range, whatever they say." She looked at him gravely. "But we can't be melded if my clansfolk won't allow it. I can't disgrace the good name of my clan."

"But if we can't be melded . . . ?"

"I'd still be your friend."

Tungdil stopped chewing and gasped, nearly choking on his mushroom. *Why didn't anyone warn me that dwarven mores are so complicated?*

He imagined what it would be like to see Balyndis every orbit and never come close to her again. Their kinsfolk would frown at them for holding hands like they were doing now.

A brisk handshake, a formal embrace—that was the most he could hope for. She would never again press her lips against his. His heart wept at the thought that another dwarf could take his place and enjoy the rights that went with the iron band. *It would be agony.*

He was so distressed that he stopped worrying about Boëndal, all thought of the Gray Range and the orcs at the Stone Gateway forgotten. He finished the ragout in silence.

"What's the matter?" asked Balyndis, squeezing his hands. "Have I spoiled things? I didn't mean to upset you."

He raised his eyes from his plate. The sight of Balyndis was so comforting that his mood brightened like the morning sun. "It's all right," he told her. "We'll be a wonderful couple. Just think, we'll have lots of lovely children and they'll all be splendid smiths." He kissed the back of her hand and she ruffled his hair. The bad dream was over.

Some time later, a steward knocked at the door and escorted them to the throne room. They passed through the imposing doorway and entered the octagonal hall, the walls of which shimmered warmly with beaten gold.

The quake had shown little respect for the time-honored room, and great cracks had opened in the ceiling, proving that solid rock was no defense against the force of a speeding comet.

Tungdil didn't take long to spot the new columns, added for purely structural reasons. The firstling masons had done their best to match them to the rest of the room, adorning them with intricate carvings inlaid with gold, silver, vraccasium, and other precious metals, but for all their efforts, it was obvious that the pillars were a late addition. Glancing up, Tungdil noticed that the majestic mosaics had been damaged and several tiles had fallen to the floor.

"There's a lot to be done," said Xamtys, noticing their glances. She greeted them from her metal throne.

Tungdil and Balyndis inclined their heads, but the queen held up a hand before they could kneel before her throne. "Let's dispense with formality. We've got business to attend to." She paused for a moment while a steward brought stools for her guests to be seated. "Tungdil, I think you should leave for the Gray Range right away. Girdlegard won't be safe until you've closed the Stone Gateway. We need you and as many of our kinsfolk as possible guarding the Northern Pass. On top of that, there's the quake damage to consider. If the fifthling stronghold was hit half as badly as we were, you'll have to work flat out to rebuild it. We know the orcs vandalized the fortifications; the quake may have flattened them completely."

"I was thinking the same," he said. "But you'll need every pair of hands to repair the firstling halls. Why not send your volunteers later, when the work has been done?"

She considered him intently. The golden rings of her

mail shirt shimmered in the light of the braziers, bathing her plump face in light. Her expression was serious. "Your generosity does you credit, Tungdil, but your new compatriots should leave at once. It's in Girdlegard's interest that they go." She turned to Balyndis. "The Steel Fingers arrived bearing news from the western border of the kingdom. The falling star continued its trajectory and crashed to earth on the far side of the range to the west. Since then, flames have been sighted every night on the horizon. According to the guardians of the Red Gateway, it looks as though a fire is raging throughout the Outer Lands." She looked from Tungdil to Balyndis. "I've sent word to the elves and men. Andôkai should hear the news within the next few orbits. It's a pity we can't tell them more."

Tungdil was busy trying to work out whether there was any connection between what the sentries had seen and Nôd'onn's warning of a threat from the west. The magus, insistent that Girdlegard was in danger, had pleaded with Andôkai to spare his life. "I dread to think what happened when the star crashed to earth," said Tungdil, remembering the craters formed by falling debris from the comet's tail. "The damage was bad enough here, but the impact of a rock of that size . . . Surely nothing could survive."

"Do you think the fire is connected with Nôd'onn's warning?" asked Balyndis, catching on.

Tungdil shrugged. "Somehow it doesn't seem likely. No good ever came of fretting, although I dare say we'll fret anyway—there won't be much else to distract us on the long march ahead." He thought for a moment. "Your Majesty, perhaps you could propose a council of the most learned minds in Girdlegard," he suggested. "Together, we stand a better chance of finding a solution." He smiled. "Why shouldn't a dwarven queen be the first to remind the other rulers of the newly pledged solidarity between dwarves, elves, and men? Your Majesty would have the honor of leading an initiative devoted wholly to the common good."

Xamtys returned his smile. "Wise words from our scholar. Giselbert chose the right dwarf to rebuild his kingdom." She turned to Balyndis. "You're free to go— the Steel Fingers are impatient to see you."

They bowed respectfully and hurried into the corridor where Balyndis's clansfolk were waiting.

Tungdil appraised the delegation of dwarves. The women among them, four in total, were dressed in traditional brown leather bodices and woolen skirts. Some of their male companions wore heavy chain mail and had weapons in their belts. They were warriors in the firstling army, proud to be chosen by Vraccas to fight for their folk. Although Tungdil was standing right in front of them, they acted as if he weren't there.

Balyndis threw herself on the tallest, stateliest warrior and hugged him tight.

"Ah, my intrepid daughter," he greeted her, laughing heartily. He laid his hands on her face. "I hear you fought the hordes at the Blacksaddle! Thanks be to Vraccas that you're safe."

Although he and Balyndis were thrilled to see each other, their reunion was dignified and restrained. Tungdil had been half expecting them to jump up and down with elation, but dwarves didn't go in for the effusiveness common among humankind. Besides, there was no need for it; the affection between father and daughter was evident in their smiling faces and shining eyes.

"How are the others?" asked Balyndis. Her expression darkened. "I heard the comet . . ."

"Missed us entirely!" said her father. "Vraccas was merciful and diverted the falling debris away from our halls. Boulders landed either side of us, and a few of our chambers were damaged by the quake, but everyone's safe. We're looking forward to hearing about your adventures— but first there's some more good news."

"More good news? And I was so worried about you!" exclaimed Balyndis, making her way through the ranks of the Steel Fingers and greeting each in turn. At last she signaled for Tungdil to join her. "Father, this is Tungdil Goldhand. He led the expedition to forge Keenfire and kill the dark magus." She squeezed his arm. "He's a good friend and, with your consent, we'd like to be melded."

Tungdil held out his hand to the warrior and met his steely gaze. "My name is Tungdil Goldhand—of what clan, I cannot say, but I'm a child of the Smith and a—"

"You're of Lorimbur's line," said the warrior, cutting him short. He ignored Tungdil's outstretched hand. "Bulingar Steelfinger of the clan of the Steel Fingers, child of the Smith and warrior of Borengar," he introduced himself. "No daughter of mine will ever be melded to a dwarf whose founding father swore eternal vengeance on the other folks. I know you fought valiantly at the Blacksaddle, but you're a thirdling, and that's all there is to it as far as I'm concerned."

Tungdil would rather have been beaten over the head with a cudgel, stabbed through the heart, or pushed into a chasm than suffer the harshness of Bulingar's words.

His vision of a shared future with Balyndis shattered into a thousand jagged shards, leaving him with a gut-wrenching feeling of emptiness.

"Believe me, I've never wanted to kill another dwarf," he said, hoping to change the firstling's mind. "All my life, I've longed to—"

"All your life?" interrupted Balyndis's father. "A dwarf of sixty cycles is practically a child! How would you know if you wanted to kill us? You were found by a magus and brought up by men. It stands to reason that you didn't hate us in Ionandar, but after a few cycles in a dwarven kingdom, your true disposition will come to the fore. What if the golden warrior is made of gilded tin?"

Balyndis's eyes flashed angrily. "Don't his actions count for anything?" she protested, struggling to control her temper. "A dwarf intent on destroying our kinsfolk wouldn't risk everything to save the dwarven kingdoms. It doesn't make—"

"Silence!" thundered Bulingar. "There's nothing to discuss! You won't be getting melded to Tungdil because we've found someone else."

Balyndis took a step back. Her cheeks, which seconds ago had been filled with color, turned a sickly white. "Someone else?" she stammered, turning to Tungdil and begging him silently to forgive her for what would surely follow.

"Cheer up, child," said a skirted personage whom Tungdil guessed was Balyndis's aunt. "We know you were upset about not getting melded, so we found you a worthy suitor. Most dwarves aren't good enough for our Balyndis, but we found one in the end."

She clapped her hands and a figure stepped out of a

side passage. The warrior was everything that a dwarven hero should be: tall, powerfully built, with a thick black beard, and finely crafted armor.

Tungdil, gazing at the mail shirt in wonder, decided that he was looking at Borengar's second-best smith. *No*, he prayed, hoping that the warrior would decide to walk away. He clenched his fists.

The other paid no attention to Tungdil's silent pleading. Solemnly, he turned to Balyndis. "My name is Glaïmbar Sharpax of the clan of the Iron Beaters, a child of your folk." He pointed to his armor. "I'm a smith as well as a warrior, and this," he held out his hand and offered Balyndis a beautiful gold ring inlaid with gleaming vraccasium, "I made for you. It's an honor to be considered worthy of a Steel Finger; I won't let your clansfolk down."

Tungdil didn't know whether to shriek or weep. His instinct and reason were pulling in different directions, the one telling him to challenge the rival, the other warning that fighting Glaïmbar would upset Balyndis and prove her father right. He didn't want to be classed as a dwarf hater, after all. While his mind continued to chafe against his fate, his heart was weeping and his soul was lamenting his loss.

She won't turn him down; she can't. Defying the wishes of the clan was as heretical as breaking Vraccas's laws. In dwarven society, clan was second only to family. Deep down, Tungdil knew this, but he refused to give up hope.

If the situation had been reversed, he would have rejected the unwelcome suitor and turned his back on the clan.

It was different for Balyndis. She had grown up in a dwarven kingdom, surrounded by family, clan, and folk. These were the dwarves who had fed, protected, and trained her in warfare and metalwork for thirty-five cycles—and she was expected to defer to their desires. If Balyndis neglected her duty and followed her heart, her family would disown her, and she would be a dwarf without clansfolk, a pebble banished from the flanks of the mountain, lonely and forlorn.

Balyndis turned to face him. Tears trickled down her cheeks, collecting on her chin and merging into a single, diamond-like droplet. "My heart belongs to you," she mouthed before turning to Glaïmbar and accepting his gift with trembling hands. With that it was settled: Balyndis and Glaïmbar would forge the iron band.

"It's time you were melded," her father told her, visibly relieved. "The future of the Steel Fingers is safe in your hands. You're young and strong, and you'll have plenty of children. And you, Glaïmbar Sharpax of the clan of the Iron Beaters, you're a fine addition to our clan. Our elders will be delighted to hear my daughter's decision." He stood between them and laid a hand on their backs, propelling them down the corridor away from Tungdil. "Come, let's eat together and make plans for the biggest celebration in history. The bride is a heroine, after all."

The Steel Fingers lined up on both sides of the corridor to let the trio pass. Balyndis turned around to look at Tungdil, but one of her clansfolk stepped between them, his helmet blocking their view. The others joined the back of the procession, and Balyndis was lost among the crowd. A moment later, the Steel Fingers rounded a corner, their jangling mail and stomping boots fading away.

Tungdil stared after them, feet welded to the ground. He tried calling himself to order, but his thoughts were spinning in all directions, hopelessly out of control.

Incapable of formulating a single clear idea, he took the only course of action left to him and wandered aimlessly through the passageways of the firstling kingdom, blind to the beautiful friezes and inscriptions on the walls. Mind in a fever, he crossed suspension bridges and wandered through grottos, stumbling from hall to hall, not knowing or caring where he was or whom he encountered on the way; all he could see was Balyndis's face. After a while he lost all sense of time.

At last, he came to rest in a dimly lit cavern and pressed his sweat-drenched forehead to the floor. Droplets splashed from the ceiling, calling the name of his beloved as they dropped to the ground. In the distance, a pickax was hammering against the rock, and the noise joined the chorus of droplets. Every sound that came to his ears seemed to echo with her name.

No, he whimpered, closing his eyes and curling into a ball. *Leave me alone.*

But the noises persisted until tiredness overcame him, numbing his tormented mind. Before he fell into a deep and dreamless sleep, he had a vision of Bulingar and Glaïmbar looming over him, and hatred and anger took hold of his heart.

Porista,
Former Realm of Lios Nudin,
Girdlegard,
Spring, 6235th Solar Cycle

*S*urely *he can't have destroyed all Girdlegard's famuli?* thought Andôkai as she made her way through the sunlit arcades of the palace in Porista. Sighing, she remembered how Nôd'onn had rooted out his rivals' apprentices, killing them with his magic or putting them to the sword.

In place of her customary leather armor she wore a close-fitting dress of crimson cloth. The skirt was slit at the sides and the low neck emphasized her figure, lending her a femininity absent from her angular face.

For orbits she had been focusing her energies on finding apprentices to school in the art of magic. *Nôd'onn can't have killed them all.* Her legs, clad in soft suede boots, strode purposefully over the beautiful mosaic floor. The last of the sun's rays filtered through the vaulted glass roof, illuminating the passageway and causing the white marble columns to shine like beacons.

She reached the base of the second-highest tower and descended the steps to the vaults, where the flow of energy was strongest. Located at the heart of Girdlegard, the former realm of Lios Nudin was the source of the force fields, a wellspring of magic energy supplying the other enchanted realms.

Andôkai sat on the floor of the carpeted room. She turned her focus inward and felt for the invisible force, sensing at once how the energy had been changed. Nôd'onn, drawing on knowledge given to him by the Perished Land, had contaminated the force fields, making them dangerous for other wizards to use.

Andôkai was an exception. Her chosen deity was Samusin, god of equilibrium, champion of darkness and light. She was a conduit for good—but also for forces commonly described as evil, which was why she could channel the tainted energy without succumbing to the poison. A practitioner of white magic would not be so lucky.

Senses keyed, she checked for signs that the force fields were recovering, but even with Nôd'onn dead and the Perished Land defeated, the magic energy flowing from Porista was under the magus's spell.

She rose to her feet. *How long will it take the force fields to cleanse themselves of Nôd'onn's evil? A hundred cycles or even a thousand? If they ever recover at all . . .*

She ascended the stairs, left the palace through the main doors and came to a halt on the steps leading down to the courtyard.

The sun was resting on the horizon, creating a shimmering tableau of color, cloud, and light. The warmth of the sunset reached as far as Porista, steeping the palace in its reddish glow and transforming the sable turrets to vibrant amber. Andôkai felt the breeze and smelled the aroma of freshly turned soil. Birds were soaring and dipping in pursuit of buzzing insects. It looked the picture of harmony and order.

Andôkai was reminded of past occasions when she and the other magi had lingered on the palace steps, waiting for the sun to set and knowing that it would rise again in a blaze of light to announce the new dawn.

While she had little doubt that the sun would continue to put on its twice-daily spectacle, she was beginning to wonder whether she would be the last maga in Girdlegard to admire the fiery orb.

For two thousand cycles the council of the magi had met in Porista, but Nôd'onn had turned his palace into a slaughterhouse, sending four of Girdlegard's magi to their deaths, killing their famuli, and destroying the magic girdle. Andôkai had barely escaped with her life.

Now, with Nôd'onn defeated, she had returned to the palace, the only building untouched by the inferno that had raged through Porista.

Andôkai had little affection for the city where her colleagues had met their deaths, but she had elected to live there for one simple reason: It was the best place to instruct apprentices in the magic arts.

She surveyed the ruined houses and rubble beyond the palace walls. Little remained of the eight thousand dwellings that had once stood proudly on Lios Nudin's plains. Faced with an army of revenants, Prince Mallen had razed the city to the ground.

On hearing of Nôd'onn's death, the first brave souls had returned to the city, and more had followed, re-assured by the sight of Andôkai's pennants flying from the flagpoles. Porista had a new mistress, who through no desire of her own, had come to preside over six enchanted realms.

Looking up, she gazed at the ever-darkening sky, watching her pennants rippling on the breeze. *Samusin, god of equilibrium, master of winds, I need apprentices. Send me famuli, old or young, with the ability to learn. If the danger is as great as Nôd'onn foretold, I won't be strong enough to combat it on my own.*

She heard a loud knock on the gates to the forecourt. Runes lit up throughout the palace, the signal for a servant to rush out and determine whether to admit the waiting person or persons.

But the palace staff had been discharged.

For want of a doorman to answer the knock, Andôkai uttered an incantation, and the gates swung open to reveal a tall slender woman and a young man.

The pair stepped into the forecourt and headed toward the steps. Dressed in black leather armor, the woman was carrying a weapons belt with two outlandish weapons that Andôkai recognized as unique to their bearer. Porista, like most ruined cities, was plagued by looters and thieves, and this particular woman preferred to be armed. She walked briskly and fearlessly, while her companion hurried after her, scanning the forecourt anxiously and hugging his pack to his chest.

A shadow fell over Andôkai.

"It's all right, Djerûn," she told her bodyguard, keeping her eyes on the couple. "They're quite harmless." She flashed him a wry smile. "Although quite frankly, I wouldn't mind if they were Nôd'onn's chief famuli." She looked up at the towering warrior, eying the demonic metal visor that always masked his face. "Even hostile apprentices would be better than none at all."

Djerûn stayed where he was, diagonally behind her. He seemed to be watching the approaching couple, but the eyeholes in his visor gave nothing away. His helmet appeared to be empty, but he was capable of fixing his enemies with terrible rays of violet light.

His stillness was also deceptive. Clad from head to toe in armor, he looked heavy and inert, but at the sight of an enemy, or if his mistress was in danger, he moved with incredible agility, running, jumping, and fighting as if he were made of shimmering silk. Few could say what lay beneath his armor—and it was better that way.

The woman and her frightened companion ascended the steps. Andôkai realized that she had been mistaken. "Narmora, who's this?" she demanded, forgetting to welcome her guest. "I mistook him for Furgas."

The half älf smiled. Like Djerûn, she was careful to hide her striking features from strangers, and her pointed ears were covered by a crimson headscarf. The daughter of an älf and a human, she had thrown in her lot with the men, elves, and dwarves, but älfar were feared and hated throughout Girdlegard, and she knew better than to expect any mercy from a baying mob. The headscarf was vital for her safety.

"Maga, I found him roaming the city. He wanted to see you, but he was too afraid to knock."

The man lifted his eyes and saw Djerûn, who stood three paces tall. His gaze traveled fearfully over the metal breastplate that mimicked the curve of bulging muscle. He took in the tionium gorget, the terrifying visor, and the ring of metal spikes encircling his helmet like a crown. "What in the name of Palandiell . . ." Stepping back, he almost tumbled down the staircase, but the nimble Narmora grabbed him by the elbow. "Djerûn won't hurt you," she assured him.

The man did his best to compose himself. "Wenslas is my name. I served Turgur the Fair-Faced," he said timorously.

Andôkai's heart sank. The only famulus in Girdlegard, and he was trained by a preening dandy. "There's no need to be afraid," she told him. "Which tier did you reach before your magus died?"

"I didn't," he said softly. "I wasn't actually a famulus. My name was on the list for the academy, and I was waiting to take the exam. I heard the Estimable Maga was looking for students, so I came to Porista."

"That's when I found him," chimed in Narmora. "He saw the ruined city, and his courage failed him, so I escorted him myself. Did I do well?"

Andôkai looked the man up and down. "I need to know how strong you are, Wenslas. You'll do the exam right away." Privately she doubted that the nervous young man had the mental fortitude to handle complicated formulae and strength-sapping rituals. *He knows nothing about magic. It will take cycles to turn him into a tolerable apprentice.* Turgur had put him on a waiting list, which meant only one thing: Wenslas was a last resort.

Turning sharply, she went into the palace. "I'll need your help, Narmora—if you can spare a little time."

"Furgas was busy when I left him—he won't mind if I stay for a while." She gave Wenslas a little shove; he side-stepped quickly around the armor-plated giant and set off after Andôkai.

The little party made its way through the deserted palace. Wenslas's boots echoed through the empty marble passage-ways, setting him further on edge. None of the stories he had heard about the tempestuous maga had prepared him for meeting the real-life Andôkai and her disquieting companions. He was about to announce that he had decided not to go through with the exam when they passed through a doorway and came to a halt in the conference chamber.

The hall, once famous for its domed roof of gleaming copper, was in ruins. It was here that Nôd'onn had revealed himself as a traitor and an enemy of Girdlegard, and his battle with the council had destroyed the ancient room. Large chunks were missing from the ceiling, some of the pillars had been smashed to pieces, and ash, blown into the chamber from the burned-out city, had mingled with rainwater, forming a thick black sludge on the marble floor.

Amid the wreckage stood the fossilized form of a man, an enduring reminder of Nôd'onn's treachery. The cruel magus had used his dark magic to turn Lot-Ionan the Forbearing to stone.

Wenslas stepped over the fallen columns and followed Andôkai to the center of the chamber where the floor was littered with splintered malachite.

"I'm going to send a charm in your direction—only a weak one, so you won't come to any harm, but enough to gauge your aptitude for magic." She signaled for Narmora to position herself behind him and catch him if he fell. "Ready?" Without waiting for an answer, she hurled a glowing blue sphere toward Wenslas, who raised his arms unthinkingly, palms outstretched to stop the missile.

The spluttering sphere hit his hands and sent him flying backward. There was a hissing noise, and he yelped in pain and shock. Narmora was behind him straightaway, holding him by the armpits to save him from the splinters on the floor.

But the glowing sphere continued on its path.

Whizzing through the air, it spiraled higher and higher, gathering speed for its next attack. Like an angry wasp, it circled above them, then swooped toward Wenslas.

"Maga?" gasped Narmora, alarmed. When no help was forthcoming, she laid Wenslas gently on the floor and prepared to face the magic weapon. Using a wooden plank as a shield, she took up position and watched as the sphere zigzagged crazily toward her. It came within half a forearm of her; then it burst.

Andôkai's eyebrows shot up in surprise. "Congratulations, Wenslas," she praised him. "I believe in challenging my pupils; it brings out their talent." She walked over and examined his scorched palms. "Don't worry about your hands; the skin will soon heal."

Groaning, Wenslas clambered to his feet. "Estimable Maga, it's no use pretending that I passed," he said dejectedly. "We both know that I didn't stop the sphere. It's nice of you to be encouraging, but I'm not a magician. If you hadn't taken pity on me, I would have been killed." He picked up his bag. "Turgur told me that I wasn't cut out to be a famulus, and he was right. If only I could . . . Oh, what's the use?" Sighing, he bowed before the maga and took his leave. "May the gods be with you."

They heard his footsteps echoing through the arcades, then Djerûn set off after him to escort him through the gates.

The maga studied Narmora's face. "So it was you," she murmured incredulously. "You destroyed the sphere." Her eyes narrowed dangerously. "How? You told me you inherited a few tricks from your mother, nothing more. Correct me if I'm wrong, but älfar can't do magic."

Narmora seemed as surprised as she was. "I . . . I didn't use a spell or anything. I just wanted the sphere to go away. I was thinking about it disappearing and then . . ." She tailed off and raised a hand to her eyes. "It disappeared, just like that," she whispered. She seemed almost scared.

Andôkai was the first to recover her composure. "Do you know what this means, Narmora?" she said excitedly, laying her hands on the half älf's shoulders. "I've found my apprentice! It won't take long before you're ready to—"

"No."

Narmora's refusal was spoken with such intensity and conviction that Andôkai let go and took a step back. "No?" she said uncomprehendingly, searching Narmora's face for signs that she might be swayed. "You can't mean that."

Narmora drew herself up to her full height. "Yes I can." She wasn't afraid of Andôkai's wrath. "I'm sure there are better candidates, and I'm willing to help you find them, but I won't be your famulus." She met the maga's questioning stare. "Remember what happened at the Blacksaddle? It's a wonder that we survived. No more adventures, that's what we decided, and I've given Furgas my word. We came to Porista so that Furgas could help you rebuild the city, and I'm here because of him. Nothing is going to separate us again." She paused, noticing the maga's baffled expression. "It doesn't make sense to you, I suppose."

She sat down on a fallen column and lowered her voice. "Listen Andôkai, I want to grow old with Furgas; I want to have children and grandchildren, and I want to see them grow up. How am I supposed to do that if I train to be a maga? I don't want to risk my life for Girdlegard; I love Furgas, and I'm happy the way I am." She lifted her loose-fitting breastplate; her figure was fuller than usual. "I'm going to be a mother," she said, stroking her bump. "The baby is due in ninety orbits."

Andôkai snorted angrily and made no reply.

The news hadn't produced the intended effect. Narmora took a deep breath. "Excuse me, Maga, it's getting late. It's time I went home to Furgas." She got up and walked to the door.

"Is there anything I can say to persuade you?" the maga called after her, undaunted. "How can I change your mind?"

Narmora glanced over her shoulder and saw Andôkai silhouetted in the light of the rising moon. "I don't intend to break my promise," she said firmly as she made her way out.

Sighing, the maga went over to the statue of Lot-Ionan, formerly a man of flesh and blood. "My poor friend, I could do with your support," she whispered absently. Her fingers stroked the smooth marble, tracing the folds of his cloak. The magus of Ionandar was dead—dead like Turgur the Fair-Faced, Sabora the Softly-Spoken, and Maira the Life-Preserver.

She turned around sadly, surveying the wreckage of the hall.

Narmora was a fool to sacrifice her talents for love of a man.

Richemark,
Southeastern Gauragar,
Girdlegard,
Spring, 6235th Solar Cycle

King Bruron stood at the gates and watched as a steady stream of loaded wagons left the storehouse. His entourage was made up of seven bodyguards and two stewards, whose job was to write down how many drums of grain were heading north.

The first wagon had left the capital at dawn, on course for the far reaches of the kingdom, where the soil had been blighted by the Perished Land. The fields and meadows were beginning to recover, and by summer they would be fertile, but there was nothing for the farmers to sow. They desperately needed seeds, not to mention food to see them through.

"Supplies are dangerously low, Your Majesty," said the first steward, noting another figure on his wax tablet. He pointed the stylus at the convoy of wagons.

"The silos are almost empty," replied the king, dressed inconspicuously in dark brown cloth as if he were an ordinary stocktaker. He watched for a moment as the last of his provisions left the capital for the provinces, the drums of grain jiggling up and down in the wagons. "I've taken the necessary measures. Yesterday King Nate received payment for five thousand drums of grain to be delivered to the northern provinces. Idoslane will supply the rest." He smiled and thumped the steward on the back. "I've been keeping count as well. None of my subjects will go hungry—another five thousand drums are on the way."

His bodyguard alerted him to a group of riders who seemed intent on cantering through the gates of the storehouse. There were thirty in total, three dwarves and the rest men, and their grim faces left little doubt as to their mood.

Bruron's smile vanished from his lips. The arrival of the delegation wasn't entirely unexpected, but it filled him with dread. It was too late to slip away unnoticed, so he would have to face his troublesome guests.

The first rider reined in his horse. No sooner was he out of the saddle than a group of servants surrounded the horse and led it away. His soldiers stayed mounted, but the three dwarves lined up beside the man. "Greetings, King Bruron," said the ruler of Idoslane with a cursory bow.

"Welcome to Richemark, Prince Mallen," the king replied warmly. "I was heartened to hear of your victory against the orcs." He turned to the dwarves and smiled. "Please extend my thanks to your commanders. The people of Gauragar won't forget how the allied army saved them from the green-hided beasts. They're very grateful." He laid a bejeweled hand on his chest. "As am I."

One of the dwarves thumped the ground with the poll of his ax. "Yet you handed the Blacksaddle to our enemies while we were fighting on your behalf. Is that how you show gratitude? I call it disloyal and underhanded, and I don't mind telling you that I expected better from a human king."

Bruron looked pained. "Those are harsh accusations, master dwarf—especially as I had no choice. I agreed to take over the watch when your kinsfolk left the Blacksaddle, but I had no way of knowing that a centuries-old agreement would force me to—"

"Betray your allies," the dwarf finished for him, the creases on his forehead deepening into furrows.

Prince Mallen studied the wagons of grain. "An agreement, you say?"

"Many cycles ago, the house of Gauragar signed a treaty with Lorimbur's folk, according to which the Blacksaddle was ceded to the thirdlings—for perpetuity and with no recourse."

"Are you sure the document is genuine?" asked Mallen.

Bruron inclined his gray head. "I'm afraid so. My archivists scoured our deepest vaults and highest towers—and the evidence confirms the terms of the agreement. The thirdlings helped my forebears to mine Cloudpiercer's riches, and the Blacksaddle was their reward." He turned to the dwarves. "The stronghold belongs to the thirdlings," he said apologetically. "What was I supposed to do?"

"Refuse?" suggested one of the dwarves.

"My forefathers signed a treaty with the thirdlings, and

it behooves me to uphold its terms. Surely the dwarves, with their fondness for tradition, can understand the situation?" His tone had undergone a sudden change, becoming sharper and more impatient; it was obvious that he considered the matter closed. "The Blacksaddle belongs to the thirdlings; I'm not thrilled about it either, but the honor of Gauragar is at stake."

Mallen looked at him squarely. "I won't presume to judge you, Bruron, but in your position I would have advised my allies of the treaty and looked for a better solution."

"I didn't have the luxury of—"

"You could have requested more time—a few extra orbits to check the treaty's terms," cut in Mallen. "Instead you allowed the dwarf killers to seize a stronghold that poses a strategic threat to our friends. We'll soon find out how Lorimbas intends to use his advantage." He locked gazes with the monarch, smiling coolly as the other looked away. It was obvious that Bruron had been offered some inducement to remind him of the treaty's terms. "I see what this is about," he whispered in the king's ear.

"You have no idea," hissed Bruron. "My subjects are starving. Grain costs money, and I'm spending a fortune to keep them alive! If my allies would waive the cost of the—"

"It's rude to whisper," boomed one of the dwarves. "We won't inconvenience you any longer—we're needed in Dsôn Balsur. But don't worry, King Bruron; we'll be sure to tell our kinsfolk what you said. No doubt the high king will reach his own conclusions about your obligations."

The three dwarves raised their hands and took their leave with a gesture that could have passed for an obscenity or a wave.

"So you sold it," said Mallen angrily as soon as they were out of earshot. "You traded the Blacksaddle for gold."

"No," snapped Bruron. "My forebears signed a treaty; I kept to the terms."

"And risked the wrath of the dwarves? What if they cut their ties with the human kingdoms?" Mallen shook his head bitterly. "I said before that I wouldn't judge you, but I've changed my mind. You're a fool for ceding the Blacksaddle to the thirdlings."

The king turned on him angrily. "How dare you—"

"I speak only the truth," broke in Mallen, weary of Bruron's excuses. "Even a king must be censured if he errs. Don't you realize what's happening in Dsôn Balsur? The dwarves lost three hundred warriors in a night! They were murdered in their sleep—duped by älfar who claimed to be envoys from Liútasil. And now a strategically crucial stronghold, complete with weaponry and supplies, is in the hands of the dwarf killers. How do you think our friends will react?"

Bruron's self-assurance vanished. "I hadn't heard," he said, concerned. "I'll tell my advisors to find a way of annulling the treaty."

"You do that, King Bruron. New friendships are easily sundered. The dwarves are valuable allies; we can't afford to lose them." He paused, deciding that he had said enough. "By the way, I came to tell you that we've started setting fire to the forests around Dsôn Balsur. The trees are harder to burn than we thought, and we'll need more pitch—but it's working. The assault on the älfar's black kingdom will soon begin."

"I have news for you as well, Prince Mallen," said the king. He hesitated. "The thirdlings want to speak with you. Their spokesman is in the capital, waiting for you to send word." He gave Mallen the name of a boarding house. "I've met a few groundlings in my time, but these ones are . . ." He checked himself and tried to mask his disquiet. "In any case, you're more experienced at handling them than me."

Mallen swung himself onto his horse. "I've nothing to say to the thirdlings. We're leaving this very orbit. A couple of orcish commanders are limping back to Toboribor and I intend to destroy their troops." He raised his hand in farewell.

"Palandiell be with you and your men," said Bruron sincerely.

"May the alliance hold strong," replied Mallen. At his command, the cavalrymen formed a guard around him and they left the storeroom in the direction they had come.

The king of Gauragar lowered his yellow-flecked eyes and examined the lists that his stewards had prepared. After a moment's consideration, he reached a decision— for the good of his kingdom.

The three cases of gold that would arrive in the capital in nine orbits' time would allow him to purchase further supplies. There was no point in throwing the thirdlings out of the Blacksaddle until he had accumulated enough gold to secure his kingdom's future.

Bruron was certain that Mallen and the dwarves would think differently if they knew the suffering of his people. *No other kingdom was ravaged as badly as Gauragar. After orbits of eating moldering wheat, my subjects shall have fresh bread. Happier times are ahead for my kingdom.*

"See to it that the silos are emptied," he told his stewards. "Tell the farmers in the northern provinces to till every inch of fertile land. And order another nine thousand drums of barley from Tabaîn. I won't have my subjects eating crumbs."

I'm sorry I wasn't in when you called."

The deep voice sounded from near Mallen's feet. The prince, unaccustomed to being addressed in such an irreverent manner, stopped admiring the red-tinged clouds above Richemark and looked down to identify the speaker. It was a heavily armed dwarf, who had slipped past his guards.

"I didn't call," he said coldly. "There was nothing to discuss." He raised a hand to reassure his guards, fearing that any action on their part would result in bloodshed.

The dwarf's armor was unlike anything that Mallen had seen. His reinforced spaulders were fitted with finger-length spikes, sharp blades glistened on his vambraces, and his gauntlets boasted sharp metal studs. Even without drawing his weapons he could wound or kill a man.

"If you don't have a name," said Mallen, "I'd be happy to choose one for you—although it might not meet with your approval."

"In which case, I'd knock you out of the saddle—and I'm loath to hurt your splendid horse." The dwarf smiled unpleasantly, the black tattoos on his cheeks rearranging themselves briefly. "If you care for your mount, you'd do well to call me Romo—Romo Steelheart of the clan of the Stone Grinders, descendant of Lorimbur, and nephew of King Lorimbas. I'm here on my uncle's business."

Mallen's gaze traveled over the dwarf, taking in his breastplate, the steel plates protecting his thighs, and the three-chained morning star on his belt. "You're dressed for war, not business. With a tongue like yours, you're bound to find enemies, I suppose."

"My enemies are your allies, and our war has been raging since the creation of the dwarves." He reached down and pulled a sealed leather roll from his boot. "From my uncle—he told me to bring him your reply." He held out the roll for Mallen to take.

It seemed to the prince that he should read the missive; if nothing else, it would apprise him of the thirdlings' intentions. He broke the seal, opened the roll, and pulled out the parchment.

He was expecting some form of blackmail, which was exactly what the letter contained. It referred to an ancient treaty between the house of Ido and the thirdlings in which the latter agreed to provide assistance in combating Toboribor's orcs.

The arrangement still stood. Idoslane's defenses depended on the dwarves' undying hatred of orcs. Dwarven warriors, renowned for their toughness, staffed the outposts in parts of the kingdom most vulnerable to the marauding hordes, but it was difficult to know which of them were thirdlings because, unlike Romo, they looked no different to ordinary dwarves.

According to the letter, the thirdlings' services were conditional on Mallen sticking to the terms of an agreement signed by his forefathers. It was the first he had heard of such a deal.

"I'm afraid your king is mistaken," he said firmly, lowering the parchment. "Tell him I don't like his scheming. First he seizes the Blacksaddle; then he tries to turn Idoslane against her allies. Nothing can induce me to pick a fight with the fourthlings." He dropped the letter, watching as it floated toward a pile of horse dung. "King Gandogar is more than an ally; he's a friend."

"How touching," scoffed Romo, seemingly unsurprised by his refusal. "Perhaps my uncle can take his place in your affections. We *demand* that you keep to the terms of the agreement. Your forebears signed the treaty of their own free will."

"I won't be held to ransom by your uncle. My forefathers weren't allied to the fourthlings and their adherence to the treaty was never tested. In fact, I can't recall any reference to an agreement with the thirdlings; it wouldn't surprise me if the document were a fake." He leaned forward in his saddle. "Tell King Lorimbas that bribery worked on Bruron, but it won't work on me. He can keep his gold."

"We didn't bribe Bruron; we paid him." Romo poked the letter with his boot, watching as the parchment sank into the brown, soggy dung. "You must be very proud of your kingdom, Prince Mallen. I suppose your cavalry is strong enough to deal with the orcs—provided you've got enough mercenaries watching your borders."

"Is that a threat?"

"A threat?" echoed Romo, feigning surprise. "My uncle merely said to tell you—"

Mallen didn't wait to hear the rest. Dropping the leather holder into the mud, he kicked his heels into the horse's flanks and rode away. He had said everything he wanted to say.

The cavalrymen, noticing their monarch's displeasure, took their leave from the dwarf without ceremony. Their places were taken by the traders and citizens of Richemark, who trampled the dung-soaked parchment underfoot.

Romo watched Mallen's departure with a contemptuous grunt. *He'll see the consequences of his obstinacy soon enough.* The dwarf was pleased that the passers-by were careful not to crowd him; they were nervous of dwarves, and his demeanor did nothing to calm their fears.

Mallen's refusal to ally himself with the thirdlings meant that Romo was obliged to continue his journey in a north-easterly direction. He could be sure that his advances would be looked on more sympathetically there.

A group of children ventured closer, stopping a few paces away and staring at him with open curiosity.

"Are you a dwarf as well?" asked the eldest among them. "Why do you look so funny?"

"For the same reason you look so ugly," he growled. Then he realized the implications of the child's words. "Of course I'm a dwarf, a very special dwarf—a warrior, if you must know." He smiled a crooked smile. "Are more of my kind in town?"

The children jumped up and down, nodding eagerly.

"What a wonderful coincidence. Can you tell me where I might find them?" He took a coin from his leather purse and threw it to the tallest boy. His right hand closed around the metal haft of his morning star. He intended to end his business in Richemark on a high.

IV

I t hasn't changed since last time," said Boïndil, gazing
at the crumbling ramparts and fallen towers that were
all that remained of the stronghold's glory. He, Tungdil,
Balyndis, and a group of twenty handpicked warriors were
marching ahead to survey the land. The gateway to the
fifthling kingdom lay before them, tall as a house and
tantalizingly close. The doors had been smashed to pieces.
Boïndil looked back at the steep path leading down the
mountainside. The remaining dwarves were about a mile
away, working their way to the top with their belongings
and supplies. "They're moving too fast," he muttered.
"They need to be more careful with Boëndal's stretcher—
and they shouldn't be making so much noise." He
dispatched a warrior to pass on the message.

Tungdil left the little group, ducked behind the weathered ruins, and darted toward the gateway, moving as
quietly as he could. Mindful of the possible dangers, he
had taken his ax from his belt and was ready to strike
at a moment's notice. A few paces from the gateway,
he stopped and crouched behind a pile of rubble.

"Hey, that wasn't the deal," growled Ireheart, setting
off after him. "What are you playing at, scholar? The first
ten orcs belong to me." He ducked down, charging from

rock to rock and sheltering behind the ruined ramparts, now almost fully visible beneath the melting snow. Balyndis and the others ran after him, rattling and clunking like an army of tinkers.

Tungdil rolled his eyes. "You couldn't be more obvious if you were singing dwarven war songs," he hissed irritably. "I've a good mind to make you take off your chain mail." He focused his attention on the dark gateway leading into the mountain; everything was still.

The silence was broken by dripping water. All around them, stalactites were melting, and not far from the gateway, a waterfall, free at last from its icy prison, was cascading down the slope. Spray rose into the air, lingering in a haze of iridescent mist.

"I'd sooner shave off my beard than take off my chain mail," protested Boïndil. "I'm naked without it." He flared his nostrils, sniffing the air for orcs. "Not a whiff of them—or their rancid armor." He turned to Tungdil and Balyndis. "Remember the orcs in the smelting works?" His eyes lit up with the memory. "They were packed in so tightly, just waiting to be killed. I couldn't swing my axes without disemboweling a dozen of them by accident. Do you think—"

"Quiet!" ordered Tungdil, conscious that Balyndis was looking at him.

She had been true to her word and joined the expedition—not as his fiancée, but as a friend. At her side was Glaïmbar Sharpax, to whom she would soon be melded.

Tungdil didn't know how to behave around her. In the space of an orbit, he had gone from being a lover to a friend, but his tortured heart refused to accept the change. "I'll go first," he said.

Stooping low, he darted off and stopped to the side of the gateway, pressing his ear to the wall and listening for sounds from within. Hearing nothing, he slipped inside and disappeared into the gloom.

Boïndil jiggled his axes impatiently. "I can't stand it!" he spluttered. His inner furnace was overheating, stoked by his fiery spirit and concern for his brother's life. "We should be seizing the Dragon Fire furnace and making my brother well. I'm going straight to the fifthling smithy, and no one can stop me—not you or a hundred orcs!" Throwing caution to the wind, he jumped up and ran through the gateway. Balyndis, swearing softly, hurried after him, followed by the others.

The tread of their boots on the rock sounded different in the tunnel. Balyndis found herself imagining that she was running across the roof of a cavern, but she pushed the thought aside.

A moment later, she and the others almost barreled into Tungdil, who had come to a halt at the end of the tunnel. "Forget what I said about keeping down the noise," he said testily. "They're bound to have heard us by now." He gripped Keenfire with both hands. "It's time to find out whether Tion's beasts are still squatting in our stronghold or whether they've found themselves another home."

"That's more like it," said Boïndil cheerily. "Dwarves don't hold with sneaking and skulking; it's cowardly and underhanded." He flashed them a ferocious grin. "Show me where the runts are hiding—I'm dying for a fight."

"How unusual," said Balyndis, cross with him for breaking rank.

They set off through the passageways, Tungdil, Balyndis, and Boïndil, who knew the stronghold from their previous visit, leading the way. The likenesses of dead fifthling chieftains greeted them, axes hefted, from gleaming palandium panels on the walls.

They soon found evidence of orcish activity: a trail of dirt and muddy prints—some booted, others unshod—leading toward the exit. It seemed the beasts had marched through the stronghold on their way to the Blacksaddle.

On reaching a many-columned pentagonal chamber, they took the passageway to the Dragon Fire furnace.

Tungdil's memories came flooding back. He heard Gandogar's booming voice taunting Nôd'onn's hordes, he saw images of his dead friends, and he braced himself for grunting orcs and squawking bögnilim—but the halls were deathly still.

"Botheration! It's empty as an ogre's skull," cursed Boïndil as they reached the smelting works adjoining the furnace. The fires had gone out beneath the blast furnaces, the chamber was cold, and the air stank of excrement and orc. "They've abandoned the halls," said Boïndil, striding toward the door. "What are you waiting for? To the Dragon Fire furnace! What's the betting it's still alight?"

Tungdil realized it was useless to reprimand his reckless friend. Consumed with worry about his brother, Boïndil was at the mercy of his temper. Finding some orcs would give him an outlet for his anger, and stop him harming the rest of the group.

Boïndil was driven by hatred for Tion's creation, which

made him a fearsome warrior—and a danger to others and himself. Unless he vented his rage, the flames of his furnace would burn higher and higher until he threw himself on whoever had the misfortune to be in his way. His fiery nature was a blessing and a curse.

They entered the Dragon Fire furnace, and immediately noticed a change in temperature.

Twenty hearths and eighty anvils were arranged around the central furnace. The vast room was filled with an odor so foul that the dwarves, covering their noses, tried not to gag. Decaying corpses lay strewn across the floor—orcs, bögnilim, a handful of älfar, and even three trolls. This was the work of Bavragor Hammersmith and the undead fifthlings who had given their lives so that Tungdil and the others could escape.

"By the beard of Beroïn, what a battle it must have been!" murmured Boïndil respectfully. "I never thought the merry minstrel had it in him."

They sifted through the bodies, hoping to give a proper burial to their friends, but nothing remained except chain mail and cloth; the valiant warriors had been overpowered and torn to pieces.

"Look!" said Balyndis, pointing her ax at the main furnace. "It's still burning!"

Tungdil breathed out in relief. With Dragon Fire, his worries about forging weaponry, armor, and other equipment for the kingdom were instantly solved. "Fan the flames! Giselbert's kingdom belongs to the dwarves!"

The dwarves shoveled coal onto the furnace, taking care not to extinguish the flickering flames. Then they pulled on the chains connected to the giant bellows and breathed new life into Dragon Fire's heart. Tungdil sent Boïndil and nine others to relay the good news to the rest of the company and guide them through the passageways.

In the meantime, Balyndis set about opening the vents to the flue. The fifthlings had sabotaged the mechanism to stop the orcs following Tungdil and the others through the chimney. She looked up at the ceiling, eighty paces above. A stone staircase led to the flue, which was blocked by a pair of solid metal plates.

"I'll need a bit of time, but I can fix it," she said, raising her voice so that Tungdil, who was standing nearby, would have to respond. "The chain came down because they destroyed the main sprocket. I'll have the mechanism working in less than an orbit."

Tungdil nodded but didn't turn round. "It shouldn't take long to clear up the forge. The bodies can go in the furnace—we'll find a use for the melted armor." He bent down and discovered tongs, hammers, chisels, files, and other tools hidden beneath the rotting remains. "We'll soon have the smithy ringing with the sound of our hammers. The fifthling kingdom has been waiting for hundreds of cycles to hear the music of the forge."

Glancing round to check no one was watching, Balyndis strode over to Tungdil and grabbed him by the arm. "Tungdil Goldhand, what did I do to deserve this?" she demanded, her brown eyes smoldering as fiercely as the furnace.

"I don't know what you mean," he said, scanning the hall intently, as if he were planning the details of the clean-up operation. Balyndis's powerful fingers, accustomed to toiling at the anvil, refused to let him go.

"Are you ignoring me as a punishment? You shouldn't treat me this way—I'm your friend!"

"My friend?" erupted Tungdil. "We were in *love*, Balyndis, we wanted to be joined by the iron band! And then you decided to pledge yourself to a stranger, just because he's a Sharpscythe or a Bluntax or whatever . . ." He broke off and looked at her hopefully. "You haven't finished with him, have you?"

She closed her eyes. "No, Tungdil. It's the law. I have to obey my clan."

"Even at the cost of your happiness?" *My happiness*, he corrected himself.

"Yes," she said simply. "There's nothing more sacred, nothing we prize more highly than tradition. Tradition has kept our society together for thousands of cycles; it allows us to live in harmony; it keeps our clans alive. Sometimes it means we have to make sacrifices, but it's all for the greater good. You'll understand when you've lived in a dwarven kingdom for a while; at least I hope you will." She let go of his arm and went to stroke his cheek, but he jerked away.

"Don't do this to me," he said bitterly. "You're making it worse." Too choked to talk, he turned away and hurried out of the forge, where he bumped into Boïndil, who was leading the procession to the furnace. The four dwarves carrying his frozen brother were just behind.

Glad of anything that might distract him from his thoughts, Tungdil set about sorting the dwarves into groups and sending them into the passageways to scour the stronghold for hidden orcs.

Over the course of the journey, Boëndal's stretcher had

been strapped to a pony or, when the terrain was uneven, carried by his fellow dwarves. They walked the stretcher to the middle of the room and set it down by the furnace. The flames were becoming brighter and fiercer all the time.

"What now?" enquired Boïndil, eying his brother's pale face. "Do you think he'll wake up?"

Tungdil laid a hand on Boëndal's brow. It felt cold and dry. "No change yet, but the furnace isn't up to temperature—we'll wait a bit longer for the pure white flames."

"And then what?" demanded Boïndil. He reached for his brother's hand and clasped it tight. "We could fill a tankard with glowing coal, add some beer, and pour it down his throat," he said hopefully.

Tungdil shook his head. "I can't make sense of the riddle, but I promise you this: We'll ransack the fifthlings' archives until we find a solution." He got up and signaled for the physicians to attend to Boëndal. "Come on," he said, thumping Boïndil's broad back. "There's work to be done."

The two dwarves left the forge, leaving Balyndis to stare after them sadly.

The following orbits saw the peaceable takeover of the kingdom continue apace.

The secondling masons lost no time in beginning the restoration work on the badly damaged chambers and corridors, with everyone lending a hand when it came to transporting the stone.

The firstling smiths fired up the blast furnaces and forged metal strips and bands to reinforce the gateways and doors. Their constant hammering echoed through the underground halls, reminding the mountain of the activity within it, six thousand cycles before.

In the early stages of the project, there wasn't any call for diamond cutting or gem polishing, so the fourthlings helped wherever they were needed and set about exploring every passageway, chamber, nook, and cranny of the kingdom.

But no matter how hard they searched, there was still no sign of a tablet or document containing the key to Dragon Fire's power. And so the orbits passed, and Boëndal continued to lie by the fire, his inner furnace cold and weak.

Tungdil and the others were barely aware of the passing time. New treasures were discovered every orbit, and the fifthlings' craftsmanship became a source of continual delight. The firstlings, who had hitherto considered themselves experts in the art of working gold and other precious metals, readily admitted that the smiths of Giselbert possessed skills in excess of their own.

After orbits of searching, Tungdil decided that nothing in the halls and chambers would help them to revive the frozen dwarf. He gathered an advance party of warriors and set off in the direction of the Stone Gateway, hoping to find something there.

If he were honest, it was also a way of escaping Balyndis, who was torturing him with her beautiful smile, her loveable manner, and her irresistible curves.

The idea of Balyndis living side by side with Glaïmbar Sharpax, her Iron Beating kinsman, was enough to make his spirit plummet deeper than the darkest mine. Worse still, it encouraged his thoughts in untoward directions, and he found himself wishing that Glaïmbar would die.

He allowed his mind to ponder the prospect. *His death would solve everything, wouldn't it?* said a voice in his ear. *If Balyndis were widowed, no one would object to her taking a suitor, whoever he was.*

Tungdil bristled. If Balyndis took a new suitor, it would obviously be him.

Everyone would be happier, whispered the demon inside his head.

Tungdil, shocked at himself, banished the voice.

He was so withdrawn and miserable that Boïndil, who had insisted on joining the expedition, couldn't help but notice.

"I suppose there's a downside to being a dwarf," commented the secondling when they stopped to rest their legs. They were sitting on the rocky banks of an underground stream, far enough away from the band of fifty dwarves for their conversation to go unheard. It gave Boïndil the courage to speak freely. "I'm no scholar," he said, puffing vigorously on his pipe until the tobacco caught light. "I don't have a knack with words, but I can listen; it doesn't take much brains." He crossed his arms and leaned back against the rock, waiting. "It's time we talked."

"About what?"

"Whatever's bothering you." He prodded Tungdil's chain mail with the stem of his pipe. "I can shout her name until you tell me," he threatened.

Sighing loudly, Tungdil cut himself a slice of dried mushroom to go with his cheese. "It's not fair," he said succinctly. Then his pent-up anguish came out in a torrent of words. "I thought we could still be friends," he said finally. "I wasn't expecting it to be so hard." His appetite gone, he put down the mushroom and took a long draft of brandy instead.

"I'd go easy on the drinking," warned Boïndil, still puffing noisily on his pipe. "You wouldn't be the first to drown yourself in brandy. I don't like seeing you like this—especially when me and Boëndal are to blame."

"How do you figure that?" asked Tungdil, running a hand over his beard to wipe away the drops.

"Remember all the things we talked about on the long march to Ogre's Death?" his friend said earnestly. "You asked about our customs, but I guess we forgot the most important ones—or maybe we should have explained them better. It's all about family, clan, and folk. The laws are there to keep order, to protect us, to keep us safe. Without them, everything, er . . ."

"Falls apart," supplied Tungdil, realizing that Boïndil was struggling.

"Exactly! So Balyndis didn't have a choice, do you see?"

"I grew up in a human realm . . ."

"Do humans choose their partners willy-nilly, with no regard for their families?" demanded Boïndil.

"No," conceded Tungdil, "but love comes first. I thought dwarves would be the same." He leaned back against the rock next to his friend. "Look, I've been thinking—the fifthlings should choose a new leader."

"What for? You're the one they want: Tungdil Goldhand, hero of the Blacksaddle, rightful heir to Giselbert's belt, and the only dwarf who can kindle the power of Keenfire."

"They need a dwarf who grew up with our lore, someone who knows the traditions and respects them. There aren't many of us, and we're miles from the other kingdoms; our future depends on us pulling together. Keenfire and I will fight if we're needed—I don't have to be leader as well."

Boïndil removed his pipe and blew smoke rings through his mouth. He waited for the blue smoke to disperse. "I understand what you're saying, scholar. I've never known anyone so wise," he said admiringly.

Tungdil reached into the bubbling stream and scooped a handful of water into his mouth. It was wonderfully clear—slightly metallic, but delicious. It tasted a hundred times better than any overland spring or river, and it slaked the thirst at once. "Is it wrong of me to wish him dead?" he asked softly, damping his hair with his hands.

"Who? Glaïmbar Sharpax?" Boïndil roared with laughter. "I've been wishing him dead since I met him; anyone who makes my best friend unhappy and pilfers his girlfriend deserves as much." On seeing Tungdil's shock, he laughed again. "What's the matter? I'm crazy, remember? My inner furnace has melted my mind." He made an effort to be serious. "Honestly, Tungdil, I'd challenge Sharpax to a duel if I thought it would do any good, but rules are made for a reason. One rash deed leads to another, and before you know it, it's a bloodbath." He thumped Tungdil on the knee. "Chin up, scholar. You'll find another maiden who'll give you a place in her heart and her bed—you'll forget about Balyndis."

"No," said Tungdil.

"It's the only way," his friend advised sharply. "You can't store up your anger forever. Believe me, I know." He handed his pipe to Tungdil, who took it gratefully.

Long moments passed as they sat in silence by the stream.

If it weren't for Glaïmbar, you and Balyndis would be happy, said the fiendish voice in Tungdil's head. *She'll be miserable with Glaïmbar. Do her a favor, and kill him when you have a chance.*

"How will you do it?"

"Do what?" asked Tungdil guiltily, sure that Boïndil could read his thoughts.

"Tell them you don't want to be leader. How will they know whom to choose?"

"Oh . . . I'll say what I said to you," he said carelessly. "They should pick a leader of proper dwarven stock."

He fell silent because Boïndil was on his feet, sniffing the air excitedly. His axes flew to his hands. "You can't say the Gray Range doesn't look after us; it gives us everything we ask for: water for our gullets—and orcs for our blades." His eyes glinted as he grinned at Tungdil. "Can't you smell the stinking runts?" He pointed to a passageway on the right. "This way—down the tunnel!"

The tunnel was labeled with an ancient inscription to signpost the route. It led upward, toward the Stone Gateway.

Their brief rest was over.

Hurriedly they packed their things and lined up for battle, with the warriors at the front. The masons, more accustomed to splitting granite than crushing orc skulls, brought up the rear with their chisels, hammers, and other tools.

The unit of dwarves moved off down the corridor at a jog. By now Tungdil could smell the beasts' acrid perspiration and the rancid fat on their armor. The foul odor was anathema to any dwarf.

"I knew they'd turn up sometime," said Boïndil gleefully as he jogged at Tungdil's side. "Nôd'onn or no Nôd'onn, they can't keep away from our borders. Girdlegard is too tempting for a band of hungry orcs."

Tungdil spotted light in the distance—they were nearing the end of the tunnel. The Stone Gateway, a miracle of dwarven masonry, awaited them on the surface, along with an unknown number of enemy troops.

"Word won't have got out that the dwarves have recaptured the fifthling kingdom," said Boïndil, tossing his black plait over his shoulder. "I reckon we can kill at least a hundred before they catch on. We'll storm out and take them by surprise."

"You'll do no such thing," his friend told him sternly. "I want to see who we're dealing with." He tiptoed to the end of the passageway and peered outside.

Two dozen or so orcs were standing in a huddle on the site of the ruined gateway. The portal was wide open, the five powerful bolts that had once protected Girdlegard from invasion in pieces on the ground. At some point during the orcish occupation, the beasts had pried the metal from the doors.

The leader of the band pointed to a flight of stairs leading up to a watchtower. They didn't seem in a particular hurry, and Tungdil had the impression they were studying the defenses.

As if to confirm his suspicions, one of the orcs bent down to inspect a fragment of bolt, while the rest set about climbing the stairs.

"How many are there?" asked Boïndil eagerly, banging his axes together. "A hundred? Two hundred? How many runts can I kill?"

Tungdil described the group.

"What? Only two dozen?" spat Boïndil. He gave the others a threatening look. "Don't even think about it! These are for me! You'll have to find your own orcs."

"They're acting strangely," said Tungdil. He quickly explained his hunch. "If you ask me, they're scouts. They must have been sent ahead to find a means of destroying the defenses forever."

It was all the encouragement Boïndil needed. "Hurrah! In that case, we'd better stop them!" He sprinted off, heading straight for the watchtower. Bounding up the stairs, he caught up with the orcs and killed three in quick succession. Only then did the rest of the troopers realize they were under attack.

Muttering under his breath, Tungdil ran to the base of the tower and stopped. Dead orcs tumbled down the stairs, landing in a heap by the door. His help wasn't needed.

By the time the rest of the dwarves caught up, twenty or so orcs had died by Ireheart's hand. The watchtower was too narrow and the orcs too broad-shouldered for close combat with a raging dwarf. At last, Boïndil started to make his way down the staircase, stepping over the muddle of dead orcs, whose efforts had been hampered by their cumbersome swords, clubs, and axes.

"Quick, I want him alive," said Tungdil, pointing to the orc who had stopped to inspect the bolt. His chance of interrogating any of the troopers would be lost if Boïndil got there first. "Four of you capture the beast; everyone else, come with me—we'll meet Boïndil halfway."

They climbed the bloodied stairs, squeezing past bodies, taking care not to slip, and steering clear of falling corpses.

Suddenly a clawed hand reached out and grabbed Tungdil by the ankle. Growling and snarling, the orc lunged toward him, but Tungdil struck out, burying his ax in the creature's right shoulder.

With a pained grunt, the orc pulled on Tungdil's ankle, knocking him off his feet. Toppling backward, Tungdil landed in the arms of the dwarf behind him, and the orc, still attached to Keenfire, came too.

He should be dead by now, thought Tungdil, noticing the wounds inflicted by Boïndil's axes. Summoning his strength, he wrenched his blade from his antagonist's shoulder and kicked him in the kneecap to stop him getting up. Then, swinging Keenfire as savagely as the confines of the watchtower permitted, he took aim at his neck. The orc's head hit the wall and bounced down the stairs; the rest of him slumped to the floor and showed no sign of movement.

"Stubborn bastard," said the dwarf behind him, glowering at the corpse.

A terrible thought occurred to Tungdil. "Shush," he commanded. Judging by the grunting and jangling at the bottom of the watchtower, Boïndil's other victims were clambering to their feet.

"Everyone back!" he ordered. "The beasts aren't . . . dead." His mind was gradually clearing. Only the Perished Land had the power to raise the dead—but its influence stopped at Girdlegard's border, beyond the Northern Pass.

It doesn't make sense . . . His success in defeating the revenant seemed to confirm that there was only one sure way to deal with the beasts.

"Chop off their heads!" he bellowed. At the bottom of the watchtower, the dwarves at the rear of the unit were fighting off the sharp claws and hastily drawn daggers of a horde of undead beasts. "They're revenants!"

The battle started all over again, only this time it was fiercer and more dangerous.

Tungdil fought his way out of the tower, brandishing Keenfire. The ax lit up, vaunting its legendary power.

Runes ablaze, the shimmering blade sliced through the air, leaving a trail of blinding light, but the spectacle seemed to bypass the orcs, who attacked with undiminished savagery. The beasts were natural fighters, quick to exploit the slightest mistake, and the dwarves, hampered by the height difference, were hard pressed to behead them.

"Aim for their throats!" yelled Tungdil, ducking and swinging his ax. He brought down his opponent with a blow to the leg and followed up with a decapitating strike.

Panting heavily, he straightened up and looked around. The battle was shifting in favor of the orcs: All around him, dwarves were being killed or wounded after assuming—mistakenly, as it happened—that they had dealt their antagonists a mortal blow.

Most of Tungdil's companions, unfamiliar with revenants, were on the defensive, slashing pluckily but pointlessly at the orcs. Their axes cleaved through flesh and bone, but the undead orcs fought on regardless, faltering only if they lost both arms. The determination faded from the younger warriors' faces as the casualties grew.

"You need to behead them," shouted Tungdil, rushing to the aid of a dwarf who was hacking frantically at a clawed hand that was closing around his throat. Green blood spurted in all directions, but the orc, caring nothing for his injuries, merely tightened his grip. With three powerful strikes of Keenfire, Tungdil felled and killed the beast.

The beasts had to be brought to their knees before they could be beheaded, which was troublesome and tiring, but the indefatigable Tungdil seemed to be everywhere at once. Inspired by his example, the dwarves regained their confidence and overpowered the undead orcs.

Victory didn't come cheap. Tungdil's unit had started with superior numbers, but fifteen had fallen and another twenty were seriously hurt. To everyone's relief, the slain dwarves showed no sign of rising from the dead to turn on their erstwhile friends.

"To the tower!" shouted Tungdil to the survivors. He and the others raced up the steps, nearly colliding with Ireheart, who had cornered the final beast. The secondling swung both his axes simultaneously into the creature's groin. Yelping, the orc sank to his knees and dropped his sword, which clattered down the stairs past the warriors' boots.

"I need to behead him, right?" he shouted. His axes sped forward, severing his antagonist's vile green head. He wiped his face, which was dripping with sweat, blood, and foul-smelling filth. "Well that was fun," he sighed happily, bending down to clean his axes on the dead orc's jerkin. "By the hammer of Vraccas, if only we could fight on narrow stairways all the time—it's the best way of making sure the cowards don't escape. I wasn't counting on fighting revenants, though—not after we defeated the Perished Land." He fell silent and counted the bodies. "There's one missing," he said grimly, a crazed glint returning to his eyes. "Unless you miscounted, scholar."

Tungdil, his mind chafing at the reasons for the orcs' longevity, wasn't prepared to enter a discussion. "We'll talk at the top," he said firmly, shooing his friend up the stairs.

Boïndil led the procession, and soon all the dwarves were gathered at the top of the fortified tower. From there they were able to survey the land on both sides of the gateway, including the track leading north out of Girdlegard.

"No sign of the enemy," said Tungdil, relieved. With the stone doors wide open and the bolts in pieces, there could hardly be a worse time to fight off an army of orcs—especially if they were revenants. He didn't feel ready; Girdlegard wasn't ready.

"What made them keep fighting?" persisted Boïndil. "Was it the curse of the Perished Land?"

Loud, brutish snarls heralded the arrival of the missing trooper, dragged and pushed by his smaller captors to the top of the tower.

"Maybe he can tell us," said Tungdil. This time he didn't need to warn Boïndil to keep his axes away from the prisoner; judging by the warrior's pained expression, the message had got through. "Bring him over," Tungdil instructed the four dwarves, who promptly pinned their victim against the battlements.

It had clearly taken considerable effort to capture the

orc, and the dwarves had set about their task wholeheart-edly. The beast was bleeding from manifold gashes, mainly to his thighs and abdomen. His jawbone had been smashed by a dwarven hammer, and nothing remained of his tusks except two jagged stumps. Any ordinary mortal would have died of such wounds.

The beast's deep-set yellow eyes darted nervously between the dwarves, taking in their bearded faces. His flat nose quivered as he sniffed the air. The rise and fall of his grease-smeared breastplate mimicked his shallow, rapid breathing.

"What brought you here?" demanded Tungdil, hefting Keenfire. The diamond-encrusted blade glittered in the sunlight, dazzling the prisoner. Squealing, the orc shied away, but his back was against the parapet. "You're right to fear my ax," said Tungdil, speaking in the tongue of the orcs. Once again, he had cause to be grateful for the cycles of study in Lot-Ionan's library.

The orc's terror gave way to surprise. "You speak orcish!"

"Where are the others? What made you immortal? How strong is the Perished Land?" He swung his ax, stopping just short of the creature's nose. "Talk, or we'll kill you."

"It's because of the water," stammered the orc. "The blood of the Perished Land turned us into . . ." He tailed off. "I'm not allowed to tell you."

Just then Tungdil, who was working on the assump-tion that the orcs had invaded from north of the border, realized that his logic was flawed. *How would an orc from the Outer Lands recognize Keenfire? Could news of the weapon have spread beyond Girdlegard? Would an orc be scared of an ax that he knew only from hearsay?* "You know this weapon, don't you?" he challenged him. "You know the weapon, and you know who I am. You've come from the Blacksaddle, haven't you?" He glared at him menacingly. "You'd better tell me about the water."

"I can't," the orc said hastily, keeping his eyes on the blade.

"Do you want me to kill you?"

"No, but Ushnotz will . . ." The orc broke off and looked around frantically. Tungdil read the signs correctly and jumped aside in time to evade the charging beast.

But neither Tungdil nor his captive had reckoned with Ireheart's smoldering spirit. Shouting wildly, the secondling warrior threw himself on the orc, using both axes to slice through his neck. Blood gushed from the headless body, which slumped to the floor.

"Bravo, Boïndil," said Tungdil sarcastically. "We can safely assume that the prisoner is dead."

"He tried to attack you," said Boïndil meekly, knowing that his friend was right to be cross. "Did he tell you what they were up to?"

"He might have done, if you hadn't cut his throat." Tungdil looked thoughtfully at the corpse. The name Ushnotz seemed familiar, but he couldn't work out why. "Search the bodies," he ordered. "And keep an eye out for anything that might link the revenants to the battle of the Blacksaddle." He bent down and rummaged through the dead orc's pockets and rucksack.

Boïndil, full of contrition for killing the prisoner, hovered behind him. "If they came from the south, they must have sneaked past our sentries," he said evenly, fixing his gaze on the surrounding peaks.

"Not necessarily—they probably got to the Gray Range before us and lost their way in the tunnels. The signposts wouldn't be any good to them because they can't read dwarven runes." He picked up the dead beast's waist bag and turned it upside-down. "They weren't carrying much, which means one of two things; either they've been traveling for orbits and finished their provisions—or they've set up camp nearby."

The crazed glimmer faded from Boïndil's eyes. For a short while his mood would be stable until he was filled again with a burning desire to hunt down Tion's hordes. A cool breeze buffeted his face, drying the blood on his beard, as he contemplated the ruins of the gateway.

"They pulled the bolts off," he said, thinking aloud. He noticed gouges around the upper edge of both doors— it looked as though someone had attacked them with a chisel. "Look, they were trying to take down the doors, but their second-rate tools weren't strong enough. They must have settled for ripping off the bolts."

"Our smiths and masons will put everything to rights," Tungdil reassured him. He hadn't found anything yet to indicate where the orcs had come from. He searched methodically, frisking the orc's clothing and removing his mail shirt and armor to check underneath. At last, a small chunk of wood fell out of the cuff of his glove. It was clumsily engraved with the insignia of an orcish chieftain, and it was darker and heavier than ordinary wood.

Boïndil leaned over to take a closer look. "It's fossilized," he said. "I wouldn't be surprised if it came from a dead glade, like the one we saw in Gauragar."

The memory snapped into place. Tungdil's last encounter with Ushnotz's troopers had taken place in Gauragar before he met the twins. While hidden in a tree, he had eavesdropped on the orcs' plan to attack the village of Goodwater. Strictly speaking, Ushnotz and his band belonged in Toboribor, the orcish enclave in the southeast of Girdlegard. *Toboribor is fifteen hundred miles away. What would Ushnotz be doing in Gauragar? And why would he send a band of troopers to reconnoiter the Northern Pass?* He shared his thoughts with Boïndil.

"It stands to reason, doesn't it? Escaping across the Northern Pass is the perfect solution for the orcs. Ushnotz lost a decisive battle, and the allied army is waiting for him to return to Toboribor. If you were a lava-livered runt, you wouldn't go home either."

"I think you're right about them leaving Toboribor," said Tungdil, nodding. He joined Boïndil at the weathered battlements, leaning over the parapet and running his fingers over grooves and pockmarks created by cycles of rain, wind, sun, and snow. Straightening up, he fixed his gaze on the legendary peaks of the Gray Range. "But if you ask me, they don't intend to leave Girdlegard: They're planning to settle here."

"What?" growled his friend. "In our mountains?" He spat on the fallen orc. "May Vraccas beat your soul with a red-hot hammer and torture your spirit with burning tongs!"

Thinking about it, Tungdil felt certain that Ushnotz had intended to occupy the fifthling kingdom. *It's lucky we got here first.* He doubted that he and his warriors could have liberated the stronghold from an army of orcs.

It was difficult to know what the troopers had been doing at the gateway. *Trying to close it or destroy it?* He wondered whether the orcish chieftain had been planning to charge a levy for crossing into Girdlegard. *A toll system would be an excellent way of securing weaponry and supplies.* Ushnotz struck him as the type to exploit a situation for maximum gain.

Tungdil, having made the connection between Ushnotz, the dead glade, and the revenants, realized with a sinking feeling that he and the others were soon to be visited by some very unwelcome guests. *How big was the orcish army? Four thousand, at least . . .*

His gaze swept the mountains, valleys, and ravines and came to rest on the mighty summit of the Dragon's Tongue.

"I promised to win back the fifthling kingdom for the dwarves," he murmured softly. "The orcish invaders brought misery on Girdlegard. I don't care how many necks we have to sever, we won't let the Stone Gateway fall to the beasts."

Boïndil nodded. "Well said, scholar. To blazes with the orcs! If they're the same lot we saw in Gauragar, they'll be stronger in numbers: The odds aren't impossible—but it's a sizeable challenge."

"We'll have to behead them, don't forget. Undead orcs are four times more difficult to kill—we lost a lot of warriors today. We won't defeat them on our own." He thought for a moment. "We can't ask the firstlings—they won't get here in time."

"What about the elves?"

"They're too busy reclaiming Âlandur and destroying the älfar. We can't rely on their help."

"Hmm." Boïndil stared at the sheer flanks of the Great Blade. "Who *can* we ask?" His eyes lit up as he thought of the perfect solution.

"The outcasts," said Tungdil, thinking the same.

"Look!" shouted a dwarven warrior, peering across the border to the Outer Lands. A milky fog had descended on the mountains, shrouding the Northern Pass in mist. "There's something down there! I saw movement on the track."

Tungdil frowned. He and his warriors were in no position to defend themselves against an army of beasts. Considering how many had been killed or injured already, they could scarcely hope to hold the gateway for longer than a peal of orcish laughter would take to echo across the pass. "Be quiet while I listen," he commanded.

They strained their ears, listening for noises in the thickening fog. The tension showed on their faces. Boïndil peered into the mist, chewing absentmindedly on his braids.

Thick tendrils of fog crept toward the gateway, slipping nervously through the opening as if afraid that the doors would close.

After listening for a while longer, Tungdil breathed out. "You must have been mistaken," he said, relieved.

"I knew I shouldn't have got my hopes up," grumbled Boïndil, letting his arms hang limply by his side.

A muffled jangling sounded from below, its source obscured by the thick veil of fog. In an instant, the tension returned.

"Sounds to me like badly forged armor," said Boïndil.

He turned to the four dwarves who had captured the orcish prisoner. "You checked the gateway for survivors, didn't you?"

They looked at each other uncertainly.

"I think so," said one of them, but he didn't sound sure.

"Which is to say, we might have missed one," surmised Tungdil, realizing that the boulders on either side of the path were plenty big enough to hide an orc. It wasn't a reassuring thought. "We'd better check."

"Let's catch him before he tells everyone in the Outer Lands that the border is open," said Boïndil, jiggling his axes. "For all we know, he might be a northern trooper, not one of Ushnotz's scouts."

Tungdil had no desire to fight off an invasion from the north, especially with Ushnotz marching on the kingdom from the other side. He signaled for Boïndil to follow him and picked out three dwarves who had acquitted themselves well in the previous skirmish. "You lot come with me, while the others keep watch." He and his warriors hurried down the stairs.

Porista,
Former Realm of Lios Nudin,
Girdlegard,
Spring, 6235th Solar Cycle

Take that, Nôd'onn, you traitor!" boomed a heavily armored man, leaping somewhat inelegantly out of the shadows to challenge the cloaked figure in the middle of the room. His voice was muffled by a helmet, which made it sound like he was speaking from inside a bucket. He struck a heroic pose. "Your cruel campaign against Girdlegard is over. With this ax I shall slay your inner demon and bring peace to these lands. Prepare to meet your death!" He raised a shimmering ax and swung it above his head. The blade left a trail of red light in the air, whereupon smoke filled the room.

Yelping, Nôd'onn backed away; the valiant warrior lurched after him, armor tinkling unheroically. The magus retaliated by bombarding him with fiery sparks.

"Your dark arts can't save you," prophesied the warrior, sparks rebounding from his breastplate. Lunging forward, he wobbled slightly before raising his weapon to deliver the final strike. Even as the ax slammed into Nôd'onn's torso, an almighty explosion sounded from somewhere, filling the room with blinding light.

When the glare finally faded, Nôd'onn had vanished, and the warrior was stamping frantically on the smoldering remains of his cloak. It wasn't until the flames were well and truly extinguished that he turned to face the front.

"And that, worthy spectators, is how your hero, the fabulous Rodario . . ." He broke off and fumbled unsuccessfully with his visor. After a time, he yanked it impatiently, and the clasp came away in his armored hand. "Of all the confounded—"

Dropping his ax, which planted itself in the floorboards a hairsbreadth away from his foot, he raised both hands to his helmet and pulled with all his might. When that failed, he flung out his arms theatrically, causing his armor to emit an ear-splitting screech.

"As I was saying," he started again. "I, the fabulous Rodario, assisted by Andôkai the Tempestuous and my loyal helpers, the dwarves, rescued Girdlegard from Nôd'onn's clutches and restored our kingdoms to their rightful rulers. Thank you for your indulgence, worthy spectators. Donations will be collected at the door."

He stepped forward to take a bow, stood on a wobbly floorboard, and tumbled off the makeshift stage. The orchestra pit, usually packed with musicians and technicians, was empty. His armored body clattered to the floor.

The audience of two burst out laughing and hurried to help him up. "Congratulations," said Narmora dryly. "Do you think you can repeat it on the night?"

"Get me out of this helmet," came Rodario's muffled voice. "I can't breathe!"

Furgas, chief theater technician at the Curiosum, examined the broken clasp. "You've ruined the mechanism. It won't be easy." He got to work on the visor and a few moments later, Rodario's aristocratic features were revealed. His pointed beard had suffered terribly from his unconventional exit from the stage. In fact, his whiskers were sticking out in all directions as if to express their shock.

"Thank you," he said gratefully. He turned to Narmora and looked at her expectantly. "What did you think?"

"A hero must wear his armor convincingly or the audience will boo him off the stage. You were swaying from side to side."

"Don't you know anything about tactics?" said Rodario sniffily. "A good warrior wrong-foots his opponents."

"Narmora has a point; you need more practice," chimed

in Furgas. He was dressed in tight black clothes and his hair was specked with powder. He tried to shake it out. "For my part, I need to work on the effects. Another flash of light like that, and our audience will be blinded. On the whole it was good, though." He thumped Rodario's armored back. "Oh, one last thing—why was Andôkai's costume so skimpy?"

"Skimpy? The Estimable Maga likes to flaunt her figure. I can't be blamed for portraying her as she is."

"Of course not," said Narmora sweetly. "But what possessed you to cast her as your mistress?" Her smile became decidedly arch. "I hope you haven't forgotten she's sending Djerûn to watch the play. You remember Djerûn, don't you? Three paces tall, bristling with weaponry and strong as ten men . . . Oh, and he's fast as an arrow as well."

The impresario turned to Furgas. "I don't like to tell you this," he said in a wounded tone, "but your wife is a heartless harridan who takes pleasure in other people's misfortunes."

"Only in yours," Narmora corrected him with a smile. "Anyway, you should be grateful to me. Don't say you weren't warned."

He narrowed his eyes and cast her a scornful glance. "My dear Narmora, I'm using my artistic freedom. Even the Estimable Maga must submit to the playwright's pen." He turned again to Furgas. "Since your wife has no compassion, perhaps you, as a caring father-to-be, will have the goodness to free me from this metal dungeon . . ." He stuck his arms out tentatively and managed to lift them as far as his waist. "How can anyone fight in this get-up?"

"Most warriors manage to stay upright," said Furgas dryly. "Wait here while I fetch my tools. You've twisted everything out of shape."

Narmora went with him to the cramped workshop where he designed and tested all kinds of incredible theatrical effects. Furgas could build props, make fireworks, cause flames to appear from nowhere, and create illusions worthy of a magus, for which he was rewarded by the audience's gasps and cheers.

He gathered up a hammer, a pair of dainty pliers, a chisel, and a crowbar, while Narmora examined his latest drawings.

"A crane on wheels," she said admiringly.

"It saves the effort of taking it to pieces and moving it by cart. We can roll it wherever it's needed." He beamed. "We're making good progress. It won't be long before Porista rises from the rubble, a hundred times more splendid than before."

Narmora kissed him impulsively. "Our child will grow up in a city built by its father," she said proudly. "Think what you've achieved here!"

"I'm glad you persuaded me to work for the maga." He put his arms around her tenderly, taking care not to squash her belly. "If it weren't for you, I might have turned down the chance to rebuild Porista. I had another offer from Girdlegard's leading actor. He wanted to reopen the Curiosum in Mifurdania, you know."

"Girdlegard's leading actor—do I know him?" quipped Narmora, ruffling Furgas's spiky black hair. "I'm proud of what you're doing. You're too talented for the theater."

"I heard that!" came an indignant shout from the stage.

"I heard *everything*! Stop delaying him, you poison-tongued witch! You'll be sorry if I expire!"

Furgas laughed and stroked Narmora's face. "The theater has its attractions—but the maga pays better." He pressed his lips to hers. "Why don't you go ahead? The hero of Girdlegard needs a hand with his armor."

Narmora unwrapped her arms from his neck, walked to the back door and opened the latch. Turning, she watched as he hurried out with his tools to rescue his friend.

Even as she stood there, she knew that Furgas meant more to her than anything in the world. Andôkai could offer her all the money and power in Girdlegard, but it wouldn't match their love. *Maybe the maga is right, and the gift of magic lies within me, but I'm happy to let it slumber.*

Her gaze fell on a sheet of foolscap half-hidden by a pile of drawings. She pulled it out and gasped. It was a design for the most beautiful cradle she had ever set eyes on. *How sweet of him to hide it from me.* She slipped out quietly and closed the door.

Inside, Furgas was attending to the trapped impresario. He worked a chisel between the buckled plates and pried apart the armor. "I don't believe there's a warrior in Girdlegard who could damage his armor as thoroughly as you."

Rodario nodded modestly. "Excellence comes naturally."

Screeching in protest, the plates returned to their original position. Furgas took up the pliers to straighten the hasps. "I'm glad you moved the Curiosum to Porista."

"What choice did I have? I needed my brilliant Furgas

to dazzle the audience with his fireworks. The Curiosum depends on your jaw-dropping, purse-opening tricks." Realizing that he had furnished his friend with grounds for a pay rise, the impresario bit his lip. "It's a shame the people of Porista aren't especially wealthy," he added hastily. "A few lucky souls are on the maga's payroll, but the rest of us make do with what we've got."

Furgas smiled to himself. "I'm sure you won't live in penury for long. You own the best theater in the bright new city of Porista at the heart of Girdlegard's only enchanted realm—and the playhouse was a gift from Andôkai, don't forget." The pliers battled with a steel fastening, forcing it into shape. Furgas finished the job with his fingers by unhooking the breastplate deftly. "There you go."

"Excellent work, my dear Furgas." The impresario pulled off his helmet, shook his hands free of his gauntlets and smoothed his tousled beard. "It was getting hot in there. Why would anyone want to be a warrior? Thank the gods that acting is a talent that appeals to women as well as lovers of the arts."

"It didn't work on Andôkai," commented Furgas, gathering his tools and setting off for his workshop.

Rodario picked up his armor and hurried after him. "O cruel Furgas," he wailed. "You break my heart with the mention of her name." He flung out his right arm dramatically. "Look, there it lies, broken into a thousand pieces. How will I find the strength to make it whole again? Have you no pity?"

"You seem to have forgotten we're not rehearsing anymore," said the prop master, returning the hammer, chisel, and pliers to their proper places. "Leave the armor on the workbench. I'll take a look at it tomorrow."

The heartbroken Rodario forgot his sorrows and deposited the armor happily on the bench. "My dear friend, an actor must exercise his talents. My words must flow freely and effortlessly like water in a stream."

"Perhaps you'd like to divert your waterway to the tavern; I'm sure the gentlewomen of Porista and their daughters will find it most refreshing." Furgas extinguished all the lamps but one, locked the back door, and propelled his friend through the theater. "Be careful about flowing too freely. We don't want hordes of husbands, fiancés, fathers, and brothers banging on our door. Remember what happened in Sovereignston?"

Rodario silenced him with an imperious wave. "I don't water every blossom," he said dismissively. He turned on his heels, picked up his cloak and tossed it over his shoulder theatrically. "But if they incline their petals prettily toward me . . . I'm too well mannered to refuse."

The Curiosum was four hundred or so paces from the palace and even closer to the market. They left through the front entrance. Furgas padlocked the door and held out his hand. "Good night, you old charmer. Sooner or later your little Rodario will end up on the end of a pitchfork or dangling from a flagpole."

"Even then its prodigious size will put other men to shame." Rodario winked at him roguishly. "I appreciate your concern." He pointed to the brightly lit windows of a tavern. "How about a beverage? I'd be flattered if the architect of the new Porista would buy me a glass of wine." His proposal was rejected. "In that case, I'll meander among the flowerbeds of Porista." He raised his left hand and placed his right on his heart. "Don't worry; I'll stick to the path."

Furgas smiled and started on his usual route home. He and Narmora had found an abandoned house near the marketplace, within easy reach of the many building sites under his jurisdiction. The physical labor was accomplished by those who were builders by trade; his job was to make their work as easy and efficient as he could. Andôkai the Tempestuous wasn't known for her patience, and she was depending on Furgas to rebuild the city overnight.

For his part, he suspected that her interest in restoring Porista had little to do with the good of its citizens. More buildings meant more people, and more people meant a greater chance of finding suitable candidates to train in the art of magic, which would spare the maga a troublesome journey in search of apprentices.

Just then a shadowy figure leaped out of the rubble and barred his path. A dagger glinted in the darkness. "Your money or your life!"

Northern Pass,
Fifthling Kingdom,
Girdlegard,
Spring, 6235th Solar Cycle

Tungdil set off in pursuit of the orc, followed by Boïndil and the trio of warriors. They were halfway down the stairs when they found themselves knee-deep in fog. Thick clammy air swirled around their legs like fast-flowing water. Tungdil hesitated for a moment, reluctant to venture any further. *Don't be ridiculous*, he told himself sternly.

Everything inside him rebelled at the notion of walking through the fog, but he knew the others were looking to him for leadership. Swallowing his misgivings, he waded into the murky air. There was something about it that reminded him of the mist-like demon that had taken control of Nôd'onn's mind. *It's only fog*, he reassured himself.

They left the tower and turned left, hurrying toward the border. The visibility worsened with every step.

Glancing back at the others, Tungdil could tell that they shared his unease. The cold air stuck in their throats, making it difficult to breathe, and small droplets of water settled on their beards, hair, and mail. Soon their vague sense of trepidation hardened into dread.

"This is worse than a laundry," grumbled Boïndil, breaking the silence. "Where's the blasted orc? Anyone would think the fog was protecting him."

Just then they heard a familiar jangling.

"Did you hear that?" said Boïndil, raising his axes. "We've got him."

The orc was nowhere to be seen.

They pressed on, but the wearer of the armor stayed ahead of them, jangling in the distance, hidden from view.

Apart from clouding their sight, the fog dulled their hearing and warped their sense of time. Tungdil couldn't say for certain how long they had been walking, and his inner compass, which worked perfectly in passageways, tunnels, and caverns, proved useless in the fog. From what he could see, it was definitely getting darker—much darker.

"Stop," he commanded. He heard four sets of boots behind him skidding to a halt. It was too dark to see his companions. "Can anyone hear the orc?"

No answer.

The hairs on Tungdil's neck stood on end. He raised his ax warily. "Boïndil?"

Suddenly the sound of armor was much closer. *Clunk, clunk.* A shadow loomed out of the mist; its contours looked orcish.

The beast lunged at Tungdil with a two-handed sword.

"At least someone can hear me," muttered Tungdil, dodging the blow. He brought his ax down smartly as the beast stumbled past. The blade connected, and the orc howled in pain; then the fog closed over him, concealing him from view. *This isn't going to be fun.*

Not wanting to give himself away, Tungdil kept quiet and refrained from calling to his friends. His priority was to find his bearings before the orc attacked again. He stepped carefully backward, expecting to come up against a wall of rock, but there was nothing behind him: He had wandered off the track.

Clunk, clunk.

This time the jangling came from the left. Alerted by the noise, Tungdil whirled round, dropped into a half crouch and launched himself at the orc. The blade cut into his enemy's leg, severing it at the knee. Shrieking, the orc dropped his sword and pitched forward.

"You might live forever, but you'll never grow another leg," said Tungdil, taking aim at his head.

Even as the ax chopped down, the orc rolled over and the blade hit the ground. With a scornful grunt, he crawled toward his sword.

Tungdil knew he had to act quickly before noise of the scuffle drew other beasts to the scene.

The orc's right hand was already closing around the hilt of his two-hander when Tungdil's ax sped toward him, cutting effortlessly through helmet and skull, and embedding itself at the base of the neck.

The orc slumped to the ground. Tungdil set his right boot on the stricken beast's breastplate and levered his weapon from the corpse. There was no guarantee that cleaving a skull vertically was enough to kill a revenant, so he positioned himself over the twitching body and severed the creature's head from its shoulders.

Stopping to catch his breath, he leaned on his ax and listened to the silence. After a few moments he was forced to the conclusion that, contrary to his hopes, Boïndil and the others weren't somewhere in the vicinity, hidden by the fog. The orc's shrieking would have drawn Boïndil to him as surely as sparkling diamonds attract a kobold. *What a sinister place.*

He set off and kept walking until he came to a wall. The gray rock was hard and brittle with ridges sharp enough to injure a careless dwarf. The wall hadn't been worked or polished, which confirmed his suspicion that he had left the dwarven track.

The mist had led him astray.

Judging by the unremitting darkness, he had wandered into a cave of gigantic proportions. Every nerve in his body was as taut as a bowstring, ready to snap at the slightest noise. The swirling mist played tricks on his mind, conjuring orcs and other phantoms in the shadows.

He tried to remember what he knew of the Outer Lands. His old tutor, Lot-Ionan, had shown little interest in discovering what lay beyond Girdlegard's borders, and the same applied to the dwarves, who stuck to their side of the mountains.

Apart from a few anecdotes told by merchants and migrants, the only descriptions of the Outer Lands were hundreds of cycles old, dating back to expeditions sent out by human kings. Most of the explorers had never returned, and in human folklore, the territory outside Girdlegard's belt of mountains belonged to the souls of the dead. Tungdil, lost in the shifting fog, shuddered at the thought. If his soul had to go anywhere, he would rather it went to Vraccas's smithy.

More determined than ever to get out of the cavern, he decided to follow the wall. Placing one hand lightly against the stone and gripping the ax with the other, he set off as quietly as possible. Deep down, he was terrified about what had become of Boïndil and the others.

After a time, his fingertips brushed against a strange set of grooves. He stopped to examine the wall. *A rune!* The symbol was unfamiliar to the dwarf, but there was no mistaking the craftsmanship. Elves and dwarves were known for the elegance of their script, but for all the symbol's ornateness, it didn't look elvish. *It could almost be dwarven*, thought Tungdil, recalling the ancient stories of the undergroundlings, who were reputed to inhabit the Outer Lands. *What if they're dwarves like us?*

He strained his ears. *Clunk, clunk.*

Tungdil whirled around in surprise. *I cleaved his neck. Surely he can't have survived?* His confusion gave way to fear. "Boïndil, is that you?" he whispered hopefully.

Clunk, clunk.

The noise was definitely getting closer. Backing away, Tungdil pressed himself against the wall, peered in both directions and filled his nostrils with cold, damp air. The only discernible odor was the smell of wet stone.

Clunk. The noise was no more than two arm-lengths away from him. He heard gravel cracking beneath a booted foot.

It seemed to Tungdil that he was surrounded by orcs. He saw them towering over him, he smelled their filthy odor, and his heart beat furiously in his chest. Turning his head this way and that, he waited for the attack that would surely come.

A squat shadow appeared before him.

"Take that, you villain!" shouted Tungdil, sprinting to the right and raising his ax. The blade connected with a steely clatter. He pulled back to take another strike, but his weapon was stuck.

"Careful, scholar," snorted a voice from the fog. "You could kill a dwarf with a blow like that."

As Tungdil's panicked eyes refocused, he realized that Boïndil was the target of his attack. The secondling had crossed his axes defensively, trapping Tungdil's weapon in a triangle of steel.

"Vraccas almighty, I thought you were an orc." It was a relief to be reunited with at least one of his companions. "Where are the others?"

"No idea. I thought they were with you."

"Did you hear me killing the orc?"

"You killed an orc without me?"

"I chopped his head off and then—"

Clunk.

Tungdil gave his friend an almighty shove, and Boïndil toppled backward into the fog. A split-second later, an orc charged out of the darkness, his sword whistling toward the spot where the two friends had been standing. Neither was hurt.

Ireheart, beard quivering, popped up behind the beast. With an ear-splitting shriek, he rammed his left ax into the creature's belly and chopped down with his right ax, hewing through its neck. The orc's torso crashed to the ground, followed by his head.

"I guess there were two of them," commented Boïndil. Sighing with satisfaction, he wiped his axes on the orc's jerkin. Viscous green blood stuck to the shabby cloth. "Shall we look for the rest of our troop?"

Tungdil nodded, relieved.

They set off together, running their hands against the wall. Their investigation revealed that the cave had three exits, one of which smelled of fresh mountain air, from which they deduced that it led to the fifthling kingdom.

It took considerably longer to find their missing friends.

Two of them were dead, mauled savagely by orcs. The third had been kept alive by the will of Vraccas, but his inner furnace was cooling fast.

"There were three of them," he whispered weakly. "Three . . ."

Boïndil straightened up sharply and listened for suspicious noises in the stubbornly murky fog.

"Which way did they go?" asked Tungdil, realizing at the same time that it was pointless to pursue the surviving orc. He was probably hurrying to join his cousins in the Outer Lands.

"I . . ." A spasm ran through the dying dwarf, and the fire went out of his eyes. His soul had been gathered to Vraccas's smithy.

"Let's get out of here," said Tungdil, hefting the dead warrior over his shoulder and securing him with a leather belt.

"Aren't we going to find the other orc?" objected Boïndil, who firmly intended to kill the final beast. He was treated to a long look that silenced further protests. Sighing, he picked up the second of their dead companions, and between them, they carried the third.

Little by little, the darkness seemed to lift, indicating that at some point they had exited the cavern, although neither remembered when. The mist retreated, revealing the starry firmament, which twinkled above them, pointing the way.

Seeing the vast stone arch in the distance, they put on a final burst of speed, stopping only when they reached the gateway. Glancing behind him, Boïndil gave himself a little shake as if to free himself from the sinister pull of the Outer Lands. "It's a wonder any of those human explorers came back alive," he said to Tungdil. "From now on, I'm keeping south of the pass."

Tungdil agreed wholeheartedly with his friend.

With the exception of the sentries, who were stationed at strategic points throughout the kingdom, everyone was assembled in the main hall, where Giselbert had held counsel, over a thousand cycles before. At one time, the walls had been clad with silver panels inscribed with the fifthlings' laws, but orcish looters had rampaged through the hall, smashing the precious metal and pocketing the spoils. The most intricate, valuable, tablets had suffered the worst.

But the artistry of the fifthlings was evident in the architecture.

A double door opened onto a circular area twenty paces across, ringed by a low wall measuring a pace in height and extending four paces backward, so as to create a circular ledge. This in turn was ringed by a wall, which extended upward and backward to form the third tier, and so the series of ring-like platforms rose away from the central stage. The arrangement reminded Tungdil of the theater in Mifurdania where he had first met Narmora, Furgas, and Rodario. The fifthlings had even thought about acoustics, and the very faintest of whispers could be heard throughout the hall. Light came from a number of metal racks filled with burning coal.

Tungdil watched from the stage as the other dwarves took their seats above. He scanned the rows; some eight hundred dwarves, including three hundred dwarf-women, had left their kingdoms to form the new fifthling folk.

He waited for the noise to settle. "Thank you for coming," he welcomed them. "There are important matters to discuss."

He told them what had happened on his recent expedition and finished by warning of a likely invasion. His listeners took the news calmly; orcs were a constant danger, and fighting against superior numbers was nothing new.

"I led you here, but Vraccas knows I never intended to be your leader," he said, turning to the second item on the agenda. "From now on, I won't presume to make decisions on your behalf. Dangerous times lie ahead, and our enemies will be quick to exploit the slightest difference among us. We need to elect a new leader, and the matter should be settled without delay. As you know, I'm a thirdling." He felt a lump forming in his throat. "Recently, I've come to realize that my lineage is a problem. Doubts have been expressed about my loyalty—on one occasion, to my face. Until my trustworthiness has been proven to everyone's satisfaction, I shall serve the kingdom as a regular warrior and smith." Raising Keenfire, he turned slowly to survey the tiers of delegates. "Which of you is prepared to lead the fifthling kingdom? Nominate yourself or a kinsman." He lowered his ax and stepped aside, demonstrating his willingness to make way for the new fifthling king.

The delegates conferred among themselves. Their deep voices echoed through the rock, bringing the Gray Range to life.

Tungdil saw no reason to explain himself further; he was almost certain that some of the delegates had frowned when he mentioned his lineage, and his announcement seemed to have elicited overwhelming approval and relief. He thanked Vraccas for guiding him so wisely.

A brown-haired dwarf-woman rose to her feet and rapped her hammer against the stone floor. The clear tone cut through the hubbub, and a hush came over the hall. "My name is Kyriss Finehand of the clan of the Good Smiths, daughter of Borengar. I understand your decision,

Tungdil Goldhand, but I, for one, never doubted your loyalty. The fifthling kingdom needs your scholarly wisdom as well as your ax." Lowering her hammer, she inclined her head respectfully, then looked up at the delegates. "Our new leader must be someone who enjoys our respect. I hereby nominate Glaïmbar Sharpax of the clan of the Iron Beaters, warrior of Borengar." She listed off the firstling's accomplishments and deeds.

As Tungdil listened, the hall spun around him, dizzyingly. His eyes clouded over, and a chill crept over his skin, but his inner furnace burned higher than ever, stoked by bitterness and rage.

Make them choose someone else, he begged Vraccas. *Anyone but him.* Through the fog of his thoughts he realized that the delegates were nodding approvingly. In the short time since their arrival in the fifthling kingdom, Glaïmbar had made a name for himself with the dwarves from the other folks—and no one would dream of questioning his lineage.

You fool, whispered a voice in his ear. *You've ruined your chances. If you were king, you could post him to the furthest reaches of the Gray Range or send him to fight a band of orcs, but now you'll have to do the deed yourself. Just be sure to do it quietly: Push him over a precipice, crush him with a falling boulder, splice his skull with an orcish weapon, chase him into the Outer Lands . . .*

Tungdil summoned all his strength and focused on Boïndil's face. The fiendish voice grew fainter, fading gradually out of earshot, but the hatred remained in his heart, and the sight of the handsome firstling made him tremble with rage. For the first time he understood Boïndil's urge to hack someone or something to pieces, and he pitied his friend.

His grim thoughts were interrupted when he realized that Kyriss had stopped speaking. She and the other delegates were looking at him expectantly.

"Our first nominee is Glaïmbar Sharpax of the clan of the Iron Beaters of Borengar's line," he announced with a catch in his voice. "Let the next candidate step forward." No one stirred. "Are none of you willing to serve your folk?" he asked, venting his bitterness. He tried to look at his rival, but his gaze was drawn to Balyndis, who was standing at his side. "In that case, we have one contender. Glaïmbar Sharpax of the clan of the Iron Beaters, warrior of Borengar do you accept the nomination?"

During what followed—Glaïmbar rising and answering with a solemn "yes", the delegates clapping and cheering as he walked to the stage, the axes rising in his favor—Tungdil's thoughts were elsewhere, focused on his beautiful, unobtainable, smith.

At last, when the delegates went down on one knee and raised their hammers, axes, and clubs to the new fifthling king, he tore his eyes away from Balyndis.

"The fifthlings have elected Glaïmbar Sharpax as their king," he said, scanning the rows of faces and refusing to acknowledge the dwarf at his side. "May he rule with the wisdom of Vraccas." He left the stage without a bow or a handshake; he wasn't prepared to humble himself in front of his rival, not as long as he lived.

Once out of the hall, he decided to walk off his anger. He started through the passageways, striding past scaffolding and building sites where the secondling masons had started to repair the ceilings and walls. His feet carried him to the outer reaches of the kingdom where he came to rest among the ruins of an orcish watchtower.

Overcome with emotion, he stood among the rubble and looked up at the stars. Tears of anger and despair streamed down his cheeks, trickling through his beard, and dripping onto his mail shirt.

"You should know better than that, scholar. Your armor will rust."

Tungdil smiled in spite of himself. "I suppose you're here to drag me to the banquet."

"Vraccas himself couldn't drag you there, so it's hardly a job for a simple dwarf like me." Boïndil glanced up at the twinkling stars. "What do you see in them, scholar? I guess they're pretty after a fashion, but I'd rather look at glittering diamonds in freshly hewn rock. Won't you come inside? We need to work on our plan—the king has given his approval."

"Oh really? You didn't waste time!" Tungdil turned to his friend. "If we leave right away, we might run into more of Ushnotz's scouts. Is that what you're hoping?"

Boïndil ran his hands over his stubbly cheeks and smoothed his beard. "Am I that transparent?" he said with a smile. "Listen, I'm not in the mood for singing either. Let's have our own celebration with Boëndal and tell him about the plan. You never know, it might be just what he needs to unfreeze his blood and get him going."

They set off through the passageways, taking the route that led to the forge where Boëndal was lying on his camp bed by the Dragon Fire furnace. Tungdil sat at the frozen dwarf's bedside and talked to him as if he could hear every word.

Their hopes that Boëndal would make a miraculous recovery were disappointed that night.

Porista,
Former Realm of Lios Nudin,
Girdlegard,
Spring, 6235th Solar Cycle

The highwayman's features were hidden beneath a mask, but Furgas recognized the voice immediately. He put his hands on his hips and confronted his assailant. "Don't be an idiot, Rodario. If the guardsmen see you—"

"Your purse," said the highwayman harshly, waving his dagger. "And make it snappy."

"What, no flowery speeches?" Furgas stepped toward him. "Put away the dagger before someone sees us; we don't want anyone rushing to my aid."

The highwayman stood his ground and ran his finger menacingly along the blade. Furgas was assailed by doubt. In view of his prospective fatherhood, it seemed best to be careful. He unhooked his purse from his belt and threw it to the ground.

"That's more like it," growled the stranger, stooping as if to retrieve the loot. All of a sudden he threw up his arms, pulled the mask from his face and roared with laughter. "You fell for it," crowed a jubilant Rodario. "How do you rate my performance now?"

"I could tell it was you," said Furgas, picking up his purse. "What's got into you?"

"Consider it payback," said Rodario smugly. He paused for a moment to draw out his victory. "I heard the two of you slandering my reputation while I languished in my armored prison. Given the choice, I would have ambushed Narmora, but—"

"It's a good thing you didn't," exclaimed Furgas. "The Curiosum would have to look for a new leading man." He took the dagger from the impresario's hand and tapped his forehead. "For someone who's quite clever, you're amazingly stupid."

"Your money or your life," said a voice from the rubble. "And make it snappy."

Furgas rounded on his friend. "Don't tell me there's more!"

The impresario was white as a sheet. "Mine was a one-act play. I'm afraid he must be real."

They turned around slowly to face a masked assailant holding a knife. The weapon glinted as it sped toward them. Skipping aside, Furgas plunged Rodario's dagger into the highwayman's arm.

The blade slid into the handle, re-emerging when the stranger stepped away. He and Furgas stared at the dagger in confusion.

"It's a prop," explained Rodario. "I'd never draw a real weapon on a friend."

With a scornful laugh, the highwayman bore down on Furgas, slashing at him with the knife, which seemed to be coated with a strange yellow fluid. The prop master retreated, ducking and spinning away from the poisoned blade.

"I'm coming, Furgas," shouted his friend, arming himself with a plank. Just then a second man stepped out of the rubble, raised a cudgel and brought it down on Rodario's head. "How unsporting," mumbled the impresario, drifting out of consciousness.

"Are you Furgas?" demanded his attacker. The voice echoed through Rodario's dazed mind. He opened his eyes; a sword dripping with yellow fluid was pointed at his chest.

"Over here," shouted the first man. "Furgas is over here."

"If you're looking for Furgas," whispered Rodario feebly, "I'm your . . ." Despite his wooziness, he made a grab for the highwayman, but his fingers closed on thin air. The maneuver earned him a kick to the head, and darkness came over his mind.

Meanwhile, Furgas had been forced against the wall by the smaller of the men. "What do you want?"

"Your money," hissed the highwayman. His companion ran over to join them. "Hand it over."

Furgas unhooked his purse for a second time that evening and cast it to the ground. "There you go. It's all I've got."

The first man picked it up and weighed it in his hand. "Good. In that case, we're done." He was about to say something further when a shadow fell over them.

Looking up, they saw the dark outline of Djerůn's armor silhouetted against the moonlit sky. The maga's bodyguard was crouching on a raised portion of wall, in his left hand a sword two paces long. A purple glow emanated from the polished visor. Then the light intensified and Djerůn let out a terrible growl.

"Palandiell forfend . . ." stuttered the smaller highwayman, transfixed by the monstrous warrior. He took a few steps backward, unable to look away. "He'll tear us to—"

Djerûn launched himself from the wall and soared through the air. Just then the second highwayman came at the astonished Furgas with his sword.

The blade rammed into his stomach, passing through his guts. A second later, the highwayman fell to the gutter as Djerûn, bringing down his sword, landed beside him and cut him lengthways in half.

The sword continued in a sweeping arc, lifting perpendicular to the floor as Djerûn whirled around and struck the other highwayman from behind. The blade caught the man above the pelvis, penetrated his unarmored midriff, and exited the other side, coming to rest in a wall.

Legs attached to his upper body by a ribbon of flesh, the highwayman slumped to the ground, whimpering unnaturally as his intestines poured from his stomach on a tide of crimson blood. A moment later, he was still.

Djerûn stepped over the corpse and retrieved his sword. Standing motionlessly by Furgas's body, he waited until the torches of Andôkai's guardsmen appeared in the distance; then, as the jangling armor grew louder, he slipped into the night.

V

Five orbits had passed since Tungdil and Boïndil left the fifthling kingdom with a company of ten warriors on their way south through the sparsely populated countryside of Gauragar. They were looking for an entrance to the underground network, the location of which was marked on Tungdil's map.

Springtime had arrived in northern Gauragar, breaking many cycles of bondage to the Perished Land. It seemed to the dwarves that everything was blossoming and burgeoning with new vitality. The flowers seemed to drip with honey-yellow nectar, and the pure country air was abuzz with industrious bees.

Not that the party, with the exception of Tungdil, took much interest in the scenery: In their view, nothing compared to the beauty of underground halls. Most were unaccustomed to daylight and resented the sunshine because it dazzled their eyes. To save their sight, they broke camp before dawn, slept in the afternoon and walked from dusk until the middle of the night.

It was Tungdil and Boïndil's second journey south from the Gray Range. On the first occasion, many orbits previously, they had set off with the newly forged Keenfire, stopping in Âlandur to throw off their pursuers, confident that neither Nôd'onn nor his orcish army would think to look for them in the home of their ancient foes. This time, they traveled due south, making straight for the nearest entrance to the underground network. Their mission was to find the outcasts, a mysterious group of dwarves who haunted the tunnels. No one knew exactly where they lived.

The company had left the fifthling kingdom in a hurry, which suited Tungdil on several counts.

For one thing, preparations were underway for Balyndis's melding with the new fifthling king, and he didn't want to add to his heartache by sticking around for the banquet. Quite apart from that, time was running out. Ushnotz's scouts had made it as far as the Northern Pass, which meant the rest of the orcish army would be following close behind. Tungdil needed to find some reinforcements and get them to the fifthling kingdom before the hordes arrived. And he couldn't discount the possibility of a separate invasion from the Outer Lands.

The journey passed mainly in silence; the exertion of marching, coupled with the weight of bedrolls and provisions, limited their conversation to the briefest of exchanges.

Boïndil, whose thoughts were with his brother, barely said a word. It had taken considerable effort to persuade him to leave his frozen twin, and he had done so only on the basis that Boëndal had no use for his axes, whereas Tungdil did.

On the morning of the sixth orbit they spotted the walls of a settlement. Adjusting his course, Tungdil made a beeline for the city. "Boïndil and I will find out what we can about the orcs. The rest of you get some sleep and be ready to leave this evening. With a bit of luck, we'll reach the tunnels by dawn."

Entering the city through the main gates, they were surprised by the lack of guards. By the time they made their way through the winding maze of narrow alleys, they were acutely aware of the silence.

"Humans are rarer than diamonds in this city," grumbled Boïndil. "Do you think they've died of the plague?"

They headed for the nearest tavern to look for some answers.

The publican, a hirsute fellow of some forty cycles with the yellowest teeth that Tungdil had ever seen, practically fell over himself to welcome them. "It's an honor to receive such distinguished guests," he said with a bow. "Hillchester welcomes you." He wiped his greasy hands on his apron. "I'll give you my best room, of course, but I expect you're in hurry to get to the market. The sun ceremony is the highlight of the cycle."

Boïndil and the others stared at him in bemusement. They weren't used to human ways.

"No wonder," whispered Tungdil. "Everyone's at the marketplace!" He followed the publican up the creaking staircase. "I'll explain in a moment," he hissed to Boïndil.

The publican rushed away and came back seconds later with a tub of water. While they washed the dust off their faces, Tungdil told them what he knew about the sun ceremony. "It's a cyclical festival with stands selling food and drink and all kinds of attractions. There'll be peddlers and hawkers and music and dancing . . . Boïndil and I will head over there now. If it's worth seeing, the rest of you can take a look later—you'll have something to tell the others back home."

"Don't wait for me," said Boïndil, shooing him away. "If we search the city separately, we'll be done in half the time."

"Only if you promise to talk to them politely," said Tungdil cautiously, remembering an earlier incident involving singed whiskers and an altercation in a tavern. It was a miracle that no one had been killed.

"Don't worry, scholar, I know how to deal with long-uns," breezed Boïndil, steering him out of the room. "See you at dusk."

"Very well," said Tungdil with a smile. "But I don't want to have to break up any fights." He closed the door behind him.

The spacious bar was remarkably empty. Sitting in the corner by the remains of the fire was a lone guest who, judging by his outfit, wasn't a regular drinker at the tavern. He was wearing an expensively tailored tunic and knicker-bockers of the finest cloth. His thin legs were clad in tights, and his fancy shoes were adorned with sparkling silver buckles. A ridiculous little hat perched on top of his bobbed black hair. He was clean-shaven and smelled as perfumed as a lady.

Tungdil couldn't help grinning at his preposterous attire. To his astonishment, the man jumped to his feet and hurried over.

"There you are! I was beginning to think you weren't coming!" he exclaimed, visibly relieved. "I'm Truk Elius. I'll show you the way." Without waiting for a response, he turned and strode to the door.

Tungdil scratched his beard. "I'm afraid I don't . . ."

"Hurry up," the man said sharply. "Come on, groundling,

your services are required. We're late enough already." His pointed shoes drummed impatiently against the floor.

"Oh," said Tungdil. He knew that most itinerant dwarves were blacksmiths, and it wasn't uncommon for humans to assume that all dwarves were metalworkers. Still, blacksmiths weren't in the habit of carrying weapons like Keenfire. The man was obviously stupid or blind. "You should probably ask someone else. I'm a bit out of practice."

"Nonsense! Any groundling could handle a job like this." The man's blue eyes narrowed to slits. "Is this about money?" he asked suspiciously. "You'll get the same as the others, and not a penny more. Another word, and I'll report you as a troublemaker; you won't be hired in Hillchester again."

Tungdil decided to play along. Metalwork came easily to him, and it would be a good opportunity to ask some questions about the orcs. Besides, he didn't want the citizens of Hillchester to think that his kinsfolk were unreliable— unlike gnomes and kobolds, the children of Vraccas could be trusted to keep their word. "I'll do what I can, but it might take longer than usual—and I'm not a groundling; I'm a *dwarf*."

Elius laughed. "After the first few strokes you'll be fine."

Tungdil had a sudden thought. "I haven't brought any tools."

"We've got everything set up for you," said Elius, pointing to the door. "Let's go."

They hurried through the alleyways, heading for the center of Hillchester. Tungdil found himself jogging to keep up with the long-legged man.

Judging by the number of people who greeted them, Elius

was a well-known personality in the town. After a while it dawned on the wheezing Tungdil that Truk wasn't a forename, as he had supposed, but an honorific title. It seemed likely that his new employer was in the service of King Bruron.

Ahead of them, the alleyway broadened, opening into a proper street. Tungdil detected the hum of several hundred voices. They were still some distance away, but Tungdil guessed from the music and laughter that the festivities were in full swing.

Truk Elius rounded a corner and came to a halt. Tungdil stared at the vast gathering of people. From his standpoint, their legs and torsos formed a single impenetrable wall. There was no way through.

His pessimism wasn't shared by Elius, who clearly thought it beneath him to make a detour around the square. "Out of the way," he shouted, stepping briskly into the marketplace. "Out of the way, citizens of Hillchester!"

The crowd separated obediently, allowing the man and his stocky companion to pass.

After a while, Tungdil noticed a big wooden stage in the middle of the square. They seemed to be heading straight for it.

Standing on the rectangular platform were four soldiers and eight civilians dressed in nothing but thin, grubby rags. Steel handcuffs encircled their wrists, and blindfolds covered their eyes.

It looks like an execution, thought Tungdil, confused. Looking around, he realized that the festivities weren't quite as harmless as he had imagined; the citizens of Hillchester were celebrating the imminent death of eight of their number—three women and five men. Elius ascended the steps to the platform, pausing when he realized that Tungdil had stopped. "Get a move on," he ordered, signaling for him to follow.

It finally dawned on Tungdil that their route through the marketplace wasn't a shortcut to the forge.

He thinks I'm an executioner! Tungdil stepped back. "There's been a mistake," he said loudly. "I'm not an executioner."

The crowd gasped.

Elius strode down the steps toward him. "What's this?" he hissed. "I warned you not to haggle. The rabble wants blood—if you don't kill the prisoners, they'll settle for yours." He scrabbled around in his purse and pressed a few coins into Tungdil's hand. "All right, here's a little extra from me. Now get up there and do your job!"

"You don't understand," said Tungdil, determined to put an end to the confusion. "I'm not an executioner. My name is Tungdil Goldhand. I'm here on a—"

"Tungdil? I don't know any Tungdils!" said Elius, taken aback. "We hired Bramdal, the best itinerant executioner in Gauragar."

The crowd's surprise turned to anger. It was clear from the shouts and jeers that they weren't prepared to wait.

Elius glared at the dwarf. "I don't care what your name is or who you are; all I need is a groundling." He grabbed Tungdil's shoulder and tried to drag him up the stairs, but the dwarf was determined not to budge. "Keep this up, and I'll have you arrested," threatened Elius. "I order you to behead them."

"No," said Tungdil, giving up on Elius and deciding to chance it with the crowd. The man seemed to fear the citizens of Hillchester, which Tungdil took as a positive sign. His legs carried him up the stairs and onto the podium.

A loud cheer went up from the assembled masses when the dwarf appeared on the stage. Tungdil looked at the rows of crazed faces, all baying for blood, and suspected that Elius was right. No one would leave the stage alive unless the execution went ahead. He and the eight prisoners were trapped.

The executioner's block was at the center of the stage. The furrowed wood was stained with patches of dark red blood and bore the marks of countless executions. A broad-bladed ax lay two paces to the side.

The guards pushed a woman to the front of the stage. After a quick drum roll, a herald read out her name and her crime.

Tungdil gathered that his first victim was a disloyal spouse. The woman's husband had died and she had been seen with a new suitor before the full period of mourning had elapsed. She wasn't a murderer or a violent criminal; her only crime was love. *Love.* He suddenly thought of Balyndis.

The woman was dragged to the executioner's block and forced to her knees. The guard's movements were forceful and precise. He pushed her head against the wood, seized her long hair and wrapped it round a metal pole. Now her neck was exposed and she couldn't turn her head or move. The drumming grew louder and faster.

A violent shove sent Tungdil stumbling forward. His hand touched the woman's back, and he felt her shaking body through the flimsy fabric of her vest. Her sobs were barely audible, which made him pity her all the more. He stared at the soft, smooth skin on her neck and shoulders; she was only a girl, condemned to death by a law that, in Tungdil's opinion, was downright absurd. *If the humans want to kill her, they should do it themselves.*

"What are you waiting for?" snarled the guard. "Hurry up and chop off her head. There's another seven to go."

"For the last time, I'm not an executioner!" shouted Tungdil, holding Keenfire in the air. "My name is Tungdil Goldhand. This blade killed Nôd'onn and freed you from the Perished Land. I'm not your henchman." He picked up the executioner's ax and held it out for the guard to take. "Here, do it yourself if you're so keen for her to die. I won't do it for you."

His speech caused an uproar. Pushing and shoving, the crowd surged forward, determined to see blood.

"Now look what you've done, you stupid groundling," snapped Elius, staring fearfully at the mob. It was clear that the soldiers were barely able to restrain the frenzied crowd.

Tungdil offered him the ax without a word.

"What are you doing? I'm not an executioner, I'm a Truk," said Elius indignantly. He stooped down and shoved his face into Tungdil's, filling the dwarf's nostrils with his perfume. "You'll rot in prison for this, groundling," he hissed with a shake of his ridiculous little hat. "Although I've a mind to throw you to the crowd."

Another cheer went up, louder and more triumphant. Tungdil and Elius swung round.

A powerfully built dwarf was limping across the stage toward them. He was dressed in black with brown leather armor and heavy boots. His features were hidden by a leather mask, and long fair braids hung down from his chin.

His footsteps thudded against the planked floor. "I was

delayed," he said tersely. Without another word, he took the executioner's ax from Tungdil and marched to the block. He didn't stop to take aim, just hefted the weapon with two hands and swung it mid-stride.

The blade cut a whistling arc through the air and connected with the prisoner's neck, killing her outright. Her head thudded to the floor, and blood spurted from the grisly stump. Her headless torso twitched a final time, showering the front row of spectators with droplets of blood, then her body fell from the block.

The black-clad dwarf sliced through her hair to free the head from the pole. He held it up for the crowd to see. The ax had chopped cleanly through skin, sinew, and bone. Bramdal certainly knew his stuff.

"Get out of my sight," hissed Elius to Tungdil, who quickly obliged. Hurrying away from the stage, he found himself a spot not far from the marketplace and settled down to wait for Bramdal. It didn't occur to him to return Elius's money; gold was gold.

The crowd cheered for a bit, then went quiet, a pattern that repeated itself at irregular intervals another seven times. Then the music started and the citizens of Hillchester laughed, cheered, danced, and celebrated while the severed heads were hoisted on flagpoles next to the stage.

A short while later, the black-clad dwarf appeared at Tungdil's side. A few specks of gore flecked his boots and his armor, but his clothes bore no trace of his grisly work. Tungdil looked him up and down. His leather mask was dangling from his belt.

"I heard about the mix-up," laughed the executioner. "It's not often I'm mistaken for another dwarf." He held out his hand. "I'm Bramdal Masterstroke." There was a pause while he waited for Tungdil to reply.

Tungdil studied his features. Bramdal Masterstroke, professional executioner, was many cycles older than he was, but his deep brown eyes were bright and shiny. Despite his gruesome trade and the many deaths he had witnessed, he seemed neither gloomy nor remorseful.

Tungdil cleared his throat. "Why do you do this?" he demanded, gesturing toward the eight heads hoisted from the flagpoles.

"Why not? Some dwarves are smiths, some are bakers, and I'm an executioner. It's just a trade." His eyes smiled at Tungdil from under the black headscarf that covered his fair hair. His cheeks were shaven except for a small circle around his mouth and chin. "Shall we go somewhere quieter?"

They set off down the alleyway.

"Which kingdom are you from, Tungdil Goldhand?" enquired the executioner in a soft, gentle voice. "I'd like to hear news of my kinsfolk. It's a rare pleasure to meet another dwarf, and you don't look like a tinker or a traveling smith. Are you an exile?"

"I was going to ask you the same," said Tungdil, thanking Vraccas for introducing him to the dwarf. In spite of the initially unpromising circumstances of their encounter, it looked as though Bramdal might be the key to locating the tunnel-dwelling dwarves. "Are you an outcast?" he demanded.

Bramdal laughed. "Yes and no. I've found a new home, faraway from the other folks. I didn't like the rules in my kingdom, so I broke them on purpose. I'm an exile by choice." He played with his corn-colored braids. "Nothing would induce me to go back. How about you?"

Tungdil was about to introduce himself properly and explain the nature of his mission and the fortuitousness of their encounter when he suddenly thought the better of it and decided to let Bramdal think that he was an outcast too. "I loved a maiden and her heart belonged to me, but she was promised to someone else. I killed him in a quarrel." The lie came easily—too easily. He looked away.

Bramdal nodded. "Not all of our laws are just, and it's time they were changed." He looked at Tungdil intently. "What if I were to tell you that there's a place where dwarves aren't tied to the precepts of family and clan?"

He stopped in front of a tavern and held the door open for Tungdil, who was digesting the news. They sat down by the fire and the executioner ordered two beers.

"Is there really such a place?" asked Tungdil, after taking a long draft of beer.

Bramdal nodded. "There is indeed, Tungdil Goldhand. It's a place where dwarves live together as equals, free from the tyranny of traditions and laws."

"Isn't it chaos?"

"We still have rules," admitted the executioner. "The king and queen make sure we stick to them, but it's basic stuff about working for the common good and not harming each other. There's nothing about clan lore and other bunkum. We're equals, and no one can tell us what to do."

Tungdil looked at Bramdal over the rim of his tankard. "So why are you in Gauragar, chopping off heads?"

"For the money, of course," the executioner said coolly. "I used to be really busy when the Perished Land was still around. With revenants all over the place, my skills were in demand. Besides, I like to help humans; it's our Vraccas-given task."

"Help them?" exclaimed Tungdil. "You've made it your business to kill them. How does that make you different to an orc?"

"I'm protecting them from themselves. I don't kill for the sake of killing; my duty is to clear out the dross. Vraccas wants us to help the humans, so I rid them of lawbreakers like the eight men and women on the stage. A quick blow to the neck, and the city is a safer place. Criminals are as dangerous as orcs."

"What about the widow who didn't stick to the mourning period? Was she a danger?"

"She broke the law, and that's the danger. It's not my place to question their laws," said Bramdal, emptying his tankard. "It's stupid to have too many laws, but it's important to keep the ones you've got. Humans, elves, dwarves—we're all the same." He cocked his head. "You didn't answer my question," he said.

"What question?"

"About your lineage."

"I'm a . . ." He stopped short, unsure of what to say. The beer and the memory of Balyndis weighed on his heart.

"Only a thirdling would hesitate like that," observed Bramdal. His voice was calm and non-judgmental. "You're not obliged to answer. In any case, lineage doesn't matter where I come from."

Tungdil leaned forward. "Do you mean you've got thirdlings in your kingdom?"

Bramdal roared with laughter, delighted by Tungdil's amazement. "Our halls are open to all exiles, regardless of where they come from—including members of the thirdling kingdom. All we ask is that everyone sticks to the rules; if they don't . . ." He laid his right hand on his ax.

The executioner's explanation only added to Tungdil's confusion. He was looking forward to seeing the outcasts' kingdom for himself. "How do I get there?" he asked. "I'd like to visit the place you speak of. Are you sure they'll let me in?"

Bramdal gave him directions to a pond that Tungdil judged to be located near the entrance to the tunnels. "Strap weights to your ankles and jump into the pool. It's important to sink to the very bottom—only then will you be admitted to the freelings' halls."

"Is that what you call yourselves?"

"Free by nature, free by name." Glancing up, Bramdal spotted a man sitting two tables to their left. "I'll be back in a moment," he said, picking up his rucksack and limping across the bar. He and the man talked in hushed tones.

Tungdil wasn't sure what to make of the instructions. Dwarves were famously suspicious of water, regardless of the depth.

He still had painful memories of traveling across Girdlegard with the twins, neither of whom would set foot on a boat, resulting in constant detours. Like most of their kinsfolk, they believed that contact with water would lead to certain death. In their opinion, any lake, tarn, river, or stream outside a dwarven kingdom was a threat.

How am I going to get Boïndil to weigh himself down and jump into a pond when he won't even tread in a puddle? Tungdil leaned back in his chair and racked his brains. He had to hand it to the outlaws—it was the perfect way of hiding their existence from the other folks. *It's going to be a real challenge.* He watched the man push a couple of coins toward Bramdal, in return for which he was handed a small object wrapped in cloth.

"What was that about?" asked Tungdil nosily when the executioner returned.

"You don't want to know. It's superstitious human stuff," replied Bramdal in a tone that was affable but firm.

Rather than press him for details that he probably wouldn't get, he tried another tack. It had occurred to him that some of the dwarf-like inhabitants from the Outer Lands might have crossed into Girdlegard, and he wondered whether Bramdal might have met one. "You've been living with the freelings for a while. Have you ever seen an undergroundling in your realm?" He ran a finger around the rim of his tankard and traced a moist rune on the tabletop. It was the mysterious symbol from the cave. "Do you know what this means?"

Bramdal raised his eyebrows. "No idea. Undergroundlings, did you say?"

It was too much to hope for. "It's just a rumor I'd heard of. Where are you heading now? The roads aren't safe at the moment. An army of orcs is marching north toward the Gray Range—we had a run-in with some of their scouts."

The executioner shook his head, braids flying to the side. "It's all right, I'm on my way south. I'm needed in the next city: The prisons are overflowing with criminals and justice must be done." He held out his hand. "It was a pleasure to meet you, Tungdil Goldhand," he said solemnly. "Perhaps our paths will cross again. I hope I've been of some assistance. May Vraccas guide you to your goal." He shouldered his rucksack and limped to the door. Outside, it was pouring with rain. Bramdal took a step back, put up his hood, and slipped away.

"Excuse me, but do you happen to know what the executioner sold to that man?" asked Tungdil when the publican collected his empty tankard. The man bent down and whispered in his ear. Tungdil's eyes widened: Bramdal was trading in body parts.

"They make excellent talismans," explained the publican. "Candles from the tallow of murderers will cure most illnesses, and a thief's little finger is good against fire. I've got one myself." He raised his hand with the empty tankards and pointed to the ceiling. A shriveled scrap of blackened flesh was fixed by a nail to the beam. With a bit of imagination, it was possible to make out the shape of a finger. "This street has been struck by lightning on two occasions, but my tavern has never been hit."

Tungdil shuddered and paid up quickly, keen to escape before he was hit on the head by a dead man's finger. He set off to tell his friends of his discovery. The outcasts would be easier to find than he had imagined—although there was still the challenge of persuading his companions to dive into a pond.

As he trudged through the alleyways of Hillchester, he realized that Bramdal hadn't told him the reason for his banishment. The word *murder* haunted his thoughts.

At last the laughter died down.

Boïndil ran a hand over his eyes to wipe away his tears of mirth, while the others lay back on their beds and struggled for breath.

"That was a good one, scholar," chuckled Boïndil. "But, joking aside, how do we get to their realm?"

Tungdil sighed. "I just told you. I was quoting Bramdal exactly."

Boïndil's grin disappeared. "Let me get this straight: You're asking me to jump into a pond." He leaned forward and sniffed Tungdil's breath. "Ha, no wonder! How many tankards have you had? Weights on my ankles, I ask you!" He noticed the grave expression on Tungdil's face. "By the hammer of Vraccas, I won't do it! Elria's curse is bad enough, but drowning ourselves on purpose . . ." He folded his arms in front of his chest and stuck out his chin, black beard aquiver. "Not in a million cycles!"

"How do we know that Bramdal's not a thirdling?" piped up one of the others. "He could have made up the stuff about the entrance to trick us into drowning."

Boïndil whipped around. "Exactly!" he said fiercely. "It's a trick! We'll get there, and he'll be hiding in the bushes, waiting for us to drown in his confounded pond. I bet he's dreaming up a way to thieve our armor."

"There might be dwarf-eating fish in the water," ventured one of his companions.

Tungdil raised his eyebrows. "All right," he challenged them. "Name me a dwarf who died by drowning."

"I've heard all kinds of terrible stories," said Boïndil balefully. "I can't remember the poor fellows' names."

"I'm not talking about *stories*," persisted Tungdil. "I want names: names of friends, friends of friends, or relatives, who died by drowning. It seems to me that Elria had plenty of opportunity to kill us on the way to the

Blacksaddle, but no one died, as far as I know." He stared into their wrinkly faces. "Well?"

No one said a word. Boïndil examined the runes on his axes while the others stared at the ceiling or rearranged their clothes.

"I won't do it," said Boïndil at last. "I don't mind *looking* at the pond, but it had better be shallow. If it's deeper than my knees, we'll head for the tunnels, like we said."

"Fine," said Tungdil, pulling off his boots. It seemed futile to discuss the matter any further, especially when he himself was beginning to doubt the wisdom of the scheme. "We'll get moving as soon as I've had a bit of sleep." He lay down on the straw mattress and dozed for a while, only to be woken by jangling chain mail. He looked up to see Boïndil standing by his bed. "I meant to tell you: I spoke to a merchant, and he reckoned he'd seen some orcs."

Tungdil sat up. "How long ago and where?"

"He said they were coming from the east—from Urgon, he thought. They were marching toward the Gray Range, and he said they were moving fast."

Tungdil leaped out of bed, fetched the map from his rucksack and laid it on the floor for the others to see. He traced the route with his finger.

"They must have turned east around here," he surmised, pointing midway between the dead glade and Dsôn Balsur. "By sticking close to the border with Urgon, they slipped past the allied army and the älfar without being seen." For an orc, Ushnotz was remarkably cunning. "Where exactly did the merchant say they were?"

Boïndil placed a finger on the map. According to Tungdil's calculations, the spot was only four hundred miles from the fifthling kingdom. Gauragar was hilly, but there weren't any proper mountains or other obstacles to slow them down. The territory suited the dwarves, but their longer-legged foes would have the advantage. Orcs were formidable marchers.

Tungdil rolled up the map and stowed it into his rucksack. Even if everything went to plan, he couldn't bank on recruiting the outcasts in time to save the fifthling kingdom. His boots were still wet, but he pulled them on regardless, and reached for his cloak.

"We're leaving," he told the others. "From now on, we only stop if we have to."

The next orbit, the dwarves had a niggling feeling that something was wrong. It wasn't tiredness or stomach cramps or any physical sensation, just a general uneasiness that made them nervous and withdrawn. All around them the grass was getting greener as if to flaunt its victory over the Perished Land, but the burgeoning vegetation did nothing to ease their trepidation, and they longed for their mountain homes.

The mood became tenser and the dwarves more irritable, but they kept themselves going with the occasional song. After a time, the path led into a forest, and the singing dried up. From then, they continued in silence, trudging bad-temperedly along the overgrown track.

Tungdil had a fair idea what was causing their edginess, but he wasn't inclined to share the news. The others would hardly be heartened to know that they were traveling through Lesinteïl, former home of the northern elves.

The älfar had conquered the kingdom many cycles ago and wiped out their cousins, before invading the Golden Plains, killing the elves, and founding the älfar kingdom of

Dsôn Balsur. Only Liútasil's elves in the dense forests of Âlandur had survived the älfar's crusade against their race.

Tungdil suspected that he and his friends had crossed into the first of the fallen elven kingdoms, and that Lesinteïl was expressing its old antipathy toward the dwarves. Either that, or the land was drenched in the sinister memory of Sitalia's slaughtered elves.

Unfortunately, he hadn't reckoned with eagle-eyed Boïndil, who spotted the remains of a statue half hidden by a thicket of brambles and creepers.

"By Vraccas, if that isn't a statue of Sitalia!" he exclaimed, bringing the little procession to a halt. "What's it doing in a godforsaken forest like this? Don't tell me we're in Âlandur already!"

Needless to say, the whole group looked to Tungdil for guidance. "There's a chance we're in Lesinteïl," their leader conceded quietly.

"Unbelievable," snorted Boïndil, aiming a kick at the elegantly sculpted marble. "First you ask us to jump into a pond, and then you lead us straight to the heart of the pointy-ears' . . ." He stopped short and corrected himself. "Straight to the heart of an *elven* kingdom. No wonder I've got the shivers; it's no place for a dwarf."

"If you've finished complaining," said Tungdil, "I suggest we carry on. You seem to have forgotten that we're friends with the elves."

"Tell that to the forest," growled Boïndil, setting off behind him. He turned and glared at a nearby tree. "Trip me up, and I'll hack you to pieces. Consider yourself warned."

It was probably coincidence, but at that moment the wind got up, whistling threateningly through the trees.

Boïndil whipped out his axes and banged them together, filling the forest with a high-pitched jangling of metal. "Was that supposed to scare me?" he shouted defiantly. "Do it again at your peril!"

Footsore and tired, the dwarves continued their journey, eating and drinking on the move. At dawn, the tops of the trees were wreathed in mist. The sun was still rising slowly as they made their way out of the forest and stopped at the edge of a meadow. The terrain was completely flat, but the grass, a mixture of dead stalks and fresh new blades, came as high as their chests.

Scattered about the meadow was the wreckage of an elven town, and beyond that, a pond, just as Bramdal had described. For some reason, the executioner had omitted to mention that the water was as black as the night. Devoid of light or sparkle, its surface swallowed every particle of sunlight. Tungdil was reminded of the dull, forbidding water of the dead glade.

Boïndil wouldn't stop shaking his head. "I wouldn't have minded if you could see the bottom, but this . . ." He pointed to the pond. "It's the work of the Perished Land."

One of the others nodded. "It's as black as pitch. I'll be darned if I dip my toe in it, let alone the rest of me."

"We need to get a proper look," said Tungdil, tramping through the grass.

Tendrils of ivy twisted playfully over scattered blocks of stone. Unlike the elves of Âlandur, the founders of Lesinteïl had favored solid, imposing buildings, but the weather and the älfar had taken their toll, and it was difficult to imagine how the town had once looked.

"Don't wait for me—I'll catch up," said one of Tungdil's companions, stopping among the ruins. Bigor Stonecolumn was a stoneworking secondling, who was drawn to masonry of any sort. He ran his calloused fingers over crumbling carvings, cracked sculptures, and once-beautiful friezes, the colors of which had faded in the sun. "Not bad for a bunch of flower-pickers," he said admiringly.

The dwarf studied the intricate workmanship and found no sign of faulty hammer strikes or careless chisel cuts. In spite of himself, he wished the elven town were still standing so that he could see it in its original glory.

Meanwhile, Tungdil had arrived at the pond. He looked around for Bigor, but the secondling was nowhere in sight. "Bigor?" he called.

"Don't worry, scholar. He'll be admiring the ruins," said Boïndil.

"Or answering a call of nature," chuckled one of the others. "The grass will be glad of some water."

Tungdil peered at the pond. In front of him were the sorry remains of a pier, and, further left, a tumbledown shrine, which, according to the worn inscription, was dedicated to Sitalia, goddess of the elves. A flight of stone steps led down to the water.

Right, here goes . . . He crouched at the water's edge, pulled off his gloves, and hesitated briefly before lowering his index finger into the liquid darkness. The water felt cold. "It seems harmless enough," he said to the others. "The pier reaches almost to the middle of the pond. With a proper run-up, we should be able to reach the—"

"Hang on a second, scholar," interrupted Boïndil. "I'm

not in the habit of questioning your decisions, but you can't seriously be suggesting that we should jump in there."

Tungdil didn't like exploiting his friend's weaknesses, but he was left with no choice. "You're not scared, are you, Ireheart?" He scooped up some water and threw it at the dwarf. "Ooo," he teased. "Can you feel it trying to kill you? It's only water, you know."

The tactic worked. Boïndil puffed out his chest, wounded honor triumphing over his instincts. "Why would a warrior be afraid of Elria?" he asked proudly. "Look, I'll dive in and prove it." He clambered onto the pier, but Tungdil held him back.

"Hold on, we can't leave without Bigor." He called the mason's name and waited in vain for an answer. "We'd better look for him. Everyone spread out."

"I reckon he's been kidnapped by the forest," said Boïndil, pulling out his axes. "Elvish trees can't stand us dwarves."

"You threatened them," commented one of his companions. "What do you expect?"

"For them to behave themselves," snapped Boïndil, hacking at the high grass to work off his temper.

They spread out and advanced in a line, sweeping the meadow for the missing dwarf, and calling his name.

Next to a marble column, shielded by head-high grass, they found Bigor, or what was left of him.

At once Boïndil and the others formed a defensive ring around Tungdil and the corpse.

Bigor's mail tunic had been pulled halfway over his head and his leather jerkin ripped to shreds, exposing his torso. His flesh was covered in bite marks and some of his bones were missing, including his ribs. The trampled grass around the body glistened moistly with blood.

"This was the work of an animal," reported Tungdil.

Boïndil glared furiously at the sea of rippling stems that blocked their view in all directions. "It was a thirdling trap," he growled. "Your friendly executioner was trying to feed us to his pet." He shifted his weight, planting both feet firmly on the ground. "The dwarf-eating monster won't be gobbling any more of our kinsfolk. I'll deal with the varmint, you'll see."

Noticing a wide channel of trampled grass, Tungdil concluded that the predator was by no means small, which led him to wonder why no one had heard it pouncing on Bigor. Judging by the dwarf's half-eaten remains, the creature had been disturbed mid-meal. *It must be lurking nearby*, he thought with a shudder. He tried to predict the creature's next move. There were two possibilities: either it meant to attack them, or it was waiting to finish its meal.

Just then a strong wind gusted through the field. Amid the rustling grass, the hiss of an approaching arrow went unnoticed by the dwarves.

Its arrival was so sudden and unexpected that the dwarf to the right of Boïndil barely realized he was hit. Staggering backward, he raised a hand to his chest and closed his fingers disbelievingly around the black shaft protruding from his mail shirt. Pierced through the heart, he slumped to the ground.

"Älfar!" came the shouted warning from Boïndil. Not wanting to offer an easy target, he threw himself onto his belly. The arrow intended for him sailed over his head and pierced the back of the dwarf behind him. Groaning, the stricken dwarf keeled over. A third dwarf took two arrows to the chest.

Seeing the arrows come thick and fast, Tungdil realized that there was more than one archer. By his reckoning, at least three älfar were hiding in the grass, making it all but impossible for the dwarves to fight and win.

"Get down and crawl," he ordered, throwing himself to the ground. He lowered his voice. "Make for the pond. We'll soon see whether Bramdal was telling the truth."

"Are you blind or something?" barked Boïndil, wriggling through the grass beside him. "This is the Perished Land! We can't—"

Tungdil grabbed a handful of grass. "Look, it's green, not gray! The Perished Land has been banished." An arrow whistled over their heads. "No more talking; I'll see you at the pond." He pushed himself carefully across the ground, intent on disturbing as few blades as possible. The älfar were bound to be looking for movement in the grass.

What brought them here? he wondered feverishly. *Lesinteïl's occupation ended cycles ago.* It was too far north for älfar scouts, especially when their troops were in action on the fringes of Âlandur and Dsôn Balsur. Tungdil could think only that they knew of some secret weapon in the fallen kingdom that they were hoping to use against the elves.

The rustling increased as if hundreds of älfar were swarming through the meadow. During his long crawl toward the pond Tungdil heard five more agonized screams.

Seized by fury, he felt like drawing Keenfire and confronting his pursuers, but common sense convinced him otherwise, thereby prolonging his life. The älfar were expert marksmen, and neither mail shirts nor solid armor could halt the arrows that sped from their bows. A dwarf, stationary or moving, was an easy target, and Tungdil knew better than to break his cover. He hoped to Vraccas that his surviving companions would stay out of sight.

Just then Samusin, commander of winds and god of equilibrium, noticed the outnumbered dwarves. The wind changed direction, blowing across the pond toward the dwarves and their pursuers.

Tungdil decided to get out his tinderbox and set light to the grass.

"Burn the meadow!" he shouted, rejoicing at the sight of the dancing flames working their way up the dry stalks and spreading like lightning. A moment later, several other columns of smoke appeared above the field. The breeze fanned the flames, sweeping them toward the älfar.

Protected by the smoke, grass, and flames, Tungdil kept crawling until he reached the edge of the pond. Glancing around, he spotted two of his companions; of the others, including Boïndil, he saw no sign.

Before he could instruct his companions to dive into the water, a shadow fell over them and a vast creature emerged from the field.

The saddled bull was barely ten paces away. It was wearing a helmet of gleaming tionium and its horns were sheathed in metal. Smoke rose from its coat, and its hooves were singed, as Tungdil could tell from the acrid odor.

There could be no doubt of its intentions. It turned to face the dwarves, lowering its broad head, scraping its hooves against the ground, and snorting aggressively. Its tail swept from side to side.

"Quick, to the pier," commanded Tungdil, drawing Keenfire. Deep down, he knew the ax could do nothing to stop the charging bull. The beast weighed at least a quarter of a ton and was made of pure muscle without an ounce of fat. "Dive into the water—it's our only chance!" They started running.

The bull watched them with fiery red eyes. Opening its jaws, it let out a bloodcurdling roar, showed them its jagged incisors and broke into a trot, accelerating as it thundered behind them, churning up the ground. Tungdil realized that the beast would be upon them before they reached the pier.

"Hey, over here, you cud-chewing brute!" A split-second later, Ireheart shot out of the grass. Grabbing the bull by its tail, he dug his heels into the churned-up soil and pulled back with all his might.

The bull charged onward, dragging Boïndil, whose boots carved two deep furrows in the ground. Suddenly it stopped and whipped around to glower at the intrepid warrior hanging off its tail.

"I'll teach you to eat my friends," shouted Ireheart, pulling one of his axes from his belt. The blade cut a deep gash in the bull's behind. "Keep going, scholar. I've got your back."

Tungdil peered into the raging wall of flames that separated the pond from the meadow, but the älfar were nowhere to be seen. After assuring himself that the coast was clear, he signaled for the others to follow and hurried onto the pier. Thereafter they were in full view of any lurking archers. From the corner of their eyes they watched as Boïndil jabbed at the raging bull with one hand and clung to its tail with the other. Bucking and turning, the beast tried to shake itself free, but Boïndil's grip was like iron and he stayed out of reach.

"I've killed bigger beasts than you," the dwarf warned him. "What are you, an oversized cow? You won't be around much longer." Swinging his ax rapidly, he hacked at the creature's legs. Crimson blood flowed from countless gashes, then the hind legs caved in, and the bull bellowed with helpless fury. "Now for your ribs," roared Boïndil.

"Watch out! They're—" With a final shriek, the dwarf next to Tungdil toppled over, a second arrow piercing his back as he fell. Gurgling incoherently, he convulsed and died.

"Älfar!" shouted Tungdil, stowing away his ax and grabbing his dead companion by the shoulders. He hoisted the body into the air and held it in front of him like a shield.

Unable to see anything, he took a step back, only to hear his other companion fall prey to the älfar's arrows. Five times he heard the same sequence of noises—a soft whirr, a jangle of chain mail, and the terrible sound of metal burrowing through sinew and flesh. The dead dwarf splashed into the water.

Tungdil didn't dare raise his head above the corpse to look for his attackers. Instead he stumbled backward toward the end of the pier. "Listen to me, Boïndil," he ordered, doing his best to shout. "You can't risk the pier: You'll have to wade in from the side."

Boïndil was standing beside the bull, both hands on his ax and aiming for the creature's sturdy neck. "I'm not getting in that water!" he shouted, swinging his ax. "This cow needs to be—"

Just then the bull tensed its mighty muscles and its head

jerked around. Its horns hit the dwarf's belly, knocking him off his feet.

Boïndil flew four paces through the air and splashed into the somber water of the pond. His weapon followed a split-second later, disappearing with a gentle gurgle. Bubbles floated to the surface, but neither dwarf nor ax reappeared.

Tungdil decided that his friend's unexpected flight was the work of Vraccas. He was preparing to launch himself after him when footsteps hurried down the pier.

Even as he lowered the corpse to gauge the distance, his right shoulder was hit by an arrow.

The strength drained out of his arm and his makeshift shield slipped even lower, exposing more of his body.

The älf dispatched another missile, this time hitting Tungdil's chest. He crashed to the ground. Groaning, he tried to crawl out from under the corpse. Whether or not he reached the end of the pier was no longer of import-ance; his only chance of survival was to enter the water as fast as he could.

His pursuers were getting closer.

Glancing up, he saw a female älf wearing a half mask, her features veiled by a strip of black gauze. She was running toward him, calling something at the top of her voice. Without stopping, she raised a sickle-like weapon not dissimilar to Narmora's and hurled it at his chest.

"My life is in your hands," he muttered to Vraccas as he snapped the shaft of the arrow and rolled off the side of the pier. "I hope Bramdal wasn't lying."

He let himself fall.

The dark surface of the pond came closer and closer;

then, just as he was approaching the water, he came to a sudden halt.

Someone had grabbed his weapons belt.

Pendleburg,
Southwest Urgon,
Girdlegard,
Spring, 6235th Solar Cycle

My uncle, King Lorimbas Steelheart of the clan of the Stone Grinders, ruler of Lorimbur's folk, sends his heartfelt condolences for the loss of your nephew. Urgon has been deprived of an exceptional king," said Romo Steelheart, inclining his head in a gesture that was barely a bow.

He was standing at the foot of a throne, and the throne was in a modest palace—in Romo's opinion, a humble fort. It was situated on the tallest of the three hills that made up Pendleburg, the capital of Urgon.

Wood was a rarity in the mountainous kingdom, and so the people of Urgon built their houses of stone. From a distance, it looked as if the city were made of thousands of colored cubes. There were no tiled roofs, only flat stone slabs on which laundry, fruit, and meat were laid to dry.

Pendleburg owed its colorfulness to the different types of rock available to the masons, who created mosaics and bold geometric patterns from the contrasting hues. Romo felt at home among the solid walls and soaring mountains, which bore comparison with the peaks of his native range.

"I didn't want to be king," said the man on the throne.

He was probably about forty-five cycles old, small and rather portly. He pointed to a portrait of a young man with long fair hair. "Lothaire was a true king of Urgon . . ." His voice cracked and he broke off, burying his lopsided face in his hands. Tears seeped between his fingers.

Romo, who couldn't abide weakness, masked his scorn by staring at the ceiling until the sobs had subsided.

"Forgive me," said King Belletain, wiping the salty tears from his clipped brown beard. "The loss is still very fresh. My dear brother, Lothaire's father, died seven cycles ago in the war against the trolls, and as for me . . ." He raised his hand and tapped his helmet. "I took a blow to the head. Since then I've had a face like a lopsided pumpkin, and I have to wear this helmet or my skull will fall apart. I thought I'd suffered enough, but the gods stole my nephew. I loved him like a son."

That was Romo's cue. From what he had seen so far, the king of Urgon would be easier to deal with than Mallen. "I don't mean to be disrespectful, Your Majesty," he ventured, knowing that if he hit the right note, Belletain would dance to his tune, "but the gods didn't kill Lothaire. It was the dwarves."

The king raised his head wearily and stared at his visitor. "Your kinsmen killed my nephew?" His hand reached for his sword. "Kneel in front of me, dwarf. Lothaire's death must be avenged!"

"Not *my* kinsmen," said Romo hastily. "I was referring to the fourthlings, the dwarves of Goïmdil whose stronghold lies to the northeast of your kingdom, the dwarves who live off the treasures of the Brown Range— treasures that belong to you." Romo took a step toward the invalid on the throne. The king's face was empty and unresponsive. "The fourthlings stood by while your nephew took arms against the magus. If they'd fought at Porista like they did at the Blacksaddle, Lothaire would have lived."

"Tell me about your folk. Don't they call you the dwarf haters?"

"Indeed, Your Majesty, which leaves me at liberty to expose their deceit," he said quickly, determined to steer the conversation to less treacherous ground. "Remember the ax that killed Nôd'onn? It was in the fourthlings' possession all along. They kept it back because they wanted to be Girdlegard's saviors. It was their intention that the human armies should be crushed." He leaned forward. "They could have defeated Nôd'onn whenever they wanted, but they let your nephew die."

Belletain gave him a long look, then roared with laughter. "I'm not falling for this nonsense. Why in the name of Palandiell would they—"

"Glory," cut in Romo. "Glory, and power. The way they saw it, the human kingdoms weren't showing enough gratitude for their defense of Girdlegard's borders. And now they're heroes, thanks to their scheming. They set themselves up as Girdlegard's saviors because they wanted to take the reins. Thousands of humans died because of the fourthlings, and you thanked them for their treachery. Girdlegard is ruled by the dwarves; you welcomed them into your kingdoms, and even Lord Liútasil has fallen for their tricks." He glanced at Lothaire's portrait. "Thankfully, the thirdlings are loyal guardians of your people. We don't want to rule your kingdoms—it's enough to guard the gates."

His speech had struck a chord, as he could tell by the expression on the king of Urgon's face.

"I need to think," said Belletain wretchedly. "If what you're saying is true . . . It hurts my head to imagine what . . ." He broke off and raised a hand to his helmet. Even the light pressure of his fingers caused the broken sections of his skull to move apart. "Leave me a while. I'll call for you when I'm . . ." He cried out, clutching the arms of his throne, and slumped to the side.

The doors flew open, admitting three physicians who set about reviving the king. One held his head, the other loosened his helmet, exposing his bandaged head, while the third unwrapped the dressing and inserted a needle into his skull. Romo watched in amazement as pale pink fluid spurted from Belletain's brain, splashing into a bronze bowl.

"Wait in your quarters," said one of the healers, whose efforts were focused on holding together his ruler's crown. "His Majesty will be incommoded for some time."

The dwarf assented with a growl, turning and leaving the chamber. Once outside, he smiled: Belletain would side with the thirdlings, and a wedge would be driven between the dwarves and their allies, just as his uncle had planned.

Porista,
Former Realm of Lios Nudin,
Girdlegard,
Spring, 6235th Solar Cycle

Narmora raced through the corridors of the palace with little thought for the unborn baby in her womb. The person whose life she valued more than any other was critically ill.

She stopped and clutched her side, gasping for breath and feeling her lack of condition. The baby was still kicking in protest at the sudden burst of speed.

Her path was barred by Djerûn, who was standing guard outside the chamber where Andôkai was tending to the two wounded men.

"Let me through," she said sharply, reaching for the handle. The metal giant stood firm, blocking the doorway entirely with his bulk. "Andôkai," shouted Narmora angrily, "tell your bodyguard to let me in or I'll force my way past him, I swear."

A muffled answer sounded from the chamber, and Djerûn snapped out of his paralysis, allowing her to pass. Narmora heard his armor creaking and groaning as if the metal were under tremendous stress.

She rushed forward and burst through the double doors. The maga was bending over Furgas's bed. His eyes were closed, his forehead shiny with perspiration, and the sheets looked damp.

Narmora hurried over. "Furgas," she whispered fearfully. "His lips . . . They're blue." Glancing down, she saw the blood-soaked bandages around his abdomen. "He's not . . ."

"No," said Andôkai quickly. "Keep your voice down; he needs absolute quiet or he won't recover from his wounds. The blade was poisoned; with what, I don't know. It's lucky the watchmen found him and brought him straight here. Samusin saved him."

The half älf kneeled before her, sobbing with relief. "Thank you, Estimable Maga. I don't know how to repay you."

Andôkai signaled for her to rise. "You won't be so eager to thank me when I've finished," she said darkly. "My magic is strong enough to keep him alive, but I don't have the power to cure him." Her clear blue eyes searched Narmora's face. "Furgas was poisoned by someone with knowledge of dark magic. The men who attacked him weren't highwaymen; they were famuli of Nôd'onn's. Furgas was brought here with a blade in his belly. It was stamped with Nôd'onn's crest."

Narmora straightened up and took hold of his cold, clammy hand, warming his fingers in hers. "Famuli? Why would the magus's famuli ambush Furgas?" She stroked his pale face. "He knows nothing of magic."

"No, but he works for me, and that's enough. Nôd'onn's famuli thought that the palace would pass to them; in their eyes, I'm a usurper." She laid a hand on Narmora's shoulder. "While the servants of evil are at large, Porista is in danger, and no one in Girdlegard is safe. Nôd'onn's famuli must be defeated before it's too late." She paused. "Listen, Narmora, I need an apprentice—someone I can rely on, someone whom I can trust with my life. What if I were to die in the struggle against the magus's supporters? Who would continue in my stead? When I'm gone, the enchanted realms of Girdlegard will fall to Nôd'onn's disciples."

Narmora closed her eyes. "If I were to help, could we heal him?" she asked hoarsely.

Andôkai interpreted the question as a pledge of support.

"I'm sure of it," she said, visibly relieved. "Together, you and I can make him well—but Furgas must be healed in half a cycle, or the poison will be his death. Your apprenticeship will be intensive." She laid a hand on the half älf's rounded belly. "Can you cope?"

"Yes," came the determined reply. "No child should be born to a dead father and a grief-stricken mother." She let go of Furgas's hand and clenched her fists. The whites of her eyes darkened and fine lines spread like cracks across her narrow face. "My nursery songs will chronicle the passing of those who conspired against Furgas. No punishment can be too great."

On the other side of the room, Rodario watched the scene in silence. His bandaged head was pounding horribly from its encounter with the highwayman's cudgel, which counted among the least enjoyable experiences of his life. He was keenly aware that Narmora hadn't looked in his direction, but he magnanimously forgave her. The father of her child was in a coma, and she had other things on her mind.

After the attack, Andôkai's guardsmen had carried him to the palace while he watched in a daze as the ruined streets of Porista passed before his eyes. In spite of his wooziness, he knew for a fact that Andôkai hadn't deemed his condition worthy of a charm or a spell. After a while, someone had cleaned his wounds and bandaged his head; he could picture the hands, but not the face.

Andôkai glanced over. "Feeling better, Rodario?"

Not wishing to appear a weakling, he mustered a valiant smile.

"Excellent," she said briskly, "I'm sure you're in a hurry to get home."

His smile became a pout. "Fine," he said proudly. "You've made it perfectly obvious that you don't want me here." He sat up cautiously, expecting his head to start spinning, but instead he felt irritatingly well. Sighing, he slipped his feet into his buckled shoes, stood up slowly and went over to Furgas's bedside.

In the meantime, Narmora had composed herself and the signs of her älvish heritage, brought on by the emotional intensity of the situation, had disappeared from her face. Her eyes returned to their usual color, and her skin was flawless again. She looked the model of an expectant mother. "Rodario," she said apologetically, laying a hand on his arm. "You mustn't think I'm ignoring you. It's just I'm a bit . . ."

Rodario waved airily. "Don't apologize; I understand."

The maga looked at him squarely. "Answer me this: Can you take over from Furgas?"

"Me?" He raised his arms in astonishment. "You're asking me, the best impresario in Girdlegard, to rebuild your city?" He was about to refuse when something made him change his mind. "I can always try."

"Trying isn't enough; I need someone who can do it," she snapped. "If you don't have the skill, I'll hire someone else."

"Never fear, Estimable Maga," he assured her. "While poor Furgas is in a coma, your city will be in capable hands." She eyed him skeptically, but he was too busy thinking about his salary to care. He gave a flamboyant bow. "As for my own affairs, they can wait. The construction of my theater, the premiere of the masterpiece that I—"

"Very well," she said, interrupting his overblown speech.

"Go home, get some sleep, and be ready to start in the morning. I don't want any extra delays." She turned to Narmora. "I'll ask for your things to be fetched to the palace; there's no shortage of space, as you know. I'll leave it to you to choose a room."

"I'll stay here with Furgas. It's big enough for—"

"No," ruled Andôkai. "Furgas needs peace and quiet. Too much noise could elevate his heart rate and push the poison through his system. Come, we've lingered long enough." She steered them to the door. "You can visit every orbit," she told Narmora. "Sit with him, hold his hand if you want to, but don't speak to him, and stay no longer than an hour. The slightest agitation could be the death of him." She opened the doors, and Djerûn shifted to let them pass. "I've got a few things to do here, but I'll join you in a moment."

Narmora accompanied Rodario out of the palace. "Would you do me a favor?" she asked. "You're an expert in disguise and dissimulation. Can you find out whether the assassins were acting alone?"

He beamed. "You've come to the right man. I'll slink through the streets of Porista at the dead of night, searching for the magus's treacherous disciples and . . ." He trailed off, remembering his encounter with the cudgel. But the thought of poor Furgas gave him the courage to play the hero in a drama without a script. "I'll disguise myself properly for my protection. Leave it to me. The city will be rid of Nôd'onn's accursed famuli sooner than Andôkai thinks."

"I'd rather you didn't tell the maga."

"You want revenge? Dearest Narmora, are you sure it's advisable in your condition?"

"Right now I feel stronger than ever; I'd fight Djerůn if I had to." She unlocked the side gate, reached for his hand and gave it a squeeze. "You'll do it, won't you, Rodario?"

He gave her a hug. "I'll do it," he said reassuringly. He looked both ways; there was no one in sight. "I promise," he said with a wave, and hurried away.

Free from prying eyes, he found the courage to open his left hand.

All the while he had been hiding a drop of the mysterious substance that, according to Andôkai, was responsible for poisoning his friend. He had been spattered with it when the second highwayman mistook him for Furgas.

Rodario raised his hand to his eyes and peered at the strange fluid. It was yellow, almost luminescent, and it reminded him of something, but he couldn't think what. He thought about what Andôkai had said about the blade. He had no recollection of a crest or any kind of symbol on the dagger; in fact, the only part of the story that he could corroborate wholeheartedly was that Furgas had been the target of the attack.

It seems like someone isn't telling the truth . . . In an instant, his reservations vanished: He couldn't wait to get to the bottom of the mystery, so long as it wasn't anything too sinister or dangerous . . .

VI

Fallen Kingdom of Lesinteïl,
Gauragar,
Girdlegard,
Spring, 6235th Solar Cycle

Tungdil's weapons belt was stretched to its limits. The leather cut into his shoulder, embedding itself diagonally across his chest. His downward journey toward the safety of the water had ended with an almighty jolt, forcing the air from his lungs, but there was no danger of him fainting; the pain from the arrow wounds kept him agonizingly awake.

Above him, his captor panted with exertion. The female älf could barely hold him, let alone lift him onto the pier. Tungdil knew from her urgent shouts that she was calling for reinforcements: In a few moments, they would reel him in like a fish on a line, and there was nothing he could do.

He was trapped.

Dangling from his belt, he watched the blood leak from his chest and shoulders and splash into the pond below. Desperate to free himself, he thrashed around with his arms and legs, praying that the älf would be forced to release her grip. At last, one of his feet made contact with the pier, and he pushed off vigorously, shuttling back and forth.

The tactic seemed to work: His antagonist groaned with the effort and said something that he took to be a curse. "You'll never take me alive," he shouted defiantly, feeling her skid across the pier toward the water. "I'd rather drown us both."

Shouts echoed across the pond as the älf's companions rushed to her aid. Before he had time to realize what was happening, he felt himself being hauled inch by inch toward the pier.

He wasn't ready to concede defeat.

The next time his boot hit the pier, he pushed back with all his might to catapult himself toward the middle of the pond. The älf and her friends clung on determinedly.

His belt was the first to give in.

The buckle, like most buckles, wasn't designed to withstand the full weight of a dwarf, especially an armored warrior. The pin cut into the leather, which promptly gave way. Moving from hole to hole, the buckle chewed through the belt, slicing it in two.

Tungdil felt a rush of elation.

Then it dawned on him: *Keenfire!* His weak fingers snatched at the disappearing belt. *I can't let the älfar get . . .*

Already he was plummeting through the water, which was as cold and forbidding as it looked from above. His chain mail weighed him down, dragging him relentlessly toward the bottom. He focused on holding his breath, a trick that he used to practice in the bath.

He seemed to fall for an eternity, sinking deeper and deeper. After a time, the darkness thickened, perhaps because of the water, perhaps because of his air-starved mind.

Tungdil could feel himself weakening. Briefly, he was tempted to open his mouth and fill his lungs with air, but his fading consciousness warned him that he would drown.

At last he saw light.

It was all around him, wrapping him in a comforting cocoon. Even as he reached out eagerly, he heard the roar of bellows. *The eternal smithy! Vraccas has summoned my soul . . .*

He got a clip on the ear for presuming to know the Smith's intentions.

Shocked, he jerked away. A hand struck his cheek, knocking his head to the side.

He saw the blurry outlines of a dwarven god, who looked surprisingly like a regular dwarf. The red halo intensified, expanding into the darkness and filling it with light.

"That's right, scholar," the Smith said testily, preparing to strike again. "I'll keep this up until you tell me to stop."

An arm sped toward him. This time Tungdil had the presence of mind to reach up with his left hand and grab the dwarf's wrist. "Stop," he coughed, trying to drag himself out of the water. Someone reached down and hauled him out. He spewed a mouthful of water, coughing, sneezing, choking, and swallowing until his lungs filled with air.

He looked up. His cheeks were flushed from coughing, and his eyelids were swollen, but he could see.

Crouching beside him and beaming enthusiastically was a dripping wet Boïndil. Their watery journey had ended on the shores of an underground lake.

Tungdil traced the noise of roaring bellows to a waterfall that was tumbling into the middle of the pond from the ceiling of the cavern, ten paces above. There was no sign of a furnace, only strings of lanterns with tinted panels that bathed the lake in a deep red glow.

The cavern itself was a mile long by a mile wide. Tungdil and Boïndil were sitting on the only section of dry rock; elsewhere the water came right up to the walls.

"Quite a drop, eh?" said Boïndil, pointing to the torrent of water. "It pitched us into the middle of the pool, and the current washed us ashore." He furrowed his brow. "Are we the only survivors?"

Tungdil nodded weakly.

"Damn the älfar," thundered Boïndil. "I'll give those cowardly murderers a taste of my axes." He thumped the floor with his hand, then remembered that he had something important to convey. "We're in the realm of the freelings; they're fetching a doctor." He inspected Tungdil's wounds. "You were lucky, scholar—assuming the arrows weren't poisoned . . ."

"I'll be fine," said his friend in what he hoped was a convincing tone. The truth was, the cavern was still spinning, but then again, he had lost a lot of blood. *Don't let it be poison.* He raised a hand and ran it over his chest, then looked for his weapons belt.

"You must have lost it on the way. The chute between here and the pond was pretty narrow; I almost got stuck." Boïndil stood up and peered into the water. "I suppose you'll have to dive for it."

"It's gone," groaned Tungdil, laying his head against the ground. He was still too dizzy to sit up.

"Gone?" echoed Boïndil, fearing the worst. "Tell me you lost it in the water . . ." He kneeled down and stared at his friend in horror. "Are you certain? Anything would be better than losing Keenfire to our enemies."

Tungdil made his report.

"That's bad news," muttered Boïndil. "Still, with a bit of luck, Keenfire could have fallen into the water while they were hauling up the belt."

"Do you think we should—"

"We've brought a stretcher," said a deep voice behind him. "We're going to take you to a doctor; Gemmil will deal with you after that."

Four dwarves with incredibly pale skin stepped into Tungdil's line of sight. Bending down, they placed him gently on a stretcher.

After studying their faces, Tungdil concluded that they looked like ordinary dwarves, only paler and without the usual dark brown eyes. One of their number was almost entirely colorless: His red eyes smiled at Tungdil from an ashen face.

Boïndil, unnerved by the pallid dwarf, placed a hand on his ax. "I'll hack them to pieces if they attack us," he promised, lowering his voice so only Tungdil could hear. He nodded surreptitiously at the back of the colorless dwarf. "Do you think he's a ghost? It doesn't seem natural."

Tungdil had considered the matter already. "On the contrary," he said, remembering the books about animal life in Lot-Ionan's library. "I've read of cave-dwelling frogs who are born with no eyes. They live in total darkness, and their skin is pure white."

"I see," said Boïndil uncertainly. He wrung out his beard and turned his attention to his plait, trailing water as he walked. "But the dwarves in the other kingdoms live in underground halls, so how come—"

"That's different. They don't stay underground forever, do they? They come up to the surface to tend their cattle, trade their goods, set out on adventures . . ." Tungdil hadn't studied science in detail, but he was sure that the loss of pigment resulted from living in darkness for a considerable time.

They exited the cavern, leaving the thundering waterfall behind them. The corridors reminded Tungdil of ancient waterways carved by rivers through the rock. Straight ahead was a small metal door that led into a simple room. Tungdil's stretcher was lowered onto a table.

"I was expecting worse," said a clear, bright voice like the ring of a hammer against an anvil. "Cut away his garments; I need to see the wounds."

Two dwarves fitted a pair of sharp-edged pliers around the bottom of his mail shirt, while a third dwarf squeezed the handles. Ring by ring, the blades cut through his armor as if it were paper, not metal. The mail shirt fell to the table in two neat halves. Next the dwarves tore open the leather jerkin, exposing his chest.

"Let's see what the älfar have done to you," said the voice. Its owner stepped into view: a delicate dwarf with snow-white skin.

The sight of the dazzling stranger sent Tungdil's memories of Balyndis up in smoke. He had never seen a more beautiful dwarf-woman.

"I'm Myrmianda," she said. Her red eyes smiled at him, traveling down his face to study the arrow shafts protruding from his naked chest. She was dressed in dark brown robes and a leather apron. A golden circlet rested on her head, holding back her long snowy hair. "Everyone here will vouch for my skill. I'm a medic—I know what I'm doing."

She leaned closer to examine the flesh around the

wounds. Her fingers were remarkably slender and delicate for a dwarf. He breathed in her scent, which was clean and fresh without a hint of sweat or smoke. If anything, he detected an aroma of herbs.

"No discoloration or swelling—Vraccas was on your side," she told him. Straightening up, she signaled to her assistants, who maneuvered Tungdil into a sitting position, pushing away the remains of his chain mail and slitting open the rest of his jerkin. "The älfar use arrows with detachable heads. We can't leave anything in the wounds, so it's no use pulling on the shafts. The only solution is to push them through."

No sooner had she finished speaking than she placed her middle and index fingers on the broken shafts and pushed the arrows through his flesh.

Tungdil clenched his jaw, grinding his teeth together furiously. It felt like red-hot pokers were passing through his shoulder and his chest. Myrmianda reached around him, taking hold of the arrowheads and pulling them from his back.

"Not all my patients are as brave as this," she said approvingly, casting the arrowheads into a tub of water and washing her bloodied hands. She took some wet moss from a bowl and placed thick compresses on his front and back; then, with the help of her assistants, she bandaged his wounds. "Blue moss," she told him. "It's the best way to stop the bleeding. We'll wait a few hours and change the dressings, and by tomorrow you won't feel a thing." She added a powdered substance to a beaker of water, and thrust it into his hand. "Here, this should boost your strength and help against fever."

"By the hammer of Vraccas, that's what I call efficient," Boïndil said to her admiringly. He was almost tempted to get himself injured so that he could profit from her skill.

The medic nodded briskly. "Thank you. I've treated a fair few arrow wounds in my time."

Tungdil was transfixed. Myrmianda spoke educated dwarfish, her accent was faultless, and she was bound to be well read; her delicate stature pointed to cycles of handling parchment rather than laboring in the mines. In short, she was nothing like Balyndis, who was twice as muscular and imposing, as befitted a smith.

He gulped down the contents of the beaker. "I'm Tungdil Goldhand," he said, pulling himself together. "And this is Boïndil Doubleblade of the clan of the Swinging Axes of Beroïn's line."

She dried her hands on a towel and placed it on a little table. "The hero of the Blacksaddle and his trusty companion," she said, inclining her head toward them. "It's an honor to meet you. As far as I'm aware, slaying Nôd'onn isn't against the rules of the dwarven kingdoms, so you must be here by chance. Did you fall into the water when the älfar attacked?"

Tungdil wished that he could be more upfront with Myrmianda, who, apart from being exceptionally beautiful, had treated and bandaged his wounds. "I'm sorry," he said awkwardly, "we can't discuss it until we've spoken to your king."

For a moment she seemed disappointed, then she flashed him a smile that brought color to his cheeks. "In that case, I was wrong. You're here for a reason, whatever it might be."

Tungdil watched as she packed away her instruments: thin-bladed knives, hooks, surgical saws, and assorted paraphernalia that would be lethal in the hands of a warrior. Myrmianda rolled them up in a cloth, secured each end with a leather strap and took her leave. "I hope you feel better soon."

A white-haired dwarf appeared at the door. His skin was whiter than white, and his eyes were the loamy brown of fresh soil. He wore a mail tunic, and an ax hung from his belt.

"May your inner furnace burn for many cycles," he said welcomingly. "My name is Gemmil Callusedhand. I'm the elected sovereign of the freelings' realm."

Tungdil and Boïndil introduced themselves. Their names made an immediate impression on the king. "I'm honored by your visit. You bring news from the other kingdoms, I suppose?"

"Bramdal Masterstroke told us about your realm," said Tungdil, launching into a lengthy explanation. He told Gemmil about the new fifthling kingdom, his meeting with the executioner, his efforts to find the exiles, and the älvish ambush at the pond. "Pardon me," he said suddenly. "I should have started by thanking you for your assistance in defeating Nôd'onn. Your warriors stopped the orcs from overrunning the underground network, for which the kingdoms of Girdlegard will be forever in your debt." He bowed as best he could with his bandaged chest. "Boïndil and I have particular cause to thank you—we couldn't have forged Keenfire without the freelings' help."

"It's as well you left a message in the tunnels," said Gemmil, smiling. "We're exiles, but even an exiled dwarf is a child of the Smith. Girdlegard's safety is our priority; we couldn't allow the magus to prevail."

"Perhaps you could tell your subjects—"

"They're not my subjects," the king corrected him gently. "The dwarves in this realm are free in word and deed. We elect a king to take decisions on behalf of our community, and, at present, that honor falls to me. In three cycles, my term of office will be over, and we'll hold another vote."

"You pass the crown between you?" exclaimed Boïndil, laughing out loud. He clearly found the notion quite preposterous. "That's a fine kind of monarchy!"

"The best," agreed Gemmil, failing to take offense.

"Your Majesty," said Tungdil, jumping in before Boïndil could insult the king again. "The freelings came to the aid of Girdlegard when it mattered. Would you be willing to fight with us again?" He summarized what he and Boïndil had seen at the Stone Gateway and outlined his fears about the army of orcish revenants marching north. "We think Ushnotz wants to seize the Stone Gateway. The new fifthling folk won't survive the invasion of four thousand undead beasts, not to mention an influx of orcs from the Outer Lands, which is exactly what will happen if the missing scout tells his cousins that our defenses are down. Without you and your warriors, the kingdom will fall before our masons can fashion its gates. Only the freelings can reach us in time."

The king frowned, his eyebrows joining together in a long white line that reminded Tungdil of a ridge of salt. "This is bad news indeed—and the loss of Keenfire makes it all the more serious. If the ax fell into the water, we won't get it back."

"If it's gone, it's gone," said Boïndil lightly, knowing

that Tungdil would be blaming himself for its loss. "We'll get Balyndis to make a new one. Keenfire was forged to wipe out evil, so it won't be much good in the hands of an älf. Besides, their axmanship is atrocious."

"It's more complicated than that," said Tungdil thoughtfully. "Keenfire is a special dwarven weapon, a symbol of our victory over Tion's hordes. Its loss will do us greater injury than any number of undead orcs." He turned to the king. "Please, Your Majesty, I entreat you in the name of Glaïmbar Sharpax, king of the fifthlings, don't let us fight this threat alone. Your warriors will give our kinsmen new courage. A doubting dwarf is easily conquered; your army will make us strong."

Gemmil came straight to a decision. "I'll send out messengers to spread the news. As soon as I've raised an army, I'll dispatch it to the fifthling kingdom." He stroked his white beard. "If the orcs attack before my warriors get there, you'll have to hold out as best you can—Vraccas willing, it won't be for long. Go back and tell your king that the freelings will answer his call."

"How many can we count on?"

"As many as I can find," said Gemmil with a shrug. His eyes settled on Tungdil's bandages. "You won't survive another run-in with the älfar. Take Myr, some of her assistants, and a few of my warriors. I can't have you traveling alone." He turned to leave.

"Can I ask a question, Gemmil?"

The king stopped at the door and nodded for Tungdil to continue.

"Our intention is to rebuild the kingdom in Giselbert's name. Would any of you like to join us?"

"And swap our freedom for the unbending laws of a dwarven kingdom?" Gemmil paused. "It's a charitable offer, Tungdil Goldhand, but we should focus on winning the battle against the orcs. After that, I'd like you to visit us properly so you can see the difference between the freelings and the other folks. I think you'll understand why most of us would prefer to stay here."

"What nonsense!" trumpeted Boïndil. "I've never heard such foolishness from a king." He stomped toward the door, stopped in front of Gemmil, and looked him in the eye. "We're just as free as you are!"

"I suppose you're allowed to do whatever you please?"

"Too right we are," said Boïndil stubbornly.

"So you wouldn't have a problem disobeying your chieftain's orders if you thought he was wrong?"

Boïndil was momentarily thrown. "Our chieftains are always right," he snapped testily, looking to Tungdil for support. The argument wasn't going as he had intended, but he was too hotheaded to back down.

"I'm glad to hear it. Wise chieftains never engage in pointless feuds about long-forgotten grievances."

"Our chieftains never forget a grievance," growled Boïndil.

"I'm sure they don't," said Gemmil. "And I expect they're happy for you to meld the maiden of your choice . . ."

The disgruntled warrior said nothing, folding his hands in front of his chest.

"I'm not trying to score points," said Gemmil earnestly. "I was merely suggesting that your laws aren't always fair."

Looking at the monarch's face, Tungdil was convinced of his integrity, and even Boïndil was appeased.

"Change isn't welcome in the old dwarven kingdoms,"

the king continued. "The chieftains and elders are too attached to the power inherited from their forefathers. I can introduce you to dwarves who campaigned for greater freedom and were banished from their kingdoms. They're freelings now, of course."

Boïndil, who had been racking his brains for a comeback, spotted a weakness in Gemmil's argument. "Let's not forget that you accept all kinds of outcasts into your realm—murderers, troublemakers, and the like. Not all of them were banished for speaking out of turn. Surely it can't be good to have criminals in your ranks?"

The king seemed suddenly eager to put an end to the debate. "We never ask why a dwarf was banished from his kingdom; all that matters is that he accepts our ethos and contributes to the common good." He stepped backward into the corridor. "You'd do well to remember that some of our so-called criminals will soon be defending your kingdom against the orcs. Whatever their misdeeds, dwarves who risk their lives for the good of Girdlegard won't be made to hump coals in Vraccas's smithy. Our god will forgive their sins."

The door closed behind him with a bang.

"Ha, did you hear that?" cackled Boïndil smugly. "He didn't answer my question. Maybe he's not so clever after all!"

"You shouldn't have provoked him," scolded Tungdil, who secretly agreed with Gemmil on a number of points. "We need his help, remember." He slid down from the stretcher and walked over to his friend, who draped a blanket over his shoulders. "At least we've got what we came for; our poor companions won't have died in vain."

They kneeled down in front of the hearth, feeling the comforting warmth of the little fire. Closing their eyes, they prayed to Vraccas to bless their fallen companions and summon them to his smithy.

Tungdil's thoughts turned to the freelings.

He was especially keen to see one of their cities. *I wonder if they've got their own architecture*, he mused. This question and a dozen others would remain unanswered until the last army of orcs had been chased out of Girdlegard, but Tungdil was determined to return one orbit and see how the freelings lived. *I'd like to stay for long enough to understand their customs.*

Tungdil was thrilled by the thought of seeing new things and discovering different ways of life. While dwarves like Boïndil were happiest in their kingdoms, Tungdil longed to know as much as possible about the wider world. He was interested, for example, in how Myr's assistants had cut through his chain mail. The sharp-edged pliers were like nothing he had seen.

Boïndil finished praying and made his way to the corner of the room where the freelings had left them some food. He shoved a hunk of bread into his mouth and beckoned to Tungdil.

"Dig in," he instructed him between mouthfuls, spraying his beard with crumbs. "It's going to be a tough march with your injuries, but at least Myrmianda can help."

I'm glad I was wounded, thought Tungdil, picturing the freeling's face. Even the soft down on her cheeks was the color of snow with a faint hint of silver . . .

He felt a pang of guilt, and the vision of Myr morphed into Balyndis. He remembered how he had given her his heart. *It doesn't count anymore*, he told himself. *She's melded to Glaïmbar.* "We'll be in capable hands," he said casually. He strolled over to join Boïndil in the corner.

"Their food tastes nice enough," said the secondling grudgingly. He could barely talk because his cheeks were fit to burst. "Still, I'm not sure I like the idea of fighting shoulder to shoulder with criminals. How do we know they weren't banished for murdering other dwarves?" He helped himself to a wedge of cheese that smelled strong enough to asphyxiate a band of orcs. "Dwarves don't get banished for no reason." He stopped munching and looked at Tungdil questioningly. "Their kinsfolk were right to banish them, weren't they, scholar?"

Tungdil nodded briefly and pretended to be swallowing a mouthful of bread. He reached for the jug of dark ale.

Gemmil's criticisms of the dwarven kingdoms had struck a chord.

He wasn't prepared to admit as much to Boïndil, but he could see the sense in the freelings' ideals. He had been brought up in a school where opinions were exchanged freely and nothing was exempt from scholarly consideration. Tungdil had been taught that ideas were fluid and ever-changing, but the outlook of the dwarves resembled their kingdoms: rigid, inflexible, and unyielding.

Boïndil stopped gulping down his food and stared absentmindedly at the wall. He seemed to be lost in thought. "Which way round is it?" he said slowly. "Does Vraccas want us to carry the spark of change to the fifthlings' furnace, or is he testing our faith?"

Tungdil could barely mask his surprise; he hadn't expected Boïndil, who was usually very traditional, to ponder such things. "It's a tricky question and I don't know the answer," he replied. He leaned forward abruptly and picked up his tankard. Pain coursed through him, reminding him of his punctured shoulder and chest. He set down the tankard with a curse. "They're going to help us, and that's the main thing. The rest will take care of itself."

Boïndil wiped his mouth and burped. "How big is their realm? Ten square miles? Fifty square miles? How many warriors do you think they can send?" He helped himself to some beer and refilled Tungdil's tankard. "I'll wager three hundred at most."

"Three hundred might be enough. We'll wait until Ushnotz and his troopers set their ladders against our walls; then we'll tip them over and shower them with stones." He clinked tankards with Boïndil. "With Gemmil's help, we'll put an end to the beasts once and for all."

"Some of the runts have fled to Toboribor," said the secondling. "I suppose it's a bit far for our armies . . . Do you think Mallen can handle them himself?"

"Without your axes?" Tungdil shook his head in despair. "I can't help wondering when you'll finally tire of killing orcs. At this rate you'll still be chasing runts when you're a frail old dwarf of seven hundred cycles."

"I'll be dead by then," he said in a matter-of-fact way that chilled his friend's blood. "A spear or an arrow will see to that. It's all right, scholar," he added, noticing Tungdil's expression, "I don't *want* to die. When I lost Smeralda, I prayed to Vraccas to kill me on the spot, but now I give thanks for every orbit. When my time is up, I want to go out as a hero, like Bavragor did." He raised his tankard to Tungdil and emptied it in a single draft.

"To Bavragor Hammersmith and all those who died for Keenfire and Girdlegard."

"Vraccas preserve the rest of us from joining them too soon," added Tungdil, downing his beer. *Don't worry,* he promised his fallen friends. *Keenfire won't be lost forever.* A plan was taking shape in his mind. When the battle was over, he would come back with a big net and sweep the bottom of the pond—and if that failed, he would retrieve the ax from Dsôn Balsur as soon as the allies defeated the älfar. Either way, he would get the ax back, but the coming battle would be fought without it. *Its loss could cost us dear.* The beer tasted suddenly bitter in his mouth.

Pendleburg,
Southwest Urgon,
Girdlegard,
Spring, 6235th Solar Cycle

You opened my eyes to the dishonesty of the dwarves," said King Belletain. "Palandiell must have sent you." He was sitting in bed, his back propped up with countless cushions. His leather armor had been exchanged for a loose purple robe.

Three physicians attended his every move, dabbing continuously at his fractured skull. Pink, viscous fluid seeped into their sponges.

Belletain pointed to the trio and snorted derisively. "Look at those crows! They circle me all the time—they're hoping I'll die." The physician standing closest to him received a violent shove. The man stumbled, bowl, sponge, and fluid dropping to the floor. "Confounded crows," the king screamed, his face flushing red. "Caw-caw, caw-caw!" He flapped his arms up and down. "I'm not your carrion! I'm not dead yet! I'm the eagle of Urgon, I'm master of you all!"

Ha, he's lost his mind. The dwarf was careful not to show a reaction. *What a stroke of luck. He'll do exactly as I say . . .*

Belletain lowered his arms. "I have news for your uncle, Romo Steelheart. I think it will please you." He assumed an air of mystery and beckoned for the dwarf to approach. "Come here, and I'll whisper in your ear. I don't want the crows to hear us."

Romo, leaning in to listen, smelled the odor of rotten gums on his breath.

"They're watching me all the time," the king continued. "I can't get rid of them, you know." He laid an arm around Romo's shoulder and tapped his index finger against the dwarf's armored chest. "It will be our secret— a secret between me, the eagle of Urgon, and you, my little falcon with the beard." He chuckled like a child. "Your king and I are going to get on famously. We'll throw the fourthlings out of their stronghold!" His eyes rolled back in his head. "The Brown Range is mine! *Mine*, do you hear? The fourthlings should be paying me, and they're squatting on my land. You were right, Romo: It's time I threw them out. My soldiers will . . ."

"Please, Your Majesty," ventured one of the physicians, "you should be resting. Too much excitement will add to the swelling in your brain. Here, this infusion will lower your blood pressure." Concerned, he examined a crack in the king's skull. The blood was flowing faster than ever.

"Caw-caw, caw-caw," chortled Belletain, raising a hand to his mouth.

The second physician tried to maneuver him back into position, hoping to make him sit upright and stem the flow of blood. Belletain punched him in the stomach. "Get back, winged devil," he raved.

"We're trying to help you, Your Majesty," the bruised attendant soothed him. "Your mind will clear when you've had some sleep. Gandogar isn't—"

"Eavesdropper!" screeched Belletain. He lunged forward and before Romo could stop him, he had seized the dwarf's morning star and smashed the three metal balls into the physician's head, shattering his skull. "No more cawing," he said triumphantly. He tossed the weapon back to Romo. "Come, little falcon, help your new friend to get rid of the other nasty crows." A malevolent smile spread over his face as he looked at the remaining attendants.

Romo weighed the morning star in his hand.

"Don't listen to him," begged one of the men. "The king hasn't been himself since the ogre cracked his skull. He won't survive without our—"

Belletain pressed his hands to his ears. "Stop their cawing! I can't bear it any longer, my little falcon. I need new birds—birds that sing!"

The dwarf took a step forward and the attendants backed away. "It's all right," he said reassuringly. "I wouldn't dream of hurting you." Just then he swung the morning star into the crotch of the man on his left and sent his spiked fist into the belly of the man on his right. They slumped to the floor, writhing in pain. "But a king's word is law." He raised the morning star and brought it down forcefully. After two brutal blows, the whimpering stopped. The three attendants lay motionless beside their monarch's bed, their heads a pulpy mess of gore and shattered bone.

"My loyal falcon," squealed the king. "The crows have stopped cawing."

"I'll send some new attendants from our kingdom," promised the dwarf, wiping his dripping weapon on the dead men's clothes. "They'll banish the pain from your skull, and they won't make a peep."

"Good," sighed the king, slumping contentedly onto his pillows. "No more cawing—what a blessing." He gazed out of the window at the grassy slopes. The sun was shining and the fields looked green and lush; there would be plenty of straw by the autumn. "Lothaire's death will be a-ven-ged," he chanted, fitting the words to the tune of a traditional Urgonese folk song. "And Gandogar's treachery will be re-ven-ged . . ." He turned and looked Romo in the eye. "Rivers of blood and mountains of gold; that's the price they'll pay," he declared firmly. "Tell your uncle that we have an agreement: If he can come up with a strategy, my warriors will do the rest. They're experienced in warfare and fleet of foot. The highest peaks, the narrowest paths, the steepest chasms—nothing can make them fall. They will go where the eagle commands them. And when they hear the truth about my beloved nephew's death, their hearts will burn with fury."

Romo bowed. "I'm glad you've heeded my warnings. Lesser rulers have been fooled by the reputation of the other dwarven folks. You're a wise king indeed." He backed away toward the door.

"Send a few lackeys to take away the bodies. I'll feed them to the other crows." He stretched out his arms cheerfully. "I can feel the wind beneath my wings. The eagle is soaring, thanks to his little friend, the falcon." He waved him away. "Come back soon. We need to finalize our plans."

"You have my word, Your Majesty." The dwarf stepped out of the chamber, closed the door carefully and let out a hearty laugh. It had cost considerable effort to hide his amusement. The next step was to surround the king with thirdling physicians, and Belletain would be welded to him for life.

My uncle will be well pleased. He set off through the corridors, whistling. He was anxious to leave at once, not least because he wanted to know if Mallen had been brought to his knees by the orcs.

Porista,
Former Realm of Lios Nudin,
Girdlegard,
Spring, 6235th Solar Cycle

Xamtys's message to the rulers of Girdlegard confirmed Andôkai in her determination to make a maga of Narmora as quickly as possible. *The firstling kingdom crushed by a shooting star, the Outer Lands engulfed in flames . . . Samusin, god of equilibrium, what danger is gathering in the west?*

At least Xamtys's news wasn't all bad. Under her leadership, the firstlings were rebuilding their stronghold and repairing the damage inflicted by the meteor and the avalanche. Xamtys had vowed to repair the fortifications in record time so that her warriors would be ready to fight off the threat. Her tone was somber but quietly confident.

Is she right to be hopeful? Can the threat be contained by an army of dwarves? The maga left the letter on the table and went to find her pupil, whom she had sent to the library to familiarize herself with scholarly script.

The half älf had a natural gift for magic, but it wasn't the same as the maga's knowledge of spells and charms. Narmora's magic derived from single syllables and an innate ability that had nothing to do with Andôkai's art.

Her älf mother had taught her a few simple formulae, but she had never encountered symbols and runes. Mornings were spent studying in the library, while afternoons and evenings were given over to practical exercises. The final hour before bedtime was reserved for Furgas. Every night she sat by his bedside, holding his hand, crying tears of rage, and vowing to wreak terrible vengeance on the villains who had reduced him to this state.

Andôkai strode into the library. The chamber was lined from floor to ceiling with stacks containing books, manuscripts, atlases, and compendia. Some of the shelves were bowing dangerously under the weight of the recorded knowledge.

It's all a question of quantity, she thought to herself. *With enough sheets of parchment, you could kill a troll.* She swept past the stacks in search of her famula.

Narmora, who had swapped her armor for loose-fitting robes that accommodated her rounded form, was sitting by a narrow window. The light shone directly on the pages of a hefty book. Particles of dust shimmered in the sun.

"It's time for some fresh air," announced the maga,

suddenly aware of the musty smell. The library was the biggest of its kind in Girdlegard, and it smelled of parchment, leather, glue, and dust. Andôkai, who preferred to devote her time to refining her combat skills, had almost forgotten the odor of books. Half an orbit in the stuffy library was enough to make her restless. "How are you getting on?"

"Some of the runes are easy to remember," said Narmora without looking up from the page. "But they stop me from learning anything else. It's as if they don't want me to forget them." She stood up. "I can't do it, maga. Half a cycle isn't enough."

"You need only learn the basics," said Andôkai reassuringly. "Thanks to your natural talent, you're ten cycles ahead of most famuli." She stopped short, realizing that the plate of food on Narmora's desk was untouched. "You're supposed to be looking after yourself," she scolded. "How do you think the baby will grow if you're not eating? You mustn't starve yourself."

Narmora looked at the meat, vegetables, and bread in surprise. "I'm sorry, maga, I got distracted . . ." She picked up the plate and set off behind the maga, eating as she went. "You look worried. Has something happened?"

Andôkai stopped in front of a bookcase, climbed the ladder and pulled out a book from the row of battered spines. "The firstlings have spotted something strange," she called from the top of the ladder. "The Outer Lands are on fire." She leafed through the book, closed it impatiently and took another volume from the shelf. "It appears that the magi have been regrettably short-sighted in their quest for knowledge. Every known fact about the kingdoms of Girdlegard and the art of magic is archived in the library, but I can't find a single book about the land beyond our borders." She gave up and left the volume on the top rung of the ladder. "The Outer Lands barely get a mention—except in relation to the explorers who ventured over the mountains. Most of them never came back."

"Surely there must be merchants who've been there," said Narmora, gazing at the rows of books. "Didn't any of the explorers keep a journal?"

They left the library.

"I think the only solution is to scour the other archives," said Andôkai, unhappy at the prospect of leaving her realm. "I'm sorry to put you through this in your condition, but I'm afraid you'll have to come too. We should be able to find what we're looking for in the universities of Weyurn. The archivists keep detailed records of every occurrence, no matter how unremarkable, in the history of the realm."

They emerged into the courtyard. The sun was high in the sky, so they retreated to the shade of the arcades and Andôkai prepared to start the lesson.

Narmora came to a halt and put down her plate. "We'll have to take Furgas with us." It was clear from her tone that she considered the matter settled.

The maga had other ideas. "The roads of Girdlegard are full of potholes. How is Furgas supposed to rest when the carriage is tipping from side to side like a boat?"

"Someone will have to look after him. You can't expect Djerûn to nurse him to health."

"No, but I'm sure his best friend Rodario will jump at the chance to sleep in my chamber, regardless of whether I forbid it, which, needless to say, I will."

Narmora stared at her incredulously. "Estimable Maga,

the impresario is an old friend, and I'm familiar with his talents: acting, orating, and philandering. On stage he makes a wonderful physician, but he isn't the real thing. Quite frankly, I'd sooner trust Djerůn than him."

"Djerůn won't be here; he's going on a mission to the Outer Lands. We need to know what we're up against and prepare ourselves accordingly. At present, our only intelligence is the firstlings' description of a fire." The maga had constructed her case in advance, realizing that she would have to persuade her famula of the merit of the plan. "Don't worry about Furgas; I'll renew the charm, and every third orbit Rodario will change the sheets. There won't be anything else for him to do." She pointed to the far end of the arcade. "Stand over there—we're going to try something new."

The half älf took up position, but she wasn't prepared to concede defeat. "Are you sure the charm will be strong enough? What if it wears off before we're back?"

Andôkai raised her arms and traced silvery syllables above her head. "Furgas would die," she said candidly, casting the charm toward Narmora, who held out her palms defensively and uttered a simple incantation.

The glittering jet of light turned a deep shade of green, slowed down and changed its trajectory, swooping upward and boring its way through the roof. The sky appeared through the marble.

The maga could hardly believe her eyes. "You changed the energy," she said in astonishment. "How did you do it?"

Narmora smiled. "I suppose I must have muddled up the runes."

A crack appeared in the ceiling and fragments of marble showered to the ground. Crackling and hissing, a green bolt of lightning swooped toward Andôkai. The charm had returned and was pursuing its target with grim determination. The maga disappeared in a cloud of dust.

A fragment of marble struck Narmora on the shoulder. Just then a searing pain ripped through her womb, stopping her breath.

She doubled over and sank to her knees, clutching her belly. Looking down, she watched in horror as a dark tide washed over her robes; warm fluid was seeping from her body, drenching the cloth.

No! She touched the sticky fabric with her hands and stared at her crimson fingers. Heat washed through her, but she was shivering with cold. "You've taken Furgas; spare me my child!" she pleaded helplessly. Her eyes turned the color of coal and dark lines appeared like cracks on her face, revealing her lineage.

She held onto a column and tried to pull herself up, but her bloodied fingers slid over the polished marble and she sprawled against the floor. Her stomach landed on a splinter of stone.

This time she knew for certain that something had burst. She curled up on the floor and screamed despairingly as she clutched her belly with shaking fingers, water streaming from her womb.

No one paid much attention to the leper in the corner whose ravaged features were hidden almost wholly by yellowed dressings. Sometimes a bronze coin flew through the tavern in his direction, whereupon he rose to his feet, bowed several times and collected it gratefully.

"Here, eat this and be on your way," said the publican,

depositing an ancient plate and a battered tankard on the table. He was careful not to touch the man's hands, having noticed the rips in his gloves. Later, he would throw away the plate, tankard, and cutlery and scrub the bench and table with precious vinegar solution. It pained him to think of the cost, but the price of refusing charity to a leper was infinitely higher—the sick and infirm were under Palandiell's protection, and she was dangerous in her wrath.

The man bowed and made an incomprehensible whimpering noise; it seemed the disease had eaten away at his tongue, rendering him mute.

Further along the bench, two women and a man, all dressed in plain garments, were talking so quietly that no one could divine the subject of their discussions. They treated the leper as if he weren't there.

"How am I supposed to know who paid them?" snapped the fair-haired woman.

"That's what I thought." The man nodded. "No one at the guild knows anything about it. Frud and Granselm wanted the money for themselves." He poured himself a goblet of wine and emptied it greedily. A look of satisfaction crept over his face. "Much good it did them, the greedy bastards."

"It's the giant's fault," grumbled the brown-haired woman. "The guardsmen you can hide from, but the giant always knows where you are. If you ask me, there's something unnatural inside that armor."

"It goes without saying," agreed the fair-haired woman. "I mean, how many men do you know who are three paces tall?" She glanced at the leper who was dozing with his back to the wall. Her eyes came to rest on his pouch of coins.

"Not here," hissed the man. "Are you crazy? If someone were to—"

"I know, I know," she said carelessly. "I'm not suggesting we should actually . . . But if any of us were to meet him in an alleyway . . . Well, he's practically dead already; I'm sure he won't object." She whinnied with laughter, and the others seemed to share the joke. "By the way," she said, suddenly serious. "Have you heard that the maga is looking for secret supporters of Nudin?"

"*Nôd'onn*, not Nudin," the dark-haired woman corrected her. "The maga has placed a bounty on their heads. I was thinking we should find ourselves some likely suspects and hand them over to the guards. Presto, the money will be ours."

"Good thinking," said the man enthusiastically. "Knowing Andôkai, she won't bother with putting them on trial. Who can we frame? It can't be anyone who's liked or admired by the citizens with coin."

"I know just the person," said the fair-haired woman, clapping him on the back. Her dark-haired companion laughed. "What makes them think that Nôd'onn still has followers in Porista?" she enquired.

"Apparently, Frud and Granselm were carrying weapons embossed with the magus's crest," explained the man. "I don't believe a word of it: They weren't exactly friendly with the magus, and they avoided magic like the plague."

"Unless they were given those weapons by whoever was holding the purse strings," reasoned the fair-headed woman, stealing a swig from her companion's goblet. "It's almost like someone wanted Andôkai to believe in a conspiracy. There's something funny about this business."

A sudden noise sent them scrambling to their feet. The leper had woken up and was coughing and sputtering. They shifted along the bench to avoid being showered with phlegm.

Still gagging, the leper hauled himself upright and staggered to the door. The other drinkers drew back and held their breath until he was safely out of the tavern. As soon as the door closed behind him, the publican rushed over with a bucket of vinegar solution and started scrubbing the table and bench.

"Quick," said the fair-haired woman, jumping up from the table. "I reckon his purse is going to need a new owner sooner than we thought." They piled out of the tavern and stopped on the pavement, listening intently.

The tinkling bell on the man's ankle, designed to warn of his approach, drew his pursuers straight to him. With a smile, the fair-haired woman whipped out her dagger, holding it flat against her forearm to hide the blade from view. She set off after the tinkling leper, while her two companions hurried after her, watching her back.

The man came into view. He was hobbling at great speed and seemed to have heard them coming. Cursing, he glanced over his shoulder and slipped into an alleyway. The tinkling stopped.

"He's seen us. After him!" They raced into the alleyway, the fair-haired woman charging ahead. After only a few paces, she tripped over a pile of dirty clothes and hit the cobblestones. The dagger flew from her hand. The man's right foot got caught in a leather band to which a small metal bell was attached. They heard the familiar tinkling.

Spitting angrily, the woman got to her feet and held up

the discarded rags. "Look at this," she said slowly. "He was only pretending to be a leper. This smells of . . . talcum powder or ointment or . . ." She ran her hands over the stains. "Paint!"

"He was spying for the maga," growled the man, checking the alleyway for signs of the impostor. "We need to catch him or we'll be finished." He sent the women in different directions and they fanned out, determined to secure the man's silence once and for all.

Rodario watched motionlessly from the doorway of a house as the fair-haired purse-snatcher tiptoed past him and continued along the alleyway, stopping occasionally to listen for telltale noises. The city was eerily quiet.

It was a relief after countless nights of eavesdropping in the dingiest taverns of Porista to finally hear something of consequence, but he hadn't allowed for the rapacious nature of the criminal mind, and his current predicament put a dampener on his mood.

There could be little doubt that the trio intended to kill him: The look on their faces and the mention of the "guild" were evidence enough of that.

So Frud and Granselm were paid to attack us, he thought, watching with relief as the woman disappeared from view. *But I still don't know who hired them, and I probably never shall.*

His mind chafed at the possibility that the daggers had been planted to make it look as if Nôd'onn's famuli were behind the attack. He wondered whether someone held a grudge against the magus's pupils and wanted them dead. *But why bother with framing them? A tip-off would suffice* . . . A smile spread over his handsome face. *What a wonderful idea for my next play—a thrilling drama full of local color.*

He was about to disappear into the alleyway when the door behind him flew open. Pale light streamed out of the house and before he had time to react, someone grabbed him and pulled him backward. The door slammed shut, trapping him inside.

"My apologies, worthy citizens of Porista," said Rodario. "I can explain . . ." His arms were bent up behind him, and someone turned him round. He saw three figures wearing malachite robes and masks. One of his captors was a woman, as he could tell from her curves. "He's a spy," hissed the man, holding Rodario in a vice-like grip. "He was eavesdropping for the usurper."

The woman leaned over and examined his face. "I know him. He's the actor in charge of the building work. The maga hired him when the other fellow was attacked."

Rodario had seen and heard enough to know whom he was dealing with. Under other circumstances he would have relished the prospect of rooting out Nôd'onn's famuli, but not now. "Worthy citizens, you're mistaken," he said, trying to extricate himself from the situation with his dependable smile. "I'm not the fabulous Rodario—although he and I are very much alike."

"Only an actor would talk so prettily," said the woman with a laugh. "It's him, all right." She nodded to the man behind Rodario. "Good work, famulus. It's our chance to discover the maga's next move." She pointed to a chair. Rodario was hauled unceremoniously toward it and made to sit down, while his hands were tied behind his back.

The woman leaned over and looked him in the eye. "We know you're in league with the maga. What does she mean by her games?"

"I'm a lowly impresario," he said sweetly. "All I want is to rebuild my theater but, after what you did to my poor friend Furgas, I've been lumbered with rebuilding the city as well." He didn't think for a moment that the famuli were responsible for the ambush, but he wanted to keep his newfound knowledge to himself.

The woman immediately corroborated his suspicions. "We didn't attack your friend," she said angrily. "If we were going to attack anyone, we wouldn't use daggers embossed with the magus's crest. What bothers us is that Andôkai is bent on telling everyone that we were involved. First she steals Porista from its rightful owners, and now she's turning the city against us. What does she mean to do next?"

"Gentle lady, your grievance is with the maga, not with me. I wasn't spying on you; I was fleeing from three unscrupulous reprobates who were after my purse. Your doorway offered protection, I took shelter, and your friend here mistook me for a spy." He looked up at her imploringly. "If you let me go, the maga will never learn of our encounter. I'm none too fond of her either—she's a cold-hearted, unfeeling woman who likes to make other people feel small." As he talked, he pulled on the rope that bound his wrists, freeing himself by degrees. One of the men had stopped watching him and was sitting by the window, peering into the street. "I could spy for you, if you like," Rodario offered boldly.

He could tell from the woman's face that she was ready to believe him, but his hopes were dashed when a fist appeared out of nowhere and punched him on the chin. "You treacherous windbag," barked the second man. "Stop trying to deceive us with your silver-tongued lies. We know the maga is up to something. Why else would she leave the palace at the dead of nigh—"

"Shush," hissed the man at the window. "Keep your voices down. Someone's outside."

"Can you see who it is?" whispered the woman.

"Three people. They're armed and they're standing outside the door."

"They're . . ." At the last second, Rodario, who was about to identify the trio as his purse-snatching pursuers, changed his mind. He gave the rope a final jerk; it was loose enough for him to break free at the first opportunity. "They're my guards," he lied, deciding to add to the confusion by claiming to be a spy after all. "They're under orders to put an end to your treachery."

The woman slapped him. "You almost had me fooled." She glanced at the men. "Kill him. We'll escape through the back."

"They've covered both exits," said Rodario quickly, managing to sound confident and disdainful in spite of his fear. "Give yourselves up and your lives will be spared. I'm sure the maga will be merciful, provided you confess."

"Confess? We haven't committed any crime. No, I'd rather die than throw myself on the mercy of the usurper." She drew a dagger from the leather belt across her shoulder and tried to plunge it into his heart.

Rodario kicked her as hard as he could in the crotch. "Count yourself lucky you're not a man!" he muttered unsympathetically when she groaned. Jumping to his feet, he grabbed the back of the chair and brought it down on the head of the man who was rushing toward him. A wooden leg snapped off, flew through the air, and shattered the crown glass window.

"They're coming!" shouted the other man, unsheathing his sword. "Death to the supporters of Andôkai!" He darted outside and charged toward them. Rodario couldn't see what happened next, but he knew from the sound of clattering steel that the famulus and the thieves had met.

Meanwhile, the woman had recovered sufficiently to launch a new attack. He fended her off with the broken chair while her companion rushed out to help his friend. Lightning crackled and Rodario caught a glimpse of a flickering red glow on the pavement outside. Voices shouted in panic; then a man let out an agonized scream.

"Die, villain!" The woman's dagger hurtled toward him.

Rodario had enough time to step aside and thrust the back of the chair into her belly. Then, flipping it over, he slammed it seat-first against her head. The chair broke apart, tearing her hood. She slumped to the ground, blood gushing from her head. The dagger embedded itself in the floorboards.

The impresario swooped down and crouched over her, clamping her arms to the ground with his knees. Her breath came in short gasps, her chest rising and falling rapidly. "It seems the gods are on my side," he laughed, ripping off her mask with a theatrical gesture.

He saw a charming little face. Blood was trickling through her long dark hair and into her eyes, which gave her a slightly rakish look. He guessed her age at twenty cycles.

"Well, pretty one, it's time for you to talk," he said,

fighting back his natural exuberance, which was urging him to celebrate his unexpected victory with a kiss. "You said you saw the maga. What was she doing?"

She tried to shake him off. "You know perfectly well what she was doing," she said, gasping for breath. Her resistance subsided, and she resorted to threats. "Let go of me this instant or I'll send you up in flames."

Rodario grinned and stroked his beard. "I'd like to see you try. Why would you use a dagger if you could attack me with magic instead? You're just a novice, aren't you?" He pulled the blade from the floor and placed the tip above her heart. "Tell me what you saw. What was the maga doing?"

"Talking to two men," she said angrily. "Why am I bothering? You know all this already." Her legs shot up and wrapped themselves around his neck, her calves pushing against his throat. Bracing herself, she pulled back with all her might.

Rodario's neck creaked in protest. Fearful that his spine was about to break, he shifted his weight.

The famula freed her arms and slid away with the slipperiness of a serpent. Scrambling to her feet, she kicked him in the crotch. "Too bad that you're a man," she said spitefully.

He doubled up, holding the dagger in front of him while he recovered from the pain.

Just then one of her companions appeared in the doorway. Blood was pouring from a gash in his arm and he could barely hold himself upright. By now the whole neighborhood was awake and people were shouting for the guards. "Quick, Nufa," he panted. "We need to get out of here."

The woman ran over and half carried him out of the

room toward the back door. Before she disappeared, she shot a final, murderous glance at the impresario.

But Rodario wasn't finished with her yet. According to the famula, Andôkai had left the palace in the dead of night to meet two men, but Andôkai was mistress of Porista; she could summon anyone to the palace whenever she liked.

Something's going on here, and I'm going to find out what. He straightened up carefully and shuffled out of the room. Little Rodario and his two plump brothers were throbbing in protest, and the pain was almost more than he could bear.

Nufa and the famulus were at the door. "Get back!" she shouted, grabbing her wounded comrade's sword and waving it threateningly at Rodario. "Next time I set eyes on you, I swear I'll kill you."

"Are you sure you don't want a part in my play?" he asked, still clutching his groin. "I'm looking for a new actress and when I see you standing there, sword in hand, so daring, so courageous . . . You'd be a natural on stage."

A dark figure landed behind her and straightened up, revealing his imposing height. There was a sound of grating metal.

"Watch out!" shouted Rodario, who, for reasons that weren't entirely clear to him, wanted to save her.

The famula ducked as a blade measuring two full paces whistled through the air. The gleaming metal sliced through the ends of her long dark hair and bit into the man's torso. The two halves of his body fell to the ground.

Rodario knew that Andôkai's bodyguard would carry out his mission with ruthless efficiency, but still he hobbled forward, positioning himself in front of Nufa. "Do as I say if you want to survive," he whispered over his shoulder. "You'd better tell me everything you know about Andôkai." She nodded, her eyes wide with fear. "Don't hurt her, Djerûn," he told the metal visor. "We need her alive."

A terrible purple light shone through the eyeholes. Djerûn waited, frozen in position. His hand was outstretched and his sword was perpendicular to the ground. The famulus's blood trickled down the blade, collected around the hilt, and splashed onto the cobbles.

" Djerûn," he said slowly, "I need you to spare her. She hasn't answered my questions, and Andôkai will be angry if you kill her. The woman can't hurt us; she's not armed." He stepped aside to prove that Nufa wasn't a threat.

There was nothing he could do to prevent what happened next.

The giant's arm shot up in a flash of metal, and his long sword whizzed over Rodario's head, past his face, and into Nufa's collarbone. Screaming in agony, she sank down, blood gushing from the wound.

"No!" cried Rodario, throwing himself onto his knees. "I'm so sorry, Nufa. I didn't think he would . . . I mean . . ." He glanced at the open wound and felt a rush of nausea.

Her bloodied fingers reached for his collar; she pulled his head toward her and whispered in his ear. "The maga . . . two men . . . a pouch," she gasped. "Dagger . . . magus's crest . . ."

He was suddenly struck by an improbable thought. "Do you know their names?"

Nufa nodded. "Gran . . ." Her eyes filled with fear. "No!" The sword brushed past his shoulder and sliced through her mouth, cleaving her skull from top to bottom.

Rodario looked at Djerûn in horror and disbelief. He stroked Nufa's arm and straightened up to face the giant. "You killed her, you monster! Don't you realize she was about to . . ." It dawned on him that the famula had been killed for a reason; another ill-considered word, and he would share her fate. "She was about to tell me the names of the other conspirators," he continued. "Andôkai will be furious."

The maga's bodyguard sheathed his sword. It wasn't possible to tell whether he had heard or understood anything that Rodario had said. There was nothing but darkness behind his visor. Turning, he strode down the alleyway and disappeared.

Rodario, shaken by what had happened, sat down on an empty barrel beside the back door and gazed at the bodies. *She would have made a good actress*, he thought sadly as he looked at the famula's once-pretty face.

Djerûn had brought the sword up and down so cleanly that the famula almost seemed to be asleep. But the giant's ruthless deed was the spark that ignited Rodario's smoldering suspicions. His worst fears had been confirmed. *I might have guessed that no good would come of spying for Narmora.*

VII

Dsôn,
Kingdom of Dsôn Balsur,
Girdlegard,
Spring, 6235th Solar Cycle

The black velvet glove caressed the diamonds on the blade, stroked the shimmering inlay of precious metals, and slid down the haft of the ax. The fingers closed around the sigurdaisy wood and lifted the weapon gently from its bed of dark brocade. "It's heavy," said the melodious voice of a male älf.

The bearer of the gift was kneeling at the bottom of the black marble steps that led up to the pair of thrones. She held the cushion aloft, but her gaze was fixed on the stairs; ordinary älfar were forbidden from looking at their rulers. "Indeed it is, Nagsor Inàste. For many miles I bore its weight."

"You should have sought our approval beforehand, Ondori," the female älf said gently. "By rights you should be punished, but the success of your mission absolves you of your guilt."

"You are most generous, Nagsar Inàste," said a humble Ondori, watching as the gloved fingers returned the ax to its cushion.

"What happened to the groundling?" enquired the male älf.

"He fell into a pond the color of the night, your Highness. His companion drowned as well. We waited two orbits, but they didn't surface. The weight of their mail must have dragged them to the bottom." Ondori's face was flushed with anger. "I almost had him, but his weapons belt broke and he fell from my grip. I wanted him to die by my hand, not in the muddy waters of a nameless ditch in godforsaken Lesinteïl. My sisters and I lost our parents to the groundling. I swore to kill him slowly and cruelly: His death was too kind." It was clear from her tone that she took scant comfort in her victory over the dwarf.

"Every älf in this kingdom lost loved ones at the Blacksaddle," the lady of Dsôn said calmly. "Does it give you the right to forsake your duty and settle a private score? No, Ondori, you were wrong to act as you did. It's as well that you returned to us with the weapon—we have a use for it already."

"You wanted to go to the Gray Range, and now you shall," said Nagsor, his voice no longer friendly. "You and your friends are to leave tomorrow. Take Keenfire with you, and join forces with the orcs. We'll see what happens to the groundlings' courage when they hear how you robbed them of their hero and their ax. The orcs will break their defenses; you will break their will."

"I beg your pardon, your Highness. Which orcs?"

"Thousands of troopers skirted our eastern border," explained the älvish lord. "They were heading north—we think they mean to seize the groundlings' hall."

Ondori was taken aback by the news. "Why didn't they stop to help us?" she asked angrily. "Surely they must have realized that Dsôn Balsur was under attack? I don't see why we should repay the stinking cowards for their treachery by lending them the mightiest weapon in the land. What will we get in return?"

"Power," chorused the voices.

"Your task is to ensure that we are party to the orcish victory," explained Nagsor. "We can't allow the orcs to defeat the groundlings without our help. You must stake our claim to the underground kingdom: The Gray Range is to be our refuge if Dsôn Balsur falls."

"If Dsôn Balsur falls?" echoed Ondori. The prospect of the älfar's defeat was so shocking that she almost forgot to avert her gaze from the all-powerful rulers. "But the humans have advanced barely half a mile. They'll never . . ."

"The humans are paying dearly for laying siege to our borders. Hundreds have died already. Their stubborn generals refuse to heed the advice of the elves, and their soldiers are easy targets for our archers." The lady of Dsôn leaned forward, as Ondori knew from her rippling hem. "But our troops are outnumbered. Every orbit the enemy grows more powerful as new recruits flock to the front, drawn by the promise of stolen älvish riches. The alliance between the men, elves, and dwarves is stronger than ever. Their purpose is clear: to destroy Dsôn Balsur. Together they can defeat us—it's only a matter of time."

Fabric rustled, and a hand settled gently on Ondori's head. She saw a gleaming blade engraved with runes. Its tip touched her forehead and cut a line from left to right. The blade came toward her again as Nagsar used the blood to trace a symbol on her brow.

"May Inàste be with you, Ondori," she said. "Bless your friends as I have blessed you, then ride to the fifth-ling kingdom. Your heart may not quicken at the prospect of aiding the orcs, but the future of our kingdom is in your hands." The lady's voice was so gentle, so melodious that Ondori scarcely felt the gash in her brow.

"What if the orcs don't want our help, Nagsar Inàste?"

"Then you must take this ax and slay their chieftain. Let them see the extent of our power. A handful of groundlings are rumored to live in the stronghold, but you will lead the charge against them. Intimidate the troopers and they will obey."

Ondori felt Nagsar lift her hand from her head, signaling that it was time for her to go.

Still kneeling and with her head bowed, she shuffled backward away from the steps, holding Keenfire on the cushion in front of her. Little by little she retreated across the black marble floor.

At last she was out of the throne room and the blind doormen stepped forward to close the black tionium doors. She stood up and inspected the legend engraved on the metal.

LOOK NOT UPON
THE EVERLASTING CHILDREN OF INÀSTE
NAGSOR AND NAGSAR
BROTHER AND SISTER
WHOSE BEAUTIFUL COUNTENANCES
TORTURE THE EYES
RAVAGE THE SOUL
AND CONSUME THE HEART WITH
DEADLY FIRE
BOW YOUR HEAD IN REVERENCE
AND FEAR

Ondori shuddered, remembering how close she had come to lifting her gaze. No one knew exactly what happened to those who disregarded the warning, but from time to time an älf would be summoned by the immortal siblings, never to be seen again, a sure sign that the penalty was death.

Ondori dislodged the dried blood from her eyelids, taking care not to smudge the symbol on her brow.

"It's time for you to leave," said one of the doormen, fixing her with his unseeing gaze. "Come with me." He marched toward her and positioned himself at her side, his movements so precise and confident that Ondori almost doubted his blindness. "Put your hand on my shoulder," he instructed her. She felt the cool metal of his ceremonial armor beneath her right palm.

The beauty of the high-ceilinged corridors was lost on Ondori's guide. Panels of gleaming silver and matt tionium accentuated the polished darkness of the wooden walls, while colorful murals, painted with the blood of the älfar's enemies, depicted glorious victories—the conquest of the elves, the defeat of the human armies, the seizure of new land, and the creation of Dsôn Balsur, the beautiful, sinister jewel in the älfar's crown.

Ondori stopped short, noticing an empty panel on the wall. The best artists among her folk had sketched the outlines of a magnificent painting showing the death of Liútasil, lord of the elves. *Will it ever be finished?*

The blood of different creatures gave rise to an impressive array of colors. Ondori spotted the insipid red of humans, the green hues of orcs and bögnilim, the bright red of the elves, and the dark crimson of the groundlings.

It took a great deal of skill to paint with blood. The artists added special herbs and essences to stop it clotting, but the mixture had to be used at once. Ondori thought of the empty easels in her parents' home. Her mother had been an accomplished artist, but the groundlings had murdered her in Greenglade, and none of her daughters felt like painting anymore.

"Keep walking," said her escort, placing his hand over her own and propelling her onward.

Soon they were at the doors leading out of the siblings' palace. Groaning, the vast panels of stonewood swung open and slammed behind her. The rumbling echo lasted for a while, then everything was still.

The älf strode across the deserted courtyard, pearl-shaped fragments of bone crunching under her boots. The perfectly round balls had been fashioned from the bones of elves, dwarves, men, orcs, and all manner of Tion's beasts. The blanched gravel covered the courtyard and the alleyways of Dsôn, cushioning the älfar's feet. The white of their enemies' bones contrasted nicely with the somber buildings of the city.

Ondori reached the edge of the plateau. An evening breeze ruffled her long brown hair and played with the edges of her mask.

Dsôn lay in the middle of a crater measuring ten miles across and two miles deep.

According to älvish legend, the hollow had been formed by a black teardrop from Inàste's eye. The elves of the Golden Plains had shoveled soil into the crater, but the älfar had defeated them and seized their kingdom, using the loose earth to create a mountain over three miles high. At its summit was the majestic palace of Nagsor and Nagsar.

Ondori gazed down at the city of her birth. Most of the buildings were made of blackwood, a wood so strong that stone foundations were unnecessary for any structure with fewer than eight stories.

The wood's special properties had enabled Dsôn's architects to exercise their talents and break away from the box-like dwellings favored by men. Seen from above, the city was a dark mosaic of sloping angles, perfect curves, elegant ornaments, twisting turrets, and cupolas, connected by luminous white streets. By day, Dsôn glittered with silver, tionium, and precious gems, but some of the alloys and gemstones were visible only in the moonlight. The true splendor of the city was apparent only after dark.

The underground halls of a dwarven kingdom are nothing compared to this, she thought sadly, watching as the blood-red sun dropped beneath the jagged edge of the crater.

She turned and looked up at the palace, a vast and extravagant tower made of bone.

The bones varied in size, some belonging to men and orcs, others to giants and dragons, while the largest came from terrifying creatures whose names were unknown. Slotting together neatly, they made up the first hundred paces of the palace's walls, into which bas-reliefs and ornaments had been carved. The walls needed constant reinforcing, owing to the crumbliness of bone, but the älfar had plenty of enemies, so the palace was never in danger of falling down.

The next eight hundred paces were made of pure elf bone, harvested from the archers of the elven kingdoms. The tower culminated in a slender spire.

In the dying light of the sun, the walls turned a rich honey-yellow, which darkened to orange and turned a deep crimson, as if the palace were drenched in groundling blood. Ondori never tired of the view.

"So you're alive?" said a voice behind her. "Does that mean we can hope for the siblings' mercy too?"

Smiling, Ondori turned to see Estugon and her other loyal friends who had accompanied her on the quest to avenge her parents. "The siblings have been most merciful. Our journey isn't over; tomorrow we leave for the north."

The others glanced at each other uncertainly. "You mean we're not being sent to the front?" asked Estugon, surprised.

"No, our orders are to claim a share of the orcs' new kingdom," said Ondori, raising Keenfire. She quickly explained their mission.

"It's hardly a punishment," commented Estugon, gazing up at the palace. She watched as the sclera of his eyes turned white, revealing his irises. Now that his dark älvish eyes were hidden, he looked as flawlessly beautiful as an elf.

"Tion has smiled upon us," he murmured, dropping to his knees. "Thank you, Nagsor and Nagsar Inàste. Your trust will be rewarded." The others followed his example and kneeled to pray.

Ondori stood before them and produced a thin-bladed knife. "Stand up so that I might bless you as our lady blessed me," she said, preparing to perform the ritual that Nagsar Inàste had performed on her. None of her friends flinched as she drew the knife across their foreheads. It was an honor, a distinction, to be marked by the immortal siblings. They would wear the symbol of Nagsor and Nagsar with enduring pride.

"We should get some rest," said Ondori. "We'll need to ride hard if we're to catch the orcish brutes."

"Another chance to kill a few groundlings," said Estugon happily. "Inàste willed us to find your parents' murderers in Lesinteïl and destroy them. May her name be praised."

"One of the groundlings still lives. My father mentioned three warriors; I saw no sign of the missing twin."

"He must have escaped."

"Whoever heard of a groundling abandoning his brother and his friends? The others came from the north; I reckon we'll find our missing warrior with his kinsfolk in the Gray Range. Nagsor and Nagsar were merciful indeed to entrust us with this mission." She weighed Keenfire in her hand, returned it to her weapons belt, and shook her head. The prospect of having to wield the ax against the orcs filled her with dread. "Why would anyone choose to fight with an ax? You'd think the groundlings would find them heavy and cumbersome. I don't want to waste my energy levering their clumsy weapon from the corpses of my foes."

She left the plateau and started down a staircase of five hundred steps, at the bottom of which her companions had left their mounts. The animals—a collection of shadow mares and a fire bull—were waiting patiently; there was no need to tether them because their obedience was absolute.

"Groundlings might be small but they're powerful," Estugon reminded her. "I suppose it comes from burrowing through rock all the time. I can't imagine them with swords or longbows—their fingers would be too short." The others joined in his mocking laughter.

Ondori went over to Agrass, her powerful fire bull, and examined its hind legs. The dwarf's axes had cut deep gouges into its flesh, and the loyal animal had been lucky to survive. Scabs had formed over the wounds and the edges were peeling away, revealing new, smooth skin. The bull's legs would be permanently scarred. Ondori patted its flanks lovingly and swung herself into the saddle.

Her companions preferred to ride shadow mares, but Ondori considered them too weak for battle. "I know what you think of Agrass," she told them, turning the bull and rubbing its powerful neck. "But your pretty horses would have died of these wounds."

The others laughed. "It's a shame he's so slow," teased Estugon, circling Ondori on his snorting mare.

The red-eyed bull watched the nervous mare and lowered its head, shaking its fearsome mask. Ondori dug her heels into its flanks to encourage it forward. Using its long horns like a shovel, Agrass scooped up the mare and rider and tipped them over as if they weighed nothing at all.

"You were saying . . . ?" crowed Ondori as Estugon lay in the dust.

The mare scrambled up, pawing the ground frantically and raising sparks. It bared its spiked teeth and prepared to strike back. Lowering its head, the bull braced itself for the charge.

Estugon called back his mare. "All right, you've proved your point," he conceded, swinging himself into the saddle. "Still, you'd never keep up in a race."

"Strength and agility are what matters," she retorted confidently. "I prefer to vanquish my enemies; I don't need to run away."

Turning back, she took a final look at the shimmering lights of her beloved Dsôn, letting her gaze linger on its sinister glow. Many orbits would pass before she next saw the city; whether it would still be standing, only Samusin and Tion could tell.

7 Miles From the Fifthling Kingdom,
Gray Range,
Girdlegard,
Spring, 6235th Solar Cycle

Myrmianda's fingers peeled back the dressings. She seemed satisfied that the wounds were healing nicely. "Well done, Tungdil," she said, head bent over his chest.

"The credit's all yours," he said, relieved. "You stopped the infection."

"You're tough enough to fight an infection on your own." She exchanged the dry compress for a new wad of moss and replaced the bandages carefully. The old compress was consigned to the campfire and went up in flames. "You'll be as strong as granite by the time you fight the orcs." At last, as Tungdil was hoping she would, she looked up and smiled.

A smile from Myrmianda was guaranteed to lift his spirits. Tungdil was fast becoming attached to the slender freeling, and Myr, as he was permitted to call her, seemed to value his company as well. No topic of conversation was too obscure or esoteric, and Tungdil was reminded of the lively discussions in Lot-Ionan's school. With Myr to talk to, the long orbits of marching became a pleasure, not a chore.

It wasn't often that Tungdil came across someone who knew as much as he did, but in Myr he found a kindred spirit. The freeling was undeniably pretty, but her mind was every bit as attractive as her face. Each was perfect in itself, and they complemented each other superbly, like an anvil and a forge.

"As strong as granite, eh?" Smiling, he stretched out his arms while she helped him into the jerkin and mail shirt loaned to him by Gemmil. "I'll hold you to that." He wandered away to join Boïndil by the fire.

"Thank you, Vraccas," he whispered. "Thank you for leading me to the freelings' realm." After the pain of losing Balyndis, he was dreading the orbit when Myr would go home. He could visit her for a time, but he couldn't stay forever—he was committed to rebuilding the fifthlings' halls. *Or am I?* The fifthling kingdom was Glaïmbar's responsibility, now that he was king.

What am I to do? Deep in thought, he stared across the fire at Myr as she packed away her instruments. The strength of his feelings surprised him.

"Got a crush on her, scholar?" teased Boïndil, who was melting some cheese in the fire. "What's the use of being clever if you can't resist a pretty face?"

There was something about his tone that prompted Tungdil to ask, "You're not jealous, are you?"

"Me? Jealous? Of course not!" Boïndil nibbled on the cheese, grunted discontentedly, and returned it to the fire. "Who do you take me for? I'm not a lovesick maiden, I'm a warrior! Warriors don't get jealous, they get . . . disappointed, I suppose." He inclined his head toward Myr. "Who am I supposed to talk to while you're chatting with *her*?" He waved the skewer above the flames. "The other outcasts aren't exactly talkative, I can tell you." Aggrieved, he slid the cheese from the skewer and stuffed it into his mouth with a thick slice of bread.

"Did you want to talk about something specifically?"

"Just things," said Boïndil indistinctly, still chomping on the bread. "About the älfar who attacked us. About the strange bull and its fearsome horns. About how we're going to manage without Keenfire. About Boëndal. About whether the runts are attacking our kinsfolk. About the rune we found in the Outer Lands." He reeled off the list, his voice increasing in volume with every word. "I've heard you, scholar, tying your tongue in knots to impress that albino rabbit. I shouldn't wonder if you've forgotten why we're here."

The conversation around them stopped. Myr, who was explaining something to a couple of freelings, broke off and stared in silence at the warrior.

Tungdil had a bad feeling about the situation. Boïndil's inner furnace was burning high, he hadn't used his axes for orbits, and he was desperate to avenge their fallen companions. But Tungdil's uneasiness also stemmed from guilt; he had upset his friend.

The warrior took another bite of cheese, this time crunching through the skewer. Too agitated to notice, he ground the wood between his teeth. "You've got a mighty short memory, Tungdil Goldhand."

"You said to forget her," said Tungdil weakly.

"I said to forget about getting melded to her," barked the warrior, who obviously deemed it unnecessary to lower his voice. "Not about everything else! Doesn't duty mean anything to you?"

"Duty?" exclaimed Tungdil. "I'm tired of hearing about duty. Everyone wants to talk about duty—Lot-Ionan, the late high king, the dwarven assembly, and now you. I've had enough! From now on, I'll decide what I'm going to do, and the kings, the chieftains, and the clans can—"

"Oh really?" interrupted Boïndil heatedly. "Is that what you've learned from the outlaws and thieves? I suppose you don't know any better—you didn't grow up in a dwarven kingdom. You're not a proper . . ." He bit off another section of skewer and clamped his mouth shut. Wood splintered between his teeth.

It was too late already; Tungdil knew exactly what his friend had intended to say. He glared at him angrily. "Go on, Boïndil. You may as well say it to my face. I know what my kinsfolk say about me in private." When no answer was forthcoming, he carried on. "Tungdil Goldhand is a thirdling, a foundling raised by men, a warrior who only became a hero because he alone could wield the ax." He stared into the flames. "If the late high king hadn't sent for me, I wouldn't be here at all. If it weren't for him, I'd be shoeing horses for the humans or earning my keep as a freeling smith. It's not my fault you're saddled with me."

Boïndil was already regretting his words. "I didn't mean it like that," he said, hoping to repair the damage. "Without you, Girdlegard would be ruled by Nôd'onn and . . ." He gave up and tried another tack. "Forget what I said," he pleaded. "I wasn't thinking straight."

Tungdil smiled sadly and laid a hand on his shoulder. "No, Boïndil, you spoke from the heart and so did I." He got up and walked away from the fire. His friend started to follow, but Myrmianda signaled that she would go.

She found him under a tree, passing a pebble from hand to hand.

"I didn't realize that being a hero was so difficult," she said, sitting next to him on the grass. "I heard what Boïndil said: You were in love with a maiden and it didn't work out."

He sighed. *Now she'll get the wrong idea . . .* "Her name was Balyndis Steelfinger. She and I were going to get melded and live together in the Gray Range."

"But she broke off the engagement because her clansfolk disapproved," finished Myr. "Listen, Tungdil, you'll get over her eventually," she soothed him. Her fingers reached for the pebble, and for a moment, they held hands. "Maybe I can mend your heart," she whispered, withdrawing her fingers slowly.

"Myr, I've been meaning to tell you . . ." Tungdil felt suddenly sick with nerves as if he were traveling through the tunnels of the underground network at breakneck speed.

Myr shuffled over until she was facing him and laid a slender finger on his lips. "It's all right, Tungdil. I'm not promised to anyone, and the decision is mine to make as I please. I've never met anyone who knows half as much as you. I don't care a jot about your lineage; I like you for who you are. Besides, I've met plenty of thirdlings who are perfectly decent dwarves." Moonlight shimmered on her pale hair and downy cheeks, bathing her in silvery light, and her red eyes sparkled alluringly. "Don't be afraid to let your heart bleed—it's nature's way of cleaning the wound." She leaned forward and pressed her lips to his brow. "Wait until you're sure that healing, not vengeance, is what you yearn for. If the warmth you feel is more than a passing spark, come to me, and I will nurse your broken heart." She sat back on her heels and looked up at the sky.

Together they contemplated the starry firmament above the Gray Range. "Thank you," said Tungdil after a while.

"I was only telling you how I feel," she said simply.

"Yes, but you're so understanding. You've done so much for me," he said fervently. "I'm really glad you're here."

"My pleasure," replied Myr with a tinkling laugh that charmed Tungdil's ears. "It's not often that I meet a dwarf like you—educated, battle-hardened, and handsome."

He lowered his head bashfully.

"Oh goodness, I've embarrassed you," she apologized. "Maybe we should talk about something else like Boïndil suggested—the älfar, or Keenfire, or even about the Outer Lands. The two of you have been there, haven't you? What's it like?"

"Foggy," said Tungdil with a wry smile. His mind traveled back to their expedition to the Northern Pass and he described how he and Boïndil had left the safety of Girdlegard and wandered for hours in the fog. A shiver ran down his back.

Myr hunched her shoulders as if she too could feel the sinister fog. "I don't know how you kept your cool in such a dreadful place—I would have charged around in a panic and tumbled into a crevasse. It's a shame we don't know more about the dwarves who live there. What did you call them? Undergroundlings?"

"They're hardly mentioned in our records." Tungdil looked at her intently. "How old are you, Myr? You know an awful lot."

She beamed. "I'm still young—104 cycles. I can't really remember my parents—they were killed by rockfall when I was a child. My adoptive parents were new to the realm.

They brought a lot of books from their kingdom. Miraculously, the volumes survived the journey through the pond, and that's how I learned to read. I studied those books until I knew every line and every rune by heart."

"No wonder you know so much."

"That was just the start," she said, smiling. "After that, I wanted to read more. I must have knocked on every door in the city, asking for books. I was so busy reading that it didn't occur to me that dwarves are supposed to be metalworkers and warriors." She laughed. "*There goes Myr, carrying her books*," she said, putting on a mocking voice. "*Isn't she skinny?*" She gave him a dig in the ribs. "Imagine my satisfaction when I found myself stitching the wounds of the dwarves who teased me for reading. I took my time with those stitches, I can tell you." She mimed pulling the needle very slowly through the skin.

"Ouch!" exclaimed Tungdil. "But tell me, did your real parents have . . . I mean, did you get your . . ." He broke off, wondering how to frame the question.

Myr seemed to know what he meant. "Did my parents look like albino rabbits? Yes, my parents and my grandparents were freelings—they were born in our realm. I think the paleness comes from—"

". . . generations of living underground," chimed in Tungdil excitedly, pleased to see his hypothesis confirmed. "Salamanders are the same." It occurred to him belatedly that the comparison was likely to cause offense. Fearing that Myr would be angry, he fell over himself to explain.

"I expect you're right," she said, sharing his excitement. "Most of my kinsfolk never venture to the surface. Why would they? Our realm is more than big enough.

We're not accustomed to living in traditional dwarven strongholds. It's a good thing the fifthling kingdom is just around the corner—I can hardly wait to find out what it's like."

"Right now, it's unfinished," said Tungdil, thinking of the construction work. He was more interested in talking about the freelings' realm. "What's your architecture like?"

"You'd like our cities—lots of multistoried stone buildings in great big grottos, with skies of rock and twinkling gems. We've got lakes as well, and some of my kinsfolk can fish from their windows. They set up their rods and wait for a bite."

Tungdil couldn't begin to imagine what life would be like with the freelings. Still, it was good that Myr had spoken of cities in the plural: Gemmil had more than one settlement in his realm. "How many dwarves—"

Laughing, she got to her feet and held out her hand. "Come on, the others will be wondering where we've got to. I've given away too many of our secrets—you'll have to visit us if you want to learn more."

Tungdil clasped her hand and allowed her to pull him up. She was stronger than she looked. *It probably comes from carrying stacks of books.*

At the campfire, Boïndil was sitting watch. He nodded as they approached.

Tungdil went over and gave him a warrior's hug. Boïndil, relieved to be forgiven, thumped him on the back. "I always talk nonsense when I've been eating cheese," he growled. "Next time you see me with cheese in my mouth, remember not to listen."

"Thanks for the tip," said Tungdil, laughing. "I'm glad

we're friends again." He lay down beside the fire and glanced at Myrmianda, who had been watching them through the flames. She smiled at him, just as Balyndis had smiled at him across another campfire, not so long ago.

Southern Entrance to the Fifthling Kingdom,
Girdlegard,
Spring, 6235th Solar Cycle

The orc touched down on the other side of the boulder and ducked out of sight. A light northerly wind blew toward him from the gateway. Flaring his nostrils, he sniffed the air.

Nothing untoward.

He peered out from behind the boulder to get a better look. The gates were wide open and unguarded. He could walk right in without anyone trying to stop him or sound the alarm.

With a satisfied grunt, he straightened up and lumbered toward the tunnel, picking his way between the scattered boulders and ruined masonry. Of the two routes into the groundlings' kingdom, the southern approach was more direct.

The other route entailed leaving Girdlegard and entering the kingdom from the Outer Lands, which Ushnotz was reluctant to do.

The orc smiled. The prince would be well pleased with him for finding the southern entrance before the other scouts.

Splashing carelessly through puddles of melt water, he stopped at the gateway, poked his head into the tunnel, and sniffed the air for groundlings.

His lips drew back in a smile. Stepping away from the gates, he unhooked his horn and sounded a long, clear signal that echoed through the range.

The prince's bugle sounded in reply, telling the scout to keep watch at the entrance until the troops arrived.

The orc decided to take a break. By locating the southern entrance, he had spared the troops a testing march over snowfields and glaciers, and it was time he had a rest.

Grunting contentedly, he retreated to the shadow of the peaks, sat down on a boulder and rummaged through his bag, bringing out a hessian sack containing the remains of a fleshling. The man had been unusually tall, too tall for one sitting, so he had saved his shanks for the journey. His mouth began to water at the festering smell; spoiled meat was particularly flavorsome.

He sank his teeth into the left shank, ripping off a sizable chunk, which he chomped through with gusto.

The taste of fleshling brought back memories of the recent feast in Gauragar when Bruron's army had tried to trap them in a glade. On Ushnotz's instructions, the orc and his fellows had drunk the dark water from the pond, broken down the barricades and run riot through the fleshlings' ranks. The victory had kept them in meat for orbits.

He tore off another strip of flesh and swallowed greedily, forgetting to chew. The meat slipped halfway down his gullet and came to a halt. Cursing, he whacked himself on the back, but the meat refused to budge. By now he was coughing and spluttering quite violently, so he reached for his drinking pouch, which slipped through his fingers and dropped to the ground. The pouch rolled down the hillside, with the orc chasing after it, taking wild, ungainly bounds. After a few seconds he gave up and raced to the clear blue pool at the bottom of the waterfall.

Throwing himself onto his belly, he lowered his head to the surface and drank. Cool water streamed down his throat, clearing his gullet.

He took another gulp and realized that he was lying on a flat slab of rock above a trough measuring half a pace across. It looked like a conduit or a drain.

Having no interest in waterworks or dwarven engineering, he lowered his head for another sip. This time he stopped in surprise, transfixed by his reflection. Staring back at him was a wrinkled face with a bushy blond beard, a silver helmet, and long wavy hair.

There was only one explanation: The pool was under the curse of the groundling god. *I shouldn't have drunk the water*, he thought frantically. *It's turned me into a groundling.* He squawked in terror. *Ushnotz will kill me on the spot.*

His panicked mind was still whirring when the watery face began to smile. A moment later, it stuck out its tongue.

The orc stopped howling and leaned toward the surface. *Ugh!* He wrinkled his nose in disgust. *I even smell like a filthy groundling!*

Eyes fixed on the gently rippling water, he stared at his reflection. To his astonishment, a second dwarven head appeared on his shoulders and, above that, two brawny arms and an ax.

A proper entrance," grunted Ushnotz in satisfaction. He climbed onto a flat-topped boulder to get a better view. "Fastok has done us proud."

Runshak took up position beside him and surveyed the

sloping ground—a few boulders and some crumbling fortifications, but no cover to speak of. His brow furrowed as
he spotted Fastok reclining near a waterfall, helmet pulled
low over his eyes and legs stretched out comfortably. "The
bungling idiot's gone to sleep," he grunted, picking up a
fist-sized stone to hurl at the dozing scout. The missile
missed its target, flying past Fastok's privates and landing
near his feet. "Hey!" bellowed Runshak. "Why aren't you
keeping watch, you soft-skinned fleshling?"

"Get the troops into formation," commanded Ushnotz,
encouraged by the hush. "Advance with caution until we
know what's what."

His troop leader, a broad-chested orc who stood two
paces tall, drew himself up and relayed the orders to the
troopers, who were strung out along the track behind him
like an enormous metallic snake. "The plateau's too small,"
he observed. "They'll have to advance in waves."

"So this is our new kingdom," muttered the orcish chieftain, lifting his head to survey the mighty peaks. "It isn't
as homely as Toboribor, but it's better than being hounded
by Mallen and his men."

His plan was foolproof: First his army would occupy the
abandoned kingdom and secure the old defenses, then half
of the troopers would stay behind to guard the gateways
while the remaining units paid a visit to the settlements in
nearby Gauragar. Ushnotz needed provisions, and he was
counting on the fleshlings to hand them over quietly. The
king of Gauragar wasn't likely to come to his subjects'
rescue; his army was weaker than Mallen's, and his troops
were tied up in Dsôn Balsur, which lay within the kingdom's
bounds. While the älfar remained undefeated, Ushnotz

would be free to consolidate his empire without interference from the fleshlings. Afterward, neither the allies nor the älfar would be able to oust him from the mountains and he would reign victorious until the end of time.

He had taken measures to ensure that the dark water wouldn't run out. Every trooper was carrying a full drinking pouch, and his quartermasters were bringing additional barrels and kegs. Ushnotz intended to empty the contents into an underground basin and create his own lake. The water was actually quite palatable, and a single sip sufficed to renew the effect.

He watched as his troopers filed onto the plateau and lined up before the gates. "My new kingdom," he said proudly, whinnying with laughter. The troopers saluted their leader, cheering, banging their shields, and raising their weapons. In spite of the commotion, Fastok was still asleep. Snarling angrily, Runshak bore down on the unfortunate scout.

"Hey!" he shouted, kicking him in the ribs. When Fastok failed to respond, he ground the heel of his boot against one of his shins. No creature could sleep through such agony, but Fastok didn't stir. Runshak frowned, his ugly features contorting suspiciously as he bent down and snatched the helmet from Fastok's head.

The scout would never rise again. His skull had been spliced from the crown to the bridge of his nose by a weapon that Runshak judged to be an ax. A second blow had parted his head from his shoulders. The killer had positioned the corpse over a crack in the rock, allowing the dark green blood to drain away. With the helmet off, the head rested loosely against the neck, rocking gently from side to side.

Runshak leaped up. "On guard!" he yelled. "We're not—"

A lone dwarf appeared in the gateway. "Come no closer," he warned him. "Vraccas's children protect these mountains. Turn back or face their wrath." He set a bugle to his lips, sounding a pure, deep note that resonated loudly through the range.

There was a loud crack and the mountain seemed to shudder beneath the orcs' feet. Ushnotz watched in horror as thin black lines zigzagged across the plateau at lightning speed, creating a network of fractures that augured badly for the orcish troops.

The ground shook again, as if struck by an almighty hammer, and the plateau caved in, taking with it a thousand or so orcs. Shrieking and snarling, they disappeared from view.

A loud splash indicated that they had landed in water. Three paces below the ground, the dwarves had extended the plunge pool beneath the waterfall to create a deep basin with precipitous sides.

The orcs were trapped. Ushnotz watched as his troopers sank beneath the surface, dragged down by their armor. Some were hit by falling debris, while others clutched at the sides of the basin, claws scraping helplessly against the slippery rock. The dark water had made them immortal, but it couldn't stop them sinking over and over again.

Since when is the Gray Range back in the groundlings' hands? thought Ushnotz, shaking with shock and displeasure. The only way around the basin was via a narrow path, barely four paces across. On the far side, directly in front of the gateway, stood Runshak. He was a tough orc, made tougher by the dark water, but he couldn't be expected to hold out against the groundlings while the rest of the army advanced four-abreast around the pool.

The groundlings were waiting for us. It occurred to Ushnotz that he might never set foot in the groundlings' kingdom, let alone claim it for himself. Of the orcs on the plateau, barely a hundred had survived, and they were looking to him nervously, reluctant to advance in case they met the same fate as their comrades.

From the pool came high-pitched wails as the orcs continued to flounder in the water, unable to die. The noise redoubled as a battalion of dwarves poured out of the gateway, their shouts and cheers echoing between the peaks.

Blind panic descended on the remaining orcs.

At the sight of the grimly determined, ax-wielding dwarves, they turned tail and fled, forgetting that the dark water had given them unnatural strength. In their head-long charge to safety, they collided with the next orcish unit, which was making its ascent. Unsettled by the noise from above and the sight of their fleeing comrades, the next wave of troopers took off down the mountainside as well. In the chaos, the shouts of the orcish lieutenants went unheeded.

Ushnotz liked to think of himself as a cunning tactician. He was about to give the order to pull back and regroup when a slender figure detached itself from the rocks.

"You're not scared of a handful of groundlings, are you?" demanded a female älf. She was wearing a half mask and a veil of black gauze. "I count two hundred groundlings to your five . . ." She paused and glanced at the flailing troopers in the pool. "Sorry, four thousand orcs."

Ushnotz rounded on her. "What's it to you?" he snapped. "Have they kicked you out of Dsôn Balsur already? Well, the Gray Range is mine." He pointed down the mountainside. "Get out of my sight before I show you what happens to älfar who trespass on my land."

"*Your* land? As far as I can see, the Gray Range belongs to the groundlings," she said with a scornful laugh. "You're lucky I'm here to help." Reaching over her shoulder, she drew an ax.

Ushnotz saw the glittering diamonds on the blade and stepped back with a snarl, almost losing his balance.

"You're familiar with the ax, I see," observed Ondori, holding Keenfire aloft. "Groundlings of the Gray Range," she called, her clear voice and the shimmering gems on the ax commanding the dwarves' attention. "Your fabled weapon is in the hands of Dsôn Balsur's älfar. Its bearer is dead."

The announcement had the desired effect. The charging dwarves stopped in their tracks.

"Well?" said Ondori to Ushnotz. "This is your chance: Send in your troopers and finish them off."

Ushnotz hesitated. "What if they've laid another—"

Ondori responded so swiftly that the orcish chieftain didn't have time to raise his sword. Keenfire whirred through the air, hewing his neck in a single blow. His head, complete with helmet, hit the boulder, bounced, and rolled down the mountainside. As if in defiance of the älf, Ushnotz stayed standing, blood gushing from his neck. Ondori kicked him in the chest, and the rest of his body followed his head.

The gory blade rose through the air, tip pointing toward

the startled Runshak, who had witnessed the death of his chieftain from afar. "Orc," Ondori called out to him. "You're their leader now. Next time I won't be so merciful: Tell your troopers to attack."

Runshak immediately gave orders for the army to attack and the orcs advanced cautiously.

Ondori bounded down from the boulder, alighting in front of the dwarves, who drew back, eyes riveted on the legendary ax. They were talking in hushed tones and their bearded faces were stamped with dismay.

The älf felt a wave of revulsion. "I killed your hero," she told them coldly. "Tungdil Goldhand and his companions met their deaths in the lonely woods of Lesinteïl, and you . . ." She tilted the ax toward one of the dwarves. "You'll die as they did, killed by the weapon that you forged."

Four dwarves stormed toward her, but their bravery was in vain. A flurry of arrows ripped through the air, and the warriors toppled backward into their comrades' arms. It was clear from the black shafts protruding from their chain mail that the älf was not alone. A unit of älvish archers was hidden among the boulders, ready to loose fire on the dwarves.

As if the dwarves weren't sufficiently intimidated, Ondori raised the ax and slashed at the nearest warrior. The blade passed effortlessly through the hastily raised shield, cleaving the arm behind it. The wounded warrior stared at his bleeding shoulder, paralyzed with shock.

"Groundlings are gifted metalworkers," she said, laughing vindictively. "See how cleanly the weapon slices through your flesh." The air quivered, and five dwarves fell to the ground.

Runshak grunted an order and the orcs charged at the defenders, weapons raised.

Ondori stepped aside, not wishing to be sandwiched between the troopers and the dwarves. The main part of the mission was over; she had staked a claim to the underground halls.

Watching in satisfaction, she saw that the groundlings were already losing ground. It was exactly as the immortal siblings had predicted: The news of their hero's death was more crushing than the sight of five thousand orcs. Without their usual confidence, they would be hard pressed to resist the invaders' superior might.

Meanwhile, orcish reinforcements were surging onto the plateau and stampeding toward the gateway, their fears forgotten now that victory was in sight.

Ondori jumped onto the rocks where her companions were unleashing their feathered missiles at the defenders. Their aim was deadly; each of the arrows killed or wounded one or more dwarves.

Slowly but surely the defenders fell back. At last their front line regrouped to form a semi-circle barely ten paces from the gateway. A unit of dwarves bearing crossbows stepped out of the tunnel.

Ondori realized that the dwarves were preparing to close the gates. "Look," she said, alerting her archers. "Feather them with arrows before they lock themselves inside."

The älfar took aim, drew back their bowstrings, and sent a flurry of missiles over the heads of the invaders. The bombardment stopped when the last dwarven archer went down.

Ondori waved angrily at Runshak. "What are you

waiting for? Get your troopers through the gates!" Once closed, the gates could only be opened with the help of siege engines, so everything depended on storming the tunnel before it was too late.

She leaned forward and followed the battle. It seemed to her that the groundlings were intent on beheading the invading orcs. Usually they concentrated on slashing their legs and shattering their kneecaps, allowing the maimed beasts to thrash about in agony and trip up their fellows. But this time they were definitely aiming for their necks.

She watched in amazement as orc after orc picked himself up from the ground and fought on. *What's going on? Are the beasts immortal?* She glanced at Ushnotz's corpse. *Is the Gray Range back in the grip of the Perished Land?*

Another bugle sounded.

This time the call came from a small band of dwarves emerging from a narrow opening near the waterfall. Ondori recognized their leader at once. *What's this? I saw him drown . . .*

"That's right," bellowed Tungdil, his deep voice carrying over the din of clashing blades. "I've come to reclaim my property and avenge my friends. I won't rest until you're dead."

The dwarves, seeing their hero, were filled with new courage. The strength returned to their arms and they fought back determinedly. The orcs responded by renewing their attack. It was clear to both sides that the battle had entered a crucial stage.

"We'll see who gets vengeance," replied Ondori, trembling with rage. "You'll die by the ax that you forged!"

Signaling to her companions to secure her path, she jumped into the melee of orcs.

Porista,
Former Realm of Lios Nudin,
Girdlegard,
Spring, 6235th Solar Cycle

Narmora kneeled down and drew her right hand over the loose, moist soil, then packed it down firmly. "Taken from me at birth," she whispered, tears leaking from her closed eyes. "You started life together, and now you're alone. We won't forget you, I promise."

Wiping her cheeks with her sleeve, she opened her eyes and began to cover the little grave with stones.

All alone in a forest beyond the walls of Porista, she took her leave from her son, burying his body, and committing his soul to Samusin. It was an älvish ritual, taught to her by her mother.

No one else was there to mark the infant's passing. Furgas, the only person who could offer some solace, was in a deathly coma, leaving Narmora alone in her grief.

She was dreading the moment when she would tell her husband that their baby boy was dead. *What will I say?* She covered the grave with another layer of stones to protect the child from the claws and teeth of hungry scavengers. His body was tiny, but perfectly formed, with miniature fingers and toes, and an adorable face. Fate had ordained that he would never grow old.

The hours wore on and the trees cast long shadows over

the forest floor. At last, as dusk began to fall, she made her way back slowly to Porista. In the distance, the familiar landscape of scaffolding and cranes heralded the city's rise from the ashes, and the maga's palace loomed on the horizon, sable turrets reaching to the sky. Narmora, head bowed, looked only at the ground.

Blinded by grief, she entered the city, insensible to the activity on the crowded streets.

In the marketplace, stalls were being dismantled, goods packed away, and coins counted into bags. People were leaving work, going home, piling into taverns that smelled of hot food, or gathering on the pavements to discuss the latest news. Narmora walked on.

After a time she became aware of the conversation around her. Everyone was talking excitedly about the deaths of Nôd'onn's famuli, Rodario's heroism, and the rapid construction of the city walls.

Next they'll be gossiping about how I killed my child, she thought grimly.

Andôkai's intervention following Narmora's botched incantation had prevented the two of them being crushed by the marble archway, but while a sprained ankle had been the only injury sustained by the maga, Narmora had paid with the life of her son.

To her surprise, Rodario was waiting for her at the palace gates. Wrapping his arms around her, he hugged her in silence. Narmora's eyes filled with tears all over again.

"Andôkai told me what happened," he said sadly, trying not to look at her flat, childless belly. She looked exactly like the old Narmora.

"I know," she said quickly, not wishing to discuss the

baby's death. "The fireball robbed me of a son and left me with a daughter. When she's old enough, I'll tell her about her twin." She tried to meet Rodario's eyes, but he was looking at her strangely. "You're not in trouble again, are you?" she asked, guessing that he needed to get something off his chest. She mustered a faint smile. "Don't tell me that the hero of Porista is being chased by the angry father of some poor impressionable girl . . ."

He looked at her warily. "We should talk somewhere else," he said, steering her back down the street. As they walked, he summarized how he had eavesdropped on the thieves and interrogated Nôd'onn's famula. His story was considerably more convoluted than the version that Narmora had heard.

"I don't know how to tell you this," he said carefully. "For all I know, the story was a fabrication, but the poor girl was dying, so I doubt she made it up." He hesitated, not wanting to add to his friend's distress. "Precious Narmora—"

The half älf glared at him. "This isn't one of your plays," she reminded him impatiently. "What did the famula actually *say*? Are the villains who stabbed my Furgas still alive?"

"That's just it," he said unhappily. "According to Nufa, the attack on Furgas had nothing to do with her. She said someone paid the ruffians to make it look like Nôd'onn's famuli were to blame."

She seized him by the shoulders. "Speak clearly, Rodario. You're not making any sense."

He took a deep breath, steeling himself for what would follow. "Nufa told me that she and her friends saw

Andôkai . . ." All of a sudden his face lit up with a radiant smile. "Ah, there she is!" he exclaimed, hailing the maga with a wave. "How reassuring for the citizens of Porista to know that Andôkai the Tempestuous is patrolling the streets!"

Narmora eyed him intently; there was something insincere about his smile.

"Is Djerûn with you perchance?" he enquired, glancing about him.

The maga went over to Narmora. "I was worried about you," she said, her face as stern as ever. "You were gone a long time, longer than expected. Your daughter won't stop crying. I'm many things, but I'm not a nurse."

"I'll be there right away," Narmora promised. "Well?" she said, turning back to Rodario. "You were saying . . . ?"

The impresario withered under Andôkai's harsh gaze. "I was telling Narmora not to worry," he said quickly. "She's got nothing to fear now those villains are dead. Well, don't let me hold you up." He yawned theatrically. "It's nearly my bedtime. So much to do, so little time. May the gods be with you!" Hurrying away, he turned a corner and was gone.

Narmora shook her head in bemusement. "Actors," she sighed.

Andôkai just shrugged. "The journey starts tomorrow. We'll head west and begin our search in the libraries of Weyurn. Your daughter can join us, of course. I've hired a wet nurse to take care of her while I help you with your studies." They walked for a while in silence. "I hope you haven't changed your mind," said Andôkai, gazing at the rows of buildings rising from the rubble. "Furgas's survival depends on you, remember."

"I hate magic," said Narmora fiercely. "Magic robbed

me of my son—if it weren't for Furgas, I'd have nothing to do with it." She glanced at the maga almost reproachfully. "I know you were trying to help, but you shouldn't have made me your famula. It's bound to end badly." She lowered her voice. "It already has."

"From now on you'll learn your formulae more carefully," said Andôkai harshly. "I suffered losses when I was a famula as well." Her stern face showed a flicker of emotion. "I'm sorry I can't offer more comfort. Magic comes at a price."

They were almost at the palace.

"Perhaps the price is higher than we know," said Narmora. She recited the incantation to open the gates, and the two women, one dark-haired and slender, the other muscular and fair, walked in silence through the palace.

On reaching the nursery, Narmora went in and closed the door behind her, shutting the maga outside.

At the sound of the door, the child woke up and let out a thin, piteous scream. Narmora bent over the cot, scooped up the tiny baby and clasped her to her breast, running her hand softly over her tiny head. The little girl's skull felt no stronger than an eggshell. Comforted by her mother's touch, Dorsa stopped crying.

After the stillbirth of her son, Narmora had been surprised by the arrival of a daughter. It hadn't occurred to her that she was carrying twins, but Samusin, god of equilibrium, had taken one of her children and let the other live. *What price must I pay for Furgas to get well?*

The little baby made a clumsy attempt to suckle her breast. "Are you thirsty, little one?" asked Narmora. She left the nursery, crossed the corridor, and knocked on the opposite door. It was opened by a young woman with bleary eyes and tousled hair. Narmora held out her daughter. "Dorsa needs feeding."

"Of course," murmured the girl, taking the baby tenderly and putting it to her breast. Dorsa took to her at once.

The half älf felt a pang of sadness as the wet nurse, singing softly, carried her baby around the room. With no milk of her own, she had to entrust her child to a stranger. Fortunately there were plenty of young women in Porista who were happy to suckle her child in return for food or coin.

As soon as the nurse had finished, Narmora scooped up her baby and returned to the nursery. She held onto her for a while, cradling her to sleep, then replaced her in the cot, tucked her in, kissed her nose and stroked her downy head.

"Sweet dreams, my darling," she whispered. "I won't be long." She slipped quietly out of the nursery and hurried to Furgas's room.

For an hour she sat there, holding his clammy hand, then she crept out of the palace to look for Rodario.

She had no doubt that the impresario had a secret—and somehow or other, the maga was involved.

Southern Entrance to the Fifthling Kingdom,
Girdlegard,
Spring, 6235th Solar Cycle

Leaping down from the boulder, the masked älf entered the scrum of armor, spears, and swords, and disappeared from view. Tungdil knew she wouldn't reappear until she was close enough to attack him, very probably from behind. It was like waiting for a serpent in a field of rippling grass.

At the same time he felt absurdly grateful. Vraccas had shown him that Keenfire wasn't lost. *I need to kill the älf.*

Boïndil, his inner furnace blazing, banged his axes together impatiently. "Thousands of fat, juicy orcs! My axes can't wait for a taste of their blood!" He glanced at Tungdil. "Ready, scholar?"

Tungdil was watching the raging battle. The odds were in favor of the orcs; firstly because the dark water made them difficult to kill, and secondly because the dwarves had only a few hundred defenders, a fact that the orcs seemed thankfully slow to grasp. It was vital to close the gateway before the invaders gained more ground.

So much for Glaïmbar's tactics, thought Tungdil, allowing himself a moment of smugness. "All right, we need to head for the gateway," he told the others. "Our priority is to close the gates. The beasts will never be able to force their way in." Drawing his ax, he ran toward the charging orcs.

Boïndil, huffing disappointedly, took off at great speed. "Can't we just kill the lot of them?" he asked breathlessly, sprinting past Tungdil. He wasn't in the least bit intimidated by the raging beasts; their snarling and grunting spurred him on. "The first ten are mine!" he shouted, raising his weapons. His right ax sliced into a green-hided thigh, the left ax swinging upward to catch the falling orc. The blade passed effortlessly through the visor, releasing a torrent of green blood. The orc collapsed without a murmur, a third strike severing his neck.

"Oink, oink," snorted Ireheart, darting forward. He slashed a path through the hordes, allowing Tungdil, Myr, and the others to follow.

Thanks to his sterling efforts, the group made rapid progress and axes whirred in all directions, felling orc after orc. Killing the beasts posed a problem because they had to be beheaded, which wasn't easy, especially since the dwarves were fighting several orcs at a time. After a while they took to working in pairs, the first dwarf felling their opponents and the second dwarf driving his ax through their necks. All of a sudden, the gateway seemed much closer.

The defending dwarves, eager to help their former leader, sallied forth to meet him.

"Get back!" shrieked Tungdil as the älfar leveled their bows. "Hold your shields above your heads. They'll . . ."

Black arrows sang through the air, finding cracks in the wall of shields and homing in on unprotected flesh. Five dwarves fell to the ground and disappeared under the boots of the snarling orcs, who surged into the space, forming a living barrier between the gateway and the rest of the group.

The defenders' maneuver had failed, leaving a handful of dwarves at the entrance of the tunnel, while the others fought frantically to keep the orcs at bay. Dwarven archers raised their crossbows and fired bolts at the beasts, but the advance continued undeterred. The bolts were lethal for ordinary warriors, but not for a rabble of undead orcs.

"We should have brought warriors, not masons and smiths," growled Ireheart, whirring his axes at giddying speed in an effort to reach the beleaguered defenders.

He was splattered from head to toe with green blood, which had an intimidating effect on the beasts. "Either that, or artisans who can fight!" His axes struck again; his victim, backing away nervously, took a blow to the neck.

Tungdil tried to count the dwarves at the entrance to the tunnel. As far as he could tell, almost everyone in the kingdom had come out to beat back the invaders, but the orcs were still advancing and had nearly reached their goal. Tungdil spotted Glaïmbar and Balyndis fighting side by side.

He pointed to the survivors of the ill-advised sally. "Head toward them," he commanded. "If we band together, we'll make it to the gates." Out of the corner of his eye he noticed that Myr and the exiles were holding their own against the orcs. In fact, the dainty medic was fighting with tenacity and strength.

Soon Tungdil's party joined the band of defenders, but their path was blocked.

The beasts surged forward, spurred on by Runshak, who was bawling orders at the top of his voice. The älfar feathered the troopers with arrows, driving them on from behind. Yelping with pain, the orcs advanced; victory was in their grasp.

In front of the gateway, the lead orcs were locked in combat with the dwarves, who were fighting valiantly but ineffectually against the invaders. Meanwhile, some of the smaller orcs were trying to sneak past and attack from behind, trapping the defenders between two fronts.

Tungdil glanced at the orcish leader. "It's time he went," he said, deciding that a change of tactics was in order. "We need to kill their chief."

Ireheart, brown eyes glinting manically, had fought

himself into a frenzy. At the mercy of his fiery spirit, he threw himself on the enemy, windmilling his axes at incredible speed.

"Boïndil!" shouted Tungdil. "I said we need to kill their chief!" He had to repeat himself several more times before Boïndil finally heard.

The group set off toward Runshak, who spotted the approaching threat and turned to the älfar, hoping to enlist their bows in his defense. Suddenly his grin froze, his mouth falling open in horror.

Tungdil saw the fear on his ugly green face and turned to discover its source.

A colossal figure loomed into view. Brandishing a sword in one hand and an ax in the other, the metal-clad giant towered over the boulder where the älfar were stationed with their bows. The orcs in the vicinity squealed in terror and scattered in all directions, falling over each other in their eagerness to escape.

A demonic visage stared out from the giant's visor, the eyeholes emitting a bright purple light. Even from a distance, Tungdil's eyes were dazzled. The giant let out a dull, menacing roar that caused the ground to quake. Tungdil's hair stood on end.

Alerted to the danger, the älfar raised their bows, but Djerûn was already upon them, sword and ax slashing through the air, severing bowstrings, cleaving arrows, and slicing through sinew and bone. In no time the boulder was strewn with bloodied armor and gory remains.

Only one of the älfar succeeded in evading Djerûn's blades, but the colossal warrior had no intention of letting him escape. Jumping onto the boulder, he pushed off and launched himself into the air, landing on the shoulders of the fleeing älf, who crumpled screaming to the ground. Without stopping to use his weapons, Djerûn stamped on his head, squashing it like a plum.

A tense silence descended on the plateau; both sides had watched the encounter with bated breath.

This is our chance! Wrenching his eyes away from Djerûn, Tungdil aimed his ax at the orcish chieftain and hurled it at his head.

Runshak heard the weapon whir toward him and turned in time for the blade to miss the back of his helmet and land between his jaws, slicing cleanly through his head. The newly appointed chieftain was dead.

"For Vraccas and Girdlegard!" shouted Tungdil, breaking the hush. "Behead the brutes! Long live the children of the Smith!"

The orcs had heard and seen enough.

After losing their unbidden allies, not to mention Runshak and the prince, the beasts were ready to admit defeat. Forgetting their undead powers, they forfeited their advantage and fled.

The panic was so great that some of them jumped on top of their spluttering comrades in the pool, while others stampeded down the mountainside, bowling over the troopers who were toiling to the top.

"You never learn, do you, scholar?" scolded Boïndil, handing Tungdil one of his axes. "What was the first thing I taught you? Never throw your ax unless you've got another in reserve!" He grinned. "Still, there's nothing wrong with your aim." Oinking ferociously, he threw himself on the fleeing troopers, slaying orc after orc.

Cries of astonishment went up from both sides as a second battalion of dwarves appeared on the far side of the plateau. The new arrivals threw themselves on the invaders, squeezing the orcs between two fronts.

Tungdil noticed that some of the warriors had white hair and pale skin. *The freelings,* he thought, relieved. Although the tide had turned in favor of the defenders, there was a chance that the orcs would remember their immortality and lay siege to the gates. Gemmil's warriors couldn't have arrived at a better time.

This is the crunch, he thought, glancing to where Glaïmbar and Balyndis were fighting.

The king and his fiancée were defending the gateway against a handful of orcs whose fury outweighed their fear. Far gone in bloodlust, the beasts threw themselves against the defenders' axes, hammers, and clubs.

Most of Tungdil's comrades were too busy chasing the fleeing army to realize that the gateway's last defenders were dangerously overextended.

Tungdil paused, his thoughts in turmoil as he watched his rival parry blow after blow. The attack redoubled, but Glaïmbar was holding his own. *Just.*

It's nothing to do with you, whispered a devilish voice in his head. *So what if he falls? He'll die a hero, and Balyndis will be free.*

The chosen leader of the fifthlings took a step backward and came up against a wall. For a second, he was distracted, and an orcish sword made contact with his wrist.

Glaïmbar can take care of himself, the voice whispered. *He's a great warrior; let him prove his worth. Hurry up and find Boïndil.*

Tungdil had almost decided to rejoin his group when Balyndis caught his eye. She was surrounded by orcs, and she looked at Tungdil pleadingly, her brown eyes begging him to go to Glaïmbar's aid.

"Botheration," he grumbled, gripping the haft of his ax. "What a pity it was his wrist, not his chest."

He set off bad-temperedly toward the gateway, but the rescue mission came to a precipitous end.

In the heat of the battle, he had forgotten to look out for the älf. A slender figure appeared out of nowhere and alighted beside him. Looking up, he saw Keenfire speeding toward his head.

VIII

Blacksaddle,
Kingdom of Gauragar,
Girdlegard,
Spring, 6235th Solar Cycle

The diamonds on the high king's helmet glinted in the sun. Gandogar knew that even the most shortsighted sentry would notice his approach, but he held his head high; he wanted to be seen. In all his 299 cycles he had never set eyes on the thirdling king, and his arrival at the court of Lorimbas marked a turning point in the history of the dwarves.

Pushing the brown hair away from his eyes, he looked up at the Blacksaddle and watched as sun and shadow strove for mastery over its slopes. The gullies and couloirs were shrouded in inky darkness, but the flanks of the mountain were gilded with light.

For Gandogar, there was something menacing about the flat-topped mountain where countless dwarves, elves, and men had lost their lives.

The battle has left its mark on this place. He shook the reins and the pony moved off. The powerful dwarf and his mount were suffering from their long journey through Sangpûr's deserts. Particles of sand had found their way into Gandogar's beard, slipped through the rings of his mail, and sneaked inside his leather jerkin, rubbing against his skin in the tenderest places. His poor pony had fared no better. There was no escape from Sangpûr's sand.

Now, as they rode through southern Gauragar, the temperature was cooler, but the air was thick with menace. The banners flying from the top of the Blacksaddle warned the high king and his fifty armed warriors that the stronghold was in the hands of its makers, the children of Lorimbur.

Bones crunched beneath the ponies' hooves. No one had buried the dead beasts after the battle; their corpses had been eaten by predators or piled up and burned. Sun, rain, and snow would take care of their skeletons, but for now their remains lay strewn at the base of the mountain, warning travelers not to linger in this place.

Second in the procession was Balendilín, king of Beroïn's folk. He had joined the expedition after Gandogar accepted his offer of advice and support. His gaze was fixed on the mountain ahead. "Should we mourn our fallen comrades or celebrate the joint victory of dwarves, elves, and men?" he asked pensively. "There's never been a battle like it: The massed ranks of Nôd'onn's army against the armies of Girdlegard, with the dwarves at the fore."

"Let's hope the alliance lasts," said Gandogar fervently.

"We can't let the thirdlings shatter our newly forged bonds." With a sigh, the one-armed king looked up at the fluttering banners. "I wonder how the mountain feels about the return of the dwarves who plundered its gold."

"Bruron had no choice but to cede the stronghold to Lorimbas," replied Gandogar evenly. "According to his envoy, Gauragar was bound by the terms of an ancient treaty."

"No choice?" objected Balendilín. "What does Bruron owe the thirdlings? Mallen is reliant on thirdling mercenaries, but he refused to surrender to Lorimbas's demands. I'd wager my one good arm that Bruron was bribed."

Gandogar tugged on the reins, steering the pony to the right of an ogre skull that was blocking their path. The stripped bone bristled with broken spears and arrow shafts, and the crown of the head provided the birds with a useful platform as they scanned the path for dung.

"You're probably right," said the king of all dwarves. "And that's precisely why a diplomatic solution is called for. Girdlegard won't be at peace until we put an end to this senseless feud." He glanced at Balendilín. "I thought you were supposed to be the voice of reason. Are you suggesting we kill him?"

"Vraccas would roast my soul in his furnace if such a thought were to enter my mind," said the secondling, laughing. His expression became grave. "No, Gandogar, neither of us are dwarf killers, although I can't say Lorimbas deserves our mercy—his machinations are undermining our alliance with the elves and men." He held the king's gaze. "The question is, how are you going to stop him? We haven't spoken to the thirdlings for hundreds of cycles, so the usual sanctions won't work."

"That's why we need to talk to them," said Gandogar firmly. "I understand your reservations, but Lorimbas and I will find a way of making peace."

A door came into view at the base of the mountain. In earlier cycles, it had been concealed by conifers, each standing fifty paces tall, but the orcs had cut down the forest to make siege engines and ladders. After the battle, the wood had served as kindling for the biggest funeral pyre in Girdlegard's history, on which the corpses of the beasts had been burned. All that remained was a multitude of stumps.

"I'm not naïve enough to think we'll ever be friends with the thirdlings," continued Gandogar, realizing that the secondling leader was unconvinced. "But it's time we put a stop to the feuding and treated each other with a little respect."

Balendilín clicked his tongue doubtfully. "By the hammer of Vraccas, I wish I could knock some sense into their heads."

They drew up outside the door. Barring their way were twenty warriors with long-handled pikes, the tips of which were pointing menacingly at the riders.

"Stop," commanded a broad-chested thirdling, fingering his morning star. His face was covered in tattoos. "My name is Romo Steelheart of the clan of the Stone Grinders, nephew of King Lorimbas." He measured the high king with his gaze. "I suppose you must be Gandogar," he said, denying him the usual courtesies extended to a dwarven king.

Balendilín studied the thirdling's face. Tattooed runes spoke of his eternal hatred of the four dwarven folks, promising death and damnation to the descendants of Beroïn, Borengar, Giselbert, and Goïmdil. The sinister effect of the tattooist's artwork was heightened by the hostility in Romo's eyes. Balendilín had no doubt that he was looking at the face of a zealous dwarf killer.

"My name is Gandogar Silverbeard of the clan of the Silver Beards, head of Goïmdil's line," said the high king. "My business is with your—"

Romo snorted derisively, and a globule of snot hit the ground by Gandogar's feet. "Gandogar can come in. The rest of you, wait outside."

Balendilín was unmoved. "The high king goes nowhere without his escort. If this is your tone, you can forgive our suspicions."

Romo shrugged, armor clunking. "It's him or no one," he said sharply. "Those are my orders. If you don't like them, you can leave." A sneer spread over his face. "Oh, I should have realized: Poor Gandogar is scared of my uncle. Don't worry; Lorimbas has given his word of honor that your king will leave our stronghold in the condition that he arrived." He stared at the high king insolently. "Is your heart made of granite or pumice?"

Gandogar ignored the warning looks from his advisor and jumped down from his pony. "I'm the high king of the dwarves, and my business is with Lorimbas Steelheart," he said firmly, striding toward the guards, who raised their pikes to let him pass. The metal tips lowered, separating Balendilín and the others from the king.

"My, my," said Romo, leading Gandogar into the cavernous heart of the mountain. "It's astonishing how a feeble fire can produce a spark of courage. You're a typical fourthling—scrawny and small."

"Brain is more important than brawn," countered Gandogar patiently. "It's better to have a sharp mind than a sharp blade."

Romo turned into a side passageway, picking his way confidently through the maze of corridors and stairs. He and his kinsmen were new to the Blacksaddle, but he plainly knew his way around. "A nice theory," he said, laughing. "But an ogre's cudgel can blunt the sharpest wit."

"On the contrary," replied Gandogar firmly, keeping his eyes fixed on Romo's back. "Ogres are particularly easy to outsmart."

His gaze fell on a beautifully crafted scabbard hanging from the thirdling's belt. It looked awfully familiar. In fact, he had last seen it on the belt of a warrior who was fighting with the allies in Dsôn Balsur. The chances of a smith forging two such scabbards were remote.

"I met him and two others in Richemark," said Romo, when the high king enquired about its owner. "They're dead." He shot a hostile glance at Gandogar. "You can have it, if you like—but you'll have to fight me first."

Gandogar clenched his fists. It wasn't easy to keep his composure when Romo was bragging about killing three dwarves. The thirdling talked about murder in the way other dwarves talked of masonry or metalwork. "With pleasure," he muttered darkly, setting his jaw.

Romo hiccoughed with laughter. "What are you going to do?" he asked scornfully. "Sprinkle me with gold dust or throw diamonds in my face?"

It occurred to Gandogar that his faith in diplomacy was possibly misplaced, but he wasn't prepared to leave without trying—if only to satisfy his conscience and prove to the allies that he wasn't to blame for the feud.

Without a word, he followed Romo into the great hall where the final battle against Nôd'onn had taken place.

Lorimbas Steelheart was standing in the middle of the room. His attention was focused on a recently repaired staircase that gave access to the walkways overhead. At last he turned to greet the new arrivals. "What have I done to deserve the honor?" he sneered.

Romo smiled and positioned himself at his side.

Gandogar looked intently at the thirdling monarch. His long black hair was streaked with gray and braided against his scalp in three tight plaits. Gandogar noticed that his beard had been dyed in three different colors, which was probably a mark of something, although he didn't know what. He also saw that Lorimbas, unlike the other thirdlings, hadn't been tattooed.

"I want a truce," he said simply, outlining his reasons for the visit. "A cessation of hostilities until the älfar have been defeated."

"That's a new one," scoffed Lorimbas. "The hostilities haven't started, and you're asking me to stop. I didn't realize our cousins were so soft."

"Don't be too harsh on him, uncle," chipped in Romo. "He might soil his breeches."

"I was referring to your efforts to turn the humans against us," said Gandogar evenly, ignoring the snickering Romo. "Open warfare we can deal with, but your tactics are pernicious and underhanded. We know what your envoy said to Prince Mallen and we know that a dwarf was seen at King Belletain's court. He wasn't there on my authority, so I assume he was sent by you."

"Mallen is a shortsighted fool," Lorimbas said breezily. "He'll soon see the error of his ways. He turned down my nephew's assistance out of misguided loyalty, but the loss of his dwarven mercenaries will come as a blow. I shouldn't wonder if he's ruing his decision already." He let his eyes travel over the ceiling. "It's a wonderful thing to be standing here after all this time. My forefathers lived in this strong-hold until you drove them out. A new era is dawning for Girdlegard." He snapped out of his reverie and glowered at Gandogar. "The decline of Beroïn, Borengar, and Goïmdil has begun." He strode toward the high king, stopping only when their noses were practically touching. "You won't weather this storm. The wind of change is blowing through the dwarven kingdoms, sweeping through the narrowest shafts and tiniest caverns. You and your subjects will be scattered, and my warriors will seize your halls." His spiked gauntlet thumped his armored chest. "The children of Lorimbur will stand guard at the gates of Girdlegard and your folks will be forgotten." He took a step back and drew his weapon. "I swear it on Lorimbur's ax."

"Is this how the thirdlings negotiate?" asked Gandogar. "I—"

Lorimbas cut him short. "*Negotiate?* Who said we wanted to *negotiate?*" He raised his ax. "I have news for you, Gandogar: Your orbits in Girdlegard are numbered—and there's nothing you can do."

Gandogar's patience, which had withstood countless indig-nities, suddenly snapped, allowing his pent-up fury to erupt into words. The king and his nephew had pushed him to the brink. "Vraccas won't abandon his loyal children to the murderous wiles of Lorimbur's unholy dwarves," he shouted, clinking blades with Lorimbas. "I dare you to fight us fairly, you backstabbing coward."

"Get out!" bellowed Lorimbas, forcing Gandogar's blade to the ground. "No one threatens me in my strong-hold! You're lucky I promised to let you go unharmed. I've a mind to kill you anyway."

"Can I do it for you?" asked Romo hopefully.

Lorimbas trembled with silent fury; he was fighting the urge to plant an ax in the high king's head. "Lorimbur's children won't negotiate with the other dwarves. Your destruction is assured."

"All right, gem cutter," said Romo, gripping Gandogar's shoulder. "It's time you went home to polish your jewels." He steered him through the door in the manner of a bailiff escorting a drunk.

The high king shrugged him off angrily. "Lay a finger on me again, and you'll regret it, dwarf killer," he growled. When Romo spat on the floor and grabbed his shoulder, he seized the thirdling's gauntlet and swung his ax against his wrist, shattering the bone. Romo's face contorted with pain, then he reached with his un-injured arm for his morning star, swinging back to strike. A bald-headed dwarf stepped in front of him and made a grab for his arm. The three-balled weapon thudded to the floor.

"Salfalur!" he exclaimed in surprise. "What—"

"Silence or I'll break your other wrist," the dwarf snapped. He turned to Gandogar. "That's the first and last time I'll save one of your kind. I want to be clear about this: Your life counts for nothing, but Romo promised not to harm you, and Lorimbas would punish him for breaking his word."

Gandogar nodded. His eyes were drawn to his rescuer's massive arms and chests. Dwarves were stocky and powerful, the fourthlings less so than most, but even the slightest dwarf was a good deal stronger than a man. Salfalur, though, had muscles to rival the battle-crazed

Boïndil. Like the other thirdlings, he was tattooed, the dark runes covering his face and his gleaming skull.

Gandogar met his eye. "At least let me thank you for—"

"I want nothing from you," growled Salfalur. "I'd sooner die in the deserts of Sangpûr than drink water from your pouch. Follow me, I'll show you out." He strode away and Gandogar fell in behind him.

Salfalur's route through the passageways of the Blacksaddle took them past chambers filled with provisions, bunkrooms accommodating hundreds of dwarves, and crowded forges echoing with constant hammering.

Some of the smiths were fashioning weapons, others were working on strange pieces of metal that served no obvious purpose. Gandogar knew that no one would volunteer the information, so he saved himself the trouble of asking and studied the objects carefully, intending to describe them to the firstling smiths.

At last they reached the door leading out of the stronghold.

"Stay away from here," Salfalur advised him coldly. "If we meet again, Lorimbas will be delighted to receive your head on a plate."

He opened the door for the high king to rejoin his anxious companions.

After enduring the company of the thirdlings, Gandogar was glad to leave the stronghold and step into the sunshine, which usually hurt his eyes. He caught himself looking forward to the dreaded pony ride home.

"Well?" asked Balendilín.

Gandogar shook his head and gave a brief account of the meeting.

"I can't say I'm surprised," said Balendilín with a sigh. "They're thirdlings, after all."

Under the steely gaze of the sentries, they turned their ponies and rode toward the south. "Lorimbas must be very sure of himself to speak so openly of his intentions," observed Balendilín, wondering what the thirdlings had in mind. Lorimbas's bold predictions augured badly for the dwarves.

Judging by Gandogar's report, the thirdlings were planning something far more serious than Bislipur's treacherous scheming. This time, the whole thirdling kingdom was ready to mobilize against the other dwarves.

Balendilín glanced back at the sinister mountain. *What we need is a spy.*

Southern Entrance to the Fifthling Kingdom,
Girdlegard,
Spring, 6235th Solar Cycle

Tungdil did the first thing that came to mind. As the älf loomed over him, he dropped the ax that Boïndil had given to him and reached up to block the blow.

Grabbing Keenfire with both hands, he wrapped his fingers around the sigurdaisy haft and dropped to one knee, muscles straining and joints creaking. The blade hovered above his head.

Stooped over him, the älf threw all her weight behind

the diamond-studded blade, arms trembling as she pushed against him. Her breath came in labored gasps.

But Keenfire seemed to sense that the second set of hands belonged to Tungdil, its rightful bearer. The intarsia shimmered, and a tongue of fire licked over the ax head, reaching for the älf's mask. Moving and twisting, she stayed out of harm's way.

"You're not getting away from me again," she gasped, kicking Tungdil in the chest.

Still clutching the shaft, he tumbled backward, and the älf, determined not to lose Keenfire, came with him.

She used her momentum to launch herself into the air, all the while gripping the ax. The soles of her boots sped toward him. He turned in time, rolling to the side as she landed beside him, missing his throat.

"Vraccas brought you here to give me Keenfire," he spluttered. His right hand shot up, punching her in the belly. Uncurling his fist, he reached for her left foot, bringing her to the ground. Her black veil lifted as she fell, revealing her chin and left cheek. There was no sign of a scar or deformity that would warrant the wearing of a mask.

Each had a hand on Keenfire's haft, and neither was prepared to let go.

They stumbled to their feet, and Ondori, reaching behind her, drew another weapon—a scythe-like blade that Tungdil recognized from their encounter on the pier. Whipping out his dagger, he squared his shoulders and waited for a weakness in her guard. Slowly they circled each other, the thickset dwarf at one end of the ax, the willowy älf at the other, separated by the length of the sigurdaisy haft. The ax head was on Tungdil's side and he could see the intarsia flickering, as if Keenfire were waiting for the opportunity to strike.

"Why won't you show your face?" he demanded. "Only cowards hide behind a mask."

"My mask shall remain in place until my murdered parents are avenged," she told him, looking at him with pure hatred. "You'll see my face before you die."

"I killed your parents, did I?"

"You killed my mother in Greenglade—you and the warrior twins."

Tungdil twisted away as the scythe-like weapon slashed toward him.

"My father you killed at the Blacksaddle," she continued, slashing at him again. This time she drew blood. She eyed his wounded throat with satisfaction. "My loss shall be avenged."

Tungdil kept his eyes on the scythe, waiting for her to strike. "I can't bring them back, but I'd be happy to help you join them," he retorted, ducking under the swooping blade and using his momentum to ram the ax head toward her.

Once again, the intarsia flared up, but the älf avoided the red-hot suspiration, only for the sigurdaisy haft to slam into her face. The mask slipped over her eyes and her veil caught alight, flames shooting through the gauze and singeing the ends of her long brown hair. Dazed by the blow and blinded by the mask, she stumbled toward him.

In less time than it takes a drop of sweat to vaporize in a red-hot furnace, Tungdil was beside her, ramming his dagger through her armor. It embedded itself to the hilt.

Tungdil bent down to claim Keenfire, but he was stopped by a shout from Balyndis. Looking around, he saw the cause.

Glaïmbar was on the ground, and standing over him was a badly wounded orc. Screaming with pain, the beast raised his notched sword and prepared to smite the dwarf.

Tungdil cursed roundly, wishing he could let his rival die. Instead, he picked up the ax that Boïndil had given him and hurled it at the beast. Whirling end over end, the ax struck the orc beneath the armpit. Green blood gushed from the wound, spattering the sprawled Glaïmbar.

The orc stumbled, dropping his rusty sword.

In an instant, Glaïmbar was on his feet, ramming the spiked end of his ax into his enemy's neck. He slit the beast's throat and raised a hand to thank his rescuer. Tungdil, who had no intention of acknowledging his rival, looked away.

You fool, the voice inside him whispered. *You should have let him die.*

Tungdil gave himself a little shake. "Where was I?" he said, turning back to finish off the älf, but she and Keenfire were gone. A trail of blood led into the heart of the battle, losing itself among the mass of dwarves and orcs. The masked älf had escaped to live another orbit and Keenfire was in her hands. *I'll never find her now.*

Tungdil remembered what she had said about her parents. *Sinthoras was her father*, he thought. He picked up an abandoned ax and threw himself on the remaining orcs, drawing strength from his frustration at losing Keenfire for a second time.

Hoping against hope that he would find the älf, he cleaved through the beasts.

But the ax and the älf had disappeared.

It was late afternoon when the battle ended. The dwarves had won a decisive victory, but the mood was subdued.

They gathered the headless bodies of their enemies and threw them into the basin, where they floated among hundreds of spluttering orcs. After killing the survivors by pelting their heads with rocks, the dwarves decided to drain the basin and let the sun do its work. Later, the bleached bones would be strewn around the Stone Gateway as a warning to invading beasts.

Tungdil stood on the plateau and scanned the mountainside below.

It seemed to him that a small dot was moving rapidly across the horizon toward the southeast. He felt sure it was the älf, in which case it was futile to think of chasing her by pony, let alone on foot.

It's Glaïmbar's fault, he told himself, kicking the ground angrily. A stone skittered down the mountainside. *I had the älf where I wanted her. Keenfire was mine.*

"I wanted to thank you properly, Tungdil Goldhand," said the object of his curses.

"Any dwarf would intervene to save his king," he replied. Too frustrated to hide his hostility, he kept his back turned. "I forfeited Keenfire," he said pointedly.

"I know," said Glaïmbar, sighing. He stood next to Tungdil. "I suppose it isn't possible to forge a replacement. Boïndil seems to think we can."

"Keenfire is irreplaceable," said Tungdil, happy to twist

the knife a little further. "We could forge a new blade, but the haft was fashioned from the last remaining fragment of sigurdaisy wood in Girdlegard." He turned to face the king. "I don't fancy fighting the threat from the west without our strongest weapon. If the älfar join forces with the new invaders, Keenfire could be used against us. Who knows how we'll fare . . ."

"Vraccas will give us the strength to prevail," said Balyndis, positioning herself at Glaïmbar's side. She looked at Tungdil reprovingly.

"Besides, you won't be fighting alone," chimed in Myr, overhearing the conversation. "You'll have our warriors as well." She finished tending to a wounded dwarf and took her place next to Tungdil.

The battle lines were drawn.

To Tungdil's satisfaction, Balyndis looked put out.

"It's time we met properly," said Myr. "I'm Myrmianda Alabaster from the freeling folk. Tungdil battled his way to our realm to remind us that we dwarves were hewn from the same rock." She shook hands with Balyndis and Glaïmbar. "I'm here at the request of King Gemmil, who raised the army of two thousand warriors that helped you today."

Glaïmbar bowed. "Tell King Gemmil that he saved our kingdom from the orcs. It was only a matter of time before they launched their next assault. We owe our lives to your king."

Tungdil surveyed the dwarves who had come from all corners of Girdlegard to defend the Northern Pass. The comrades-in-arms were working together to gather their dead.

Four hundred warriors from the fifthling kingdom had fallen in battle. Their bodies would be laid in the great hall for the fifthlings to pay their respects. After an orbit, the fallen warriors would be placed in the burial vaults. The freelings had suffered heavy losses as well, and barely a thousand of Gemmil's warriors had survived. The others would rest in peace beside their fifthling comrades.

"How many are planning to stay?" asked Tungdil.

"You'd better ask her," said Myr, pointing to an armor-clad warrior almost twice her size. "Sanda Flameheart is Gemmil's wife." She called her over.

As Sanda approached, the others noticed the dark lines and menacing runes on her face. Her whole visage was covered in intricate tattoos, the like of which Tungdil, Balyndis, and Glaïmbar had never seen. The symbols spelled out terrible threats against the other dwarven folks.

Glaïmbar's fingers tightened around his ax.

"There's nothing to worry about," Myr hastened to reassure him. "Sanda was born a thirdling, but she's served our army for over two cycles. She's a popular queen and a respected commander—and she's certainly not a dwarf hater, in spite of her tattoos." She greeted Sanda with a hug. "Thank goodness you got here when you did. We weren't expecting you so soon."

"We came through the underground network. Some of the tunnels were damaged, but Vraccas kept us safe." She laughed. "Gemmil couldn't wait to get rid of us—he was convinced we'd be late."

"He was right to worry," said Glaïmbar, trying not to stare at her tattoos. "We owe our victory to you." His eyes were riveted on her face.

Sanda smiled broadly, answering his unspoken doubts with a warmth and friendliness at odds with the sinister runes. "I know what you're thinking, King Glaïmbar. It's no wonder you're confused. Here I am, talking to you as an ally, with the promise of your destruction etched across my face." She held out her hand. "I'm a thirdling on the outside, but at heart, I'm a child of the Smith. I wasn't born to hate."

Glaïmbar hesitated briefly before taking her outstretched hand. "Lineage isn't everything," he said firmly, as if to convince himself. "Tungdil Goldhand has shown us that."

"Tungdil and I aren't the only thirdlings who weren't born to hate the other dwarves. My story is long in the telling, but later, when we've raised our tankards to slain enemies and lost friends, I'll tell you how I came to leave the kingdom of my birth."

"Sanda, this is the hero of the Blacksaddle," said Myr. She cast a sideways glance at Balyndis. "Tungdil is a *dear* friend of mine already."

Balyndis bristled visibly, as Myr had hoped she would.

"We were wondering how long you were planning to stay," continued Myr. "King Glaïmbar and the future queen, Balyndis, have invited the freelings to join their folk."

Sanda laid a powerful hand on her weapons belt. "We'll stay until the danger has passed." She turned to Glaïmbar. "Too many dwarves were killed in the battle. You could do with reinforcements at the gateway, I imagine?" She smiled as he nodded. "As for moving to the fifthling kingdom . . . None of my warriors intend to stay at present, but they're free to change their minds. Who knows, maybe

the fifthling kingdom will gain a thousand extra axes."
She looked at him levelly. "Naturally, anyone who chooses
to join the fifthlings will submit to your command. As
regards the rest of us, we'd like to be treated as guests."

Tungdil could tell that she meant what she said. The
freelings were happy to help, but they wanted their
independence.

"Could you spare a moment later?" he asked Sanda.
"I was hoping you might know something about my
parents."

"With pleasure," she promised. "Now, if you'll excuse
me, I need to attend to my troops." She hurried away, the
others watching in silence.

"I can't pretend that it's easy for me to trust her,"
admitted Glaïmbar. He turned to Myr. "When did you
say she arrived in your realm?"

"Two cycles ago. I don't blame you for being wary, but
Sanda is an upstanding dwarf." She shifted her weight,
nudging closer to Tungdil and allowing their arms to touch.
Tungdil pretended not to notice and stood his ground,
willing Balyndis to see that he too had forged a bond with
another dwarf.

"Those who seek to become freelings must submit to
certain tests," continued Myr. "Sanda passed with flying
colors and she's proven her worth on countless occasions."

"She's obviously popular with your king," observed
Balyndis. "It seems to me that Glaïmbar is right to be
suspicious. If I were a thirdling spy, I'd make friends with
my enemies before I betrayed them."

Myr's face hardened. "Don't let Sanda hear you talking
like that, or she'll challenge you to a duel. Warriors are

very particular about their honor . . . Besides, she's my friend." Her red eyes bored into Balyndis like daggers; from now on, it was war.

"I hope Vraccas helps me to conquer my doubts," said Glaïmbar, sighing. "I daresay we're honored to have the freelings as our guests." He decided to steer the conversation to safer ground. "Tell me, Tungdil: Is Djerûn here for a reason?"

Tungdil reached for the leather cylinder hanging from his shoulder and pulled out a scroll. Andôkai's bodyguard had waited until the end of the battle to hand him a letter. Since then, he had been standing patiently by the waterfall, his armor gleaming majestically in the setting sun.

Tungdil unfurled the roll of parchment and began to read aloud:

Dearest Tungdil

The purpose of this letter is to secure the services of the finest smith in Girdlegard.

Djerûn requires a new suit of armor and a tunic of chain mail. Enclosed are his measurements and the composition of the alloy, for the attention of Balyndis Steelfinger.

When she comes to fitting the armor, Balyndis must bind her eyes and gauge the fit with her fingers. Make her promise to remain blindfolded until Djerûn is fully clad in his armor. This I ask for her own safety: No one must look on Djerûn's face.

As for the cost, tell her to name a sum and I will pay.

Djerůn will be heading west across the Red Range. His instructions are to assess the situation in the Outer Lands and determine the nature of the threat. If the danger is real and not a figment of Nôd'onn's imagination, we need to know what to expect.

By the time you receive this letter, Narmora and I will be in Weyurn, where we hope to find record of migrants from the Outer Lands. Perhaps they will tell us something about their homeland.

Vraccas be with you,

Andôkai

Tungdil lowered the letter and handed Balyndis the notes regarding the giant's measurements and the composition of the alloy. "It's lucky that Djerůn turned up when he did," he observed. "He couldn't have arrived at a better time. Thank goodness Andôkai worships Samusin. Her bodyguard restored the equilibrium."

The smith scanned the list of metals and glanced at the giant. "How will he know what I'm saying? I can't speak his tongue."

"Andôkai will have thought of that," replied Tungdil.

Balyndis turned to leave, but he laid a hand on her shoulder. "Hang on," he said, pulling her back. "I need you to promise not to look at Djerůn's face."

"I wouldn't look at his face for all the gold in Girdlegard," she retorted sharply, shaking him off.

Tungdil watched as she hurried away, followed by Glaïmbar. They exchanged a few words before Glaïmbar took charge of the clean-up operation and Balyndis attended to Djerůn. Tungdil gazed at her sadly. He wanted to call out and apologize for his childish behavior. He was already sorry for his rudeness: For some reason, he couldn't keep a check on his thoughts and emotions when Balyndis was around. If he was honest with himself, he still loved her, in spite of his growing feelings for Myr.

Do I really like Myr? Or am I just trying to punish Balyndis for choosing Glaïmbar? Sometimes he wished that he were back in Lot-Ionan's school; life had been simpler then.

Myr seemed to guess what he was thinking. She slipped her hand into his. "Isn't it time we went to see your friend?" she asked. "I'd like to help him if I can."

Tungdil was too wrapped up in his thoughts to realize whom she meant, but then it dawned on him. "Come on," he said, squeezing her hand impulsively. "Let's see what you can do for Boëndal."

They hurried through the passageways of the fifthling kingdom and arrived in the forge.

Boïndil was sitting on a stool beside the Dragon Fire furnace, regaling his frozen brother with stories about the battle against the orcs. Every now and then he thumped a battered helmet that he had stolen from an enemy head.

"But it wasn't the same without you. Nothing's the same without you," he finished sadly, noticing Tungdil and Myr.

Boïndil had been trying to stay cheerful for the sake of his twin, but found it impossible to hide his feelings from the others. The truth was, it smote his soul to see Boëndal in a death-like sleep. He stood up and smoothed his black beard. What he was about to say didn't come easily to a warrior. "Myr," he began, "I saw you tending to the wounded on the battlefield, and I saw you cure Tungdil. You're the best doctor I've ever known." He swallowed. "I'm begging you: Bring Boëndal back to life. Cure my brother, and I'll protect you with my life. Nothing and no one will ever hurt you." He made room for her at Boëndal's bedside.

"I'd be honored to help," Myr said simply. "You don't need to promise anything in return." Perching on the secondling's bed, she laid a hand on his forehead, then lifted his eyelids to look at his pupils. "I can't examine him properly in his clothes," she told the others. "Let's get everything off except his apron. I need to see if the blood is still flowing to his limbs."

Tungdil and Boïndil stripped the sleeping dwarf. The next hour passed in silence as Myr examined every inch of her patient's body. Nothing escaped her scrutiny. "Your brother was blessed by Vraccas," she pronounced. "His limbs are cold, but not frozen, and his skin looks healthy enough."

"So he's basically all right," said Boïndil eagerly.

"I was worried he might have frostbite." She lowered her head to listen to Boëndal's heart and breathing. "It tends to affect the toes and fingers—the digit freezes, blackens, and eventually falls off. Sometimes the patient is too numb to realize what's happening. It's a nasty condition and impossible to treat." She listened intently. "Extraordinary! His heart is beating, his lungs are working, but his body has slowed right down. His inner furnace must be burning very low." A smile spread over her face. "That's it! Fetch me a tub of warm water—and some beeswax!"

"Warm water?" queried Boïndil doubtfully. "We tried that before. It didn't work."

"Patience," she said mysteriously.

The tub was brought in. Myr produced a strip of leather, rolled it up to make a tube, and secured it with some cord. She placed an end between Boëndal's blue lips and sealed his mouth and nose with warm wax, forcing him to breathe through the tube. "Right," she declared purposefully. "Let's get him into the water."

Soon the dwarf was submerged in the tub, his arms and legs weighed down with lead.

"This will thaw him out and melt the ice in his brain," she explained, fetching a shovel load of glowing coals from Dragon Fire. The hot coals hissed as they splashed into the water, warming the bath. Myr was careful not to let them fall on Boëndal.

Tungdil checked the temperature with his hand. "It's pretty hot already."

Boïndil leaned over, frowning anxiously. "You'll boil him like a sausage if you're not careful." He glared at Myr as she stepped forward to empty another load of coals into the tub. "Put them back, Myr. You'll stew him alive."

"I thought you wanted me to cure him," she retorted. "Hot water won't hurt him. He has to be immersed completely or his brain will clog with ice. I know what I'm doing, Boïndil."

She raised the shovel to tip out the coals, but Boïndil made a grab for the handle, forcing her to stop.

"I said *enough*," he growled, squaring his shoulders to prove he meant business. "I won't stand by while you turn my brother into broth. You'll have to think of another cure."

Her red eyes stared back at him fearlessly. "I'm the expert on this, Boïndil Doubleblade." She tried to wrench the shovel away from him. He hadn't reckoned with her resistance and pulled back too sharply.

A large piece of coal separated itself from its white-hot neighbors, slid to the edge of the shovel and launched itself into the tub. Steam rose as it sank through the water.

Tungdil, determined to save his friend from harm, plunged his hand into the tub and tried to catch the glowing coal. His fingers swept the water in vain.

The fiery missile plummeted toward Boëndal's bare chest and struck the skin on a level with his heart.

Tungdil watched as the dwarf's body twitched. "Did you see that?" he asked the others. "Boëndal just . . ."

At that moment, the sleeping twin opened his eyes, sat up with a jolt, and tore the tube from his mouth. After a few gasps of air, he started coughing.

"Lift him out," said Myr, holding up some warm towels to swaddle the dripping dwarf.

Boïndil wiped his brother's face gently and waited for the coughing fit to pass. "You're awake," he said excitedly, throwing his arms around him.

Boëndal tried to say something, but his voice was just a croak. He had to clear his throat a few times, and even then he could speak only in a feeble whisper. "What h . . . happened?"

Thrilled by his friend's recovery, Tungdil was about to launch into an account of everything that had happened since the avalanche, but Myr stopped him.

"All in good time," she said firmly. "Boëndal, we need to find you something to wear, then you should try to eat and drink a little. Your stomach needs to get accustomed to food again—no meat, no beer!" Her tone was so emphatic that no one, not even Boïndil, dared to object. "Give yourself time to adjust. You're going to be just fine." She smiled at him warmly.

Boëndal looked at her in bewilderment. "Who are you?"

"Myr melted your inner cold," explained his brother. He clasped the freeling to his chest, overcome with gratitude. "Forgive me for doubting you. I promised to protect you if you healed him, and I will. Vraccas can smite me with his hammer if I ever forget my debt!"

She laughed to see his bearded face light up with boyish excitement. "I forgive you," she said happily.

Tungdil made no mention of what he had observed. In his opinion, it was the falling coal, not Myr's bath, that had woken Boëndal. Still, an apology was in order, and Myr might be glad of extra protection. He turned back to the bed. "How are you feeling, Boëndal?" he asked.

Speaking seemed to cost the twin a great deal of effort. "My fingers are still numb," he said ponderously. "I can feel them tingling. Thank Vraccas the White Death didn't take me."

Myr reached for his left hand and massaged the fingers carefully. "Does that feel better?" Boëndal nodded. "Good," she said, relieved. "The blood is coming back, so you won't lose your fingers. You should start to perk up this evening, and by tomorrow you'll be fighting fit. Just be sure to keep warm." She smiled at him. "Great things lie ahead for you, Boëndal Hookhand. Vraccas went to a lot of trouble to keep you alive." She dried her hands on the corner of one of his towels and yawned. "I hope you don't mind if I excuse myself. I'm ready to drop."

Boëndal took her hand. "Thank you," he whispered

gratefully. "Whoever you are, wherever you come from, thank you for saving my life. From now on, your enemies will be my enemies. I'm forever in your debt."

"My name is Myrmianda Alabaster. It's kind of you to thank me, but I don't need a reward: It's enough to see you awake." She stroked his hand gently. "You're warming up nicely." She made sure that he was wrapped in the towels and stayed at his bedside until the clothes and food arrived. Once dressed, Boëndal wolfed down the meal while Boïndil sat beside him and started to recount their adventures, beginning with the forging of Keenfire and the journey to the Blacksaddle.

"Come on," said Tungdil to Myr. "Let's find you somewhere to sleep." They took their leave of the twins and hurried out of the forge. "There's usually plenty of space in the halls, but what with the wounded and the other freelings . . . Still, we're bound to find somewhere."

"Tungdil, I'm dead on my feet. Can't I sleep in your chamber? I won't be a nuisance, I promise. The floor will do just fine."

"Nonsense," said Tungdil. "You can have my bed while I keep looking. Are you sure you don't want something to eat?"

She shook her head.

It was only a short walk through the passageways to Tungdil's chamber. He opened the door and ushered her in, then stepped back outside.

"Can you give me a hand?" asked Myr, tugging tiredly on her chain mail. "I can barely lift my arms."

"Of course," he said with a smile. "You know what the problem is? You need more muscles."

He walked in and showed her to the bed. "It's not too soft, which means it's perfect for us dwarves." It occurred to him that softer beds might be customary in the freelings' realm. "You can pad it out with blankets, if you like."

"No," she said, suppressing a yawn. She lifted her arms over her head. "I'd fall asleep on a bed of nails right now. Do you think you could . . . ?"

He took hold of the bottom of her tunic and pulled it carefully over her head. Underneath she was wearing a padded jerkin with a V-shaped neckline that revealed her plump white breasts. Embarrassed, he draped the tunic on the rack designed to take his mail. "Sleep well, Myr."

"Mm, that feels good," she said, reaching up and stretching luxuriously. She kicked off her boots and slipped into bed. "I'm going to sleep like a rock." She smiled at him. "Thank you for letting me have your bed." Her red eyes shifted to something behind him.

Tungdil glanced at the half-open door in time to see a shadow speed down the corridor.

"I'll be dreaming of you," whispered Myr, brushing her lips against his cheek and closing her eyes.

The kiss had a paralyzing effect on Tungdil's mind. At once he forgot everything, including his intention to speak to Sanda Flameheart . . .

Balyndis was hammering furiously. Sparks flew in all directions, showering the furthest corners of the forge, while the Dragon Fire furnace continued to exude an incredible heat.

Sweat was streaming from her body, even though she wore nothing but a thin linen shirt and lightweight leather breeches beneath her smith's apron. Her head was covered with a scarf to protect her hair from sparks.

The hammer rose and fell until the troublesome metal cracked. Cursing, she picked it up with her tongs and tossed it into a cart, where it landed on top of her previous four efforts. Later, the metal would be melted down to make weapons and tools.

She waited until the jangling echo had faded from the forge.

I may as well give up, she thought despondently, leaning against the anvil. She dipped a wooden ladle into the bucket of water beside her and took a sip. *I can't afford to be angry. It's making me careless.*

She was furious with Tungdil on two counts: First, for refusing to see her point of view, and second, for carrying on with Myr. To top things off, Myr seemed very comfortable in the role of his girlfriend. *Too comfortable.*

And Tungdil's ploy was working: She was jealous.

Why can't he see that I love him?

Clan law had forced her to betroth herself to Glaïmbar, but her heart still longed for Tungdil, even though she knew her fiancé to be a worthy dwarf. She had spent a good deal of time with Glaïmbar, who genuinely adored her. He knew of her feelings for Tungdil, but he wanted to love her and treat her well.

Balyndis took another sip of water. *I mustn't be too hard on him; he doesn't understand our traditions.* Tungdil's upbringing in Lot-Ionan's school was the root of the problem. He was a dwarf at heart, but when it came to love, he behaved like a man. It didn't help that his pride was hurt as well.

Maybe one orbit he'll understand that I couldn't defy the will of my family and my clan. She got up and looked for something to distract her thoughts. *Vraccas knows it wasn't easy for me.*

She took out Andôkai's letter and left the forge for the smelting works.

Fires blazing, the blast furnaces were spewing out iron, steel, and bronze, from which the smiths fashioned tools, armor, and replacement parts for all manner of things. The new fifthling kingdom was taking shape.

Balyndis chose one of the smaller furnaces that was designed for smaller quantities of metal. She went in search of the elements for the armor, as listed in Andôkai's letter, and loaded them into carts. Together the metals would form the basis of Djerûn's plate mail, just as the maga had prescribed.

Astonishingly, Balyndis, who was a master smith, had never heard of the compound.

"Drat!" She held the sheet of parchment in the air. Her sweat had drenched the paper and the ink had run in places, making it difficult to decipher the maga's flowing script. *Is that tionium—or palandium?*

It took a great deal of effort to make sense of the instructions and she privately doubted that the formula would work. It sounded too unlikely. If she had understood correctly, she was supposed to add small quantities of tin, copper, and mercury to the steel, followed by an equal quantity of vraccasium and . . .

Tionium or palandium? Or tionium and palandium? The metals had similar properties, but tionium was black in color and belonged to the dark lord Tion, whereas palandium was silvery-white and four times cheaper. The goddess Palandiell was worshipped in the human kingdoms, so her metal was popular with Girdlegard's smiths.

I don't know what to do. The formula is too vague. She ascended the steps leading to the hatch at the top of the furnace. The flames were burning fierce and white, fuelled by coals from the Dragon Fire furnace. The tin and other metals had been added already.

I can't ask Andôkai, Balyndis thought glumly, weighing the tionium in one hand and the palandium in the other. She hesitated for a moment and read the formula again, but she was still none the wiser. By now the other metals were beginning to coalesce. She had to act fast.

Pulling on thick leather gloves to protect her hands from the rising heat, she dropped the black metal carefully through the hatch and followed it with the palandium. *Andôkai worships the god of equilibrium; Samusin will balance everything out.*

She turned a winch to lower the lid over the hatch and keep in the heat.

Back on ground level, she worked the enormous bellows and pumped air into the furnace, fanning the flames. Every now and then she opened a hatch and tossed in some white-hot coals from Dragon Fire until the furnace had reached the requisite temperature. She retreated to a safe distance of four paces.

A chimney channeled the foul-smelling gases away from the underground halls, drawing them through a duct in the ceiling to the surface.

Balyndis waited until she was sure that the metals had

combined, then, taking a long stick, she broke the clay seal at the base of the furnace.

Golden and gleaming, the liquid alloy streamed forth. Balyndis skimmed the slag from the top as it flowed through a clay conduit on its way to a cart lined with firebricks. Surrounded by the heat of the furnace, she felt completely at home. Beads of sweat formed on her skin, evaporating almost instantly. She watched in anticipation as the alloy cooled and dulled.

Picking up a pair of tongs, she took hold of the red-hot hook on the end of the cart and pulled the precious load along the rail that led from the smelting works to the forge. "Right," she said to herself. "Let's see what happens when Samusin entrusts a formula to a dwarf . . ."

Wind Chime Island,
Kingdom of Weyurn,
Girdlegard,
Late Spring, 6235th Solar Cycle

Towering waves crashed toward the shore, dashing themselves to pieces on the rocks.

A host of tiny droplets rose high above the roiling lake and lingered, almost suspended for an instant, before dropping into the waves below and disappearing without trace. The air glistened moistly above the cliff, shrouding an ancient temple built in honor of Palandiell.

Inside the building, Narmora gathered the shawl about her shoulders and shivered. Even the thick walls of the former temple did little to muffle the constant pounding of waves against the shore. The change of season had brought storms to Wind Chime Island, with spring doing battle with summer, and winter seizing the chance to sidle in.

"What possessed you to store your books here?" Andôkai asked the chief archivist, a balding man of some sixty cycles. His costly robes looked shabby and ill-fitting, and his nose was permanently red, owing to a fondness for drink. The maga eyed him reprovingly. "It's too damp for a library."

"I'm afraid the timing of your visit is most unfortunate. The damp spell will be over in a couple of orbits. Wind Chime is known throughout Weyurn for its temperate weather." Bowing respectfully, he led the women through the stacks to a cabinet measuring seven paces high and crammed with books. "The official records from the last hundred cycles," he said with a flourish. "Births, marriages, and deaths."

"Do you keep separate records for migrants?" asked Narmora, hoping to limit the scope of the search. She had no desire to spend longer than necessary on the island, to which she had taken an instant dislike. Besides, she was worried that Dorsa, a delicate child by nature, would catch a chill. "We're looking for settlers from the Outer Lands," she explained.

The archivist thought for a moment. "With a bit of luck and Palandiell's blessing, you'll find what you're looking for in the south wing." He wiped his nose on his sleeve. "These records deal only with Her Majesty's subjects. Outsiders, including migrants from the rest of Girdlegard, are listed in the other wing." He set off down the corridor to show them the way.

Narmora lagged a few paces behind, watching as Andôkai, brandishing a decree from Queen Wey, attempted to commandeer the library staff and anyone else with the power of reading to help with her quest.

In word and deed, Narmora was a model famula—hard-working and loyal. Since the accident, she had applied herself more diligently than ever to her studies, delighting the maga with her progress.

But Narmora's motivation for learning magic had changed. The threat from the west and the future of Girdlegard were secondary concerns. After the whispered conversation with Rodario that night in Porista, Narmora had returned to Furgas's bedside and sworn an oath of revenge that required her to bide her time and study patiently while disguising the rancor and fury that filled her thoughts.

The little party reached the south wing of the library. Andôkai turned to her famula and pointed to the stacks on the right. A wooden stepladder led up to additional shelves behind a balustrade. "You start on this side, and I'll work toward you. The others can take the lower shelves."

Narmora nodded and ascended the creaking steps to the narrow gangway. A low rail protected careless readers from tumbling ten paces to the floor. Andôkai waved to her from the other side and pulled out a folio. Dust scattered everywhere as she turned the first page.

Narmora reached for a volume as well and began to read, her eyes roving over the spidery handwriting without attending to the meaning. *How could you go to such lengths to bend me to your will?* She leafed through the volume, seeing nothing but the maga's betrayal on every page.

The story recounted to her by the ashen-faced Rodario pointed to a single, terrible, explanation: Andôkai had orchestrated the attack on Furgas as a means of recruiting Narmora as her famula. The maga's strange behavior, the deaths of the highwaymen, Djerûn's determination to silence Nôd'onn's former famula—it all added up.

She turned the page absentmindedly.

You'll be sorry for teaching me your art, she thought grimly, glancing at Andôkai. She was prepared to bide her time until Furgas was cured and the threat from the west discounted or defeated, but sooner or later the maga would pay for her treachery, and Djerûn himself would be powerless to help her. Narmora felt nothing but loathing for the woman who had put her husband in a coma and killed her baby son.

Anger simmered inside her, and she turned her mind to other thoughts, afraid that her älvish heritage would betray her hidden rage.

"I think I've found something," called Andôkai suddenly.

Her dutiful famula hurried over.

"Seventy cycles ago, a group of travelers arrived in Gastinga," the maga continued. "It says here that they came from the Outer Lands. Their children or grandchildren should still be alive." She summoned the archivist and enquired about the location of the place.

"It's here on the island," he said. "It takes two orbits to get there. I'll loan you one of my assistants to show you the way."

"Splendid," exclaimed Andôkai, satisfied. "Samusin has rewarded us for the long and wearisome journey from Porista."

The man cleared his throat. "Perhaps the Estimable Maga could refrain from invoking foreign gods in the library; it's a consecrated building."

Andôkai turned her head slowly and jutted out her angular chin. "I'll speak the name of my god whenever and wherever I please. Samusin saved me from Nôd'onn and lent me his power in the fight against the Perished Land. My fellow magi, devotees of the gentle Palandiell, didn't fare so well. It seems to me that my *foreign* god is more deserving of your respect." She gestured to the shelves. "And don't lecture me about desecrating your temple. Palandiell left here when you filled her house with books." She started down the ladder. "I want to ride within the hour. Tell your man to be ready." Her boots clacked harshly against the tiled floor.

Narmora raised her eyebrows and smiled sympathetically at the archivist, before following the maga out of the room. "I'm going to check on Dorsa," she told her mentor. "Who knows, I might be in time to stop Rosild unpacking our trunks." Without waiting for the maga's approval she hurried through the corridors of the vaulted building, once home to Palandiell's priests before the temple was converted to a library and a new place of worship built in honor of the goddess.

She found her daughter in the arms of Rosild, the nurse-maid employed by Andôkai for the duration of the trip. Rosild was still young and her breasts were plump with milk. It was a mystery to Narmora why the maid had agreed to leave her own small child and her family to accompany them on their journey. *Unless she was forced* . . .

"She's a thirsty wee thing," said Rosild. She smiled proudly.

"See, she's putting on weight." She handed the baby to Narmora, who noticed the difference at once. The maid seemed to be gathering the courage to say something. She took a step forward. "There's something else I've noticed," she said nervously.

"She's filling out nicely—"

"No, I don't mean that." Rosild adjusted the blanket to reveal Dorsa's right ear. "Maybe it's just me, but the tip of her ear looks pointed." She paused, waiting for confirmation or perhaps a word of praise. "It's only a little thing, but she'll be teased for it later," she added when Narmora was silent. "We used to trim the ears of our hunting dogs at home. I don't see why it wouldn't work on a—"

"No," said Narmora firmly. "No one lays a hand on my daughter. She'll look fine when she's older, I'm sure." She tucked the ear under the blanket. "I don't want you speaking of this to anyone, do you hear?"

Rosild nodded, her gaze lingering briefly on Narmora's red headscarf. She looked away quickly.

"Very good, Rosild. Pack our trunks—we're leaving in an hour."

With her daughter on her arm, she left the chamber and made herself comfortable in the great hall where a fire was roaring in an open hearth. The warmth drove out the cold of the wind and the spray, and Narmora and her child enjoyed the respite.

"We'll be back in the sunshine soon," she assured the sleeping Dorsa.

Gastinga, the village that they were heading for, lay further inland, and Narmora was looking forward to escaping from the damp.

The journey to Wind Chime Island hadn't been easy. Following the quake, the lakes that covered fifty per cent of Weyurn's surface had overflowed, their waters combining to form great reservoirs. The flooding had claimed a handful of casualties, and the survivors had taken their misfortune in their stride, as Narmora and Andôkai had observed. Most had abandoned their homes and moved to one of Weyurn's many islands. The majority of Weyurnians lived on the lakes.

Narmora didn't like the thought of it. To her mind, the islands seemed dangerously impermanent, and she was sure that some of them pitched and rolled with the waves.

It was said that a few of the smaller islets floated across the lakes like croutons in soup. The islanders floated with them, putting down anchor wherever the fishing was particularly good. Narmora felt queasy at the notion of drifting to and fro.

When the first log, a vast piece of timber bigger than the average man, had burned to a cinder, Narmora piled on more. Physically, she wasn't strong enough to shift the logs from the woodpile at the end of the hall to the hearth in the middle, so she used magic instead. As if lifted by an invisible hand, four logs rose in the air and traveled through the hall, lowering themselves dutifully onto the flames and catching fire.

By now, simple spells came easily to Narmora, and she performed the conjuration while singing softly to Dorsa in the tongue of her mother, a beautiful, melancholy language that Furgas loved to hear.

The thought of Furgas reminded her to send a prayer to Samusin and Tion, entreating them to keep him well.

Rodario had sworn solemnly to do everything in his power for Furgas, and on this occasion she believed him. He knew as well as she did that Furgas was in a critical state.

"Andôkai told me to fetch you," said Rosild behind her. "She's ready to leave."

Narmora stopped singing abruptly.

"What a lovely song," observed the maid. "What language was it? I couldn't make sense of the words."

"I made it up," said Narmora, clasping the sleeping Dorsa and rising to her feet. "It's nonsense really, but Dorsa seems to like it." She left the room, taking care not to meet the maid's gaze.

"You'll have to teach it to me," decided Rosild, shouldering her bags and following her mistress outside.

Fifthling Kingdom,
Girdlegard,
Late Spring, 6235th Solar Cycle

Balyndis ran her hand over the mail-clad arm, feeling the powerful wrist and the formidable muscle beneath her fingertips as she groped her way toward the shoulder. She checked the alignment of the spaulders and breastplate. Fitting armor to a warrior over twice her size was quite a challenge, and wearing a blindfold made things worse.

Orbits had passed while she hammered the plates into shape. Some required hinges, while others were simply laced together—although the instructions called for metal cable instead of standard leather thongs.

He won't be undressing in a hurry, thought Balyndis,

who was beginning to wonder whether Djerûn ever removed his armor at all.

The final adjustments could be made only while the giant was wearing the suit, so Balyndis had blindfolded herself securely, remembering how Tion's beasts had screamed in terror on seeing Djerûn's face. To make doubly sure, she kept her eyes closed whenever her head was turned toward him.

The maga's measurements were incredibly precise. Most of the plates fitted perfectly, and a tap of the hammer brought the others into line.

Once the fit of the armor had been verified, Balyndis could set about patterning the armor as the maga had prescribed. Some of the runes were to be engraved, others etched with acid, and thin strips of gold and silver hammered into the grooves.

Since starting work, Balyndis had noticed a strange noise, similar to a growl, that seemed to be coming from Djerûn, although his chest was completely still.

To Balyndis's surprise, his warm breath smelled fresh. She had expected him to stink like an orc, so either the smells of the smithy were masking the stench, or Djerûn was cleaner than she had thought. There was no obvious evidence of perspiration, whereas a man wearing a full suit of armor could be smelled from a hundred paces or more.

Balyndis worked swiftly. She strapped the plates around his arms and instructed him to flex his muscles while she listened intently. The joints were perfect—no grating or creaking to indicate rubbing or stress.

Relieved, she climbed down from the platform and returned to the anvil. Lifting her blindfold, she reached for

Djerůn's helmet. The shiny demonic visor contrasted strikingly with the matt surrounds, and a thin strip of black tionium emphasized the ferocious eyes. Proudly, she wiped the helmet with a cloth and added a drop of oil to the hinges.

"All done," she called, not knowing whether the giant could understand her. "If this isn't enough to frighten your enemies, I don't know what will." She tied the blindfold around her head and picked up the helmet, remembering to collect the skullcap, made of leather-lined mail. With her free hand, she felt her way along the rope leading back to the giant.

Just then disaster struck.

Balyndis stepped on something, probably a lump of coal. Her foot slid away from her.

She skidded, overbalanced, and flung out her arms to break her fall. The helmet whizzed past her, one of the spikes coming within a knife's edge of her eye. It snagged on her blindfold and pulled it off.

The next Balyndis knew, she was sprawled on the floor, arms stretched in front of her, skullcap and helmet clutched in one hand. Raising her head, she looked up and froze.

Djerůn was leaning against the anvil in front of her—and her blindfold was off.

Balyndis had seen some unpleasant sights in her time. She had fought in gruesome battles, dueled with hideous orcs and plug-ugly ogres, and waded in rivers of blood and spilt intestines. As a warrior, she was unshakable; but the visage before her filled her with terror.

Her mouth opened in a silent scream.

Massive fangs protruded from Djerůn's jaws, strong enough to bite through the toughest sinew and crush the strongest bone. The giant's skull resembled that of a human, only many times bigger, and his skin looked pale and sickly, revealing the yellow blood in his pulsing veins. He had no ears, and his nose consisted of two triangular holes.

His enormous eyes bored into the stricken dwarf. Slowly, he straightened up, walked over, and reached out an armored hand, the fingers of which could crush boulders.

He knows I've seen him. Dear Vraccas, he'll kill me. Balyndis tried to run away, but her stomach was cemented to the ground.

His fingers closed around her mail shirt and lifted her into the air. Trembling, she let go of the skullcap and the helmet, but Djerûn caught them before they hit the floor. He strode toward the platform, deposited Balyndis on top of it, and placed the skullcap and helmet in her hands. His little finger stretched toward her, sliding the blindfold over her eyes.

She blinked in confusion. *He spared me!* The strange growling noise resumed, which she took to mean that Djerûn was ready for her to continue. In any case, it was clear that she was never to mention that she had looked on his face.

Taking a deep breath, she commanded her trembling fingers to be still. A little clumsily at first, then with more assurance, she fitted the skullcap and lowered the helmet over his head, removing her blindfold as soon as the terrifying visage was hidden behind the gleaming visor. Sighing with relief, she got down from the platform and took a few paces back to admire her work.

Djerûn drew himself up to his full height.

Balyndis felt a rush of admiration for the giant. He seemed to like his new armor—and if he didn't, he made no objection. The maga's illegible writing had forced her to deviate from the instructions on several occasions, but Djerûn seemed happy with the result.

She had half expected her improvised formula to end in disaster, but the armor looked fine. *Vraccas and Samusin be praised!*

Bowing to acknowledge her skill, Djerûn picked up his weapons, returned them to their sheaths, and marched to the door, his armor gleaming darkly in the flickering light from the many hearths.

Satisfied with her efforts, but relieved that the job was done, Balyndis wiped the perspiration from her face and noticed that her arms felt like lead. The constant hammering had sapped her strength.

I'll drink a tankard to a job well done, she decided. She left the forge without getting changed and headed to the tavern to celebrate with a tankard of good, strong beer before bed.

Congregated around the bar were some smiths and a few masons, whose hair, beards, and garments were covered in powdered stone. They clinked tankards with Balyndis and congratulated her on Djerûn's new armor.

"Have you heard?" asked one of them excitedly. "We've repaired the Stone Gateway. The doors are locked and bolted again."

"That's fabulous news!" she said, joining in the general jubilation. "You must have been busy while I was in the forge." She shook the mason's hand enthusiastically, raising clouds of dust. "No more orcs, bögnilim, or other invaders.

To think that the northern border is secure." Her heart swelled with pride at the thought that northern Girdlegard was safe because of the dwarves. "To the children of the Smith," she cried, raising her tankard. "To the children of the Smith!" replied the others. They raised .their tankards, and a few moments later, one of the dwarves burst into song.

"The bad times are over," murmured Balyndis happily, taking another long sip and wiping the foam from her lip. "The Northern Pass is sealed, the dwarves stand united, and we've found some new friends." She raised her tankard again, this time nodding at a pale dwarf who was celebrating with the group. "How do you like it here?"

"For the most part, very well. I wonder what Tungdil will make of our realm. I think it's harder for a freeling to adapt to the rules than the other way round."

"Oh," said Balyndis, instantly deflated. She wondered whether Tungdil's decision to leave the kingdom had anything to do with her. *I should really speak to him.* "So Tungdil was serious about visiting the freelings? When does he go?"

"He left four orbits ago," said one of the masons. "He and the twins set off for Trovegold as soon as the Stone Gateway was secure."

Balyndis was shocked that he had left without saying goodbye. *Is he punishing me for accepting Glaïmbar?* She had an unpleasant thought. "Was the freeling doctor with him?"

The mason nodded.

Of course she was.

The others stared in surprise as she emptied her tankard and left without a word.

Wind Chime Island,
Kingdom of Weyurn,
Girdlegard,
Late Spring, 6235th Solar Cycle

It didn't take long for the carriage to convey its unusual passengers to Gastinga.

They broke their journey only once, and that was to make way for a battalion heading west. Under Andôkai's interrogation, the commander told them proudly that he and his men were on a royal mission to investigate a possible threat to the kingdom from the Outer Lands. The maga wished them luck and waved them on their way.

"None of them will make it back," she predicted as the battalion marched past. A few of the men turned their heads and peered into the carriage. "They won't know the territory, and they're trained to fight on water," she said, drawing the curtains. "They'll never survive a battle on land." She knocked on the roof of the carriage to tell the coachman to drive on.

As the road bore to the left, Gastinga emerged through a gray haze of rain.

A collection of tiny houses with clapboard roofs cowered against the ground, sheltering from the swirling winds. Lush green grass surrounded the buildings, and a few boys were watching over a little herd of white cows. Neither the children nor the animals seemed to mind the rain.

So much for it being warmer here. Narmora checked to make sure that her daughter was properly swaddled in her bassinet. Dorsa seemed to like the movement of the carriage—at any rate, she was fast asleep.

Following the guide's instructions, the coachman drew up outside a house and the guide jumped out to fetch the village mayor. The poor fellow was dragged away from his midday meal and marched through the rain to the carriage, where he waited by the window, his flat shoes sinking into the waterlogged grass.

Andôkai seldom bothered with salutations and social niceties when dealing with the lower ranks. "We're looking for relatives of settlers who arrived here seventy cycles ago," she said without preamble. "Where can we find them?"

"At least have the decency to introduce yourself," said the poor man, trying belatedly to exert some authority. "What do you want with them?"

The maga stared at him scornfully. "My name and my business needn't concern you; suffice to say, I'm more important than a mayor. I assume from your reaction that the family is known to you. Kindly tell me where they are." She locked gazes with the man until he looked away. "Is there a reason why we can't see them?"

"No," he replied, raising his arm and pointing down the road. "It's the last house on the left." He hunched his shoulders and hurried back inside.

Narmora noticed his wife and children peering at them through the window, noses pressed to the crown glass pane. They had probably never seen a carriage of any description in their lives.

With a crack of the whip, the coachman drove away.

The wheels of the carriage were still turning when Andôkai jumped out, followed closely by Narmora. The maga hammered on the door until a man of some fifty cycles opened up. His surprise and displeasure changed to undisguised hostility as he studied the women in silence, waiting for them to speak.

"Are you going to let us in?" demanded the maga. It was an order, not a request.

"What for?" he growled. "Your carriage is twice as big as my house." He looked them up and down, trying to guess the reason for their call. "What do you want?" he asked in a heavy dialect.

"We'd like to talk to you, if we may," said Narmora politely. "It's raining out here, and our cloaks are getting wet."

"In that case you'd better talk quickly," snapped the man.

"Listen to me, peasant," said Andôkai, her temper fraying. "We're here to protect Girdlegard from a threat from the Outer Lands." She glowered at him murderously. "If you know what's good for your wife and children, you'll let us in without delay."

A woman's voice sounded from inside the house, and the man, swearing sullenly, stepped aside to let them pass.

They found themselves in a cottage barely bigger than a hut. The walls were black with soot, and seven children were cramped into the tiny room, the youngest barely half a cycle old; the eldest had seen eight cycles at most.

Sitting at the table was their mother, dressed in a coarse linen tunic and a woolen jacket. She looked nervously at the strangers whose cloaks alone were worth more than her house.

Tallow candles permeated the room with a smell of burning fat. The children slept in bunks stacked in a corner of the room, and a ladder led up to an alcove, separated from the main room by a curtain, which was all the privacy that the parents could afford.

To Narmora's surprise, the heap of blankets on one of the lower bunks rolled over and coughed. On closer inspection, it turned out to be a wrinkly old woman whose shriveled body was barely visible among the sheets.

"Thank you for letting us in," said Narmora, nodding kindly at the wife, a woman of forty cycles or so. "Are you descended from the travelers who arrived here from the Outer Lands?"

The woman looked questioningly at her husband, who was standing, arms folded in front of his chest, by the door. He shrugged and turned away.

"I don't understand, madam," said the woman to Narmora. "We're honored by your visit, to be sure, but . . ." A worried look crossed her face. "It's not bad news, is it? You're not going to make us leave Weyurn . . ." She got up, cradling the baby in her arms. "I know we haven't made much of the land here, but the soil isn't right for farming. My husband is a good man, but the fields are like bogs—"

"It's all right, woman," Andôkai said sharply. "We're here to find out about your homeland, not to drive you off your land." She pulled up a stool and sat down, using her cloak as a cushion. "What are people in the Outer Lands afraid of? Evil spirits? Ferocious beasts? The dark power of an evil magus?"

"My homeland?" The woman gave the baby to her husband and sat down, visibly relieved.

Narmora produced four gold coins from her purse and laid them in the woman's chapped hands. "Here, take these," she said gently. "Don't feel obliged to earn the money by embroidering your tale. We're interested in the truth."

The woman stared at the shiny gold coins. "So much?" she said uncertainly. "We could live on these for a cycle. Nothing I can tell you is worth that much."

Her husband strode over and pocketed the coins. "Who are we to refuse their generosity? The money was weighing on her purse."

"Is your husband from the Outer Lands as well?" enquired Narmora.

The woman shook her head. "He's from Weyurn. Aspila is my name. My mother was just a girl when she crossed the Red Range. Her mother left the Outer Lands because of the war."

The maga cleared her throat. "Let's not get distracted," she said tersely. "Did your mother tell you legends about terrifying creatures? Maybe she told you a story about a creature so terrible that no one believes it exists . . ."

Alarmed by the maga's harsh manner, Aspila turned to Narmora. "The war was started by the amsha," she said, resuming her story. "No one knows where they came from. Before anyone knew it, they were massed at the border, and the kingdom was at war. The king and his army could do nothing to stop them, so my grandmother took her daughter and fled. The amsha killed my grandfather and his three brothers, and my grandmother was all alone. She and my mother settled in Weyurn." She paused and frowned. "Can you think of another word for amsha?" she asked her husband. "Amsha is what they call them over there."

"What does it matter?" said Andôkai impatiently. "Since you're intent on telling me about a war that doesn't interest me in the slightest, I may as well ask *her*." She turned to the woman on the bunk. "Are you her mother?"

Aspila looked confused. "But the amsha are a threat. They're gods—powerful gods. Before the invasion, people thought they were a myth, a scary story to make their children behave. Then they found out they were real."

At last she had the maga's attention.

"Why didn't you say so?" snapped Andôkai. "Start from the beginning. What exactly are the amsha?"

Aspila wrung her hands awkwardly, struggling to find the right words. "I don't know what they're called." She looked to the ceiling as if the answer were hanging from the rafters beside the mangy leg of ham.

Narmora smiled and endeavored to compensate for the maga's harshness. *Samusin must be proud of me today.* "Why don't you tell us the rest of the story?" she suggested. "We might be able to work it out."

The woman nodded and began her tale.

In the beginning, the deities created themselves, each more magnificent, splendid, and courageous than the next. Before long, two of their number, Tion and Vraccas, or Kofos and Essgar in the language of my mother, got into an argument about which of the deities was the best.

Kofos insulted Essgar and provoked his wrath. The god of the smithy left his forge and struck the arrogant Kofos with a red-hot hammer. Ten times he hit him, and ten times a piece of the deity fell to the ground and came to life in the form of a god. The amsha—ten living fragments of the dark lord Kofos—were born.

After the tenth blow, Kofos lay stricken on the ground, and Essgar heeded his pleas for mercy.

When Kofos picked himself up, he was surprised to see ten miniature versions of himself flocking around his feet. The bold little fellows demanded to be eaten, insisting that they belonged together as one.

Kofos had no intention of obliging. Laughing scornfully, he raised his boot to crush them. The amsha took flight and swore to avenge themselves on Kofos and his creation.

The ten gods stuck together and devoted themselves to their goal, namely the destruction of Kofos's work.

That was the start of the amsha's campaign.

Intent on punishing Kofos, they hunted the creatures known as orcs, wiped out trolls and ogres, and slaughtered the beasts that Kofos had created to torment our people. Their strength increased by the orbit as they harnessed the power of the beasts they destroyed.

In time, they gathered a following of warriors who saw them as gods of peace. Only the amsha's disciples were spared the fire of their wrath.

Aspila broke off her story to fetch some water.

Narmora breathed out in relief. "Orc-killing, Tion-hating gods aren't much of a threat to our kingdoms. Prince Mallen would welcome them with open arms."

"There's more to the story, madam," said Aspila. "The

amsha are still on a quest to wipe out evil. They were chipped from the body of a god by a red-hot hammer, and fire is their element. The heat they exude is so ferocious that the ground burns beneath their feet. Sometimes they stop for a while, and everything around them turns to ash. I've heard of lakes and rivers drying up as they pass. Everyone is afraid of them. When they invaded, the king summoned the best magicians, the purest creatures, the most honorable men and blameless women. He thought that if he gathered a band of beings who were free from evil he could keep the amsha at bay."

"Did it work?"

Aspila shook her head. "I don't know, madam. My grandmother left before the amsha reached her village."

Narmora remembered the comet that had passed over Girdlegard and enquired whether Aspila knew of a similar incident.

"Oh yes," said a quavery voice.

To the visitors' astonishment, the old woman sat up in bed and looked at them with lively eyes.

"Kofos was struck eleven times, not ten. The last blow was so powerful that the eleventh amsha was catapulted into the firmament and shot through the skies like a ball of fire. My mother used to say that the missing amsha would come back to find his brothers, and the eleven deities would light up the skies with their wrath."

Andôkai placed her fingertips together. The old woman's story fitted with the firstlings' reports of a blazing fire in the west. She glanced at Narmora, who was thinking the same. "Thank you," she said, feigning disappointment. "You tell a good story—not exactly

what we were looking for, but you've earned the coins."
She got up and left.

"May the gods be with you," said Narmora, taking
another coin from her purse and pressing it into Aspila's
hand. "Don't neglect your farm—the money won't last
forever."

She ran the few paces to the carriage and slammed the
door behind her to keep out the rain. The coachmen drove
off before she had time to sit down.

Andôkai was staring through the rain-streaked glass.
Narmora could tell that she was worried. In spite of what
she had said to Aspila, the story of the amsha was exactly
what they were looking for: It proved that Nôd'onn's
warnings were real.

Perhaps we were wrong to kill him, thought Narmora
uneasily. She stroked her sleeping daughter's cheeks. *The
rulers of Girdlegard would never have agreed to a truce*,
she reasoned. *The magus betrayed them and caused the
deaths of thousands of dwarves, elves, and men*. A terrible
thought occurred to her. *Our purest creatures have all
been killed*. Bands of marauding orcs had slaughtered the
last remaining unicorns in the woods of Mifurdania. No
other creature in Girdlegard was as good or pure.

"Avatars." Andôkai's plait unfurled from her hood and
draped itself over her shoulder as she pressed her head
against the window. "If there's any truth in the legend,
the amsha are avatars—manifestations of the divine in
earthly form, which is to say, god-like beings that can't
be destroyed by ordinary weapons." She looked at
Narmora. "You know what that means, don't you?"

"From now on, I'll have to study twice as hard," she

said gravely. Her thoughts turned to little Dorsa. *I want you to have a proper homeland, not a barren desert of soot and ash.* "Should we tell the rulers of the other kingdoms?" she asked, keeping her eyes on her daughter's face.

Andôkai was struck by her famula's reluctance to meet her gaze, but she decided not to pry. "It's for the best. I'll call a meeting of all the leaders of Girdlegard when Djerůn returns from the Outer Lands. The news is too important to be communicated by letter. The kings and queens of Girdlegard will discuss the matter in Porista. Perhaps by then Queen Wey will have tidings of her warriors." She turned to Rosild and looked at her menacingly. "Not a word of this to anyone, or you'll never suckle another child. The people of Girdlegard will learn of the threat from their leaders, not from an idle-tongued girl. No one will hear about the avatars until I've found a means of combating the threat."

Rosild paled and nodded hastily, swearing in the name of Palandiell not to breathe a word of what she knew.

"Good," declared Andôkai. "Let's make haste to Porista. Narmora, you and I have work to do."

"Of course," said the half älf vaguely, still gazing at her child. She was thinking about how the maga had unwittingly earned herself a reprieve: The avatars had to be defeated before Furgas's suffering could be avenged. She turned to the maga and smiled.

Rodario's former leading lady was still a consummate actress.

PART TWO

I

D o you think you'll regret your decision?" asked Myr, looking determinedly ahead. As she walked, she slathered her fair skin with bluish ointment from a little pot to keep off the sun.

Tungdil sensed that something was bothering her. Either she didn't want him to visit the realm of the freelings, or she was embarrassed to be seen with him, or she was worried about him leaving the fifthling folk. *Maybe she blames herself . . .*

"I won't regret it," he said after a while. He kept walking, eyes fixed on the horizon as the sun sank lower and lower, bathing Girdlegard in fierce red light. "You don't think I left because of you, do you?"

"Left the kingdom, or left Balyndis?"

Tungdil had to think for a moment. "Left Glaïmbar and Balyndis," he said firmly. "At any rate, it wasn't because of you—which isn't to say you don't matter to me. You're different to other dwarf maidens; you're a breath of air for my scholarly soul." He turned his head and they gazed at each other for a moment. Her red eyes were full of hope.

"I need time, Myr. I can't make sense of what I'm feeling because my heart and mind are so confused." He smiled wryly. "It will do me good to get away. It's why I left the fifthling kingdom—to figure out what I want. Besides, I'm curious to see how the freelings live."

She averted her gaze, focusing on a point in the distance. They had been marching toward the pond for orbits. "It's all right," she said, nodding slowly. "I can wait."

Tungdil's train of thought was interrupted by a sudden noise. He turned round to see Boëndal doubled up with laughter, arms braced against his thighs, howling with mirth. Tears were streaming from his eyes.

Tungdil smiled. "I haven't seen anyone laugh like that since the joke about the orc who wanted directions from a dwarf. What did you say to him?"

Boïndil shrugged. "Nothing. I was telling him about the realm of the freelings and he laughed in my face," he reported in a slightly wounded tone. "I explained how we had to jump into a p—"

His words were drowned out by another roar of laughter as Boëndal sank to his knees, shaking with mirth. For a moment, conversation was impossible.

"Look what you've done to me," spluttered Boëndal. "I was nearly frozen to death, and now you've practically killed me with your jokes." He stood up and brushed the dirt from his breeches. "A pond!" he muttered, still hiccoughing with laughter. "As if a dwarf would dip a toe in Elria's accursed water!" Wiping the tears from his eyes, he looked up and saw their faces. At last it dawned on him that Boïndil was serious. "No," he said, horrified. "We're not really going to . . . ? I mean, all the way to the bottom?" He was too traumatized to say the words "water" or "pond".

Boïndil clapped him on the back. "It's all right, brother.

Tungdil and I jumped in last time, and it's over before you know it. If you get scared, just look at the fish."

Boëndal cast a skeptical look at Myr. "It can't be the only way into your realm," he said suspiciously. "How are your warriors going to get home? Don't tell me they're going to jump into the water like an army of frogs."

She grinned, showing her pearly white teeth. "There are other entrances, but Gemmil told us to keep them secret. I took Tungdil and your brother by a different route, but they were blindfolded first." She returned the pot of ointment to her pack and led them into the woods surrounding the pond. "I'm sorry, Boëndal, but you're going to have to take the plunge. It's not as bad as it sounds."

"No," said Boïndil crossly. "It's much, much worse. I had brackish water in my ears for orbits, and Elria was laughing in my head."

"At least it proves that dwarves don't necessarily drown in deep water," said Tungdil, trying to make them see the bright side.

Boëndal frowned, all trace of amusement vanishing from his face. His mood was grim as they marched through the forest that was formerly home to Lesinteïl's elves, and he continued to scowl as they stole through the meadow on the lookout for enemies. By the time they discovered the bleached bones of their murdered comrades, his brow was creased in a permanent frown.

The party collected the scattered remains and buried them under a pile of stones. With the skeletons laid to rest, the dead dwarves would be free to warm their souls in Vraccas's smithy.

It was dusk when they stepped onto the pier. Each of

them held a chunk of granite as large as a dwarven head—
Myr had advised them to use the debris from the elves'
ruined temple to speed their journey to the bottom of the
pond. They gathered at the end of the pier.

"I'll go first," said Myr, beaming at Boëndal, who was
eying the water suspiciously. She stepped off the pier and
disappeared into the darkness below.

"She's gone," he said anxiously. "Are you sure we
should . . ."

"Ha, you were brave enough to fight Nôd'onn, and
now you're scared of a pond," his brother said airily.

"Weren't you thrown into the water by a bull?" asked
Tungdil, raising an eyebrow.

Boïndil waved a hand dismissively. "That was last time."
He stepped to the edge of the pier and looked down at
the water with distaste. "Accursed pond. It's dark and
cold," he grumbled, leaping into the air and landing in
the water with an almighty splash. He disappeared.

"I suppose I've got no choice," sighed Boëndal, resigning
himself to his fate. He took a deep breath, closed his eyes,
and held his nose. A moment later, he was gone.

It was left to Tungdil to bring up the rear. The water
closed over his head and he found himself staring into
inky blackness. It was only because of the pressure in his
ears that he knew that he was sinking, pulled down by
the weight of his armor, his ax, and the granite.

He heard the sound of a waterfall, and a moment later
he was falling with the cascading water, which pushed him
under the surface of the pool. The current brought him up
again and deposited him on the bank.

Coughing and spluttering, he clambered to his feet. The

twins were there too, and he could tell from their noisy expiration that their lungs were filled with water. Myr was tightening her belt, which had loosened when she jumped.

"Next time I'm going a different way," spluttered Boëndal, shaking himself vigorously and spraying water in all directions. He and the others were soaked through, and water was streaming from their undergarments and collecting on the floor. "How am I going to dry my chain mail?" he growled, running a hand over his chest. "You'd better have some good oil."

Myr ran a hand through her bedraggled hair and laughed. "We'll find you some warm clothes," she promised, striding to a vast oak door with thick iron bands. She knocked loudly. "And I'm sure I can get you some oil."

A panel opened and a pair of red eyes peered at Myr and the others. The dwarf disappeared, then the bolts slid back and the door swung open, admitting them to the freelings' realm.

In the next chamber, Gemmil was waiting to greet them. He shook hands with them one by one, although the twins seemed a little wary.

"Did Sanda and her army get there in time?" he asked anxiously. Myr gave a brief account of how the orcs had been defeated. "And the fifthlings have repaired the Stone Gateway," she recounted. "For the first time in a thousand cycles, the northern border is secure."

"My heart weeps for our fallen comrades," the freeling leader said gravely. "Before you go, we'll raise a tankard to our victory and remember the dead." He pointed to a pile of blankets. "Wrap yourselves in those. You'll catch a chill."

"Clothes would be more practical," grumbled Boïndil.

"You'll find clean outfits in your lodgings," the king told him, opening a door at the back of the room. Outside a wagon was waiting for them. Tungdil and the others clambered in, and they set off, juddering and rattling, along the underground rail. Some time later the wagon stopped and everyone got out. The king led them through a magnificent hall to a double door.

"Follow me," he said, pressing his ring against the runes engraved in the door. The symbols pulsed with light and the doors swung open, spilling pale light toward them. "Enter, friends. Welcome to the realm of the freelings."

Tungdil and the twins stepped forward and found themselves on a broad ledge, from which a flight of steps led down to Gemmil's realm. Tungdil heard an awed "Vraccas almighty" from Boëndal behind him. They stared down in amazement.

Below them was a vast city with buildings of all sizes lined up in a grid of symmetrical streets, alleyways, and squares. By Tungdil's reckoning, it covered two square miles, and the roof of the cavern was at least a mile and a half high.

On the outskirts of the city, two waterfalls fell from a height of four hundred paces into a reservoir that supplied a network of canals, some of which led to gardens and allotments, others disappearing into openings in the rock.

From above, the city's inhabitants looked tiny, no bigger than cave ants. Tungdil, straining his ears, heard a soft murmur of voices, the sharp ring of countless hammers, and other noises that he knew from human cities.

Rows of houses shaped like cubes lined the gentle slope

at the far end of the cavern, at the top of which sat a small, but ornately fashioned stronghold. Light came from shimmering moss that covered the walls of the cavern, bathing the city in a gentle, brown glow. There were burning buckets of coal suspended from masts at various points throughout the settlement, with polished sheets of metal reflecting the light of the fiery flames.

"It's incredible," said Tungdil to Gemmil, who was standing at his side. "I never imagined your realm would be so big."

The king pointed down at the city. "Trovegold is one of five—"

"Five?" interrupted Boïndil in astonishment.

"One of five major cities," Gemmil continued proudly. "Five thousand freelings inhabit this place, five thousand souls living in freedom, unencumbered by the rules of family and clan, blessed by Vraccas, and bound only by the will of the Smith."

Boïndil puffed out his cheeks, but Tungdil signaled to him to keep quiet. "Where will we be staying?" he enquired.

Gemmil pointed to a house in the city center. "Those are your quarters," he said. "You'll be staying with Myr. Her house is in the thick of things so you'll get a proper taste of city life. Sanda and I live in the stronghold, but I'll call for you tomorrow and show you around." He nodded to Myr and bade them good night.

"Follow me," she said to the others, starting down the steps. "It's an honor to have you as my guests."

Tungdil and the twins brought up the rear.

With every step, the city increased in size, and soon the neat grid of streets became a maze of roads and buildings, although Tungdil could still detect an under-lying symmetry. A fresh wind swept the smoke away from the smithies and workshops and provided the city with good, clean air.

Soon they were walking through streets and alleyways. Dwarven ballads echoed from inside a couple of taverns, and on the pavements, freeling traders were hawking anvils, tools, jewelry, and other wares. A steel statue of Vraccas towered ten paces above the ground, glittering with gold and vraccasium and studded with sparkling gems.

No one stopped or questioned them. Their presence went almost unnoticed, except for the occasional greeting directed at Myr.

"Have you seen their funny beards?" whispered Boïndil. "I swear I saw an old dwarf with a completely naked chin. And they're wearing perfume—I can smell it." He wrinkled his nose. "By the hammer of Vraccas, they'll soon be speaking elvish and growing pointy ears."

"Where are their weapons?" hissed Boëndal. "Most of them aren't wearing mail. It's a rum sort of place."

"Why would anyone wear mail?" asked Myr, stopping in front of her house. "Our realm is safe from orcs and other beasts. Wearing mail is completely unnecessary. It drags you down."

"*Unnecessary?*" snorted Boïndil, turning to his companions. "What kind of dwarf goes without chain mail and axes? It's like walking around with no breeches or boots!"

"For you, maybe, but not for us." For the first time Myr sounded put out. It was hard not to be offended by Boïndil's gruff and forthright manner. In fact, his tactless comments were liable to cause as much damage as his blades.

She unlocked the door and stepped inside. "Come in and go straight upstairs—I don't want you ruining my carpets," she said, shooting Boïndil an angry look. She disappeared into another room.

"Carpets?" muttered Boïndil incredulously. "What next? Scented water for our hands?"

"Don't be rude," said Tungdil. "We're guests here, remember?" He led the way up a flight of stone steps to their quarters. As Gemmil had promised, there was a selection of dry clothes.

They picked out the right sizes and peeled off their wet undergarments.

As soon as Tungdil was changed, he took a closer look at their quarters and found another, narrower staircase. He went up the steps and came to a hatch. A moment later, he was standing on Myr's roof.

Amid the noise from the city he heard scraps of conversation. Mostly it was boring, like complaints about the price of vegetables, but every now and then someone would mention the new arrivals or start a discussion about the other kingdoms.

As far as Tungdil could tell, the majority of freelings weren't enamored with the idea of reestablishing contact with a traditional dwarven kingdom. They were outlaws, after all.

It works both ways, I suppose, he thought, somehow comforted by the realization that both sides had their doubts. He took a step forward to get a proper look.

Some of the dwarves had pale hair and pale skin, others

looked no different to Tungdil and the twins. They greeted each other respectfully, exchanged pleasantries, and went their separate ways.

After a while, an octagonal temple caught his eye. It was situated near the statue of Vraccas, and its five tall chimneys released plumes of white smoke, infusing the air with a smell of herbs and hot metal that dispersed on the wind. Tungdil guessed that the priests were conducting a ceremony in honor of the Smith.

The pale smoke reminded him of the strange mist that had surrounded them in the caves of the Outer Lands where he had discovered the mysterious rune. *I wonder if the undergroundlings pray to Vraccas as well?*

"We're in time for evening prayers," said Myr, behind him.

Startled, he took a step forward, coming dangerously close to the edge of the roof. Myr reached out and grabbed him. He swayed backward, knocked into her, and flung out his arms to stop her falling.

For the time it takes a drop of beer to fall to the floor, they were locked together in a tight embrace. Tungdil, feeling the warmth of her body and the curve of her breasts, was glad that he had taken off his mail.

He cleared his throat and stepped away. "Evening prayers?" he queried casually. Turning to look at the temple, he saw the doors fly open.

Five dozen dwarves dressed in the garb of the Smith filed out and took up position on the steps; their places had clearly been allocated in advance. Everyone seemed to know exactly where to stand. The last dwarf, carrying a steel sledgehammer, came to a halt beside an anvil of pure vraccasium.

"It's how we praise Vraccas at the end of an orbit," she explained. "I told the twins to come up and watch."

Boïndil squeezed through the hatch. He wasn't wearing his precious chain mail, but his axes were dangling from his belt. "The best seats are taken, are they? In that case, I'll stand at the back." He peered at the temple. "What are they doing?" he asked, staring at the priests. Myr explained the ritual. "Oh," he said. "In our kingdom we pray on our own. We give thanks together only on special occasions."

"It's pretty well organized," remarked Boëndal, stepping onto the roof. "What happens next?"

A horn sounded, its deep, rich tone echoing through the streets and summoning the citizens of Trovegold to the statue in the square.

The crowd kept swelling until the square was full of bobbing heads, some dark, others white as snow. Tungdil spotted more dwarves on top of the other buildings, which were flat roofed like Myr's. Everyone in the city stopped what they were doing and turned to face the statue. Myr and the others looked expectantly at the priests.

The dwarf behind the anvil lifted the sledgehammer into the air, holding it above his head as if it weighed nothing at all. "Vraccas, hear our prayers of praise and adoration," he called loudly, lowering his arms to smite the anvil.

The metal rang out, producing a clear, high note, and gleaming sparks flew through the air, leaving comet-like trails and landing in braziers on either side of the steps. The staircase lit up with bright white flames.

The priest in the middle of the group tilted back his head and began to sing. His voice was rich and vibrant.

When the first verse was over, a second priest joined in, and so on and so forth until half the priests were singing.

What started as a solo became a stirring chorus of many singers, which swelled again as the hammer struck the anvil and the remaining priests joined in. Tungdil, who had never heard the like of it, felt a shiver run down his spine.

The hymn of thanks stirred the heart of every dwarf in Trovegold, including Boëndal and Boïndil, who had lumps in their throats. Forgetting their reservations, they dropped to their knees and adopted the freelings' collective method of prayer.

Thrilled by the atmosphere, Tungdil watched in awed silence, wishing the singing would last forever, and knowing that it would end.

The priests finished the final verse and fell silent. The hymn reverberated through the cavern, returning as a faint echo that gradually melted away. The priest struck the anvil for a third and final time, the choir filed back into the temple, and the congregation rose to their feet. The spell was broken.

"So that's that," whispered Boïndil as the temple doors closed. "What about morning prayers?" he enquired hopefully, turning to Myr.

The firstling smiled. "You'll have to lead your own prayers in the morning. The next service takes place tomorrow at dusk." She shooed him downstairs. "I don't know about you, but I'm going straight to bed after dinner. You should probably get as much rest as you can. Gemmil will want to show you every last alleyway in Trovegold; he's very proud of our city."

A few moments later, they were seated around a table of sand-colored rock, ready to sample Myr's cooking. Some of the dishes were unfamiliar to Tungdil; the twins eyed the food with obvious suspicion.

Myr didn't seem to mind. "Boiled moss, tuber-leaf salad, and sautéed cutlet in dark beer sauce," she explained. "They're traditional dishes from the five dwarven folks— adapted and improved by us." She gave them each a generous helping, and they tucked in heartily, their appetite overcoming their doubts.

"Mm," said Boïndil happily, holding out his plate for more. "The meat tastes good. It's not goat, is it?"

"It's prime loin of gugul. You won't find any in Trovegold—we hunt them in the tunnels."

Boïndil looked at her blankly.

"It's a type of beetle," explained Myr. "They're as long as you're tall, and pretty nippy. They make a lovely roast." She pointed to the morsel of cheese on his fork. "Beetle cheese. Gugul milk curdles on contact with air, so it's simply a question of salting and stretching it." She gave him another serving and handed back his plate.

Boïndil's fork was poised in mid air. He stared dumbly at the cutlet, wondering what to do.

"Lost your appetite, have you, brother?" teased Boëndal, taking another mouthful and licking his lips. "It hasn't done Myr any harm, so it's hardly going to kill you." He picked up his tankard and emptied it in a single draft. His burp was unusually restrained; he was on his best behavior because of Myr.

"Do you like our beer?" she enquired eagerly.

"It's delicious," he said approvingly, helping himself to

more. "It's got an interesting aftertaste—a hint of malt or spice or something."

"We spice the beer with—"

Boëndal removed the tankard from his lips and held up a hand to quiet her. "Don't," he said. "I'd rather not know if you flavored it with powdered maggot or caterpillar blood or Vraccas knows what. It tastes too good for you to spoil it." He carried on drinking, and Myr said nothing, smiling to herself.

Dessert was a pale creamy dish that tasted a bit like honey. Tungdil found a husk in his bowl that looked suspiciously like the casing of a maggot, but he finished his serving and kept the discovery to himself.

Boïndil requested seconds, but this time he didn't enquire what went into the dish. Tired, sated, and slightly tipsy, they swayed up the stairs and tumbled into bed.

"I'm glad we came with you," murmured Boïndil, loosening his belt and letting out a big belch to make space in his belly. "If we stay much longer, I won't fit into my mail shirt. Myr's cooking tastes too good."

The other two laughed. "I'm glad you came as well," said Tungdil seriously. "I thought I might be traveling on my own."

"After all we've been through?" exclaimed Boïndil. "We'll always be here for you—especially if you insist on risking your life among outcasts and criminals. Someone has to watch your back!"

"Outcasts and criminals," echoed Tungdil thoughtfully. "I haven't seen or heard anything to suggest that the freelings are any less respectable than the other folks."

Boëndal yawned and crossed his arms behind his head.

"You seem to be forgetting that they were banished from their kingdoms—which means they, or their parents or grandparents, were guilty of a crime." He gave Tungdil a hard look. "The same goes for Myr."

"Myr saved your life," snapped Tungdil testily.

"I know, and I won't forget it. That's why Boïndil has sworn to protect her—but it doesn't change who she is."

"That's not the only oath we've taken," said Tungdil, thinking of the vows of friendship pledged after the battle of the Blacksaddle. "We wanted a unified Girdlegard, and that means *all* men, elves, and dwarves, the freelings included. Gemmil spoke of five main cities—five cities the size of Trovegold! We need to ally ourselves with the freelings for the sake of Girdlegard and the security of our borders." He met Boëndal's eye and held his gaze with dwarven tenacity. "It's our responsibility to find out more about them and their customs before we come to any decisions about whether our differences can be bridged." He paused, fixing the twins with a steely stare. "To be honest, they seem a good deal more welcoming and forgiving than some dwarves I know."

Boëndal looked up at the ceiling. "Vraccas will open our eyes to the truth," he said elliptically, settling down to sleep.

Sighing, Tungdil stared glumly into the darkness. *I'd have more luck bending steel than changing a dwarven mind.* He was grateful to the twins for coming with him to Trovegold, but he wished they were a little friendlier toward their hosts. Even Boëndal, who was usually quite reasonable, seemed to have ruled out the possibility of forging a lasting bond with Gemmil's dwarves. *Why does it have to be so hard?* he thought wearily.

"What are we going to do about Keenfire?" asked Boïndil, breaking the silence. "You're not going to let the hollow-eyes keep her, are you?"

"Why don't you ask Glaïmbar?" said Tungdil snidely. He closed his eyes. "I'll get the ax back. We don't need it right now, and it won't be much use to the älfar, but I won't delay too long: Keenfire belongs with the dwarves."

"Hurrah," cheered Boïndil, sensing a new adventure. "You can count me in!"

Kingdom of Dsôn Balsur,
Girdlegard,
Early Summer, 6235th Solar Cycle

Ondori breathed in the smoke billowing over her homeland and shuddered, remembering the red-hot flames that had burned her face. The struggle for Keenfire had left her horribly disfigured and given her another reason to wear a mask.

From her vantage point in the watchtower, originally constructed by the elves of the Golden Plains, she gazed at the thick bank of smoke in the south.

Dsôn Balsur was on the brink of defeat.

Firebombs rained into the dense woodland from allied mangonels, spilling petrol, oil, pitch, and sulfur, and setting light to everything, including the silicified wood of the fossilized trees. Already the allies had burned a wide path through the forest toward the bone palace. They were a fair few miles from Dsôn Balsur, but the remaining distance consisted largely of flat, open land.

Ondori turned to face the capital. Midway between Dsôn Balsur and the forest lay the stronghold of Arviû, from whence reinforcements were marching toward the front. Soon every last älf would be fighting for the kingdom.

She ran a hand over her quarterstaff. *We'll make the allies pay for their victory*, she vowed. *They've had enough of our arrows; let's see how they like our staffs.*

She left the tower and descended the fifty paces to the ground. Every step was slow and considered, her movements hampered by the damage inflicted by Tungdil's dagger. The pain was a constant, humiliating reminder of her disastrous mission to secure the groundlings' kingdom. She had failed on all counts: The groundlings were ensconced in their stronghold, her parents' murderers were still alive, and she had failed to learn the secret of the orcs' unnatural power. Forced to flee the battlefield, she had stopped only to snatch up a drinking pouch, knowing that wasted hours looking for streams or rivers could lead to capture or death. It was only much later, when she uncorked the pouch, that she realized her mistake: The water was stagnant, brackish, and unpalatable, but she drank it all the same.

The immortal siblings, after hearing how the five-thousand-strong orcish army had been defeated by a handful of dwarves, had banished her to the front, where she was to die in defense of her kingdom. To her relief, the siblings had confiscated Keenfire: She never wanted to touch the accursed weapon again.

Ondori was content with her fate. Death would come as a release, the last chance of heroism at the end of life of abject failure. *Although I can't avenge my parents when*

I'm dead, she thought bitterly. At least the immortal siblings had granted her a final favor: A hundred warriors, all failures like herself, were at her command.

She emerged from the base of the tower and swung herself onto her fire bull. Her eyes wandered over the waiting group of älfar—warriors of both sexes whose courage had been found wanting.

"Listen to me, weak-hearted warriors," she said harshly. "I'm taking you behind enemy lines. Your mission is to kill ten elves, dwarves, or humans before you die. Anyone who flees the battle will be chased by my arrows or Agrass's horns." She patted the thick black neck of the fire bull. "Acquit yourselves well: Tion's judgment awaits you when you get to the other side, and eternal agony is the price of failure. Those who prove themselves worthy will receive the blessing of the immortal siblings, the mark of which I bear."

She nodded to the warrior at the head of the procession, and the troop set off on a southerly bearing. Ondori rode at the back, keeping a careful watch for defectors.

It took less than an orbit to reach the forest where the allies' firebombs were whizzing through the trees.

Another mile, and they'll be marching across the plains, she thought, dismally. She had foreseen the fall of Dsôn Balsur from the watchtower, but the reality of the situation came as a shock. The allies were closer to victory than she had thought.

A warrior in black armor emerged from the trees. "The immortal siblings want you to destroy the mangonels and kill those responsible for the bombardment," he told her tersely. His manner indicated all too plainly that he considered her unworthy of respect. He handed her a scroll detailing the strategy for the attack. "My band will distract them while you and your troop set light to the oil drums. We'll figure out the rest from there." His gaze rested on her mask. "Are you too ugly to show yourself?" he demanded, reaching out to tear off her mask and veil.

Agrass let out a belligerent snort and turned his head so that his left horn grazed the warrior's chest. The älf paled and took a step back.

"It's a pity you're a coward," Ondori told him coldly. "If you were to see my face, you'd know . . ." She trailed off, remembering that Keenfire had stolen her looks. ". . . that I'm ready to die," she finished lamely.

"No one's stopping you," he hissed, disappearing among the trees.

After relaying her orders to the troop, she led them in a westerly direction, looking for a safe route into the forest where they wouldn't be spotted by enemy guards. Four miles later, they found a suitable place and rested until midnight, before stealing their way toward the camp.

Ondori stopped and cursed. She and her troop were perfectly placed to attack, but the camp was guarded by a battalion of groundlings and elves.

There was a constant screeching and groaning as wind-lasses turned, tightening the ropes to pull back the wooden catapults. Dripping pouches were placed in the metal cups at the end of each arm and the contents set alight with a burning torch, whereupon the arms were released and a hail of fiery missiles hissed through the night and crashed among the trees. The burning petroleum turned the forest into a sea of twisting flames.

"Tion wants us to die gloriously," she whispered to the

others. "See the groundlings and the tree-loving fairies? Their destruction is our salvation." She gripped her quarterstaff and held it aloft like a lance. "Prepare for attack. And don't forget, I'll be watching you—desertion is punishable by death."

A few moments later, they heard shouts from the other side of the encampment. Horns sounded the alarm, warning the dwarves and the elves of an älvish incursion. The diversionary tactic seemed to work.

"Now," she said loudly, and her warriors rushed forward, keeping low to the ground. In the darkness, they were all but invisible, and their boots moved noiselessly across the forest floor. The elves and dwarves, expecting an attack on the opposite flank, were taken by surprise.

Ondori waited until all her warriors were engaged in combat. When she was sure that no one had slipped into the undergrowth, she left her hiding place and threw herself into the scrum.

The elves had no chance to use their bows and were forced into close combat. Dwarves rushed to their aid and surrounded their hated enemies, swinging their axes and hammers with grim determination.

Ondori's heart sank as she watched the elves and dwarves close ranks to ward off the invaders.

Soon dwarven axes were slashing at the älfar from behind a wall of shields. The elves lined up in rows behind them, ready with their spears. The älfar came to a standstill three hundred paces from the barrels of oil.

"What's the matter with you?" Ondori shouted angrily, stabbing her quarterstaff into the back of a retreating älf. "Don't let up!"

Just then a dwarf cried out in agony and sank to his knees, breaking the wall of shields. The tip of an elven spear protruded from his chest.

"Did you see that?" shouted a dwarven voice. "The pointy-eared villain stabbed him in the back!" There was an almighty crash and an elf slumped to the ground, felled by a ferocious blow from a morning star. "Children of the Smith, the pointy-ears have betrayed our vows of friendship!" howled the dwarf, voice cracking with grief and rage. "Death to the traitors!"

Ondori heard an elven curse, and a moment later, an arrow sang through the air and came to rest in a dwarven skull. The sturdy warrior's face was frozen in astonishment as he fell to the ground. An elf sprawled on top of him, a dwarven ax in his back.

Two dozen dwarves turned as one and advanced toward their supposed allies, who raised their weapons to block the attack. At first the elves parried and checked the dwarven axes, but soon both sides were locked in combat.

Ondori could hardly believe her luck. *The dwarves and elves need more than a promise of friendship to bridge an age-old rift . . .* She bellowed at her warriors to resume the attack, and the älfar surged forward, finding the gaps in the allies' defenses and slaughtering elves and dwarves alike.

Ondori, trusting in Tion to watch over her warriors, left the battlefield and rode toward the undefended encampment. The men loading the mangonels stared at her in horror as she galloped past and seized a burning torch from the hand of a guard.

Lowering his head, Agrass charged into the pile of oil

barrels, destroying them with his horns. The burning torch landed in the middle of the spillage, turning the foul-smelling oil into a fiery lake. More barrels exploded, further fuelling the flames.

Ondori didn't stop to watch. She was busy cutting down the men at the mangonels, none of whom were trained warriors. They put up little resistance to Ondori and her fire bull, and their deaths were painful, but swift.

With one exception.

Unbeknown to Ondori, one of the men had escaped the bloodbath and sheltered behind a mangonel's wheel. He waited until she rode past, then hurled his spear, hitting her in the back. The tip pierced her heart. Ondori gasped, fighting for breath as she wrenched the weapon from her chest. Slumped in her saddle, she listened to the man's receding footsteps and waited for death to take her soul.

After a while, the pain in her chest subsided and she was able to sit up. She raised a hand to the exit wound and ran her fingers over her flesh. The wound had closed. *I'm not dead*, she realized in amazement. *Tion has made me immortal like the orcs* . . . In a flash of understanding, she remembered how she had drunk of the orcs' foul water. *Tion be praised*, she thought, resolving to tell the immortal siblings of her discovery.

But first she would carry out her orders and destroy the mangonels. Steering Agrass to the edge of the blaze, she lowered her quarterstaff and dragged it across the ground to the mangonels, cutting a furrow through the forest floor. A river of burning liquid flowed toward the wooden siege engines.

Soon flames were licking at the timber and creeping

hungrily along the ropes. *My work isn't finished,* she thought proudly, pressing gently against the fire bull's flanks and cantering back to the battle. *Let's find more elvish souls for Tion to torture . . .*

Roaring, Agrass charged through the enemy lines, tossing elves and dwarves into the air like rag dolls. His powerful, metal-sheathed horns pierced everything they encountered—shields, armor, and guts. Shaking his head furiously, he sank his pointed teeth into his victims' torsos, ripping out chunks of leather, metal, and flesh.

To Ondori's astonishment, she and her warriors triumphed over the battalion of elves and dwarves. *They brought it on themselves,* she thought gleefully, remembering how the allies had turned on each other. She touched the mark on her forehead. *Tion is with me.*

The flames from the burning mangonels were clearly visible throughout the forest by the time the survivors alerted their allies to their plight. But the humans came too late.

Elves and dwarves lay dead or dying on the battlefield and, on seeing the new arrivals, the remaining älfar slipped into the forest and disappeared among the gloomy boughs. Arrows and crossbow bolts whizzed past them, missing their targets.

A few paces away from the clearing, Ondori stopped and looked in satisfaction at the inferno raging in the enemy camp. Agrass snorted and swung his head to the left. "A fugitive?" she asked. The fire bull raked a metal-plated hoof against the ground. *Who could it be?* she wondered. *An elf for Tion to torture, or a deserter who deserves my wrath?*

The bull slunk through the trees. In the faint moonlight,

Ondori spotted four squat figures running through the undergrowth. *Groundlings,* she thought, surprised. *It's not often you see them running from a fight.*

A moment later, she was upon them.

Hearing Agrass's hooves, they turned to face her, weapons raised.

"Clear off, and we'll spare you," growled their leader from behind a metal visor. He gave his morning star a menacing swing.

"Spare me?" she spat scornfully. Just then she realized that one of them was holding a bow. The string snapped back and she dodged the arrow, which buried itself in a tree. "A fairy bow?" she exclaimed, confused. "What would a groundling want with a . . ." Her eyes widened. "A morning star and a fairy bow . . . It was you! You started the quarrel on purpose." She peered at the band. "Who are you?"

"I said, clear off," snapped their leader. "We're stronger than you, and we're not afraid to prove it."

Ondori was tempted to put the matter to the test, but an angry mob of humans, emboldened by fury, had summoned the courage to pursue her through the trees. She could tell from the clunking armor, raised voices, and flickering torches that the men were approaching fast.

"Are you thirdlings?" she asked sharply. "Why don't you send an envoy to Dsôn Balsur? Together we could defeat our common foe."

"Clear off, or die," their leader threatened.

Ondori decided that it wasn't the time or the place to risk her life against four groundlings. Her failure at the Blacksaddle had been redeemed in part by her success on the battlefield, and a foolhardy skirmish with a band of groundlings would do little to improve her stock. Tugging on the reins, she turned and rode off to find the rest of her band, leaving the four dwarves behind her.

Nagsor and Nagsar will welcome the news of the groundlings' rift.

The thirdlings' intervention, though unexpected, was welcome. Ondori had no idea what they were plotting, but it was bound to mean trouble for the other dwarven folks. *We'll have to keep an eye on them*, she decided. *With luck, the children of Inàste will profit from their game.*

Porista,
Former Realm of Lios Nudin,
Girdlegard,
Autumn, 6235th Solar Cycle

We can't wait forever, Estimable Maga," said Narmora, looking up from her reading. "Wasn't Djerůn supposed to be home by now? I thought you told him to be back within eighty orbits."

The fair-haired maga nodded wearily. They were sitting opposite each other in the library, Andôkai with her right elbow propped on the armrest of her easy chair. She rested her forehead on her palm, feeling the weight of the thoughts that had been troubling her since Weyurn. "He's been gone 132 orbits," she murmured. "It isn't like Djerůn to be late; something must be stopping him . . ." She stood up fretfully. "I'd understand if he were an ordinary warrior, but Djerůn is—"

"He's the king of Tion's creation," finished Narmora. "I know the legend. 'The son of Samusin', my people call him. He keeps order among Tion's beasts, destroying the weak and hunting the cowardly."

"I keep forgetting your mother was an älf. In that case, I'm sure you understand that whatever is keeping him must be tremendously powerful."

"How do you . . . I mean, where did you find him?"

"I saved him from a band of men. I couldn't bear the thought of a magnificent creature like Djerûn dying at the hands of fame-seekers and glory-hunters, so I rescued him, and he became my bodyguard. Over a hundred cycles have passed since then . . ." She snorted angrily, snatched up a candlestick, and hurled it against the shelves. "To blazes with it all! We'll never find out what's happening in the Outer Lands."

"Didn't Weyurn's warriors have anything to report?" enquired Narmora, eager to learn the contents of the maga's correspondence.

Andôkai smiled wryly. "They've disappeared, as I said they would." She took a scroll of parchment from the folds of her crimson robe. "According to Queen Xamtys, they left via the Red Range and haven't been heard of since. Her sentries are on the lookout for survivors, but it doesn't look good. Xamtys thinks the fire is spreading in the Outer Lands. There's a bright red glow across the border, and it's getting closer all the time." She pointed to the rows of books. "The combined wisdom of Girdlegard's scholars, and what does it tell us? Nothing!" She paced to and fro, stopping behind Narmora. "You've worked hard," she said, resting her hands on the half älf's shoulders. "I wouldn't have thought it possible that a student could make such progress. We might be strong enough to fight the avatars after all."

"We don't know for sure that the avatars are to blame for the fire in the Outer Lands." Narmora took the letter from the maga and read it, uninvited. "Hmm," she said thoughtfully. "Queen Xamtys says no one is crossing into Girdlegard from the west. She thinks something must be stopping traders and beasts from leaving the Outer Lands."

"Which confirms our theory that the avatars are getting closer," said Andôkai, straightening up and returning to her chair.

Relieved that the maga was no longer standing over her, Narmora gave herself a little shake. She could feel the imprint of Andôkai's hands on her shoulders, red with the blood of Furgas and her son.

The maga pulled out a sheet of parchment and inked her quill. "I hope to Samusin that Djerŭn is still alive, but I can't delay any longer. If we don't hold the meeting now, the dwarves, elves, and men won't arrive before winter, and they're bound to get stuck in the snow."

"They'll come as soon as they can," Narmora assured her. "There's plenty to discuss." According to reports, cracks were appearing in the great alliance. News had reached Porista of a dispute that had arisen between the elves and dwarves during a battle in Dsôn Balsur. Both sides were refusing to take arms against the älfar until the other apologized, but neither was prepared to accept the blame. The destruction of the siege engines was a further obstacle to the allies' progress, granting the älfar a dangerous reprieve.

Narmora recalled the rumors about King Belletain's army.

"We'll have to ask the king of Urgon why his warriors are marching north. There's speculation that he means to attack the fourthlings, but he's probably after the trolls. Isn't his physician a dwarf?"

"Belletain is a cretinous cripple," pronounced Andôkai, lowering her quill. "He took over from his nephew Lothaire, whom the people loved and admired. Belletain has profited from his nephew's popularity, although it's more a case of pity than respect. A mad king and an adoring populace—it's a dangerous mix."

"If you don't mind, I need to check on Dorsa," said Narmora, straightening up and striding to the door. "I'll be back in time for my lesson." She left the library and hurried through the empty corridors of the palace.

Dorsa was tucked up in her cot. For a moment, Narmora feared that the weight of the blankets had crushed her little chest, which was ridiculous, of course. The little girl was sleeping peacefully, tiny arms beside her head. Her breathing was calm and regular, which set Narmora's mind at ease

"How you've grown," she whispered, stroking the baby's downy head.

Her daughter was an endless source of comfort, proof that everything would be all right. A single smile from Dorsa was enough to banish all her doubts. Narmora could gaze forever at her sweet dimpled cheeks and tiny mouth, but sometimes another face would haunt her, the face of a tiny, lifeless baby moldering under a pile of stones.

She stooped down to kiss the pointy tip of her daughter's left ear. Dorsa smiled in her sleep. "Sleep well, my darling," she whispered softly. "Your brother's death will be avenged."

She left the nursery on tiptoe and crossed the corridor to Furgas's room. Hearing the door open, Rodario leaped to his feet, dagger in hand. "Oh, it's you," he said shamefacedly. His forehead was lined with creases from the sheets, indicating that he had been asleep.

"Honestly, Rodario," she said briskly. "What would the maga think if she found you in the palace with a dagger? You'll have to do better than this; I'm relying on your talents as an actor." She paused to kiss Furgas and caress his pale cheeks. "Andôkai has called a meeting about the avatars," she continued.

Rodario sat up straight and ran a hand over his pointed beard. "Listen, Narmora . . . Do you really mean to kill her?"

She glared at him angrily, so he hastened to elaborate. "She's our only maga," he said diplomatically, trying not to rile her. "It won't make you any friends."

"No one will know it was me," she said confidently, wetting a cloth and squeezing it gently over Furgas's cracked lips. "Andôkai has taught me well; I know how to cover my tracks."

"Hmm," said Rodario, unconvinced. He took a moment to find the right words. "The problem is this: If you avenge yourself on the maga, Girdlegard will be at risk. How are we supposed to defend ourselves if, or more likely, *when*, we're attacked?"

She looked at him sadly. "What's wrong with you, Rodario? You're shielding the woman who tried to kill your closest friend."

"Andôkai never intended to kill him, just to put him in a coma." He slumped into his chair. "Sometimes I think I shouldn't have told you," he said, sighing melodramatically.

"I don't wish to incur your fury, myopic angel of death, but Andôkai is our one and only maga."

"Aren't you forgetting me?"

"You?" said Rodario incredulously. "I don't doubt you're a fast learner, but you're hardly Andôkai the Tempestuous." He shook his head. "You're not ready, Narmora. Wait a few more cycles until your studies are complete. You might feel differently then."

"I didn't realize you were an authority on magic," she sneered. "My son is dead, Furgas is in a coma, and their suffering will be avenged." She nodded to the door. "Goodbye, Rodario, and thank you for looking after Furgas. I hope you enjoyed the sleep."

"Spare me your barbs, and think of Girdlegard. Some of us are relying on the maga to save us from our foes." He stepped smartly into the corridor and closed the door.

Narmora sat down beside Furgas. Slipping her right hand into her bodice, she felt for the gemstone hanging from her neck. She had been wearing the pendant since the battle of the Blacksaddle.

If only Rodario knew my power . . . Still clasping the gemstone with her right hand, she placed her left hand on Furgas and ran her fingers over his stab wounds. As she closed her eyes, a green glow suffused his bandages, permeating the fabric and irradiating the flesh below. The glow intensified, shining brightly over the infected flesh, and leaving healthy pink skin that grew back over the wound, leaving no sign of inflammation or scarring.

Narmora took a deep breath. It was beyond her means to revive her husband from his coma, but she knew how to heal his wounds. She left the bandages in place so that the maga wouldn't notice.

"Thank you," she whispered gratefully, letting go of the stone. "Our time will come, you'll see." She hurried away to resume her schooling.

The transition was practiced and flawless; with every step toward the library, Narmora became the obedient student whom the maga had come to trust.

Trovegold,
Underground Network,
Kingdom of Gauragar,
Autumn, 6235th Solar Cycle

Tungdil was sitting cross-legged on Myr's roof, sipping a tankard of beer and looking down at the statue of Vraccas.

Another busy and inspiring orbit was drawing to a close. Since arriving in Trovegold, Tungdil had experienced all manner of new things, and he was looking forward to seeing more. He used the pre-dinner lull to sip his beer and review what he had learned about the underground realm.

As Myr had predicted, the king had insisted on guiding Tungdil and the twins through every street and alleyway in Trovegold to show them the richness of freeling life. They had visited allotments, workshops, and smithies, and walked the length of the irrigation system, which was fed by a pair of waterfalls.

Since then, they had made the acquaintance of numerous freelings, some new to Trovegold, others born in the city, but all unstinting in their praise of Gemmil's realm. Tungdil had searched their faces for signs of melancholy or sadness, but almost everyone seemed genuinely content. He could see why they were drawn to Trovegold, which was more than could be said for the twins. Boëndal and Boïndil were looking forward to returning to the fifthling kingdom with its familiar customs and laws.

He heard heavy footsteps behind him. Jangling chain mail identified the visitor as one of the twins. Unlike Tungdil, they insisted on wearing armor wherever they went.

"You're thinking of staying, aren't you?" said Boëndal, sitting down next to him and putting his tankard on the floor.

Tungdil sighed. "Is it that obvious?"

His friend chuckled. "Even my brother has started to realize that you might not come home. For him—well, for us, really—staying isn't an option. He threw up his hands. "Yes, I know we're all hewn from the same rock," he said, preempting Tungdil's objections. "But the freelings are *outcasts*." He paused to take a glug of beer. "Outcasts and thirdlings," he added in a muted but truculent voice. "I'm sorry, Tungdil, but it isn't a place for upstanding dwarves."

"You're impatient to leave, I know," said Tungdil, refusing to enter into a discussion about outcasts and thirdlings, a category to which he belonged. "Your brother's inner furnace is overheating. He won't be happy until he's worked off his temper on a couple of orcs. He can't hunt gugul forever."

Boëndal grinned. "He's been catching them with his hands. You wouldn't want to be bitten by a gugul—their teeth are pretty sharp. The other hunters respect him, even though they think he's mad." He raised his tankard to the statue. "Here's to Vraccas for steering our path to Trovegold. I'm glad we've seen a freeling city, but Boïndil and I want to leave." He looked at Tungdil intently. "The sooner the better," he said firmly. "We're worried."

"You mean about the dispute with the elves? It shouldn't have happened, I agree. Broken trust is difficult to repair, but I'm sure they'll find a way. It might delay the conquest of Dsôn Balsur by a cycle, but we'll triumph in the end. The älfar are surrounded—there's nowhere for them to go."

"What?" exclaimed Boëndal, astonished. "Don't you want to be out there, fighting with them? Think what a difference it would make if the hero of the Blacksaddle were to lead an army of dwarves against the älfar! You could make peace with the elves, win back Keenfire, and—"

"Confounded Glaïmbar," cut in Tungdil irritably. "I wouldn't have lost the ax again if it weren't for him. To think the king of the fifthlings couldn't defend himself against a wounded orc! I don't know how you expect me to get it back. The älf could be anywhere by now." He didn't like to be reminded about Keenfire and he wished the others would stop mentioning it all the time.

Boëndal looked at him thoughtfully. "Anyone would think you were ready to spend the rest of your life telling stories about the battles you fought in the good old cycles when you were a hero. You're not old yet, Tungdil. What about the future?"

Tungdil swallowed his irritation. "I've done my bit for Girdlegard," he said calmly. "From now on, I want to be a regular dwarf who does regular things. I don't intend to sit by the fire; I'd like to work in a forge or find a way of using my knowledge."

"Like Myr you mean? Is that what's keeping you here? Nothing kills the spirit of adventure like a maiden, they say."

Tungdil took a deep breath. "I don't know," he said sadly. "Myr isn't a bit like Balyndis. We talk for hours and hours about books and ideas. I couldn't have that kind of conversation with Balyndis—she isn't scholarly at all. But it's her I dream about, not Myr."

He looked his friend in the eye. "What if I do something awful to drive Balyndis and Glaïmbar apart? I don't want to be a schemer or murderer like Bislipur and the other thirdlings. I'm scared of hurting Glaïmbar and becoming just like them." He emptied his tankard and set it down with a thud. "I need to forget about Balyndis so I can stop hating Glaïmbar. I think it's better for everyone if I stay here with Myr."

His friend nodded sympathetically. "Very well, scholar. If you're sure . . . But I can't promise that Boïndil won't try to abduct you." He and Tungdil laughed briefly, but their hearts weren't in it.

"What if Girdlegard were in trouble?" asked Boëndal. "Would you come if I asked you to?"

"Of course," said Tungdil simply. "But I can't see it happening. When will you leave?"

"Tomorrow morning before sunrise. Andôkai has summoned the leaders of Girdlegard to a meeting in Porista." He produced a roll of parchment. "According to Glaïmbar, you, me, and Boïndil have been chosen for the high king's entourage."

"I'm sure Gandogar will manage with you and Boïndil," said Tungdil emphatically. "What's the meeting about?"

Boëndal shrugged. "No one knows. It's confidential, apparently, but the maga probably wants to haul everyone over the coals. To be honest, I don't blame her—we pledged an oath of friendship, and now we're killing each other . . ." He laid a hand on his friend's shoulder. "Farewell, Tungdil Goldhand. May Vraccas bless you and bring peace to your soul. I hope you live happily in Trovegold." They stood up and clasped each other affectionately.

"I'm not looking forward to telling my brother," Boëndal said gloomily. "Maybe Myr should sprinkle some herbs on his dinner to calm him down."

"It's all right, I'll tell him myself," promised Tungdil. They went downstairs to the kitchen and found Boïndil at Myr's shoulder, watching hungrily as she prepared the meal. Two gugul were laid out on the kitchen table, gutted and ready to cook.

"Caught with my own fair hands," he said, beaming. He rolled back his sleeves for his scratches to be admired. "I didn't use axes, just wrung their necks. I tried telling myself they were orcs to make it more exciting—but it didn't really work." He saw their glum expressions. "What's wrong? No bubbles in your beer?"

"You and Boëndal are leaving tomorrow," said Tungdil simply. "I'm staying because . . ."

Boïndil frowned, lowering his head and squaring his shoulders aggressively. "I'll knock you down and drag you away if I have to. This had better be a joke."

"No, I'm staying in Trovegold . . ." began Tungdil. "For

the time being, at least," he continued, alarmed by the look on Boïndil's face. "I'm hoping to persuade Gemmil to send freeling troops to Dsôn Balsur. I can't ask for his help and run away."

Boïndil harrumphed and crossed his arms belligerently. "Why not? Maybe I should talk to him."

"Not on your life!" laughed Tungdil. "Although your natural charm would probably settle the matter quickly."

"Especially with a bit of help from your axes," added Boëndal with a smile. "Come on, brother, leave the negotiations to our scholar. Gandogar needs us in Porista."

Boïndil strode up to Tungdil and smothered him with a hug. "Look after yourself—and don't keep me waiting."

"I won't," promised Tungdil halfheartedly. He glanced at Boëndal, who was staring fixedly at the disemboweled gugul. He was obviously uncomfortable with the charade.

Myr, guessing that the others were keeping something from Boïndil, couldn't help smiling at the thought of having Tungdil to herself. "I'll cook a proper feast tonight," she promised. "The twins will need plenty of energy for the journey." She tied an apron around her waist. "Maybe Gemmil will let you use the tunnels to save a bit of time. I can ask him, if you like."

Boïndil grabbed the beetles by the tail and lowered them into the vat of bubbling broth. "Not until we've eaten," he ruled.

II

Trovegold,
Underground Network,
Kingdom of Gauragar,
Autumn, 6235th Solar Cycle

Tungdil got up the next morning to find two empty beds. His friends had left without waking him.

Myr was waiting with a special breakfast to fuel his inner furnace: pancakes with cranberry syrup, warm gugul, and a variety of smoked meats.

"You just missed them," she said when he asked about the twins. "They had breakfast, packed some provisions, and that was that." She sat down beside him and watched him eat. In the end, she couldn't help herself: A question was burning a hole in her soul. "You've decided to stay in Trovegold, haven't you? You told Boïndil you'd catch up with them later because you didn't want to cause a scene."

"Yes, Myr, I've decided to stay." He searched her inscrutable red eyes. "I'd like to stay with you, if I may."

"Have you reached a decision?" she asked eagerly. "Do you want me to heal your heart?"

He gazed at her beautiful face, the silvery down on her cheeks, and her plumps lips. *She wants me to kiss her*, he realized.

"I need more time." He jumped to his feet, seized with a sudden urge to leave the house. His brusqueness took him by surprise. "I'm going to the allotments—I've been thinking of ways to improve the irrigation." Stopping briefly to kiss her forehead, he hurried from the room.

You idiot, he cursed himself. He wished he were a proper dwarf who could fall in love with the maiden selected by his clan. *I'd be a lot happier*, he thought dismally. *Balyndis is happy—isn't she?*

He took the path leading to the waterfalls, visible from the other side of town. He watched them cascade into the basin, garlanded with spray. Droplets of water splashed against the surrounding rocks.

On reaching the sluice system that regulated the flow to the canals, he spotted Sanda Flameheart, Gemmil's companion and commander-in-chief of the freeling army. Sanda was talking to the dwarves in charge of monitoring the water level and adjusting the sluice. Tungdil stopped for a moment.

The king's muscular consort finished briefing the workers and turned to leave, but, noticing Tungdil, raised a hand in greeting and hurried up the hill to meet him.

The menacing tattoos on her forehead were unmistakable proof of her dwarf-killing past. Not even her billowing fair hair could soften the menace of the runes.

"May Vraccas keep the flames of your furnace burning," she greeted him warmly. She didn't seem the least out of breath, despite marching uphill in a leather bodice, plated mail, and a skirt-like arrangement of metal tassets that reached almost as far as her ankles.

"Vraccas be with you," he replied. "Are you going to battle? I thought no one wore armor in Trovegold."

She smiled, but the overall effect was more menacing

than cheering. "I'm a warrior, Tungdil. I don't feel comfortable without my mail—I'm sure your friends felt the same. Besides, Trovegold isn't as safe as sweet little Myr would have you believe. Cave trolls and bögnilim have a habit of getting caught in the tunnels." She laid a hand on her ax. "Thanks to my warriors, they never pass our gates."

He noticed that her downy cheeks were streaked with gray, indicating that she was older than he had thought. "You haven't lived here long, have you?"

"Just over two cycles—it's no big secret." She looked at him shrewdly. "You don't know what to make of me, do you? You and I are both thirdlings, but we've chosen not to kill our own kind."

"I've never killed a dwarf in my life."

"I have," she said frankly, "but I didn't much enjoy it. I was a dwarf killer because I grew up with dwarf killers, and killing was all I knew. Deep down, I knew it wasn't right." She sat down on the soft carpet of moss and gazed at the city. Tungdil sat beside her. "In the end, I had to make a choice."

"So you chose banishment?"

"I chose death. If my clansfolk were to find me, they'd kill me on the spot. I used to be a high-ranking warrior, as you can probably tell from my tattoos, but I forfeited the respect of the thirdlings. In their eyes, I'm the enemy—another dwarf for them to kill." She gazed up at the stronghold. "Trovegold is my home now. I found someone who was willing to take me for who I am. Starting over is the hardest thing I've ever done, but I've made a new life with the freelings." She turned to Tungdil. "You wanted to ask me about your parents. What were their names?"

"I don't know," he said with a shake of the head. "I was a baby when my foster father, Lot-Ionan, bought me from some kobolds who came knocking one night at his school. I can't remember a thing about my parents. I didn't realize I was a thirdling until the battle of the Blacksaddle."

She looked up sharply. "How old are you?"

"Sixty cycles, maybe more. I'm not sure. Why do you ask?"

Sanda was staring at him intently. "I've been trying to figure out why your face looks familiar. You look exactly like her!" She turned away, eyes fixed on the city. "Sixty cycles ago something happened that made me leave my clansfolk and flee the fifthling kingdom. It hardly seems possible but . . ." Her gaze lifted to the statue of Vraccas. "It's the will of the Smith," she whispered gratefully. "My decision saved Girdlegard. All my suffering wasn't in vain!"

Tungdil laid a hand on her shoulder. "What is it, Sanda? Do you know my parents?" he asked, heart beating wildly.

She laid a hand over his and looked at him tenderly. "I knew your father, Tungdil. His name was Lotrobur, and your mother was Yrdiss. They called you Calúngor. Yrdiss was promised to another, and her love for Lotrobur was born of an ill-fated flame, but their feelings were too strong to ignore. You were born in secret. Your father tried to smuggle you out of the kingdom because he knew Yrdiss's guardian would kill you if he could." She took a deep breath. "I followed Lotrobur through the tunnels. My orders were to kill father and son."

"Did you . . . ?"

"No. I caught up with him, we fought, and I won." Her eyes glazed over as her mind traveled back to the past, and the events of sixty cycles ago came to life. "I raised my ax," she continued, tapping her weapons belt. "I was going to cleave his skull with this very blade, but I heard you crying. It was a pitiful whimpering, but it softened my resolve. I looked into your father's eyes and decided that I never wanted to kill another dwarf. It was then I realized that I'd never been a proper dwarf killer." She lowered her eyes and stroked her weapon. "So I helped him up and told him to hurry."

Tungdil said nothing, waiting for her to continue.

"When I got back, I told them that Lotrobur had run away. That was when they showed me the corpses—your mother's body and your father's head. I wasn't the only one who'd been ordered to kill them. Yrdiss's guardian, your great-uncle, had murdered them and thrown you into a chasm. Vraccas couldn't save your parents, but he let you live because he knew a glorious future lay ahead of you. He shaped your fate and led you to the magus." She smiled at him fondly. "And now he's brought us together, sixty cycles later."

Tungdil swallowed. "What was my great-uncle called?"

"Salfalur Shieldbreaker, King Lorimbur's right-hand dwarf. He's still alive, as far as I know. Your father was his best friend, which is how he met your mother. If things had happened differently, he would have taken over from Salfalur as commander-in-chief. Lotrobur was our second-best warrior, after Salfalur."

"Is that when you left?"

"I became a mercenary in Idoslane until I met a dwarf who told me about a group of exiles living underground. Every dwarf needs kinsmen, so I made my way to Trovegold."

Tungdil took her hand and shook it vigorously. "Thank

you, Sanda. I can't tell you how much it means to know the names of my parents—although I wish they hadn't died because of me."

"I wish they were alive to meet their famous son," she said sincerely. "But you're not to blame for their deaths. The laws are at fault—Lotrobur and Yrdiss loved each other, but she was promised to another against her will. The freelings have done away with forced marriages. That's another reason why I like this realm."

Tungdil got to his feet. "Will you drink with me to my parents?"

"It would be an honor," replied the commander. They made their way to the nearest tavern and raised their tankards to Yrdiss and Lotrobur. Sanda seemed happy to talk about Tungdil's parents, for whom she had nothing but respect.

Listening to her stories, Tungdil, who had no memory of his parents, felt an overwhelming urge to avenge their deaths. His hatred for Glaïmbar was supplanted by hatred for a thirdling by the name of Salfalur.

After a few tankards, he summoned the courage to ask Sanda to help him with his axmanship. *I'll be the best warrior in the history of the thirdlings,* he decided. *Salfalur will pay . . .*

Porista,
Former Realm of Lios Nudin,
Girdlegard,
Late Autumn, 6235th Solar Cycle

The maga's distinguished guests were greeted by the magnificent architecture of the new Porista. Under Rodario's supervision, the city had risen from the rubble, the ruined buildings restored to their former glory. A bright future lay ahead for the realm.

By the time the last of the delegates reached Porista, the city had begun to resemble a military camp. Flags and banners fluttered above the streets and houses, marking the territory of the different kingdoms. To no one's surprise, Liútasil's banners were situated as far away as possible from the crests of the clans in Gandogar's entourage.

The shops and hostels of Porista welcomed the visitors. For the first time since its destruction, the city was booming. Takings were up, and the streets and alleyways were full of men, elves, and dwarves.

But the tension was palpable.

Everyone had heard about the conflict between the elves and the dwarves, and no one could say for certain whether the old enemies would talk peacefully or go for each other's throats. A repetition of the incident in Dsôn Balsur would put paid to the great alliance, not to mention the assembly. The other delegates were relying on the threat of the maga's magic to bring order to the proceedings.

When the appointed orbit dawned, the leaders of Girdlegard descended on the palace. The meeting was to be held in the conference chamber, where the council of the magi had met for the last time. There was no sign of the battle that had claimed the lives of Lot-Ionan, Maira, Turgur, and Sabora. The cracked flagstones and fallen pillars had been cleared away, and the gleaming copper dome and pristine marble testified to the skill of Porista's artisans. In the eastern corner of the chamber stood Lot-Ionan, whom Nôd'onn had turned to stone.

Waiting to greet the delegates was Narmora, dressed in an embroidered robe that matched her crimson headscarf and went perfectly with her eyes. Andôkai stayed out of sight; by arriving last, she intended to underline her power and signal to the kings and queens of Girdlegard that she outranked them all.

"Scrubs up nicely, doesn't she, brother?" boomed a voice that Narmora recognized instantly as belonging to Boïndil. It seemed to be coming from somewhere behind the delegation from Weyurn. "It's nice to know she made an effort on our behalf."

As the last of the Weyurnians entered the conference chamber, the dwarves came into view. At the head of the procession was King Gandogar, flanked by the twins. Representatives from the four allied kingdoms made up the rest of the deputation.

She welcomed the high king first, then turned to the twins, who shook her hand vigorously. "Do you still dream about me?" she asked Boëndal with a smile.

The dwarf shuddered. "Vraccas protect me from älvish nightmares," he said, pulling a face. "You look older, Narmora. I thought Andôkai would teach you the secret of everlasting youth."

"I've had a lot on my mind," she said evasively, unwilling to share her worries with every kingdom in the land. "I'll tell you about it later." She spotted Balyndis at the back of the delegation. Standing beside her was a broad-chested warrior whom Narmora didn't recognize. "Where's Tungdil?" she asked the twins.

"Tungdil?" said Boïndil. "He's—"

His brother cleared his throat. "He stayed behind in the fifthling kingdom," he said, conscious that Gemmil might not thank them for revealing the freelings' existence. In his opinion, it was a strictly dwarven concern. "He couldn't join the delegation. Sentry duty, I'm afraid."

Narmora nodded sagely, although Boëndal was obviously lying. Gandogar, overhearing, avoided her gaze.

"I wouldn't mention him to Balyndis," said Boïndil moodily. "They're not together anymore. She forged the iron band with the king of the fifthlings. It's a touchy subject."

I'm not the only one to whom fate has dealt a bad hand . . . "Thanks for the warning," she said aloud. "The assembly is about to begin. We've put you next to the door—as far away as possible from the elves." Stepping aside, she ushered them into the hall.

When the last dwarf had taken his seat, she left her post, entered the chamber and closed the doors behind her. The benches and tables were arranged in a semi-circle with Andôkai's throne-like chair at the center. Narmora sat down on the only remaining seat and waited for her hated mentor.

On the other side of the chamber, Liútasil was talking in hushed tones to two members of his delegation. Every now and then they looked up, glowered in the dwarves' direction and continued their whispered conversation.

I wonder what they're plotting, thought Narmora, wishing she could read their thoughts. She watched their lips move soundlessly and discovered to her astonishment that every word, every syllable was perfectly audible inside her head. Unfortunately, she couldn't make sense of the discussion—elvish was nothing like älvish, and she had never learned the elven tongue.

Just then a powerful gust blew open the double doors.

Everyone in the chamber swiveled round and the dwarves reached for their weapons, prompting the elves to raise their bows.

Andôkai was standing in the doorway. Like Narmora, she was dressed in a crimson robe, but the cut and embroidery were more elaborate. In her left hand she held a sheathed sword.

Proudly she surveyed the assembled delegates. "Rulers of Girdlegard, welcome to Porista," she called. "Kings and queens of dwarves, elves, and men, I welcome you and your courtiers to my palace." She swept past the benches to her chair, from which she gazed down at the other rulers. At the back of the chamber, the doors swung shut, as if of their own accord. "I have something to tell you, something that bodes ill for our kingdoms." She paused for a moment, allowing her words to take effect. "Ten powerful avatars are laying waste to the Outer Lands. They were created from the flesh of Tion, hewn from his body by the red-hot hammer of Vraccas. These creatures see it as their mission to destroy the darkness created by the god from whom they were born, an objective that most in this room would approve of, were it not for the trail of destruction they leave in their wake. The avatars are demigods, fiery beings who scorch the ground and care nothing for human casualties. At their service is an army of warriors who share their commitment to destroying Tion's creation, whatever the cost."

The delegates' faces mingled fear and alarm.

"I'm sure you all remember the comet that passed over Girdlegard and brought death and destruction to a number of our kingdoms," continued Andôkai, looking gravely at her audience. "It wasn't a comet. The ten demigods have a long-lost brother who descended from the skies to join them in the Outer Lands. According to legend, the eleven brothers can only be defeated by beings with pure hearts and noble souls. It seems we must prepare ourselves for an attack."

Queen Wey, a woman of some fifty cycles dressed in a long blue robe trimmed with diamonds, was the first to speak. "If what you say is true, we need a fighting force more powerful than the allied army at Dsôn Balsur." She inclined her head toward the maga. "Most of all, we need your help."

"You shall have it," promised Andôkai. "But I can't guarantee that my famula and I can defeat them. An army is exactly what—"

"An army of innocents," exclaimed Nate, the fur-wrapped king of Tabaîn. His eyes were as green as lily pads, and his thinning hair was the color of ripe corn. "You said they can only be defeated by pure souls," he continued. "I propose we raise an army of maidens and youths unsullied by the pleasures of the flesh. We can train them to fight."

"Poppycock," yapped King Belletain, apparently addressing his goblet. He gave it a playful spin. A dwarf at his side monitored his every movement, watching for early signs of a seizure. "I say we use children. Stick them in a mangonel and fire them at the comet-gods. That should do it."

"Supposing the men and women were pure to begin with, would they retain their purity if we trained them to fight?" enquired the bronzed queen of Sangpûr. Despite wearing several layers of clothing, Umilante was suffering from the cold. The climate in Porista was decidedly frosty compared to her desert realm.

"We could pull their legs until they're long and stringy and sharpen their heads to a point. Put them in a trebuchet, and *whoosh*!" Belletain made a hissing noise like a flying missile and stuck out his index finger, aiming for the goblet. "*Ker-plung!*" The goblet crashed to the ground. "See, it works!"

The king of Urgon's ramblings went uncommented on by everyone else in the room.

Prince Mallen turned to King Nate. "Your suggestion strikes me as plausible—but perhaps Lord Liútasil can offer some advice." He turned to the elven lord. "These demigods . . . Have your people heard of them? How might one defeat them?"

Before the auburn-haired lord could reply, the elf to the left of him jumped up and stabbed a finger at the dwarves. "What about the traitors in our ranks? The groundlings cut down our archers." He glowered at them furiously. "You can't use the threat of the avatars to get away with your crimes."

Boïndil jumped to his feet. "Take that back, you pointy-eared liar, or I'll—"

"Sit down, Boïndil!" roared Gandogar, as Boëndal and Balyndis reached forward to drag the furious warrior into his seat.

"Or you'll what?" the elf asked mockingly, taking a step toward him. "Come here and kill me, if you dare. Everyone knows the dwarves are cowardly murderers.

I'll warrant you've been killing our archers and blaming it on the älfar all along!"

Andôkai, eyes glinting dangerously, rose to her feet. "Quiet!" she barked furiously and was instantly obeyed. Her magic was feared by the dwarves and the elves. "I suggest we focus on the important issues. We can deal with your feuding later, if we must."

Her words were still echoing through the chamber when someone hammered on the doors. Andôkai signaled to Narmora to deal with the unexpected interruption.

She opened the doors to find herself face to face with Rodario and an unknown dwarf. A penetrating smell of perspiration rose from the visibly exhausted warrior whose leather jerkin was stained with rings of sweat.

"Apologies for the interruption, my dark-hearted beauty, but this little fellow and his diminutive companions desire an interview with the maga," explained Rodario with customary flamboyance.

The dwarf seemed dissatisfied with the introduction. "My name is Beldobin Anvilstand of the clan of the Steely Nails of Borengar's line. Queen Xamtys's deputy, Gufgar Anvilstand of the clan of the Steely Nails, sent me here to speak with the maga directly." He pointed to something behind him. "The long-un tried to turn me away, but I showed him who we've brought."

Peering over his head, Narmora saw a makeshift stretcher surrounded by twenty dwarves.

The stretcher, made of planks of wood and steel shields with wheels attached to the bottom, was bowing dangerously under the weight of a warrior of colossal proportions. Traces of bright yellow liquid covered the giant's visor and parts of his armor. In his left hand he held his sword, the blade of which was broken and spattered with orc blood. Hair and scraps of flesh were stuck to the cudgel in his other hand. The dwarves hadn't been able to wrench the weapons from his grip.

"We don't know what's wrong with him. A sentry found him near West Ironhald. We didn't know what to do with him, so we thought we'd bring him here."

"You did wisely. Bring him in." Narmora opened both doors and hurried to the front of the room. "Estimable Maga, there's someone to see you."

The dwarves pushed the stretcher into the chamber and came to a halt beside Narmora. Turning toward the dwarven delegation, they saluted the high king and Xamtys before leaving the room. Their mission, a feat of dwarven endurance, was complete.

"Djerûn!" cried Andôkai, laying her sword on the table and hurrying over to examine his injuries.

"Get back!" shouted Balyndis, leaping up and drawing her ax. "Get back! It isn't Djerûn!"

Andôkai froze and turned to the smith, seeking an explanation, but it was already too late.

The colossal warrior awoke from his paralysis and rammed his broken sword into the maga's unprotected midriff. Jumping down from the stretcher, he drew a second sword with his left hand and swung his cudgel toward Narmora, who leaped aside, landing among King Nate's delegation. A fearsome roar echoed through the chamber and the giant's visor emitted a blinding violet glow.

"Djerûn!" groaned the maga, staring at the hilt of the sword protruding from her belly. She took a step back, pulled out the blade and reached for her sword. Murmuring an incantation to close the wound, she braced herself for the next assault.

It came sooner than she expected.

The armored giant went for his victim with murderous zeal. Blows rained down from his cudgel and sword with preternatural power and speed. Andôkai had crossed swords with her bodyguard in training, but nothing had prepared her for this. She had never encountered such savagery.

Her stomach had barely stopped bleeding when her right shoulder was struck by a blow from above. The cudgel smashed through her collarbone and sent her flying to the ground. The incantation on her lips became a piercing scream of pain. The sword entered her belly for a second time and she gave an agonized groan as the giant rotated the blade by 180 degrees.

By the time Djerûn's helmet crashed against her head, there was nothing she could do. The steel spikes pierced her skull, blood streamed into her eyes, and everything darkened around her.

The delegates, who had been following the duel in stunned disbelief, leaped belatedly to the maga's aid. Ireheart led the charge against the giant, followed by his fellow dwarven warriors, then the humans and elves. Arrows perforated the giant's armor; axes and hammers pounded his breastplate and hacked through his chain mail. At last, the violet light went out behind his metal visor and he sank to the ground, blood gushing from countless wounds.

Nine men, three dwarves, and four elves went with him to their deaths. Queen Wey was lucky to evade a fatal encounter with his cudgel, and Umilante's many layers of clothing saved her from his deadly sword.

Boïndil, not satisfied that the giant was dead, continued to batter his helmet. "By Vraccas, he was tough," he panted, wiping his face with his sleeve to clear away the saffron-colored blood. "Curse my inner furnace. Now I'll never know what he looked like underneath."

Narmora crouched beside the critically wounded maga. Those around her assumed she was trying to save her mentor, but the half älf had other ideas. There wouldn't be another chance like this.

"I know a charm that would save you," she whispered in the maga's ear. "But I've decided to let you die. You killed my son and put my husband in a coma. You deserve to suffer for your scheming and lies."

Andôkai coughed weakly and closed her eyes. "Furgas won't recover without my help," she hissed, grabbing Narmora by the collar of her robe. "If I die, Furgas dies with me."

Narmora made no attempt to shake off the maga's trembling hands. She reached for her necklace and produced the jagged splinter of malachite. "Does this look familiar?" she asked, eyes darkening to fathomless hollows as she spoke. "It's the key to Nôd'onn's power. He wore it in his flesh until Tungdil cut him open and spilled his guts. I found it at the Blacksaddle and made it my talisman. I didn't realize how powerful it was." She slid the gemstone from the chain. "Samusin have mercy," she cried for the benefit of the others. "The maga is dying!"

She laid her hands slowly on Andôkai's chest. Her lips moved as if she were summoning healing energies for the maga's recovery, while her fingers pressed the splinter of malachite through the bodice of her dress. The long, pointed shard bored deeper and deeper, a green halo encircling the maga's body as the malachite pierced her heart.

Narmora, still mumbling strange incantations, waited as the maga's life force drained away. The halo was fading fast.

The half älf leaned over her mentor. "Look at me," she whispered in the dark tongue of the älfar. She tilted Andôkai's head toward her. "Narmora is your death. I will take your life and drain you of your magic. None of this need have happened if you'd left us alone."

The maga tried to lean forward, but all she could manage was a feeble groan. Her eyes glazed over.

After checking that her hands were hidden by her robes, Narmora withdrew the splinter and pocketed the malachite. Her bloodied fingers were unlikely to attract suspicion, given the maga's injuries and the pool of blood that surrounded her body. Straightening up, she turned to address the delegates.

"Andôkai the Tempestuous is no more," she announced, voice cracking with feigned grief. She raised a hand to wipe away a nonexistent tear. "Girdlegard's last maga is dead."

A horrified silence descended on the chamber.

"You shall take her place, Narmora," said Gandogar calmly, stepping forward. "You were her famula; you shall lead us in the battle against the avatars."

"You're doomed already," said a gruff voice from the doorway. "You can't beat the avatars with magic or an army. You'll never find a way of halting their advance."

The dwarves, elves, and men turned to the doorway and hefted their weapons, readying themselves for the next unwelcome surprise.

Before them was a lone dwarf. His face was covered in intricate tattoos and he was armed to the teeth. In his right hand was a three-balled morning star. "My name is Romo Steelheart of the clan of the Stone Grinders, nephew of Lorimbas Steelheart, king of the thirdlings and ruler of the Black Range. I have a proposal to make to Lord Liútasil and the delegations from the human kingdoms." A second dwarf, broader and more muscular than Lorimbur's brawny nephew, appeared behind him. Sunlight gleamed on his bald head.

"The thirdlings want to help us fight the avatars?" whispered Queen Wey, surprised.

"What kind of proposal?" muttered Balyndis to Glaïmbar. She had a fair idea that it wouldn't be good news.

"Call it an offer you can't refuse," said Romo, grinning maliciously. "My uncle knows how to combat the threat from the west." He swung his morning star in the direction of the dwarven delegation. "I'll explain once they've left. My uncle refuses to negotiate with the dwarves of Beroïn, Borengar, Giselbert, and Goïmdil."

Trovegold,
Underground Network,
Kingdom of Gauragar,
Late Autumn, 6235th Solar Cycle

Sanda ducked just in time, allowing the blade to sail over her head as she dropped to one knee and lunged forward.

The blow was dealt with such precision and power that Tungdil didn't have time to avoid the blunted ax.

Neither his weapons belt, his chain mail, nor his leather jerkin did anything to slow the blade as it thudded against his ribcage, winding him momentarily and bringing tears to his eyes.

"Stop!" shouted Myr in alarm, hurrying over to inspect his chest. "You're supposed to be coaching, not killing him," she scolded, as Sanda picked herself up from her knees and smiled at Tungdil without a hint of contrition.

"Don't make such a fuss, Myr," she said coolly. "He's only bruised his ribs. Pain is an excellent teacher." The commander-in-chief made no secret of her dislike for the pale-faced medic. "He's learned an important lesson, and he'll live to fight again." She turned to Tungdil, expecting him to agree.

"It was careless of me," he admitted, yelping internally as Myr proceeded to prod his ribs.

"They're broken, not bruised," she hissed. "Your muscles are in danger of squeezing out your brain. A blunted ax isn't a toy, you know."

Sanda's tattoos, animated by fury, rearranged themselves across her face. She swung her ax playfully, but there was menace in her eyes. "It's a good thing you're here to advise me, Myrmianda. I'll remember not to tap my blunted weapon against your delicate little head." Snorting angrily, she abandoned the training session, leaving Myr and Tungdil to show themselves out of the stronghold.

"I thought I was a decent warrior," said Tungdil, who had been practicing his axmanship every orbit in preparation for fighting Salfalur. Groaning, he lowered himself onto a marble pew. "Even the twins said I was passable, but Sanda is in a different league. Boïndil could learn a thing or two from her, I reckon."

"You'll get there in the end," she soothed him. "Lift up your shirt: I need to palpate your ribs."

Palpate. He felt like kissing her on the spot. It was such a fine, scholarly word.

"She's fought more battles than you've seen cycles— she's three times as old as you, remember." She clicked her tongue disapprovingly at the sight of the bruise on his chest. "No more training today," she ruled. "We're going home so I can ice your chest. Once the swelling has gone down, we'll put some ointment on the bruise."

Tungdil struggled clumsily to his feet. He had been injured more times than he cared to remember, and it never got any less painful. Slowly, he and Myr left the stronghold and made their way down a winding path that afforded excellent views of the city.

Tungdil remembered the heated exchange between Sanda and Myr. "Why doesn't she like you?" he asked. "I didn't think Sanda was a dwarf hater."

"You don't have to be a thirdling to dislike other dwarves," she said with a smile. "The feeling is mutual."

"Why don't you like each other?" he persisted.

She winked at him cheekily. "Why do you think, Tungdil Goldhand? What could possibly cause a quarrel between two female dwarves?"

He grinned. "Don't tell me you were vying for the affections of a handsome warrior!" He glanced back at the stronghold. "It wasn't Gemmil, was it?"

Myr blushed and turned her pretty face toward the waterfalls. "I'm from Gemtrove, our southernmost city. Gemmil was one of the first dwarves I met when I moved to Trovegold. We were getting on really well—until Sanda muscled in. I wasn't afraid to tell her what I thought of her, and she made it fairly clear that she didn't like me. At least it's in the open. I'd find it hard to be civil to a thirdling spy."

"You don't mean that, do you?"

"I most certainly do. The thirdlings hate the descendants of Lorimbur's brothers, the freelings included. They don't care that we've cut our ties with the other kingdoms—we're still enemies in their eyes. Spies like Sanda are sent to snoop on defectors and gather intelligence about our realm."

"What does Gemmil think? Don't say you haven't told him."

"Oh, I've told him, all right."

"What did he say?"

"He laughed it off. Gemmil is blinded by love, but I've recruited some friends to keep an eye on Sanda. She can't do anything without us knowing."

"That's why she hates you?"

"She hasn't found out yet. No, Sanda hates me because she thinks I'm after Gemmil. She said I was pretending to like you because I wanted to trick her into feeling safe." She turned her red eyes on Tungdil and seemed to read his thoughts. "I'm not interested in Gemmil. I like you, Tungdil Goldhand."

It wasn't his intention to kiss her, but he found himself pressing his lips against hers. They were soft, tempting, and sweet, with a taste like spiced honey. A tingle of excitement ran through him, and he felt strangely lightheaded.

Myr hesitated for a moment before kissing him back. At last he pulled away and they looked at each happily, smiling in contented silence as they strolled through the streets of Trovegold.

Maybe she's the one for me, he thought while he waited for Myr to buy a few things for dinner. *Surely I'm over Balyndis by now*. Myr smiled at him before turning back to order a punnet of stone fruit. His heart gave a little leap like it used to do for Balyndis. *Yes*, he decided, relieved. *Myr is the one for me*. The rest of the way home, he had his arm around her shoulders.

After a quick nap, a hearty dinner, and a pause to apply Myr's ointment, which helped to soothe the pain, Tungdil left the house and allowed himself to be guided through the city by Myr. After a while they reached the far wall of the cavern and joined crowds of dwarves flocking into a tunnel. Tungdil pestered Myr to tell him where everyone was going, but she told him to wait and see.

They strode through a beautifully hewn gallery, and Tungdil spotted a blue light ahead. The hum of conversation grew louder as they approached.

At last the passageway opened into an artificial cavern. Tungdil and Myr were standing at the highest vantage point, at the top of a series of terrace-like platforms. Carved into each platform was a long marble pew, and most of the dwarves were seated already. The bottommost terrace was a large stage, clearly visible from everywhere in the room. The walls were studded with blue crystals that provided ample light.

"A play!" said Tungdil. "Just wait until I tell Rodario. I bet he'd love to perform in Trovegold." Myr looked at him blankly. "Sorry," he apologized. "I forgot you hadn't met him. He's an impresario—and a philanderer. He was part of the expedition to forge Keenfire."

"We're not here for a play," she told him. "Every cycle we hold a singing competition in honor of Vraccas. Each of our five cities sends a choir. It's a big occasion." She pointed to the stage where the members of the first choir were preparing to sing. The assembled dwarves stamped their boots against the stone floor to show their appreciation. A thunderous rumble echoed through the room. Myr reached for Tungdil's hand. "You'll love it, I promise."

The concert began.

The first song was nothing like the mystical hymns of the priests at the temple. The baritone and bass voices sang of underground riches, beautiful caverns and grottoes, hidden treasure, and the hundred-and-one shades of gray in a single piece of rock. The themes were quintessentially dwarven, and other verses dealt with forging axes or building bridges over chasms.

Soon the choir raised their powerful voices to the heroes of yore, singing of glorious deeds and great victories over Tion's minions. Tungdil listened to the stirring words.

On he marches, axes raised
While our singers sing his praise
The fearless warrior will not rest
Helped by Vraccas in his quest.

For Girdlegard he gives his life
Murdered by a deadly knife
As he crumples to the ground
Let these halls with song resound
To praise our dwarven hero.

His savage killers surge ahead
Trampling on the valiant dead
Dwarven fighters bar their path
Sealing off the mountain pass.

More invaders flood the gates
But our warriors never rest
Helped by Vraccas in their quest
And our singers sing the praises
Of our warriors, axes raised
Long live our dwarven heroes!

To Tungdil's surprise, one of the songs was dedicated to the battle of the Blacksaddle, while another darker ballad described the loss of Keenfire and the battle for the fifthling kingdom. He found the lyrics deeply affecting—so much so that his mood became quite melancholy. Thankfully, the ballad was brief, and the next number was a drinking song. Soon he was humming along to a ditty about the elves, taught to him by the twins.

Created by Sitalia from dew, soil, and sun
In elegance and beauty second to none
But appearances aren't everything
As every dwarf knows
If you meet an elf
You'll come to blows.

Pointy ears and a pointy chin
Sticking-out ribs and much too thin

Their skin is smooth, they smell like flowers
They talk to trees, they sleep in bowers
They can't grow beards, they spurn our wealth
Three cheers to Vraccas for not making me an elf!

Gullible humans admire their grace
Tricked by the charm of the elfish face
But appearances aren't everything
As every dwarf knows
The stuck-up elves
Love no one but themselves.

Pointy ears and a pointy chin
Sticking-out ribs and much too thin
Their skin is smooth, they smell like flowers
They talk to trees, they sleep in bowers
They can't grow beards, they spurn our wealth
Three cheers to Vraccas for not making me an elf!

And now we come to the moral of the song
The elves are weak and the dwarves are strong
Ask any maiden and her choice is clear
A dwarf's mighty hammer outdoes an elfish spear!

In the intervals between choirs, musicians came onto the stage with horns, flutes, goat-leather bagpipes, and drums of all shapes and sizes.

Tungdil barely noticed the passing hours; he was too caught up in the music to feel tired. A shiver of pleasure ran down his back.

"Thank you," he whispered to Myr. "Thank you for

sharing this with me. Thank you for everything." He kissed her. "If I were to offer you a ring, what would you say?"

She smiled. "Thank you, Tungdil Goldhand."

Seven orbits later, Tungdil was sitting in Myr's library, reading an account of the freelings' origins.

The history of the realm was chronicled on numerous stone tablets in the temple, and Myr had gone to the trouble of transcribing the inscriptions and collating them in manuscript form. She had incorporated sketches of the city, including views from the stronghold and the plateau. Another manuscript described her home city of Gemtrove, which, as Tungdil gleaned from the sketches, was an architectural masterwork.

Myr's meticulous draftsmanship rivaled anything he had seen in Lot-Ionan's books. *She's a real scholar*, he thought admiringly as he leafed through her work.

Just then someone knocked at the door.

Assuming it was a patient for Myr, he stayed in his armchair, but the knocking became more insistent, eventually reaching a volume impossible to ignore. Cursing Sanda for breaking his ribs, he got up slowly and went to investigate the source of the racket.

"What are *you* doing here?" he exclaimed, staring in astonishment at the pair of bedraggled warriors on the doorstep.

"Confounded water!" thundered Boïndil. "Next time those avatars decide to fall out of the sky I hope they have the decency to vaporize the freelings' pond." He wrung out his beard, dripping brackish water all over Myr's steps. "We've come to fetch you, scholar." A strand of duckweed had attached itself to his hair. He pulled it out and stamped on it angrily. "Nasty Elrian mischief! She nearly got me this time."

Boëndal dried his eyes on his sleeve before realizing that the fabric was wetter than his face. "I swore never to enter that water again, but how else were we supposed to find you?" he said, aggrieved.

They hovered on the doorstep uncertainly. Last time Myr had been quite insistent about keeping the carpet dry.

"It's good to see you both," said Tungdil, shepherding them into the kitchen where they could drip to their heart's content on the floor. "Start from the beginning. What brings you to Trovegold?" Miniature lakes formed around the twins' feet as water streamed from their garments onto the tiles.

"We're taking you to Porista," said Boïndil, making himself at home. He was already tucking into the leftovers from lunch. "Mm, I'd forgotten about Myr's cooking."

"Does Andôkai need me? Is it about Keenfire?" asked Tungdil, as baffled as before.

"No." Boëndal paused for a moment to wipe his face on a dishtowel. Boïndil took it from him and dried his beard. "It's losing its shine," he murmured peevishly. "I should probably grease it. Beards aren't supposed to get wet."

His brother returned to the matter in hand. "You won't believe what's happened while you've been here in Trovegold." He gave a brief account of the conference, the news from the Outer Lands, and the events leading

up to the maga's death. "Narmora has taken the reins—
no one else in Girdlegard knows anything of the magic
arts. And Gandogar wants you to be there when Romo
outlines his proposal to Liútasil and the men."

Me? Once Tungdil had overcome his initial surprise,
he realized why he had been chosen to represent the
dwarves. *The thirdlings banned the dwarves of Beroïn,
Borengar, Giselbert, and Goïmdil from attending the
meeting.* "He chose wisely. I'm a thirdling, so Romo will
have to let me in."

Boïndil finished scooping out the contents of a beetle
carapace and replaced it on the sideboard. "By the way,
I've got a bone to pick with you. Why didn't you tell me
you were planning to stay in Trovegold? It isn't nice to
lie to an old friend."

Tungdil smiled and held out his hand. "No hard feelings, Boïndil. I was afraid you might drag me away by
my beard."

"Too right I would!" chuckled Boïndil, helping himself
to a dumpling. He dipped it in some cold gravy and popped
it in his mouth. "One of these is worth four dozen runts,"
he said approvingly. "Although there's nothing to stop me
fighting *and* eating."

Tungdil was brooding over the news. "It doesn't bode
well for Girdlegard," he muttered. A new challenge and
the awkwardness of seeing Balyndis awaited him in Porista,
whereas in Trovegold he led a peaceful scholarly life with
Myr, interrupted only by training sessions with Sanda and
the occasional afternoon in the forge.

He glanced into the adjoining room and glimpsed the
diamond-studded weapons belt given to him by Giselbert

Ironeye. It was hanging on the wall beneath two crossed axes—his own work, of course.

Boëndal followed his gaze. "It doesn't bode well," he agreed, although it wasn't clear whether he was referring to the changes in Girdlegard or in his friend.

"You're living the scholar's life, are you?" mumbled Boïndil, picking up another dumpling and waving it vaguely in the air. "No chain mail, comfortable boots— are you sure you haven't put on weight?"

Tungdil laughed and fetched three glasses of beer. "I doubt it. I'm taking lessons in axmanship from Sanda Flameheart. You should see her muscles; she'd lay you out cold in a fight."

"It's easy to impress a novice," said Boïndil, smiling. "She probably hasn't fought a true warrior. I'd show her who's boss." He swallowed the dumpling, washed it down with a draft of beer, and belched loudly.

"It's time to dust off your weapons belt," said Boëndal earnestly. "I hope you're not too settled here. Gandogar needs you in Porista; no one can go to the meeting but you."

Boïndil, always the pragmatist, pushed past him and unhooked the belt and one of the axes from the wall. He handed them to Tungdil. "Don't make me force you," he said with a wink. "Are you ready?"

The front door opened, and Myr walked in, carrying her medicine bag. "Vraccas almighty, we've been flooded!" she said in mock horror. "I thought they'd fixed the sluice for the canals . . ." She put her hands on her slender waist and followed the trail of water to her guests. "So it was you!" she said, pretending to be cross. "I see you found the kitchen." Laughing, she hugged Boïndil and then Boëndal. "I smell dumplings," she commented, sniffing the air. "That's strange—they've disappeared . . ."

"It's your own fault," protested Boïndil. "You left them unguarded."

"I assume you didn't come here to steal my food," she said, noting their earnest faces. Boëndal explained the purpose of their visit. "If Tungdil's leaving, so am I," declared Myr. "I'll accompany the three of you as far as Porista, and we'll see from there. I can't bear to separate our freshly melded hearts."

"Freshly melded?" exclaimed Boëndal. "Congratulations! May Vraccas bring you happiness and wealth." He shook hands with them vigorously. "We should have brought a present."

Boïndil responded to the unexpected news by choking on a handful of cranberries and would have died an inglorious and untimely death, were it not for Myr, who thumped him on the back. The red-faced warrior took a sip of beer. "To the happy couple," he gasped.

Tungdil showed them the ring on the middle finger of his right hand and the smaller version worn by Myr. He had forged them himself. "We had the ceremony in the temple." *And no one was there to stop us*, he added silently.

"In that case, we'll take *two* scholars to Porista," said Boëndal, smiling. "All the better for Girdlegard and the dwarves."

Myr beamed. "I can't wait to see a human city. How am I going to find enough parchment for all my sketches and notes?" She hurried upstairs. "We'll set off as soon as I've packed a few things . . ."

"Personally, I'd rather dry out first," said Boïndil, tapping his foot against the floor. His boot squelched unpleasantly. "There's no point in getting blisters."

Before they left, Tungdil paid a final visit to the stronghold and took his leave of Gemmil and Sanda. As usual, he was greeted warmly, and Sanda offered him a drink. He gave as full an account as possible of the situation in Porista. "It's essential I go," he concluded.

Sanda had been listening attentively. "I know Romo Steelheart. His uncle dotes on him. He's a dedicated dwarf killer, one of the worst I've ever met. He was trained by Salfalur himself. Entrusting Romo with the fate of Girdlegard is like asking an orc to look after a playground. Lorimbas is up to something serious." She glanced at Gemmil. "Romo doesn't make deals; he's there to enforce his uncle's will. He won't back down." She turned back to Tungdil. "Romo and his associates can't be trusted. The meeting could be an ambush—or worse. You'll have to watch your back."

"I'll remember your advice," he thanked her with a bow. "Myr and I will return to Trovegold as soon as we can."

"Myr's going with you?" asked Sanda, taken aback. Almost immediately she recovered her composure and smiled.

Tungdil decided that she was probably pleased at the prospect of not being watched for a while. *Except Myr says she doesn't know about the surveillance* ... Arrangements had already been put in place for Myr's friends to keep an eye on Sanda during her absence.

"Perhaps you could give the high king my regards," said Gemmil. "I'd like to pay a visit to Gandogar once Girdlegard's safety has been assured. I think a meeting would be useful. I don't suppose many of the freelings would be interested in rejoining their folks, but a trade relationship would benefit us all. I'll leave it to you to describe our realm and assure him that we're not a band of criminals and murderers. May Vraccas be with you on your journey."

"I'll talk to Gandogar for you," promised Tungdil. "He'll hear nothing but praise from me."

He left the modest hall and was halfway down the stairs when footsteps sounded behind him. Turning, he found himself looking at the tattooed features of the queen.

"You won't like what I'm going to tell you," she said gravely, "and you probably won't believe me, but be warned: Whatever happens on your journey, keep a close eye on Myrmianda." She glanced about nervously to satisfy herself that they were unobserved.

Tungdil frowned and took a small step away from her. "I don't follow." His eyes searched her face, looking for an explanation. "What's Myr got to do with anything?"

"I'm not at liberty to tell you," she said obscurely. "Myrmianda is who she is because of her family. You mustn't breathe a word of what I've told you, especially not to her." A sentry appeared at the top of the steps and watched them from afar. "I know she's spying on me," she whispered. "Myrmianda could outscheme a gnome. For your own sake, don't trust her." She held out her hand. "This is for Gandogar," she said loudly. "May Vraccas protect you and your friends."

Looking into her eyes, it seemed to Tungdil that she was telling the truth. *She's a thirdling, though, and Myr thinks she's a spy*, he reminded himself as he continued down the stairs. *I don't see why she'd try to drive us apart—unless she's plotting something in Trovegold or conspiring with the thirdlings in Porista . . .*

Barely an hour later he was marching through the tunnels toward the surface with Myr and the twins.

When he looked into Myr's warm, red eyes, the conversation with Sanda seemed ridiculous. Soon afterward, when Myr kissed him lovingly, he forgot what the thirdling had said.

Porista,
Former Realm of Lios Nudin,
Girdlegard,
Late Autumn, 6235th Solar Cycle

I did it for you, Furgas. Narmora kneeled at her husband's bedside, pressed her forehead against his cold hand, and buried her face in the covers. *I punished her and took her power so that I might cure you. It won't be long until Dorsa can meet her father.*

She got up, kissed his colorless lips, and slipped out of the room. She could feel the warmth of the malachite crystal around her neck. The stone had absorbed the maga's magic, transferring her power to Narmora, who intended to use the crystal to cure Furgas—as soon as she learned how.

The half älf's satisfaction at killing her hated mentor

had been disappointingly brief. With Furgas critically ill and Girdlegard in danger, she hadn't been able to enjoy the victory as much as she had hoped. She ran a hand over her bodice, feeling the malachite splinter beneath the fabric.

Rodario emerged from one of the passageways and walked alongside her. They hadn't seen each other for orbits; in fact, they had barely spoken since Andôkai's death. "I keep thinking about what happened," he began. "An awful business."

"Ideal for one of your plays," she said tersely.

"Too dramatic," he countered. "Even for me. My valued spectators would storm out of the Curiosum if I were to tell them that Girdlegard's only maga was dead, killed— in all probability—by Tion's descendants, the devious avatars, more dangerous than anything our kingdoms have ever—"

She stopped and glared at him. "You've been eavesdropping on the assembly!"

"I wasn't eavesdropping. I just happened to overhear." He assumed a look of wounded innocence. "The walls are extremely thin." His hand slapped the sturdy marble. "Well, some of them are . . ."

She set off again, with Rodario walking determinedly alongside her.

"I suppose you know what would really upset my spectators?" he said softly.

"The abysmal acting?"

"No, my sharp-tongued beauty." He barred her way. "The calculated murder of the maga by her famula, who committed her heinous crime in front of Girdlegard's assembled kings and queens, none of whom realized what was unfolding before their eyes."

"Are you out of your mind?" hissed Narmora, rounding on him.

"An excellent question—and one that I was saving for you. I saw what you did, Narmora."

"And what would that be?"

As a longstanding friend of Narmora's, Rodario refused to be intimidated. "I followed the dwarves into the conference chamber. I was standing beside you, in case you needed help. I saw what you did with the crystal."

"I see." Her dark eyes seemed to look right through him. "And what are you going to do about it?"

He pouted. "Nothing. Provided that—"

She stuck her chin out scornfully. "The fabulous Rodario, a blackmailer."

"Oh please," he said dismissively, "I'm too classy for blackmail, and besides . . ." He took a step closer and looked her in the eye. "I'm Furgas's friend. Whether I'm your friend or not is another matter. You're not the old Narmora anymore."

"How could I *not* change?" she said, her haughtiness evaporating. "Andôkai deserved to die—you of all people should know that. I've studied hard to get this far—I can handle the avatars."

"No one, not even the most diligent famula, can become a fully fledged maga in the space of half a cycle." He tilted his head to one side and stared at her bodice, eying the spot where the shard of malachite was hidden. "Unless of course . . ."

She strode past him in the direction of the conference chamber. "If you've got something to say, I recommend you say it," she snapped.

"Fine," he said calmly, setting off behind her at a leisurely pace. "I'm going wherever you're going. I want to be privy to all your decisions. From now on, I'm here to advise you—like Furgas would, if he were well."

She laughed. "How do you think the kings and queens of Girdlegard will like the idea of sharing their confidences with an impresario? Not everyone wants to be featured in your plays."

He jogged to catch up with her. "That's easily solved," he said brightly. "You'll tell them I'm your famulus." He raised his right hand and looked at her solemnly. "Think of the benefits—I can help with your lines. Listen, Narmora," he said sincerely, "I want to be your friend. You need someone you can trust, someone you can share your thoughts with. I'm offering you my help."

They hurried through the arcades in silence. At the door to the conference chamber, Narmora stopped and turned to Rodario. "You're right, a friend is exactly what I need." She smiled, and for a few heartbeats she was the old Narmora, leading lady of the Curiosum. "Come on, it's time to save Girdlegard." She threw open the doors and walked in.

The leaders of the other kingdoms were waiting for her. Only the dwarves were missing. In the interests of Girdlegard, they had agreed to absent themselves from the assembly, as per Romo's churlish instructions. Narmora had promised to brief them later.

The half älf sat down on the throne belonging to

Andôkai, while Rodario claimed the chair beside her and tried to look the part. "This is my famulus, Rodario," she introduced him. "The late maga discovered his talent for magic and schooled him in the mystic arts. He will continue his studies under me."

Rodario rose and gave a deep bow. The combination of his aristocratic features and fine robes would have dazzled a lesser audience. "My gifts as an actor are well known, but Andôkai made a secret of my apprenticeship. I'm delighted to announce that my growing skill as a weaver of enchantment will be placed in the service of our new maga, Narmora the Unnerving, as she leads the fight against Tion's fiery avatars. With my help—"

"A fat lot of good he'll do," jeered Romo, cutting short the impresario's speech. He glanced at Narmora. "She won't defeat the avatars either. Not even the famous Andôkai could halt their advance." He stood up, crossed the chamber and came to a halt beneath the copper dome, armor glistening in the intersecting rays of sunlight from the lofty windows. His companion, a taciturn, almost man-high dwarf, watched impassively from his seat.

Prince Mallen of Idoslane leaned back in his chair and shook his head. "And I suppose Lorimbas is the only one who can stop them?"

Romo bowed. "Greetings, Prince Mallen. My uncle was wondering how your kingdom was faring. We saw the smoke rising over Idoslane from our watchtowers across the border. It must be hard without our mercenaries to beat back Toboribor's orcs."

"Enough of this childishness," snapped Narmora.

"We're here to listen to your proposal—although, frankly, it seems a waste of time."

The thirdling bridled and was about to retaliate when someone hammered on the door.

Remembering the last interruption, Narmora rose uneasily from her throne and walked to the door.

"The hero of the Blacksaddle!" exclaimed Rodario, who had followed her. He couldn't contain his surprise. "What an honor!"

Narmora held out her hand and Tungdil clasped it warmly.

"I wish the circumstances were more favorable, but it's good to see you," he said with a smile. He was accompanied by the twins and a pale dwarf with white hair and red eyes. "This is Myrmianda Alabaster, my spouse," he said briefly. "I'm here for a reason. I'd like to take part in the discussions on behalf of the dwarven folks."

"No," growled Romo, his face contorting with rage. His tattoos looked darker and more menacing than ever as he glowered at the unknown dwarf. "The terms are clear: The descendants of—"

"I'm a thirdling," said Tungdil politely, raising the ax in his right hand. "If I understand correctly, the dwarves of Lorimbur aren't excluded from the proceedings." He rapped his weapon against the floor, the metal ax head clattering against the flagstones. "Either the meeting is open to thirdlings, or you and your companion are barred as well." He stared fearlessly into the eyes of the furious dwarf. "Very well," he said, claiming the chair previously occupied by Gandogar. "The three of us will stay. I hope I haven't missed much.

Tell me, Romo, how exactly is your uncle going to stop the avatars?"

Mallen, eyes sparkling with amusement, gave his friend an encouraging nod. He and the other rulers, with the exception of Belletain, were heartened by Tungdil's early victory in the war of words.

Romo, though, had regained his composure. "I see you haven't brought Keenfire," he said, hoping to humiliate his new adversary. "I heard a rumor that it was stolen."

"It's on loan to a mortal enemy," said Tungdil lightly. "She's sworn to kill me, so I know she'll bring it back." He cocked his head. "I thought you said Keenfire couldn't help us?"

Mallen chuckled.

"It *can't*," Romo growled. He let his gaze travel over the faces of the assembled rulers. "My uncle saw the comet in the firmament and knew at once that the avatars were here. I expect you were wondering why we retook the Blacksaddle. Our archives are hidden in the stronghold, and we wanted them back. It was worth it: We learned from our forefathers' writings how the avatars can be destroyed. There's a secret weapon."

"Little maids," interjected Belletain, his dull eyes fixed on the thirdling. "Sharpen their heads, that's the important bit. Take as many as you like."

"No, worthy Belletain, there's no need to sacrifice the maidens of Urgon," said Romo. "As you know, my folk were created by Vraccas, but we despise the rest of his creation, including the avatars, who were brought into being by the hammer of the Smith. The Vraccas-hewn, Tion-bodied demigods must be destroyed."

Queen Wey cleared her throat. "In the name of Elria, how?"

"If I were to tell you, you'd defeat them, and where would be our reward? With Lorimbas's help, Girdlegard can defeat the avatars. That's all you need to know." He waited in silence for the protests to die down.

"What kind of reward did you have in mind?" enquired Tungdil, looking at Romo through narrowed eyes. He feared the worst.

"Nothing too unreasonable," replied Romo. The men and elves leaned forward in anticipation, but Romo's words were addressed to Tungdil alone. "The dwarves of Beroïn, Borengar, Giselbert, and Goïmdil must leave these lands without delay. Once they're gone, the thirdlings will save Girdlegard from the avatars and send warriors to defend the gates of the other four kingdoms. Our folk is numerous and powerful." He smiled maliciously. "The children of Vraccas must decide whether Girdlegard shall be destroyed."

III

T he thirdlings are crafty," said Gandogar, looking into
the worried faces of the other dwarven monarchs.
"It's not war they're after. They want to kick us out of
Girdlegard by other means."

Boïndil clenched his fists. "I'd like to give Romo a taste
of my axes."

"It wouldn't help," Tungdil reminded him.

"No, but it would make me feel better." The warrior
snorted impatiently. "I'm angry enough to kill an army
of runts and stamp on their plug-ugly—"

"Shush," said Boëndal. "Some of us are trying to think."

Gandogar and the rest of the dwarven delegation were
seated at a table in one of the palace's many rooms. Laid
out before them was a map of Girdlegard. Hours had
passed since they started discussing what to do about
Romo's proposal, and still no one had come up with a
viable solution. They had until dusk to reach a decision,
and the light was fading fast.

"Why didn't he want us there when he told them about
the weapon?" asked Balyndis.

At the sound of the smith's voice, Tungdil reached for
Myr's hand as if to prove to himself that he loved her.

He felt as if he were dangling over an open mineshaft, with only Myr to stop his fall. Looking up, he saw that Balyndis was holding hands with Glaïmbar. *I've moved on*, he told himself firmly, although he couldn't help thinking that Balyndis looked pretty. His heart sped up a little. *Because I'm agitated*, he reasoned. He was furious at the thirdlings for exploiting Girdlegard's predicament for their own ends.

"I expect he was hoping to win over the elves and men before Narmora had time to warn us," said the one-armed king of the secondlings. "Neither he nor his uncle reckoned with Tungdil's appearance."

"One–nil to the children of Vraccas," commented Boïndil confidently, running a hand through his sleek-looking beard. He had greased it with leftover fat from Myr's kitchen, and he didn't seem bothered by the residual smell of meat.

"It's not over yet," warned the high king, feeling the weight of his crown. He rested his chin on his hands. "We underestimated Lorimbas. He's a hundred times more dangerous than Bislipur. Unless you can come up with a better solution . . ." He paused, looking hopefully at Balendilín, who was silent. "In that case, Vraccas forgive me, but I'll have to give the order for our kingdoms to be cleared."

"Never!" protested Boïndil, smashing his fist against the table. "If you banish us to the Outer Lands, the thirdlings will steal our strongholds and—"

"Girdlegard will be saved," said Gandogar in a commanding voice. "Boïndil Doubleblade, I know how you feel. I don't want to give our strongholds to the

thirdlings either, but what of our Vraccas-given mission?"
He looked each of them in the eye. "I want you to remember
the Smith's first commandment: Our duty is to protect the
inhabitants of Girdlegard. If we're obliged to leave our
kingdoms, so be it."

The high king's speech was followed by a long silence
as everyone searched for an alternative.

"Couldn't we attack the thirdlings and seize the secret
weapon?" suggested Queen Xamtys.

Balendilín shook his head. "The Black Range is
uncharted territory. None of us could lead an army safely
through the passageways and tunnels. There isn't time to
plan an attack, even if the elves and the men were to help.
Besides, Lorimbas would be ready for us—and some of
his warriors are garrisoned at the Blacksaddle. If we march
on the Black Range, he'll attack us from behind."

"Perfect timing on their part," observed Tungdil, leaning
back in his chair. "They probably think we've got no
choice." He smirked.

"What's this?" queried Gandogar, sitting up. "Is Tungdil
Goldhand proposing another act of heroism?"

"Not exactly. I was thinking the thirdlings could
help us."

Boëndal and Boïndil exchanged glances, guessing what
their friend had in mind. Balyndis looked at them questioningly, and Boïndil flashed her a confident smile.

Tungdil stroked the coin-shaped patch of gold embedded
in his hand; it shimmered in the light of the setting sun.
"I got to know the freelings during my stay in their capital.
Some are thirdlings like me, and, like me, they aren't
possessed of Lorimbur's murderous hatred." As he said

the word "hatred", his gaze settled briefly on Glaïmbar.
"They know their way around the thirdling kingdom," he
finished, looking away.

"I'm sure they'd be happy to help," agreed Myr. "They
could lead . . ." She trailed off, discouraged by the delegates' response.

Everyone around the table was staring at her with open
curiosity.

She was a pale aberration, a dwarf without chain mail,
whose smooth white skin was unlike anything in Vraccas's
creation. It was true in some respects that she resembled
alabaster, but the comparison wasn't favorable. Alabaster
was soft, crumbly, and practically useless. It had nothing
in common with the granite from which the founding
fathers had been hewn.

"How can we be sure the thirdlings in Trovegold are
any better than Romo?" someone demanded grimly. The
others were thinking the same, but it was Balyndis who
voiced their concern. "Don't take it personally, Tungdil.
Your loyalty is beyond question, but we *know* you. We
can't trust thirdlings whom we've never set eyes on."

"What about Sanda? She's the queen consort," he
protested. Before he could continue, he was silenced by a
kick from Myr. Given her distrust of the freeling
commander, it seemed prudent to leave the matter there.

"I know plenty of thirdlings," volunteered the pale-
skinned medic. "I'd trust them with my life." She knew
from their scornful looks that she was wasting her breath.

"We can't stake our future on the dubious loyalties of
thirdlings," decided Gandogar, ruling against the proposal.

"Your Majesty, the thirdlings in Trovegold are an

invaluable asset," ventured Balendilín, hoping to change the high king's mind. In his view, Tungdil's suggestion was their only hope. "With knowledgeable guides, we could launch a surprise attack."

Tungdil nodded gratefully at the one-armed secondling. "Gemmil's realm is vast—much bigger than I'd imagined. The number of freeling cities defies belief." He rose to his feet, knowing that the next words he uttered could change the dwarves' course. "The freelings came to our aid and defended the fifthling kingdom against hordes of orcish revenants. Two thousand warriors battled for our cause. It took King Gemmil a matter of orbits to send an army to the range." Tungdil looked at Gandogar beseechingly. "They can help us, Your Majesty. They're a force to be reckoned with."

Gandogar bowed his head, closed his eyes, and covered his face with his hands. No one could tell whether he was praying or deep in thought.

Silence descended on the chamber. Myr squeezed Tungdil's hand and smiled at him nervously.

At last Gandogar uncovered his face and sighed. "We're leaving," he said evenly.

Boïndil let out a shriek. "Leaving? We can't give up our kingdoms without a fight!"

"Are you sure, Your Majesty?" persisted Balendilín. "We'll be leaving our strongholds in the midst of winter. What about the womenfolk and children? Our losses will run to hundreds before we encounter the first band of orcs. What kind of future awaits us in the Outer Lands? Even the fog is dangerous."

"I know," sighed Gandogar. "I'm aware of the risks.

I'm condemning our kinsfolk to a perilous march over icy passes and narrow ridges and treacherous winter snow. Believe me, Balendilín, I'll mourn the death of every dwarf. Vraccas will hold me accountable." His eyes welled with tears. "But our sacrifice won't be in vain. We'll leave in the knowledge that Girdlegard is safe—our kingdoms will still be standing when we return."

"The thirdlings won't relinquish our strongholds," objected Balendilín. "It's war either way. If we fight them now, we might prevail, but later . . . The thirdlings will wipe us out, Your Majesty. They'll ensconce themselves in our strongholds and bombard us with boiling pitch, boulders, and arrows. We'll perish at the bottom of our own defenses." He leaned over the map and placed a finger on the Black Range. "Strike now, and—"

Gandogar rose to his feet, trembling with rage. "Enough!" he bellowed. "I'm the high king and I've made my decision. We can't risk a war with the thirdlings, do you hear? The avatars are wily and powerful—they killed the maga, and they'll strike again. The decision stands: We're leaving Girdlegard." He raised the ceremonial hammer and brought it down so heavily that a crack appeared in the table. "Tungdil," he said, his voice still edged with anger. "Go back to the conference chamber and tell Romo we accept the deal."

Tungdil got up, bowed, and left the room with Myr. "It's all wrong," he muttered to himself. *I don't know why Gandogar thinks the avatars are so wily. Why target Andôkai when the thirdlings are the threat?*

"What's the matter?" asked Myr. "Do you think it's a mistake for the dwarves to leave?"

Tungdil stopped mid-stride, as if colliding with a wall. He turned to Myr and kissed her fervently. The satisfied expression on his face seemed at odds with his earlier despondency.

"What's the matter?" she asked breathlessly, puzzled by the rush of affection.

"I'll tell you later," he promised. She waited outside while Rodario opened the door and ushered Tungdil to his chair.

Romo had ordered a tankard of beer and was slurping noisily. His companion peered intently at Tungdil. A look of astonishment crossed his face, and he averted his eyes.

"If it isn't King Gandogar's message boy!" exclaimed Romo with a malicious laugh. He wiped his beard on the back of his sleeve. "Has the high king reached a decision?"

"Yes," replied Tungdil levelly. "King Gandogar wishes it to be known that he agrees to the unscrupulous terms laid down by your uncle." He heard gasps from the other delegates, some of whom seemed relieved, while others were clearly shocked and saddened that the dwarves were being blackmailed into giving up their kingdoms. Tungdil left his chair and, drawing himself up to his full height, stopped in front of Romo. "Know this, Romo Steelheart: If Girdlegard falls, you and your uncle will die by my hand," he threatened, tilting his ax toward him.

Lorimbas's nephew saw at once that it would be foolish to provoke his challenger. To the astonishment of the delegates, Tungdil's threat met with something akin to respect.

"Tell King Gandogar that his decision has been noted and will be conveyed to my uncle. Your fears about

Girdlegard's future are unfounded. Once the thirdlings are in control of the ranges, nothing will breach our defenses." He took his morning star from the table. "We'll keep out the vermin—the avatars, the beasts, and the Vraccas-loving dwarves." He got up, hooked the weapon over his belt, and set off toward the doors, followed by his taciturn companion, who glanced over his shoulder at Tungdil. Romo stopped in the doorway. "The thirdling annexation of the dwarven kingdoms begins in eighty orbits. After that time, any dwarves in our ranges will be killed." He cast a roll of parchment to the floor. "Here's a list of chattels. The items in question must be left at our disposal. Tell Gandogar we'll deal with his kingdom first."

The delegates watched as the sturdy figures receded into the distance, their unwieldy armor echoing through the shadowy corridors long after they disappeared from view.

Led by Gandogar, the dwarves rejoined the discussions as soon as Rodario brought word that Romo and his companion had left the chamber.

"These are dark times for Girdlegard," said Mallen, stepping forward to shake hands with the dwarves. "We're saving our kingdoms and losing the dwarves. It's a high price to pay. Perhaps we should fight the thirdlings instead."

"No," replied Gandogar firmly. "We can't waste precious time. The dwarves will return when the danger is over."

"You can count on our support," promised Mallen. There were no words to express his gratitude, so he inclined his head respectfully instead.

"If the thirdlings break their promise, you won't be the

only one after their blood," said Liútasil to Tungdil. "We'll kill them faster than it takes eleven demigods to burn Sitalia's forests. If the thirdlings have deceived us, the elves will make them pay." He turned to Gandogar. "From now on, the selfless dwarves and their noble high king will be immortalized in our songs. No one in Âlandur will speak ill of the four dwarven folks who sacrificed their king-doms for our safety." The lord of the elves bowed before the dwarf of all dwarves, showing his deference. One by one the monarchs followed his example and bowed before leaving the room.

"I'll accompany Romo in person and find out the truth about their weapon," said Narmora, preparing to leave. "If they've lied, they'll have an angry maga to deal with as well as a dwarven hero and an elven lord. Gandogar and the other monarchs can take care of the survivors." Signaling for Rodario to follow her, she withdrew to her wing of the palace.

The deputations from the dwarven kingdoms took their leave. Most were hoping to drown their sorrows in beer and mead.

At last only Tungdil, the twins, and Balyndis were left.

Boïndil remembered something that had been puzzling him. "Balyndis, how did you know it wasn't Djerûn?"

"I never forget a piece of metalwork," she said, smiling. "Especially not a suit of armor like that. The etchings and engravings on the breastplate weren't my work—they were passable imitations, but nothing more." Her face fell. "Unfortunately, I didn't spot the forgery in time." She stepped forward and gave Tungdil a tentative embrace. "May Vraccas bless your melding with a warm hearth and a casket of gold," she said in a strained voice. "We won't see each other for a while, I suppose."

Closing his eyes, he filled his nostrils with her scent. He hadn't missed it until now, but it was so familiar, so precious. He knew it was the last time he would hold her in his arms.

I still love her, he thought forlornly, clasping her to him and pressing his lips against her brow. "Vraccas be with you," he murmured, too choked to say anything else.

For Balyndis it came as a shock to see the truth in his eyes, and Tungdil was startled to see the tenderness and sorrow in her face. She still loved him; she loved him in spite of the way he had shunned her. He reached for her hand, but she took a step back and shook her head. "Glaïmbar is waiting," she said in a smothered voice, turning away.

He watched her go, remembering all the other goodbyes, too many goodbyes. "Myr is waiting too," he whispered.

"We're still here, you know, scholar," said Boïndil with his usual lack of tact. He looked at him intently. "You and Myr should join our deputation. How about it?"

Boëndal suspected that their friend had other plans. He was sure he had seen a hint of a smile playing on Tungdil's lips. "Have you thought of a way to foil the thirdlings?"

"Maybe," said Tungdil cagily, laying a hand on Boëndal's shoulder. "I haven't quite conquered my doubts—but I'll come straight to you and Boïndil when I'm ready."

Boëndal grinned. "I knew you weren't destined to spend your orbits in an armchair! Vraccas has sent a spark of heroism to relight your fires. Whatever you're planning,

count us in: We'll storm the Black Range if we have to."
He set off with his brother in the direction taken by
Balyndis.

Tungdil wandered through the palace, vacillating
between confidence and doubt. Soon he was hopelessly
lost, but he kept walking, deep in thought. Balyndis's
farewell was playing on his mind.

His wounds from their separation were as painful as
ever. He realized now that scarring wasn't the same
as healing, and even Myr was a salve, not a cure—she
took his mind off the pain, but she couldn't make it go
away. It wasn't that he didn't love her; he just loved the
smith more.

*How can you think about Balyndis when the future of
Girdlegard is at stake?* He shivered at the thought of the
decision he had to make. *Vraccas give me wisdom.* It took
a while for him to regain his bearings among the endless
passageways and chambers of the palace. At last he found
himself outside the conference chamber.

Striding past an archway, he noticed three short figures
at the end of a shadowy corridor. One was small and
dainty, the next was broad-shouldered, and the third was
noticeably taller and larger.

That sounds like . . . Myr! Tungdil stopped in his tracks
and hurried back to the corridor. "Hello, Myr!" he called
cheerfully. "Don't tell me you got lost as well!"

The smallest of the three figures gave the biggest dwarf
a shove. Tungdil heard a muffled shriek, followed by a
clatter of weaponry, and a sickening thud.

His warrior's spirit ignited. Whipping out his ax, he
sprinted down the corridor and threw himself between the

dainty freeling and the other dwarves. "Back off," he said menacingly, noticing the gashes in Myr's left cheek. Blood was streaming down her face, streaking her pale complexion. *Now it's personal* . . .

Romo, holding two thick tomes in one hand, reached for his morning star with the other. His gauntlet shimmered red with Myr's blood. "Lorimbur be praised," he spat. "Not everyone has the privilege of killing Girdlegard's favorite dwarf." He threw the books to his companion. "Take these, Salfalur. My uncle can't wait to read them."

Salfalur! The dwarf who killed my parents! Tungdil stared at the powerful dwarf, who caught the books, and turned to flee. The tattoos made his ferocious features look doubly sinister, almost demonic.

"No," shrieked Myr, pulling a dagger from her belt. She launched herself at the brawny thirdling. "Give me back my work!"

Salfalur waited unflinchingly for the dagger to thud against his chain mail. The tip broke off. Raising an armored fist, he punched the little dwarf's wounded face. Myr flew back as if struck by Vraccas's hammer, hit the wall, and slumped to the ground. "Come on, Romo," commanded Salfalur. "We're leaving before the maga and her famulus catch up with us."

Romo roared with laughter. The chains of his morning star whirred menacingly, the spiked balls circling above his head. "And let the scumbag live? I've never spared a child of Vraccas, and I won't start now."

At last Tungdil shook off the paralysis induced by finding Salfalur and seeing Myr hurt. He saw the morning star coming and ducked.

"You've killed your last dwarf, Romo Steelheart," he growled, ramming the sharp end of his ax into the thirdling's thigh. He drew the weapon back and used the momentum to lunge at him with the blade.

Cursing, Romo dodged the blow and hobbled backward. Features distorted by hatred and rage, he stared at his bleeding thigh. "Die, you traitor!" he thundered, taking the morning star in both hands and swinging it at Tungdil again and again.

Tungdil knew that the haft of his ax, albeit reinforced with steel, was no match for the morning star. Rather than risk losing his only weapon, he focused on staying out of reach.

The metal balls cannoned into the walls of the passageway, sending shards of marble flying through the air, but Romo's assault continued unabated. Cursing and panting, he pursued his adversary with relentless zeal.

Stepping backward, Tungdil stumbled over Myr and was punished for his carelessness by a terrible blow. One of the steel balls crashed into his arm, while another collided with his broken ribs. Bent double with agony, he focused his energy on keeping hold of his ax.

"How many blows to fell a hero?" jeered Romo, circling the morning star above his head and preparing to strike. "Two at the most, I'll warrant . . ."

The balls spun toward him.

Tungdil reached up and deflected them with his ax head. They hit a door and crashed through the timber. One of the chains got stuck in the wood and refused to yield to Romo's increasingly vigorous efforts to pull it free.

"How many strikes to fell a thirdling?" said Tungdil,

dealing a one-handed blow to Romo's torso. The blade cut through his chain mail and buried itself in his flesh. Blood spurted from the wound.

Romo had no intention of conceding defeat. Abandoning his morning star, he thrust both gauntlets simultaneously into Tungdil's face. Tungdil tumbled to the ground. His eyelids swelled, narrowing his vision, and blood trickled from a gash above his right eye.

Romo pulled the ax from his torso and held it aloft. "More than you think!" he thundered, preparing to strike.

Harsh yellow light filled the corridor.

"Take that!" shouted a melodramatic voice behind Tungdil. He felt a rush of hot air as flames shot toward Romo, turning him into a living torch.

The thirdling's beard was ablaze and his skin was charred and cracked. A nauseating smell of burning flesh filled the air.

Romo made no attempt to extinguish the flames. He took another step toward Tungdil and raised his arm to strike. Just then a figure cannoned into him from behind and his ax careered sideways. The blade embedded itself in the floor half a hand away from Tungdil's chest.

Growling, Romo shook off his assailant.

"Huzzah!" shouted Ireheart, leaping up and brandishing his axes. "Come here so I can give you a taste of my blades!"

"Stop," called Tungdil. He clambered to his feet and pulled the morning star from the ruins of the door. "He's mine."

Romo parried the first blow, but Tungdil struck again,

and the metal balls slammed into the thirdling's head, neck, and throat. He wobbled, but didn't fall.

Tungdil landed three hefty strokes in succession until at last Lorimbas's nephew lay motionless on the floor. *I never wanted to be a dwarf killer*, thought Tungdil, dropping the morning star onto his enemy's body. *But Romo deserved to die.*

"That was no fun," complained Ireheart. "He'd been burned to a cinder and injured already. Where's the challenge in that?" He glanced around eagerly. "What happened to the chunky one? He'll put up a better fight."

Meanwhile, his brother, assisted by Tungdil and Rodario, still glowing from his debut as a famulus, was attending to Myr.

Tungdil, ignoring his own wounds, scooped the unconscious freeling off the cold flagstones and carried her back to their chamber where he tended to her until Narmora took charge. In short order, the maga restored the dwarf to her former condition, allowing her skin to grow back as smooth as ever, with no evidence of damage to the silvery down on her cheeks.

Next Narmora turned her healing energies to Tungdil and mended his broken ribs. Lifting his arms gingerly, he discovered that the pain was gone. "Magic gives me goosebumps," he said.

"*All* magic, or just Samusin's magic?" the maga enquired.

"You pray to Samusin?" said Tungdil, surprised.

"I was born of an älf—the other gods won't have me. Listen, Tungdil, there's no need to worry about Myr. She's sound asleep and she won't wake before morning. You may as well look for the missing thirdling."

"Salfalur," he said grimly, picking up his ax and hurrying over to the twins who were hovering in the doorway with the impresario. "Thank you for your help back there," he said to Rodario. "Can you tell us the fastest route out of Porista?"

"My dear dwarf, I *built* this city," bragged Rodario. "Well, I oversaw the building of it," he appended, edging closer to the truth. "Furgas drafted the plans."

Boïndil frowned. "So you're more a caretaker than an architect . . ."

"I know this city like the back of my hand." He tugged on his sleeve to hide the miniature tinderbox, a sophisticated device that threw flames at the tug of a cord. Several dwarves and humans had witnessed his fiery attack on Romo and were convinced of his magic powers.

"Still doing party tricks?" laughed Boëndal. "You're supposed to be a famulus, not a street magician."

"It worked, didn't it?" the impresario retorted touchily. "You wait, women will love it. I've got everything: thespian charm, writerly eloquence, natural good looks—and now mastery of the mystic arts."

Boïndil roared with laughter. "Not to mention the wandering eye of a philanderer."

"Come on," said Tungdil, smiling in spite of himself. "We don't have time for your nonsense, Rodario."

"My nonsense? I've never been so—" He saw the determined look on Tungdil's face and set off through the labyrinthine corridors of the palace with the dwarves in his wake.

The city wasn't destined to sleep that night. Every street, every house, every chamber was searched by patrols of men, elves, and dwarves, but there was no sign of Salfalur.

The thirdling had vanished, and with him Myr's notes about Trovegold and the other cities. Soon Lorimbas would know every detail about Gemmil's secret realm.

Porista,
Former Realm of Lios Nudin,
Girdlegard,
Late Autumn, 6235th Solar Cycle

Tungdil was sitting at Myr's bedside when she woke with a start. The delicate dwarf took a few moments to remember what had happened. "Did you stop them?" she asked weakly.

He shook his head. "We couldn't find Salfalur. He disappeared."

"We've got to warn Gemmil! The thirdlings will know everything about our realm." She looked up at the ceiling and thumped the wall. "If only I hadn't brought the books with me! I never thought my penny-pinching could cause such trouble. What if Lorimbas invades?"

"Your penny-pinching?"

"I only brought the books with me because I wanted to fill the empty pages. I knew I'd have lots to write about, and paper is expensive. It's my duty as a scholar to chronicle everything I see and hear. I'm the eyes and ears of Trovegold. I can't allow our history to be forgotten." She ran a hand tentatively over her forehead, remembering her encounter with the wall. "Warriors never leave home without their weapons. I never go anywhere without my books."

He stroked her smooth cheeks. Belatedly she realized that she wasn't in any pain. She raised a hand to her face.

"You won't find a scar," Tungdil told her with a smile. "Narmora is a maga. She healed my ribs as well."

"A maga?" echoed Myr, impressed. She lay still for a moment and closed her eyes. She seemed to be searching for evidence—an inner voice, a hidden clue that might reveal the workings of the maga's power. "I've read about magic," she said, a little sheepishly. "I thought maybe you could feel it."

"It's strange, isn't it?" he agreed with a grin. "There's something odd about magic—it doesn't suit us dwarves."

He was glad to see that Myr had made a full recovery. It seemed to confirm that he had made the right decision about melding his heart to hers. Just because he loved Balyndis didn't mean he wasn't genuinely fond of Myr. They were soul mates, brought together by their love of learning. As soon as he taught her to appreciate metalwork, they would make a perfect pair.

Except you still love Balyndis, his inner demon reminded him slyly.

Tungdil responded by leaning over and kissing Myr.

Nice try, laughed the demon.

Myr smiled uncertainly. "It was horrible, Tungdil. I found the thirdlings in our chamber, rummaging through my things. Romo—I think that's what he said his name was—bashed me on the head and knocked me out. The next I knew, I was dangling from his shoulder. He threatened to kill me if I made a noise. Thank Vraccas you came along and saved me."

"It was nothing," he said modestly. "Anyway, I probably wouldn't be here if it weren't for your skill as a surgeon. Remember how we met? I had an älvish arrow in my shoulder, and another in my chest—you pulled them out and healed me." He paused and looked at her gravely. "As soon as you're well enough, we'll be on our way. Meanwhile, there's something I need to deal with. I've asked for an audience with Gandogar."

"With Gandogar? Why?" She tried to sit up in bed, but slumped sideways against his shoulder. "It's all right. I think I'm still dizzy from being bashed on the head or colliding with the wall—or both."

He held onto her. "You'll probably say I'm crazy, but I think it's a cunning ploy."

She looked at him, startled. "What's a ploy?"

"I think the thirdlings don't know anything about the avatars," he explained. "If you ask me, they know we're running scared, and they're taking advantage of the situation. This could be their ultimate victory—it's safer and more effective than a war. One in two of our kinsmen will die on the march to the Outer Lands. The paths are treacherous, it's deepest winter, and we'll have avalanches to contend with."

"Not to mention hunger," she said sadly.

"The thirdlings' demands are designed purely to kill the maximum number of dwarves. They're trying to trick us into leaving Girdlegard by spinning us a story about a secret weapon." He looked into her red eyes. "The thirdlings are lying, and I can prove it. From what Boëndal told me about the first meeting, Romo didn't say anything about the avatars, only about a threat from the west. He was stringing us along."

"If I were Gandogar, I'd want better evidence than that," objected Myr. "What if Romo was referring to the avatars when he—"

"Maybe he was," cut in Tungdil. "The question is, why would the avatars kill Andôkai if Lorimbas were the threat?" He smiled. "First Romo was talking about stopping them, next he was going to destroy them. Which is it?"

"Stopping, destroying—it's the same to a warrior like him. He wasn't the sort to care about distinctions."

"That's not all, though. He couldn't give any details about the weapon. No wonder—it doesn't exist!"

"What if the secret to stopping the avatars is so straightforward that he'd be giving away their bargaining power? Or maybe he likes being awkward."

"He could have told us *something*—like whether it's an ax or a trebuchet or runes to be carved above the western gates," insisted Tungdil, who felt like he was arguing his case before a judge. It seemed to him that Myr was being deliberately contrary.

"You're right to distrust him, but think how the dwarven monarchs will react. He's promising to save Girdlegard, and you're saying we can't be helped."

"Why would they believe Romo? He hasn't given them any proof," said Tungdil moodily. He thought for a moment. "You're right though. Sometimes the truth isn't welcome."

"If I were Gandogar, I'd give Romo the benefit of the doubt. Imagine what it would be like watching Girdlegard go up in flames and knowing you could have saved it. I wouldn't want to live with the guilt."

"You'd rather send thousands of dwarves to their deaths? Come on, Myr, you can't agree to the banishment of the folks when there's a good chance the thirdlings are lying! Even if we make it back to Girdlegard, we'll have to fight or trick our way into our kingdoms. Meanwhile, Lorimbas and the thirdlings will be laughing themselves vraccasium-red." He stood up. "I know you don't agree with me, but it's my duty to alert the high king to a possible plot."

"You need more evidence," ruled Myr. "You haven't persuaded me." She pressed her lips to his hand. "Vraccas be with you."

We appreciate you sharing your suspicions," began Gandogar.

Tungdil knew at once what the high king was going to say. *Myr was right*, he thought. *I need more proof.* He didn't bother to listen to rest of the speech; Gandogar's objections were much the same as Myr's.

He glanced at the other delegates: King Balendilín, King Glaïmbar, and Queen Xamtys looked worried and dismayed. *They must be wondering how to break the news to their clansfolk. How do you explain that the high king wants everyone to leave their kingdoms and risk their lives for a weapon that might not exist?* He bowed and took a seat, even though Gandogar was still speaking.

The dwarf of all dwarves didn't seem offended by his rudeness. "I'll go down as the worst high king in history, I know, but I've been left with no choice. Vraccas commanded us to give our lives for the safety of Girdlegard." He stood up. "It's settled: The dwarves will leave their kingdoms. Tungdil, you'll have to tell Gemmil to abandon his realm. Now that the thirdlings know the location of the underground cities, they're bound to attack." He raised his hand in parting and left the chamber. The other delegates followed his lead.

Tungdil covered his face with his hands. He couldn't bear to think about the hardships awaiting his kin.

The footsteps died away and the chamber was still. It didn't occur to him that anyone was left, so he was startled when a hand squeezed his shoulder. Uncovering his eyes, he turned and looked into Boëndal's bearded face.

"You mustn't give up, scholar." He stepped aside, revealing a small band of dwarves looking grimly determined. "Not everyone thinks you're wrong. The kings and queens chose not to heed you, but your efforts weren't in vain. We saw the strength of your conviction, and we believe you."

One by one the delegates introduced themselves. Between them, they represented all four folks.

"Well?" said Boïndil expectantly. "I hope there are enough of us. I'm assuming you've got a plan."

"I *had* a plan," he said, thanking Vraccas for his small band of followers. A smile spread across his face. "But I've thought of a better one."

One of the delegates cleared his throat. "I won't do anything to hurt my king, my clansfolk, or my family."

"You're an honorable dwarf." He scanned their faces. "I'd sooner chop off my head than put any of our kinsfolk in danger." He beckoned them closer. "But I do have a mission for you. With your courage and Vraccas's blessing . . ."

"He'll bless us all right," said Boïndil confidently.

"In that case, the thirdlings are in for a shock." And he told them what he had in mind.

Narmora leaped out of bed, rushed down the corridor, and ran into Furgas's room. A moment later, Rodario was by her side.

"Did you hear him scream?"

"Fetch Myr," she said tersely. "She'll know what's wrong."

Rodario hurried away.

It's happening too soon, thought Narmora distractedly. *I don't know how to cure him yet.* She wiped the sweat from Furgas's face.

A pink blotch appeared on the cloth. Thin lines of blood were trickling from Furgas's closed eyelids and mingling with his sweat. *I don't know how to counteract the poison. I need more time.*

She waited impatiently for Myr, who turned up a few minutes later with Tungdil.

Myr examined her patient thoroughly, listening to his heartbeat, checking his breathing and smelling his skin before inspecting the contents of the chamber pot. "He's feverish," she announced, looking up at Narmora. "All the symptoms point to poisoning. He's in a bad way, Estimable Maga. His heart is gathering speed like a runaway trip hammer—he'll die if you don't slow it down."

The maga shivered. "I've been working on a charm,

but . . . I was wondering if you could give him something to ease the pain."

Myr raised her eyebrows. "You can't cure his symptoms with your magic? The toxin must be awfully strong."

"Can you help him or not?" demanded Narmora more sharply than intended. "You said we need to slow his heart."

"I can't do anything without knowing the make-up of the poison," she said sadly. "His life is in your hands." She packed her things and waited uncertainly next to Tungdil, until the maga dismissed them with a nod.

As soon as they were gone, Narmora slipped her hand beneath her bodice and pulled out the shard of malachite, running her finger over its surface and sloughing off the dried blood. *It's the only way.* She washed the gem quickly, opened her bodice, and focused her mind, channeling her magic energy into the malachite.

The stone began to glow, becoming warmer against her skin.

Samusin, keep me from harm and save Furgas from suffering. She placed the tip of the stone on the pale skin below her sternum and tensed her muscles, preparing, as Nudin had done before her, to absorb the malachite's power.

Take my life, if you have to, Samusin, but let him live. She closed her eyes and drove the malachite into her chest.

The pain was unbearable.

A viridescent sun exploded within her, dousing her in a caustic tide that seared, froze, and swelled her veins, gathering inside her until she was sure she would burst like a rotten fruit. Suddenly it stopped.

Narmora fell to her knees and retched. A puddle of green vomit collected on the floor. The next wave of nausea purged her stomach of its contents, the stinking torrent of malachite vomit narrowly missing Furgas's bed.

"Who are you?" called a voice.

She retched again, raised herself on trembling arms, and turned her head, looking for the speaker. "Is someone there?" she gasped.

"I can teach you things that will make you more powerful than any maga or magus in history," the voice whispered. Nudin appeared in a corner of the room. He smiled at her warmly. His robes belonged to another, long-forgotten era.

"You can't be . . . We killed you at the Blacksaddle!"

"I'd like to help you," he said, morphing suddenly into the familiar bloated figure of Nôd'onn. His smile became a smirk. "All Girdlegard will cower in awe of you," he promised. The air above Furgas's bed seemed to shimmer, bringing forth the misty demon that Tungdil had slain at the Blacksaddle. "Poor soul, he's dying," whispered the mist, caressing Furgas's cheeks. "You can save him. I've given you the power."

Narmora was dazzled by a bright green light. She closed her eyes, and when she opened them again, the mist was gone and the room was silent except for Furgas's muffled groans.

I must have imagined it. She looked down to see that the wound had closed without leaving a scar or a telltale malachite glow. The skin was flawless and a single droplet of crimson blood marked the place where the stone had entered her breast.

Furgas cried out in agony, his body convulsing with pain.

"I'm here," she said weakly, clutching the bed and stumbling to her feet. She laid a hand on his dressings. *Now we'll see the extent of my powers.*

In a clear voice she uttered the first of many incantations, taking her time over the syllables that came unbidden to her lips as she commanded the poison to leave Furgas's body.

At once she heard a hissing noise.

Sulfur-yellow vapor rose from the motionless body and melted into the air. Meanwhile, tiny yellow droplets appeared on Furgas's skin, dancing like spilt water on a stove. Soon the sheets were drenched in yellow.

Furgas's chest was rising and falling rapidly. He started to moan.

Am I killing him? thought Narmora in alarm, starting to lift her hand.

"Keep going!" commanded a voice beside her. "You have the power to cure him, Narmora. His eyes will open, you'll see." Nôd'onn smiled at her encouragingly. "Trust in me and the power of the stone. You're a maga: He's in good hands."

Narmora could see him clearly now. He bore no trace of the wounds inflicted at the Blacksaddle. "You're an illusion," she said firmly. "Be gone!"

Nôd'onn pointed to Furgas's stained bandages. "You've got to keep going," he told her.

Narmora turned her attention back to Furgas. Strange words of healing surfaced in her memory and she continued her incantations.

Poison was still seeping from Furgas's pores, but suddenly he stopped groaning, drew a sharp intake of breath, and lay still.

"No!" cried Narmora despairingly, rushing to the head of the bed and stroking his face. "What have I done?"

Furgas opened his eyes and looked at the ceiling in surprise. At last he noticed Narmora and raised a hand to her face. "Narmora . . ."

She swallowed, then threw her arms around him, laughing and crying. Furgas sat up and clasped her tightly. "You're back," she sobbed happily. "Thank Samusin, you're back!"

Furgas seemed bewildered by the outburst of affection, but enjoyed it all the same. "I remember now . . ." he said slowly. "We were attacked . . . What happened after that?" He kissed her shiny black hair and took her head in his hands so that he could look at her properly. His gaze fell on her slender waist. "How long have I been asleep?" he asked, startled.

"Stay there! It's time you met your daughter," said Narmora, racing off to fetch Dorsa.

She handed the baby gently to Furgas, who was weeping with joy. "She had a brother, but he didn't live," she said. Her eyes glistened as she recounted the events leading up to the accident that killed their child.

Furgas stroked his daughter. "At least we've got Dorsa," he said gruffly, kissing her tiny head. He pulled Narmora to him. "I love you, Narmora. I love you both. After the orbits of torment, this moment is all the more precious."

Narmora gave him a lingering kiss. "Get some sleep, my darling. Everything else can wait until the morning.

I'm afraid there's a long road ahead if our family is to live happily in Porista. We'll need my talents and your technical wizardry." She snuggled closer, holding her breath for a second as Nôd'onn appeared at the end of the room. The apparition faded away.

Kingdom of Dsôn Balsur,
Girdlegard,
Late Autumn, 6235th Solar Cycle

Hosjep was sitting atop the largest mangonel, banging nails into the sturdy timber and wrapping rope around the framework to absorb the impact of the throwing arm.

All around him, carpenters were at work in their lofty perches, twisting rope, adjusting leather buffers, and hammering nails into wood. On the ground, others were chopping and planing raw timber to make beams and struts for the next consignment of mangonels.

Many orbits had passed since the älfar burned down the siege engines. The nighttime raid had led to huge losses for the allies, not to mention a standoff between the elves and the dwarves, but the biggest casualty was morale. The savagery of the älfar's attack had dented confidence in an allied victory, prompting mass desertions. Many of Hosjep's fellow workers had abandoned their posts.

Hosjep had been tempted to join them, but the money was too good. Under normal circumstances, he wouldn't have ventured within a hundred miles of Dsôn Balsur, but the army had secured his services with the promise of gold. He had already been paid more than he earned in an average cycle.

He looked across at the swathe of scorched earth bordered on both sides by gloomy forest. From his vantage point, he could see that the allies were barely a mile from the plains. Soon the army would be able to advance unhindered.

Beyond the forest, the stronghold of Arviû blotted the landscape like a malignant cyst, its dark walls casting a shadow across the verdant plains.

To cheer himself up, he imagined what Dsôn Balsur would look like when the älfar were gone. *Beautiful*, he thought, his spirits lifting a little.

From the stronghold, the grassy plains extended for miles, dipping on the horizon to form a crater, from which rose a tapering tower, shimmering bone-white in the sun. This then was the heart of the älvish kingdom, the target of the allied campaign.

Hosjep picked up his hammer and returned to work. *I wouldn't want to be a soldier,* he thought with a shiver. *This is close enough for me.*

Hours later, he was still clambering over the enormous mangonel, but the gathering gloom brought an end to the orbit's work. He began to climb down carefully. Without a rope to hold onto or a net to catch him, the slightest clumsiness could see him falling ten paces to the ground.

Down below, the latest recruits had arrived and fires were being lit. The soldiers had dug a moat around the camp, filled it with rags dipped in pitch and tar, and set light to the mix. Any älf that tried to breach the ring of fire was liable to burn to death. The order had been given for more pitch and tar to be added every hour. The foul-smelling concoction had been mixed to a sticky gloop to ensure it served its purpose rather than leaching into the soil. No one minded the stench or the acrid smoke—it was better than dying at the hands of the älfar.

Hosjep was in good spirits. The siege engines would soon be back in action, reaching toward the stronghold of Arviû with their powerful arms. Barrels of oil and petroleum were arriving from the human kingdoms, and in ten orbits the army would have sufficient fuel to finish the campaign. All in all, the allies were in an excellent position.

But fear, superstition, and rumor prevailed.

Time for some hot grub and a tankard of ale. After a solid orbit's labor, Hosjep was looking forward to his bed of fresh hay. He jumped onto the mangonel's throwing arm and started to walk carefully to the ground. His eyes were drawn to the ring of fire around the camp. The flames were cowering fearfully at the bottom of the ditch.

He stopped in his tracks.

Every light in the camp was burning low. The camp-fires were dying, the candles on the makeshift tables were sputtering, and the oil lamp above the commander's tent was barely alight. A moment later, the camp was plunged into darkness.

Hosjep listened to the silence. Everyone was waiting and praying for the moment to pass.

Every light had retreated, including the moon and stars. *I've never seen it so dark.* It seemed to Hosjep that the camp had been dunked in black ink, making it impossible to see further than his nose.

The horses flared their nostrils and tried to break free.

Whinnying in terror, they strained against their hitching posts, pulling until the wooden stakes jerked out of the ground.

Hosjep heard the sound of splintering timber, then thousands of hooves stampeded through the camp, trampling tents and soldiers. The spooked horses could see no better than the men, but their nostrils told them to run. Hosjep clung to the arms of the mangonel as the fleeing herd collided with the frame. Great clouds of dust rose from the churned-up ground, mixed in with cold cinder from the fires. At last the deafening stampede was over and the whinnying faded: The horses were out of the camp.

"Get in formation!" commanded an officer, apparently undaunted. He had to shout to be heard above the welter of screams and shouts. "Third company to me, pikemen at the front—" An armored body hit the ground.

The soldiers didn't need eyes to know what had happened.

"Run!" shouted someone. A weapon clattered to the ground and footsteps raced away. "They're here! They're in the camp!"

Hosjep pressed himself against the mangonel, lying flat against the throwing arm between the uprights of the frame. If the darkness were to lift, he wanted as little as possible of his profile to be visible from the ground.

Death descended on the camp.

It started with a single, drawn-out scream of agony, then the slaughter began. Hosjep heard noises that would haunt him for the rest of his life, tortured wails and terrible weeping, blown to him on the cruelest of winds.

The älfar seemed to know exactly where to find the

soldiers. Arrows ripped through the air in all directions, and Hosjep was hit by a stray missile that embedded itself in his leg. He clenched his jaw and swallowed the pain.

Time dragged on, but at last the clattering of swords and screams of the wounded died away. The moon and stars broke through the cloud, revealing the carnage below.

Corpses were strewn several deep across the battlefield, covering the ground like a gory carpet of torsos, limbs, and blood.

Älfar stepped lightly over them, looking for survivors. The living were pulled out from under the dead and killed in the cruelest fashion.

Hosjep surveyed the slaughter, eyes welling with tears of helpless rage. *Ye gods, have mercy. They've killed them all . . .* Try as he might, he couldn't see a single dead älf. *How could you forsake your children, Palandiell?*

Down below, an älf was riding over the bodies. Her mount, a bull with monstrous horns, wore a metal visor, and its eyes emitted a fearsome red glow. She shouted an order, whereupon a band of älfar waded through the corpses, slitting their throats and collecting their blood. Meanwhile, another band threw pitch and petroleum over the frames of the mangonels.

I've got the choice of being slaughtered or burning to death, thought Hosjep wretchedly. Given the options, he decided to wait until the älfar torched the mangonels, then pull the arrow from his leg and stab himself through the heart. *I'd sooner kill myself than fall into their hands.*

Just then the bull raised its head, looked straight at him, and snorted impatiently. Its rider followed its gaze. She was wearing a mask and a black gauze veil that obscured her features. Hosjep watched as she raised her quarterstaff and barked an order. An archer raised his bow and took aim at the mangonel.

The arrow hit him in the left shoulder. He lost his grip, rolled off the throwing arm, glanced off a strut, and landed on the soft carpet of bodies below.

"Get back! Get back, you devils!" he wailed, floundering among the corpses. Already an älf was beside him. Snatching up a sword, Hosjep thrust it forward, stabbing the älf in the guts.

The älf stayed standing.

Then to Hosjep's horror, he took hold of the sword and pulled it from his torso. Dark, almost black blood poured from the wound, but within an instant the flow dried up.

He healed himself. Hosjep wriggled backward. *No wonder I couldn't see any älvish casualties . . . Palandiell, what have we done to be punished like this?*

"Listen, wight," said the älf on the bull. "Your gods took mercy on you and spared your life. Return to your kingdom and tell your monarch what you've seen. The immortal siblings wish it to be known that the älfar will not yield. Tion has blessed us with new powers." The bull took a step closer. "I'm sure you can testify to their effect— unless you'd like another demonstration . . ."

"No!" Hosjep shrank away from her. "I'll do as you say and tell Prince Mallen."

"Then go," she commanded.

Hosjep struggled to his feet and ran for his life, ignoring the pain in his shoulder and leg.

Turning her bull, Ondori congratulated her warriors.

The little band had passed the test. After drinking the

dark water, the warriors had ridden into battle and survived their wounds. *Sitalia's fairies will be next*, she thought grimly. *Âlandur, prepare to meet your doom . . .*

She looked down at the trampled bodies, imagining the wonderful sculptures that she would make from the skeletons. Any leftover bones would be transported to the capital and added to Nagsor and Nagsar's tower.

Kingdom of Gauragar,
Girdlegard,
Late Autumn, 6235th Solar Cycle

The autumn weather refused to smile on Tungdil and Myr. Most of their overland journey was spent in the pouring rain.

Myr, fearing they would catch a chill from sleeping outside in damp clothes, insisted on gathering herbs for an infusion to protect them from the cold. Knowing that they couldn't afford to lose time to illness, Tungdil knocked back cup after cup of the stuff.

Unfortunately, he started the regimen too late and developed a nasty cough that left him tired and weak. The pair had no choice but to break their journey at an inn, where they could sleep on a dry mattress out of the rain until the first big storm had passed.

The innkeeper's wife could barely conceal her astonishment at the appearance of two such unusual guests. "I'll make you some hearty broth, Mr. Goldhand," she promised when he was safely tucked up in bed. "I've got plenty of herbs in the kitchen. They work wonders against coughs and colds."

"Really?" said Myr enthusiastically. "I'll make an infusion. We'll have him back on his feet in no time." She snuffed out all but one of the lights, placing the remaining candle in a holder, which she left on the table by his bed. "I'll be back soon," she said soothingly, bending down to kiss him. "Try to get some sleep." In the doorway, she stopped and looked at him with an odd expression.

Tungdil lay on his back, sinking into his mattress of wool and straw, and looked sleepily at the shadows cast by the candle on the whitewashed walls.

The more he looked at them, the more menacing they became, closing in on him steadily like wild beasts as he lay, unarmed and unarmored, between the sheets. It felt like he were at the mercy of a vague, intangible evil, like the sinister fog in the Outer Lands.

"Confounded candle," he grumbled, reaching over to snuff it out. His fingers, weak from the fever, groped clumsily for the wick, brushing against it without extinguishing the flame.

Though he had barely touched the candle, it was sitting so loosely in the holder, that it toppled over, landed on the floor, and rolled, still burning, under his bed. A moment later, the straw poking out beneath the mattress was on fire.

"Damn and double damn." Tungdil tried to get up, but succeeded only in falling out of bed. He watched as the mattress went up in flames.

"Myr!" he shouted. "Myr, the bed's on fire!"

Silence.

"Fire!" His shouts turned to coughs. Glowing embers flew in all directions, spiraling through the chamber and settling on the floor and furniture, spreading the blaze. Soon the room was unbearably hot. "Fire!" he shouted desperately. Exhausted and feverish, he lay on the rough floorboards, unable to move.

The crackling grew louder and the fire began to hiss and roar. The whole room had become an oven, and still no one came to his aid.

Do you want me to die here, Vraccas?

At last the door flew open. Tongues of fire licked greedily toward him, fanned by the rush of air. "Mr. Goldhand?" called a gruff male voice. "Are you there?"

"I'm here!" he croaked. "Here, by the bed!"

A bucket of water arced through the air, sloshing against the floor, and spattering Tungdil's beard. A moment later a muffled figure wearing a dripping blanket charged into the chamber, grabbed Tungdil by the wrist, and dragged him out of the inferno to the safety of the landing.

"Tungdil!" At once Myr was beside him, crouching over him anxiously. She seemed more upset by the incident than he was. Upset and slightly guilty. "What happened?"

"It was my fault," he whispered in a rasping voice. "I knocked the candle . . ."

"Take Mr. Goldhand downstairs," interrupted the sooty-faced man. "I need everyone out of the corridor so I can put out the flames."

The innkeeper's wife helped Myr to carry Tungdil downstairs to the main tavern. "This is for you and your husband," said Myr, handing the woman a gold coin. "I can't thank you enough. Tungdil would have burned to death without you." Black smoke was still billowing from the landing. "We'll pay for the damage, whatever it costs."

The woman thanked her and hurried away to help her husband.

"What am I to do with you, Tungdil Goldhand?" said Myr. "I leave you alone for two seconds, and you set fire to the bed!" She hugged him tightly. "You gave us both a nasty shock."

"Where were you?" he asked, wrapping his sooty arms around her.

"We were preparing the infusion. The housemaid was making such a din with the pots and pans that we didn't realize that the room was on fire until the innkeeper shouted for help." She swallowed and buried her head in his chest. "Get some sleep," she said tearfully. "I'm never going to leave you alone again. Not ever." *You're all I care about. I've learned my lesson. Thank goodness you didn't die.* She hugged him tenderly.

IV

The fire was put out before the flames could consume the rest of the inn. Only the roof above the upstairs chamber and the chamber itself were destroyed in the blaze.

Two orbits later, after plenty of rest, regular doses of Myr's herbal infusion, and generous helpings of the land-lady's broth, Tungdil was ready to start walking again. Myr knew of a secret entrance to the underground network, and they covered the final miles of the journey at breathtaking speed.

On arrival in Trovegold, they went straight to the strong-hold to make their report to the king.

Sanda Flameheart was with Gemmil when they were ushered into the room. She seemed delighted to see Tungdil, but her relief turned to trepidation when he recounted the news from Porista. From time to time she glanced suspiciously at Myr, who ignored her steadfastly, perhaps because she hadn't noticed or because she didn't care.

"Our realm is in great danger," judged Gemmil. "If we don't leave our cities, the thirdlings will take them by force."

"Glaïmbar said that you're welcome to join the fifth-lings," Tungdil told him. "Your warriors saved his kingdom from the orcs. He said it's the least he can do to give you passage and assistance over the northern pass. He knows the fifthlings can't repay their debt, but they'll do what they can to help."

Gemmil could tell from Tungdil's tone that he doubted the wisdom of the proposal. He also realized Tungdil had spoken of the fifthlings as if they weren't his folk. It probably wasn't deliberate, but Gemmil suspected that he didn't consider himself a fifthling anymore. Tungdil had rebuilt the fifthling halls, as Giselbert had requested, but the Gray Range had ceased to be his home.

"You think we shouldn't leave Girdlegard," said Gemmil, tackling the matter head-on.

"I think leaving would be a mistake," said Tungdil forthrightly. He proceeded to list the key points of his speech to Gandogar and the delegates.

This time his arguments didn't fall on deaf ears. "Those are all good points," said Gemmil. "Still, you can't know for sure that Romo was lying. How are you going to stop the thirdlings from poaching our strongholds without putting Girdlegard at risk?"

"I can do it—with your help," replied Tungdil. "Think of the thirdlings' proposal as an ordinary business deal. Would you pay for something without asking to see it first? Lorimbas is asking us to buy a diamond in a poke." He could tell from the king's face that he agreed. "Wouldn't it be better to verify that the item exists? We need to know that the thirdlings are capable of stopping the avatars. If they aren't, Girdlegard will need every warrior at her disposal. We'll be sealing her fate if we leave."

Gemmil turned to Sanda. "What do you think?"

"Sixty cycles is the blink of an eye in dwarven history," she said slowly. "No one mentioned a secret archive when I was in the Black Range. We talked a lot about the Blacksaddle because our ancestors are buried in its chambers, but there was never any mention of an archive or a weapon. Lorimbas's story doesn't ring true."

"A great deal can happen in sixty cycles," argued Myr. "Think how much has changed in Trovegold in the past sixty orbits. You can't presume to know what the thirdlings are thinking or doing. We need better evidence than that." She eyed Sanda scornfully before turning to Gemmil. "I think you should be careful. For all we know, Lorimbas could be telling the truth."

Tungdil was taken aback. "Whose side are you on?" he said indignantly.

"Yours, of course," she said soothingly, taking his hand. "Fearlessness and daring are excellent qualities in a warrior, but an overhasty decision could be the ruin of Girdlegard, not just the dwarves." She gave his fingers a little squeeze. "I'm your very own voice of reason. I'll offer good counsel and be right behind you, whatever you decide."

"There's another thing you should consider," said Sanda. "Are you prepared for a life like mine? If you defy the high king, you'll be punished. You won't be Tungdil Goldhand, hero of the Blacksaddle; you'll be an outcast. This isn't a minor infraction of the rules; it's rank disobedience, possibly treason. Your sentence will be harsh." She took a deep breath. "They could banish you for good. You might never be allowed back to the fifthlings."

Tungdil smiled at Myr. "As soon as I arrived here, I felt like Trovegold was my home. I like being with dwarves who follow Vraccas without enslaving themselves to petty rules. Besides, my heart is melded to Myr's." Though he spoke with conviction, he couldn't help thinking of Balyndis. *She made her decision; I made mine*, he added defensively before his inner demon could comment.

You don't fool me, a small voice mocked him.

Gemmil looked him in the eye. "You seem to know what you're getting yourself into," he said levelly. "Why don't you tell us what you propose? You can count on the freelings to play their part."

Tungdil told them his plan.

Borengar's Folk,
Eastern Border of the Firstling Kingdom,
Girdlegard,
Early Winter, 6235th Solar Cycle

It was snowing again. In no time the nine towers and twin ramparts of East Ironhald, recently rebuilt by the firstlings, were covered in glittering white.

Everyone, no matter how young or old, had helped to clear the debris and restore the stronghold to its former glory. Even the gully leading up to the stronghold boasted six new fortified gates.

The masons had learned from the mistakes of their predecessors, and the fortifications, including the towers and bridges, were designed to withstand three times the previous winter's snowfall.

Barriers had been erected further up the mountainside. Thick stone slabs and long mounds of rubble protruded from the slope, ready to trap the White Death before it smothered the dwarves below.

At the base of the gully, the first of the six gates, built to withstand snow and ice, formed a formidable defense against invaders, including Lorimbas Steelheart and his dwarves.

Tasked with searching the portal for a lever, handle, or secret mechanism, Salfalur could find only a freshly polished block of stone that had once bidden visitors—*friendly* visitors—to enter. The inscription had been chiseled off.

"No luck," he called out to Lorimbas. He and his warriors were wearing thick woolen cloaks, hats, and scarves over their armor to protect them from the biting cold. The king, as a mark of his status, had draped a fur stole over his shoulders and was wearing the royal helmet. "The gates won't open," explained Salfalur. "We'll have to climb over."

"Confounded firstlings," thundered the king, his voice echoing through the valley. "They did it to spite us."

The heavyset commander trudged through the snow toward him, sinking deeper with every step. "It's only a minor setback, Your Majesty. Xamtys's stronghold will soon belong to Lorimbur." He shouted for ropes and grappling hooks to be brought to the base of the gates.

Climbing equipment wasn't usually to be found in dwarven kit bags, not least because dwarves weren't suited to dangling from ropes, but after receiving reports from two of his units, Salfalur had come prepared.

According to the bulletins from the north and northeast of Girdlegard, the gates to Glaïmbar and Gandogar's kingdoms had been locked. The entrances had been barricaded so thoroughly that not even a mouse could get through.

"I wouldn't count on it," muttered Lorimbas angrily. "Xamtys will have copied the others, I bet." He was already expecting to receive news from the south that the secondling stronghold was impregnable too. It was like forging hot metal on an anvil, only to have the hammer snatched from his hand. Even more frustratingly, there weren't any dwarves for him to kill.

"Normally I'd ask Vraccas to guide your hand and bless your hammer, but I know how little you care about the Smith," called a loud voice that seemed to come from the mountain. Just then a dwarf appeared on the parapet above the gates. "I'll keep it short. Greetings, King Lorimbas Steelheart of the clan of the Stone Grinders, ruler of the thirdlings."

Salfalur recognized the figure immediately and signaled to Lorimbas, who clenched his fists in fury. "Tungdil Goldhand, I presume. You murdered my nephew."

"Your nephew tried to kill an innocent dwarf," retorted Tungdil. "He chose his own fate. Ask Lotrobur's murderer if you like."

"I'll skin you alive," thundered Lorimbas, drawing his ax.

"You'll have to catch me first," said Tungdil, laughing. "In case you hadn't noticed, shouting won't open the gates." He leaned over the parapet confidently, reminding Lorimbas that he had the upper hand. "Incidentally, you might want to keep your voice down. The White Death will come thundering down the mountainside if it hears you screeching like a hairless orc." He made a show of scanning the surrounding peaks. "I didn't realize the Red Range was so dangerous. How many warriors have you brought? Five thousand? And where's the famous weapon that you promised the men and elves?"

"It's none of your business. Get out of my kingdom!"

"I'm the one on the inside; the kingdom belongs to me. I'll open the gates on one condition: that you show me the weapon and tell me how it works."

The thirdling king raised his ax menacingly. "We had an agreement! Gandogar will be furious when he hears about this. He'll hew your miserable—"

"I'm a thirdling," said Tungdil, undaunted. Drawing his ax, he pointed it at Salfalur. "Ask him, if you don't believe me. He killed my mother and father and threw me into a chasm, but Vraccas saved me and brought me here to save Girdlegard from your lies." Tungdil clasped his ax in both hands and drew himself up to his full height, standing tall and proud like a true custodian of the gates. "Where's the weapon, Lorimbas?"

Salfalur gave a signal, and a band of thirdlings prepared to scale the walls.

Tungdil smiled. "Is that how you're going to fight off the avatars, with climbing ropes and grappling hooks?" He paused. "There's something you should know: I'm not alone." Boïndil appeared at his left, and Boëndal on his right, weapons aloft, and faces grimly determined.

"This is definitely in breach of the agreement," said Salfalur. "I know those two; they're secondlings!"

"Not any more," chimed in Boïndil, twirling his axes

impatiently. He was clearly spoiling for a fight. "We're freelings now."

Gemmil appeared on the parapet. "They're with me."

On Gemmil's signal, the rampart filled with dwarves carrying shields, clubs, axes, and other weapons. Some of them deposited rocks on the edge of the parapet, ready to hurl them at the thirdlings in the event of an attack.

"A few of my warriors from Trovegold," explained Gemmil. "The battalions from Gemtrove and the other cities are guarding the stronghold. Ten thousand dwarves, six gates, twin ramparts, nine towers, and a bridge lie between you and Xamtys's halls."

"You'll have me to reckon with as well," said a crimson-cloaked Narmora, stepping up to the parapet.

"And me," called Rodario grandly, trying to look as imposing as possible. He was wearing a magnificent new robe for the occasion. "My name is Rodario the Fablemaker, apprenticed to the mighty Narmora the Unnerving, and second only to the maga in skill and power."

Tungdil swung his ax above his head. "King Lorimbas, the choice is yours: Attack, and expose your warriors to dwarven bombardment and the wrath of a maga and her famulus, against whose magic no mortal army can prevail, or show us the weapon and explain how it works."

The king scanned the ranks of the defenders. "The weapon isn't here," he said, scowling. "Our first priority is to take possession of our territory and secure our position."

"Fine, but you and your warriors will have to wait until you've convinced us that the weapon really works. I hope for your sake that it doesn't take long—it's cold outside."

He pointed to the right. "There's a cave over there. It should be big enough for half your army. The others will have to make do with blankets."

"Psst, scholar," whispered Boïndil. "How are we going to know if the weapon really works?"

Tungdil grinned. "Did you see the look on Lorimbas's face? I thought Salfalur was going to scale the gates and tear me to pieces!"

Boïndil looked at him blankly. "So what?"

"In other words," whispered Boëndal, "Lorimbas and Salfalur are furious with us for seeing through their scam." He smiled, relieved that their decision to follow Tungdil had been rewarded. "You were right, scholar. Lorimbas lied to the other rulers. The weapon doesn't exist."

Tungdil took little satisfaction in his victory, knowing that the news augured badly for Girdlegard as a whole. "Narmora is our only hope. She'll have to delay the avatars while we raise an army of innocents to fight them. The dwarven rulers and other monarchs must be informed."

"Don't get ahead of yourselves," shouted Lorimbas from below. "I'll have the weapon for you in two orbits. Prepare yourselves for a surprise."

"We're happy to wait—if waiting will save our homeland," Tungdil called back. He lowered his voice so that only his friends could hear. "They're bound to attack. They're going to use the time to find a way of breaking our defenses. Tell the sentries to be vigilant. We need to brace ourselves for an assault."

Boïndil banged his axes together. "I'm not afraid of them. I don't like the notion of spilling dwarven blood, but what choice do we have? Vraccas forgive us for raising our axes against his creation, but the thirdlings have brought it on themselves."

"Clansfolk!" Lorimbas's voice cut through the mountain air. "Thirdling clansfolk who have strayed from the Black Range, deserters like Sanda Flameheart who left the thirdling ranks, your crimes will be forgiven. Turn back to the thirdlings before it's too late."

"More lies, Lorimbas?" called Tungdil. "Your trickery won't work." Out of the corner of his eye he watched as Sanda glanced nervously from Gemmil to Myr, but her face betrayed no emotion. He couldn't help recalling Myr's warning. "Fine, Lorimbas, you've got two orbits. I can't wait to see the secret weapon that can destroy a band of demigods."

He backed away from the parapet until he was out of sight, with Narmora and the others following suit. He didn't know whether to feel satisfied that his strategy had proven successful, or dismayed that his worst suspicions had been confirmed. All along he had been secretly hoping that Lorimbas would surprise him by unveiling a mighty weapon capable of saving Girdlegard from destruction.

He was joined by Narmora, who seemed to guess what he was thinking. "What are we going to do now?" she asked. "We can't fight a battle on two fronts." Her dark, almost fathomless, eyes gazed toward the west. "After orbits of calm, the past few nights have been worse than ever. Judging by the fire on the horizon, the avatars are dangerously close." She was glad that she hadn't brought her daughter with her. There could be no doubt that Dorsa would be safer with Rosild in the palace than with her parents in the western range, but it didn't make the separation any easier to bear.

"Can you stop the avatars?" asked Tungdil.

She gave a wry laugh. "What can anyone do against eleven miniature deities?" She looked crushed. "Andôkai studied for over a hundred cycles and never attained the skill and knowledge she sought. I was her apprentice for half a cycle." She lowered her voice. "No one knows how to stop them. We know nothing about them, except that they're lethal. Nôd'onn was right, Tungdil. He warned us about the avatars, and we killed him. The only magus with the power to destroy the avatars is dead." She took a deep breath. "We won't have many peaceful orbits like this. We shouldn't spoil it with gloomy thoughts." She turned to leave. "I'll tell Furgas to load the catapults."

"Tell the sentries in West Ironhald to inform us of any developments," he said. "I only hope we can resolve things with Lorimbas before the avatars reach the border and Xamtys and her clansfolk are burned to death."

Narmora nodded and took her leave.

"She cured Furgas even though she said she couldn't," Myr said thoughtfully. "Her powers must be increasing, don't you think?"

"I hope she can handle it. We need her to be strong in spirit." Tungdil took her in his arms. "What will become of us, Myr? Will we be killed by Lorimbas or Salfalur, or reduced to ashes by a band of demigods? Is this the end of our adventure?"

She stroked his cheeks. "I'm a medic, not a seer. I can't foretell the future, but I'll always be right behind you. After what happened last time, I won't be letting you out

of my sight. You could have died because of me, and
nothing is going to stop me being there if you need me—
not Salfalur, not the avatars, nothing." She looked at the
dwarves thronging back to the warmth of East Ironhald.
"I'll make sure my medicine bag is properly stocked. I'll
need it, if Lorimbas attacks."

"They won't breach the gates."

"What if they don't have to?"

She glanced across at Sanda, who was giving orders to
the guards behind the fortified wall.

"She'll ruin everything," murmured Myr. "Someone
needs to keep an eye on her, and it had better be me."

The two orbits were over in no time.

Tungdil, Narmora, and the twins took up position on
the ramparts and waited for Lorimbas to spin them another
story or launch an attack. "Any idea what they've been
doing?" Tungdil asked a sentry.

"Singing—standing right here, and singing. Songs about
battles, songs about the other dwarves, most of them highly
offensive . . . They wouldn't shut up." It was clear from
his tone that the lyrics had incensed him. "We couldn't
sleep because of the noise. But the main thing is, they
couldn't bring down the gates with their voices."

"They've started again," said Boëndal, pointing to the
crowds of thirdlings emerging from the cave. "They're
singing their hearts out."

The thirdling warriors lined up in rows, the front row
as long as the gates were wide. Still singing, they marched
toward the mouth of the gully with Lorimbas at their
head. He came to a halt some thirty paces from the gates.

"I thought you were going to show us the weapon, Lorimbas," called Tungdil sarcastically. "Don't say you forgot!"

"There never was a weapon, Tungdil Goldhand, you traitor," bellowed the thirdling king. "Know this before you die. Your wise dwarven friends, the oh-so-clever humans, and the snotty-nosed elves fell for our ruse. The avatars don't exist."

"So now you're pretending we were never in danger," scoffed Tungdil, signaling to Gemmil's warriors to heft their weapons. "I can't fault your resourcefulness. What have you lined up next?"

"Your destruction. Right now four thousand warriors are marching on West Ironhald. They'll storm your defenses from the west, while I lead the rest of my army to victory from the east. No dwarf, no maga, and no god can stop my conquest of the dwarven kingdoms. My spies have served me well."

"Where's the fat one?" hissed Boïndil suspiciously, scanning the enemy ranks. "I can't see him anywhere. What's happened to the others? There were five thousand of them not so long ago. A thousand are missing at least."

"You're right. Something funny is going on." Tungdil turned back to Lorimbas. "If the avatars don't exist, how do you explain the fire burning on the horizon, night after night? Can you do magic, Lorimbas?"

The thirdling king chuckled. "Oh yes, I can do magic, even without your maga's powers. I can conjure dwarves to the Outer Lands and harness the power of sulfur to make gullible dwarves like you quake in their boots at the sight of my mighty conflagration."

"But how did you . . ."

"A real hero would have explored the Blacksaddle and uncovered its secrets," Lorimbas taunted him. "You were in our stronghold, and you never suspected how valuable it was. We've got our own system of tunnels, built by our ancestors many cycles ago. From the Blacksaddle, we can attack in all directions. I heard you were expecting trouble from the west, so I invented a threat."

"You're lying, Lorimbas."

"The whole of Girdlegard is shaking like a leaf because I set off a few fireworks in the Outer Lands," crowed Lorimbas.

"What about the comet? No catapult in Girdlegard has the power to—"

"The comet was real, all right. A happy coincidence for us. It landed in the Outer Lands and left a big crater. Some of my spies saw it fall. They didn't spot an avatar, unless he was made of lava." He slapped his thigh and shrieked with laughter. "To think you took the comet as a sign that Nôd'onn was right! You would have done anything I said to protect yourself from the imaginary threat."

"You made the dwarves leave their kingdoms," murmured Tungdil.

"What happens next is up to you. Either open the gates and leave with your lives—or wait for us to cut you down. My warriors will show no mercy."

Narmora stared at the thirdling king. *All lies . . . I lost my child, Andôkai died by my hand, and Furgas was in a coma, all because of his scheming . . .* Her eyes darkened to fathomless hollows and she lifted her arms, causing the dwarves around her to shrink away. "Lorimbas Steelheart, you will die for your treachery," she called menacingly.

"Not as soon as you think, witch," he retorted, raising his horn to his lips. A moment later, the ground caved in, causing the fortified wall to collapse.

The defending dwarves crashed to the ground. Most of those on the parapets were crushed by stone blocks the size of a fully grown dwarf or buried under falling debris.

No sooner had the final block come to rest than the thirdlings surged forward, clambering over the rubble and throwing themselves on the startled defenders whose leaders had fallen with the gates.

Worse was to come.

Amid the commotion, Trovegold's warriors heard picks and hammers breaking through the frozen ground behind them. Soon they were confronted with the missing thirdlings, as one thousand warriors led by the ferocious Salfalur emerged from a hastily built tunnel and attacked from the rear.

The first battle began.

By dusk, the bodies of three thousand defenders lay strewn between the first two gates, and the thirdlings were singing victory songs to Lorimbur.

Tungdil and the twins had managed to drag the wounded Narmora from the rubble and carry her through the second gate before the thirdlings noticed. Gemmil, Sanda, and nine hundred badly shaken warriors had also survived the assault.

Eyes closed, Narmora was concentrating on healing her wounds. The skin grew back faster than water rising in a well. She leaped to her feet. "I'm going to make that treacherous thirdling pay for his—"

"No, Narmora," said Tungdil. "We're abandoning the first five gates. I don't want to lose more of our warriors to the thirdlings' underhanded tactics. Save your strength for defending the stronghold."

Narmora was about to reply when Myr ran up. "Come quickly, maga," she called. "You'll never guess what the sentries have found on the western border."

"More warriors for me to tend?"

"Just one," said Myr. "It's Djerůn, Estimable Maga. At least, I think it is . . ."

"Great," snorted Boïndil. "First Andôkai, now Narmora. Where the heck are these Djerůns coming from?"

"More to the point, who are they being sent by?" muttered Tungdil. "You're a genius, Boïndil!"

"Thank you." The secondling paused. "Er, why?"

The little group hurried after Myr, who was racing across the bridge to the stronghold.

"You raised an excellent question, and I don't think Lorimbas will have an answer for it—which is worrying . . . Very worrying." He exchanged glances with Myr, who seemed to share his concern.

Djerůn, or rather, what was left of Djerůn, was lying on the floor.

His armor looked old and battered, with countless scratches, scorch marks, and dings. It was obvious from the broken-off swords, lances, and spikes embedded in his mail that his journey had been fraught with danger.

He was smeared all over with bright yellow blood, and he hadn't stirred since their arrival.

"Hmm," said Boïndil, scratching his beard. "Can anyone speak Djerush?"

All eyes were turned on Narmora.

"I'm sorry," she said. "The maga didn't teach me his language. She took the secret with her when she died."

"Where's my mistress?" rasped a strange voice inside her head.

"Listen!" exclaimed Boïndil. "Did you hear him growling? Come on, buckethead, speak a language we understand!" Fearlessly, he took a few steps toward him. "You'd better not be an impostor." He leaned over and peered at the visor. "Balyndis would know from the metal-work . . ." His stubby fingers reached for the beak of the visor. "I'll take a peek at his face."

"Tell him to stop," said the voice to Narmora, who finally realized that Djerûn was talking to her. "You've changed, half älf. There's something inside you—something that belonged to Nôd'onn."

"Ha, listen to him growl," said Boïndil, laughing. "Don't you dare bite me," he warned the armored giant, menacing him with the blunt edge of his ax. "I'll wallop your metal skull so hard you'll—"

"That's enough, Boïndil," snapped Narmora. "I've . . . I know what he's saying after all." Her lips moved effortlessly, forming strange syllables that came to her of their own accord. *It must be the malachite*, she thought.

"It's not the malachite, it's the energy within it," said Nudin, appearing at Djerûn's side. "It's more powerful than you think." Suddenly he was gone.

I must be hallucinating, thought Narmora, blaming it on the fall from the parapet. *I'm probably still concussed.* "Your mistress is dead, Djerûn," she told the giant, hoping that the others hadn't noticed her distraction. "She was murdered by a giant, a giant wearing your armor. Can you tell me what happened?"

"Are you the new maga?"

"Why won't he get up?" asked Boïndil impatiently, prodding him in the chest with the haft of his ax. "Maybe he's asleep. Are you sure he's not snoring, Narmora?"

"Be quiet," his brother shushed him, tugging him away. "Do you *want* him to eat you alive?"

"He's not armed, is he? What's a half-dead giant going to do to a warrior like me?"

"If he doesn't stop prodding me, I'll rip through his chain mail and tear him in two," Djerûn told Narmora. "Answer my question: Are you the new maga?"

"It wasn't my choice." She paused. "The late maga's legacy will abide in me forever. They call me Narmora the Unnerving."

"You were her famula and you worship her god. Narmora the Unnerving will be my new mistress."

"She sent you to the Outer Lands. What did you see?"

"My strength is fading, mistress. I need your help."

"Did Andôkai have an incantation or a—"

"I don't need magic, mistress," he said, lifting his head a little.

"Hoorah!" whooped Boïndil, edging closer. "Old buck-ethead is alive! Assuming it's really him . . ."

"Boïndil!" chorused the others disapprovingly. He shrugged

moodily and kept quiet, although no one believed for a moment that the silence would last.

"I need your blood, mistress."

"My blood?"

"The blood of a maga is more nourishing than my prey. It will give me power—and bind me to you."

"Everyone out," said Narmora, trying to hide her agitation. "I need to heal Djerûn's wounds. The incantation is powerful—I don't want anyone getting hurt." The others traipsed out reluctantly, dragging the protesting Boïndil with them. As soon as Narmora was alone with Djerûn, she kneeled beside him, heart thumping in her chest, and rolled up the sleeve of her robe.

Djerûn raised a hand to his visor and flipped it open. It was all Narmora could do not to run away. Like Balyndis, she was filled with terror at the sight of his face. She held out her wrist.

"It will hurt, mistress," he told her. Without warning, his head sped forward and he sank his teeth into her arm, slitting the flesh from wrist to elbow. His lipless mouth sucked the wound.

Narmora felt instantly light-headed. Every drop of blood seemed to be draining from her body. At last, when she was certain she would faint, Djerûn released her and she sank to the floor, murmuring an incantation to close the wound.

Djerûn's eyes shone violet, the light becoming brighter and stronger, more dazzling than the sun. Beneath his armor, something was rustling, cracking, clicking. A lance dropped to the floor from his breastplate, followed by a hail of broken sword tips, arrow heads, and spikes.

"Your blood is good, mistress," roared Djerûn with the energy of a young god. "You taste like Andôkai, only powerful, more powerful. You're a good maga—strong and full of healing." He got to his feet like a warrior raring for battle after a good night's sleep. Bowing his armored head to Narmora, he began his account . . .

Andôkai sent me to look for the avatars.

I crossed the Red Range, marched across the flatlands, and came upon a raging fire and a band of dwarves. My mission was to look for avatars, not groundlings, so I continued on my way.

Next I came to a crater, four times as big as the gully and full of glowing, bubbling rock. The land beyond was charred and barren. I kept walking until I found the strewn remains of human soldiers—Weyurnians, as I realized from the crests on their blackened armor.

Soon afterward, I saw an army.

The warriors carried white banners with ten different crests and their armor was white, so white it hurt my eyes. Their mounts were whiter than any horse in Girdlegard.

I watched them from a distance to find out who they were and where they were going, but they discovered my hiding place and came for me with their swords.

For every warrior I killed, four others took his place, and four became eight. At length they overwhelmed me and brought me before seven beings, each surrounded by a ring of light that dazzled my eyes. They were wreathed in purity and I couldn't see their faces.

They asked me where I came from, and I didn't reply, so they tormented me with kindness, love, and warmth.

But I didn't die like they hoped.

Summoning my strength, I broke away, anxious to tell my mistress of what I had witnessed.

They called after me that the good, pure souls of Girdlegard should fear no more. Soon, they said, the evil that had inhabited our kingdoms for cycles would be banished, and Tion and the spirit of evil would plague Girdlegard no more.

I ran for many suns and moons until I found the hidden path to the firstlings' stronghold.

Narmora stroked her arm, marveling at the smooth, healthy skin. *So that's why the avatars are marching on Girdlegard. They think we're still in the clutches of Nôd'onn and the Perished Land. No one's told them that the magus was defeated.*

"Thank you, Djerûn," she said pensively.

"What about the dwarves, mistress?

"What about them? They were thirdlings."

"Not the dwarves near the fire, I mean the others. Some of the warriors from the White Army followed me. They must have found the dwarves by now—the thirdlings, and the dwarves on the mountain tracks."

The maga nodded. She didn't much care what happened to the thirdling fire-raisers, but she was concerned about Xamtys and her dwarves. She left Djerûn and walked out into the corridor where Tungdil and the others were waiting.

As soon as she opened the door, they looked at her expectantly. She could see the curiosity in their eyes. "We were right to fear the avatars. They're on their way."

Their curiosity turned to shock.

The angry little midgets might listen to reason," said Rodario, feeling the weight of the silence. "We need to tell them that the avatars are real."

Tungdil, Gemmil, Narmora, the twins, and various dwarven dignitaries were in a meeting to discuss the coming threat. Meanwhile, Salfalur and his warriors were barreling through the firstlings' defenses.

Three hundred thirdlings had died in traps rigged by Furgas, but nothing could deter the fanatical dwarf killers. Very soon they would succeed in conquering the stronghold, and the last resistance to their treachery would be crushed. But neither Lorimbas nor his warriors suspected that the avatars were real.

Boïndil burst out laughing. "Trust you to want to talk them into submission! Just imagine: the fabulous Rodario—"

The impresario raised a hand to silence him. "*Rodario the Fablemaker*," he corrected him. "Perhaps my short-legged, hotheaded friend could take the trouble to address me by my proper title."

Boïndil put his hands on his hips. "Since when have you been a wizard? You're just a cheap conjurer with the good fortune to be acquainted with Furgas, a technician of dwarven intelligence and skill!" He tapped his forehead in mock excitement. "Maybe you could hold a poetry reading for the thirdlings! Remember how you tried to talk the runts to death?"

"There's no need to be rude, Master Ireheart. It was merely a suggestion."

"A bad one."

"In your opinion."

"Useless, actually."

"You can do better, I suppose?"

"Quiet, both of you," cut in Narmora. She glared at Rodario. "He's right, by the way. Talking to the thirdlings won't change anything."

"Gang up on me, why don't you?" he said, offended. "I was merely suggesting that we should explain the situation. The thirdlings have guarded the Black Range for cycles. They might be murderous traitors, but they've done their duty in defending the Eastern Pass."

Boëndal made a clicking sound with his tongue. "I suppose he's got a point. We could give it a go, but we'll need some proper proof. The thirdlings won't be any more inclined to trust us than we trust them."

"I've sent word to Xamtys that the thirdlings were lying," said Tungdil. "I've warned her about the avatars— I'm praying that the message will get to her in time."

The door flew open. "You're needed at the inner gates," gasped the agitated dwarf. "Come quickly! They've nearly broken through."

"I hate to say it, but Lorimbur's children know a thing or two about fighting," growled Boïndil, jumping up, axes at the ready, and following the dwarf. "Luckily I'm here to show them that you don't need marks on your face to be a good warrior." He laughed. "Let's give the thirdlings some new tattoos."

In spite of the bluster, Tungdil could tell that his friend wasn't nearly as excited about slaying thirdlings as he was about killing orcs, bögnilim, and other beasts. Deep down, he doubted that they could hold the gates. *The Red Range is living up to its name; the gully will be awash with blood before the orbit is out.*

The dwarves' hopes rested with Narmora's magic, Djerûn's strength, and Furgas's technical expertise. Tungdil, after witnessing the first battle, had been awed by the thirdlings' discipline, power, and axmanship.

No matter what happens, Salfalur won't leave here alive. Tungdil was determined to kill him, whatever the cost. Taking up his ax, he left the hall and hurried over the bridge to the highest of the nine towers from which he could survey the action.

It was an incredible sight.

Fighting wasn't the thirdlings' only talent. Lorimbas's warriors had built a three-sided tower out of the rubble of the fallen gates. The front edge of the tower was pointing straight at the twin ramparts of East Ironhald; and from Tungdil's vantage point, it looked like an enormous guillotine.

The structure, built at an angle, was supported by struts to which ropes had been attached.

Tungdil watched as fifty warriors stepped forward, took hold of the ropes and pulled. The struts came away, the tower tilted forward, slowly at first, then faster and faster until it hit the ramparts, smashing through the fortifications like a colossal blade. The stronghold had been breached, allowing the thirdlings to charge forward.

"The freelings shouldn't have let them build the tower," said Boïndil, gazing down at Gemmil's dwarves. He frowned. "Fighting isn't their forte. In terms of pure numbers, we've got the advantage—not that you can tell."

They left the tower and waited for the system of platforms and pulleys to lower them to the ground. "Xamtys had better hurry or Lorimbas will be sitting on her throne," said Boïndil darkly as they hurried to the defenders' aid.

Tungdil spotted the broad-shouldered commander in the front line of thirdlings. His long-handled hammer curved through the air, felling freelings with every stroke. "I'll deal with Salfalur," he said, closing his fingers around the haft of his ax. "You take Lorimbas."

Molten slag poured down on the invaders from above, followed by a torrent of petroleum, which ignited as if by magic as it neared the thirdling troops.

On the left flank of the defending army, the sky was dark with fiery smoke. Narmora and Rodario were doing everything in their power to keep the thirdlings at bay. In the maga's case, the magic was real, whereas Rodario relied on conjuring tricks and imaginary curses. Meanwhile, Djerûn endeavored to protect them from attack.

But even the colossal warrior did little to deter the thirdlings, who jabbed at him from a distance with lances and pikes.

Despite their efforts, the invaders had yet to reach the

ramp leading to the inner rampart. The thirdlings would have to breach the gates, ascend the highest tower, and cross the bridge to conquer Xamtys's halls. While the gates still stood, the thirdlings could kill as many defenders as they liked without taking the kingdom for themselves.

Tungdil fought his way to the front, keeping Salfalur in his sights. Just then he heard a piercing scream. *Myr!*

Turning, he spotted her at the gates. She was sprawled on the ground, a few paces from her medicine bag, and Sanda Flameheart was standing over her, threatening her with a single-balled flail. Behind them, the gates to the inner rampart had opened slightly. The thirdlings saw their chance.

Myr was right, thought Tungdil, pushing his way through the throng of warriors to rescue his companion. *Sanda is a traitor, and I fell for her act.*

Before he could reach her, Ireheart jumped in and sent Sanda crashing to the ground.

Tungdil hurried to help Myr. Her right cheek bore a fiery handprint, the thumb and four fingers burning red against her smooth, pale skin. Blood was trickling from her mouth and nose. "She opened the gates," she croaked as Tungdil helped her to her feet. "I couldn't stop her."

"It's not your fault," he said, kissing her brow and thanking Vraccas for Boïndil's speedy intervention. "Quick, we need to close them." They hurried through the gates.

Tungdil cursed when he saw the traitor's work. Sanda had sabotaged the mechanism, and the chain lay abandoned on the ground.

By now, Sanda had scrambled to her feet and was

batting away Boïndil with ease, which enraged the zealous warrior. His eyes glazed over as his fiery spirit took hold of his mind and spurred him on. "I swore to protect Myr," he growled, slashing at her furiously. "No one lays their murderous hands on my brother's healer and gets away with it."

"I wasn't trying to kill her," she told him, forced by his whirring axes to focus harder on her defense.

"Traitor!" He raised his right arm and feigned a blow.

"*I'm* not the traitor! *She* was the one who opened—" The ax veered sharply and struck her armpit. There was a sound of metal on metal, then the crunching of bone as the blade passed through her chain mail and into her arm. The stunned Sanda was still gasping with pain when Ireheart's boot connected with her kneecap, smashing the joint, and sending her crashing to the ground.

"Liar!" screeched Myr, whipping out her dagger.

Tungdil held her back. "Look at her, Myr! She can't hurt you now."

"It was Myr," gasped Sanda, trying to stem the blood with her other hand. "I tried to stop her, but I came too late." She swallowed. "Lorimbas is her father. "

"And I'm the mighty Vraccas," sneered Boïndil. "We're not stupid, you know."

"It's the truth," murmured Sanda, propping herself against the wall. Boïndil's blow had severed the vessels in her armpit, and her tunic was drenched in blood. "I'll never forget when she first arrived in Trovegold. I knew at once who she was, but she swore me to secrecy. She said her father would kill my clansfolk if I breathed a word to Gemmil or anyone else."

"Enough of your lies!" Myr pointed at her accusingly with the dagger. "Haven't you caused enough trouble? *You're* the thirdling, not me!"

"Remember what happened in Porista? She made it look like Romo and Salfalur abducted her because she needed to hand over the information about Trovegold without arousing suspicion. Why else would they have spared her life?" Sanda closed her eyes and spoke in a whisper. "I don't suppose she mentioned that she's been melded twice before. The first dwarf died of a fever; the second was on his sickbed when his chamber went up in flames." She looked at Tungdil, who gazed into her eyes and saw nothing but honesty and concern. "I realized she was after Gemmil, so I asked him to meld me instead."

Tungdil was busy reviewing what had happened in Porista, how he had fallen ill, and what Myr had said to him after the fire. "Myr, that time at the inn when I nearly died in the fire," he said slowly. "You didn't have anything to do with it, did you?" Her red eyes looked at him uncertainly. He grabbed her by the arm and pulled her aside as if she were a naughty child. "Promise you had nothing to do with it!"

Her eyes brimmed with tears. "Tungdil, I . . . You can't take her word over mine," she protested halfheartedly.

"Promise you had nothing to do with it, and I'll never mention it again."

She looked at the ground. "You've got nothing to fear from me, Tungdil. After the fire, I realized that I couldn't . . . I didn't mean to fall in love with you, but . . ." She started to cry.

"Myr, tell me you're not Lorimbas's daughter," whispered Tungdil. He had never felt so betrayed. He forgot about the battle and the threat from the avatars; nothing seemed to matter anymore.

She sniffed and dried her eyes on her sleeve, then looked him in the eye. "Sanda is right. I was sent by my father, Lorimbas Steelheart, to spy on the freelings and prepare the way for a thirdling invasion. I've always been pale-skinned; nature gave me the perfect cover. I had only to change my eye color and invent a story about my provenance. No one thought to question my origins. Then *you* came along." She reached for his hand. "I was supposed to kill you, but my heart wouldn't—"

Her gaze shifted, and her eyes filled with fear. Grabbing his shoulders, she spun him around and took his place just as something rammed into her from behind, throwing her forward. Tungdil reached out to catch her. Her mouth opened, lips moving silently, but she could barely breathe.

Standing behind her was Salfalur. He was clutching his hammer, the haft of which was tipped with a metal spike as long as a human arm. The end was resting against Tungdil's chest, having passed through Myr.

"I would never have . . ." she sighed, clutching at him. "You mustn't think too badly of me . . ." Her dainty body went limp in his arms. In spite of the pain, she seemed to smile at Tungdil as she died.

Salfalur drew the spike from her body. It made a soft popping noise as he pulled it clear.

"Are you satisfied now?" Tungdil laid her down gently

and drew his ax. "You killed my parents, and now you've killed my wife."

"*Your* wife?" Salfalur was still clutching his hammer and staring at Myr. "She was *my* wife, not yours." With his free hand he touched the blood dribbling down the haft, then rubbed it between his fingers. "Myr was my wife, and she died because of you. I'll make you die a thousand deaths."

"She was your . . ." Aghast, Turgdil stepped back, then pulled himself together.

"Let's settle this now," he said grimly, preparing to fight.

They circled, waiting for the other to strike.

Salfalur was the first to attack. In his arms, the mighty hammer looked no heavier than a broom.

Tungdil braced himself, but the blow never came. In the background, Lorimbas was sounding the retreat. Looking up, Tungdil saw a battalion of firstling warriors on the parapets—Xamtys had marched ahead with half of her army to save her kingdom from falling to their dwarven foes.

Salfalur was torn between continuing the duel and doing his job as commander-in-chief. At last he lowered his hammer. His brown eyes contained a silent promise to resume the duel in another place, at another time.

Tungdil nodded.

Nyr wasn't the last to die that orbit. Sanda Flameheart was mortally wounded.

Gemmil held her in his arms while Boïndil stood beside them, not knowing what to say.

"It's all right," she said, her breath coming in little

gasps. "I know you didn't mean it, Boïndil Doubleblade. I've heard about your curse."

He kneeled beside her, distraught. "I'm . . ."

"You don't have to explain; I forgive you." She stretched her bloodied fingers toward him.

Boïndil took her hand and held it in silence until she passed away. "Vraccas must hate me," he muttered. "Why can't he kill me and be done with it?" His face was expressionless, but his eyes welled with tears. "I should have settled for stunning her, but my fiery spirit made me cut her down. First Smeralda, now Sanda . . ."

Gemmil stood up and signaled to some dwarves, who hoisted the dead queen gently onto their shoulders and carried her into the stronghold. "Sanda was right: You mustn't blame yourself. You fell for Myr's lies, and Vraccas gave you a heart of fury. It's not your fault." He rested a hand on the secondling's shoulder to show there was no animosity between them; then he followed the others to the firstling halls.

An ill-fated orbit, thought Tungdil, gazing at Myr's lifeless body. Her leather jerkin was crimson with blood. He gathered her up and picked his way through the dead and wounded toward the retreating army.

"Lorimbas!" he called loudly. "Your daughter is dead, slain by Salfalur's hammer." He bent down and laid her gently on the ground. "She's yours to take if you want to bury her."

Lorimbas stepped forward, accompanied by a score of warriors. Salfalur wasn't among them. "Curse you, Tungdil Goldhand," he said, kneeling beside his daughter and stroking her pure white hair. "You murdered my nephew, and now you've killed Myr. Everyone I ever loved is dead because of you." He lifted her up tenderly. "We'll never make peace. You're like your father. He started this misery, and it will end with your death."

"Lorimbas Steelheart!" Xamtys hurried toward them, followed by a cluster of dwarves. "I'm afraid this is all that remains of the army that you sent against West Ironhald."

"The firstlings are better warriors than I thought." He shot a contemptuous look at the survivors, who were covered in gashes and burns.

"The firstlings didn't do this," said one of them, wincing as he spoke. "It was the avatars, Your Majesty."

"What?" Lorimbas frowned. "What do you mean, the *avatars*? Is this why the dwarf-queen spared you, because you promised to lie?"

"No, Your Majesty, I wouldn't deceive you."

"The avatars don't exist," shouted Lorimbas. "They're a legend, a legend designed to frighten small children, stupid beasts, and foolish dwarves!" He hugged his daughter to his chest.

"We were marching east," said another dwarf. "The firstlings had turned round and were on their way home. We could see them in the range ahead of us; then the cavalry attacked from behind. They were mounted on white horses and unicorns, and they rode straight into us as if we were unarmed. They were fearless." He swayed, and one of his companions had to steady him. "Then the demigods attacked. They were as dazzling as sunlit snow, shinier than a polished diamond, and five times hotter than a dwarven forge. They were everywhere at once, attacking us with . . ." He paused.

"I don't know what exactly," he whispered wretchedly. "I was struck by a cloud of light. It knocked me over, but I got up before it could hit me again. Then I ran for it. After a while, me and the others caught up with the firstlings. They made us surrender our weapons."

At last he had Lorimbas's full attention. "What happened to the rest of the army?"

The warrior bowed his head, revealing charred skin and a few blackened strands of hair. "I don't know, Your Majesty. The wind was coming from behind—it was warm with glowing ash."

"We sent a scout to the Outer Lands," chimed in Tungdil. "He told us the same story. Queen Wey's soldiers were destroyed by the avatars as well. It's not a legend, King Lorimbas."

The thirdling king hugged his daughter more tightly, smearing his armor with blood from her chest. "They can't be real," he whispered. "We made them up. It's simply not possible . . ."

"What now, Lorimbas?" asked Xamtys bluntly. "Do you want to fight me for my kingdom, or will you join us at the western border to halt the avatars' advance?"

He stroked the silvery down on his daughter's cheeks. "Everything I dreamed of has been destroyed. I don't want Girdlegard to suffer as well." He turned toward Tungdil, but something prevented him from looking him in the eye. "When this is over, we'll fight to the death. I should have wiped out your line when I had the chance." He bowed his head toward Xamtys. "I hereby declare a truce between the children of Lorimbur and the dwarven folks. I swear on my daughter, whose blood stains my hands, that the

have the combined strength of all the dwarven folks to draw on. It's the perfect time to strike."

Tungdil nodded. "I've sent word to Gandogar, Glaïmbar, and Balendilín. Their troops will take a while to get here, but when they do, Lorimbas will see what he's up against. We're bound to come to an arrangement." He bent over the table to examine the map. "We need to deal with the avatars first."

"I've got five thousand warriors," said Xamtys.

Tungdil looked at Furgas, Narmora, and Rodario. "How much time do you need?"

"I'm ready," said Narmora. "There's nothing I can do until they get here. I've got enough magic energy to take them on." She was lucky that the dwarves knew very little about the workings of magic, otherwise they would have wondered how she could summon the strength to attack the avatars without channeling fresh energy from the force fields. The malachite was lending her formidable strength.

Furgas spread some sketches on the table. "I've dismantled the catapults here"—he pointed to the site of the battle with the thirdlings— "and moved them to West Ironhald. I had enough helpers to get everything up and running. We can blot out the sun if we fire all at once."

"Excellent. How about you, Rodario?" asked Tungdil. "Sorry," he corrected himself quickly before the impresario could protest, "Rodario *the Fablemaker*."

"How kind of you to remember my title," Rodario thanked him sourly. Rising to his feet, he assumed the air of a great orator. "You see before you the greatest living avatar-trap. I have agreed to draw the demigods to me, to make myself the target of their wrath, to sacrifice myself so that my maga, Narmora the Unnerving, can use her powers to full advantage without fear of attack." He cleared his throat. "Naturally, I'm deeply honored to be an integral part of the heroics, but if anyone would like to share the glory . . ." There was silence. "Anyone at all? . . . I thought as much," he muttered grimly, sitting back down. "The poor supporting actors always get killed off. I hope Girdlegard honors my memory."

"You're not going to die, Rodario," said Tungdil. "I'm sure you'll be treading the boards of the Curiosum in no time at all."

"I can see it already," said Boïndil, swallowing the last of his beer. "*The Incredible Story of How Rodario the Fablemaker Saved Girdlegard from the Fiery Avatars.* You'll need a few jokes to liven it up. Did you hear about the orc who asked a dwarf for directions?"

"Go on," said the impresario eagerly, reaching for his quill.

The discussion was cut short by news that Lorimbas's warriors had arrived. Xamtys led the others to the entrance hall where they watched from the gallery as the thirdlings, bristling with weaponry and covered from head to toe in heavy armor, streamed through the doors below. Entire units were composed of grim-faced tattooed warriors, the thirdling elite. It was obvious from their expressions that they resented entering the kingdom as allies. For a moment the stronghold was silent except for jangling mail and the steady thump of booted feet.

"Are you sure they're not dangerous?" ventured Rodario nervously. "If I were an avatar, I'd give myself up."

"If you were an avatar, Girdlegard would be safe," commented Boïndil. He sniffed loudly and snotted on the warriors below, missing a ferocious tattooed thirdling by a dwarven whisker. "The famous dwarf killers. I know they're on our side, but I'm not inclined to trust them. I recommend you watch your backs."

Tungdil straightened up and clapped the twins on the shoulders. "We're needed in West Ironhald. It's time to save Girdlegard—this time without Keenfire's help."

They traveled through an underground tunnel beneath Xamtys's halls to reach the fortifications on the other side of the range.

West Ironhald was a perfect copy of its counterpart on the eastern flanks of the range. Queen Xamtys had rebuilt the walls to match the improvements made to East Ironhald, ensuring that both strongholds were sturdy enough to withstand the winter snow. Six fortified walls barred the steep-sided gully leading from the Outer Lands to West Ironhald, protected by twin ramparts, nine towers, and a bridge.

Tungdil and the others were greeted by a remarkable sight: Lined up on the ramparts beside the firstlings were Gemmil's freelings and Lorimbas's thirdlings. The three groups, divided by history, tradition, and outlook, had been brought together by a common goal: the protection of Girdlegard against invaders. Shoulder to shoulder they waited for the avatars to arrive.

Tungdil took up position in his favorite observation post and surveyed the thirdlings from the highest of West Ironhald's nine towers. According to his estimates, Lorimbas had summoned over twenty thousand warriors. *Xamtys was right. It would take more than the firstlings and freelings to defeat the thirdling army.* He turned back to the gully and looked for signs of the enemy, although he didn't know what to expect.

It was nearly dusk when he spotted a fierce white light at the end of the gully. Steadily the light drew closer, like a pure white sun rolling toward the range, sending its scorching rays skyward and lighting up the clouds.

Even from a distance, Tungdil could tell that it was dazzlingly bright. He could barely look at it without screwing up his eyes.

"This is it," said Narmora, joining him in the tower. She placed her hands on the parapet and stared at the glow. "Suppose we were to tell them that Nôd'onn and the Perished Land have been defeated? They might call off the invasion."

"How would we get them to listen to us?"

"With the help of a maiden."

"Is Djerǔn hungry again?" enquired Rodario, stationing himself beside the maga. "Don't be foolish," she reprimanded him. "The avatars respect purity, so they won't kill an innocent maiden—well, I'd be surprised if they did." She turned to Tungdil. "We need someone to walk out and tell them that Girdlegard is safe. I'd do it myself, but I'm not sure the avatars would listen to a follower of Samusin."

"Will they listen to anyone?"

"We won't know unless we try," she said. "Sometimes the simplest solution is the best."

That night, a young dwarf wrapped in white furs left the stronghold. At only twenty-four cycles, Fyrna Goodsoul of the clan of the Ore Finders was a child by dwarven standards. Xamtys had chosen her from the group of volunteers—young dwarves who were yet to be melded.

The wording of the message had been given to her by Narmora. "Stick to the script," the maga reminded her. "If they want to negotiate, tell them you'll pass on their demands. Don't mention our army or our plans."

The young dwarf listened attentively and set off briskly through the gully, heart quickening as she left the safety of the fortified walls.

The dwarves watched as she hurried through the sweeping gully and disappeared from view. All they could do was wait and pray.

The bright light moved closer and closer.

Some time around midnight, when the moon was high above the range, the light came to a halt, sparking a flurry of excitement among the anxious dwarves.

"They've found Fyrna," whispered Xamtys. "Vraccas, protect the dear child."

Narmora rested her elbows on the parapet and leaned forward, focusing on the glow. "I hope it's enough to dissuade them from invading."

"Look!" shouted Boïndil, tugging at Tungdil's sleeve. "It's fading!"

"Vraccas be praised!" cried Xamtys. "I'll melt down every ingot in my kingdom in honor of the Smith."

As they watched, the light faded to a faint glow on the mountain slopes; then the gully was shrouded in darkness once more.

It worked! Tungdil smiled and turned to Narmora. "You were right! The simplest solution turned out to be the best!"

Everyone in the stronghold and on the ramparts was watching as well. As soon as the light went out, they cheered and hugged each other. Firstlings, thirdlings, and freelings, together they rejoiced, their differences forgotten—temporarily, at least.

"Let's see what Fyrna has to say." Tungdil shook the maga's hand and went to fetch a mug of hot spiced beer before hurrying back to the tower to wait for the plucky firstling to return.

The night wore on.

At dawn, the sun rose over the ridge, warming the shivering dwarves with its soft yellow rays. Their confidence grew.

But there was still no sign of Fyrna Goodsoul.

By noon, snow clouds were gathering over the gully, and Xamtys dispatched a band of warriors to hunt for the missing dwarf. It wouldn't be safe to leave the stronghold once the weather closed in.

Several hours later the warriors returned with Fyrna, unconscious but alive. The maga examined her and diagnosed a mild case of frostbite from sleeping in the snow.

"She'll be fine," said Narmora, after reviving Fyrna's

fingers and toes. She patted the dwarf on the cheek to wake her and handed her a beaker of hot lichen tea.

Fyrna gulped it down. "I failed, Your Majesty," she said, shivering. She bowed her head wretchedly. "I'm sorry, Queen Xamtys."

"Sorry? What's the matter with her?" spluttered Boïndil, peering over the parapet. "The avatars have gone. There's no sign of them anywhere—unless they're too darned pure for me to see."

"Shush," growled Boëndal, giving him a warning prod.

"I got as close as I could, like you told me to, but the light was really bright. In the end, I called out, and a creature of pure light flew toward me and asked me what I wanted." The young firstling glanced at Narmora. "I repeated the words you taught me, Estimable Maga, but the creature just laughed. The noise went straight through me; it was high-pitched and cruel." She took another sip of tea. "The creature said not to worry, it would be over really soon. Then it touched me, and I . . . The next thing I knew, I was here."

Tungdil looked at his friends' worried faces. "If they're not here or in the gully, where are they?"

"In the tunnels," rasped a voice behind them. King Lorimbas had joined them and heard the end of Fyrna's story. "One of my tunnels comes up in the gully."

Tungdil shuddered. "They'll go straight to the Black-saddle. Your guards won't be expecting them—and the rest of your army is here."

An appalled silence descended on the group. In their

minds, they could see the pure light hovering over the Blacksaddle while the avatars poured out of the stronghold, laying waste to Girdlegard as they hunted for an evil that didn't exist.

"What are we waiting for?" said Boïndil after a time. "We know where we're needed!"

Blacksaddle,
Kingdom of Gauragar,
Girdlegard,
Early Winter, 6235th Solar Cycle

Theogil Hardhand gripped the chain with both hands and pulled as hard as he could. The block and pulley system made lifting the driverless wagon relatively easy. He hoisted it into the air and swung it away from the rail.

The real question was how it had got there.

He had arrived at the depot to find an empty wagon blocking the rail. He guessed it had rolled through the tunnel from a disused platform, in which case it was lucky it hadn't collided with a convoy of dwarves. At any rate, it had to be shifted: The last few thirdlings were preparing to leave the Blacksaddle to join Lorimbas in the west.

"Let's get you moving," he muttered, pushing the wagon with one hand. It was linked by a cable to a runner on the ceiling, so he barely had to steer.

He stopped at the rear of the hall where the extra wagons were kept. Carefully, he lowered it to the ground, unhooked it from the cable, and placed his hands on the back to push it the final few paces. Just then he heard a noise.

It seemed to be coming from the tunnel, and it sounded like a convoy of wagons rattling down the rails.

New arrivals? he thought in surprise, ticking off the battalions in his mind. Every single thirdling unit was either waiting to depart from the Blacksaddle or already en route to the west. Lorimbas's summons had caused consternation among the thirdlings, but orders were orders, and the warriors had left without delay.

He abandoned the wagon and made his way carefully to the mouth of the tunnel. Holding his breath, he listened intently until he was sure of the source of the noise. It was as he thought. The rumbling and clattering was getting louder.

Darned fools, he grumbled irritably. *What's the point of having a braking zone if they can't be trusted to leave a proper gap? They'll cause a pile-up.*

He hurriedly tossed a few extra sacks of straw onto the buffers in the hope of saving the passengers from serious harm, then he took up position in the signal box, intending to throw the lever as soon as the convoy arrived. By diverting the wagons onto different platforms, he could reduce the risk of a crash. He couldn't help wondering why the wagons were heading in his direction at all.

Staring into the dark mouth of the tunnel, he waited for the lead wagon's lanterns to come into view.

A few moments later, he glimpsed a light—a light so bright that he wondered briefly whether the sun had fallen through the rock. No dwarven lantern could cast a glow like that. As the wagons drew nearer, Theogil turned away, dazzled by the glare.

What is it? A new invention, perhaps? Keeping his back to the tunnel, he decided to rely on his hearing instead.

At last he heard screeching metal as the brake blocks pressed against the narrow wheels, forcing them to slow. The wagons' arrival was heralded by a sudden rush of air.

Theogil detected a strange smell that wasn't dwarven or human, and had nothing to do with elves or beasts. The wind tugged at his beard, set his chain mail aquiver, and brought him the odor of oiled weaponry, polished metal, and clean hands. All in all, it smelled somehow pure. The first wagon shot out of the tunnel, illuminating every corner of the hall.

"Put the darned thing out," he shouted. The brightness was so unbearable that his eyes brimmed with tears and he had to close them. Thereafter he worked in darkness, pumping the lever up and down and switching the points in time with the clattering of each wagon. "Everyone out," he ordered, raising his voice above the din. "Get the wagons off the rails or we'll have a collision."

The light intensified, becoming so bright that he could see the red of his eyelids. The light shone straight through them, as if he were looking directly at the midday sun.

He felt a sudden wave of heat, and someone grabbed him by the shoulder, and pulled him away from the lever. "Hey, you're burning me!" he protested, feeling the searing pain in his shoulder. He opened his eyes and blinked.

The creature in front of him was made of pure light. It was as tall as a human and wreathed in a white halo that was painful to behold. The air in the hall seemed to shimmer. "Greetings, undergroundling," the creature greeted him in a kindly voice. "Don't be afraid. I won't hurt you if your soul is true."

Theogil reached for his club and took a step backward. "Who are you?" he asked gruffly. "And who said you could use our wagons?"

With his free hand, he unhooked a horn from his belt and held it to his lips, but before he could sound the alarm, the creature stretched a hand, sending a bolt of light toward the horn, which ignited with a roar.

Theogil dropped the bugle before his beard went up in flames. He knew without a shred of doubt what was happening: The avatars had arrived.

In proper dwarven fashion, he gripped the club with both hands and brandished it menacingly. "Be off with you. You've no right to bring death and destruction to these lands."

"I beg your pardon," the creature said politely, "but our mission is to stamp out evil in all its forms. A dwarf-girl told us that Nôd'onn has been destroyed, but we've heard of other creatures, creatures that worship Tion or were fashioned by his hand." The avatar took a step closer, and Theogil, who had spent countless orbits in the forge, was forced to draw back from the heat. "Honorable undergroundling, descendant of the worthy Essgar, tell us where we can find the älfar. Our soldiers will wipe out their army and burn their evil souls. You'll never have anything to fear from them again."

"Be off!" commanded Theogil, raising his club. "We'll deal with Inàste's pointy-ears ourselves. No one asked for your help. You wipe out good as well as evil."

"Only the pure can look on us and live. Those who perish were found wanting."

Before Theogil could react, the avatar's hand was resting on his head. "Are you pure, undergroundling, or will you perish in our flames?"

Theogil felt crippled by the terrible heat. Red-hot metal seemed to press against his temples, cutting through his skull, and desiccating his brain. His arms grew heavy and fell to his sides, and his fingers unfurled, letting go of the club.

"You should have told the truth," the creature admonished him. "Why didn't you tell us about the orcs? Toboribor is the name of their kingdom, is it? And what of the ogres? I see mountains swarming with ogres . . . The realm of Borwôl, northeast of here . . ." He laughed, satisfied. "Our army will be busy in Girdlegard. Soon the men, elves, and undergroundlings will be freed from Tion's beasts." The creature released its searing grip on his head. Dazed, Theogil stumbled back and steadied himself against a metal rail. "Don't interfere with the will of the deities," the avatar warned him, stepping back. "Anyone who stands in our way is an ally of evil."

Theogil shielded his face with his hands to block out the light and peered through his fingers at the rest of the hall.

Warriors were descending from the wagons and forming

orderly lines. Their armor and banners were white, and they didn't seem to mind the glare, which was so intense that Theogil was afraid his eyes would shrivel in their sockets. He blinked, just in case.

The commotion in the depot came to the attention of the thirdlings in the other halls.

Theogil spotted a group of sentries creeping down the wide stairway. As soon as they saw what was happening, they sounded the alarm. A bugle call echoed through the passageways and galleries of the Blacksaddle, calling the children of Lorimbur, few of whom remained in the stronghold, to arms.

The avatar paused and marched back to Theogil, who reached for his club. "Poor stubborn undergroundlings," the creature said sadly. "We should be allies, but you've chosen to oppose us. We can't be held responsible for your deaths."

"Our deaths? I'll teach you to respect a dwarven warrior," growled Theogil. He let out a ferocious war cry and bounded forward, swinging his club.

Even before he reached his fiery antagonist, the heat became unbearable. His chain mail burned red against his skin, the air reeked of scorched leather, and his sinew and blood evaporated faster than a drop of water in a fire.

Nothing remained of Theogil Hardhand but a mound of ashes and a few blackened bones. A moment later, they too were crushed and scattered by the pounding boots of the avatars' soldiers as they charged the defending dwarves.

Kingdom of Gauragar,
Girdlegard,
Winter, 6235th Solar Cycle

Boïndil trudged through the freshly fallen snow that lay
like a coating of icing sugar over the fields, trees, and
tents. He was the last to arrive at the meeting, and he
made his way straight to the campfire and helped himself
to a tankard of warm beer. Like the others, he was keen
to have a nice, restful evening in preparation for their
arrival at the Blacksaddle at noon the next orbit. They
were expecting to find the avatars in the dwarven
stronghold.

"They've got a funny way of wiping out evil," said
Boïndil vehemently. "You can tell they're descended from
Tion; nothing good ever came of *him*." He drained his
tankard and went back for more. His pinprick eyes settled
on Tungdil. "Any news from our scouts?"

"Only that the avatars' cavalry has arrived in the stronghold," chimed in Lorimbas. "They rode part of the way
underground, and the tunnels collapsed behind them."

"How do you know?" asked Boïndil.

"Because of the cracks on the surface," explained the
thirdling king. "Most of our tunnels have been destroyed.
Anything left standing after the comet and the earthquake
has been brought down by the avatars and their army."

Xamtys nodded. "I heard the same from my scouts.
The underground network around the Red Range is
dangerously unstable. Balendilín, Gandogar, and Glaïmbar
will have to send their armies overland."

"It won't be easy," said Tungdil, turning back to the

map. In his mind, he charted the rest of the avatars' route, which, assuming they stuck to their current course, would take them straight to Dsôn Balsur. "From their point of view, it makes perfect sense to attack the älfar," he said. "They're the biggest threat to our safety, especially with the added power from the dark water. I'd say they were a worthy target for a band of demigods."

"It's a pity the avatars are so destructive," said Xamtys. "I mean, it's almost tempting to let them get on with it. They're capable of wiping out the älfar, which isn't true of us. Ever since the älfar butchered an entire camp of allied soldiers in Dsôn Balsur, the human soldiers have been deserting in droves. No one wants to face the älfar."

"I'm not surprised," said Tungdil. "The dark water has made them deadlier than ever." He paused. "I've heard from our scouts that the snow around the Blacksaddle has melted completely, while the rest of Gauragar is covered in thigh-high drifts. Are you ready to take on the avatars, Narmora?"

The maga looked at the flickering flame of the lantern overhead. "I keep wondering whether my kind of magic can stop them," she said slowly. "My way is the way of equilibrium, the balancing of darkness and light. My power comes from both, but it might be better to attack them with pure light." She looked away from the flame. "We'll soon find out."

"I'll be right beside you, maga," said Rodario in a voice that he hoped was suitably comforting. "I'll make them believe I'm the most powerful magus in Girdlegard so you can attack them without endangering your valuable person." He took a swig of beer and grimaced: It was too bitter, too strong, too malty for his taste. "At least that's the aim," he added quietly. He lowered his voice again. "I hope you'll erect a statue in my honor when I'm dead."

His comment was met with silence from the maga, who pretended not to hear.

Tungdil noticed that Djerûn had positioned himself behind his new mistress, ready to spring into action at the first sign of danger. His damaged armor made him more intimidating than ever, the scratches and burn marks proving that neither swords nor fire could bring him down.

Tungdil, thinking about it more carefully, realized that Djerûn's escape from the avatars didn't make sense. The experience of those who had encountered the demigods confirmed the legend in every detail. The avatars were in possession of magic powers capable of destroying all forms of evil. There were two categories of survivors: those who had the good fortune to escape their attention, and those who satisfied their cockeyed notion of purity.

But Djerûn is still alive, and they had every reason to kill him. He's a creature of evil, and he's powerful, which makes him a hundred times more dangerous than orcs, bögnilim, or ogres. A shiver of excitement ran down his back. *He survived their attacks, and he survived for a reason.*

Without a word to the others, he went over to the giant warrior and ran a hand over his armor, following the lines and curves of the scorched intarsia and studying the symbols etched by Balyndis at Andôkai's behest. *Is that the answer?*

Rodario cleared his throat. "May I ask what you're doing, illustrious hero of the Blacksaddle? I know it's hard for a dwarf to resist a good piece of metalwork, but don't you think we should deal with the avatars first?"

Tungdil ignored him and turned to Narmora. "Maga, ask Djerůn what happened when the avatars attacked."

"Ask him yourself," she said. "He understands you." She listened to the giant's response, which she alone could understand. "I see. He says they attacked him with their magic."

Tungdil took a step back and thumped Djerůn's armor. "So why did he survive? The thirdlings were clad in armor and they perished in the avatars' fires." He turned to the others. "Djerůn is precisely the sort of creature they're out to destroy. They must have done everything in their power to kill him, and what did they achieve? Practically nothing—except cover him in soot. His only injuries were inflicted by their army."

"You think he was saved by his armor," said Boëndal. He could tell from Narmora's expression that she was thinking the same. "Andôkai must have found a counter-charm to protect him."

Narmora shook her head. "She would have told us. Why keep it to herself?"

"Maybe she didn't want to get our hopes up," suggested Rodario. "Maybe she sent her knight in shining armor to see what happened when the avatars attacked. She was probably going to tell us when she knew for certain that it worked."

"Not Andôkai—she cared too much about Djerůn to

put him at risk. The avatars weren't supposed to find him, but they did." She signaled for Tungdil to step away from the giant. "We'll try a little test." After warning Djerŭn, she raised her arms and began an incantation.

"Steady on, Narmora," protested Boïndil. "You can't set fire to Djerŭn in a tent!" The maga continued, undeterred. A tongue of fire pulled away from the lantern above her and flew into her outstretched hands, turning from orange to ruby-red. The flame grew and expanded until it was the size of a human head, then it cast itself, hissing and spluttering, against the giant's armored chest.

There was a loud explosion, and Djerŭn was wreathed in flames. At once the runes on his armor pulsed with light, and the fire went out. Djerŭn didn't so much as flinch.

"Fine, I'll take it up a notch," murmured Narmora, raising her right arm and summoning tongues of fire from every lantern in the tent. They gathered in her fingers, forming a red-hot fireball that she hurled at his chest.

Again the giant was surrounded by flames. This time, the force of the impact brought him to his knees, but he straightened up as soon as the flames had died. He growled softly.

"He says he felt the heat, but it couldn't hurt him," explained Narmora, who was visibly surprised by what had occurred. She clicked her fingers, and the flames returned to the lanterns, restoring light to the tent. "You'd better not say I was going easy on him," she told them. "The fireball was hot enough to melt any normal metal." She stepped up to the giant, inspected his breastplate, and laid a hand on the metal. "It's warm," she said, shaking her head incredulously. "The runes are still alight, but there's no sign of warping." She turned to the dwarves. "I think we can safely say that Balyndis has forged a suit of armor that works against magic as well as swords."

Tungdil breathed out in relief. "Vraccas knew what he was doing when he gave us a talent for metalwork. He's given us another chance to protect our lands." Kneeling, he gave thanks to the dwarven deity.

The other dwarves, with the exception of Lorimbas, followed his lead.

The thirdling king let his eyes glide contemptuously over their bowed heads. He felt like cleaving their necks with his ax, but he was their ally—for the moment, at least. *Vraccas won't save you from Lorimbur's children,* he vowed.

Tungdil was the first to rise. "We need to summon Balyndis," he announced, buoyed by the thought that help was at hand. "Send word that we need the instructions for Djerûn's armor." He wondered whether Vraccas was testing his character. *I tried to get away from her, but it doesn't seem to work.*

"We'll need ten thousand suits," said Boëndal, leaning on his crow's beak. "I'm no coward, but I don't fancy our chances of fighting them without the magic armor. We'd be throwing away our lives."

Tungdil gave orders for four messengers to leave immediately for the Gray Range via four different routes—it was crucial that the message got through. "We'll decide what to do when we see the situation at the Blacksaddle tomorrow. I'd rather not fight without the armor, but we may not have a choice." He pointed to the menacing black lines on the map that designated the kingdom of Dsôn Balsur. "The avatars are rumored to draw their power from the evil they destroy. Once the avatars wipe out the älfar, they'll be stronger than ever. Who knows if the armor will still work."

"Stop fretting," said Boïndil cheerfully. "I can't wait for Balyndis to forge me a fine new suit of armor. I'll teach the avatars not to tangle with the dwarves. By the way, the first ten are mine."

"There are only eleven of them," Boëndal reminded him. The others laughed.

Grinning, Boïndil clinked tankards with his brother. "Tough luck," he said, chuckling. "You'll have to work it out among yourselves."

Their high spirits lasted until mid-afternoon the next orbit when the Blacksaddle came into view.

As they approached the mountain, they realized that the gloomy clouds in the gray winter sky weren't loaded with snow, as they had thought, but with smoke. And there was no doubt about the origin of the fire.

The mountain without a peak had become a blazing pyre.

The very rock of the Blacksaddle was burning, the mountainside a sheet of red-hot fire, with tongues of flame rising from every crack and vent. Black smoke cut off the sunlight, obscuring the sky, and turning the noon hours into dusk. Vast chunks of rock broke away from the Blacksaddle and plunged to the ground. The snow had evaporated and the soil around the mountain was powdery and dry. As they watched, the flames grew fiercer, leaping as if to ignite the sun.

"It doesn't seem possible," gasped Xamtys.

"How did they do it, maga?" asked Boïndil. "Did they turn the Blacksaddle into coal?"

Narmora's eyes narrowed. "It's a warning," she said. "A warning to anyone thinking of following them. They're showing us their power."

"What a disaster," sighed Rodario. "How am I supposed to recreate it on stage?" He looked hopefully at Furgas, who shrugged.

Tungdil shouldered his ax. "Let's take a look at the damage."

The devastation was complete.

At five hundred paces from the Blacksaddle, the snow turned to slush. Three hundred paces later, they were walking on firm, dry earth, raising clouds of dust with their boots. At a distance of a hundred and fifty paces, they came to a halt. Any closer, and they were liable to be killed by flying rock. Scattered in the dust were fragments of axes and clubs, scorched bones, and warped armor caked with charred flesh. The Blacksaddle's defenders were no more.

Lorimbas gazed at the devastation, eyes wet with tears. "To you they were thirdlings," he said quietly with a catch in his voice. "But to me they were friends—friends, whose deaths must be avenged." The sight of the burning Blacksaddle ignited the fires in every thirdling heart: For Lorimbas and his dwarves, the war had become personal.

"We're done for," muttered Rodario, kicking at the

powdery gray earth. "Surely we're all agreed that it's no good fighting them without Balyndis's armor?"

"We may have no choice," said Lorimbas grimly, looking at the gray trail left in the avatars' wake. A vast path of dusty earth, a hundred paces across and bordered on both sides by snow, was proof of the direction they had taken: The army was marching north. Lorimbas bent down and picked up an ax head; it was still attached to a charred fragment of haft. "Goldhand is right. We need to stop them before they reach Dsôn Balsur and wipe out the älfar. They're powerful enough as it is."

"Who would have thought it would come to this?" remarked Boïndil. "All this time we've been trying to kick out Inàste's children, and at last there's someone who could do the job for us, but instead of letting them burn down Dsôn Balsur, we're going to jump to the älfar's defense."

"It doesn't seem right," agreed Tungdil, "but we can't let the avatars get to Dsôn Balsur. In any case, we're not defending the älfar; we're postponing their death." He glanced at Lorimbas. "Can you spare ten thousand warriors? I want to outflank the avatars and squeeze them between two fronts."

Lorimbas nominated his elite battalions for the advance guard, which would consist of Tungdil, Narmora, Rodario, and the twins.

"We'll cut off the White Army before it reaches Dsôn Balsur," explained Tungdil. "Meanwhile, Lorimbas, Gemmil, and Xamtys will attack with the rest of our troops from the rear. Narmora will take care of the avatars." He thumped Boïndil on the back. "How's that for a challenge?"

"No challenge is too big for a dwarf," said Boïndil, although he didn't seem terribly confident.

It was late afternoon when Tungdil set off with ten thousand thirdlings on a northerly bearing. By the time they left the Blacksaddle, the once legendary mountain resembled a broad-based hill, fifty paces in height and riven with cracks and fissures; by evening, when they stopped to rest for a while, it was gone. A few flames remained to mark the spot where the powerful Blacksaddle had once stood. Tion's demigods had razed it to the ground.

Tungdil was intent on catching and passing the avatars' army. At night, its bright white glow was visible for hundreds of miles against the black firmament, but the dwarven warriors were still hopelessly behind.

It seemed the White Army could march without rest. Their soldiers were on the move from dawn until dusk, racking up the miles, while Tungdil and the others were feeling the strain of ten orbits of constant marching.

"Another ten orbits, and they'll be there," said Boïndil, sitting down by the campfire to examine his blisters. "We can hardly keep up with them, so how are Lorimbas, Gemmil, and Xamtys supposed to get there in time? We've got ten thousand elite thirdling warriors, and we're falling off the pace."

Tungdil pored over the map. The other dwarves at the campfire were thirdling generals; it was hard to tell from their tattooed faces what they were thinking. "We said we'd strike here," he said, lowering the stem of his pipe over an area south of Dsôn Balsur. He did some quick calculations. "If we hurry, we can catch them right on the border. It's the earliest possible chance of attack. I'll send word to the others to tell them of the change of plan."

The thirdling generals listened in silence.

"It's risky, but it's the only way," agreed Boëndal. "They'll speed up as soon as they see the border. They'll want to push on to the capital as fast as they can."

"I know, but we won't catch them beforehand," ruled Tungdil, turning his attention to a written report from one of the scouts who was tracking the enemy army, unbeknown to the avatars.

So far, the invaders had laid waste to four towns en route to the älfar's kingdom. The inhabitants had refused to join the army, in return for which the avatars had plundered and burned their homes.

According to the report, few had survived, for the most part children and young girls whom the avatars had spared. Everyone else had been burned to a cinder like the thirdlings at the Blacksaddle. Forests, fields, meadows, marshes—everything the avatars encountered was destroyed. The demigods were leaving a trail of ashes and scorched earth.

It seemed to Tungdil that the men and dwarves, while far from pure, had done nothing to merit such a fate. *I don't think much of divine justice, if that's what it is. Not even the älfar have wreaked such destruction on Girdlegard.* He threw the bulletins into the fire and watched as the paper crumpled. His thoughts returned to the Blacksaddle and the dwarves who had died in the blaze. *The avatars are worse than älfar, orcs, and bögnilim combined.*

That night he dreamed of Balyndis and Myr.

They were fighting for his favor, Balyndis, equipped with a blacksmith's hammer and a pair of metal tongs, and Myr wielding daggers. The duel was interrupted by Salfalur, who killed them both with his hammer. Tears streaming down his tattooed cheeks, he turned on Tungdil and charged . . .

Tungdil woke with a start.

Boïndil was crouched next to him, shaking his shoulder. "Come on, scholar. The White Army is on the move. Anyone would think they'd got wind of our plans."

Muttering and cursing, Tungdil clambered to his feet, put on his weapons belt, stuffed his blanket into his rucksack, and jogged to the front of the thirdling battalions. The thirdling generals had set off without him. If it hadn't been for Boïndil, he would have woken by the campfire to find everyone had gone.

He felt the eyes on his back as he made his way to the head of the army. Boïndil was right: He would never trust a thirdling in battle, even though he was a thirdling himself.

82 Miles Southwest of Dsôn Balsur,
Kingdom of Gauragar,
Girdlegard,
Winter, 6235th Solar Cycle

Ondori turned her fire bull and looked proudly at the unit of four thousand warriors marching behind her through the night.

They were stronger than ever, having partaken of the dark water and profited from its life-preserving power.

The immortal siblings had ordered Ondori to lead the troops against Âlandur and wipe out the elves. The älf couldn't have wished for a more glorious mission. A duel with Lord Liútasil would give her tremendous pleasure and she was happy to delay her private campaign against the dwarves. Besides, with the help of the dark water, she could settle her score with Tungdil whenever she wanted.

With a bit of luck, and Tion willing, Ondori was hoping to put an end to Sitalia's elves. If the initial attack went well, she and her warriors would march on the rest of the kingdom and raze the leafy elven settlements to the ground. The immortal siblings' palace would be clad from top to bottom in shiny white elf-bone, and Liútasil's skull would be skewered at the top.

Hmm, what do we have here? At the foot of a lone hill she could make out the faint glow of a poorly hidden campfire. *Careless wayfarers.* She signaled for two dozen warriors to join her. *With any luck, they'll be elves . . .*

They stole through the valley toward the hill. A shelf protruded from the hillside, affording shelter from rain and snow. At any other time, it would have made the perfect place to rest for a while, but the gods had deserted the travelers that night.

Ondori reined in her bull and slid noiselessly to the ground. She heard snores from her victims and smelled the strong tobacco on their clothes. After a few paces, she came to a boulder and ducked behind it, keeping to the shadows as she peered at the camp.

Groundlings, she thought in astonishment, eying the ring of stocky warriors asleep around the dying fire. Their sentry was perched on a rock, facing away from her, and smoking a pipe. Every now and then he dipped his tankard into a cauldron over the flames and took a sip of the steaming brew.

Ondori did a quick headcount and came to twenty dwarves in total. *What are they doing here? They can't be spies or scouts; they're in the middle of nowhere.*

She signed to her warriors that she wanted to question one of the groundlings; the others could be killed. Then she focused on the fire, willing the flames to die down. The fire flickered briefly and went out.

Cursing, the sentry clambered to his feet, placed some tinder on the embers and kneeled on the ground to blow on the flames.

Ondori detached herself from the shadows and crept toward him. Her movements were silent, and he didn't have time to react. Out of nowhere, a scythe-like blade sliced through his throat and he toppled over, landing in the dying embers and dousing them with blood.

The thud of his falling body caused one of his companions to stir. Three black arrows winged toward him as he raised his sleepy head. He sank back against his mattress, as if overpowered by fatigue.

The älfar murdered their way systematically through the ring of sleeping dwarves, slitting their throats, ramming their narrow daggers between their eyes, and running their swords through their chests.

Crouching beside the lone survivor, Ondori disarmed her victim and rapped her quarterstaff against the ground.

It was only when the dwarf sat up sleepily that Ondori realized she was female. The little creature reached for her ax—to no avail.

"Lie still," whispered Ondori, holding the dwarven ax above her head for her victim to see. She hurled it into the snow. "Scream, and we'll kill your friends, then you. Is that clear?" The dwarf nodded, and Ondori detected the sound of grinding teeth. "What are you doing here?" the älf demanded.

"Hunting älfar."

Ondori glowered. "Trust a groundling to lie." She peered at her victim's face. "I've seen you before. You were at the mouth of the tunnel to the Gray Range; you shouted for Goldhand to help you—and I got away." She smiled balefully. "You're a queen, aren't you? Queen of the mob who moved into the halls. Are you sending an army to fight us? Are you scouts?"

"I don't know what you're talking about," the dwarf said stubbornly. "Our orders are to find out what's happening at the front. We're supposed to make a deal with the elves."

Ondori raised her quarterstaff sharply and pressed a hidden catch. A blade shot out from one end and came to rest on her captive's throat. There was a click as she locked the mechanism to prevent the blade retreating. "I want the truth, groundling." She swung her quarterstaff so that the blade hovered over the body of the dwarf to her right. "Think of your friends," she whispered threateningly. "Do you want them to die?"

Her captive bristled. "You won't hurt them, no-eyes," she said fearlessly.

Ondori rammed the blade into the heart of the seemingly sleeping dwarf. The trick worked: It was plain from her captive's face that she blamed herself for the death of her friend. "That leaves eighteen of you, including yourself. How many more lies are you going to tell me?"

"You monster!" Without warning, the dwarf thrust aside the quarterstaff and charged at the älf, who dived to the ground and rolled away nimbly to escape the dwarf's powerful hands.

"Too slow," crowed Ondori, kicking her under the chin. The dwarf fell backward and lay limply on the ground.

Inàste is smiling on me today, thought the älf. *The immortal siblings will be pleased to see my prisoner.* Dusting the snow from her clothes, she got up, only for the apparently unconscious dwarf to whip out a dagger and ram it into her calf. The blade tore through the leather upper of her boot and brought her to the ground.

"To arms!" shouted the dwarf, scrambling toward the älf. She pointed the dagger at Ondori's throat. "We've got an intruder in the camp!"

"Don't kill her!" shouted Ondori, swallowing her pain. "We need her alive!" She grabbed the dagger-wielding arm. The solidly built dwarf threw all her strength into avenging her dead companion.

Four älfar rushed to Ondori's aid and grabbed the dwarf from behind, tossing her roughly to the ground. Each held a leg or an arm, but the dwarf was still intent on breaking free.

Ondori tore a strip from the cloak of a dead dwarf and tied it around her calf. The wound would heal of its own accord. "Mountain vermin," she hissed, ramming the blunt end of her quarterstaff into the dwarf's belly with all her might. "We're taking you with us. You're a queen consort and a good friend of Tungdil Goldhand." She gave the order for the captive to be bound. "Something tells me you're going to be very useful."

She limped away, followed by her warriors and the dwarf. Their captive was as stubborn as a donkey, and they had to drag her through the snow. The älfar themselves left no tracks.

Ondori was glad to get back into the saddle. Her calf was still throbbing; the dark water, though able to close any wound, had no effect on the pain. She took the end of the rope with which they had trussed their captive and threaded it through a loop on Agrass's saddle to tether the dwarf to her mount.

She and her unit resumed their journey toward Âlandur. After a time, Agrass shook his head, nostrils flaring in the wind. Ondori understood the warning and sat up in the saddle. Turning, she saw something in the west.

What in Tion's name is that?

A long band of light was moving through Gauragar, and it seemed to be heading straight for her homeland. It was traveling fast enough to reach the border in less than two orbits.

Have the humans found a new way of setting fire to the woods? she wondered, surprised that the invaders had regained their courage so soon. She quickly discarded the idea: There was no lamp in Girdlegard, not even an elven lamp, that could give off such a light. It wasn't fire either; it was too brilliant, too white.

"Groundling!" Her foot connected with the back of the dwarf, who had come to a halt beside the bull. "Is this your doing?"

The captive glared at her murderously and shrugged. "It might be."

"In other words, no." *It looks like a tide of molten palandium . . .* In Ondori's mind, there could only be one answer to the riddle: Andôkai.

The humans must have convinced the maga to come up with a spell that would aid their armies against the älfar. But the explanation wasn't entirely satisfactory. Andôkai the Tempestuous was known for her stormy temper and her fondness for cataclysmic winds. She liked to surprise her enemies with sudden gales or cyclones; it wouldn't be her style to light up the sky like a beacon and alert the älvish army to her approach.

What's going on? Ondori had a bad feeling about the light, which was beginning to hurt her eyes. "Halt!" she shouted. "We're turning back." She pointed at the luminous band. "Dsôn Balsur is under threat. The elves can wait."

Two of her guards rode off on shadow mares to spread the word among the troops. The other two stayed at her side. Eyes still fixed on the glow, she touched the symbol of Nagsor and Nagsar on her forehead. It was throbbing as if the skin were inflamed.

"Ondori," said one of her guards, pointing south. "What's that over there?"

She stared into the distance and spotted a faint glow in the darkness. It was another strip of white light, this time much further away. "It's not a threat at the moment," she said confidently. "Keep an eye on it, though. We don't want anyone to slip past us and attack from the north."

"Looks like we've got two armies to deal with," observed the guard, smiling. "The immortal siblings will thank us for bringing them their bones."

Ondori rubbed her forehead, hoping to soothe the pain. "We can be sure of their gratitude." She felt strangely ill at ease at the sight of the approaching light. "We should hurry. We need to find out who they are."

At daybreak, Ondori stood watching the soldiers in their gleaming white armor. The first rays of sunlight glinted on the polished metal, blinding her eyes. She couldn't decipher the runes on their banner, but she knew for certain that the soldiers weren't from Girdlegard.

"Twenty thousand foot soldiers and two thousand five hundred riders," said one of her guards, surveying the unknown enemy. "The immortal siblings should be warned."

"Our scouts are bound to have seen them," Ondori assured him. She screwed up her eyes, dazzled by the glare. "They're sparkling like an army of diamonds. As soon as the sun goes in, we'll attack from behind, take some prisoners, and retreat."

Ondori had fought soldiers from every army in Girdlegard, but none wore uniforms such as these. *Where are they from?* It seemed unlikely that the human generals could raise an army of foreign mercenaries without the rest of Girdlegard knowing. Älvish spies had been eavesdropping on the enemy camps in Dsôn Balsur for a good many orbits.

"Whoever they are, they'll get a proper älvish welcome," she said darkly, returning to her troops. They followed the strange army at a distance until dusk, waiting for the sun to set.

As the light began to fade, she ordered her guards to tie the dwarf to a tree and fill her mouth with snow to stop her dying of thirst.

"We'll be back soon," Ondori assured her. "As soon as we've finished here, we're taking you to the immortal siblings." She waggled her leg tentatively. The dark water had healed the gash in her calf and there was nothing to show that a dagger had sliced through her flesh.

She climbed into the saddle and rode at the head of her troops.

When they were close enough, she took cover and surveyed the tail end of the army. The situation wasn't to her liking. The soldiers' armor had absorbed the sunlight, and, despite the gathering gloom, was shining as brightly as ever, forcing Ondori to take an unusual precaution. She ordered her warriors to don strips of black cloth designed to protect them from snow blindness.

Peering through slits in the fabric and still half dazzled by the light, they launched a stealth attack from the rear.

Even as they advanced, Ondori began to doubt the wisdom of the scheme. The blessing on her forehead was burning against her skin, and Agrass, rather than charging the enemy and trampling through the ranks, was snorting and bucking nervously.

The battle got off to a disappointing start.

The soldiers must have anticipated their attack; at any rate, they showed no sign of panic.

As soon as the first enemy rider went down, struck by an älvish arrow, the back row of infantry raised their shields to form a wall, which rose to a height of three paces as the cavalrymen followed suit. Lances and halberds appeared through the cracks.

At that moment, a midnight sun flashed into the sky above the älfar, bathing them in cold white light. Ondori cried out and clutched her forehead. It felt as if liquid fire were coursing through the blessing inscribed there and searing her brain. The attack faltered.

"So you are the älfar of whom we've heard tell," said the sun. "I can sense your corruption. You carry the spirit of Tion within you and you live to further his works." The sun became hotter, brighter. "All that is over. The älfar shall threaten Girdlegard no more."

A wave of heat rolled over the älfar, and a third of the troops caught alight. The burning warriors threw themselves to the ground, writhing in agony, trying to put out the flames—but to no avail.

Ondori watched as the fiery presence drew closer and waited until it was almost above her, then dived beneath her bull, praying not to be trampled beneath its hooves.

Eyes closed, she felt the searing heat pass over her like the fiery breath of a dragon. Crackling flames engulfed the warriors around her and a stench of burning hair, clothes, and flesh filled the air. Agrass kicked out frantically, striking her in the side, then the terrible rush of heat was over.

Ondori sprang to her feet and stared at her scorched

and dying bull. The flames had melted its metal visor, sealing its fate.

"Pull back!" she shouted. "Make for the woods!"

Her voice was barely audible above the shouts and jeers of the unknown soldiers as they seized their chance and attacked. Riders on stallions charged fearlessly at the dark ranks of the älfar, cutting them down with their swords.

Ondori watched in horror as her warriors took blows to the limbs and torso and lay where they fell. The power of the dark water offered no protection against the dazzling riders' swords.

We're no stronger than ordinary mortals. Aghast, she turned to flee. There could be no hope of victory against an enemy as powerful as this.

Leaping over the bodies of her fallen comrades, she ran for the ash-covered trees.

Hampered by the undergrowth, the riders stopped their pursuit. The foot soldiers blundered on, but none could match her speed. Ondori kept running, spurred on by the memory of the heat, oblivious to her aching lungs and throbbing legs. At last she reached a clearing and slumped to the ground, exhausted.

Soon after, she was joined by the rest of her unit, who arrived in dribs and drabs. There were ten of them in all. The others had been cut down or consumed by fire.

"What happened?" gasped one of the warriors.

Ondori couldn't answer. Her lungs were screaming for air and her forehead was on fire. She reached up to touch the skin above her mask and her flesh fell away, exposing the white of her skull. Her fingers were covered in sticky black ash.

She wiped them on the ground, digging her hands into the soil and crying with rage and agony. The noise reverberated through the night.

Suddenly a pair of battered boots stepped into view. "What have we got here?" growled a deep voice. A heavy object collided with the back of her head and she slumped to the ground, unconscious.

VI

21 Miles Southwest of Dsôn Balsur,
Kingdom of Gauragar,
Girdlegard,
Winter, 6235th Solar Cycle

I know her because of the mask," said Tungdil, staring at the älf, who was lying, wrists and ankles bound, in the snow by the fire. He and the others were waiting for her to open her eyes "She's the one who stole Keenfire. She came after me in the Gray Range and swore to kill me."

Boïndil was gripping one of his axes, ready to dispatch their captive at the first sign of trouble. "I'm tired of waiting," he complained.

"We're only waiting because you walloped her over the head," his brother reminded him.

"In that case, I'd better wake her," he said promptly, taking a handful of snow and hurling it at her face. They had stripped her of her mask to reveal a slender, well-proportioned countenance, universal to älfar and elves. Tungdil was particularly interested to see the burns on her face; some were the work of the avatars, but the rest had been left by Keenfire.

The clump of snow bounced off and landed on the ground, leaving a few stray crystals that melted on the älf's warm skin.

"Hmm," said Boïndil. "She knows what it's like to get

burned, so maybe fire will do the trick." He bent down and picked up a glowing ember in his glove.

The älf's eyes flew open. "Put it down," she hissed.

"Ha, I knew it! The scheming no-eyes is awake!" crowed Boïndil, lowering his ax toward her face. "Do as we say or I'll chop you up like a sausage."

Tungdil stepped forward. "Now I know your face."

"Tion will curse you for stripping me of my mask," she spat back. "You and your friends are doomed."

Rodario shook his head. "Listen to the ferocious little polecat with the triangular ears." He eyed her bonds. "You can spit as much as you like, but we've trimmed your claws." He struck what he hoped was an intimidating pose. "My name is Rodario the Fablemaker, famulus to Narmora the Unnerving, and second most powerful magician in Girdlegard. I could destroy you right now if I wanted, but I'll spare your life if you—"

"Where's Keenfire?" broke in Boïndil to the indignation of the impresario, who punished him with a theatrical glare.

"It wouldn't help if I told you," she hissed.

"Perhaps not," replied Tungdil, "but don't be surprised if someone else gets hold of it. The heart of your kingdom is about to fall."

"To the White Army?" She raised her head and stared at Tungdil, her eyes full of hope. "Does Keenfire have the power to stop them?"

"Ah, so it's in Dsôn," he concluded.

The älf fell silent, trying to make sense of the situation. While pretending to be unconscious, she had heard the dwarves discussing the invaders. It seemed to her that they were trying to halt the White Army's advance. "You're not on their side," she reasoned. "Why are you trying to stop them? Don't you want Dsôn to fall?"

"Who would have thought it?" exclaimed Rodario, surprised. "The little pussy cat doesn't know who they are. Haven't you heard the legend of the avatars?" On seeing the älf's puzzlement, he proceeded to explain the history of the demigods, throwing in the odd fantastical detail here and there to make the avatars seem more terrifying. He pointed into the distance. "And your warriors were consumed by the avatars, fiery crusaders of purity descended from Tion, the god to whom you pray. Is that not deliciously ironic?"

"They won't stop until every last one of us is dead," said Ondori slowly. At last it made sense: her nervousness before the attack, the searing pain in her forehead, the failure of the dark water . . . And she knew without a doubt that Dsôn Balsur would fall to the invaders. *Unless* . . . "A bitter irony indeed. Our survival depends on those who seek to destroy us."

"Actually," began Tungdil, looking at her gravely, "we're asking you to join us. We need to fight together if we're to drive them out."

"We can't fight them, groundling," she said with a shudder, remembering the murderous wave of heat and light. "It's like asking a snowball to put out the sun."

"It depends on the size of the snowball," he replied, cutting her bonds. "Forget the enmity between us and hurry back to Dsôn to tell your leaders what you've heard. We'll need every warrior in Girdlegard if the avatars are to be stopped."

"I will deliver your message." Ondori picked up her mask and slipped it over her head, hiding her scars.

A woman in black leather armor appeared before her. Her face was slender, too slender for a human. "My name is Narmora the Unnerving. Andôkai the Tempestuous was my teacher," she said in älvish. Her accent was abysmal and her pronunciation atrocious, but Ondori understood. "Tell the immortal siblings that the älfar must join our troops. We won't fight your battles unless you're prepared to risk your lives as well." Her eyes darkened with menace. "We can always stand by and watch the avatars raze your homeland to the ground. I'd be happy to provide directions to the royal palace. Tell Nagsor and Nagsar to think very carefully before refusing our request."

She's one of us. Ondori nodded reluctantly. "I'll tell the immortal siblings," she rasped, shaking the ropes from her wrists. She straightened up.

"Swear on your blood that you'll do it," the maga said darkly, grabbing the älf's left arm and cutting a gash in the back of her hand. She held the glistening blade in front of the älf's face. "Break your word, and I'll destroy you. My magic will follow you like a huntsman follows his prey."

Ondori nodded meekly. Narmora's threat was all too believable. "I swear I'll do it," she stammered. "You can trust me, I promise. There's a groundling near here . . ." She quickly described the place where she had left her captive, then hurried away, vanishing into the night.

"What the blazes did you say to her," asked Boïndil suspiciously. "Do you have to speak in that tongue?"

"It depends on whether you want to help a poor dwarf who's waiting to be rescued," she said, smiling. Her eyes had returned to their normal color. "I'll send Djerûn to fetch her—unless you'd rather go."

She needn't have asked. No dwarf could stand by when one of their kinsfolk was in trouble, so Boïndil left with Tungdil, his brother, and thirty volunteers to release the captive dwarf.

They soon found the place.

Someone had gotten there before them, as they could tell from the melted snow and footprints in the sludge. A rope was wrapped around the tree trunk, marking the place where the dwarf had been tied up.

"The avatars beat us to it," said Tungdil, trudging around the tree in the hope of finding something that might identify the missing dwarf. Amidst the footprints, half buried in the slush, he found a broken necklace of beautiful steel links and gold balls.

He recognized it at once

"Balyndis," he gasped, picking up the chain and wiping it lovingly on his jerkin. The avatars had kidnapped his one true love, and with her, the instructions for forging Djerûn's armor.

"One darned problem after another," grumbled Boïndil. "I don't mind a challenge, but this is a joke."

Boëndal laid a comforting hand on Tungdil's shoulder. "It's a sign that we have to destroy them, scholar. Don't worry; we won't let your Balyndis come to any harm."

"She's not my Balyndis, remember?" Tungdil fastened the necklace around his wrist, over the neckerchief given to him by Frala, his childhood friend who had died at the hands of the orcs. *I'll get her back regardless, even if I have to take on the avatars myself.*

"I know she forged the iron band with Glaïmbar," Boëndal said simply, "but she'll always be your Balyndis." He paused, hesitating. "I wish Vraccas would make her properly yours."

So do I, thought Tungdil sadly.

Tungdil and the twins led the unit of ten thousand thirdlings on a forced march to outflank the avatars' army. On reaching the forest on the outskirts of Dsôn Balsur, they came to a halt. Tungdil ordered the bulk of the warriors to block the path that the allies had blazed through the woods. Two battalions of a thousand warriors apiece hid in the trees on either side. After a while, the masked älf appeared and told them that her kinsfolk had agreed to a temporary ceasefire. Most of the dwarves had guessed as much, having been neither struck down by quarterstaffs nor feathered with treacherous arrows.

Others before them had met with a harsher fate. Tungdil and his comrades were appalled to see that the älfar had erected sculptures made of human corpses to mark their victory over the allied troops. The branches were festooned with flags made of human skin, embellished with symbols painted in blood. The summer months had taken their toll on the artwork, but the autumn frosts had saved them from further decay, and a fine layer of snow covered the sculptures and flags like a clean white cloth, hiding the grisly details. Tungdil and his friends were tempted to leave the älfar to their fate.

If the thirdlings were nervous, they didn't show it. Their tattooed faces looked unerringly to the south as they waited in silence for the avatars to arrive. Shield in one hand and weapon in the other, they stood shoulder to shoulder in disciplined rows.

The sight of the thirdling warriors made a big impression on Boïndil who, like his brother, refused to move from Tungdil's side. Without discussing the matter, they had decided that Tungdil needed protection from Lorimbas's warriors, and they saw it as their duty to watch his back. The dwarven folks had united against the avatars, but they still regarded each other with mutual distrust.

The afternoon was almost over when a scout came running to make his report. "They're here," he panted. "The avatars are coming, but Lorimbas's unit is half an orbit behind. I saw them on the horizon."

Tungdil thanked the scout and sent him to join the thirdling ranks. "Half an orbit until Lorimbas gets here," he told the twins. "We'll have our work cut out." He remembered how quickly the avatars had dispatched the unit of four thousand älfar. *We'll be lucky if we survive.*

"It won't be easy, but it's not impossible," said Boïndil, trying to be upbeat. He had drawn one ax, now he drew the other.

Several hours later, a warm wind blew in from the south; the avatars were approaching.

Tungdil instructed his runners to take a message to the leaders of each battalion. "Tell them to stay in formation. When they see the fire coming, they need to lift their shields, drop to the ground, and let the flames pass overhead."

They heard thundering hooves. The avatars' cavalry swung round and came to a halt in two long lines. An advance guard of foot soldiers raised their swords and spears, ready to form a buffer between the horses and the enemy in the event of a counterattack.

The dwarves watched impassively, waiting for the light to become stronger and brighter before tying scarves around their heads to protect their eyes.

A gleaming figure detached itself from the enemy ranks and hovered above the ground. Slowly it glided toward the dwarves, leaving a trail of melted snow in its wake.

Ten paces from Tungdil, it came to a halt. The light was too bright for him to make out its features.

"You are the dwarves," said a voice of infinite kindness. "For thousands of cycles you and your forebears fought for Girdlegard and defended its borders against Tion's hordes. We share a common goal. Why do you seek to destroy us?"

"You and your brothers must leave these lands," called Tungdil. "Your presence is harmful to Girdlegard, to the ground beneath you, to our villages and towns."

"We have a mission, Tungdil Goldhand," the voice replied amicably. "Girdlegard is infested with älfar, ogres, and orcs. We won't leave these lands until Tion's beasts have been destroyed and their master humiliated. Ridding you of this plague will give us new strength. The time will come when Tion himself won't be safe from our wrath." The avatar edged closer and the temperature rose a few degrees. "Let us pass, and no harm will come to you or your kinsfolk." His shimmering hand pointed to the north. "Our quarrel is with the inhabitants of the city, not you."

"Think what your strength will do to our lands. We can't allow you to boost your powers." Tungdil raised his shield, expecting to be dazzled by ferocious white light.

"Our mission is to protect Girdlegard from harm, and you're harmful to Girdlegard. We can't let you pass, not even if—"

Djerûn charged forward. He covered the distance in three giant strides and grabbed the avatar by the neck, wrapping his hands around his throat and tightening his grip.

The avatar screamed and enveloped itself in searing light. Djerûn was bathed in fire, but he didn't let go. The smell of hot metal filled the air, and shouts went up from the enemy ranks.

Just then there was a loud ripping noise, like a curtain being torn in half. It was accompanied by cracking bones.

The light disappeared, and Djerûn roared in triumph. When the dwarves looked up, he was holding the avatar's head in one hand, and his body in the other. The avatar's face, clearly visible against the gray sky, looked unmistakably human. It belonged to a man of some thirty cycles whose beige robes were drenched in blood.

The colossal warrior tossed the avatar's dripping remains through the air, and they hit the snow, bouncing a few times before coming to rest. Contrary to expectations, the avatar's head didn't reattach itself to his body in a blaze of supernatural light. The man was an ordinary mortal.

"Knock me down with a hammer," gasped Boïndil. "Did you see how he wrung his neck? As easy as killing a chicken!"

"He was just a man," whispered Narmora, laughing in relief. "Djerûn must have known from the smell. The light and fireworks were meant to trick us; they're conjurers, not avatars."

Tungdil's worries—not least how he was going to rescue Balyndis if he didn't survive the orbit—melted away, and he laughed out loud.

The merriment spread through the ranks and soon the forest was echoing with mocking dwarven laughter that continued long after the cavalrymen began their charge. The riders no longer looked so intimidating; the death of the avatar had robbed their armor of its sheen.

Boïndil raised his ax and his shield. "Aim for the horses' knees, and let the riders come to you," he shouted, spoiling for a fight. Confidence had returned to the dwarven ranks.

Shouting a ferocious war cry, Tungdil and his eight thousand warriors ran out to meet the charge.

The speedy death of the first avatar, whose remains disappeared under the stampede of dwarven boots, was followed by a grueling battle with the enemy army.

Incensed by the fate of their leader, they threw themselves vengefully upon the dwarves, who struggled against the cavalry's superior maneuverability and speed.

The horses crashed through their ranks with such force that gaps appeared in the rows of shields, allowing enemy foot soldiers to surge through the openings and wreak havoc with the dwarven defenses.

"Fall back!" yelled Tungdil, ordering the surviving warriors to retreat to the forest. At once the hidden units of thirdlings leaped out from the trees to beat back the enemy troops. "Don't let up," Tungdil urged them. "It's almost sundown; your king will be here soon."

At that moment, a second luminous figure appeared

before them, but this time the avatar was careful not to come too close.

Hovering three paces above the ground, it stayed behind the enemy lines and bombarded them with fireballs. It took all Narmora's power to deflect the missiles and hurl them back at the enemy troops.

The avatar, realizing he had found a worthy opponent, gave the command for his soldiers to stop the magic at its source.

Calling for the twins to follow, Tungdil rushed to Narmora's aid, but the enemy soldiers got there first, and the half älf disappeared in a melee of bodies and swords.

"We've got to save her," he told the others. Boïndil led the attack, with Boëndal and Tungdil behind, and between them they cut a path through the enemy troops. Thanks to Boïndil's twin blades, Boëndal's crow's beak, and Tungdil's ax, they proceeded in a straight line, aiming for the spot where Narmora had last been seen.

By the time they reached her, she was under attack from all sides. Meanwhile, the avatar was bombarding her with curses and spells.

The thirdlings were putting up a spirited defense, and Djerůn was standing among them, sword in one hand, cudgel in the other, killing knots of soldiers with every blow. But it was only a matter of time before the maga's defenses crumbled—as the enemy was aware.

A heavily perspiring Narmora was tracing symbols and spells in the air. "I'm not strong enough to beat the avatar," she gasped. "I can't hold him off for much longer, and Djerůn can't get close enough to attack." She deflected a fireball and sent it crashing among her assailants, a dozen of whom perished in the blaze.

Tungdil wondered whether he should order the thirdlings to clear a path for Djerůn to tackle the avatar. *But where are the other nine?* Since the start of the battle he had been steeling himself for a wave of fire to wash over his warriors, as the älf had described. *What are the avatars up to? Why are they letting us kill their troops?* He decided to stop worrying and take charge of the attack. He and the twins led the way, with the thirdlings at the rear. Despite being heavily outnumbered, Lorimbas's warriors inflicted heavy losses on the enemy troops, but the odds were stacked against them.

As evening drew in, Tungdil's counterattack ground to a halt. Suddenly, help arrived on the scene.

A dark shadow crossed the sky, rippling overhead like a vast flock of birds. It was followed soon afterward by metallic jangling as hundreds of black-fletched arrows embedded themselves in enemy mail.

"It's about time the blasted no-eyes decided to help," snorted Boïndil, blocking an enemy sword. He knocked the weapon from the soldier's hand and drove an ax into his unprotected thigh. "I won't be sorry when this is over. Avatars, thirdlings, and älfar . . ." He aimed a blow at the next soldier's hip, cutting through his armor and slicing into his flesh. "I'm starting to feel dizzy from keeping tabs on them all."

Boëndal raised his crow's beak and swung the poll against a helmed head, crushing the skull. The soldier fell backward against his comrades. "Stop whirling about like a spinning top and focus on what's ahead," he instructed his brother. He wiped the sweat and blood from his face with the end of his beard. "Head straight for the avatar."

Älvish arrows whistled and whined through the air, bringing death to the enemy troops. The avatar's soldiers seemed to realize that the tide had turned against them, and the bulk of the army began to retreat, shields raised against the feathered storm.

The time had come for Djerûn to attack. Leaving Narmora, he surged forward, killing anyone foolish enough to bar his path, his sword and cudgel sweeping left and right with deadly force. Within moments he had fought his way through to Tungdil and the twins.

Lifting off with unexpected agility, he soared seven paces through the air, flying over helmets, heads, and shields and touching down at the heart of the action, within striking distance of the avatar.

The glowing figure unleashed a bolt of crackling white luminescence at his chest. The magic energy thudded against his breastplate, causing the runes on his armor to pulse with light, but Djerûn was unharmed. Ricocheting back toward the avatar, the bolt seared through the pack of enemy soldiers, allowing the armored giant to advance.

Once again he called upon his incredible strength, thrusting his metal-clad arms into the light. For a few moments the glow intensified, then an agonized scream rent the air, and the light was extinguished.

Roaring, Djerûn brandished his victim's body; the head was twisted unnaturally to the side. A purple glow emanated from the warrior's visor, like a radiant expression of pride. He seemed to enjoy his victory, holding the corpse on high and showing it to the enemy troops. At last he tossed him away like an unwanted toy.

The dead man flew through the air, landing on the pikes and halberds of the enemy army.

There was silence on the battlefield.

The avatars' army had accepted the death of the first avatar as an unfortunate accident, but the death of the second was irrefutable proof that the avatars were neither invincible nor immortal. The dead wizard's blood trickled down the shafts of the weapons like that of an ordinary mortal. There was nothing divine or pure about him.

"Attack!" shouted Tungdil exultantly. "Don't let them regroup!" His ax slammed into a shield, cutting through the metal and severing an enemy wrist. A man fell screaming to the churned-up ground.

The battle began again, but this time Tungdil's warriors had victory in their sights.

Even as the älfar emerged from the trees and threw themselves on the enemy, dwarven bugles heralded the arrival of the rest of the army with Lorimbas, Xamtys, and Gemmil at the fore. Meanwhile, Djerůn was in mortal danger.

The White Army's pikemen had made it their mission to bring down the avatars' killer and they closed in on the giant, lunging at him with their long-handled weapons and retreating out of range. From time to time he cut down a pikeman, only to be attacked by another four.

Boïndil noticed Djerůn's plight. "We'd better help old buckethead. He's overextended." Glancing at Tungdil and Boëndal, he saw agreement in their tired faces. "It would be a shame to lose him after everyth—"

"Look out!" shouted Boëndal, hefting his crow's beak

and hurling it through the air. The powerful weapon ripped toward a rider who was charging, spear in hand, toward the giant's back. The rider saw the crow's beak coming, and ducked just in time.

Meanwhile, Djerûn was too busy fighting the pikemen to notice the thundering hooves. Startled, he turned at the last moment, and the spear pierced his side. The rider paid for his bravery with his life, the giant's cudgel smashing against his chest.

At once the pikemen surged forward, falling on the injured giant and forcing him to the ground. Tungdil and the twins lost sight of their ally.

"Quick!," shouted Tungdil, alerting the maga to the danger.

Narmora fixed her eyes on the skirmish, but Djerûn was lost from view. "I can't see him," she called back, sending a flickering tongue of fire in the direction indicated by Tungdil. "Wait, I'll burn a path." The dwarves nodded and readied themselves to sprint after the next fiery bolt.

Neither Tungdil nor the twins had any inkling that the maga wasn't prepared to come to the giant's rescue. Djerûn had been useful on occasions, not least by revealing that some types of armor were resistant to magic, but he had played a key role in the plot against Furgas, and Narmora could never forgive him for that.

If he dies, he dies. If he lives, it won't be long before he falls in another skirmish. She gazed after Tungdil and the others, who were leading a unit of thirdlings to save the injured giant. *They can risk their lives if they want to. I'm not wasting my magic on him.*

*   *   *

Getting past the pikemen was the toughest challenge yet.

The advancing dwarves came to a halt in front of a bristling mass of long-handled halberds and pikes. Steel pike heads pointed menacingly toward them, keeping them at bay. Every now and then a weapon sped forward, injuring any who sought to cleave the shafts and cut a path to Djerûn, who was somewhere behind the blockade.

"That does it!" snorted Ireheart. "I'll teach them what it means to rile a dwarf!"

His levelheaded brother pulled him back. "They'll run you through like a pig on a spit." He was stopped from saying anything further by the arrival of a band of tall archers, who took up position next to them and leveled their bows. A flurry of arrows ripped toward the enemy with deadly effect. A path opened up between the pikemen, nearly two paces wide.

"Go on then," said a voice that Tungdil recognized as Ondori's. "Hurry!"

"I don't like it," said Ireheart suspiciously. He leaned across and whispered in his brother's ear. "What if they shoot us in the back?"

"You'd die, of course," said Ondori, smiling. "But we're not going to shoot you. For the time being, we're on the same side." Looking up, she saw that the gap had closed so she ordered her archers to loose another hail of arrows. "Hurry, Goldhand." She raised her bow and nocked an arrow to the string. "The pikemen won't kill you; I want that pleasure myself." Her gray eyes were cold with hatred.

Remembering Djerûn's plight, Tungdil had no choice but to trust her. He sent a quick prayer to Vraccas and charged into the breach, followed by Boïndil, Boëndal, and the thirdlings. Even though he had promised himself he wouldn't, he glanced over his shoulder to check on the älf.

She was standing ramrod straight, a nocked arrow pointing at his heart. Even as he stared, the bow string released and the arrow shot toward him. Closing his eyes, he braced himself for the feathered missile to hit. Nothing happened. By some miracle, the älf had missed her mark.

She lowered her bow and pointed ahead.

Turning back, Tungdil saw the outstretched body of a soldier, felled by a single arrow. In his distraction, he had almost impaled himself on an enemy pike. *It's my own fault for not trusting her. She hates me too much to let me die.* He leaped over the pikeman and threw himself into battle. But Djerûn was nowhere to be seen.

Ireheart, thrilled to be in striking distance of the pikemen, rampaged through the enemy ranks. In the crush of bodies, the pikemen were forced to rely on short swords, which gave little protection against hefty dwarven clubs, axes, and hammers. Suddenly the battle shifted in favor of the dwarves, who weren't in the mood for sparing lives. The enemy was shown no mercy. By nightfall, the avatars' army had been destroyed and the woods of Dsôn Balsur were strewn with corpses.

It was then they found Djerûn.

He was lying among the dead soldiers, and he didn't stir when they called his name and shook him by the shoulder. Yellow blood was trickling from countless holes in his armor, forming a vast puddle around his battered body. Tungdil shouted for Narmora's help.

"I don't want anyone closer than ten paces," she told

them. "You mustn't see what I'm doing—the magic could kill you." She bent over Djerûn's head and covered herself with her cloak. Then she opened the visor.

The purple glow had gone out, and the sockets in his terrible skull were empty and lifeless. Narmora felt neither sorrow nor satisfaction at his passing: Djerûn was a killing machine—Andôkai's killing machine. *He shouldn't have done what he did to poor Furgas.*

Closing the visor, she lifted her cloak and got to her feet. "He's dead," she announced. "Two avatars died by Djerûn's hand. May his name live on in our memory." She made her way over to Tungdil. "Any sign of Balyndis?"

Boïndil shook his head crossly. "I don't understand. What the blazes have they done with her?"

"I'd like to know where the other so-called avatars have got to," said Tungdil distractedly. He was frantic with worry for the missing smith. "Djerûn killed two, which leaves another nine."

"Maybe there were only two in the first place," suggested Narmora. "I've had a look at their bodies, and they seem like ordinary humans to me." She showed the dwarves some artifacts that she had found on the bodies. "Amulets, rings, crystals . . . If you ask me, they weren't demigods at all. Take away their paraphernalia, and they'll be helpless."

"You mean they made all that light with a few magic trinkets?" said Boïndil, amazed.

The maga nodded. "It was some kind of spell. They wanted to make us think they were gods." She pointed to a dead soldier. "See the moonstone on his gorget? It's charmed. Without the moonstone, the armor wouldn't glow."

"What a con," growled Boïndil, turning to the impresario, who had just joined their group. "They're as bad as you, pretending to be something better than they are."

"I think I deserve a little more respect," protested Rodario. "I convinced them I was a real magus—and I nearly got killed for my pains." For once he seemed to be telling the truth; his robe had been slashed to ribbons, but he was otherwise unharmed.

Without warning, the älf appeared alongside them, like a sinister suspiration of the night. Ireheart whipped out an ax and brandished it menacingly. "Get back, älf. The battle's over and we're enemies again."

"If our alliance were over, you'd be lying face down on the ground," she said scornfully. "I came to tell you that I know what happened to the other avatars. Several orbits ago I saw two lights in the distance—one heading for Dsôn Balsur, and the other traveling west. I think they've split their troops."

"Without us noticing?" Boïndil laughed.

"Groundlings will sleep through anything. I could creep up on a dwarven encampment and slit a dozen throats without waking a soul." She gave him a long, hard look. "Trust me, I know."

Fortunately, Tungdil and Boëndal grabbed their friend before he could throw himself on Ondori. He struggled vigorously and hurled curses in the älf's direction.

"Where would they be heading?" asked Tungdil. "Why

would they be going west? It's the wrong direction for ogres or orcs." He thought about what he knew of the legend. "One part of the story is true. They seem to get their magic power by destroying evil. They must be looking for something evil to destroy."

Narmora went white. "Porista," she whispered.

"Porista?" echoed Rodario, taken aback. "Porista is a nice enough place—in fact, I rather like it. The people are friendly enough—although some of the men are overly jealous."

"I wasn't referring to the population," Narmora said sharply. "Lios Nudin is the wellspring of Girdlegard's magic. The source of the energy is in the vaults. Nôd'onn corrupted the force fields to stop the other magi using them, but Andôkai wasn't affected because she prayed to Samusin, god of light and dark. She taught me to do the same."

Tungdil had an idea what the avatars were planning. "And the force fields are still corrupted, even though Nôd'onn is dead?"

Narmora nodded.

"It sounds to me that Porista would make a good target," said Tungdil.

"How much damage can they do?" asked Boëndal. "The force fields may be tucked out of sight like the stratum of rock beneath a mountain, but aren't they also vital? What if the avatars destroy them?"

"They can't do that, can they?" asked Tungdil, alarmed.

"I don't know for sure," Narmora admitted. "I expect we could find an answer, but the archives are in Porista . . ." She gasped and looked at Furgas. "Dorsa!"

"The alliance still holds," Ondori said coolly. "You should be grateful to the avatars; they've earned you a reprieve."

Tungdil gazed at the carnage around them. *This is just the beginning, Vraccas.*

Of the thirty thousand dwarves, including twenty-two thousand thirdlings, only twenty thousand or so had survived the first battle. And now they would have to lay siege to a city and take on nine magi and an unknown quantity of warriors.

Tungdil knew he couldn't count on the humans or the elves. The former had been fatally weakened by the defeat at Dsôn Balsur, and the latter would never agree to join forces with the älfar. He decided to send a messenger to Âlandur anyway.

We're the only ones who can stop them. It's up to us. Tungdil turned in the direction of the Gray Range and gazed into the darkness. "The defense of Girdlegard is our Vraccas-given duty," he said staunchly. For some reason, he was certain that Balyndis was still alive. *We'll find her in Porista.*

Boïndil nodded. "Girdlegard needs us, scholar. It's getting to be a habit." His eyes traveled from Ondori to the thirdlings. "I wouldn't mind more reliable allies."

An älvish scout said something in a low voice to Ondori, who passed on the message to the rest of the group. "We've found tracks," she told them. "A band of riders, no more than twenty in total. They're riding west—probably toward Porista. We found a footprint near the spot where they mounted their horses. It looks like a child's."

Tungdil breathed out in relief. "It wasn't a child; it was a dwarf—a dwarven smith who knows how to forge armor capable of withstanding the avatars' fire."

"If I were an avatar, I would have killed her on the

spot," declared Rodario in a manner that struck the dwarves as rather heartless.

"You mean why bother to take her with them? I expect they realized that she isn't an ordinary dwarf. For all we know, they've heard about the magic armor. With Balyndis's help, they could shield themselves and their soldiers from Narmora's curses. A real avatar wouldn't need armor, but a mortal magician would be glad of the protection." Tungdil looked at the others determinedly. "We need to rescue Balyndis before we attack Porista. Without the secret of Djerûn's armor, we can't defeat the avatars. They'll burn us to a cinder. A small group of us need to infiltrate the city and rescue our smith."

"I'll come too," volunteered Ondori. Her motivation was entirely selfish; she wanted to keep them alive until she got her revenge.

Furgas and Rodario exchanged looks. "We know a few hidden passageways," murmured Furgas. "I'll show you the way."

"But only if you rescue Dorsa," added Narmora. "I don't want her to be hurt in the fighting. I've lost a son, and I've no intention of losing a daughter." She glared at Tungdil. "Give me your word."

In spite of the extra risk on an already risky mission, he acquiesced, although deep down he was surprised at Narmora. *She's changed. It was probably studying under Andôkai that did it.* He looked sadly at Djerûn's motionless body. He would miss the fallen warrior, and not only because of his strength.

Then he had an idea.

187 Miles East of Porista,
Kingdom of Gauragar,
Girdlegard,
Winter, 6235th/6236th Solar Cycle

The ringing of the hammer filled the morning air. Tungdil was in a small forge in Klinntal, a village en route to Porista. He had laid out Djerůn's armor on a workbench. According to his estimates, the metal would suffice for three metal suits—one for him, and one each for the twins—provided he was careful.

Much thought had gone into deciding which parts of Djerůn's mail lent themselves to being refashioned into smaller, dwarf-sized items. He had begun by making detailed drawings, showing the positioning of the intarsia and runes. Only then had he started to break apart the breastplate, spaulders, and greaves.

"How are you getting along?" asked Boëndal, who, along with his brother, the village smith, and the smith's apprentices, was helping out in the forge. The men were very impressed by Tungdil, who wielded the hammer with uncommon precision, power, and speed.

"We're nowhere near ready," sighed Tungdil. "The tools aren't up to scratch and the hearth doesn't draw very well. I wish the flames were hotter . . ." The hammer swooped down, forcing the metal into shape. "I haven't got time to customize the armor properly. I'm afraid it's going to pinch."

"I don't care if it rubs all the flesh from my bones, so long as I'm safe from the avatars' magic," growled Boïndil. He finished stamping a rune into a finished section of armor and weighed it critically in his hand. "We won't be able to move as fast as usual. It weighs a ton." He turned to his brother. "From now on, anyone who throws his only weapon will owe me a sack of gold," he said, remembering how his brother had cast his crow's beak at Djerûn's assassin. "There's simply no excuse."

Nine orbits had passed since they started their journey through snow-covered Gauragar. They had buried Djerûn, still clad in his chain mail and helmet, in Dsôn Balsur. After a little persuasion, Boïndil had agreed not to peek behind his visor, and the giant warrior had taken his secret to the grave.

Since then, Tungdil, Ondori, Rodario, Furgas, and the twins had been marching as fast as possible toward Porista. The main army was following at a distance, with Narmora to protect it from magical assault.

Boëndal tapped his weapons belt. "Point taken," he said. "You don't need to lecture *me* about throwing my only weapon: I've got an ax in reserve." He waved his tongs at Tungdil. "You'll get your gold from our scholar, I'll warrant."

Tungdil peered at the breastplate emerging from the beaten metal. He threw some water onto his sweaty face and shook the soot from his long brown beard. He was too busy thinking about his work and worrying about Balyndis to pay attention to the twins.

He hadn't been especially talkative over the past few orbits. He couldn't stop turning things over in his mind and trying to gauge his feelings. After giving his heart to two dwarf-women and being let down, he didn't know what to think. Myr had betrayed him, then saved him from Salfalur's hammer, and Balyndis had spurned him in

favor of Glaïmbar, yet she hadn't stopped loving him—nor
he her. He had twice gone from happiness to despair, and
in quiet moments he succumbed to a creeping melancholy
that prevented him from taking pleasure in anything
around him. Deep down he wanted to rail against Vraccas
for making him suffer.

Pain and loss had accompanied him on every step of
his journey, and sometimes—in his darkest moments—he
found himself wishing that he would die in battle so that
his soul could be gathered to Vraccas's smithy.

"Is something the matter, scholar?" asked Boëndal,
concerned.

Tungdil shook the water from his beard. "I'm fine," he
said, forcing himself to smile. He untied his leather apron
and pulled it over his head. "I could do with a bite to eat
and something to oil my throat."

"I'm dying for some good, strong beer," agreed Boïndil.
He sighed. "Why do the long-uns brew such watery rubbish?"

They left the forge and strolled to their lodgings. Klinntal
didn't have a hostelry, so they were staying in a farm-
house. A smell of roast meat and freshly baked bread
wafted toward them.

Inside, Furgas was dozing on the bench by the table,
and Ondori was relaxing by the fire.

The meat came courtesy of the älf and her bow.
According to the villagers, there was never any game to
be had in winter, but Ondori always found something, a
deer or a brace of hares. She was a formidable hunter
who treated all living creatures as prey—in her eyes, men,
orcs, and wild animals were little better than vermin.

She didn't look up to acknowledge the dwarves. Her

sharp knife was sculpting limbs and carving faces for movable figures made from the remains of her prey. Earlier, she had made a flute for the farmer's daughter, and everyone agreed that it produced a pleasant sound.

Tungdil suspected that she was more accustomed to working with the bones of men, elves, and dwarves. It made him queasy to think that somewhere an älf would be making music on a dwarven shinbone.

But it didn't stop him or the twins from feasting on the meat. Hammering metal was hungry work, and the best way of maintaining their strength without proper dwarven victuals was to eat a lot of meat.

Furgas woke up, stretched, and glanced over at Rodario, who was studying Ondori and taking notes. "An interesting character," the impresario murmured. "She's helping the others because she wants to kill them herself. It adds an excellent twist to the plot. It's very suspenseful!" He flipped the notebook shut.

"This isn't one of your plays, you know," said Furgas, who saw it as his duty to keep reminding his friend of the seriousness of the task ahead.

"I'm aware of that, thank you," retorted Rodario. "No rehearsals, no prompts, no audience, and worst of all, no coin." The farmer's wife came in, set down a stewpot, and left in a hurry, unnerved by the presence of the älf. Rodario helped himself to a mug of herbal tea. "If anyone had predicted that I'd be roped into fighting the forces of darkness instead of setting up my theater, seducing women, and following my calling on the stage, I would have thought they were mad." He sighed and breathed on the steaming tea. "The curtain went up, and I found myself at the heart of a drama that could cost me my life."

"Feeling sorry for yourself, Rodario?" teased Boëndal.

"It's probably the weather. Too much gray isn't good for the soul." He jabbed a finger at Tungdil. "He's no better. I don't think he's said a word since we got here. Has anyone got a good joke? You didn't finish the one about the orc and the dwarf."

Tungdil sipped his warm beer. "I'm sorry I haven't been more lively."

Boïndil clinked tankards with him. "It's all right, scholar. It stands to reason that you're more worried about Balyndis than anyone else. True love never rusts, as they say." He checked himself, realizing that he was hardly improving the mood. "Why do I have to be so tactless?"

"Honesty is a virtue," said Tungdil. *There's no denying that I love her,* he thought, waiting for his inner demon to contradict him. But the taunting voice was silent now that he had stopped lying to himself. *I love her and I always will. It wouldn't be right to join the iron band with another maiden when my heart belongs to someone else. No dwarf-woman will ever hold a candle to her.* He took another draft of beer, stood up, and picked up his tankard. "There's work to be done."

It took two orbits to finish the breastplates to a reasonable standard. After a further four orbits, the spaulders, greaves, and helmets were ready as well. The gauntlets still needed to be assembled, but they decided to do it en route.

They walked fast and stopped seldom, racing across Gauragar until at last they spied Porista.

Even from a distance, it was obvious that the city had changed hands.

White banners with strange symbols fluttered from the palace and tents had mushroomed in the streets, over-shadowing the houses. Soldiers were patrolling the borders and stopping anyone wanting to enter or leave.

"They've got it all worked out," commented Furgas, pointing to the cranes that were swinging their long jibs over the city. It seemed the building work was making good progress in spite of the new regime. "The fake avatars have obviously taken a liking to my machines."

He was about to make another comment when the ground moved beneath their feet. At first it was only a slight tremble, but it soon became so vigorous that snow rained down from the trees. The shaking stopped abruptly.

Tungdil looked over his shoulder at the ground behind him.

As he watched, a ripple ran through the earth, spreading outward from Porista, like the movement caused by a pebble in a lake. Tungdil spotted branches swinging crazily in the distance, shedding their coating of snow. At last the ground was still. "They've found the wellspring," he said. "The question is, how much damage will they do?"

Boïndil wiped the clumps of snow from his shoulders. He wasn't wearing a gorget, so most of it slipped down his neck, melting against the warmth of his skin. "A little tremor like that won't do much harm."

"I'd rather they didn't interfere with the force fields at all," said his brother. He turned expectantly to Rodario and Furgas. "It's time for the long-uns to make themselves useful. Show us how to get in."

Furgas pointed north. "We started building a new sewage system. The old drains collapsed in the quake, so we dug them out and strengthened the walls. The first section is complete—it starts outside the city and runs five hundred paces toward the marketplace."

"Is there a door or something at this end?" asked Tungdil, adjusting his suit of armor. It was oppressively tight, and even the helmet restricted his view. The twins were suffering as well.

"I don't know how old buckethead put up with it," came a hollow voice. Boïndil had put his helmet on. "Blasted thing! I've trapped my beard. I won't have any whiskers left at this rate."

"We didn't want predators coming into the city from the drains, so we built a hidden entrance with a wooden door. The avatars won't have found it, I'm sure." He started to move off, but Ondori barged ahead.

"I'll go first," she said, nocking an arrow to her bow and stealing forward. The others followed at a distance of ten paces.

"My dear little warriors," hissed Rodario when they were approximately halfway to the door. "Anyone would think you were trying to attract attention. I've never heard so much squeaking, clattering, and jangling. Did you forget to oil your joints?"

"Speaking of which," said Boïndil, pushing back his visor. "How did Djerûn move so quietly in a full suit of metal?"

"The sooner you discover his secret the better," snapped Rodario. "Personally, I'd rather not be captured by the avatars. Hmm, I wonder if this will work." He stooped down, picked up a handful of snow, and rubbed it into the hinges of Boïndil's suit. The metal squealed in protest. "Same to you," said Rodario crossly.

Boïndil gave him a vigorous shove, and he disappeared backward into the snow. "Keep that word-weaving meddler away from me," growled the angry secondling. "His brilliant ideas will get us all killed. Maybe we should send him to the other side of the city to distract attention from the rest of us."

Rodario jumped up and gave himself an irritated shake. "Fine, Mr. Hasty-ax, that's exactly what I'll do," he announced self-importantly. "I'm an innocent citizen of Porista, a theater director, no less. They won't have a problem letting me into the city, my cocky little friend."

"Don't be silly, Rodario," said Tungdil. "It's safer with us."

"I appreciate your concern, but I happen to disagree. I'll see you at the marketplace. No doubt I'll be fully cognizant of the avatars' whereabouts by the time you arrive." He turned on his heels and strutted off.

"Good riddance," growled Boïndil. "I've had enough of his blather."

Tungdil gazed after him, wishing he would change his mind. The silver-tongued actor had proven his usefulness on numerous occasions in the past.

"You can bet he'll be fine," said Furgas with a grin. "He's bound to make it to the marketplace. Anyone who can seduce a maiden and sweet-talk her father is resourceful enough to look after himself." He set off again, following a trail of arrows traced by Ondori in the snow.

The symbols were the only evidence that the älf had

passed that way. Her feet left no prints and in the dying light of the orbit she melded with the darkness, disappearing from view.

"Is she really Sinthoras's daughter?" whispered Boïndil. "I don't want to find a black-fletched arrow in my back. She's a double-dealing, dwarf-killing no-eyes. We'll have to kill her before she kills us."

Tungdil was inclined to agree. "We'll bide our time. Don't do anything unless I say so—the avatars are enough of a challenge without Ondori going for our throats."

They stole toward Porista's newly erected defenses. In places, the walls were still unfinished, but they were high enough to keep out invaders.

At the base of a half-finished section of wall they discovered the entrance to the sewage system described by Furgas. The wooden gates were as high as a man, but to the casual observer or sentry they were completely hidden by a large mound of snow. The älf was crouched at the entrance, listening for enemy guards.

"Hmm," said Boëndal disapprovingly. "A great big tunnel leading straight to the city . . . You're opening yourselves to attack."

"We thought about that," Furgas assured him, smiling. "In the event of danger, we can close off the sewer by lowering the grates. The avatars won't have activated them, which is just as well for us."

He bounded down the bank, and the dwarves stumbled after him, wishing they were back in their chain mail. Their new armor was considerably heavier and more restrictive as well.

Furgas, an expert in all things technical, set about

picking the locks, his deft fingers teasing open the mechanism. There was a gentle click, and the door swung open, allowing the little party to enter the sewer.

Furgas closed the door behind him and made sure it was locked. Then, lighting a small lantern to help him find his way through the darkness, he led the others through the tunnel.

After only ten paces, he stopped and pointed at five deep grooves in the ceiling, each three or so paces from the next.

"The grates are up there—big metal barriers as thick as my arm. You can do what you like to them, but they won't shift an inch. No one could ever invade Porista through the drains."

"Isn't that precisely what we're doing?" commented Boïndil, trying not to skid on a frozen puddle. "If you ask me, there's a flaw in your plan."

Furgas gave a low laugh. "I'm sure the gods knew what they were doing when they made me forget to lower the grates."

They felt their way forward slowly. Ondori was somewhere in front of them, hidden by darkness. Suddenly she appeared at Boëndal's side. "You may as well speed up a bit," she said, startling Furgas so badly that the lantern jigged up and down. "There's no one here apart from us. It's all clear until we get to the door." She melted back into the darkness, only reappearing when they reached the bottom of a narrow staircase.

"We built the stairs so that workmen can make sure nothing is blocking the sewers. Someone will be responsible for coming down here at regular intervals to check. The manhole is covered by a slab of stone. It's easy to open from above, but it might take a bit of force to lift it up."

Ondori went ahead and signaled for them to follow. There wasn't enough room for anything but single file, and no matter how hard they tried, they couldn't succeed in shifting the stone.

Furgas peered through the cracks. "They've fastened the bolts."

"It's good to know that someone cares about security," said Boïndil, thumping the stone. "I'm afraid it's pretty solid. We'll have our work cut out."

Ondori signaled for them to be quiet.

There was someone on the other side of the manhole. They heard bolts being thrown back, then a muffled groan as the slab began to wobble.

"Do you think it's Rodario?" Boëndal asked Furgas in a whisper.

"May as well lift it up and see," said his brother, pushing against the slab. The others joined in while the älf raised her bow.

At last the slab lifted and hit the floor with a thud. Looking up, they saw a man with a grimy face and, beside him, a bucket of waste. He seemed understandably surprised to see them emerging from the sewers.

"Is that you, Mr. Furgas?" he stuttered. "Where have you—" He stepped back to let them out. "Quick, you'd better hurry or you'll be seen."

"This is Ertil," said Furgas, introducing him to the others. "He runs the kitchens for the laborers."

"Can he be trusted?" demanded Ondori without lowering her bow.

"An elf," gasped Ertil respectfully. He looked up at

the tall, slim archer, hoping to catch a glimpse of the elves' fabled beauty, which was praised in countless human songs. To his disappointment, her features were hidden by a mask.

"He's trustworthy," said Furgas hurriedly, to prevent Ondori from loosing her bow. "I daresay he'll be able to tell us what happened."

The man nodded. "That I can, sir. It's a good thing I needed to empty my bucket." He took another look at the strange group, then tipped the contents of his bucket into the street. "I don't want you dirtying your boots if you leave the same way."

They replaced the stone slab and hurried down the alleyway to Ertil's house, keeping to the shadows.

He unlocked the door, lit a couple of candles, and brought them some water. "Fifteen orbits ago they got here. They were shining like stars—nearly went blind just from looking," he said. "They spread out through the city, killing the guards who tried to stop them. The ones in charge—shimmering, glowing creatures—went straight to the palace, and we haven't seen them since. They haven't actually *done* anything—you could almost forget they were here, except no one goes anywhere near the palace. They say the city belongs to the amsha."

"Did anyone try to resist?" asked Furgas.

"We didn't dare," said Ertil, staring at the floor. "Ten thousand soldiers they brought with them. We didn't know what to do."

"It's not your fault," Furgas assured him. "The shimmering creatures you mentioned—how many of them are here?"

"I saw five, but others saw more. I was probably blinded by the glare." He looked at Furgas. "Who are they, sir? I don't know what they're doing in the palace, but it's upsetting my horses. They've been restless and fidgety for a couple of orbits. Is the Estimable Maga going to rescue us soon?"

"She's on her way," said Furgas soothingly. "She sent us here to reconnoiter the territory. You'd better not tell anyone you've seen us."

The man nodded gravely.

"Was there a dwarf-woman with them?" asked Tungdil, desperate to know what had happened to Balyndis. "Did you see where they took her?"

"A dwarf-woman. Funny you should mention it." He pointed toward the palace. "There was another group got here only seven orbits ago. I know because I was passing the gates on my way to market and I saw them riding like demons. If I hadn't gotten out of the way, they would have ridden right over me. They disappeared into the palace, and the dwarf-woman was with them."

"Any news of my daughter?" asked Furgas. "Do you know where she is?"

Ertil shook his head. "No one has left the palace as far as I know."

"That's something, at least," snorted Boïndil. "We'll deal with her and Balyndis together, and beat a quick retreat."

Boëndal peered out of the window, hoping to spot Rodario. "There's nobody out there," he said. "The streets are empty. Rodario will stick out like a stain on a clean leather jerkin."

"Don't worry," said Furgas. "He'll be fine."

"We can't wait forever," Tungdil reminded him. "We need to rescue Balyndis before the avatars learn the secret of Djerůn's armor." He could already imagine them torturing his beloved smith.

"I say we go right away. I can find my way around the palace without Rodario's help—but I suggest you grease your hinges first."

Ertil fetched a bottle of sunflower oil and the dwarves set about silencing their creaking armor, while Boïndil muttered unhappily about the inferior quality of the oil.

Furgas got up and went to the door. Their perilous mission could begin.

Ondori went ahead, followed by Furgas and the armored dwarves. Ertil was instructed to keep an eye on the entrance to the sewers and look after Rodario until they got back— assuming they weren't captured.

They hurried as quietly as possible through the city's hushed streets.

Furgas was beginning to get worried about Rodario. *He should be here by now. I hope he's all right . . .*

VII

Straight to the stage with no rehearsals. Rodario strained his eyes, peering at the guards at the entrance to the city. *I bet they don't use retractable blades.* Screwing up his courage, he picked up a bundle of firewood that he had gathered as a prop, and set off toward the gates. From a distance he could make out nine soldiers in shimmering armor. They were clustered around a brazier, warming their hands.

"Stop," commanded one of them, blocking his path. The rest of them continued to talk among themselves. The soldier's spear pointed at Rodario's stomach. "Where are you from?"

"From there," he said, pointing to a field behind him. He gestured toward the city and added a few garbled sentences to give them the impression that they were dealing with a simpleton. "Freezy-cold outside," he babbled, holding up his bundle of wood. "I needs foods for my fire."

The act seemed to work. "Did you hear that?" the guard called to the others. "We've found the village idiot." He picked up a burning log and placed it on top of the wood. "Here, take this as well. Our fire isn't hungry."

Rodario smiled dumbly and gave a grateful bow,

allowing the burning log to fall into the snow. Mumbling under his breath, he took a step forward and stooped to pick it up, at the same time dropping the rest of the firewood in front of him. He repeated the procedure again and again, making his way past the guards who were roaring with laughter and hurling logs down the street.

Obligingly, he scampered after the flying wood like a dog in pursuit of a bone, but as soon as he reached the corner, he stopped laughing and threw away the wood. *That was easy.* He slowed to a brisk walk, not wanting to draw attention to himself.

He knew Porista's narrow streets like the back of his hand, and his path took him past the Curiosum. He came to a sudden stop. Mournfully, he ran his hand over the locked door and recited the words on the sign: "Company On Tour. Grand Re-opening In The Spring. Prepare To Be Amazed And Astonished By Girdlegard's Biggest Talent, The Fabulous Rodario."

"It's a pity, isn't it?" said a gentle voice behind him. "I would have liked to meet this Rodario."

"The fabulous Rodario," he corrected her, turning round. He was expecting to see an old dame on a tour of the city's hostelries, but the speaker was a woman of his age, wrapped in expensive furs. A hood protected her hair from the light snowfall.

Rodario smiled his famous smile. "He's supposed to be very good."

"You've been away from the city," she observed, eying his torn robes and stubbly chin. "It's the wrong weather for traveling on foot."

"When your horse is stabbed to death, you don't have much choice," he said, concocting a story that he hoped would stir her pity. "I was attacked by a pair of high-waymen. They killed my stallion and stole my saddlebag and purse."

"Let me guess: You're a nobleman visiting his mistress in Porista." She smoothed a strand of brown hair and smiled at him playfully. "I'm afraid I didn't catch your name . . ."

He hesitated, sensing that she hadn't believed his story. *A hard nut to crack. Still, I like a good challenge.*

Realizing that she was staring at something behind him, he turned around to see what it was. *Of course!* He laughed. It was a life-size portrait, painted next to the entrance. In fact, he had commissioned the work himself. Luckily the guards hadn't recognized him.

"Why didn't you tell me?" she asked, stepping toward him. "Why would the fabulous Rodario want to spin me a yarn?" Her dark green eyes sparkled mischievously.

"I took a fancy to the story," he said quickly. "Anyway, I'm curious to know why a beautiful lady would be wandering the streets of Porista by herself. I don't remember your face, yet I know every—"

"Every woman in Porista," she finished for him. "In that case, I'm probably ruining my reputation by talking to you."

"I was going to say *everyone*, not every woman," he corrected her. "I came to Porista in the employ of Andôkai the Tempestuous and her successor Narmora. My friend Furgas and I were in charge of rebuilding the city after it was . . ." He swiveled, watching as she paced around him, fur robes trailing in the snow. "In any event, I know the city well." He reached out and took hold of her arm, stopping her mid-circle. "How is it I haven't laid eyes on you when every cobblestone must be jealous of your favor?"

She smiled, this time like a young girl receiving a compliment from an admirer. "Was that a line from one of your plays?"

"Words can't do justice to your beauty," he whispered, encouraged by her response. *Ha*, he thought smugly. *I haven't lost my touch.*

He shifted his gaze for a moment and looked at the street leading to the marketplace. For a while he had forgotten what had brought him to Porista. There was nothing that might justify prolonging the conversation, even though he was eager to further his acquaintance with the mysterious stranger. It was a long time since he had exercised his talents in the art of seduction.

Stop it, he told himself sharply. *The others will be waiting.* Taking her hand briskly but chivalrously, he pressed his lips to her delicate white glove. "Where can I find you? I'm on my way to a secret rehearsal, and I mustn't be late, but I could see you afterward." He gazed into her dark brown eyes.

"You're running away already?" She snatched her hand from his and took a few paces back. He detected a look of disappointment on her face. "Good evening, Rodario. I look forward to seeing you on the stage." She shot him a sizzling look and disappeared into the falling snow without turning around.

"Your address!" he called after her. "Where shall I send the tickets?" His shouts went unanswered. *I suppose it wasn't to be.* Disappointed, he hurried down the street to the marketplace.

Snow was falling thickly, hiding him from prying eyes. He reached the spot where the stairs led down to the sewer and stopped: The manhole cover had been unbolted. A light dusting of snow covered the footprints.

They didn't wait for me! He stomped his foot indignantly. *I bet that hotheaded secondling persuaded them to go.* He rubbed his pointy beard. Wounded pride made him more determined than ever to handle things by himself. He set off toward the palace. *I'll show you,* he thought, imagining how the dwarves would thank him when he freed them from the avatars and rescued Balyndis and the child.

Without stopping, he checked that his props were in place. They were essential for his transformation into the fearsome conjurer Rodario the Fablemaker, a role that he played with aplomb.

Hidden in the pockets of his robes were little bags of powder that, when brought into contact with fire, produced brightly colored flames, acrid smoke, and various shades of fog. His phials of acid, four in total, were stored safely in a padded case.

But most important of all were the flamethrowers, designed by Furgas to fit into his sleeves.

They had two main components: a miniature tinderbox attached to his cuff, and a leather purse of lycopodium spores fixed to the inside of his elbow. Pressing the pouch caused spores to shoot out of the purse and at the same time activated a mechanism that pulled the flint backward and produced a spark, thereby igniting the seeds as they exited his sleeve. It had worked on orcs, and it was bound to work on ordinary soldiers. Sometimes technology was as effective as magic.

On nearing the palace, he remembered that he couldn't just waltz through the gates. He knew the secret formula, having been left in charge of Furgas while Andôkai and Narmora were away, but the avatars would surely notice if an uninvited visitor strolled through the gates. *Is there another door?*

"Rehearsal over so soon?" said a voice behind him.

He whirled round and came face to face with the beautiful stranger. "Let's just say that my illustrious colleagues were more interested in the refreshments than my script," he said, delighted to see her again.

"Then perhaps you would do me the honor of joining me for dinner and telling me about your play." She smiled at him seductively and he found himself assenting. In his imagination, he was stripping her of her garments one by one. He was willing to bet that she smelled of cream and silk.

"I'm not very presentable," he said regretfully. "I've only just arrived and I haven't had time to freshen up or shave."

"So I see," she said, looking him up and down. "It won't take long to fix: I can lend you some suitable clothes." She stood alongside him and he offered her his arm. "I'm Lirkim," she told him, pulling him along.

"How far is your boarding house?" he enquired. Having given private performances in a number of the hostelries, he was keen to avoid a scene. The last thing he wanted was to encounter an angry husband or father, especially with Lirkim around.

She stopped outside the palace gates and shook her head. "I'm not staying in a boarding house, Master Rodario." She uttered a strange incantation and traced a symbol elegantly in the air. The gates swung open. "We're here."

He stood frozen to the spot. "You're with the avatars? I didn't realize they'd brought their courtiers as well."

"Is there a problem?" she enquired. "The avatars won't hurt you if your intentions are honorable, which I'm sure they are." Since their arms were still interlinked, she waited until he was ready before leading him through the gates.

Now he was seriously worried—not for himself, but for the others, who wouldn't be able to get in. He thanked the gods for his good fortune. *What luck!* He smiled. First he would enjoy a night of passion, or at least a good bath and a decent meal, and later he would search the palace for Balyndis and Dorsa. *I'll be a hero! Ha, I can't wait to see the look on Boïndil's face . . .*

"What now?" enquired Lirkim. "A moment ago you were terrified, and now you're grinning from ear to ear."

"No wonder," he said quickly. "I can't wait to see inside the palace. It's an incredible honor."

A look of puzzlement crossed her face as they made their way up the broad steps past the sentries. "But you were in charge of rebuilding the city. Surely Andôkai must have invited you inside?"

"You'd think so, wouldn't you? I'm afraid the maga made a big secret of the palace. She was worried about people leaking information that might facilitate an enemy attack, especially after the avatars sent someone to assassinate her in her own halls."

"Where is she at the moment?"

"You're referring to her successor, Narmora, I assume? She left for the north. Her instructions were to continue with the building work in her absence." He automatically started walking to Furgas's old chamber, but Lirkim pulled him back.

"Where are you going? You're supposed to be my guest."

He laughed awkwardly. "I wasn't thinking." Several guards strode toward them and greeted Lirkim. On seeing Rodario, they stared in surprise.

Nodding jovially, he smiled as if they were old friends. Their armor was studded with fragments of moonstone, but the metal had lost its brilliance. It seemed the warriors glowed only at the avatars' behest.

Rodario was filled with a confidence bordering on reck-lessness. He was no safer in the palace than in a cave of orcs, but he felt as if Palandiell were clasping him to her breast. Lirkim led the way to the servants' quarters, summoned two maids whom Rodario had never seen before, and instructed them to attend to his needs.

"I'll tell the kitchens that I'm dining with a guest." She peeled off a glove and held out her milky wrist. "I'll see you in an hour."

"I look forward to it, my lady," he said, kissing her soft skin. *Cream and silk*, he thought.

Needless to say, Furgas had never intended to enter the palace through the main gates, which he assumed would be guarded. Their arrival in the forecourt would doubt-less cause a stir. "Narmora mentioned a couple of side gates. She took me through one of them. It's visible only to magi, but I should be able to find it again."

Boïndil scowled. "Let's hope so," he muttered darkly.

"Patience, brother," said Boëndal. "We can't storm the gates, fight our way through to Balyndis and Dorsa, and beat a quick retreat. It takes more than a couple of axes to scare a magician."

Furgas ran a hand along the wall. "This is the spot." He recited an incantation. Nothing happened.

"Are you sure it's here?" Tungdil touched the wall carefully, but there was no sign of unevenness, much less an opening.

Ondori repeated the words, and the outlines of a door appeared in the wall.

Boïndil whirled round. "How did you do it?"

"Just get inside," she said disdainfully. "Groundlings know nothing of magic." She glanced at Furgas. "Humans are just as bad."

"And you're an expert, are you, beanpole?" said Boïndil, bristling. He had no intention of taking orders from an älf, especially if she treated him with such flagrant disrespect.

"Compared to you," she said. "Hurry up, you're in the way."

Boëndal pushed his brother through the door to stop him from arguing. One by one they stepped into a garden at the northern end of the expansive palace grounds. There was no one there to stop them.

"We can't afford to dally," said Ondori. "Sooner or later someone will notice your footprints and the hunt will be on."

Furgas went to the front of the group and led them to the servants' quarters, which he assumed were deserted.

Suddenly he stopped and pressed himself against the wall. The dwarves froze, aware that their armor might give them away.

They heard the soft voice of a woman. "I'll tell the kitchens that I'm dining with a guest," she said with a slight accent. "I'll see you in an hour."

"I look forward to it, my lady." There was no mistaking the voice.

"Rodario," whispered Boïndil in astonishment. "How in the name of Vraccas does he do it?"

"How do you think?" whispered Furgas, grinning. They heard a door close. Peering round the corner, Furgas saw a woman in white furs striding away from the room. "I say we leave him to it and stick to our plan."

"He's getting dinner as well!" hissed an indignant Boïndil.

"Be quiet," Ondori told him.

"Be quiet yourself," he growled belligerently. "If we'd killed your parents a couple of decades earlier, you wouldn't be here at all."

The älf said nothing, her gray eyes looking daggers at him. Boïndil refused to succumb to her murderous glare.

Furgas raised a hand. "She's stopped," he whispered. Ondori stepped forward and raised her bow. "Hang on . . . she's off again."

The älf handed the bow to Furgas. "Wait here. I'll find out what he's up to," she said, making for a door that led inside. She listened for a moment, then opened it quietly.

Rodario was sitting in a tub of warm water, washing away the grime of the journey. The mud and dust of

Gauragar dissolved into the perfumed foam, and a couple of pine needles floated to the surface, a reminder of the forest where they had slept the previous night. He picked up a razor and, holding a mirror in one hand, shaved the stubble from his incredibly handsome face.

"Never assume you're alone," said Ondori, staying his hand in case he slit his throat. "So you found your way into the palace?"

He breathed out in relief. "For the love of Palandiell," he gasped. "You're as bad as Narmora with your sneaking about." She released his hand and he continued to shave. "It's nice of you to join me—are you the only one?"

"They're waiting outside. I wanted to find out what you're planning."

"Tell the others not to worry," he said in a self-important tone. "In a few moments I shall be dining with a beautiful woman who happens to be part of the avatars' entourage. I'll ply her with wine, engage her in small talk, flirt with her a little—and she'll be putty in my hands." He put down the razor and stroked his cheeks. "She'll tell me where to find Balyndis, how to get to Dorsa, and what we can expect from our phony gods of fire." He checked his cheeks for stray whiskers and smiled at himself in the mirror. "I'll save the child and the dwarf, and Boïndil will be indebted to me for the rest of his life. An excellent plan, don't you think?"

She smiled behind her mask. "Not bad, considering you came up with it on the spot."

"It was my intention all along," he said indignantly. "Anyway, what about you?"

"Sounds like there's nothing left for us to do." She

glanced at the conjuring equipment stacked on one of the chairs. "You stick to your plan, we'll stick to ours. Who knows, we might find Balyndis and Dorsa first."

He picked up his razor and drew it through the foam. "You'll be grateful when I save you," he predicted. "Now get out of here before the maid comes back." She didn't reply, and when he looked up, she was gone. "I know exactly what she and Narmora could do with—a pretty anklet with a bell." He ran the razor over his cheeks, smoothed his pointed beard, and smiled; Lirkim wouldn't be able to resist him.

He's going to save *us*?" said Boïndil disbelievingly. "Only in one of his stupid plays! He's dreaming."

"It sounds like a sensible plan," said Tungdil, wondering how the impresario did it. He had a habit of making an entrance at the critical time. "Rodario might be able to help if we run into trouble later."

"*Might*," snorted Boïndil. "An anvil *might* fall over in the breeze." He didn't believe for a moment that their mission would fail.

Furgas preempted a quarrel by steering them into a passageway. "Let's find Dorsa. We'll try the nursery first."

A short while later they were standing outside the door. Once again it fell to the älf to steal into the room and assess the situation while the dwarves waited as quietly as their armor allowed.

She ushered them in. "All safe—unless the child is a threat."

Furgas hurried past her and peered into the cot where his daughter was sleeping peacefully. There was nothing to suggest she had been hurt. Tungdil, Boïndil, and Boëndal looked on in silence and shared the father's relief.

Ondori signaled to them that someone was approaching. The door opened and a woman came in. Before she had time to realize what was happening, the älf grabbed her from behind and set a knife to her throat. "Not a sound," she whispered savagely.

"It's all right," said Furgas. "It's the nursemaid." Ondori hesitated, then released her grip.

"Rosild!" Furgas threw his arms around her. "Thank goodness you and Dorsa are all right. What happened?"

Well, sir . . ." she stuttered, still recovering from the shock. "They marched in and took over the palace. I didn't know what to do, so I told them Dorsa was my daughter. They said I could stay here if I cooked for the palace guards."

Boïndil could scarcely believe his ears. "Just like that? A bit gullible, these avatars."

"I have to taste the food to prove it's not poisoned. If anyone gets gut ache, Dorsa and I will be killed. My nerves are in shreds."

Furgas laid his hands on her shoulders. "Poor Rosild, your ordeal is nearly over. We'll get you out of here as soon as we can."

"First we need to know what's happened to Balyndis." Tungdil stepped forward. "Do you know where she is? She was brought here seven orbits ago, someone said."

"Do you mean the dwarf-woman?" She furrowed her brow. "A band of soldiers turned up at the palace. They seemed agitated about something and they were carrying a prisoner—a child or a gnome, I assumed. It didn't occur to me they'd captured a groundling."

"A dwarf," said Boïndil.

"I meant a dwarf," she corrected herself. "They took her to the big chamber with the copper dome. I haven't seen her since."

"Get ready to leave," Tungdil instructed her. "Don't let the guards see you packing and try to avoid suspicion. Once we've rescued Balyndis, we'll need to get out of the palace as fast as we can. Be sure to bring blankets for Dorsa—it's cold outside." Rosild paled slightly, but nodded. Tungdil looked into the grave faces of his companions. "I suppose this is it. For Vraccas and Balyndis!"

Rodario had eyes only for his charming hostess. Lirkim was wearing an exquisitely embroidered dress made of shimmering white material that reached to her calves. Her face looked more beautiful than ever in the light of the candelabra.

"Even the candles look dull and lifeless compared to you," he said appreciatively, raising his glass. He could feel his sleeve slipping down his arm and threatening to reveal the tinderbox strapped to his wrist. Gesturing expansively, he encouraged the fabric to fall toward his hand, taking care not to spill his wine. "To a goddess whose beauty will never fade."

"Very chivalrous, my eloquent friend, but wait two decades and my skin will resemble a fishing net." They clinked glasses and gazed at each other, her green eyes telling him that she accepted the compliment nonetheless.

Rodario was enjoying the opportunity to make use of his talents. Farmer's daughters, innkeeper's wives, and rich gentlewomen were easy to impress, but with Lirkim, flirtation was an art. It gave him high hopes for her love-making, which he intended to sample that night. But first he had to obtain a few key pieces of information so that he could leave her sated, asleep, and smiling, while he completed his mission and got one over on the dwarves.

He adjusted his sleeves and rounded the table to refill her glass. A drop of red wine splashed from the decanter and landed on her shoulder.

"How careless of me." On the spur of the moment he decided to kiss away the droplet with his lips. She did nothing to stop him and turned her head so that he could press his mouth to her soft, snowy skin. "Oh, there's another one," he said, lifting her long brown hair and kissing her neck. To his satisfaction he saw a shiver of pleasure run down her back. *I'm irresistible*, he thought smugly, returning to his seat. *The sparks of passion are flying; how long until the fire is lit?*

His sleeves rode up again. He swore silently and pulled them down to cover the tinderboxes. He was wearing the contraptions only because he had nowhere to put them except his pockets, and Lirkim would notice the bulge. Later, he would have to distract her sufficiently so that he could remove his props before he stripped off his clothes.

"Only two droplets?" she asked teasingly, turning back to her plate.

His eyes twinkled. "We'll see what happens next time. Incidentally, where did you get the wine?"

"It's from the maga's cellars. It pays to be on the right side: The winner takes all."

"Do you think the avatars mind that you're dining with Narmora's former aide?"

"Former?" she queried, eying him intently.

Rodario felt suddenly queasy. *Has she guessed?* "Well . . ." He cleared his throat. "I'm a citizen of Porista, and Porista belongs to the avatars, so I'm assuming I work for them."

"I applaud your wisdom. It will save you a lot of trouble." She laughed a tinkling laugh. "No, the avatars don't mind. Their enemies are right to be terrified, but innocent people have nothing to fear."

"I imagine the maga's servants were relieved," he remarked, trying to steer the conversation to Dorsa. "Didn't Narmora have a personal maid?"

Lirkim nodded and popped a morsel of meat into her mouth. He waited while she chewed her mouthful and swallowed it down. "Yes, Rosild and her baby daughter are still in the palace. She's an excellent cook. Nothing much has changed, as you can see."

"The avatars aren't nearly as frightening as I'd heard," he said, trying not to look relieved by the news that Rosild and Dorsa were well.

"Really?" Lirkim rested her cutlery on her plate. "What have you heard?"

"Everyone says they're mythical creatures, fiery beings that scorch the earth beneath their feet . . ." He stopped short. "It doesn't make sense, if you think about it."

"Of course it doesn't, otherwise Porista wouldn't be standing now. What else have you heard? It sounds like good material for a play."

"For several plays." Passing off the story as hearsay, he described what he had seen in Dsôn Balsur, including everything from the cloud of fire to the soldiers' shining armor. He didn't mention the deaths of the avatars. Lirkim listened attentively and seemed amused. "According to some, they even captured a dwarf-woman," he added. "Personally, I don't believe it. What would the avatars want with a dwarf?" He speared a piece of meat on his fork.

"Much of what you say is true," she said, smiling. She took a sip of wine, prompting him to toast her again and refill her glass. He had been plying her with alcohol for over an hour, and he was gratified to see that her cheeks were a healthy red. "The rest is smoke and mirrors." She clapped a hand to her mouth and looked worried. "Forget what I said."

"Don't worry," he said, laughing it off. "I'm not going to report you to the avatars. I'm sure they're capable of conjuring as many illusory dwarf-women as they please."

"Oh, she's real enough. They took her prisoner because she had a secret." She laughed girlishly. "But groundlings are tough little characters."

"A secret, you say? Don't tell me the celestial avatars are interested in turning iron into gold?" He chuckled contentedly to set her at ease.

"The avatars don't need gold." She clinked glasses again with Rodario. "No, the dwarf-woman knows how to make a special . . . It's old news, anyway. Things have moved on." Her eyelids were getting heavier and she reached for his thigh. "Well, my fabulous Rodario, perhaps we should . . . ?"

"Absolutely," he said eagerly. "Who cares about a dwarf-woman's secrets?"

"The avatars don't." She got up and wrapped her arms around his neck. "Soon they'll be so powerful that even the gods will fear them. They'll take whichever lands they like and rule over vast swathes of territory. They'll be mightier than the mightiest kings, all-powerful and invincible, and Girdlegard . . ." She bit her lip, a gesture that Rodario would normally have found incredibly alluring. "But enough of that."

Rodario was never slow to show off his manhood, but Lirkim's description of the avatars had roughly the same effect as ice in his breeches or an angry husband in the room. His ardor was gone.

Just then the door flew open with a bang.

There's the husband, so where's the ice? He knew from the sound, a sound he had heard on countless occasions, that the person was furious—as furious as a cuckold had every right to be.

A fair-haired man of thirty cycles burst into the room. He was wearing white robes and carrying a short staff like a shepherd's crook. Behind him were three soldiers whose faces Rodario recognized from his arrival at the palace earlier that evening. The cozy little dinner had reached a premature end. "Are you married?" he hissed at Lirkim, who shook her head and seemed taken aback by the intrusion. "I guess the avatars don't approve of my presence after all . . ."

"That's him," cried one of the soldiers, pointing his sword at Rodario. "I told you, Fascou, it's definitely him."

"Move away, Lirkim." The man in the robes looked at her sternly.

She put herself between the soldiers and Rodario.

"No, Fascou, you're not going to hurt him. Go back to tinkering with the force fields and leave us alone. You've got the groundling to entertain you; let me have my fun."

"Come on, Lirkim," he said soothingly. "You've had a bit to drink, but the man you're protecting is our enemy. His name is Rodario and—"

"The fabulous Rodario," she said thickly. "I know. He's an impresario and he owns the Curiosum. He's—"

The man stepped forward and held out his hand, beckoning to her. "His name is Rodario the Fablemaker, and he's apprenticed to Narmora."

The soldier nodded. "That's right, I saw him on the battlefield. Throwing fire, he was, and melting my comrades like butter in the sun."

Rodario couldn't believe it. His biggest dream was to be recognized by strangers, for his reputation to extend beyond the confines of a particular city or realm. At last he had attained true celebrity—and it was likely to end in his death.

A good actor never disappoints his audience . . . Standing tall, he grabbed the astonished Lirkim with his left hand and flung his right arm toward the white-robed man. "Rodario the Fablemaker is my name!" he proclaimed, letting out an evil-sounding cackle. "Stay where you are! Move and this innocent woman will . . ."

Suddenly, faster than a gust of wind can snuff out a candle, a blinding light appeared before him. Dazzled, he saw nothing but brilliant whiteness. He let go of Lirkim, who had turned into a fiery sun.

* * *

Furgas led the group confidently through the dark corridors of the palace. At last they reached the great hall. The avatars obviously weren't worried about the dwarf escaping because the doors had been left wide open.

"What if it's a trap?" asked Boëndal, but Ondori was already inside, reconnoitering the room. She returned in an instant.

"We've found the groundling," she reported, stepping aside to let them in.

It was immediately clear why no one was guarding the hall.

Balyndis was lying on the floor in the middle of the room. Her legs and arms had been broken, and bits of bone were poking through her skin. She was smeared with blood and pus, and her bare chest was covered in cuts and burn marks. Clumps of brown hair lay scattered on the flagstones. Her hands and feet were shackled and chained to the floor.

Tungdil's eyes welled with tears. *What have they done to you?* He kneeled down and placed his hand on her brow. *She's feverish.* Raising his ax, he smashed through her chains. She didn't acknowledge his presence or register the noise: Her eyes were closed.

"I'll teach them to torture a dwarf," growled Ireheart, enraged by the sight of the suffering Balyndis. His eyes glinted wildly. "By the ax of Beroïn, I'll rip them to pieces with my hands."

Boëndal took off his coat and gave it to Tungdil to wrap around their motionless friend. "It's bad enough what they've done to her body. What about her mind?"

"The fact that she's alive is proof of her resilience—she's

still holding out, despite what they've done to her." Tungdil picked her up and balanced her on his shoulder. "They would have killed her if she'd cracked."

He made up his mind to show no mercy to the false avatars, who claimed to be fighting in the service of good. Nothing could justify their treatment of those who stood in their way.

He turned around and froze. On the other side of the hall, in the eastern corner, was his foster father, Lot-Ionan.

"But it's impossible," he whispered. He took a few uncertain paces toward the magus before realizing his mistake: He was looking at a statue. His beloved Lot-Ionan, who had raised and schooled him, had been turned to stone. Nôd'onn had killed him.

The spell can't be reversed. He remembered what Andôkai had told him, and a sob rose in his throat as he thought of Lot-Ionan and Frala and the happy times in the magus's realm. He stroked the statue tenderly and walked away. Now wasn't the time for mourning, only revenge.

They hurried back to Rosild who was waiting anxiously with Dorsa in her arms. She found an extra blanket and they wrapped it around Balyndis to protect her from the cold. Furgas volunteered to carry the unconscious dwarf. Their presence in the palace hadn't been detected.

The procession was led by Ondori, followed by the dwarves, Furgas and Balyndis, and Rosild and Dorsa. Slowly but surely they edged toward freedom and at last they left the palace and entered the grounds, steering a course for the hidden gate.

* * *

The double-dealing hussy! She's an avatar! Rodario was obliged to behave in a deplorably unchivalrous fashion. He aimed a kick at what he believed to be Lirkim's posterior, although he couldn't be certain because of the glare. She stumbled forward. There was a crash, and the light went out.

He aimed his flamethrowers at the soldiers and shouted a few improvised incantations. When he heard their cries, he followed up with a couple of phials of acid and threw himself under the table.

He firmly expected to be transformed into a heap of ashes, but nothing happened. There was an overwhelming smell of burning, but it was coming from several paces away.

Gradually, his vision cleared. The three soldiers were lying dead or dying on the floor, and the white-robed avatar was no more, one of the phials having hit him on the head and the acid eaten away most of his skull and face.

"Ha!" Thrilled by his unexpected victory, Rodario emerged from his hiding place. "That'll teach you to pick a fight with Rodario the Fablemaker!" Lirkim was resting face down on the table, her plate and two platters hidden beneath her chest. She had hit her head and knocked herself out. "You've only got yourself to blame," he rebuked her. "I don't take kindly to being played."

I knocked out two avatars! He put his hands on his hips and laughed like one of his characters on the stage. *I'm taking you with me. My friends will be interested to hear what you've been up to with the force fields.*

He grabbed the woman by the shoulders, sat her up,

and proceeded to divest her of her powers by removing her jewelry and putting it in his pockets. Then he gave her another good draft of wine and cracked the empty decanter against her head to make doubly sure that she wouldn't wake up, which seemed unlikely, considering she was already inebriated and stunned.

Hoisting her over his shoulder, he was suddenly aware of a commotion in the corridor. With a sinking heart he realized that the palace guards were on their way. *I suppose the flamethrowers weren't terribly subtle.* His valor melted like an actor's make-up in the sun.

His feet took him to the window. He could see figures in the garden—small figures. He opened the catch. "Hello down there! Guess what? I've purloined an avatar!" He pointed to her posterior. "I'm afraid her pseudo-divine friends have taken umbrage. Perhaps you could be so kind as to—"

"Stop talking and jump!" yelled Boïndil, signaling frantically. "We know a way out."

"I'm usually very courteous," he said apologetically to the unconscious Lirkim before tossing her out of the window. She dropped through the air and came to rest in the snow. A moment later he landed beside her. After assuring himself that her heart was still beating, he threw her over his shoulder and hurried after his companions, who were busy conjuring an opening in an apparently solid wall.

Leaving the palace behind them, they raced through the deserted streets. Snow was falling heavily, covering their tracks, and it was impossible to see further than five paces.

"What luck," remarked the impresario, panting under

the weight of his burden. He saw Balyndis on Furgas's shoulder and Dorsa in Rosild's arms. "The gods are on our side tonight. Balyndis, the baby, and an avatar—what a haul!"

"Avatar?" snorted Boïndil. "What are you blathering about now?" Weighed down by his heavy armor, he was almost as breathless as the impresario, who wasn't accustomed to carrying anything but his quill. To his relief, the three dwarves slowed their pace. Furgas, by contrast, showed no sign of tiring.

"Her name is Lirkim. She told me she was a courtier—at least, that's what I assumed she was, and she didn't correct me. A friend of hers burst in on us while we were having a cozy dinner, and I saw through her disguise."

"Ha, what kind of an avatar would allow herself to be captured by an actor," jeered Boïndil, wheezing.

Rodario's captive murmured something, and the others heard the words "avatar" and "eoîl". Ondori listened carefully, then cuffed the woman roundly. "It was an incantation," she explained. "I didn't want her causing trouble."

"Save your breath for running," panted Tungdil, who already had a stitch.

At last they reached the marketplace and found Ertil, who was waiting for them behind a stack of empty kegs. He was just unbolting the hatch when Ondori whirled round and stared into the swirling snow.

Something was awry. The flakes were melting and turning to slush. A moment later, raindrops pattered against their armor.

"Quick, get in," she said, nocking an arrow to her bow.

Furgas carried Balyndis to safety and Rosild hurried after him, followed by Rodario and his captive.

A gleaming gold sphere whizzed toward them through the rain, expanding and becoming brighter as it sped toward Boïndil, who was last in line for the stairs.

Even as he closed his visor, the sphere slammed into his chest, turning him into a blazing fireball. Tungdil and Boëndal felt the heat through their armor, and Ondori screamed in pain.

Crackling, the unnatural fire died down. Boïndil was still standing, miniature flames licking his spaulders and greaves. They sputtered and expired— Djerûn's armor had proven its worth.

"They're here," shouted a man's voice through the darkness. A moment later, he appeared before them in a column of light. "Hurry!"

"Ha, so your magical piffle paffle didn't work! I can't wait to see the color of an avatar's—sorry, conjurer's—blood!" Boïndil threw himself on the avatar. His brother charged after him, brandishing his crow's beak.

"For Balyndis!" shouted Tungdil, joining the fight.

The self-declared demigod hurled lightning at his attackers to keep them at bay, but no curse or firebrand could match the strength and determination of three angry dwarves.

Tungdil felt like a lump of ore in a blast furnace. The armor protected him from the flames, but the metal was getting unbearably hot. He was sure he would roast inside his breastplate if the avatar weren't dealt with soon.

The blades of the dwarves' weapons were red with heat,

and the hafts were already in danger of igniting. Even as the wood began to crumble, Tungdil and the others came in striking distance of their foe.

It was hard to see the avatar in the dazzling light, but they made out his outline. Boïndil landed two powerful blows, and the glow faded to reveal a man of some sixty cycles, with blood spilling from his thighs. He was staggering backward, sword in front of him to fend off the dwarves.

He didn't stand a chance.

His flowing white robes offered no protection against the long, curved spur of the crow's beak and the red-hot blades of dwarven axes. Weapons slashed at him from three sides until at last he lay bleeding and groaning in the gutter. Boëndal made certain that he was dead by smashing his skull with the butt of his weapon, then they hurried to the sewers and locked the hatch.

"We got him," Boïndil told the others, who were looking at the trio expectantly. "But it's darned hot in here."

"Where's Ondori?" asked Rodario, hoisting Lirkim over his shoulder and hurrying after Tungdil.

"Ondori!" The dwarves hadn't noticed her absence. "I heard her screaming, but . . ."

"She must have died in the fire," said Boïndil, smiling darkly. "Serves her right." He stomped to the head of the procession. "I was wondering how we were going to get rid of the one-eyed murderess. Still, I'd rather have killed her myself."

No one expressed regret at the passing of Ondori—but no one could say for certain that she was dead.

*   *   *

Incredibly, they managed to rejoin the army of firstlings, thirdlings, freelings, and älfar unscathed. Some of the units had advanced to within ten miles of Porista.

Tungdil went straight to Narmora, who healed the worst of Balyndis's wounds and did her best to alleviate the pain, leaving the rest to Balyndis's almost indestructible dwarven constitution.

The maga had barely finished treating Balyndis when she heard a baby crying. At once, Narmora the Unnerving vanished, and the anxious parent came to the fore. A moment later, the little family was reunited, with Narmora hugging Dorsa, then Furgas, then Dorsa again. The dwarves couldn't help but feel moved, and even the ferocious Boïndil wiped a tear from his whiskery cheek.

Tungdil spent the rest of the orbit at Balyndis's bedside. He washed her carefully, sponging away the soot and dried blood, then salved her burns and squeezed some water between her lips. Her eyes remained closed.

Toward evening, Boëndal burst in. "We're ready to interrogate the prisoner," he announced. "Narmora wants you there—we need to find out as much as we can."

Tungdil squeezed the smith's hand and stood up reluctantly.

"Listen, Tungdil," said Boëndal as they left the tent. "Glaïmbar will be eternally grateful to you for saving Balyndis, but she'll never . . ."

"I know," his friend said sadly. "She won't leave him—but I'll always love her, and she'll always love me. It's no use fooling myself—I loved her even when I was melded to Myr." He sighed. "Boïndil was right—some dwarves are better off on their own. I couldn't meld myself to another maiden. I'd only make her unhappy—and Balyndis too. Still," he added pensively, "I'm glad Vraccas chose the three of us to save her. I hope she'll accept my friendship after how I treated her."

Boëndal nodded and led the way to a disused collier's hut where Lirkim was imprisoned. Waiting inside were Narmora, Boïndil, and Rodario, the latter with a bucket in hand.

"Let's get started." The impresario emptied the bucket over the chained and fettered Lirkim, who was lying face down on the floor. Her eyes flicked open as a rush of cold water hit her back. "We meet again," said Rodario, crouching beside her. "You weren't awake when I left the palace, so I brought you back here. Don't try any of your magic or you'll be killed on the spot. Understand?"

Lirkim tried to look up, but all she could see were boots, ankles, and a collection of weapons, all pointing at her head. "My right arm hurts," she said in a muffled voice.

"Hmm, I think it may have broken when . . . I mean, I think you broke it when you fell." Rodario was doing his best to sound cold and unfeeling, although he didn't feel any real enmity toward the prisoner. He refused to believe that anyone so beautiful could be responsible for thousands of deaths. "Did you hear what I said?

"No magic, I promise." She was trembling and her voice sounded shaky. The air was bitterly cold and her clothes were soaked through.

"Tell us what you're doing to the force fields," commanded Rodario. He picked up a blanket, but a grim-faced Tungdil snatched it away.

"We found the force fields when we were riding to Dsôn Balsur. The eoîl traced the magic back to Porista and found a way of channeling its power." She coughed. "I don't know what he's planning, but he told us that we'll soon be more powerful than any being or god."

"Who are you?" demanded Narmora. "We know you're human, so don't deny it. Lie to us, and you'll pay with your life."

Lirkim nodded wearily. "There are seven of us: three women and four men. Seven magi—and the eoîl. We came together four hundred cycles ago—by pooling our power, we gained the strength to crush any ruler or army who stood in our way. We used the legend of the avatars to make people fear us. No one ever came close to defeating us—until now."

Boïndil kicked her foot. "What's an eoîl?"

"An eoîl is an . . . I can't explain it, but he's a real god—the rest of us are human."

"A god?" Boïndil snorted. "Spare us your fairytales: He's a trickster, a flimflamming charlatan like you."

"No," insisted Lirkim. "He's a god. There aren't many gods where I come from, but they're powerful, very powerful. Everyone is afraid of them—if you attack Porista, as I assume you're planning to do, you'll see for yourselves how powerful he is. The eoîl will destroy you. He turns fields into deserts and oceans into saltpans. I'm just a maga, but he's . . ."

"You get your power from the evil you destroy," threw in the maga.

"The eoîl taught us to draw on the evil in the souls of

our enemies for curses and charms. When we heard about Girdlegard's force fields and the dark magic, we—"

"You didn't come here for Nôd'onn? You knew about the force fields?"

"The eoîl knew about them. He told us that the spirit that inhabited Nôd'onn was still alive."

"I've had enough of this nonsense!" growled Boïndil, drawing his axes. Boëndal pulled him back.

"So you came to Porista because of the magic, but you don't know more than that," said Tungdil, summarizing the information. She nodded. "What were you doing with the dwarf-woman?" he demanded.

"The other magi found her," she explained. "She was tied to a tree, which aroused their suspicions. They took on the appearance of dwarves and offered to help. She mentioned something about special armor." Lirkim was shivering so badly that every word was punctuated by her chattering teeth. "We realized what she was talking about when our army was defeated in Dsôn Balsur and Timshar and S'liniinsh were killed by an aneoîl. She wouldn't tell us how the alloy was made."

"Did you torture her?"

"It was the eoîl who tortured her. He despises undergroundlings."

Tungdil was intrigued by the name that Lirkim had given to Djerûn. It implied a connection with the eoîl. He decided to probe the matter further.

"They both kill creatures of darkness," she replied in answer to his question. "Their motivation is different, of course. An aneoîl kills beasts that are weak or imperfect; an eoîl seeks to root out evil." Craning her neck, she peered at Narmora. "It was the eoîl's idea to send an aneoîl to your mistress. He knew it would work."

Narmora laughed mockingly. "This eoîl of yours seems to have made a big impression on you, but he underestimated my power."

"And mine," chipped in Rodario.

Tungdil was heartened by their captive's readiness to talk. It seemed unlikely that she was lying: The gloom of the collier's hut and the gravity of the situation were powerful incentives for her to tell the truth. *We've killed four and taken one captive, which leaves two humans and an eoîl.* He started to feel more confident again. *I'd like to talk to her about the Outer Lands. She's bound to know something about the undergroundlings . . .*

Narmora thought for a moment. "How close is the eoîl to achieving his goal?"

"He said it wouldn't take long. Yesterday he was talking of nine or ten orbits," came the sobering reply.

"He knows we've got Lirkim," Tungdil pointed out. "He'll probably redouble his efforts. We need to come up with a plan to take Porista, or Vraccas knows what will happen when the eoîl destroys the wellspring."

Boëndal looked him in the eye. "What do you think *would* happen?"

"Remember the rippling earth near Porista?"

Narmora nodded anxiously. "I can feel the change. The magic is draining from the force fields. I'd say the source is drying up."

"Or someone is using the magic for another purpose," said Tungdil. "We need to stop the eoîl before he destroys the force fields. I don't know what he's up to, but

Girdlegard might not recover." He looked at the others. "Let's meet again at sunrise. Our mission is to retake Porista." He turned to leave.

"What will we do with her?" asked Boïndil, pointing to their prisoner whose lips were blue with cold. "I don't want her weaving any jiggery-pokery behind our backs."

"I took away her amulets—she's can't do anything without them," broke in Rodario. "*I* found her; *I'll* decide her fate,"

Narmora shook her head. "No, Rodario, it's too risky. She's an avatar, and they don't deserve our mercy. They're too dangerous."

"Please, I'm begging you," whimpered Lirkim, struggling to move her frozen lips. "Don't kill me. I couldn't hurt you if I tried." She looked up at their faces. "Rodario is right. I'm powerless without my amulets."

Boïndil snorted disbelievingly. "Why should we believe you?"

"Listen, Narmora," said Rodario seriously. "You can't kill her; it's not right."

"I think we should keep her alive until we've captured Porista," agreed Tungdil, eying the prisoner with disdain. "Who knows, she might come in useful as a bargaining tool—assuming the eoîl cares about his allies." It was true that Lirkim was a useful asset, but Tungdil was mainly motivated by his reluctance to kill an unarmed human.

Narmora stretched a hand and a bolt of lightning shot out of her fingertips, hitting Lirkim in the back.

The prisoner shrieked, arching her back and tearing at her shackles, which stayed firmly in place. The bolt had burned through her gown and blistered her skin, leaving a hand-sized mark on her back. Gasping, the former avatar slumped against the floor as the pain died down.

"She wasn't lying," pronounced the maga, bending down to pluck a strand of hair from their prisoner's head. "See this hair, Lirkim? With it I can weave a curse that will find you, no matter how far you run. I recommend you don't provoke me if you value your life." She left the hut, followed by the dwarves. Four of Lorimbas's warriors stayed behind as guards.

Rodario went outside and returned with a handful of snow, which he placed on the blistered skin. Lirkim flinched.

"Thank you," she whispered with a sob. "Thank you for saving my life."

He unlocked her shackles, helped her up and led her to a mattress. She took off her wet clothes and slipped under the sheets.

"Why did you ask me to dinner with you in Porista?" he asked softly.

"The usual reason," she replied. "You're a handsome man, and I wanted some entertainment. I was going to let the evening run its course."

What an evening it would have been . . . Rodario realized that he was starting to feel sorry for her, so he reminded himself of the thousands who had died in Dsôn Balsur. Lirkim seemed delicate and vulnerable, but she was capable of terrible things. *Four hundred cycles, and still so youthful and charming* . . . "You mentioned the spirit that corrupted Nudin and made him turn traitor." He waited for her to nod. "Is it still alive?"

She shrugged and he guessed what she would say before

her blue lips began to move. "I don't know, but the eoîl knows everything. He knows the spirit and he senses where it is."

Rodario, hearing a noise at the door, turned in time to see a shadow pass the window. *An eavesdropper!*

He jumped up, ran to the door, and peered into the falling snow, but all he could see was a dark shadow disappearing into nothingness. He looked in vain for footprints, but the snow was unmarked.

Narmora? Surely not . . . He went back into the hut and closed the door. *Something very strange is going on . . .*

VIII

Western Entrance to the Fourthling Kingdom,
Kingdom of Urgon,
Girdlegard,
Winter, 6235th/6236th Solar Cycle

Captain Vallasin stomped through the ever-deepening snow. Clad in leather armor, with a woolen cloak wrapped tightly around his shoulders, he headed for the nearest sentry. "Well?" he called from a distance, to save himself the walk. "Any news?"

"No, captain," shouted the soldier. "The gates won't budge."

Vallasin's spirits sank even lower. He stopped in his tracks, raised a hand, and returned to his tent, where a mug of hot tea was waiting for him by the fire.

The same ritual had unfolded every few hours for more than forty orbits, and there was still no progress. Every time he went out, the sentry would tell him that the gates were still closed.

He glanced around the tent, hung his cloak on a hook, and plonked himself onto a folding chair. His aide-de-camp handed him a mug of tea. Even with the fire, it was cold inside the thin tent walls, and a fierce wind gusted continually through even the slightest gap in the canvas.

"Have they—" The aide-de-camp stopped mid-question, guessing from the captain's expression that the news wasn't good.

"It can't go on like this!" exploded Vallasin. "Ten thousand men camped outside a deserted dwarven kingdom, and we can't get past the doors!"

He took a sip of tea and stared glumly at the stack of letters from Pendleburg. Scarcely an orbit went by without Belletain asking for news of the campaign. So far the captain's response had always been the same: no progress.

Vallasin was aware that his career was at stake. He had worked hard to attain his rank, but the unhinged king of Urgon could easily decide to entrust the mission to someone else. "There has to be a way."

"Our technicians can't get to the hinges," his aide-de-camp reminded him politely. "Levers, chisels . . . Nothing will work."

Vallasin held up a royal letter. "His Majesty won't take no for an answer." He got up and paced angrily from the tent pole to the door. "What am I supposed to tell the poor beggars freezing off their backsides in the snow? Forty-seven dead! Forty-seven! And why? Because of a broken promise and a pair of locked gates."

According to a treaty between Belletain and Lorimbas, the thirdlings were supposed to clear the way for Vallasin's soldiers to search the dwarven stronghold and carry off the gold. Instead their path was blocked by a pair of solid granite gates that withstood the force of battering rams and blunted the strongest pick.

I'm sick of bloody waiting. Vallasin had marched his men to the Brown Range on Belletain's orders and readied the troops for attack. A thirdling relief army had materialized soon afterward, and the two armies had waited impatiently outside the locked gates until the dwarves had packed up and left without a word. Vallasin saw no point in waiting, but orders were orders, and Belletain wanted them to stay.

He heard the clip-clop of hooves outside the tent.

"Another letter from Belletain," he growled. "How many more times does he want to hear that we're stuck in the cold?"

A rider entered the tent. He was covered from head to toe in powdery snow, and his breath had frozen against his scarf, forming a sheath of ice around his face. He took a sealed leather cylinder from his saddlebag and handed it to the captain. "For you, sir."

Vallasin signaled for his aide-de-camp to give the frozen rider a hot mug of tea while he broke the seal and took out the parchment.

He was about to add it to the pile without reading it and return the cylinder to the rider with a pre-prepared report when he noticed that the letter was longer than usual.

Judging by the first few lines, he wasn't being demoted, as he had feared.

"What's this?" he murmured. "New orders from our esteemed king. Belletain wants us to leave." Relieved and heartened, he summoned his officers to the tent.

"Gentlemen," he said, when everyone was present, "King Belletain has advised me that the situation has changed. As you know, Lorimbas Steelheart broke his promise, so our alliance with the thirdlings is over." He rolled up the parchment. "It's time to break camp and leave this inhospitable range. I want everyone out of here by dawn tomorrow."

"Where are we going, sir?" asked one of the officers.

"South," he replied, pointing to a map. He traced a route through Idoslane. "King Belletain wants us to take the enemy by surprise. They won't be expecting us."

"Poor them," observed one of the men, raising a laugh from the others.

"All the better for us," said Vallasin, pleased to see their enthusiasm. Personally, he was of the opinion that it wouldn't be easy, especially once they left the safety of Urgon, but at least they could take a shortcut through Idoslane. Prince Mallen was unlikely to object, and it was by far the quickest route. "The march will be tiring—we need to move fast."

After dismissing the officers, he sat down and composed a brief letter to the king. This time he was sure that he and his little army would chalk up a victory in his name. The odds were in his favor—provided he acted before it was too late.

10 Miles from Porista,
Former Realm of Lios Nudin,
Girdlegard,
Winter, 6235th/6236th Solar Cycle

Balyndis fought her way out of the darkness that had settled over her mind. Looking up, she expected to see the vast copper dome of the conference chamber, a sight that no longer filled her with awe. After everything she had endured, she felt like taking a sledgehammer to the gleaming cooper roof.

Slowly, it dawned on her that the ceiling was made of white canvas. The sun was high in the sky, so it was almost midday.

Bewildered, she looked around and saw a shock of brown hair on the bedspread. Its owner was snoring lightly, and she knew at once who it was. *Tungdil . . .*

Reaching out, she laid a hand gently on his head so as not to wake him. She realized that he had been keeping vigil by her bedside. *Vraccas heard my prayers.*

She lifted up the sheets and blankets and peered at her chest. A shimmering layer of balm covered a rash of angry burn marks. *Narmora must have fixed my broken bones.* She ran a hand reverently over her limbs, remembering how the bones had protruded through the skin.

Tungdil sat up with a start. A smile spread over his face when he realized that Balyndis was awake. She thought he looked somehow older and more serious, and she guessed that whatever had happened since their last meeting had taken its toll

"How are you?" he asked gently, squeezing her hand.

"The maga is a miracle worker," she whispered. "The pain is almost gone." She pulled him toward her and hugged him tight. Silently, they clung to each other until he freed himself gently.

"I'm forever in your debt," she said solemnly.

"I did what any friend would do," he replied. "Balyndis, I'm really sorry about how I treated you before." He had thought long and hard about what he wanted to say. "I could blame it on wounded pride or jealousy, but there's no excuse for acting like a spoiled gnome." He took her hand again. "Can we be friends?"

"I've always seen you as a friend, Tungdil Goldhand," she said, moved by the honesty of his apology. "Nothing will ever change that."

"No, I suppose it won't," agreed Tungdil with a wry smile. He gazed into her eyes and they looked at each other lovingly. "To tell you the truth, I didn't rescue you single-handedly—you've got Boëndal, Boïndil, and Furgas to thank as well." He told her of their daring incursion into the palace and their successful escape.

Balyndis stroked her shorn head. "This älf . . . The one who came with you . . ." she began, voice shaking with rage. "I'm willing to bet she's the villain who killed my friends and tied me to the tree for the avatars to find me." She quickly recounted all that had happened. "Not long after the älfar had gone, a dwarf untied me from the tree. I was so relieved to see a dwarven face that I dropped my guard and said too much. The dwarf turned into an avatar. After that, they took me to Porista and tried to make me talk." She stopped, eyes welling with tears. "But Vraccas gave me the strength to keep the secret." She let out a muffled sob. "I couldn't have lasted much longer, Tungdil."

He held her in his arms and stroked her shorn head until the sobs subsided. "It's over now, Balyndis. You're safe." He was willing to bet that Ondori was still alive. She must have foreseen that alliances would count for nothing as soon as Balyndis made her report.

"What's so special about Djerůn's armor?" She listened intently to Tungdil's explanation. "In that case, I need to get back to the Gray Range," she said without a thought for her weakened state.

"The Gray Range?" echoed Tungdil. "What for?"

She rapped her fingers against his breastplate. "The armor can only be forged in the Dragon Fire furnace. I made the alloy with tionium and palandium. There isn't another furnace hot enough to meld the two."

Tungdil considered the situation: The Gray Range was hundreds of miles away, conditions were atrocious, and Balyndis was weak from her ordeal. "It can't be done," was his bleak conclusion. "Nine orbits from now the eoîl or chief avatar or whatever his name is will destroy the force fields. We need to storm the city before it's too late."

She looked at him sadly, knowing that the task ahead was full of dangers for her friend. "I suppose it's up to you and the twins to stop them." She noticed an imperfection in his armor and frowned. "Tungdil Goldhand, is this your workmanship?" she demanded.

"I was in a hurry," he protested, hoping to be excused.

She got up, threw on some clothes—human garments hastily tailored to dwarven proportions—and donned a cap. She held out a hand and beckoned to him. "Come on, then!"

"Where to? You're supposed to be in bed!"

"I've never seen such shoddy metalwork," she told him, smilingly. "Fetch the twins. I'll soon have you shining brighter than an avatar. You can't fight the eoîl in second-rate armor."

Laughing, he took her hand and led her to the makeshift forge, stopping off to collect the twins, who were delighted to see Balyndis back on her feet.

The heat of the forge, the high-pitched ring of the hammer, the weight of the tongs, and the clang of the chisel brought Balyndis's talent to the fore. Tungdil shared her pleasure at being back at the anvil, their hammers rising and falling in unison as they beat the imperfections out of the metal blow by blow.

Boïndil sang in time with the beat of their hammers, and his brother joined in, whereupon Tungdil and Balyndis raised the tempo. The solemn hymn became faster and faster until the twins dissolved into laughter.

For a brief moment, surrounded by the smell of hot metal and the warmth of the forge, the four friends enjoyed each other's company without worrying about the avatars and the eoîl.

Soon they realized that the dwarves outside had taken up their song.

The freelings and the firstlings were singing a verse in turn, belting out the words and trying to outdo each other in volume and tempo.

The competition ended in enthusiastic applause, and a single voice, deep and melancholy, cut through the noise of the camp.

> *Above the dark mountain*
> *A star aches with longing in a sky full of*
> *Stars that he could call to*
> *But he can't*
> *Stars that he could turn to*
> *But he can't*
> *Stars that he could join with*
> *But he can't*
> *The dark mountain, the jealous mountain*
> *Won't let him cross the sky.*

The light-hearted atmosphere was gone.

Tungdil realized that the singer was one of Lorimbas's dwarves. He was reminded of something that Sanda had said about the thirdlings. *Some of them aren't born with hatred in their hearts.* He considered the words of the song. *I wonder if the dark mountain stands for Lorimbas and the other thirdling kings who perpetuated the feud?* He prayed to Vraccas that he might live to see the orbit when dwarves from all five ranges would come together in friendship and peace.

"What a sad song," commented Boïndil. "I feel like drinking myself to death." He fastened his greaves to his shins and nodded approvingly. "They don't pinch anymore."

"Two more orbits, and you'll be ready," Balyndis assured him. "The avatars don't deserve to live a moment longer than necessary, but the armor is worth the wait."

"It certainly is," agreed Boëndal, checking the fit of his spaulders. "Besides, nothing can save the eoîl." He was visibly impressed by Balyndis's workmanship, especially since she was still recovering from her ordeal.

"I don't like it when they use their flamethrowers," complained Boïndil, stroking his braided beard. "It gets confounded hot in my suit. I might dip my whiskers in water to stop them from catching alight. I'd be sorry to scorch them."

"*There* you are," said Rodario, stepping into the forge. "Three feisty dwarves, preparing to save Girdlegard from the forces of evil. Hmm, strictly speaking, the avatars are trying to do the same." He paused and hooked a finger around his chin. "The audience will never understand. How am I supposed to explain that the dwarves, which is to say, the forces of good, are fighting their enemies—also on the side of good—to stop them destroying evil?"

"You'll think of something," Tungdil assured him. "Any useful information from the prisoner?"

"Not really . . ." He picked up a pair of tongs and twirled them in his hand. "I've been thinking about what she said earlier. According to Lirkim, the eoîl is convinced that the evil spirit that corrupted Nudin is still alive."

"What?" gasped Balyndis, staring at him aghast.

"It's been bothering me as well," said Tungdil. He raised his beautifully forged but otherwise unremarkable ax. "We can't fight the spirit without Keenfire, and the älfar won't give it back. To be honest, it's hard to see how the eoîl could be right. You were there when I destroyed the spirit, and nothing was left."

"It can't be very strong or it would have shown itself. The dark water is all that remains of the Perished Land's power." Rodario set down the tongs. "All the same, I'm worried. You'll have to take the eoîl alive."

Boïndil roared with laughter. "He's their leader, remember? He's stronger and more powerful than the rest."

"I took my avatar alive—and I wasn't wearing fancy armor," retorted Rodario, omitting to mention that Lirkim had been neither sober nor conscious.

"Why do you want us to spare him?" asked Boëndal, more diplomatically.

Rodario decided to tell the whole truth. "Lirkim told me that the eoîl knows how to find the spirit."

"So you *did* find out something . . ." Tungdil mulled the situation over. "Maybe the avatars' invasion is a blessing in disguise. With the eoîl's help, we'll be able to find the spirit and destroy it for good." He nodded. "You're right, Rodario, the eoîl must be taken alive."

"Why didn't he explain himself properly from the start?" complained Boïndil, turning the grinding wheel to sharpen his axes. "It's all very well capturing the eoîl, but what are we supposed to do with him—put him on a leash and let him drag us through Girdlegard until he tracks the spirit down?" He hooked his fingers into his belt. "We'll find the spirit lurking in a pool of dark water," he predicted. "Either that, or in a dead glade. Remember what the humans told us about people going mad? It could be the spirit of the Perished Land infecting their minds."

"Let's focus on taking Porista and defeating the avatars," said Tungdil. "The other business can wait." He picked up his vambraces and the other finished items and walked to the door. Smithing was a hungry business, and it was time for some food.

Later they were summoned to the assembly tent, where Queen Xamtys was waiting to share some good news.

"Balendilín, Gandogar, and Glaïmbar are back in their strongholds—they're sending troops to Porista. Prince Mallen is drumming up volunteers, and King Belletain has cleared his fuddled mind and fired his thirdling doctor. He's sending an army through Idoslane as well. Unfortunately, none of the reinforcements—except maybe Belletain's ten thousand warriors—will get here in time."

"Ten thousand warriors should do the trick," said Tungdil confidently. "Furgas has promised us some for-midable siege engines. We'll start the bombardment in four orbits' time. First we'll focus on their army and cut it down to size; then we'll smash our way into the city. Two entry points should be sufficient—Furgas and Rodario know the weak points in Porista's defenses."

"We'd rebuilt it all so nicely," wailed Rodario. "You'd better not hit the Curiosum." He stood up. "I'm going to check on Lirkim." He pulled back the thick pelt that served as a door. "Maybe I can persuade her to . . ."

Just then a bright light pierced the evening sky, and a gray sun shot out of the winter clouds, plummeting toward them.

Alerted by the sentries, dwarves poured out of the tents, brandishing weapons and shields. Narmora stood among them, arms raised, as she muttered an incantation to deflect the fiery ball.

The spell came too late.

The sun turned a deep shade of green and paled a little, before smashing into the collier's hut. Malachite flames shot out of the door and windows, towering to a height of four spears. The rickety shed collapsed.

A moment later, dwarves were on the scene, dousing the blazing wreckage with buckets of snow to save the nearby tents.

Rodario stared at the inferno and knew at once that his prisoner was dead. "Lirkim," he whispered, dismayed. He seldom brought happiness to the women he met.

Lirkim's death proved that the enemy wasn't to be trifled with; the eoîl was capable of detecting and punishing treason beyond the city's walls. Thereafter, the dwarves and their allies poured all their energy into building the siege engines. Furgas had designed them so that the throwing arm was strong enough to hurl spliced tree trunks, boulders, and blocks of wood spiked with nails. They didn't have petroleum or oil, so they were counting on flattening the enemy instead.

According to the älfar, the enemy was preparing to defend the city from the inside, meaning no attempt would be made to meet the allies outside the walls. Rather than risk their lives on the battlefield, the avatars were waiting for the allied army to storm the city, which was bound to result in heavy losses for the älfar and dwarves. Both sides were still busy with their preparations when the weather suddenly changed. The temperature rose and fog descended on the city, making it impossible to see beyond a couple of hundred paces.

The dwarves seized their chance.

Drawing on their knowledge of mining, they dug a tunnel from the encampment to the sewage outlet, known to Tungdil and the others from their rescue mission.

Their aim was to take the avatars by surprise. An elite battalion of thirdlings and älfar would enter the city through the sewers and clear the way for an allied task force, consisting of Tungdil, Boëndal, Boïndil, and some handpicked firstlings and freelings. Meanwhile, the rest of the army, led by Narmora and Rodario, would attack the city on two flanks to create the illusion that the allies were storming the city with a conventional assault.

"We'll aim the missiles at the ramparts and the gates," decided Furgas. "I'd like to spare the population as far as possible. The avatars have caused enough suffering, and there'll be more casualties when the fighting spreads to the streets."

The plan met with everyone's approval.

Tungdil and the others woke on the seventh orbit, knowing that Girdlegard's moment of reckoning had come.

The morning sun was a hazy presence behind the clouds. It wasn't snowing, but the sky looked gray and pregnant, with swathes of mist obscuring their view.

Tungdil went to find Balyndis, who was still too weak to leave the camp. They hugged each other like old friends, so that only the shrewdest observer would have noticed the depth of their emotion.

"Farewell, Balyndis," whispered Tungdil, filling his nostrils with her scent. "We'll meet again in the eternal smithy, if not before."

She gulped. "I'll pray to Vraccas for the hero of the Blacksaddle to prevail."

"Of course he'll prevail," cut in Boïndil. "The avatars will quake in their boots when they see us." He shook hands with Balyndis, and his brother followed suit; then it was time for them to join the älfar and thirdlings.

Boïndil eyed them with suspicion. "You'd think they were made for each other," he muttered grimly. "Black souls, black tattoos, black armor . . . It's a wonder they haven't joined forces against us."

One by one they dropped down and advanced on their hands and knees through the tunnel. Tungdil and the twins soon discovered the difficulties of crawling in a full suit of armor as they disentangled their spaulders from tree roots and emptied their greaves of cold, wet soil.

After a time the tunnel started shaking, from which they deduced that the bombardment was underway.

Above ground, Furgas's siege engines were hurling boulders and tree trunks at the enemy army. Every hit was accompanied by a tremor that shook the hastily built tunnel, raining loose soil and the occasional clod of earth on the crawling dwarves. The low roof was unlikely to survive the bombardment, even without a direct hit.

Tungdil and the twins couldn't afford to worry about the situation. Fear was a distraction, and they couldn't turn back.

At last they reached the end of the tunnel. The älfar and thirdlings were waiting at the mouth of the sewer.

"Ha," growled Boïndil. "The drains are blocked with scum already."

"Only because you're here," snapped a thirdling, baring his teeth.

Boïndil stepped forward menacingly, but Tungdil pulled him back. "You asked for that," he said crossly. "Besides, we're fighting the avatars, not them."

Boïndil lowered his axes and muttered something unrepeatable under his breath. "You're lucky," he said to the thirdling, shooting him a warning look.

They waited until the drain was packed with warriors; then Tungdil gave the order for the hatch to be opened.

Everything went to plan. The avatars hadn't expected them to try the same strategy twice.

Fifty älfar led the way, stealing like shadows as they searched the streets for enemy guards. Soon afterward, Tungdil heard a low whistle.

It was the signal for the thirdlings to file through the hatch. Once on the surface, they spread out and swarmed toward the palace, brandishing axes, cudgels, and flails.

Tungdil and the twins brought up the rear.

*   *   *

Furgas followed the trajectory of the missiles and carefully adjusted the angle until he was satisfied with the result. The fog made it difficult, but not impossible, to trace the projectiles' course.

Hoping to spare the houses, he focused the bombardment on the city's defenses, flattening watchtowers, blasting through the gates, and tearing down ramparts, sending dozens of enemy soldiers to their deaths.

The avatars' army, unable to return fire, waited helplessly, longing for the moment when the allied warriors would storm the city and the battle could begin.

"No sign of the avatars," commented Balyndis, who had left the camp to watch the action from the relative safety of the siege engines.

Furgas nodded, sharing her relief. He gave the order for another round to be fired.

Ropes were released and counterweights dropped, then the throwing arms shot up, hurling boulders through the air. The missiles arced toward the watchtowers, smashing the roofs and killing those inside.

"It doesn't make sense," said Furgas. "They managed to kill Lirkim with a fireball, but they haven't done anything to stop us attacking their men."

Dwarves rushed forward to reload the siege engines, which took considerable time and strength. Furgas wasn't the sort to stand by idly. "I'd hate to give them ideas," he said, turning a windlass, "but the siege engines would burn like tinder."

Balyndis fixed her eyes on the city walls, which stood two hundred and fifty paces from their position. A crack had opened up in the defenses. "Exactly what I was thinking. I'd say they're not too worried about their army; they're busy with something else."

"The force fields," he said, peering toward the city. Usually, the pitched roofs of the houses were visible above the parapets, but everything was shrouded in fog. "I bet they're tampering with the force fields. Pass the message to Xamtys, Gemmil, and Narmora. It's time to start the assault."

Beyond the city walls, a shimmering green arrow soared above Porista, shining brightly through the fog. It came from the bow of an älf, signaling that Tungdil's party had reached the palace. "They're through," shouted Furgas. "Bombard the gates!"

From the ranks of the freelings and firstlings, a line of warriors jogged forward and set their ladders against the ramparts. Their eyes were bound with cloth to protect them from the dazzling light. The first stage of the two-pronged assault had begun.

Already Lorimbas and Rodario were leading the attack on the northern gates, hoping to split the avatars' army and draw them away from the palace.

Furgas marveled at the rows of dwarves rolling toward the city. No mortal adversary could resist such a force— but Lirkim had said that the eoîl was a god.

Among the dwarves he spotted the tall, slender figure of Narmora, dressed in full armor and a bright crimson cloak. He prayed to Palandiell to keep her from harm. *Don't punish her for worshipping Samusin. Her intentions are good.*

Tungdil and the others reached the palace without encountering a single guard.

It doesn't make sense, he thought, wondering why no one had tried to stop them. *Maybe it's a trap* . . . He strode past the main gates; they couldn't be breached by force, and scaling the walls would be folly.

The palace was still protected by a powerful spell that trapped unwanted visitors like flies in a spider web, tying them to the masonry with magic bonds. The bleached bones of previous intruders were enough to persuade even the most unflinching thirdling that it was best to try another route.

Tungdil led the warriors through an alleyway to Furgas's secret doorway. Remembering how Ondori had recited the incantation, he pronounced the words carefully, and sure enough, the masonry began to move. The door opened a crack, enough for an arrow to whiz through and hit a thirdling on the shoulder.

"It had to happen sometime," growled Boëndal, sheltering behind the wall.

"Every dwarf loves a challenge," laughed his brother. "I hope we find some proper warriors in the palace. My axes are hungry for flesh."

The foremost thirdling laid four shields on top of each other and tied them together with his belt. He waited by the narrow opening while a queue of warriors formed behind him, each carrying a stack of shields, ready to form a wall to protect the remainder of the group.

They appeared to be acting on their own initiative—at any rate, none of them waited for instructions. Tungdil wasn't convinced that they would listen to him anyway: Lorimbas had ordered them to cut a path to the avatars, and they were apparently determined to do it on their terms.

"Let's go," said a tattooed warrior, glancing back at Tungdil. The thirdlings stormed ahead.

Arrows hissed through the air, but the reinforced shields fulfilled their purpose. Protected by the wall of metal, the remaining dwarves streamed into the palace gardens where the avatars' soldiers awaited them.

The brightness wasn't so dazzling with the cloth in front of their eyes, and Tungdil had the impression that the soldiers' white armor looked duller than before. The power of the moonstones seemed to be waning.

The thirdlings advanced in formation, and the battle began. It quickly became apparent that the sides were well matched. For every fallen soldier, two more threw themselves into the breach, fighting with a strength born of desperation to hold back the invading dwarves.

"Look!" shouted Ireheart, pointing to the second-highest tower. "Did you see that?" A faint light was shining from the windows. Its source was wreathed in fog, but the glow was clearly visible. "It might be an avatar!"

"Looking for avatars, are you?" thundered a man. Turning, they saw a glowing figure on the parapet of the tower behind them. The magus raised his hands and a pair of glowing fireballs appeared in his palms. "Defenders of evil, prepare to die!"

The burning spheres blazed toward them, speeding through the thirdling ranks.

Narmora raced up the ladder. Rocks showered haphazardly toward her, but none of the missiles found its goal.

She reached the parapet and drew her weapons. The first consisted of a short metal haft to which scythe-like blades had been mounted on each end; the second was a straight-bladed version of the same. The blades' inner and outer edges were deadly sharp. She wore metal baskets on her wrists to protect her fingers from enemy swords.

Launching herself from the parapet, she landed among the soldiers and hewed through their ranks. In recent battles she had fought with magic, not weaponry, and she was eager to test herself in combat, using Sunbeam and Crescent, her mother's blades.

Her älvish nature came to the fore. Ducking, wheeling, and slashing, she was everywhere at once. To her satisfaction, her proficiency was noted and admired by others of her kind.

The dwarves scaled the parapets more slowly. By nature less nimble, they clambered steadily up the ladders and were easy targets for the soldiers' rocks. Undeterred, they threw themselves into battle.

The avatars' soldiers were quick to adapt to the different fighting styles of the älfar and the dwarves, and they soon showed their mettle. The allies' hopes of a quick victory faded, and the battle swayed to and fro. Narmora, realizing the seriousness of the situation, decided to use her magic to cut a path through the enemy troops.

At the same time she knew she had to be ready for the avatars to retaliate, but so far there hadn't been any sign of them.

A cold wind blew into the city, clearing the morning mist. Narmora glanced over to the palace and saw two shimmering figures at the top of a sable tower.

They're up to something . . . Raising her left blade, she blocked a sword and sent it smashing into an enemy soldier before ramming her weapon through the aggressor's belly and skewering him effortlessly on the end of her blade. "Xamtys," she called to the firstling queen, withdrawing her bloodied weapon and pointing to the tower. "Can you manage on your own? I need to see what's going on."

The dwarven queen swung her four-pronged mace into a soldier's knee and smashed it against his skull as he fell, crushing his right temple. The scream died on his lips as he toppled over the parapet. "They're tougher than we thought, but Vraccas will see us through," she called, gesturing for Narmora to go. "We'll be fine without you, Estimable Maga."

Narmora took off, landing with both feet on a soldier's breastplate and knocking him into the weapons of his friends. Dropping low, she took off again and bounded over their heads. Before they could recover, she was down the stairs and running through the streets.

With every step her apprehension grew. Something about the force field was making her uneasy, and the disagreeable feeling intensified as she hurried toward the palace.

The magic energy was reaching for her, or rather, reaching for the shard of malachite buried beside her heart. No one but the eoîl knew about the gemstone, and his knowledge gave him power. She decided to kill him before he gave away her secret and brought her into conflict with Furgas and the dwarves.

It won't come to that. She picked up the pace, sprinting through the deserted streets.

"You've got to stop them," said Nudin, appearing beside her. "Everything is at stake."

She stumbled and stopped. "How did you . . . ?

"You can't stop now," he said urgently. "Hurry, they're about to start the ritual. You're a half älf, remember. They're committed to wiping out evil, and that includes you. I don't want to be alone, Narmora. Don't let them take our power . . ."

The apparition glimmered, fading out of sight.

"Where are you?" Narmora whirled round, sweeping the street with her gaze: There was nothing but terraced houses.

"Estimable Maga!" called a voice. "Thank Vraccas I've found you." An exhausted messenger hurried toward her. "Rodario the Fablemaker needs you on the northern front. He and the thirdlings are outnumbered."

"Tell him he'll have to manage," she said coldly. "I can't endanger Girdlegard to save the lives of Lorimbas's dwarves. The avatars must be stopped."

She left him standing and ran down the street as fast as her long legs could carry her. She didn't much care if the avatars' soldiers wiped out the thirdlings. She was worried about her own life—her life, and the life of her innocent daughter.

Tungdil leaped into action, trusting to the efficacy of Djerûn's armor.

He saw the first fireball speeding toward them, and threw himself into its path. Boëndal stepped in front of the second.

The world around them disappeared in a blaze of white light and roaring flames. Tendrils of fire licked their visors, but the charmed metal and powerful runes protected their eyes from the deadly heat.

Vraccas, give me the strength to pull through. Faster than an ax could sever an orcish arm, the temperature shot up, and beads of sweat formed on Tungdil's forehead, evaporating straightaway. A few strands of hair, poking out from his leather skullcap, brushed against his helmet, releasing a smell that reminded him of a freshly shod horse.

It lasted no longer than the angry fizzle of a burning coal in water, but Tungdil waited impatiently for his vision to clear.

Most of the thirdlings were sprawled on the ground and some of their cloaks were on fire, but everyone was alive.

"I say we kill him before he roasts us like cave crabs," wheezed Boëndal, opening his visor and taking a gulp of fresh air.

His brother was already storming toward the palace, followed by a knot of thirdlings, who cut down the sentries and disappeared inside. Tungdil and Boëndal ran after them as best they could. Balyndis had made their armor less restrictive, but the suits were far heavier than ordinary dwarven mail.

They pushed past the thirdlings and scrambled up the stairs, hoping to take the avatar by surprise.

He spotted them first.

A ball of fire whizzed toward them, engulfing them in roaring, hissing flames. Sweat vaporized from their pores, but the heat couldn't kill them. They heard the avatar curse and saw a flash of white robe disappear around the corner.

"He's running away!" bellowed Ireheart. "Ha, call yourself an avatar!" He hurled his ax, pinning the cloth to a wooden cupboard.

"What did you say about letting go of your ax?" asked Boëndal, sprinting past him with his crow's beak. He turned the corner.

Tungdil was hot on his heels. "You owe us a sack of gold."

"I've got two axes; it doesn't count!" protested Boïndil, hurrying after them. "Leave him to me!"

The avatar-conjurer was a dark-haired man of fifty cycles dressed in black robes. He whirled round and pointed his left hand at Boëndal. White lightning left his index finger and shot toward the dwarf.

"Die, undergroundling!" This time the avatar kept his finger pointed at his victim, allowing flames to crackle over his breastplate. He seemed to realize that the armor offered no protection against the heat.

The tactic paid off.

Slowly, Boëndal's fingers uncurled, and his crow's beak thudded to the floor. He took a step forward, stumbled, and hit the unyielding marble without stopping his fall. At best he was unconscious, at worst he was . . .

"What have you done to my brother?" shrieked Ireheart, hurling his other ax to distract the avatar from Boëndal. The flames fizzled out. Boïndil kept running and grabbed the crow's beak, swinging it over his head. "You'll die for this."

The avatar-conjurer sent another bolt of lightning toward Boïndil, but the dwarf was already upon him.

Shrieking with rage, Ireheart spun round and rammed the spur of the crow's beak into the avatar's belly, hitting him with such force that the weapon embedded itself in his guts. With another terrible shriek, the dwarf jerked the crow's beak to the side, slicing his waist.

The avatar-conjurer didn't have time to speak, groan, or express his surprise. He fell, blood and guts spilling from his belly as he hit the marble floor.

Tungdil kneeled beside Boëndal and fumbled with his visor, gagging on the smell of charred flesh. Hot steam and white smoke rose toward him. He fanned the air frantically and looked anxiously at his friend. The sight stopped his breath. *Vraccas have mercy.*

Boëndal's face was a welter of oozing blisters, his features burned beyond recognition. Nothing but a few scorched whiskers remained of his bushy beard. Tungdil knew without looking that the rest of his body was covered in burns as well. "Lie still," he told him, and Boëndal's singed, lashless eyelids flickered at the sound of his voice. "I'll get some snow for the burns."

"Boëndal," murmured his brother, appalled. "I . . ."

"Hurry," whispered Boëndal. His blackened lips struggled to form the words. "Find the other avatars—don't let them do the same to you." He swallowed and tried to continue, but his voice gave out.

"Follow me," said Tungdil determinedly. "We can have one each."

Boïndil stood up. "I'll take the eoîl."

They jogged through the palace, looking for the staircase to the second-highest sable tower. The remaining thirdlings—thirty in all—came with them; the others had been cut down by the palace guards or killed by the avatar's firebolts.

They pushed on quickly, their progress unhindered by the surviving avatar and his guards. It seemed the eoîl was happy to give them the run of the palace, which added to Tungdil's unease.

Suddenly, a man stepped out of a doorway and hurried toward them. "Stop!"

"Die, wizard!" shouted Boïndil, raising his axes. His inner furnace was burning furiously, but somehow, miraculously, he recognized the man. "The fatuous Rodario!" At the last second, the crow's beak jerked to the side, thudding against the wall and splintering the marble.

"Rodario! What are you doing here?" asked Tungdil, surprised. "I thought you and the thirdlings were . . ."

It was clear from the impresario's appearance that the past few hours had taken their toll. His robes were torn and bloodied, although the blood wasn't his. An angry bruise graced his right cheekbone and he was glistening with sweat.

"Lorimbas and his troops are dead," he gasped, leaning against the wall and catching his breath. "They were decimated in the battle. We ran straight into the enemy's traps, and Narmora left us to it. I asked for her help, but she was needed in the palace. I was hoping to find her here." He lifted his arm, rubbed his eyes on his winged sleeve, and blinked. "Xamtys said to tell you that she's holding her position, but the enemy units from the northern front are on their way to help their comrades. She won't last for long." His expression was uncharacteristically grave. "I think Narmora is trying to kill the eoîl so they won't have a leader. At this rate there won't be anyone left when Balendilín, Gandogar, and Glaïmbar's armies arrive."

"It's down to us to stop them." Tungdil glanced down the corridor. "Do you know the way to the second-highest tower? We think the eoîl and the last avatar might be hiding at the top."

Rodario grinned. "I'd be delighted to take you there: In my experience, it's generally safest in the eye of the storm. If you're going to cuckold a man, you should stay in his bedroom; the dangerous part is trying to leave." He pointed to a wide door leading away from the corridor. "You went right past it. Incidentally, the tower in question is situated above the wellspring."

They ran to the door and a thirdling warrior yanked the handle and leaped away. "A monster! They've magicked a monster to guard the tower!"

Snarling and rasping, the creature barreled toward them through the doorway, pulling out the wooden frame and fracturing the marble wall. Through the cloud of powdered stone they saw the outlines of a monster that was clearly the creation of an unhinged god.

The four-legged creature towered above them, filling the six-pace-high corridor from ceiling to floor. It had a human body, with vast white wings and four stringy arms that allowed it to strike its enemies from afar. It wasn't armed, having no need for swords or axes since its hands were equipped with bird-like talons, each as long as a dwarven arm and deadly sharp.

"Ye gods," stammered Rodario, staring at the creature's fang-lined jaws. He took a step backward. "If you ask me, this is a job for a warrior."

"Scholar," whispered Boïndil. "What is it? How do we kill it?"

The creature lowered its lizard-like head and peered at the dwarves with clear, pupil-less eyes. A forked purple tongue flicked toward them.

Tungdil had no recollection of any reference to such a creature in Lot-Ionan's books. "It's not from Girdlegard. They must have brought it from the Outer Lands—what it is, I don't know."

The creature flapped its powerful wings as best it could in the confines of the corridor, whipping up a hefty gust. The dwarves let go of their shields as the wind threatened to lift them into the air. Rodario was caught off guard and blown over.

Following its first, relatively harmless, display of power, the creature attacked.

Two long arms shot out and grabbed a couple of thirdlings, closing its talons around their heads and smashing their helmed skulls like eggshells. It loosed its grip, dropped the twitching bodies to the floor, and hissed in satisfaction.

The thirdlings, determined to avenge their dead comrades, threw themselves on the beast, whose claws turned out to be surprisingly hard. The thirdlings' axes bounced off them, allowing the creature to bat away their blows.

"As soon as it's sufficiently distracted, we'll make a run for it," said Tungdil. He didn't want to waste time on the monster when its masters were still at large.

"But I want to fight it," protested Boïndil, his inner furnace spitting flames. "It's the biggest challenge I've ever seen!"

"Wait till we find the eoîl," said Tungdil, hoping to console him. He signaled to Rodario. "The thirdlings can deal with the monster. You're coming with us."

"I see, you want me to be your decoy," muttered Rodario. "Oh well, someone has to do it." He shook the dust from his robes and sprinted after the dwarves, who had spotted a gap between the monster and the stairs.

Almost instantly, a talon swooped within inches of his head. The impresario ducked, racing past the dwarves to the bottom of the tower.

The creature resorted to cunning and flapped its wings frantically, creating a wind that swirled through Rodario's robes, causing him to topple backward and trip up the dwarves. In the resulting confusion, they failed to foresee the next attack.

The creature's fourth arm sped toward them, hitting Tungdil's spaulders and cutting five deep grooves. Continuing on its trajectory, it smashed into Boïndil, hitting his breast-plate level with his collarbone. One of the talons pierced the metal, eliciting a shriek of pain and rage, but the hardy dwarf had the strength to raise his weapon and hew through the talon, leaving the tip embedded in his chest.

"Is that the best you can do?" he shouted scornfully. "I'll kill your masters, then come back and chop off your wings." He spat at the creature's feet.

Rodario and Tungdil had to grab him by the arms and drag him away. Somehow they reached the broad stair-case leading up to the tower and kept running until the steps narrowed and the monster could chase them no more. Tungdil stopped to inspect the broken talon in Boïndil's chest. It was at least the width of two fingers.

"You'll lose too much blood if I try to pull it out," he judged. "I think we should leave it alone."

"I'll be fine," said Boïndil through gritted teeth. "It doesn't especially hurt and it can't have penetrated further than a fingertip or so. It's a good job I was wearing my jerkin." He tried to smile. "Just don't let anyone wallop me in the chest." He looked skeptically at the spiral staircase winding up the tower. It presented a considerable challenge to a dwarf in full plate armor, especially one with a hole in his chest. "This could take a while," he said, placing his right foot on the next step and beginning the arduous ascent.

The tower was an architectural masterpiece.

The steps extended four paces from the walls of the stairwell without a rail or central pillar, and the tower itself was ten paces wide, leaving a gap of two paces at the core of the spiral. The slightest clumsiness was liable to end in a long and probably fatal fall. Winter sunshine filled the stairwell, lighting the steps.

Rodario noticed a cable, about the diameter of a finger, dangling in the empty shaft. It seemed to be suspended from above, for what purpose he could not guess. *It's probably for a bell or a gong or something.* He dismissed the matter from his mind.

"What do they want with so many steps?" grumbled an out-of-breath Boïndil when they were two-thirds of the way to the top.

"It reminds me of a dwarven stronghold," teased Rodario.

"Dwarves build towers for a reason. They're crucial to our defenses, whereas this one . . ." He banged the crow's beak impatiently against the wall. "You can't do anything with this one. No platforms, no storerooms, no nothing— it's useless."

"Aren't you forgetting the fabulous view?" puffed Rodario, who was sweating profusely like the dwarves.

"The magi probably came here on clear nights to observe the celestial spectacle."

"I wouldn't climb all these steps just to gaze at some stupid stars," growled Boïndil. "Besides, think of all the equipment you'd need. It would take all night to lug it to the top." He blew out heavily. "The architect was a fool."

When they reached the top of the stairs they saw that the sunshine wasn't coming from above, as they had supposed, but from a cleverly positioned mirror that caught the light from three windows and channeled it into the stairwell. Next to the mirror was a door leading out to a parapet. Rodario stuck his head outside and a cold breeze ruffled his hair. "They're still fighting," he reported. "And unless I'm mistaken, another army is arriving from the north." He peered into the distance. "Do you think it could be another battalion of älfar? The armor looks very dark."

"It's probably Belletain," said Tungdil, elbowing him aside. "They're coming from the right direction, but I can't see the crests."

"Who cares where they're from, so long as they're on our side." Boïndil's legs were shaking and he leaned against the wall. "I'll be all right in a second," he said.

Rodario looked at the crimson tracks on the floor. Blood was trickling between the plates of Boïndil's armor, having leached through his jerkin. Contrary to his claims, the warrior was seriously wounded. The impresario nudged Tungdil and pointed to the blood.

"You'll have to stay here," said Tungdil, worried about his friend. "You won't be any good to us if you collapse in front of the eoîl. You're in no state to fight."

Boïndil was unbending. "Nice try, scholar, but you said the eoîl was mine." He took up the crow's beak and marched with dwarven stubbornness to the door. "What are you waiting for, Sir Prattlemouth?" he demanded, winking to show that Rodario shouldn't take offense. "Open the door!"

The impresario was staring at the cable, which ran from the top of the stairs across the floor and out of the tower through a hole in the wall. A pile of dust indicated that the hole was quite recent. *Did the avatars put it there?* His deliberations were interrupted by the last of the avatars.

The door flew open and a shimmering creature appeared before him, filling the tower with light.

"I knew you were here," said a woman's voice. She hurled a bolt of blue lightning at Boïndil, who wobbled under the double strain of the heat and his wounded chest. She saw that he was struggling and smiled. "Your armor won't save you. It's too late to stop the eoîl."

Rodario summoned his courage. "Desist, shining conjurer, or I, Rodario the Fablemaker, first-grade apprentice to Narmora, will take your life." He uttered a few nonsensical words, waved his arms, and activated his tinderboxes, firing burning lycopodium spores into the air.

The avatar wove a counterspell, reciting an incantation capable of defusing the most powerful magical firebolt. It had no effect whatsoever on Rodario's props. Shrieking in pain, the startled avatar went up in flames.

The bright light went out, and Rodario and the dwarves saw that their enemy's hair and robes were on fire.

"Ha, not so confident now, are you? Let's see how you like this . . ." Encouraged by his success, the impresario hurled a phial at the avatar's chest.

It hit her robes, bounced off, and exploded on the floor. Luckily for him, the avatar was so intent on putting out the flames that she stepped forward obligingly and put her right foot in the puddle. Smoke rose as the acid ate into her leather sole and burned the bottom of her foot.

"Good work, famulus!" whooped Boïndil. With a terrible laugh, he swung the crow's beak at the avatar's shoulder, impaling her on the spur. He maneuvered her to the ground, and, in an instant, Tungdil was beside them, ax raised and ready to strike.

The avatar did the first thing that came into her mind.

Instead of attacking the dwarves with firebolts, which wouldn't have worked because of their suits, she focused on the ax, casting a spell to wrest it from Tungdil's hands toward Boïndil's head, causing the blade to smack into his helm.

Boïndil let out a muffled groan. The blow wasn't enough to crack his skull, but he stumbled sideways, landing inelegantly on his rear. The weight of his armor carried him backward, and he skidded onto the steps.

"Scholar, I'm . . ." Clutching desperately at the air, he tumbled into the empty stairwell.

"No!" Rodario darted forward and made a grab for the dwarf, catching hold of a leather strap that instantly broke. He watched in horrified disbelief as the dwarf plummeted down the shaft of light, becoming smaller and smaller until he disappeared from sight.

Tungdil rammed his armored fist into the avatar's face, punching her again and again until her features were a bloody pulp and her limbs stopped twitching. Drawing his dagger, he stabbed her through the heart. "I'd kill you a thousand times if I could." His eyes welled with tears as he raised his ax and planted it in her body to punish her for Boïndil's death.

Visor and face specked with blood, he straightened up and strode outside to tackle the eoîl.

"Where are you?" he called, looking both ways. He pressed himself against the wall and advanced along the circular ledge. Rodario followed behind him.

The shimmering figure ahead of them was attaching a diamond to a crystal container dangling by a cable from the flagpole.

"You made it all this way," said a warm voice that left them wondering whether the speaker was male or female. Shining fingers tugged on a rope and the crystal container shot to the top of the flagpole, jigging up and down in the wind. "I admire you for your persistence, but I won't be distracted from my purpose. If you continue to oppose me, you and your friends will die."

"What difference does it make? You've killed thousands already." Slowly, Tungdil stepped toward the eoîl. "How can you claim to be fighting for good if you wipe out everyone who gets in your way?"

"I don't expect you to understand. You're too wrapped up in the details to see that casualties are inevitable in the fight against evil. I'm not afraid to make sacrifices for the greater good."

Rodario eyed him scornfully. "You're only interested in power. Lirkim told me that you're planning to carve up Girdlegard—I suppose that's why you killed her."

"Killed her?" The eoîl sounded surprised. "Is Lirkim dead?"

"You killed her yourself."

"On the contrary, I was planning to rescue her—she and the others were loyal friends. I'm sorry about what happened to them, but I don't need them now. They wanted territory and power, and I promised to give it to them. I'm interested only in the destruction of evil in all its forms. Sadly, undergroundlings aren't generally counted as *evil*." The bright oval that was the creature's face tilted slightly as if to focus on something behind them. "If you want to know who killed Lirkim, I suggest you ask her."

"Don't look," said Tungdil, gripping his ax. "It's bound to be a trick."

Rodario glanced over his shoulder. "Narmora?"

IX

Porista,
Former Realm of Lios Nudin,
Girdlegard,
Winter, 6235th/6236th Solar Cycle

The half älf was standing right behind them. Her eyes were two dark pits and fine lines zigzagged like cracks across her face. "Don't listen to him." She pushed past Rodario and took up position next to Tungdil. They heard her utter a single magic word.

A dark green bolt shot from her mouth, hitting the astonished eoîl who toppled backward and hit the floor. "Your trail of destruction ends here." She raised her arms, and green lightning flew from her fingers, crackling toward the eoîl.

Tungdil watched with bated breath. *Surely it can't be that easy to kill an eoîl?* He tensed his muscles, ready to charge at the eoîl with his ax. Meanwhile, Rodario gripped his last phial of acid and prepared to hurl it at the luminous figure, should Narmora's magic fail.

The eoîl, surrounded by malachite lightning, got to his feet and let out a tinkling laugh. His shoulders shook with mirth. Narmora lowered her head, summoning her strength to intensify the attack.

To no avail.

The eoîl raised his hand gracefully and pushed aside the web of lightning. The bolts disintegrated, setting him free.

"You'll have to explain to your friends where you got your power," he said mildly. "No ordinary being would be capable of channeling so much energy—but you've got a secret, haven't you? Maybe you should tell them."

"Silence!" she screeched furiously, opening her mouth to begin another spell. An apple-sized ball of light sped toward her and exploded against her chest. Screaming, she dropped to her knees and wrapped her arms around her stricken body.

"You're carrying it inside you," he said triumphantly. "You're giving shelter to what's left of the demon. What will your friends say, half älf?" He hurled another ball of light toward her, and she writhed on the ground, moaning. "Why did you kill Lirkim?"

"Enough!" bellowed Tungdil, striding toward him. "I won't be distracted by your lies. Vraccas told his children to guard these lands, and I'll fight you to the death."

With Narmora incapacitated, the eoîl turned back to the dwarf. "You're determined and you're spirited," he said approvingly. "I like that, undergroundling, which is why I'm proposing a deal." He reached down to pick up the cable. "Let me go about my business, and I'll order my warriors to lay down their arms. Girdlegard won't come to any harm—with the help of the wellspring, I'll rid your lands of evil, and every impure soul within the five ranges will perish in my flames." He pointed to the crystal tube. "Their energy will be channeled through this stone and converted to good. Afterward, I'll be strong enough to take on the lord of darkness himself." The luminous oval turned to Tungdil. "It won't take long, then I'll leave you in peace. I'm giving you and your kinsfolk a better world—a world without älfar or beasts. Nothing that bears a trace of evil will survive the stone of judgment. Isn't that what you want?"

Although the proposal was appealing, Tungdil couldn't bring himself to trust the eoîl. He decided to probe a little further. "What will happen to the force fields? If you drain the wellspring, Girdlegard will be thrown into chaos and you'll devastate the land. We've seen the effects of your meddling already."

"Change means risk. Thanks to your smith, I can use the source to give me power. She gave away the secret of your armor."

"Balyndis didn't tell you anything."

"No one can resist my power. The undergroundling endured unimaginable pain—she won't remember what she said." The eoîl glanced over the parapet. "Älvish reinforcements," he observed. "The immortal siblings are with them—I can feel their dark power. They know I intend to wipe them out. Their dark-hearted leaders aren't as indestructible as they claim." He turned back to Tungdil. "Which will it be? Will you let me destroy the älfar—or do you want your friends to die?"

Rodario suddenly grasped what the eoîl was up to. The cable was made of Balyndis's special alloy, and the eoîl was using it to connect the diamond to the spring. *I need to distract him.* "The decision isn't ours to take," he said. He took a sideways step, holding the phial behind him and dropping it on the cable at the point where it left the wall. "Tungdil can't agree to anything without the backing of the other kings. He can't speak for the dwarven rulers, let alone the men and elves, so if you don't mind, I'm afraid we'll have to—"

The eoîl raised his hand, and the impresario lifted several paces off the ground and slammed against the wall of the tower. He toppled forward and slumped over the parapet, too dazed to move.

"I didn't ask for his opinion," snapped the eoîl. "Well, Tungdil, what do you say?"

"I can't agree to your proposal."

"There's a thin line between courage and folly." Pointing at Tungdil with his right hand, he uttered a magic formula, but nothing happened. The acid had eaten through the cable, cutting the link to the spring.

"Courage and folly can defeat the most powerful conjurers," retorted Tungdil, rushing forward and swinging his ax to cut down the eoîl.

Even as he raised his weapon he was overtaken by a pair of dark figures, who ran past him on either side. They were dressed in magnificent suits of black tionium with elaborate älvish helmets, and their swords were as delicate as they were deadly, with razor-sharp, finger-width blades.

Before he had time to regain his composure, Tungdil was knocked off his feet from behind. He fell, rolled over, and prepared to fight.

"You again?" He looked into the masked face of Ondori.

She lifted her black veil and smiled coldly. "The immortal siblings will handle the eoîl. It's no job for a groundling." She thrust her quarterstaff toward him, hitting his helmed head. Tungdil was momentarily deafened, but amid the ringing in his ears he heard her whisper, "I told you it would end this way. Look at me: Ondori is your death." She said something in a strange tongue, then leaned forward again. "I'm going to take your life, groundling." A blade shot out from the end of her quarterstaff and pressed against his throat. "To blazes with your soul."

With that, the fight against the eoîl faded into insignificance as Tungdil focused his energies on survival.

Ondori raised the quarterstaff, preparing to pierce Tungdil's throat, but he rolled to the side as best he could, gasping as the blade nicked his skin. He smelled the blood trickling from the right of his throat, a strong coppery odor, characteristic of dwarves.

Ondori kicked out, striking him just as he tried to right himself like a clumsy beetle. He flew through the air, landed and ducked beneath her blade, coming dangerously close to the parapet. Straightening up, he was just in time to anticipate the next assault.

"You killed my parents, groundling." The tip of the quarterstaff sped toward him, and he batted it aside with his ax, only for her to flip the haft of her weapon into his visor. His head jerked back with a sickening crack. The blow would have broken the neck of a human, but it wasn't enough to fell a determined dwarf.

"My friends killed your father—and I'll kill you too." He slashed at her with his ax, fully expecting her to block the blade with her quarterstaff. "I warned you the first time, and I'm a dwarf of my word." He hooked his ax around the staff, jerked the älf toward him, and swung his blade to the right.

The tactic paid off. Ondori, desperate to keep hold of her weapon, wasn't quick enough, and the ax cut into the back of her right hand, almost chopping it in two. Dark blood gushed to the marble floor.

"I'll sculpt a tombstone for my parents with your bones!" She stabbed at Tungdil with her staff, ramming it into his leg. He stumbled against the parapet and reached down to yank the weapon from his thigh. The blade had cut through his armor and pierced his flesh to the bone. A scream rose inside him, but he gritted his teeth, clamping his jaws until he thought he would explode.

Reaching for her belt, Ondori drew another set of weapons similar to Narmora's crescent blades, and rushed forward to finish him off.

The duel was a fight to the death. The dwarf and the älf were both injured, but neither could land the decisive blow. They were fighting so energetically, so determinedly, that there was no time to follow the battle between the immortal siblings and the eoîl. A moment of inattention on either part would result in death.

Tungdil, limping badly, began to slow. His right leg, already unsteady, gave out completely as Ondori swung both weapons at his chest. He stumbled, falling toward his foe.

A scythe-like blade slid through the join in his breastplate and sliced through his jerkin, piercing his ribs. Weakened from his previous injury, he blacked out for a second, opening his eyes in time to see Ondori towering over him, ready to land another blow.

Mighty Vraccas, he prayed silently. *Don't abandon the elves and men. For the sake of Girdlegard, grant me the strength to prevail.* He thrust his ax toward Ondori, but she batted it aside.

"Good, but not good enough," she taunted him. Her foot sped into his face, preventing further resistance.

Kneeling beside him, she set a blade against the lower edge of his helmet and pressed it against his throat. "Die, Tungdil Goldhand." Her scarred face glowed with triumph as she contemplated killing him slowly, sinking the blade little by little into his neck, and making him suffer as she and her parents had suffered at his hands. But time was short and she decided to settle for inflicting a speedy but brutal death.

"I'd kill Sinthoras and your mother again if I had the chance," he mumbled. After the last kick, his mouth felt swollen and numb.

"You'll never kill another älf." Ondori tensed her muscles, preparing to land the final blow.

Just then the tower moved. Tiles, sections of roof, and wooden struts broke free and rained down on Tungdil and Ondori.

Shocked, she raised her arm again, but the second-highest tower in Porista was bathed in searing white light.

Tungdil, lying on his back, peered past the älf to the top of the tower. A column of light pierced the gray winter sky, topped by a white fireball ten paces across. *It's too late. The eoîl has done it.*

Magic energy rose from the vaults of the palace, pulsing through the column as the power of the wellspring was sucked toward the sky. The tower and the ground beneath it continued to shake.

I knew it. The eoîl shouldn't be meddling with the order of the gods. Tungdil seized his chance and grabbed Ondori's wrist before she could lower her blade.

Ramming her elbow into his helmet, she threw her

weight behind the weapon, forcing it toward his neck. Shaking with effort, they pushed against each other, summoning the last of their strength. Ondori, it seemed, was the stronger.

The blade nicked his neck and the älf breathed out triumphantly. "Nothing can save your pathetic little life. Die, groundling!"

Overhead, the white sun sucked the last of the energy from the wellspring in a long, thirsty gulp. The column of magic flickered and paled.

A split-second later, the sun exploded with a clear high tinkle, purer and brighter than the ring of a hammer on an anvil, louder than a thunderclap, and more piercing than the wail of a child. The city was steeped in light, every man, dwarf, and älf resplendent in the glow.

Ondori's black eyes were transformed, becoming streams of pure light. Her face contorted. "In the name of Tion, what . . ." Silvery light shimmered from her pores.

Tungdil was mesmerized by the transformation taking place before his eyes. Suddenly, a dark mist rose from the älf and floated skyward. A wave of heat radiated from her body, and she opened her mouth in a bestial scream, but no sound came out. There was nothing left of her but swirling ash that scattered on the winter wind. Her clothes and her weapons had disintegrated as well.

Just then Tungdil spotted Narmora. She had risen to her feet and was stumbling forward, wailing and screeching. Light glowed from her chest, turning to pale white flames as if her flesh were made of straw. Her screams died as she tumbled to the floor in a fiery plume.

Shocked, Tungdil looked away. There was nothing that

could be done for her. He looked in vain for the immortal siblings and their imposing black armor. *Was the eoîl right?* He pulled himself up and peered over the balcony to see how Porista had fared.

Following the explosion, the magic energy had risen above the tower, fanning out and surrounding the palace like an upturned bowl. It continued to radiate outward, picking up speed and moving through houses and temples, unhindered by marble, wood, or flesh.

The fighting had stopped on the ramparts and in the streets. Everyone was staring at the searing wall of light.

The first unit of älfar flared with light, disintegrated and perished like Ondori. A cloud of black mist rose from the city, collecting around the diamond at the top of the flagpole. Tendrils of smoke wound themselves playfully around the precious stone, streaking the air and forming strange aerial creatures.

Outside the city, the älvish reinforcements fled in panic, some running, others spurring their shadow mares, all desperate to escape the searing light.

Nothing could protect them from the eoîl.

Tungdil watched as the dark figures were consumed by light, the evil inside them rising to the diamond on the mast. The bell-like radiance continued to spread outward until its furthest edges glimmered on the horizon. Black mist wafted toward the palace, collecting overhead.

Just then a tremor ran through the tower. The earth was shaking again.

Glancing to the parapet, Tungdil saw the charred remains of Narmora. Lying beside her blackened ribs was a shimmering green jewel. *It was true!*

"Magic should be banned," mumbled Rodario, slowly coming to. He straightened up, saw Narmora's charred remains, and raised his hands to his eyes. "Palandiell be with us, he killed her!"

"She was killed by the evil within," said a voice.

The eoîl stood up, letting go of the two ends of the cable. The radiant aura disappeared.

Now they could see that their antagonist was a tall, slender maiden in pure white robes. The sword in her left hand was dripping with the dark blood of the immortal siblings. The tips of her ears pointed up through her long fair hair, and her face was too narrow and beautiful to be human.

"The stone of judgment has done its work." She inclined her head regally toward Rodario and Tungdil. "Those who passed the test have nothing to fear." Her blue eyes shifted to the cloud overhead. "The essence of evil," she explained. "Don't worry, I'll convert it to good." She smiled serenely.

Rodario raised himself to his full height and glanced at Tungdil, hoping to discover what the dwarf had in mind. "You're an . . . elf."

"I'm an eoîl, purer and nobler than my lowly cousins," she said disdainfully. "I was touched by the hands of Sitalia herself."

"Give back the magic energy," demanded Tungdil, undaunted. The pain seemed to fade as Vraccas restored his courage. At last he had a flesh-and-blood opponent: a pointy-eared eoîl who cared nothing for the suffering she inflicted and had the presumption to think that she was better than everyone else. Such arrogance was typical of her kind. "Give it back before Girdlegard is shaken to pieces."

She shook her head, sending ripples through her silky hair. "The magic is gone. The stone of judgment has absorbed its power." She raised her right hand and pointed to the sky. Black clouds were blowing toward Porista from all directions, turning the dull winter afternoon to deepest night. "See?"

Toboribor's orcs in the south of Idoslane, Borwôl's ogres in the northeastern reaches of Urgon, the last of the älfar in Dsôn Balsur, and other nameless beasts in the far-flung reaches of Girdlegard had been destroyed by the stone. There was nothing left except the darkness of the souls, billowing toward Porista.

Already a vortex of energy was swirling down from the cloud and wrapping itself wraith-like around the crystal, which devoured the darkness. At once the diamond lit up, illuminating the heavens like a star. The transformation had begun.

Rodario, his jauntiness gone, hobbled slowly over to Tungdil. Narmora's death had affected him deeply, even though he knew of her misdeeds. "What are we going to do?"

The dwarf thought for a moment. "Remember what Lirkim told us about her power?" he whispered.

The impresario bent over and picked up Ondori's quarterstaff, pretending to use it as a crutch. "She said the magic was stored in her amulets."

Tungdil studied the eoîl and counted two rings and an amulet hanging from her dainty neck. "Do you think she's got any energy left?" He glanced at the flagpole. "There's a good chance she won't be able to use her magic until she channels the energy from the stone." He unbuckled his greaves and tied a makeshift bandage around the wound. He wanted the eoîl to think that they had abandoned the struggle and embraced the new order. "Don't do anything until the darkness has been absorbed. We can't get rid of the eoîl and leave the evil in the air." He pulled the bandage tight and knotted it in place. "Wait till she reaches for the diamond, then go."

The tower shook again, the blocks of marble groaning under the strain.

"And then what?"

"We pray to Vraccas that we're right about the amulets."

Rodario smiled wryly. "I meant, what are we going to do with the diamond? I'm assuming we'll defeat her."

"We'll cast it into the wellspring and see what happens." His brown eyes were grimly determined. "I can't think of a better idea right now. The eoîl won't hand over the diamond willingly, and she can't be allowed to hold so much power. With the energy from the diamond she'll be unstoppable, and she doesn't seem terribly levelheaded."

Rodario tightened his grip on the quarterstaff. "I've run out of props," he said, patting his empty pockets. "I'm not cut out to be a warrior. I'd rather fight with lycopodium flames and burning acid than a blade."

"I thought you wanted a starring role? *Rodario the Fablemaker, Impresario and Warrior, Defeats the Mighty Eoîl.* How's that for a title?"

"I wouldn't mind if I'd rehearsed. I've got nothing against a bit of ad libbing, but I don't want to fall off the stage."

The dwarf thumped him on the back. "You'll be fine." He glanced up at the sky where the last black wisps were streaming into the crystal tube. "We'll let her think that I can't walk properly on my own. Pretend you're going for help, and on my signal, we'll attack. Whoever gets to her first will have to deal the fatal blow." The two friends shook hands.

"I can't carry you on my own," Rodario said loudly. "You stay here, and I'll go for help. You shouldn't be walking on that leg." He frowned, looking every inch the anxious friend. As always, he played his part to perfection, hobbling forward with the help of the quarterstaff as if he were badly wounded.

The eoîl seemed barely aware of their presence. She was staring, transfixed, at the diamond, which was sparkling with magic light. Her face was so beautiful that Tungdil felt unwell.

Daylight returned and gray banks of snow filled the sky, emptying their cold white cargo on the roofs of Porista. The sinister clouds had gone, the dark magic channeled through the rune-inscribed crystal tube and transformed into positive energy by the diamond.

"My work here is done." The eoîl hurried to the flagpole. "I promised that I would leave Girdlegard, and leave I shall. For the first time in cycles, these lands are free from evil."

Tungdil gave the signal and strode toward the eoîl.

"Leave the diamond where it is," he said threateningly. "It's too much power for a single soul."

It was clear from her expression that she hadn't expected to be challenged. "Still determined to thwart me, are you?" She raised her left arm. "I've never met anyone so intent on dying."

A long thin object whirled through the air, striking the right of her chest and knocking her backward against the parapet. Rodario, much to his surprise, had succeeded in felling the eoîl with his quarterstaff.

"Ha!" he shouted, drawing a sword. "Some demigod you are! We know the truth about you, elf. You're powerless without the magic of the stone."

Tungdil reached the flagpole and slashed the ropes with his ax. The crystal tube containing the diamond dropped into his hand. He threw away the cable and stuffed the tube behind the buckle of his belt. "You'll have to fight me for it." He limped toward her. "I haven't forgotten the innocent souls who died in your fires. Don't expect any mercy."

A trickle of blood left her mouth and landed on her pure white robes. She drew the quarterstaff from her side and stepped away from the parapet. A crimson halo radiated from the right of her chest. Drawing her sword, she threw herself on the dwarf, who struggled to match her incredible speed. The sword and ax met in a ringing din.

The eoîl's delicate beauty belied her strength. Each blow was delivered with the force of a dwarven warrior, and Tungdil swayed, struggling to keep his balance because of his wounded leg.

Rodario rushed to his aid, swiping at the eoîl with his sword. "You're a nifty fighter, but you can't—" The eoîl stepped nimbly aside, dodging the awkward attack. Without taking her eyes off Tungdil, she jabbed her sword with startling rapidity at the impresario, stabbing him in the belly. Rodario doubled up, screaming in agony as she rotated the blade before whipping it out.

Tungdil swung his ax.

The blade whizzed toward her, heading straight for her wounded chest. The eoîl raised her sword to check the blow.

The ax smashed down, shattering the delicate sword and continuing its trajectory. A split-second later, the ax head embedded itself in the eoîl's chest.

The force of the blow knocked her sideways and she stumbled into the parapet and overbalanced, pulling Tungdil, still holding the haft of his weapon, toward the edge.

He unfurled his fingers, allowing the ax—and the eoîl—to fall. Leaning over the parapet, he watched her descent.

Twice she knocked against the sable walls of the tower, staining them crimson as she scraped against the stone. Her fall ended at the base of the tower, her dainty body smashing against the ground.

Tungdil stared down at the sprawled eoîl and released his pent-up breath. *The gods weren't with you.* His hand patted the diamond hidden behind his belt.

"I told you I needed more time to rehearse." Rodario groaned and gripped his belly, trying to stem the blood. "Still, at least I didn't fall off the stage."

Tungdil hobbled over and assessed his injuries at a glance. "The blade entered on the left, low enough to miss your organs," he reassured him. "I'll go down and . . ." He broke off as footsteps and jangling armor sounded from the tower. "It's not over yet." Placing himself in front of the injured Rodario, he drew his only weapon, a dagger, and turned to face the eoîl's guards.

A small figure in plate armor burst through the door, crow's beak on high.

Realizing that the eoîl had been defeated, he lowered his weapon and pushed back his visor to reveal a wrinkled face and a thick black beard.

He stared at Tungdil and then the dagger. "For pity's sake, scholar, what did I tell you? Never throw your only ax!"

There wasn't time to swap stories.

The two dwarves rushed down the stairs, past the crater made by the eoîl, and into the vaults of the palace. Tungdil followed Boïndil, who knew the way to the wellspring.

"I think it stopped my fall," he panted. "It took ages to hit the ground and I remember praying to Vraccas to save me; then suddenly I slowed down and floated like a feather." He pointed down the stairs into the darkness. "The source is down there. I reckon I fell on top of it. I was practically roasting by the time I reached the bottom."

"The armor must have saved you," said Tungdil. "Girdlegard owes a lot to Balyndis; she'll be proud when she hears."

The earth shook beneath them. This time the quake continued for a few seconds, covering the dwarves in a dusting of stone. The tower was showing signs of stress, and Tungdil spotted what looked like a crack in the wall. The shaking receded, but the ground was still moving.

"Is it far?" he asked through gritted teeth. The pain in his thigh was almost unbearable, and he had to remind himself that Boïndil with his wounded chest was faring worse.

"We're not there yet, scholar." Boïndil wished that the masters of Porista had installed a pulley system like the moving platforms in Xamtys's stronghold that carried the firstlings up and down in the blink of an eye. "I suppose the wand-wielders used their hocus-pocus to fly up and down." He offered his uninjured shoulder to his friend.

At last they reached the bottom of the staircase and hurried to the center of the vaulted basement where the carpet had been cut away to reveal an array of symbols engraved on the floor. Tungdil had been expecting to find a pool or a hole in the flagstones, but there was nothing. Magical springs were clearly different to the normal variety.

Boïndil examined the stone floor and held a hand above it tentatively. Nothing happened. "It's stopped working."

Tungdil produced the crystal tube containing the diamond. "Let's hope we can get it started." He placed the stone gently over the runes on the floor, and they waited with bated breath.

The trembling continued; in fact, it seemed to intensify. Cracks were spreading through the base of the tower, and fragments of stone rained from the vaulted ceiling, crashing around them.

"The tower won't take much more," said Boïndil, running his hand along the wall. "When it goes down, it will take the other towers and the conference chamber with it. Scholar, we need to get out."

Tungdil was staring at the runes, willing them to come alive and pulse with light. The diamond looked dull and lifeless. *Maybe I need to smash the tube.*

"Give me that," he said, reaching for the crow's beak. Taking aim, he brought the butt of the weapon against the glass, smashing it to pieces. The diamond survived unscathed, but nothing happened. "What's wrong with the accursed thing?" bellowed Tungdil. "In the name of Vraccas, come alive!" He whacked it again with the crow's beak. "Come alive, why don't you!"

After the third blow, the dwarves gave up. Doubtless there was a way of releasing the magic energy, but neither of them knew how.

The shaking was becoming more violent.

Boïndil grabbed his friend by the shoulder. "We'll be buried alive in a moment," he growled. "Quick, let's go."

Tungdil grabbed the diamond and they hurried out of the vaults as fast as their heavy legs and ravaged bodies would allow.

At the door to the tower, they found the corpse of the monster, surrounded by a ring of dead dwarves, and a little further, they discovered the remains of the avatars' guards, but of the älfar there was no trace. The palace was deserted.

Wheezing and panting, they hurried down the sweeping stairs into the courtyard, running to catch up with Rodario, who was being carried to safety by a couple of dwarves.

This time they made straight for the gates, knowing that the runes had lost their power. The bleached bones of intruders who had been stuck by magic to the walls now lay scattered on the ground. Porista had lost its magic.

The next ferocious quake proved too much for the tower.

Turning, they watched as the glorious palace of Lios Nudin was broken apart. The tower above the wellspring was shaking like corn in the wind, tilting wildly from side to side. Suddenly, the walls crumbled and the uppermost third of the tower broke off.

The deadly chunk of masonry crashed into the highest tower, smashing through its walls. The tower collapsed, raining chunks of marble over the palace and destroying the copper dome. One by one the sable towers crashed to the ground.

Clouds of dust rose from the debris, rolling toward them like a vast brown wave and obscuring their view. Chips of marble flew through the air, and the sound of splitting stone echoed endlessly through the city.

Crouched behind the outer walls, they waited for the devastation to end. Dust clogged their eyes and nostrils, clinging to them like thick brown fog. Those who hadn't thought to cover their mouths and noses were already coughing and struggling to breathe.

At last the ground stopped shaking and everything came to rest.

Tungdil wiped the dust from his eyes and washed his face with a handful of snow. *Vraccas protect us.*

Nothing remained of the palace's former splendor. Tons of marble had flattened its lofty chambers, burying cycles of scholarship under its weight. It was as if the pillaged wellspring had used the last of its energy to destroy the seat of Girdlegard's mystic learning, which served no purpose now that the magic was gone. In any case, no one in Girdlegard knew anything of the mystic arts; the last of the magi was dead, and there was no one to take her place.

Thoughtfully, Tungdil closed his fingers around the diamond. *What am I going to do with you?*

He heard the tread of many feet and the familiar sound of jangling chain mail. Through the mist, the firstling queen and her warriors, accompanied by Gemmil and his dwarves, marched toward them. Tungdil spotted Balyndis's smiling face at the front of the parade.

Xamtys had survived the battle with only minor injuries and her four-pronged mace glistened with enemy blood. "Thank Vraccas you're all right! When the tower came down, we feared the worst."

"Who knows what the rest of Girdlegard looks like," Tungdil said grimly. "For all we know, Porista may have come off lightly compared to the other cities." In spite of his bleak mood, he couldn't help smiling at Balyndis.

She came over and gave him a careful hug. "We routed the avatars' army."

"And we routed the avatars," rasped Rodario. "You missed the performance of a lifetime. Tungdil and I defeated the eoîl. The blasted creature was an—"

"Apparition," said Tungdil quickly. "The eoîl was made of mist, like the spirit that corrupted Nudin." He spoke loudly and deliberately, hoping that Rodario would take the hint. If the dwarves found out that an elf maiden was to blame for the destruction, the fragile truce between the dwarven kingdoms and Liútasil's folk would be endangered, and even the humans would start to take sides. In the eyes of some, the crimes of an individual justified the punishment of an entire kingdom or folk.

Xamtys wasn't fooled. "How did you defeat the apparition without Keenfire?"

"A fatal error on the part of the eoîl," explained Rodario, playing along with the deceit. "He assumed human form, which is to say, he made himself mortal. You should have seen the battle—he fought like a devil, but I stabbed him in the chest and our twice victorious hero dealt the final blow."

Snow was still falling, pushing the clouds of dust to the

ground. The air cleared and the little group could breathe again.

Xamtys shot Tungdil a knowing look, but allowed the story to stand, preferring not to challenge their victory in front of the jubilant troops. "How about we get these three to camp?" she said, eying Tungdil, Rodario, and Boïndil's wounds. "My warriors will take care of the dead."

Tungdil started off, supported by Balyndis, and promptly trod on something small and hard.

Without really knowing why, he bent down and fumbled in the snow until his fingers closed around a finger-length shard of stone. He picked it up: It was green, slightly charred, and specked with frozen blood.

Narmora's malachite! He pocketed it quickly before anyone could see. "Just a bit of stone," he told Balyndis. "Nothing valuable, I'm afraid."

The news of the victory spread quickly through Porista.

Relieved citizens pressed their faces to the windows to watch the dwarves march past. It wasn't long before they poured out of their houses to clap, cheer, and supply the warriors with food and hot drinks. In no time, Rodario and the dwarves found themselves at the center of an unexpected victory parade.

Tungdil and his kinsfolk thanked the citizens for their kindness. It wasn't in their nature to celebrate in front of strangers, but their tired, bearded faces revealed their contentment.

Rodario was altogether less reserved, waving majestically from his stretcher and playing to the crowd.

"Fellow citizens, prepare yourself for the story of how I, the fabulous Rodario, and my trusty companion, Tungdil

Goldhand, defeated the godlike eoîl. I look forward to seeing you in my theater." He raised his voice. "Long live the dwarves and long live Porista!" The crowd roared approvingly and cheered the handsome hero.

Boïndil shook his head in disbelief.

"What?" said the impresario shamelessly. "I have to use these opportunities. I'll be reopening the Curiosum in a while."

Tungdil was busy thinking about what to tell Xamtys and the dwarven kings. He was inclined to stick to the story about the mist. *If Rodario keeps quiet, no one need know that the eoîl was an elf. Sometimes it's better to hide the truth.* He certainly didn't intend to confess that the accursed shard of malachite was in his possession, but the diamond was a different matter. He needed the others' help to keep the magic in safe hands.

With the city behind them, the full extent of the damage was revealed.

The quakes had opened deep, dark trenches through the frozen fields, and in some places the ground had opened up and swallowed everything for hundreds of paces. Fortunately, the dwarven encampment had survived the tremors, a deep crack that passed through its middle somehow having zigzagged round every single tent, preserving them all.

"Xamtys and Gemmil's losses weren't too bad," said Balyndis, helping Tungdil to lie down. She was doing her best to distract him while a physician examined his wounds. "The älfar took the pressure off the firstlings and free-lings, but the thirdlings weren't so lucky. The northern front was a bloodbath. The avatars' soldiers were massed behind the walls. The thirdlings are good warriors, but only a handful survived."

The physician removed the dressing from Tungdil's leg and opened the wound to check for infection.

"What of Salfalur?" growled Tungdil, gritting his teeth against the growing urge to scream.

She shook her head. "He and Lorimbas died in the battle. Our warriors are looking for their remains."

Tungdil's relief was mingled with disappointment. It was a fitting end for a dwarf killer, but it robbed him of the chance to avenge his murdered parents—and poor Myr. "Do you think the news has reached the eternal smithy? I'd like his victims to know that he's dead."

"I'm sure they do," she said, bending down to kiss him on the forehead. For a moment they allowed themselves to feel at one, united by the love that would bind them together for the rest of their lives.

Just then the fur drape at the entrance to the tent was pulled back, and Furgas charged in. He scanned the wounded dwarves, spotted Tungdil, and rushed to his side. His eyes were red from crying.

"Tungdil, thank goodness you're all right!" He clasped the dwarf's hand and shook it vigorously. "They said you might know where to find Narmora. I've been looking for her everywhere. One moment, she was fighting at the gates, and then she . . ." A tear trickled down his cheek and his lower lip quivered. "Where is she, Tungdil?" he whispered thickly. "I've just buried my daughter. I can't bury my wife."

A chill came over Tungdil. *Even little Dorsa wasn't spared.*

Inside he railed at the eoîl and the implacable stone of judgment. It was true that Narmora's daughter was quarter älf, but no baby deserved such a fate.

"She died in a duel with the eoîl," said Tungdil. He wanted Furgas to remember Narmora as a heroine who had given her life in the fight against evil. "She tried to save Dorsa from the power of the diamond, but the eoîl was too strong. None of us could stop him draining the force fields."

Furgas let out a despairing howl and buried his hands in his face. His loud sobs echoed through the dwarves' hearts, bringing tears to Tungdil's eyes. Furgas had paid more dearly than anyone for the avatars' defeat. Balyndis, moved by his grief, put her arm around his shoulders.

"What was the point?" he asked in a muffled voice. "What was the point of all that suffering?" He raised his head and looked accusingly at Tungdil. "We went to war to save Girdlegard, because you said there was a threat." He jumped up and pointed to the door. "But what happened? Nothing! My wife died in vain. The avatars wanted to free us from evil, and what did we do? We fought them." He sat down slowly. "If we'd helped them, it would never have come to this. Narmora and Dorsa would be alive . . ."

"Furgas," Tungdil said soothingly. "You've lost the two people most precious to you, but the stone of judgment doesn't work like that. The eoîl wouldn't—"

"We could have shown them the way to Toboribor and led them to Borwôl. We could have taken them to every single evil creature in Girdlegard without endangering innocent lives, and they would have wiped the beasts out with their army. They only used their murderous magic because we attacked them—and it cost me my wife and child." He got up and looked at Tungdil bitterly. "We attacked them because you told us to. We followed the dwarves' advice and we trusted you—everyone in Girdlegard trusted you—but this time you were wrong. Palandiell save me from the charity of the dwarves."

He turned away, ignoring Tungdil's pleas. Pulling the tent flap back angrily, he disappeared outside.

"Let him be," advised Balyndis. "It's no wonder he can't think straight when his heart is full of grief. Give him some time."

The physician cleared his throat to get their attention. "I'm afraid there's a shard of metal in your bone. I'll have to get it out." He handed his patient a metal bar wrapped in leather. Tungdil smiled and tried to give it back, but the physician shook his head. "You'll need it. It's a painful business."

Tungdil put the bar between his teeth and Balyndis squeezed his hand while the physician's assistants exposed the bone by pulling back the flesh with metal hooks. A pair of tongs closed around the shard and the physician began to pull. Tungdil didn't have time to clamp his jaws around the bar; his mind had shut down.

Porista,
Former Realm of Lios Nudin,
Girdlegard,
Winter, 6235th/6236th Solar Cycle

The citizens found a use for the fissures resulting from the quakes and saved themselves the effort of breaking open the frozen earth to bury the enemy dead.

The avatars' soldiers were tossed unceremoniously into the trenches and packed down with rubble from the palace, of which nothing remained intact.

Faraway from the men, the fallen dwarves were laid to rest in individual graves. Firstlings were buried next to thirdlings, and thirdlings next to freelings, a fitting end for the comrades-in-arms. Tungdil refused to believe that Vraccas would close his smithy to honorable dwarves of any provenance who upheld his commandments. For the first time in history, the folks were at peace.

Boëndal Hookhand of the clan of the Swinging Axes would return to the Blue Range as a hero, but not in the way that Boïndil and Tungdil had hoped. Too severely burned for the healers to help him, the plucky secondling had died of his wounds.

Boïndil and Tungdil laid him on a shield and carried him, still dressed in his imposing armor as befitted a warrior, through the encampment and into Porista. The funeral procession came to a halt on the southern outskirts of the city. A group of firstlings had volunteered to help Boïndil carry his twin to the secondling kingdom where he would be laid to rest in his beloved Blue Range.

"I couldn't bury him here," said a broken-hearted Boïndil. The loss of his twin was a blow from which he would never recover. Part of his soul had died. "He wanted to be buried at the High Pass. He'll always be keeping watch over Girdlegard and protecting our kingdom from Tion's hordes."

Bowing his head, Tungdil looked sorrowfully at his dead friend and touched his cold, scorched fingers. He wasn't afraid to shed a tear. *Forgive me for missing your funeral,* he apologized. *I'll visit your grave when my work is done. I hope to bring good news* . . . He turned to Boïndil and embraced him as they mourned the loss of the brother and companion with whom they had shared so much.

"Who's going to calm my fiery furnace now?" sniffed his twin forlornly. Salty tears rolled down his cheeks, adding to the glistening pearl at the bottom of his beard.

"I'll join you again soon," promised Tungdil in a choked voice. "We'll drink a tankard or two to Boëndal and remember the old times. He's in the smithy, you know, with Sanda and all the others who died in the fight against the avatars. Vraccas will have given him a proper hero's welcome."

They bade each other farewell; then Boïndil signaled to the firstlings to help him lift the shield. Tungdil made his way dolefully back to his tent, where an anxious Rodario was waiting for him.

"He's gone," he sighed.

"I know," said Tungdil. "He left just now."

The impresario shook his head. "I mean Furgas, not Boïndil. The best prop master in Girdlegard has vanished without trace." He shrugged sadly. "I don't know what to do."

Tungdil poured himself and his guest some tea. "With the Curiosum?"

"Who cares about the Curiosum!" snorted Rodario. "Admittedly, the special effects won't be the same without him, but Furgas was my *friend*." He took a sip of his tea.

"The poor fellow has been through such a lot. First he was attacked and poisoned, then his son died before he woke up from the coma, and now, half a cycle later, he's had to bury his baby daughter and as for Narmora . . . there's nothing left but ash. Both dead in a single orbit!" He sighed again, this time more deeply. "Can a heart survive such sorrow? What if he tries to . . ."

"I'm sure he'll be fine," said Tungdil, doing his best to sound convincing. "If he wanted to take his own life, he'd have done it in Porista, where his children and his wife met their end. I expect he's gone away for a while to clear his mind."

Rodario hoped fervently that the dwarf was right. "Fine, I'll go with your theory, hero of Porista. It's cheerier than mine."

"Do you know what, Rodario?" confessed Tungdil. "I'm tired of being a hero. Furgas was upset and he said a few things that got me thinking." He reported their exchange and took another sip of tea. "The thing is, he was probably right: maybe I *should* have helped the avatars rather than oppose them," he concluded sadly.

"I beg to differ," said Rodario, watching the steam rise from his tea. "It must have slipped my friend's mind that five towns were destroyed when the avatars marched on Dsôn Balsur. Five towns, and forty thousand men, women, and children! Think how many would have died if they'd marched on Toboribor and Borwôl as well! Besides, the so-called avatars wanted to carve up Girdlegard among themselves. Lirkim said they'd be mightier than kings, omnipotent and invincible. We wouldn't have lasted more than a couple of orbits with them at our helm." He sipped his tea. "No, Tungdil, we did the only thing we could. We saved our homeland and we rid the people in the Outer Lands of a band of tyrannical magi, not to mention an unhinged eoîl." He nodded at Tungdil and smiled. "Furgas was right to be angry, but he was wrong to be angry with you. Girdlegard is indebted to Tungdil Goldhand and the dwarves; there isn't enough gold in these ranges to repay you."

Applause sounded from the door. The dwarven monarchs—Balendilín, Gandogar, Gemmil, Glaïmbar, and Xamtys—were gathered at the entrance to the tent, accompanied by Prince Mallen.

"Well said," agreed the ruler of Idoslane. "Actors are prone to exaggeration, but it's impossible to speak too highly of the dwarves. The men and women of Girdlegard won't forget their obligation to the children of the Smith."

"To *some* of his children," Tungdil corrected him. He studied the faces of the four dwarven kings and the firstling queen. His mood was somber. "The freelings and the thirdlings defended Girdlegard in our darkest hour, and the firstlings played their part as well, but the rest of you allowed yourselves to be fooled into leaving Girdlegard. A dwarven king should be strong enough and wise enough to stand his ground."

Gandogar bowed his head. "Tungdil is right; I shouldn't have ceded to the thirdlings. I won't fail the dwarves again."

He left the doorway and walked to the center of the tent. Everyone took a seat. After all that had happened, the dwarven rulers had plenty to discuss, and Mallen had indicated that he wanted to share some news as well.

"Before we start, I'd like to ask Tungdil Goldhand to be my counselor," said Gandogar solemnly. "We've all seen the folly of ignoring your advice."

Tungdil was flattered by the offer; the king of all dwarves wanted him, a thirdling, an exile, and a foundling to be his personal counselor. But the Nôd'onn-slaying, eoîl-killing hero had other things to accomplish before he could consider accepting such an offer. The high king agreed to let him think the matter over.

It was Mallen's turn to speak. "The tidings I bring will please some and grieve others, but mostly, I think, you'll be shocked." He paused, looking gravely at the circle of expectant faces. "When King Belletain requested permission for his troops to cross my land, I knew his help would be welcomed in Porista and, not realizing his intentions, I agreed. As you know, his army never got here." He took a deep breath. "Instead of heading west to Porista, Belletain's army went east—toward the Black Range." He produced a crumpled letter from his robe. "When I realized what had happened, I demanded an explanation, and Belletain wrote to tell me that King Lorimbas had failed to honor his treaty with Urgon, and he, Belletain, had been deprived of the fourthlings' gold. By way of compensation, he ordered his soldiers to raid the thirdlings' stronghold and carry off their gold." He handed the letter to Gandogar. "King Gandogar, there was an alliance between Belletain and Lorimbas—an alliance against you."

"Are the soldiers still there?" asked Xamtys, while the high king stared at the letter in shocked disbelief.

Mallen shook his head. "I sent scouts to the Black Range. The gates were open when they got there and the watchtowers were deserted. Inside, the corridors and halls were strewn with the corpses of dwarf women and children. Belletain had ordered his soldiers to show no mercy to Lorimbas's folk."

Tungdil didn't want to believe what he was hearing. "There must have been some survivors," he said hopelessly.

"Dwarven kingdoms are full of passageways and secret vaults," said Xamtys with conviction. "The thirdlings are probably in hiding."

To the dwarves' dismay, Mallen shook his head. "My scouts reported that most of the passageways have collapsed. The kingdom was all but destroyed in the quake. I'm not saying there weren't survivors, but their number will be small."

"A whole folk, all but wiped out," murmured Tungdil. He had always dreamed of a time when the dwarves could live together without fear or suspicion. *But not like this, Vraccas.* He turned to Gandogar. "You asked me to be your counselor, Your Majesty. My advice would be to send an army to guard the Black Range. Without Lorimbas and his warriors, the Eastern Pass is open to attack."

"I'm sure the surviving thirdlings will welcome your help," said Gemmil. "It could be the beginning of a new era, an era of peace for the dwarves. The most zealous dwarf killers are dead and buried in Porista—the others can't afford to continue the feud."

"Belletain's treachery won't go unpunished," said Mallen. "The rulers of Girdlegard shall hear of how he turned his back on the allies for the sake of some gold. The mad king of Urgon must be stopped before he takes it into his addled head to invade another dwarven kingdom."

The dwarves agreed wholeheartedly.

"There's something I'd like to tell you," said Tungdil. "I haven't mentioned it until now because the fewer who know, the better." He produced a small leather pouch containing the diamond and placed it on the table. "As kings and queens, you deserve to hear the truth." He took out the stone. "This is the last remaining source of magic in Girdlegard. The diamond is powerful enough to turn a magus into a deity. The eoîl was in the process of channeling its magic when Rodario and I cut him down."

"I was merely the sidekick," demurred Rodario with a smile.

Everyone crowded around to examine the twinkling surface of the beautiful gem.

Gandogar, king of the gem-cutting fourthlings, was an authority on diamonds. "It's magnificent," he said admiringly. "The craftsmanship is dwarven in quality, but a gem like this would be mentioned in our chronicles. The technique is different too." He picked it up carefully and held it in front of the candle. The flame, seemingly enamored by the flawless surface, leaned toward the diamond, which caught and amplified the light.

The awed silence was broken by Tungdil. "The eoîl spoke of undergroundlings. He probably got the diamond from dwarves in the Outer Lands."

Gandogar set down the stone.

"You say it would give a magus almost limitless power," said Mallen, frowning. "With luck, none of our enemies will learn of its existence, but it needs to be under constant guard."

"Exactly," said Tungdil. He turned to Gandogar. "You've

had a look at the stone, and I've made a few drawings." He got up, walked to his desk, and picked up a sheet of parchment. "I've written down the exact measurements and sketched the cut. I propose we make copies and give them to the rulers of Girdlegard. The seven human monarchs, the dwarven rulers, and Liútasil will each receive a diamond to guard." He looked at them earnestly. "Build vaults, set traps, employ sentries—do whatever is necessary to ensure the stone is safe." Tungdil's plan met with approval.

"How will we know which of us is guarding the original?" asked Xamtys.

"We won't—that's the idea. I'll keep the diamond until Gandogar has made the replicas. Then we'll put them in a pouch, add the original, and shake them together. After that, we'll trust to Vraccas and draw the stones at random. You might draw a replica, you might draw the original, but neither you, nor I, nor anyone who chances to learn of the stone's existence will be able to tell." He turned away from Xamtys to address the other monarchs. "This is Girdlegard's biggest secret. Only the members of this council, Lord Liútasil, and the other human rulers must know of the stone."

Balendilín stroked his beard. "Without the diamond, we'll never have another magus or maga. The only magic in Girdlegard is hidden in the stone. How long do you propose we hide it?"

"I don't know, but maybe in time we'll entrust the diamond to a human, an elf, or a dwarf and start a new line of magi. The right individual would know how to identify the stone." He returned the diamond to its pouch and stowed it behind his belt. "If you ask me, we'll be better off without any magic for a while." No one was inclined to disagree.

Next they made arrangements for sending an allied army to the ruined thirdling kingdom with the dual purpose of rescuing survivors and sealing the Eastern Pass. In future, the dwarves would have to travel between the ranges on foot because the underground network had been destroyed by the quakes.

The meeting ended late that night. Prince Mallen was the first to leave, followed by Queen Xamtys and the dwarven kings. King Glaïmbar stayed behind to talk to Tungdil.

The fifthling monarch held out his hand. "How can I ever repay you, Tungdil Goldhand? First you saved my life in the Gray Range, then you rescued Balyndis from the avatars."

Tungdil shook hands with him gladly. He couldn't bring himself to hate Glaïmbar for stealing Balyndis; it seemed wrong to harbor grudges when fortune had treated others more harshly. "I came to the aid of a dear friend. You would have done the same."

"If I were to ask you what you wished for more than anything, what would you say?" asked Glaïmbar levelly, looking him in the eye.

"I would ask you to give up Balyndis so she could follow her heart," he answered honestly. "But since it's not in your power, I won't." He gripped the king's hand. "My greatest wish is that you look after her, honor her, and make her happy."

"You're a better dwarf than me, Tungdil Goldhand," said Glaïmbar, shaking his head in wonder. He turned to leave, then stopped and looked back at Tungdil. "They should have made you king," he said sincerely. The tent flap closed behind him.

Tungdil gazed after him, deep in thought. "Perhaps," he murmured, smiling. "But I was the one who turned down the crown." He poured himself another mug of tea.

He knew it was time for bed. Before he could take the diamond to Gandogar in the fourthling kingdom he had to travel north to Âlandur and east to Dsôn Balsur. A good deal of snow, sludge, and mud would pass beneath his boots before the coming of spring.

He smiled, remembering how Rodario had looked at him in horror when he announced his intention to travel alone to the älfar's kingdom.

"What in the name of Palandiell do you want in that confounded place? Don't tell me you want to look for survivors! You saw for yourself that the stone of judgment worked."

Tungdil had told him that he wasn't interested in the älfar; he was after his ax.

He carried his tea to his mattress, removed his fur cloak, and slipped beneath the covers.

Before he fell asleep, he got up again to throw a few logs on the camp stove to banish the winter chill. *It's my duty to see this through*, he thought sleepily, closing his eyes.

X

Tungdil peered up at the lofty branches laden with snow. All winter the boughs had bowed and sagged beneath the extra weight, proudly refusing to break. With the worst of the winter over, the sun was strengthening, freeing the trees from the snow.

Springtime beckoned, and soon Girdlegard would be awash with color. His old friend Frala used to love the first orbits of spring.

So many of my friends are dead, he thought gloomily as he made his way between the mighty trunks.

On his previous visit to Âlandur, he and his company had been given a cool reception by the elves, but this time his presence seemed to go unnoticed.

He hadn't seen a soul since he first set foot in the elven kingdom two orbits ago, following the narrow path deeper and deeper among the trees. He wondered when he was going to be met by Liútasil, the elven lord with claret-colored hair.

The answer came sooner than expected.

On rounding a corner, he came to the end of the path and entered a clearing. In front of him was a vast green tent that seemed to be made of satin. An elven archer was posted at each of the corners, and Liútasil, dressed in ceremonial robes, hailed him from the door. Smiling warmly, he shook the dwarf's hand.

"Congratulations, Tungdil Goldhand. Everyone in Girdlegard must have heard of your victory." He gestured for Tungdil to enter the tent. "Come in. We thought you might like somewhere to rest your weary legs."

Tungdil bowed to the elven lord. "Thank you." Stepping inside, he was struck by the splendor of the tent.

Dwarves and humans built their tents with canvas and plain wooden poles, but Liútasil's shelter was made of satin and elegant pillars of aromatic wood, each carved with intricate hunting scenes and embellished with runes. Tungdil wondered how he could bear to dismantle such a beautifully crafted tent.

It was pleasantly warm inside, thanks to a pair of stoves, and decorative lanterns hung from the ceiling, casting a pleasant glow. To Tungdil's surprise, the air smelled neither of soot nor burning tallow.

Two chairs and a table had been placed at the center of the tent, and steam was rising from an array of hot dishes.

"You must be hungry from your journey," said the elf, signaling for Tungdil to be seated. "I suppose you're here to scold me for not sending my archers to Porista."

Tungdil took off his heavy winter coat to reveal the suit of armor that had saved him from the avatars' firebolts. He took a sip of warm beer. After orbits of cold victuals and water, it was good to thaw his insides. He was ready to bet that the elves had prepared the brew with him in mind: It was spiced with pine needles and tasted stronger and maltier than the smooth ales favored by Liútasil's kind.

"No one blames you for not sending your archers. It was curiosity that brought me here." He paused. "If you'd joined the allied army, you would have fought alongside the älfar, and no one could demand that of the elves. At least, that's what the humans are saying. The dwarves put it down to the trouble in Dsôn Balsur. They didn't resent your absence—no child of the Smith would willingly act as a buffer between the älfar and the elves." He piled his plate with victuals, none of which looked familiar. "All things considered, the allied army was better off without you." He popped a morsel into his mouth, hoping it would taste like meat, which—thankfully— it did.

The elf could tell that Tungdil had a different theory about his motives for staying away. "Well," he prompted. "Why do you suppose we didn't come?"

"I don't *suppose*," said Tungdil, looking him in the eye. "I *know*. You see, the reason you didn't help us was because of the eoîl. It's all right," he reassured him, "Rodario and I won't tell anyone that the avatar-conjurers were taking orders from an elf. We don't want any more feuds." He paused to measure the effect of his words. The guilty expression on Liútasil's face indicated that his suspicions were correct. "Lord Liútasil, you owe me the truth. Who was the eoîl?"

Liútasil's fork hovered by his mouth, then he set down his cutlery and left the meat on his plate. "I admit it, Tungdil, you're right. My archers would sooner die than take up their bows against an eoîl. Her most fervent supporters wanted to ride to Porista to join her army, but thank Sitalia I convinced them not to go. The eoîl and her confederates were wrong to take the lives of innocent humans."

"She *was* an elf, then. Did she come from Âlandur?"

Liútasil pushed away his plate and poured himself a goblet of mulled wine. "Eoîls don't have kingdoms or homes. They're mythical beings, part of our legends." He took a long draft of wine and began his tale.

Sitalia, daughter of Palandiell, created my people from light, pure earth, and dew.

She taught my ancestors the art of healing and told them the secrets of nature and life. Her first commandment was respect for life in all its forms, and she frowned on destruction. Music, dance, poetry, painting, sculpture, those were our pastimes, and we knew nothing of hardship or war.

My forefathers' endeavors met with incomprehension and hostility from the humans and dwarves. Sitalia, realizing that her children were unhappy, gave them a new home where they could live in seclusion among the trees. The eldest of our kind were touched a second time by the hand of their creator, and they became our teachers, the higher elves.

Meanwhile, the dark lord Tion grew weary of the gods' creations. His fellow divinities had applied themselves to the creation of good, so he rebelled by spreading evil. He buried his creation in the earth like a seed, knowing that it would grow and multiply with weed-like speed. Orcs, ogres, trolls, kobolds, bögnilim, giants, and other dark creatures were born.

Cycles later, the evil was brought to the surface by salt miners, gold diggers, and dwarves.

Tion gave wings to the evil and cast it into the air to be carried on the wind.

Worse was to come.

The lord of darkness mixed his evil into lakes and rivers, and those who drank thereof were robbed of their innocence. Envy, greed, hatred, and lust entered the hearts of the elves, dwarves, and men. Next, Tion pierced the flesh of the other gods' children with a thorn that he called age, and the races of Girdlegard became mortal.

His dark work was noticed by Sitalia, who removed the thorns from the higher elves before the damage was done. And so the eoîls were created.

Liútasil emptied his glass. "So you see why no child of Sitalia could take up arms against an eoîl. They're as old as time, created by Sitalia herself. The eoîls are the source of our knowledge, Sitalia's warriors, fighting Tion in all his forms. They're sacred beings, worshipped and revered." He paused. "Sitalia would kill us if we dared to challenge an eoîl."

Tungdil nodded, although the explanation seemed decidedly flawed. He took another mouthful. "Did this particular eoîl deserve to be worshipped? She wasn't very complimentary about the elves. According to her, you're lesser beings."

The elf smiled good-naturedly. "The eoîls think we're inferior because we're tarnished by age. *They* live as long as they like."

"Or as long as we let them," said Tungdil, picturing the eoîl's body at the bottom of the tower. "Are the other eoîls like the one in Porista? It's odd they're not mentioned in our chronicles."

"The eoîls are no business of the men and the dwarves. We rarely speak of our history to outsiders." He refilled his goblet. "Most eoîls are peaceful beings. I'm personally acquainted with two of their kind—pure souls who devote their time to teaching the arts. Painting and singing are their passions, not destruction."

Tungdil was surprised and encouraged by Liútasil's willingness to answer his questions. "The eoîl in Porista was more powerful than any magus," he began. "She drained the energy from Porista, but I was wondering . . . Can elves work magic too? There's no knowing what danger could be heading our way, and perhaps the next magus will be an—"

Liútasil shook his head. "No, Tungdil. You won't find a magus in Âlandur. Sitalia doesn't grant us the gift of magic anymore."

"There's no chance of an elf being born with magical talents?"

"I've waited cycles for such an occurrence," he confessed. "Four hundred cycles, to be precise. Every baby in Âlandur is tested for magical ability, but to no avail. Thankfully, the älfar have been destroyed, so we don't need a magus to protect us anymore." He smiled. "No wonder they call you 'scholar'. At this rate there won't be anything you don't know."

"I wouldn't want to know *everything*—it would make life very dull." The dwarf sipped his beer and plucked up the courage to try a strange-looking fruit. It tasted of berries and mint. "I wanted to ask you about the älfar, actually. Who are the immortal siblings? I saw them in Porista. I'm not sure what happened to them after they attacked the eoîl." He leaned over the table. "Do they live forever like eoîls? Are they free from the thorn of age as well?"

Tungdil could tell that Liútasil wasn't prepared to answer. Elves and älfar had more in common than the proud archers of Âlandur liked to admit. He thought about Narmora, remembering how she had worked magic even before her transformation through the malachite. "The älfar can extinguish flames with their thoughts. They move soundlessly, they don't leave footprints, and they meld with the dark." An unpleasant thought occurred to him. "Can the immortal siblings work magic? *Real* magic?"

"What do you mean?" Liútasil seemed puzzled.

"Could the immortal siblings have used magic to leave the tower and hide from the stone of judgment?"

Liútasil sat up straight and looked him in the eye. "The immortal siblings are as much of a mystery to the elves as to the dwarves or the men. I'm afraid I can't help you." He thought for a moment. "In my opinion, they might be able to work real magic—but I doubt they could escape the power of the stone." He raised his goblet. "I'd like to propose a toast—to the destruction of the älfar!" He clunked his glass against the dwarf's tankard.

Tungdil decided not to probe any further. Liútasil's sudden evasiveness warned him that further questions would be unwelcome. "I won't breathe a word of what you've told me," he assured him. "But there's one last thing I need to ask: What will you do if Girdlegard is attacked by another eoîl?"

The elven lord pressed his fingertips together. "Nothing, Tungdil Goldhand. To do anything would be folly." He picked up his cutlery and resumed his meal.

They ate in silence, savoring the elven feast, then Tungdil gave his account of the battle, the death of enemies and friends, the destruction of the thirdlings, and the power of the diamond. He made no mention of his intention to travel to Dsôn Balsur, merely saying that he was planning to join Gandogar in the Brown Range.

At last it was time for Liútasil to leave the tent so that Tungdil could get some sleep. Before he went, he promised the dwarf that he would take good care of his diamond when it arrived. He handed Tungdil a little backpack. "It's a tent," he explained. "You won't have to worry about wind, rain, sun, snow, or frost. From now on you'll sleep so soundly that you'll think you're in a dwarven hall. I'll pray to Sitalia to pardon you for the death of the eoîl."

They shook hands and Tungdil was left alone in the tent. He finished his beer. *I killed an immortal elf.* He let out a little burp and grinned. *I guess that makes her mortal.*

Former Kingdom of Dsôn Balsur,
Girdlegard,
Spring, 6236th Solar Cycle

Tungdil came to the end of the path that the allies had burned through the forests of Dsôn Balsur and crossed the plains to the fortress of Arviû. From there he continued to the lip of an enormous crater left by the fist of an angry god—or so it seemed to Tungdil.

Looking down, he surveyed the deserted city of Dsôn, one-time capital of the älfar. No dwarf had ventured this far into the älvish kingdom; in fact, only the älfar and their prisoners had ever seen the fabled city, and no one would have thought it possible that an outsider could get there without drawing his ax.

The only impediment to Tungdil's progress was his leg, which hadn't recovered from his duel with Ondori. Since crossing the border, he had disappeared up to his boots in mud and battled his way through waist-high grass, but he hadn't encountered another living soul.

There was no sign of the älfar. Every step of the way he had steeled himself for finding survivors or receiving a black-fletched arrow in his back, but it was deathly still in the älvish kingdom. It seemed the stone of judgment had done its work.

There was something grimly fascinating about the architecture below. It had nothing in common with elven art, and its sinister darkness was palpable from his vantage point two miles above the city.

The most formidable structure, a white tower made of bones, rose from a solitary pinnacle at the center of the crater. From a distance, the pale needle seemed to pierce the clouds, and Tungdil knew at once where he would find his ax.

Vraccas be with me. He began his descent into the darkness of the city below.

As soon as he left the rim of the crater, the light dimmed and he felt an unpleasant chill. The strange city had an indefinable aura of horror, and he tightened his grip on his ax. Every sense was keyed and his ears detected the slightest noise—loose shutters rattling, squeaking metal, groaning wood, and the whistling of the wind around the sinister roofs.

He reached the bottom of the crater and continued along streets of pale white gravel that crunched beneath his boots. Every step seemed deafening and it took all his courage to keep going. From time to time, gray smoke rose from the roofs and ash rained down on him as if the dead älfar were determined to hinder his advance.

His nervousness surprised him. He checked his surroundings, looking left and right, peering down alleyways and bracing himself for attack. *I've fought orcs, slain beasts, and killed an immortal elf, so why am I scared of a deserted city?*

He walked and walked, realizing that the älvish city was much bigger than it had seemed. It was evening by the time he reached the base of the pinnacle and started up the steps. At last, panting with exertion, he got to the top just as the sun disappeared below the rim of the crater, plunging the city into darkness. Towering into the sky, the palace of bones shone blood-red in the setting sun, while down below the roofs of the houses glimmered with symbols and runes.

The hairs on his arms and on his neck stood on end. *What if the ghosts of the älfar haunt the city at night?* He waited, ax hefted, but nothing happened, although the runes continued to glow.

The wind was getting up. Samusin seemed to take pleasure in terrorizing the dwarf.

Gusts passed between the bleached bones of the tower, and every now and then Tungdil heard a mournful whistle like the muted scream of a soul whose bones had found no rest. Eye sockets glared at him accusingly from weathered skulls. Tungdil's instincts warned him to venture no further.

Heart pounding wildly, he strode to the entrance, pushed past the open door, and stepped into the tower.

The outer cladding of bone was obviously intended as decoration or as a sign of älvish power, for the tower was made of wood and stone. The passageways were hung with portraits, and Tungdil knew without looking too closely that the pictures weren't painted on canvas or with ordinary paint. Like their elven cousins, the älfar were natural artists, masters of the easel and brush, but they put their painterly talents to darker use.

He heard a sudden noise behind him. Somewhere in the tower, a door had slammed, and the noise resonated through the high-ceilinged passageways, lingering in the air. The last remaining lamps—the others had run out of fuel—flickered dangerously.

"Who's there?" He turned round and swallowed. "Come out and show yourself!" Silence reigned.

With growing dread, he continued down the passageway and came at last to a lofty door of tionium inscribed with mysterious älvish runes. *It's bound to be here . . .*

He pushed the door open and peered into a chamber of black marble. The chamber was hall-like in its proportions and peopled with strange statues made from the bones of many creatures. Some were painted, others bound with gold wire or tionium, or inlaid with gems and precious metals. Pictures, mosaics, and bizarre weaponry decorated the walls. At the center of the chamber, steps led up to a pair of empty thrones.

The glittering of diamonds alerted Tungdil to the ax.

Keenfire was hanging from the wall behind the thrones, abandoned and neglected, the symbol of an älvish triumph against the dwarves. For the älfar, the ax was useless.

Tungdil went over and reached for the haft. "So here's where you've been hiding." He gave it a gentle yank and Keenfire came away from the wall. After wiping it carefully with his sleeve, more because it had been in the hands of the älfar than because it was actually dirty, he took a few experimental swings, testing the balance. It was perfect. "No one will ever take you from me again," he whispered lovingly. "But I've got a job for you."

He reached into his pocket, pulled out the shard of malachite, and placed it on the third step leading up to the thrones. If any last remnants of evil—a wisp of Nôd'onn's soul, a trace of a dark spirit or any other demonic force—had escaped the stone of judgment and was sheltering in the malachite, it was about to be destroyed forever.

Tungdil raised the ax, swung it once around his head, and brought it down with all his might.

Light pulsed through the intarsia and the diamonds came to life, just as they had when Tungdil had taken on Nôd'onn in the Blacksaddle. A trail of light followed the swooping Keenfire as it smashed into the stone. The malachite broke apart, shattering into tiny pieces that scattered over the dark marble floor.

Now the mission is really over, Vraccas. It was a relief

to know that the last of the evil that had corrupted Nôd'onn and Narmora had finally been destroyed.

There was one thing left to do.

He took the lamps from their holders and hurled them against the walls. Oil spilled over the timber, splashing against the portraits and spattering the statues. Lowering his torch, he let the flames creep hungrily through the fuel.

Tungdil left the chamber and made for the exit, lighting fire after fire on his way. He was determined to raze the tower to the ground. There would be nothing left of the älvish city by the time a dwarf, elf, or human ventured this way.

Outside the tower, he looked back at the roaring flames. He was tired and he could feel the miles in his legs, but his desire to avoid sleeping in the älvish capital spurred him on.

Summoning all his energy, he made his way down the stairs and through the streets, lighting fires along the way.

Even as he began his ascent to the lip of the crater, a third of Dsôn was on fire, and the blaze was spreading, fanned by the wind sent by Samusin to confound and torment him.

The palace of the immortal siblings was burning like a giant torch. Red-hot debris fell from the walls, rolling down the hillside and setting fire to the buildings below. Soon the city would be an inferno.

Tungdil sat down and watched in satisfaction as the tower collapsed in a burst of flames. He could hear the sound of breaking timber even through the roaring fire. So far, there hadn't been any screams.

The last bastion of evil, and no one's here to save it from destruction. He got up, shook his weary legs and started up the steep stairs, determined to leave the darkness of Dsôn behind him. He was already looking forward to seeing the rising sun.

"The dead must be avenged," said a deep voice ahead of him. A broad figure appeared on the path and swung his weapon, aiming for Tungdil's chest.

The startled dwarf tried to block the blow with Keenfire, but his attacker was unexpectedly strong.

The weapon smashed against the haft of his ax, knocking him backward. He hit the ground hard and skidded a few paces, picking up speed down the muddy slope. He lost his helmet and came to a halt.

Even as he sat up, his attacker came at him again. The glare from the fire was so bright that Tungdil could only see his silhouette. *Too small for an älf, too big for a dwarf.*

The weapon whizzed toward him again, but this time he saw it and made no attempt to parry the blow. Nothing could stop a powerful war hammer. It flew past his head as he dropped to the ground.

Tungdil recognized the weapon, but its owner was dead. *He fell at Porista.*

Sliding his ax across the mud, Tungdil took aim at his attacker's right ankle. The blade met with resistance and Tungdil heard a groan. "Salfalur?" he asked incredulously.

He paid for his success with a blow to the chest. His breastplate, much stronger than his usual chain mail, protected his ribs and saved him from death.

"Well guessed, Tungdil," came the reply. "You should have known better than to believe I was dead. I swore to kill you, remember?" The hammer swung into view, on course for Tungdil's head. Tungdil jerked away at the last moment and the hammer smashed into the ground, spattering him with mud. He crawled back quickly, bracing himself against the side of the crater. "It wasn't easy to find you, Tungdil, but I never break my word."

Struggling upright, Tungdil faced his enemy. The thirdling was holding his war hammer in both hands and the runes on his face seemed to come alive in the flickering flames. Tungdil decided to save his breath; Salfalur would show no mercy, and neither would he.

Before the thirdling could strike, Tungdil swung his ax. Thanks to Keenfire, he felt confident of winning the duel, although his tired body seemed less certain.

Salfalur parried the blow with the haft of the hammer, let go with one hand and smashed his armored fist into Tungdil's face.

The spurs on Salfalur's knuckles tore through his skin and for a moment Tungdil saw stars, but he didn't let go of his ax, gripping it tightly even as the thirdling punched him a second time. Tungdil didn't have time to avoid the fist and it hit the left of his face, grazing his eye. Pain seared his mind and his vision went pink with blood.

Bellowing with rage, he thrust Keenfire forward, jerking it under the thirdling's chin.

Salfalur jumped away, only to swing his hammer and go back on the attack. Tungdil was hit in the chest again, but this time his breastplate caved in, pushing against his ribcage and making him gasp for breath. The combined power of Salfalur and his mighty weapon sent him flying several paces through the air. At last he hit the ground, panting frantically.

He heard Salfalur rush forward, ready to attack. In the glow of the fire, the thirdling looked like a living spark from the furnace of a vindictive god. His face was contorted with rage.

The sight of the furious thirdling gave Tungdil the will to fight.

I'm not dying here in Dsôn. Stubbornly, he hauled himself up on his ax and, flinging his arm out to the side, set off at a run toward his antagonist. The pain was excruciating, but he shut it out.

Shouting, they charged toward each other, each determined to deliver a fatal blow.

At last they met, weapons colliding with a steely clatter, the blade of Tungdil's ax snagging on the hammer. The joint force of the two blows sent both weapons spinning out of the antagonists' hands.

Keenfire flew to the right, the hammer to the left. Tungdil stumbled to fetch his ax, while Salfalur ran after his weapon.

Tungdil bent down, picked up the ax and turned, determined not to lose sight of his enemy. For the third time the hammer slammed into his chest. Salfalur had got there first.

The head of the hammer found the dell in his breastplate, and his sternum cracked. Pain shot through him as he flew through the air and dropped to the ground, flailing on his back like a beetle. His mind dimmed and a chill came over him, even though the crater was filling with warmth from the burning city.

Footsteps hurried toward him. "Ha, look at the dirty

thirdling who betrayed his own folk. It was worth dragging myself out of the mud in Porista and following you all those miles." The thirdling's shadow fell over him. "You deserve to die in agony, but this will do. Myr has been avenged at least."

"The dwarf killers have been wiped out," gasped Tungdil. "Your kinsfolk are dead. You'll be more alone than I ever was."

Salfalur kneeled beside him in the mud. "We haven't been wiped out, Tungdil. Our eyes and ears are in every clan in every kingdom and none of your friends know they're there. As soon as they get my summons, they'll join me in their hundreds and we'll found a new kingdom and seize the Black Range." He grabbed Tungdil's chin. "But you won't be around to see us throw your friends out of our stronghold. The children of Lorimbur will continue the feud, but your line is dead. It's time you joined your mother and father."

Tungdil tried to clear his mind. He was on the cusp of blacking out, but he couldn't allow himself to sink into eternal sleep. "You seem to have forgotten something," he mumbled, struggling to speak with the thirdling's hand around his mouth.

The smooth, tattooed skull came closer and Salfalur peered at him mockingly. Behind him, a house collapsed in a blaze of flames and sparks shot out, dancing around the thirdling's head and giving him a demonic look. "Hmm, let me think . . . You're lying in the mud, dying of your wounds. What could I possibly have forgotten?"

"The warrior's first commandment," gasped Tungdil. "Never let go of your ax." He sat up with a jerk, raising his right hand and striking with all his might. Keenfire bit horizontally into the skull of the startled Salfalur, embedding itself in the bone.

The thirdling went down as if felled by an arrow. His body twitched frantically, determined not to die, but his glazed, bloodied eyes showed that his soul had already departed.

Boïndil taught me well. Unable to rise, Tungdil lay in the mud, racked with pain.

Looking up at the stars and with one hand on Keenfire, he waited for death to claim him from the burning älvish city.

But death never came.

Tungdil, still sprawled on the path, listened as the flames retreated from the edge of the crater and returned to the city in search of wood.

He could sense that death was watching him like a scavenger hoping for food, but something was holding the darkness at bay.

Little by little the pain subsided until he felt confident enough to fall asleep without worrying that he might never wake up.

When he opened his eyes, the sun had barely moved in the sky and he felt rested but hungry. He sat up as best he could in his buckled armor, then unfastened the straps and took off his breastplate.

Carefully he touched his chest. The bones were intact and the pain had gone. His fingers came into contact with the pouch containing the diamond. He pulled out the stone and held it to the light.

Was I saved by the grace of Vraccas or by the diamond?
He glanced at Salfalur's corpse and was surprised by its
rotten state. Birds and maggots had stripped the flesh from
his face, and his body was bloated with gas as if death
were mocking the once proud warrior. *How long have I
been asleep?* He got up and staggered backwards.

Dsôn had vanished.

Every last building in the city had been razed to the
ground, leaving nothing but ash. Stone foundations were
the only indication of where the älfar's gruesome tower
had once stood.

There was no sign of smoke and the roaring fire had
fallen silent. He prodded the ash gingerly with his finger:
It was cold.

Gathering his damaged armor, he hurried up the path.
The mud had hardened to dirt, and he felt strong and
healthy, his wounds completely healed. He decided that
Vraccas had kept his inner furnace burning while he was
asleep. *The stone can't work magic on its own, and I'm
certainly no magus.*

On emerging from the crater, he spotted an army of
humans and elves approaching the city from the south,
no doubt alarmed by the smoke. Sunlight glittered on their
banners and armor.

There's nothing left for them to do, he thought. Rather
than wait for them to arrive, he struck out at once on a
northeasterly bearing.

The journey to the Brown Range took many orbits.

Tungdil enjoyed the solitude and had plenty of time to
think. He thought about Balyndis and Myr and what had
happened between them, the thirdlings, the future, and

where he wanted to go—to the freelings, to the fifthlings, or to Gandogar.

As he crossed the border into the hills of Urgon, his plan took shape.

His march through Urgon coincided with the preparations for the coronation. The fate of King Belletain was the talk of the boarding houses where Tungdil sought shelter and food. The mad king's betrayal of the allied army had cost him the support of his subjects, and lost him his throne.

Tungdil was pleased to be back among humans. It reminded him of happier times in Lot-Ionan's school when he had been nothing but an ordinary dwarf with a love of books and a talent for metalworking.

The journey through Urgon took him through green valleys, over lofty summits, and through narrow mountain passes that tested his agility as well as his endurance. At last he arrived at the fourthling kingdom. The sentries took him straight to Gandogar.

The fourthlings' talent for cutting and polishing gemstones was on full display in the stronghold. The passageways were decorated with pictures composed of brightly colored gems: blood-red rubies, deep blue sapphires, moss-green emeralds, black tourmaline, pink quartz, finely worked agate . . . Every inch of the fourthling stronghold seemed to sparkle and shimmer with precious stones.

Tungdil, disheveled from his journey through Gauragar and Urgon, his clothes dusty and his boots worn, entered the throne room and inclined his head, revealing his sunbleached hair.

"Tungdil Goldhand!" Gandogar hailed him from his throne of pure quartz. He seemed exceedingly relieved. "Thank Vraccas you're alive. How are you?" He signaled for him to sit. "Salfalur turned up in Porista," he continued, while stewards hurried in with refreshments for the tired and thirsty dwarf. "He killed a dozen of our warriors before he disappeared. We were worried he . . ."

Tungdil emptied his tankard in a single draft. "He's dead, Your Majesty," he interrupted. "He came after me and ambushed me in Dsôn." He pulled Keenfire from its sheath and rapped his knuckles against the ax head. "I claimed what was mine from the älfar. Dsôn is a dreadful place and they'd hidden the ax in a tower of bones. After I'd found it, I . . ." It occurred to him that it might be better to keep the details of his duel with Salfalur to himself. "Well, I came back here."

"You were gone a long time. Every orbit we kept waiting and hoping for news, but spring went by and no one knew where you were."

Tungdil tried not to show his surprise. "Urgon is a kingdom after my heart, I thought I'd see a bit of the land . . ." He decided to change the subject. "I suppose you've finished the replicas?"

"You made an excellent job of the drawings." Gandogar called for his master jeweler, who carried in the diamonds on a crystal tray lined with black velvet. The gems were beautifully arranged as if strung together on a necklace. To Tungdil's untrained eye, they looked identical. They seemed to resemble each other in every detail.

He took out the real diamond and placed it among the others. "It's impossible to tell the difference." He counted the gems: fourteen in total. "You've made too many," he said. "Seven human monarchs, five dwarves, and Liútasil— thirteen."

The fourthling king and the master jeweler compared the diamonds and nodded. "They're perfect," declared Gandogar. "But we haven't made too many, Tungdil. Five for the dwarven monarchs, including one for the future king of the thirdlings— and an extra one for you. If anyone is worthy of the diamond, it's you. Don't feel obliged to accept—we can destroy it if you'd rather."

"No," he said quickly. "I'd be honored."

Gandogar picked up the corners of the velvet cloth, allowing the diamonds to slide into the middle. Tungdil lost sight of the eoîl's diamond among its lesser fellows. The high king gathered the corners and shook the cloth, allowing the diamonds to jostle for position. At last he let go of one end and the stones bounced onto the tray. "Summon the messengers," he commanded.

The doors to the throne room flew open, and an elf, seven men, and four dwarves were ushered in. One by one they stepped forward to choose a diamond. Some barely glanced at the tray, while others took their time as if they hoped to pick the magic diamond.

Two stones remained on the tray. Gandogar asked the master jeweler to offer them to Tungdil. "I'd like you to choose," he said.

Tungdil reached for the right-hand stone, wavered for a moment, then picked it up.

Gandogar took the last diamond. "These gifts are a sign of our unity," he said, turning to the messengers. "Take them to your rulers and tell them these words:

Like these stones, so will be our thoughts. Remember these diamonds in times of trouble and honor the alliance. Henceforth, our hearts shall beat as one for Girdlegard." He waved them away. The messengers bowed and took their leave, and the doors closed behind them with a bang.

"Right, I've got a question for you, Tungdil Goldhand." The high king signaled for Tungdil to be seated. "You've had some time to reflect on your journey. Will you be my counselor?"

Kingdom of Idoslane,
Girdlegard,
Summer, 6236th Solar Cycle

Tungdil didn't need to tell his legs where to take him; he had traveled this way a hundred times before. The journey was full of memories, sad memories.

Summer had brought the promise of an excellent harvest to Idoslane. The fields were full of vegetables and crops, and bees buzzed between brightly colored flowers. A warm wind caressed the lush green meadows where the cows were grazing. They turned their big brown eyes toward the wayfarer, before lowering their heads to focus on the grass.

It looks exactly the same. Tungdil rounded the final bend in the road and came to a halt. Even from a distance, he could see the wreckage of Lot-Ionan's gates. Strewn among the bushes were scraps of rusty armor and gnawed bone, all that was left of the orcs who had done battle with Tungdil and the twins on their previous visit. *No,* he thought somberly. *Some things have changed.*

The orcs were gone for good. Judging by their remains, they had infested the kingdom, but the stone of judgment had put an end to their evil souls. Prince Mallen had sent an army into the caves of Toboribor and his men had struggled through the hot, dark passageways without finding a single orc.

Guarding Girdlegard isn't easy. He thought of his dead friends and of Boëndal buried at the High Pass. He had visited the secondling's grave with Boïndil and they had wept for their lost companion and twin. Boïndil's inner furnace seemed to have cooled and the glint in his eye had gone. It seemed to Tungdil that he resembled his brother more closely, and even his speech was calmer and more considered. *Death leaves its mark on the living as well.*

He approached the dark entrance to the tunnel, climbing over the wreckage of the gates and entering the cool, earthy passageway.

After a few paces, he stopped. The tunnel was still blocked where he and the twins had cut away the struts and brought down the roof on the heads of the furious orcs who were baying for their blood. Tons of rock had crashed to the ground, barricading the tunnel. The only way into the school was to burrow through.

Tungdil stroked the frayed neckerchief that he wore around his wrist. It was a present from Frala, the warm-hearted kitchen maid who had been like a sister to him, and who had died in the orcish massacre with her daughters, Sunja and Ikana.

A lump came to his throat and he forced himself to swallow, but the sadness was lodged inside him. *It's time I cleared up around here.*

It was a monumental task. Orbit after orbit passed as he inched his way forward with a pick and a shovel, carting out the rubble and building new struts. He threw the crushed remains of the orcs into a pile and burned their bones, allowing their ashes to scatter on the wind. A single skull marked the site of the battle, a reminder of the dwarven victory and a warning to future invaders.

At last he reached a section of tunnel that had survived the skirmish with the orcs. The struts and the walls looked perfectly stable, so he continued on his way.

From time to time he found an orcish skeleton. Falling debris accounted for most of the casualties, but some of the beasts had starved amid the rubble. Tungdil guessed from their gnawed bones that they had resorted to eating each other, though one of the skeletons bore no signs of damage. He eyed the creature's skull with distaste. *You were the last orc standing, were you? Even feasting on your comrades didn't save you in the end.*

He dragged the bones out of the tunnel and lit another fire, determined that nothing should remain of Nôd'onn's hordes. Next he began a search for the skeletons of the men and women who had lived at the school, but all he found was a small collection of bones, which he decided to bury on top of a little mound opposite the gates. He found a boulder and sculpted it into a tombstone, then forged their names in metal letters and hammered them into the stone.

Laying down his tools, he sat on the mound and gazed at the hills and the human settlements. Never had the kingdom of Idoslane looked so peaceful. He wiped the sweat and tears from his eyes.

A familiar figure came into view, hurrying down the path, spotting him on the mound and running to meet him.

He got up to welcome the visitor. "I wasn't expecting you," he said, giving Balyndis a powerful hug. "I suppose they sent you to talk me into settling in one of the kingdoms. Did Gandogar think I'd agree to be his counselor if you asked on his behalf?"

Balyndis let her backpack slide to the ground and sat down on the mound. Sighing, she rubbed her ankles. "I should have brought a pony. It's a long way on foot." Noticing the tombstone, she gave Tungdil another hug. There was no need for words.

They sat in silence, watching the clouds as the blue sky turned red, then black and the first stars appeared overhead.

"Everyone says hello," said Balyndis at last. "It would take too long to list all the names. You've got a lot of friends, you know. And Rodario wants to know about the orc who asked for directions." She smiled. "I don't think he got it."

Tungdil laughed. "He'll have to wait for the punch line." He was silent for a while. "I'm afraid you'll have to tell the high king that I haven't decided how much longer I'm staying. I can't work out where I belong. My heart belongs to the dwarves, but I like the company of humans, and sometimes I think I'm more like a human than a dwarf. They're not as rigid in their thinking."

"What about the freelings?"

"I can't go back to Trovegold—not now. It reminds me of things I'd rather forget." He looked at her gravely. "As soon as I've made my decision, I'll let Gandogar know. Maybe I'll go to the Outer Lands and look for the dwarves who carved that strange rune. If Gandogar needs me, he has only to say."

She tried to smile. "It's sad, you know. For the first time in history, we've got a real hero, and instead of living with his kinsfolk and sharing his wisdom with the high king, he worries about what to do with himself." She tilted back her head to look up at a star that was shining more brightly than its fellows. "Maybe it's part of being a hero. If you didn't question yourself, you might get bigheaded."

"Tell me about the dwarven kingdoms," he said. "I'm tired of thinking about myself."

Balyndis thought for a moment. "There isn't much to report. The feud with the thirdlings is over, and the dwarves are united at last. A combined army from all five kingdoms is guarding the Eastern Pass."

He was about to tell her about Salfalur's threat, but he changed his mind. "What about the freelings?"

"Still free," she reported. "King Gemmil decided to carry on as before. He'll welcome any dwarf who wants to settle in his realm. It's better that way. The freelings wouldn't be happy in our kingdoms—but we'll trade with each other and keep in touch."

"Any news from the rest of Girdlegard?"

She shrugged. "Everything's back to normal—except the beasts are gone. Even the dark water has disappeared and it's fine to drink from the lakes. Every last bit of evil has been destroyed." She sighed. "It's almost too good to be true."

Tungdil remembered how the malachite had shattered before his eyes. *There's nothing left that can harm us.* "The dwarves will see to it that Girdlegard stays safe."

"Oh," said Balyndis, uncertainly. "I almost forgot. There's a rumor that the diamond for Queen Isika hasn't arrived. No one has seen the messenger or his guards."

"What do you mean?" Tungdil shook his head incredulously. "What if it's the ma . . ." he broke off, remembering that Balyndis knew nothing of the magic stone. "But it's a symbol of friendship!"

"People are saying it was stolen. Queen Isika is scouring Rân Ribastur for the thieves. You can't sell a stone like that—the culprits will be captured."

Tungdil tried not to think about it. He was tired of being a hero. *Someone else can deal with it . . .* "What about you, Balyndis? How's life in the fifthling kingdom?"

"It's going well. We've rebuilt the halls, just as you said we should." She flashed him a wonderful smile. "You'd be proud if you could see it—even Giselbert would be proud. Glaïmbar is doing his best to be a good king and he's getting there, Tungdil."

There was a short silence. "Is he a good husband as well?"

She swallowed. "He did everything he could."

He stopped gazing at the stars and looked at her sharply. "*Did?*"

"He let me go," she said tremulously. "One morning he put his arms around me, looked at me solemnly, and told me he was lifting the iron band." She paused for a moment, regaining her composure, and Tungdil saw doubt, hope, and fear in her beautiful eyes. He could hardly believe what he was hearing. "I asked what I'd done wrong."

"What did he say?" said Tungdil, his throat suddenly dry.

"He said that he promised someone to make me happy and he couldn't keep his promise without letting me go. He told me to follow my heart." She hid her face in her hands, crying tears of relief. "I prayed to Vraccas every night, asking him to bring us together. Is it wrong of me to be glad?"

Even the stars seemed to be rejoicing. *Thank you, Vraccas, thank you.* Tungdil wanted to jump up and shout the good news across Gauragar. *Vraccas has given me my heart's desire.* Restraining himself, he stroked her short hair, remembering her ordeal at the hands of the eoîl. She lifted her palms from her tear-streaked face and looked at him tenderly.

"No, it's not wrong to be happy," he assured her, pulling her close. Silently, he thanked Glaïmbar, whose selfless gesture commanded his unconditional respect. He kissed Balyndis, disentangled himself gently, and bent on one knee. "Balyndis Steelfinger of the clan of the Steel Fingers, daughter of Borengar, will you meld your heart to mine and stay with me always, even if we live a thousand cycles?"

Balyndis dried her tears. "My heart has been melded

to yours for as long as I've known you, Tungdil Goldhand. It's yours to keep."

They embraced, squeezing each other tightly, while the moon rose above them, casting a silvery glow over Idoslane. Nothing could separate them now.

Dramatis Personae

DWARVES

Firstling Kingdom

Xamtys Stubbornstreak II of the clan of the Stubborn Streaks, queen of Borengar's folk.

Gufgar Anvilstand of the clan of the Steely Nails, Xamtys's deputy.

Balyndis Steelfinger of the clan of the Steel Fingers, smith and custodian of the gates.

Bulingar Steelfinger, father of Balyndis.

Glaïmbar Sharpax of the clan of the Iron Beaters, warrior.

Fyrna Goodsoul of the clan of the Ore Finders, messenger.

Beldobin Anvilstand of the clan of the Steely Nails, messenger.

Secondling Kingdom

Balendilín Onearm of the clan of the Firm Fingers, king of Beroïn's folk.

Boëndal Hookhand and **Boïndil Doubleblade,** known also as **Ireheart,** of the clan of the Swinging Axes, warriors and twins.

Thirdling Kingdom

Tungdil Goldhand, scholar and warrior.

Lorimbas Steelheart of the clan of the Stone Grinders, king of Lorimbur's folk.

Romo Steelheart of the clan of the Stone Grinders, Lorimbas's nephew.

Salfalur Shieldbreaker of the clan of the Red Eyes, thirdling commander-in-chief.

Theogil Hardhand of the clan of the Iron Knuckles, sentry.

Fourthling Kingdom

Gandogar Silverbeard of the clan of the Silver Beards, high king and leader of Goïmdil's folk.

Freelings

Gemmil Callusedhand, king of the freelings.

Sanda Flameheart, queen consort and freeling commander-in-chief.

Myrmianda Alabaster, medic and scholar.

Bramdal Masterstroke, executioner.

HUMANS

Andôkai the Tempestuous, maga and ruler of the enchanted realm of Brandôkai.

The fabulous Rodario, actor and impresario.

Furgas, theater technician and prop master.

Narmora, actress and wife of Furgas.

Dorsa, their daughter.

Rosild, nursemaid.

Prince Mallen of Ido, sovereign of Idoslane.

King Belletain, sovereign of Urgon.

King Bruron, sovereign of Gauragar.
Queen Umilante, sovereign of Sangpûr.
Queen Wey IV, sovereign of Weyurn.
Queen Isika, sovereign of Rân Ribastur.
King Nate, sovereign of Tabaîn.

Truk Elius, functionary in Hillchester.
Hosjep, carpenter.
Aspila, poor woman in Gastinga.
Ertil, cook in Porista.
Lirkim, courtier in Porista.
Nufa, famula of Nudin/Nôd'onn.
Vallasin, head of Belletain's army.

OTHERS
Ondori, älf from the kingdom of Dsôn Balsur.
Estugon, älf.
Djerůn, bodyguard in the service of Andôkai.
Liútasil, Lord of Âlandur, kingdom of the elves.
Ushnotz, orcish prince of Toboribor.
Runshak, Ushnotz's troop leader.

Acknowledgments

Tungdil and his dwarven friends are on the move!

The first expedition was a great success, with the little fellows proving their mettle in a victory against the odds. Soon the dwarves' supporters were demanding to know what happened next. Well, a sequel can't simply rehash the first book: It has to be as good, if not better, while covering new ground. I wanted *The War of the Dwarves* to be accessible to readers who aren't familiar with Tungdil and his friends, so I based the story on two new developments: the simmering conflict between the dwarven folks, and the impending threat from the west. Prepare yourselves for some surprises: The story gets very, very dwarven, and you won't know what's coming next . . .

Thanks are due to Angela Kuepper, my editor, as well as to Nicole Schuhmacher, Sonja Rüther, Meike Sewering, Tanja Karmann, and Dr. Patrick Müller, all of whom read the book in its early stages. A special thank you to Sally-Ann Spencer, translator and friend of the dwarves, who did a great job. Thanks also to my German publisher, Piper Verlag, for giving Tungdil & Co. a good home, and to Orbit for introducing them to the English-speaking world.

extras

www.orbitbooks.net

about the author

Markus Heitz was born in 1971 in Germany. He studied history, German language, and literature and won the German Fantasy Award in 2003 for his debut novel, *Shadows Over Ulldart*. His *Dwarves* series is a bestseller in Europe. Markus Heitz lives in Zweibrücken.

Find out more about Markus Heitz and other Orbit authors by registering for the free monthly newsletter at www.orbit-books.net

if you enjoyed
THE WAR OF
THE DWARVES

look out for

WINTERBIRTH

by

Brian Ruckley

Preface

They say the world has fallen far from its former state.

In the beginning there was but one race. It failed the Gods who made it and, though it wounded their hearts to do so, they destroyed it. In its place they fashioned five which they put in the world to inhabit it, and these were the races of the Second Age: Whreinin and Saolin, Huanin and Kyrinin, and Anain.

The sky turned a thousand thousand times and beneath the gaze of the Gods their children prospered. Cities, empires, rose and fell. But at last the Huanin and Kyrinin wearied of the cruelties of the wolfenkind, the Whreinin. Despite the will of the Gods they made war upon that race, and they destroyed it utterly and it passed out of time and history. For this deed are the Huanin and Kyrinin named the Tainted Races. And upon that deed were the hopes of the Gods broken, for they saw that what they had made was flawed beyond mending, marred by an unyielding vein of discord and hubris. The Gods took council upon the highest peaks of the Tan Dihrin, where the rotating firmament grinds sparks from the mountain-tops, and they chose to look no longer upon the failure of their dreams and to suffer no longer the rebellions of their children. They left the world, departing to places beyond the thoughts or imaginings of any save their own kind, and with them went much that was best in the peoples they abandoned.

This is how the Second Age ended and the Third began. It is how this came to be a Godless World. That is what they say.

Prologue

The solitude of the wild goats that made their home on the rock faces above the Vale of Stones was seldom interrupted. The Vale might be the only pass through the high Tan Dihrin, but it was a route that led nowhere: the bleak and icy shores of the north were home only to savage tribes. There was nothing there to draw traders or conquerors up from the lands of the Kilkry Bloods to the south.

When a sudden river of humanity began to flow up and over the Vale of Stones, it therefore sent unease darting through the herds of goats on their precipitous territories overhead. Bucks stamped their feet; does called for their kids. Soon, the cliffs were deserted and only the mute rock was left to witness the extraordinary scenes below, as ten thousand people marched into a cold exile.

The great column was led by a hundred or more mounted warriors. Many bore wounds, still fresh from the lost battle on the fields by Kan Avor; all bore, in their red-rimmed eyes and wan skin, the marks of exhaustion. Behind them came the multitude: women, children and men, though fewest of the last. Thousands of widows had been made that year.

It was a punishing exodus. Their way was paved with hard rock and sharp stones that cut feet and turned ankles. There could be no pause. Any who fell were seized by those who came behind, hauled upright with shouts of encouragement, as if noise alone could put strength back into their legs. If they could not rise, they were left. There were already dozens of buzzards and ravens drifting lazily above the column. Some had followed it all the way up the Glas valley from the south; others were residents of the mountains, drawn from their lofty perches by the promise of carrion.

A few of those fleeing through the Stone Vale had been wealthy—merchants and landowners from Kan Avor or Glasbridge. What little of their wealth they had managed to salvage in the panic of flight was now slipping through their fingers. Mules were stumbling and falling beneath overladen panniers, defeated by the desperate whips of their handlers or the weight of their loads; the wheels and axles of carts were splintering amidst the rocks, cargoes spilling to the ground. Servants cajoled or threatened into carrying their masters' goods were casting them aside, exhaustion overcoming their fear. Fortunes that had taken lifetimes to accumulate lay scattered and ignored along the length of the Vale, like flakes of skin scoured off the crowd's body by the rock walls of the pass.

Avann oc Gyre, Thane of the Gyre Blood and self-proclaimed protector of the creed of the Black Road, rode amongst the common folk. His Shield, the men sworn to guard him day and night, had long since abandoned their efforts to keep the people from straying too close to their lord. The Thane himself ignored the masses jostling all about him. His head hung low and he made no effort to guide his horse. It followed where the flow carried it.

There was a crust of blood upon the Thane's cheek.

He had been in the thick of the fighting outside Kan Avor, his beloved city, and survived only because his own Shield had disregarded his commands and dragged him from the field. The wound on his cheek was little more than a scratch, though. Hidden beneath his robes, and beneath blood-heavy bandaging, other injuries were eating away at his strength. The lance of a Kilkry horseman had pierced the Thane through from front to back, breaking as it did so and leaving splinters of wood along the tunnel it drove through his flesh. He had a fine company of healers, and if there had been time to set his tent, to rest and tend to his wounds, they might even have been able to save his life. Avann had forbidden such a delay, and refused to leave his horse for a litter.

What was left of the Thane's armies came behind. Two years ago the warriors of Gyre had been one of the finest bodies of fighting men in all the lands of the Kilkry Bloods, but the unremitting carnage since then had consumed their strength as surely as a fire loosed upon a drought-struck forest. In the end virtually every able-bodied man—and many of the women—of the Black Road had taken to the field at Kan Avor, drawn not just from Gyre but from every Blood: still they had been outnumbered by more than three to one. Now barely fifteen hundred men remained, a battered rearguard for the flight of the Black Road into the north.

The man who rode up to join his Thane was as bruised and weary as all the rest. His helm was dented, the ring mail on his chest stained with blood, his round shield notched and half split where an axe had found a lucky angle. Still, this man bore himself well and his eyes retained a glint of vigour. He nudged his horse through the crowds and leaned close to Avann.

"Lord," he said softly, "it is Tegric."

Avann stirred, but did not raise his head or open his eyes.

"My scouts have come up, lord," the warrior continued. "The enemy draw near. Kilkry horsemen are no more than an hour or two adrift of us. Behind them, spearmen of Haig-Kilkry. They will bring us to bay before we are clear of the Vale."

The Thane of Gyre spat bloodily.

"Whatever awaits us was decided long ago," he murmured. His voice was thin and weak. "We cannot fear what is written in the Last God's book."

One of the Thane's shieldmen joined them, and fixed Tegric with a disapproving glare.

"Leave the Thane be," he said. "He must conserve his strength."

That at last raised Avann's head. He winced as he opened his eyes.

"My death will come when it must. Until then, I am Thane, not some sick old woman to be wrapped warm and fed broth. Tegric treats me as a Thane still; how much more should my own Shield?"

The shieldman nodded in acceptance of the reprimand, but stayed in close attendance.

"Let me wait here, lord," said Tegric softly. "Give me just a hundred men. We will hold the Vale until our people are clear."

The Thane regarded Tegric. "We may need every man in the north. The tribes will not welcome our arrival."

"There will be no arrival if our enemies come upon us here in the Vale. Let me stand here and I will promise you half a day, perhaps more. The cliffs narrow up ahead, and there is an old rockfall. I can hold the way against riders; spill enough of their blood that they will wait for their main force to come up before attempting the passage twice."

"And then you will be a hundred against what, five thousand? Six?" Avann grunted.

"At least," smiled Tegric.

An old man fell in the crowds that surrounded them. He cried out as a stone opened his knee. A grey-haired woman—perhaps his wife—hurried to help him to his feet, murmuring "Get up, get up." A score of people, including the Thane and Tegric, flowed past before she managed to raise him. She wept silently as the man hobbled onwards.

"Many people have already died in defence of our creed," Avann oc Gyre said, lowering his head once more and closing his eyes. He seemed to shrink as he hunched forward in his saddle. "If you give us half a day—if it has been so written in the Last God's book—you and your hundred will be remembered. When the lands that have been taken from us are ours again, you will be named first and noblest amongst the dead. And when this bitter world is unmade and we have returned into the love of the Gods I will look for you, to give you the honour that will be your due."

Tegric nodded. "I will see you once again in the reborn world, my Thane."

He turned his horse and nudged it back against the current of humanity.

*　　*　　*

Tegric rested against a great boulder. He had removed his tunic, and was methodically stitching up a split seam. His mail shirt was neatly spread upon a rock, his shield and scabbarded sword lying beside it, his helm resting at his feet. These were all that remained to him, everything he had need of. He had given his horse to a lame woman who had been struggling along in the wake of the main column. His small pouch of coins had gone to a child, a boy mute from shock or injury.

Above, buzzards were calling as they circled lower, descending towards the corpses that Tegric knew lay just out of sight. His presence, and that of his hundred men, might deter the scavengers for a while longer, but he did not begrudge them a meal. Those who once dwelled in those bodies had no further need of them: when the Gods returned—as they would once all peoples of the world had learned the humility of the Black Road—they would have new bodies, in a new world.

From where he sat, Tegric could see down a long, sloping sweep of the Stone Vale. Every so often he glanced up from his stitching to cast his eyes back the way they had come. Far off in that direction lay Grive, where he had lived most of his life: a place of soft green fields, well-fed cattle, as different from this punishing Vale of Stones as any place could be. The memory of it summoned up no particular emotion in him. The rest of his family had not seen the truth of the creed as he had. When Avann oc Gyre, their Thane, had declared for the Black Road they had fled from Grive, disappearing out of Tegric's life. In every Blood, even Kilkry itself, the blossoming of the Black Road had sundered countless families, broken ties and bonds that had held firm for generations. To Tegric's mind it was a cause for neither regret nor surprise. A truth as profound as that of the Black Road could not help but have consequences.

An old man, dressed in a ragged brown robe and leaning on a staff, came limping up the Vale. He was, perhaps, the very last of the fleeing thousands. Though they were close to the highest point of the pass, the sun, burning out of a cloudless sky, still had strength. The man's forehead was beaded with sweat. He paused before Tegric, resting all his weight upon his staff and breathing heavily. The warrior looked up at the man, squinting slightly against the sunlight.

"Am I far behind the rest?" the man asked between laboured breaths.

Tegric noted the bandaged feet, the trembling hands.

"Some way," he said softly.

The man nodded, unsurprised and seemingly unperturbed. He wiped his brow with the hem of his robe; the material came away sweaty and dirty.

"You are waiting here?" he asked Tegric, who nodded in reply.

The man cast around, scanning the warriors scattered amongst the great boulders all around him.

"How many of you are there?"

"A hundred," Tegric told him.

The old man chuckled, though it was a cold and humourless kind of laugh.

"You have come to the end of your Roads then, you hundred. I had best press on, and discover where my own fate runs out."

"Do so," said Tegric levelly. He watched the man make his unsteady way along the path already trodden by so many thousands. There had been, in the gentle edges of his accent, no hint of the Gyre Blood or the Glas valley where Avann had ruled.

"Where are you from, old father?" Tegric called after him.

"Kilvale, in Kilkry lands," the man replied.

"Did you know the Fisherwoman, then?" Tegric asked, unable to keep the edge of wonder from his voice.

The old man paused and carefully turned to look back at the warrior.

"I heard her speak. I knew her a little, before they killed her."

"There will be a day, you know, when the Black Road marches through this pass again," Tegric said. "But then we will be marching out of the north, not into it. And we will march all the way to Kilvale and beyond."

Again the man laughed his rough laugh. "You are right. They've driven us from our homes, cast even your Thane out from his castle, but the creed survives. You and I are not fated to see it, friend, but the Black Road will rule in the hearts of all men one day, and all things will come to their end. This is a war that will not be done until the world itself is unmade."

Tegric gazed after the receding figure for a time. Then he returned to his sewing.

A while later, his hand paused in its rhythmic motion, the needle poised in mid-descent. There was something moving amongst the rocks, back down the pass to the south.

He carefully set aside his tunic and half-rose, leaning forward on one knee.

"Kilkry," he heard one of his warriors muttering off to his left.

And the shape coalescing out of the rock and the bright light did indeed look to be a rider. Nor was it alone. At least a score of horsemen were picking their way up the Vale of Stones.

Tegric laid a hand instinctively on the cool metal of his chain vest. He could feel the dried blood, the legacy of a week's almost constant battle, beneath his fingertips. He was not afraid to die. That was one fear the Black Road lifted from a man's back. If he feared anything, it was that he should fail in his determination to face, both willingly and humbly, whatever was to come.

"Ready yourselves," he said, loud enough for only the few nearest men to hear. They passed the word along. Tegric snapped the needle from the end of its thread and slipped his tunic back on. He lifted his mail shirt above his head and dropped its familiar weight onto his shoulders. Like smoke rising from a newly caught fire, the line of riders below was lengthening, curling and curving its way up the pass.

The horsemen of Kilkry were the best mounted warriors to be found in all the Bloods, but their prowess would count for little where Tegric had chosen to make his stand. A titanic fall of rocks from the cliffs above had almost choked the Stone Vale with rubble. The riders would be greatly hampered, perhaps even forced to dismount. Tegric's swordsmen and archers would have the advantage here. Later, when the main body of the pursuing army came up, they would be overwhelmed, but that did not matter.

He glanced at the sun, a searingly bright orb in the perfectly blue sky. He could hear the buzzards and the ravens, could glimpse their dark forms gliding in effortless spirals. It did not seem a bad place, a bad day, to die. If, when he woke in the new world the Black Road promised him, this was his last memory of his first life, of this failed world, it would not displease him.

Tegric Wyn dar Gyre rose and buckled on his sword belt.

II The Third Age: Year 1087

Mist had draped itself across the village, so that water, land and air had all run together. The domed huts were indistinct shapes, bulging out of the morning vapours here and there like burial mounds. Dew lay heavy on the cut slabs of turf that covered them. A lone fisherman was easing his flatboat out into one of the channels that meandered through the reedbeds around the village. There was no other sign of life save the wispy threads rising from the smokeholes of one or two of the huts. Not a breath of wind disturbed their ascent as the trails of smoke climbed high into the air before losing themselves in the greyness.

One larger hut stood apart from the others on raised ground. A figure emerged out of the mist, walking towards it: a youth, no more than fifteen or sixteen. His tread left deep prints in the mossy grass. Outside the hut he stopped and gathered himself. He stood straight and looked around for a moment. He breathed the damp air in and out, as if cleansing himself.

As the deerskin that hung across the opening fell back into place behind him, the interior was cast into a deep gloom. Only the faintest light oozed in through the small hole in the centre of the roof; the peat fire had been dampened down to embers. The youth could make out the indistinct forms of a dozen or more people sitting motionless in a semi-circle. Some of their faces were touched by the glow of the embers, lighting their cheeks a little. He knew them, but it was an irrelevance here and now. On this morning they were one; they were the will of the place, of Dyrkyrnon. In the background, all but beneath the reach of even his acute hearing, a dolorous rhythm was being chanted. He had never heard the sound before, yet knew what it was: a truth chant, a habit borrowed from the Heron Kyrinin. They were seeking wisdom.

"Sit," someone said.

He lowered himself to the ground and crossed his legs. He fixed his eyes on the firepit.

"We have sat through the night," said someone else, "to give thought to this matter."

The youth nodded and pressed his thin lips tight together.

"It is a heavy duty," continued the second speaker, "and a sad burden that we should be called upon to make such judgments. Dyrkyrnon is a place of sanctuary, open to all those of our kind who can find no peace or safety in the outer world. Yet we came together to determine whether you should be turned out, Aeglyss, and sent away from here."

Aeglyss said nothing. His face remained impassive, his gaze unwavering.

"You were taken in, and given comfort. You would have died at your mother's side if you had not been found and brought here. Yet you have sown discord. The friendship and trust you were offered have been repaid with cruelty. Dyrkyrnon suffers now by your presence. Aeglyss, you shall leave this place, and have no discourse with any who make their homes here. We cast you out."

There was a flicker of response in the youth's face then: a trembling in the tight-clenched jaw, a shiver at the corner of his mouth. He closed his eyes. The peaty smoke was thickening the air. It touched the back of his throat and nose.

"You are young, Aeglyss," the voice from beyond the smouldering fire said, a little softer now. "It may be that age will teach you where we have failed. If that should be the case, you will be welcome here once more."

He stared at the half-lit faces opposite him, a cold anger in his look.

"You came to us out of a storm," said a woman, "and you carry the storm within you. It is beyond us to tame it. It is too deep-rooted. When it is gone, or mastered, return to us. The judgment can be rescinded. You belong here."

He laughed at that, the sound harsh and sudden in the still atmosphere. There were tears welling up in his eyes. They ran down his cheeks but did not reach his voice.

"I belong nowhere," he said, and rose to his feet. "Not here, and therefore nowhere. You are afraid of me, you who more than any should understand. You talk of comfort and trust, yet all I see in the faces around me is doubt and fear. The stench of your fear sickens me." He spat into the embers. A puff of ashes hissed into the air.

Aeglyss cast about, trying to find someone in the enveloping darkness of the hut. "K'rina. You are here. I can feel you. Will you deny me too?"

"Be still, K'rina," said someone.

"Yes, be still," Aeglyss snarled. "Do as they tell you. That is the way of it here: tread softly, always softly. Disturb nothing. You promised to love me, K'rina, in my dead mother's place. Is this your love?"

Nobody answered him.

"I loved you, K'rina. Loved!" He spat the word as if it was poison on his tongue. He could not see through his tears.

"I only wanted . . ." The words died in his throat. He sucked a breath in. "This is not fair. What have I done? Nothing that another might not do. Nothing."

The shadowed figures made no reply. Their obdurate will lay between him and them like a wall. With a curse that almost choked him, Aeglyss turned and strode out.

After he had gone, there was a long stretch of quiet. Almost imperceptibly at first, then louder, there came the sound of stifled sobs from somewhere in the shadows.

"Save your sorrow, K'rina. He is unworthy of it."

"He is my ward," stammered the woman.

"No longer. It is for the best. He has too much in him that is wild and cruel. We cannot free him of it, for all that we have tried."

K'rina subsided into silence, muffling her grief.

"He's right in one thing," someone else said. "We are afraid of him."

"There is no shame in that. He is stronger in the Shared than anyone we have seen in years, even if he lacks the knowledge to use that strength as he might. When he was only playing cruel games, whispering in ears and working a child's tricks, we might overlook it. But now . . . the girl still cries in the night. If he remained amongst us there would be greater sorrow in the end."

"Wherever he goes in the world, there will be greater sorrow," said a man with wild, dark spirals etched upon his face. "It would have been better to put an end to him. Blood will fill that one's footprints. Wherever he goes."